19/8/2016

Slough Library Services

Please return this book on or before the date shown on your receipt.

To renew go to:
Website: **www.sloug...**
Phone: **01753 5351...**

LIB/6198

Slough
Borough Council
www.slough.gov.uk

3013050364565 0

SPECIAL MESSAGE TO READERS

THE ULVERSCROFT FOUNDATION
(registered UK charity number 264873)
was established in 1972 to provide funds for
research, diagnosis and treatment of eye diseases.
Examples of major projects funded by
the Ulverscroft Foundation are:-

- The Children's Eye Unit at Moorfields Eye
  Hospital, London
- The Ulverscroft Children's Eye Unit at Great
  Ormond Street Hospital for Sick Children
- Funding research into eye diseases and
  treatment at the Department of Ophthalmology,
  University of Leicester
- The Ulverscroft Vision Research Group,
  Institute of Child Health
- Twin operating theatres at the Western
  Ophthalmic Hospital, London
- The Chair of Ophthalmology at the Royal
  Australian College of Ophthalmologists

You can help further the work of the Foundation
by making a donation or leaving a legacy.
Every contribution is gratefully received. If you
would like to help support the Foundation or
require further information, please contact:

THE ULVERSCROFT FOUNDATION
The Green, Bradgate Road, Anstey
Leicester LE7 7FU, England
Tel: (0116) 236 4325

website: www.foundation.ulverscroft.com

Zoë Miller was born on the south side of Dublin, where she now lives with her husband and three children. She began writing stories at an early age. Her writing career has also included freelance journalism and prize-winning short fiction.

You can discover more about the author at www.zoemillerauthor.com

THE COMPROMISE

Childhood friends Juliet, Rebecca, Rose and Matthew grew up in a small village outside Dublin. Now privileged, wealthy and powerful, they appear to have it all. But when Juliet is involved in a suspicious accident and lies trapped between life and death at the bottom of a cliff, a secret that has been hidden for years threatens the seemingly perfect lives of the close-knit group. For the beautiful, fragile Rose, Juliet's accident draws unwanted attention to the sins of the past. For her husband, the ruthlessly ambitious Matthew, it removes a critical obstacle from the path of his political career. And as Rebecca discovers more about what happened to her friend, she begins to wonder if she ever knew the real Juliet . . .

ZOË MILLER

◆

THE
COMPROMISE

Complete and Unabridged

CHARNWOOD
Leicester

First published in Ireland in 2013 by
Hachette Books Ireland
Dublin

First Charnwood Edition
published 2014
by arrangement with
Hachette Books Ireland
A division of
Hachette UK Ltd.
London

The moral right of the author has been asserted

All characters and places in this publication, other than those clearly in the public domain, are fictitious. All events and incidents are the product of the author's imagination. Any resemblance to real persons, living or dead, is purely coincidental.

Copyright © 2013 by Zoë Miller
All rights reserved

A catalogue record for this book is available from the British Library.

ISBN 978–1–4448–2203–8

Published by
F. A. Thorpe (Publishing)
Anstey, Leicestershire
Set by Words & Graphics Ltd.
Anstey, Leicestershire
Printed and bound in Great Britain by
T. J. International Ltd., Padstow, Cornwall

This book is printed on acid-free paper

This book is dedicated with lots of love and thanks to my family and friends

Acknowledgements

I'd like to express huge thanks and appreciation to all those who have helped my dream become a reality:

The brilliant team at Hachette Ireland, who constantly pull out all the stops and work so hard behind the scenes, in particular Ciara Doorley, for her fantastic, insightful editing, Joanna Smyth, for her patient and endless assistance, also Breda, Jim, Margaret, Ruth, Bernard, and Siobhán. And Hazel Orme, for her superb copy-editing skills.

My wonderful agent, Sheila Crowley, for her warm encouragement and constant belief in me, and the marvellous support from Becky, Laura and the Curtis Brown team.

I truly appreciate the privilege of working with you all.

This book is dedicated to my circle of family and friends, who all deserve tremendous thanks for amazing encouragement and stellar support: in particular Derek, Michelle, Declan, Barbara, Dara, Colm and the especially precious Cruz. I love you all so much and thank you from the bottom of my heart for always being there for me. Also my extended family, who still talk to me and keep me on their invitation lists even if I don't see them half as often as I would like: Margaret and Pat, Peter and Margaret, David and Denise, Kevin and Hazel, Clare and Patricia, Rita and Pat, and Denis and Mary.

One of the themes of *The Compromise* is the value of female friendship, and I would like to take this opportunity to express heartfelt thanks and appreciation to some lovely ladies for being in my life and for laughter, fun, and wonderful support: Angela, Mary and Kate; Eileen, Mary and Anne; Kathleen and Alice; Majella; Geraldine and Joan; Brd, Margaret and Pauline T.

Thanks also to my work colleagues and circle of writer friends — you know who you are!

And lastly but by no means least, a big thank you to all my lovely readers for trusting enough in me to buy my books, and for all the wonderful messages that come via Twitter and Facebook and through www.zoemillerauthor.com. It means everything to me. I really hope you enjoy *The Compromise*.

Zoë xxx

Prologue

Dublin, Saturday, 17 March, 7.15 a.m.

It is one of those pristine, pearly mornings when the world is hushed, the opalescent sky goes on for ever, everything seems sparkling and brand new, and you don't expect anything bad to happen. Even the sea is calm, from the far-off horizon where it hazes into the sky, right up to where the incoming tide foams lightly against the pewter cliffs.

As he jogs around the headland track, the whole day lies ahead of him, waiting to be lived and filled with possibilities. He will shower when he gets home, and bring his pregnant wife a cup of tea. Later, he might paint the nursery. They might go shopping for a Moses basket. Or out to dinner. But for now there is just this: the cool, early-morning breeze on his face, the salt-scented air filling his lungs, the sound of his footfall on the earth, and then the glimmering sun, breaking free of a hazy cloud to send bright yellow flurries across the rippling expanse of water. The vital energy of it all surges through his veins and he feels he could run on for ever.

Then, out of the corner of his eye, he sees something odd, something out of place, an aberration in this calm, still morning. His stride falters. He stops. He hears his breathing, loud in his ears. His heart skips a beat.

3

It is far down, near the base of the cliffs. It looks like a heap of dark clothes, but the sudden chill running up his spine tells him it is something else. He reaches for his mobile, with him at all times, powered up and switched on in case his wife goes into early labour. A call to the emergency services will put him through to the coastguards: the area officer's pager will go off, and he will raise the cliff rescue team, maybe the helicopter.

He dials, knowing that that is only the beginning. Other calls will be made, shattering peaceful lives, like boulders crashing into a pond. His wife will still be sleeping, so he decides to keep a vigil, on the headland, until the person is safely rescued.

He hopes he or she is still alive and hasn't been lying there all night, alone. He sits down and waits, a light sweat cooling his skin, and all about him the morning unfolds, the gulls stretch their wings as they wheel into the breeze, and the sun floods the sea with bright light. He thinks of his unborn child, waiting to join the world, innocent and new, and his heart turns over. As soon as he is home, he will tell his wife he loves her very much.

Part One

Juliet

1

Dublin, Friday, 16 March, 7.30 p.m.

In the beginning there is nothing at all. It's like the moment I wake up and everything is a blank sheet. Then I taste fear in my mouth.

The tail end of a nightmare?

I struggle into wakefulness. I hear the slap of waves beating against the rocks and the hiss of shooting spray. It's the sound of the sea and the familiar backdrop to my evening stroll around the cliff top. There's no need to be fearful because, any minute now, I'll wake up under my duvet.

Something cool puffs against my face and my skin tautens. It shimmies up from my chin. It flows over my nose and cheeks, and across my forehead. It's like a breath and it carries the damp, briny scent of the sea. A breeze. A *breeze?* My eyelids flutter, heavy and sluggish. With an effort, I prise them open. But instead of my shadowy bedroom ceiling, I'm staring up at the night sky.

I *am* dreaming. That's how it feels. I see the stars, sprinkled like fairy glitter across the heavens. A crescent moon gleams, suspended in the sky like a sail on the high seas.

How beautiful it is.

The dream suddenly alters and shifts to another night, a night buried so deeply in my heart that I never venture there. But now the gateway is unlocked and I'm free-falling into it. I'm there again, lying on my back and looking up at a star-studded sky. Music, laughter and the click of castanets float across the distance and mingle with the hiss of waves on a sloping beach. This time the breeze is warm and sweet-scented, and it flutters up from my toes to my scalp. Sand grains rasp against my back and hips. Hard, unfamiliar skin slides against mine. My finger-nails skid across the planes of his powerful body and I look over his shoulders to where palm trees are blackly silhouetted against the sky.

So this is what it's like . . . I cling to him and let desire take over as we mesh together, time and time again. Then comes a sparkling moment when everything swells inside me until it reaches a perfect peak and I'm spinning freely over the edge of the universe.

Little did I know that that was the start of my downfall and the end of my freedom.

That long-ago night fades. In my dream the breeze is coming in flurries, a little stronger, more insistent. Once again I'm staring up at the night sky while the incessant sea shifts and murmurs in the foreground, as though it's alive and breathing and whispering its secrets to me. There is a rapping noise, like seawater spattering off the jagged rocks that jut out from the base of the cliffs. And then the unmistakable sucking sound as the pull of the moon draws out the tide from hidden nooks and crannies.

How come it sounds so close? Usually I'm hearing it at a distance, the clamour muffled by the long drop that plummets from the walking trail at the top of the cliffs to the sea. And why is this dream so real? I should be awake by now, stretching in my bed, not feeling a chilly breeze on my face.

And feeling nothing else at all . . .

Not even my heart jumping into my throat, as it surely should be, because this is one hell of a bad dream . . .

And then, a thought so terrible I can't go there: *If it is a dream . . .*

2

The night was thick with long shadows, and a cool breeze snatched at Rebecca Ryan's hair as she wove through the silent car park towards the Seagrass Hotel.

Glass doors to the lobby glided apart at her approach, and when they closed behind her, she might have been in another world. The warm air that wafted about her and the dazzle of chandeliers bouncing off pale marble walls was so much at odds with the dark, chilly night outside that she felt momentarily disoriented.

She took a breath, ignored the butterflies in her stomach, and told herself she could do this.

As she stepped across the lobby, traces of expensive scent lingered in the air. She glanced to the long table at the side. It was cleared of everything except a white tablecloth and empty champagne buckets. She tightened her grip on her overnight bag as her ears were assaulted by the sound of popping corks, the laughter and buzz of a wedding party. She was glad that the lobby was quiet, with just a low hum of conversation from a handful of guests scattered on big squashy couches, the rest still in the banqueting room, having dinner.

She had timed it perfectly.

'Good evening, Madam,' the receptionist said. Her uniform was pristine, and Rebecca felt tatty in her jeans, furry boots and leather jacket, even though the latter had been an expensive gift to herself during a trip to New York back in the Celtic Tiger days. When she saw her reflection in the long mirror behind the reception desk, she winced. With warm blonde hair — thanks to her hairdresser — good cheekbones and expressive eyes, she'd sometimes been likened to a younger version of Joanna Lumley. However, this evening, her face pale and tight, she didn't look remotely like the sparky actress. She forced a smile, smoothed her hair, straightened her shoulders, and looked a hundred times better.

'Have you a reservation?' The receptionist exuded a brightly glossed confidence in the way only a twenty-something could. Rebecca fumbled with her bag and produced her confirmation email. She'd never had such confidence at that age. Few of her generation had.

Except, of course, Juliet.

The receptionist slid a registration form across the polished marble and went through the usual patter. 'Can I confirm that it's single occupancy, Mrs Ryan?'

'It's Ms Ryan and, yes, that's correct.'

'My apologies. It's just that you ticked Mrs on the registration form.'

Mrs. For a moment Harry is standing by the reception desk in a far-off holiday hotel, organising their passports and key cards, smiling as he begins to propel her case. 'Let's be having you, Mrs Ryan.'

A fresh crump in her stomach. Harry had been gone six years already. He had been fifty-three. Sometimes it felt like six days or six

11

weeks. Other times it felt like six decades. Almost as though he had never been. And there were times, like tonight, when she missed him so much and would have given anything to have him there, at her back. She kept her expression neutral as she said, 'Old habits.'

The receptionist gave her a bland smile. 'The Seagrass has a special rate for those attending the Johnson-Maguire wedding. You're here for the evening reception?'

'That's right.'

'The wedding party is in the Blue Water salon on the first floor. The dinner will be over shortly and then they'll be welcoming the evening guests.'

'Perfect,' Rebecca said.

It had been a last-minute decision to accept the invitation from an old friend of Harry's to join the celebrations for his son's wedding in the north County Dublin hotel. At first Rebecca had had no intention of being there: if things had been different, her family and friends would have been gathering in the south of France, where Danielle, her daughter, had planned to get married. Then she'd decided it would be better to mingle with old acquaintances than sit at home trying to keep her mind off a cream shot-silk wedding dress, muffled in layers of tissue, Danielle's stifled sobs, and the flight tickets to a honeymoon in the Maldives, which she guessed hadn't been cancelled.

Not to mention the other curve balls that life was throwing at her.

Rebecca tucked her key card into her bag, followed the directions to her ground-floor room, and told herself she could handle it. She'd even timed it so that she could shower, change, put on a happy face and look as though she hadn't a care in the world when she joined the party.

She still found it hard to believe that, less than three months ago, life had been almost perfect as she'd sat at the table in Verbena View, Juliet's home, for a pre-Christmas gathering. She had been with the people who were closest in the world to her: darling Danielle and her fiancé Conor, Rebecca's older sister Rose and husband Matthew, with their son James, and Juliet, her best friend, whom she'd known for most of her life. Her twin sons, Kevin and Mark, who both worked abroad, were missing, and of course, Harry, who had practically grown up with her, Rose and Matthew in the rough-and-tumble of Lower Ballymalin Gardens. Her heart had swelled as she looked around the table and counted her blessings.

Juliet's table had been simply but festively dressed in red and silver, with candlelight casting a subtle glow over arrangements of fat red berries and crystal glasses. Best of all was the banter and laughter that flowed between them all, lifting Rebecca's heart.

'You must be counting the weeks now,' Rose had said to Danielle. Rose! She might be a far cry from the Rose of yesteryear, elegant now in black velvet and Cartier diamonds, as though she'd just stepped out of a *Tatler* society page, but to Rebecca she still bore traces of the quiet ten-year-old girl who had felt their parents' tragic

13

death more keenly than the younger Rebecca. Rose had gone on to become a self-effacing teenager, and equally modest adult, afraid to expect too much from life, lest it be taken away from her.

'Yes, the wedding's less than three months away.' Danielle, beautiful in silver Ben de Lisi, blonde hair shimmering in the muted light, diamond engagement ring glittering, exchanged a smile with Conor.

'Three months?' said Rose's son, James, in mock dismay. 'I guess the band better get in some practice.'

James had joined Juliet's annual Christmas bash for the first time in quite a while. Rebecca wondered if that was why Rose was slightly flushed. Her son was bass guitarist in The Name, a globally successful rock band and, beside his tall, rather rakish figure, she was bursting with pride and adoration. Even Matthew, who had recently featured on a short list of Ireland's most influential businessmen, seemed happy enough to take a back seat to his mega-successful son. The Name would be playing at Danielle's wedding in the south of France on St Patrick's Day.

'Too right you'd better,' Rebecca said. 'Especially for the first dance. I can't imagine The Name do much romantic stuff.'

'You won't hear any bum notes, Rebecca.' James flashed his aunt a grin. 'We can do a rather good 'Wind Beneath My Wings'.'

'Is that the best you can think of?' Danielle said, exaggerating her horror.

'Hmm. What about 'Always And Forever'?' James suggested. 'Or what's that one from *The Bodyguard?*'

'Yeah, right.' Danielle sniffed. 'Conor and I will pick something suitable.'

'Whatever you choose, I don't think James will let you down,' said Matthew.

'You heard the man, little cuz.' James smiled. 'Whatever you want, we'll deliver.'

'I fervently hope you do. Danielle deserves nothing but the best. Now who's for more bubbly?' This was from Juliet, oozing warmth as they lingered at the table long after the meal was over.

Juliet, unlike Rebecca and Rose and their husbands, had been born into a life of power and privilege. She made light of this, letting it roll off her back. She'd thrown all her vibrant energy into her colourful career and had never married, despite a constant string of admirers, some of whom Rebecca had been aware of and others whom Juliet had kept discreetly under wraps. Juliet had a brother in Florida, whom she rarely saw, and had come to regard Rebecca and Rose and their families as her own. Tonight she was a sparkling hostess as she joked and laughed, refreshing wine glasses and passing *petits fours*. The deepening twilight pressed against the wide patio doors and now and again, when Rebecca looked down the table, she saw them all reflected in the glass, the people she loved so much, their faces superimposed on the dark mauve sky.

Now Rebecca reached her room and rum-maged for her key card. If only she could have held all the people she loved in a protective bubble of happiness. But time had ticked by. James was the first to rise to his feet and break up the party, and then everything had changed.

Soon after Christmas, Danielle's wedding was off.

'I don't want to talk about it, Mum,' Danielle had said, her blue eyes hard and dark-shadowed, when she'd shown up at home unexpectedly on a cold January evening, announced that she and Conor had split up and asked to stay for a couple of nights. 'It's not up for discussion. Not now, not ever.'

Rebecca had clutched at her throat. 'Oh, Danielle! Darling! How terrible. Did you? Or was it Conor?' Then words had failed her.

Danielle had merely shaken her head, ignored her embrace, and begun to climb the stairs to her old bedroom.

'Darling, talk to me! Surely it's better to share it,' Rebecca had said desperately, glancing at Danielle's ringless finger as if for proof. 'At least let me know if there's anything I can do.'

'How could you do anything?' Danielle had snapped, in an unusually sharp tone, which had betrayed the depth of her pain. 'Sorry, Mum. I just can't talk about it right now. You'd be a lot better off living your own life and leaving me to look after mine. I can handle it. And if Conor calls, looking for me, I'm not here. Right?'

'Understood.' Rebecca had been devastated by the stony look on her daughter's face and deeply hurt that Danielle hadn't confided in her.

A couple of days later, Danielle had bolted to

Rome with her broken heart, and even though they had stayed in regular contact, Rebecca was none the wiser about what had gone wrong. She just hoped Danielle wasn't holed up alone in her apartment tonight, drowning her sorrows on what would have been the eve of her wedding.

That had been the first shock, and Rebecca would have coped with it: life had dealt her far crueller blows. Then, in the last couple of weeks, Rose and Matthew had embarked on a challenging campaign that had the power to shatter their hard-won comfortable lifestyle. Rebecca feared for their happiness.

As if all that wasn't fraught enough, the previous weekend Juliet . . .

Rebecca closed her bedroom door and leaned against it, fighting a stab of anxiety. Out of nowhere, her friend had begun to talk about setting herself on a collision course with Matthew and Rose. It would leave Rebecca tiptoeing through a minefield and perhaps, eventually, having to choose between her family and her friend.

3

Friday, 16 March, 8.00 p.m.

I'm coming back from somewhere dark and heavy, as though I've been asleep. There is the cold of hard stone against the back of my head, and something sharp, like a flint, is pinching the top of my skull.

I've been here already, staring at the night sky from this position, with the hiss of the sea, perilously close, and the salt-laden breeze riffling my face. Can you dream the same dream twice? For this has to be a dream. Or, rather, a nightmare.

Soon I will wake up, laughing with relief, in my bed. Bring it on, I urge. I've had enough of this stupid nightmare. My face is cold and it's getting a bit boring.

For a long time, nothing happens. There is just the spatter of water on the rocks, the plaintive call of a sea bird, and the breeze on my face. A drift of shredded cloud wafts across the face of the moon and I am spellbound once more by the perfect beauty of the night.

Then a solid wall of panic slams into my head. My eyes have adjusted to the night and I can make out something dark and solid rising on my left, blocking out a segment of the starry sky.

It looks exactly like the angle of a steep cliff face.

Oh, God. Oh, dear God.

If my heart is pumping in blind terror, I can't feel it. Neither can I feel my legs. Or my arms. Or anything below my face. I open my mouth to scream but no sound comes out. I feel detached, though, as if the nightmare is happening to someone else. I pounce on this and will myself to believe it.

It has to be a nightmare. A nightmare in which I'm imagining myself lying far too close to the sea, by the base of the cliffs, staring up at the night sky, unable to move or feel anything below my head.

It can't be real.

For these are my cliffs and my sea. No harm should come to me here. This is the breeze I feel most evenings as I stroll around the headland track, looking out across the vast expanse of the bay. I close my eyes and see the way the light falls across the surface of the sea. It looks fresh and vibrant in the early morning, sleepy and tranquil in the late evening. I often wonder at the secrets it holds. Some days the water is the clearest aquamarine; on others it is a stony grey ripple, but it is always beautiful.

I see a photograph of it, enlarged and framed, on a wall somewhere. I know that wall: it's in my office at the university. *What university?* I see, like translucent ghosts, the blurry shadows and shapes of people who stop to admire it, and hear their muffled voices as though I'm listening to them from under water.

'It must be the Seychelles . . . '

'Nah, it has to be Thailand. When were you in Thailand?'

19

'Look at the luminosity of those colours — almost like a painting!'

'It's the Irish Sea off Howth, where I live.' That's my voice. I hear the note of pride even at this remove.

'You lucky thing.'

'Yes, I walk there most evenings. There's a great track that goes all around the headland.'

'Oh, wow. That's cool.'

'Yes, it's so invigorating . . . better than a week in a five-star hotel.'

'Wish I had that on my doorstep.'

'You can join me any evening.'

Laughter. The clip of heels. The sound receding. A door closing.

The image fades. I'm thrust back into the grip of the cold, hard, inky black nightmare. Soon I'll wake up in my bedroom, surrounded by my things.

My bedroom: ivory sheets, plump pillows, a deep pile chocolate-brown carpet that feels like marshmallow under my bare feet. A stand-alone dressing-table, with crystal atomisers of my favourite perfumes. A walk-in wardrobe in which all my clothes are neatly arranged. Draped gowns and tailored suits, figure-hugging jeans and casual tracksuits. Shelves of shoes, boots and high-heeled sandals. A multitude of bags and cases. The wardrobe of a busy person leading a full, active life.

I will slip out of bed and stand under the shower, then put on my cream towelling wrap. I will go into the kitchen for breakfast — on one wall, big patio doors look out to sea. On fine days you can fold them back and soak up the warmth. I will make porridge, then a poached egg on toast. The taste is almost in my mouth. I deserve it after this horrendous nightmare.

The image shatters as hard reality crashes into my head. Why can't I feel my legs?

Where are they? *My* legs.

It's not only my legs I can't feel, it's my arms. Why can't I feel them?

Voices float out across the cold air above my head. A dog barks and from the yipping sound it makes, the owner is dragging it along against its will. I hear the tinny clink-clink-clink of an empty can, as though it's bouncing off a series of rocky outcrops. It comes closer and closer until it clatters past within a few feet of me. I hear a splash. Then silence.

Perhaps it fell down the cliff face and landed in the sea.

Did that happen to me? Did I lose my footing and bounce down the cliff face to where I'm lying helpless now, staring up at the indigo sky?

It's not just a dream or a nightmare. It's going on too long. I should have woken up by now. I can't figure out how long I've been here, how I got here, what day it is, what time, how this happened, or how I'm going to get back up that cliff to my life . . .

Help will come. It *has* to. Someone must know I'm here.

What's the last thing I can remember? The *very* last thing?

4

In their four-bedroom red-brick period house, set in landscaped gardens on Belgrave Park, Matthew Moore strode ahead of Rose to the front door. 'I don't know how you managed to arrive home late tonight of all nights,' he flung over his shoulder. 'You know how important it is for me.'

She almost laughed at the way he had assumed she'd be following in his wake. Which, of course, she was. As she had done for most of their marriage. Rose had long ago accepted she hadn't a rebellious bone in her body. 'You've a lot more balls than I have,' she'd once said to Rebecca.

Rebecca had responded with a sympathetic look.

Matthew activated the security system, his fingers stabbing the wrong buttons so that he had to start again. 'Bloody hell, what's *wrong* with it?' he fumed.

Rose watched the grim set of his jaw and remained silent as he finally keyed in the correct code and she found herself propelled outside. Standing in the porch, as Matthew turned the key in the complicated lock, she glanced back through the leaded-glass panel into the hallway where she'd left on a lamp. Every instinct urged her to crawl back into the house, go straight up the stairs to bed and blank out the world with a sleeping pill. But there was no escape from the reception being hosted by the CEO of the American Ireland Youth Association on the eve of St Patrick's Day, so she followed him down the granite steps to the driveway.

She hated these functions. Matthew loved them. He revelled in the undercurrents of power and one-upmanship that ricocheted around such a gathering under the cover of bonhomie. They made her nervous and edgy. Especially tonight, with so much at stake.

She'd have to get used to these occasions, she told herself. There'd be a lot more high-level socialising and strategic shoulder-slapping in the coming weeks. Recently their lives had taken a surprising turn, the shock waves of which she was still struggling to absorb.

'Why are you so tetchy?' she said, as they took the flagstone path beside the drive to his car. 'The invite was eight for half past so we're okay. And,' she looked at him, 'I'm not the only one who arrived home late. You were so late you barely had time to jump into the shower. What kept you?'

'I had to go back to the office to finish a report,' Matthew said brusquely, as he opened the passenger door of the Mercedes. 'So, you see, I was working. I wasn't out dining and whining with the ladies who lunch. And neither will I be drinking tonight as I need a very clear head.'

Before she stepped into the car, she glanced up at him. The front garden, surrounded by mature trees and shrubs, was alive with night-time shadows. For a moment, framed in the wash of the garden lamplight, her husband seemed like a tall, dark stranger, and Rose shivered, despite the *faux*-fur stole she was wearing over her Helen McAlinden taffeta gown.

'You're very bold,' she said, her tone deliberately light. 'What you've just said wouldn't go down too well with the ladies in question. Never mind me.'

'Ah, Rose, sorry about that and thanks for your concern,' he said, in his warm, public voice, the one that had been labelled beguiling and charismatic. 'Don't worry your pretty little head — I can take care of the ladies. You just smile and look good.'

'I always do,' she said. She'd spent years perfecting the art of smiling and looking good, which, tonight, was a definite advantage.

She slid into the passenger seat and the door clunked shut.

'Off we go,' he said, looking suddenly youthful.

Rose was reminded of the young John F. Kennedy lookalike she'd first seen lugging a heavy schoolbag up the mean streets of Lower Ballymalin Gardens in another lifetime. The couple in the plush Mercedes purring through the tree-lined avenues in one of south Dublin's most exclusive neighbourhoods bore no resemblance to the young Rose and Matthew: they'd got together as teenagers on cobbled streets where small terraced houses had no gardens and pavements were narrow, where the lucky few found work in the nearby upmarket village of Howth. Matthew's parents had eked out a living on his father's disability pension, but his mother had decided her only child was bound for better things: she had taken on a cleaning job to pay for extra tuition over and above the basic education offered in the local vocational school. Quiet, anxious-to-please Rose was only too happy to hang around windy street corners listening to the boy with the dreams.

Sometimes the teenagers got together to spend summer Sundays on the beach at Howth, or took the bus to the summit to picnic and play spin-the-bottle on the grassy slopes. And while Rebecca played hard to get in her romance with Harry, Rose and Matthew had always been together, bound by his ambitions to take on the world.

When Matthew landed a job at the bank, justifying his parents' sacrifices and faith in him, he said it was only the beginning.

They married in their early twenties on a tiny budget, had a week's honeymoon in Donegal, then set up home in a little house on the edge of Dublin; the deposit had devoured most of their savings. It had been a dream come true for Rose: she couldn't quite believe Matthew loved her enough to *marry* her.

Sometimes she still found it hard to believe. Now, almost a lifetime later, she could hardly remember the wedding, or the small reception. She had James, their son, but the journey from penny-pinching suburbia to affluent Belgrave Park had been full of dark twists and turns.

Matthew had long left the bank behind him. By degrees, he had become a charming, confident and hugely successful businessman. With hard work and ruthless focus, he had confidently embraced the growing opportunities in new technology as Ireland had slowly emerged from the recession of the 1980s. He'd founded Tory Technologies in the early 1990s and the company was still showing a healthy profit in spite of the current recession, as was his portfolio of investments, wisely diversified to include commercial investment property in Switzerland, as well as vineyards in Spain and stud farms in Argentina.

Matthew had also scaled the social ladder and was quite at home in the corridors of power, thanks to his judicious networking, his courting of senior politicians, and his state agency membership. His profile had gone into orbit, and Rose wondered what he continued to see in her, his quiet, unassuming wife. Was he still happy with her . . . or were some of his needs being met elsewhere?

She'd been a stay-at-home wife and mother, keeping house and ironing shirts, going to cookery and flower arranging classes, and helping with community activities. When Matthew had insisted they get a part-time housekeeper on their move to Belgrave Park, and Mrs Barry had arrived, Rose had volunteered at the Children's Hospital.

Now, thanks to Matthew's drive and ambition, there were more rollercoaster rides to come: he was planning to campaign as an independent candidate in the forthcoming presidential election. The prospect filled Matthew with elation and Rose with alarm.

'So the campaign starts in earnest tonight,' Rose said.

'I've learned a lot from following last year's contest,' he replied, as the car halted at a pedestrian crossing. 'I'm a good candidate, and I've got the right men to advise me.'

The previous year Ireland had been plunged into a hotly fought contest, which resulted in the surprise election of David Doolin, a forty-something television broadcaster, whose Saturday-night show was a constant winner in the ratings war. A household name, he had swept to a landslide victory. A celebrity president, some had said. He hadn't lasted long: just as he was becoming disenchanted with presidential protocol, American television moguls had asked him to front a prime-time weekend show.

Suddenly a fresh election campaign was on the agenda, and Matthew was running as an independent. The last thing Rose wanted was the spotlight that a career in politics would shine on their lives. At first she'd thought it would blow over, that he didn't really mean it. But it had taken on a life of its own. She did her utmost to rein in her anxiety, to conceal it beneath the smiling mask she wore in front of everyone, even Rebecca.

'Besides, we've no skeletons in the cupboard,' Matthew said.

'Haven't we?' she said, her breath faltering in her throat.

Without hesitation, he met her eyes. 'No, we haven't,' he said firmly. His were clear and steady, warm with reassurance. Matthew's face was a little craggier with the passage of time and it suited him. Tonight he was wearing his navy Paul Smith coat over his suit with a careless ease that belied his humble origins; it set off his short, silvering hair attractively. 'Look, Rose, I want this opportunity more than anything else in the world. This is my ultimate dream.'

'I want you to have it but — '

'No buts.' He smiled. 'We can do it, us, together. Trust me.'

He looked the part, she thought, swallowing. He looked every inch the perfect candidate. He looked like someone you could trust with your life.

At least for the moment she could be sure Matthew wasn't having an affair, despite his late nights at the office, sudden trips abroad, and the mobile phone that was never out of his sight. He wouldn't risk it now, when he had so much to lose, would he?

They joined the stream of traffic surging around Ballsbridge, Rose feeling as though she was snagged in a swiftly moving current. She remembered the packet of pills concealed in her silk clutch. They'd saved her from many a bad moment, but no way could they blot out the feeling of impending doom clawing at her chest. In spite of their success, or maybe because of it, Rose lived with constant dread: the fear of being found out.

She also felt torn in two. While she wanted Matthew to have his dream, she wanted her life to stay as it was. Surely he had achieved more than enough already, she fretted, as they swept in

28

through the entrance of the Four Seasons Hotel, slightly late. How far did he need to go to prove himself to himself?

'Do you think Juliet might be here?' she asked, a little breathless, as she watched his face carefully.

There was a short, tense silence.

'I've no idea,' Matthew said. 'Did she tell you she was coming?'

'I thought she might have been invited,' Rose said. 'I thought all the presidential hopefuls were coming tonight and that it would be a sort of informal get-together . . . '

Matthew gave a short laugh. 'Ah, Rose, you're so funny. It'll be more like an ambush, with the opponents circling each other like gladiators in the arena. Some of my rivals will be here but my guess is Juliet will stay away because she'll want to avoid me.'

'Really?'

'I might have known she'd put her name in the hat once she heard I was interested in the race. I'm still trying to figure out if she's serious about running or just trying to rattle me.'

'And why would she do that?' Rose asked, her grip tightening on her clutch. She wondered if it had been the other way around. Had Matthew entered when he'd heard Juliet had been approached?

'She's always enjoyed challenging me,' Matthew said.

Surely he meant that *he* enjoyed challenging *her*, Rose thought, remembering some of their verbal spats.

A friendly but pointed rivalry had simmered between them, right from the time Juliet had joined their group of Ballymalin friends, changing the comfortable dynamic with her exotic air and sheen of privilege. At the time, Rose had been secretly relieved that her wedding was just weeks away, with no time for Juliet to pose any real threat. Still, Matthew had always been unable to disguise his envy of Juliet's privileged background, and their rivalry set Rose on edge. Tory Technologies had become involved in a charity programme only when Matthew had seen the plaudits Juliet was gathering for hers.

They paused in the line of cars waiting to disgorge their occupants. Up ahead, Rose saw doors opening and closing, designer-clad ladies and men in dress suits stepping out. The wealthy and privileged, with their ultra-perfect lives. Just as they would appear to the people in the queue behind them. She felt Matthew's gaze on her face.

'Juliet knows that I know she'd be a shoo-in,' he went on. 'With her profile, intelligence, and avant-garde, all wrapped up in a beautiful package, she's the one we'd all have to watch. And she ticks most of the boxes of her successful predecessors. Just think,' he laughed, 'we could be going head to head.'

Is that what he really thought of Juliet? A beautiful package? 'I don't think that's remotely funny. And,' she continued, her voice shaking, 'Juliet's hardly squeaky clean either.'

'Either?' Matthew shot her a glance. 'Relax, Rose. There's absolutely nothing to worry about where Juliet's concerned,' he said. 'Or me. It'll all be fine. I promise. Juliet's not going to upset any apple carts. She has too much to lose. Hey, here we go,' he said, excitement in his voice as he spotted the journalists and camera crew gathered outside the hotel entrance. 'And, darling,' he took his hand off the steering wheel long enough to squeeze her arm, 'you look wonderful. As beautiful as ever. I'm so proud of you, and I'm sorry if I was snappy earlier. My nerves got the better of me.'

The car door opened, and Rose put her knees together before she got out. She could almost hear Juliet's voice in her ear, talking about the perils of flashing her thighs or, worse, her knickers as she got out of a car. She stepped out on her diamanté heels and, although she felt like slinking quietly into a corner, she drew herself to her full height and smiled. There was a camera flash, then another. Matthew gave the car keys to the valet and took her arm, angling her towards the cameras and pausing briefly to allow for another couple of photographs.

It was starting. Matthew Moore was suddenly front-page news, and the idea chilled her to the bone. Life as they knew it would soon be turned on its head.

Oh, God, take this cup away.

5

A filament of memory detaches itself from the thick shadows in my head. 'I'll leave them until later,' I say, looking at the wine glasses on the counter.

Two empty glasses, red wine staining them. Surely it was this evening if I can see it so clearly. I'd had a visitor. Someone who knows where I am. Because if the glasses were on the counter, not even rinsed, they had just been used, and I had left the house in too much of a hurry to put them in the dishwasher.

'Let's get going before the light fades too much. Otherwise we could walk off the edge of the cliff . . . ' There is laughter in my voice as I pick up my key.

Everything else is a blank.

Nonetheless, relief floods through my head. Whoever I was with has gone to get help. Soon I'll be out of here and back in the familiar routine of my life. Okay, I've had some kind of accident. I missed my footing and tripped over the edge, perhaps where it was crumbling away. I wonder if I broke any limbs in my fall.

This will make a right mess of things. I haven't got time to be laid up with broken legs or fractured arms. Worst-case scenario, I might have injured my spine, and that's why I can't feel my

32

limbs. Right now I can't remember my name but I know, with a deep-felt certainty, that I'm a busy person with a packed diary.

I have a sudden image of the calendar pinned to the corkboard in the kitchen. It's a daily appointment calendar, specially designed for me, with personal photographs adorning each month, birthdays already printed in their respective boxes. Out of nowhere comes the knowledge that some-body gave it to me last Christmas.

'So you won't have to worry about forgetting your important dates, like my birthday, for instance.' I hear a girl laugh, as I unwrap the ruby foil while twinkling lights from a nearby Christmas tree glint on the shimmering paper.

Did I worry about forgetting? Who is the girl? I sense she means a lot to me.

'I know you put reminders into your phone,' she says, 'but this will show what's coming up in advance. Especially the wedding of the year.'

Wedding? Whose? I struggle to recall the details but they're elusive, and then to remember who was with me, drinking wine. I wonder how long I'll have to wait for help to come.

The breeze ruffles my hair — it'll be ruined. My *hair?* Why does it matter if it's ruined? Something tells me I had it done today. Or was it the day before?

Highlights and a trim. Make me gorgeous. Make me sexy. Out of nowhere memory flashes and I hear my careless laughter. I see myself staring into a brightly lit mirror, an enormous black gown swathing me, my face pale, white plastic parcels clinging to my head in carefully aligned tiers.

Suddenly I see his reflection sitting beside me, a greying-white wig curling around his head and falling to the gathers of his black gown. The judge, against whom no sin may be committed because . . . because . . .

Because he loves me so much.

He dissolves as someone moves in and peels off my black gown to reveal me sitting with my hands neatly folded, in a cherry-red shirt that sets off my hair. Funny, I'd expected to see myself with the jet-black urchin crop I'd worn for years. But the image I'm staring at is pale blonde tints washed with pink, which adds a touch of sexiness to my short, jazzy style.

'There you are, Juliet, all done.'

Juliet. My name. I clasp it to me as though the knowledge will make up for the cold of the stone at the back of my head and the absence of light, heat, shelter, arms and legs.

Juliet Jordan. Daughter of the late Mr Justice Henry Jordan.

Part of the fog blanking out swathes of my memory lifts away and pictures of my life are dancing in front of me, not linear, in date order, but rather like a film jerking from forward into rewind.

I stride along the cliff top. My hair is damp with sweat as I reach the finish line of a mini-marathon; I spring out of a limousine, dashing into a building to avoid the rain; I march down a grey tunnel to the interior of a plane — I'm pulling a small case, laughing at the tell-tale clink of my duty free. I feel water slide off my skin as I swim with a dolphin in the blue ocean. My eyes adjust to a blindingly white ski slope that rushes to meet me. I drive along a motorway with the top down on a sunny day, singing along with Rihanna.

I mount a wooden podium. Rows of upturned faces look at me with interest. There is an expectant hush. Who are these people? I must have something to say that interests them. As I speak, a ripple of laughter runs around the room and there is a burst of applause.

My arms shrug into red shirts and cashmere jumpers. They embrace friends. My hands light candles, arrange flowers, toss a cloud of flour into a mixing bowl, and raise a glass of wine to my lips; I have nimble fingers that fly across a keyboard, call up a friend on my mobile, switch on a microphone and angle it towards my mouth.

My mind races and I grasp at floating tendrils of my life. I see my home as though I'm looking through a mist. Verbena View. I've known it all my life and I especially love the kitchen. I would give everything I have to be there right now, warm, the scent of herbs mingling with that of the freshly baked scones on the cooling rack, and the view of Dublin Bay through the patio doors.

When I get home, I will never complain again of not having enough time for a decent holiday. I will quite happily spend the rest of my days there, for it is the most beautiful spot in the world. I will never complain about anything ever again. Or be short with Rose. Or not have enough time for Rebecca.

Rose and Rebecca? My surging thoughts halt

and backtrack . . . My friends. Rebecca more so than Rose, who was always a little wary of me, and still is on account of Matthew . . . Who's Matthew? The name makes me feel uneasy but I can't think who he is.

Suddenly I see Rose standing primly by the sewing box, as her sparrow-like, grey-haired grandmother pins up the hem of my mother's ivory ballgown in my parents' bedroom at Verbena View. She stares at me with solemn eyes that are too big for her thin, pale face. Now Rebecca sidles into the room. She has been in the kitchen, where the housekeeper has given her a glass of milk and some soda bread. Rebecca is younger, nearer to my age, seven, but bigger than me, and her hair is in tight plaits. It's the first time they've come to our home with Mrs O'Malley, the dressmaker my mother occasionally uses. Their shoes are a little worn and their clothes look like they've been washed too often, but they're spotlessly clean.

I smile at Rebecca, and my face freezes: I've just remembered that their parents died in a train crash and they are newly orphaned — my mother must have told me — and they are now living with their grandparents. I can't imagine how horrible it must be to lose both parents and it makes me feel all heavy inside.

My father comes in, his bulk and sheer vitality reassuring. He offers them a lift home but Mrs O'Malley shakes her head. When I watch them marching proudly down the garden path, and Rebecca puts her arm through Rose's, I wish I had a sister. Or a best friend who would put her arm through mine. I feel ashamed of my thoughts, because I have so much and I still want more. I turn away from the window and run into my father's study.

All these fractured glimpses of my life flash around me with lightning speed, yet so real that I want to reach out, catch one and bring it close so that I can somehow slot myself back in there. *Be there, in my life.*

How did I get here? Although some fragments of my life gleam crystal clear, others are smudged. I try to think back to earlier this evening and what might have happened to me.

Let's get going before the light fades too much. Otherwise we could walk off the edge of the cliff . . .

Something's floating at the back of my mind, just out of reach. I know it's significant but it slides away from me every time I try to fasten on it. It's something I said, words coming out of my mouth that shouldn't have. Was I goaded into saying them? Pushed into a corner where I dropped my habitual guard?

Pushed.

Pushed?

I thought I was already cold, but now an icicle of terror spears through my forehead. How come that word resonates with me? Was I pushed? Over the edge of the cliff? Or is my muddled mind playing tricks on me?

But how else did I get here? I'm usually careful, and I know the track around the top of the cliffs like I know the back of my hand. Could a sudden gust have caught me unawares? Am I imagining it or was there pressure on my shoulders? I have a fleeting recall of shock as I slewed off balance. Then I'm plummeting into empty space . . .

Noooo . . .

6

Feeling as though she was observing it from a distance, Rebecca smiled brightly as she circulated through the stylish gathering in the Blue Water salon, catching up with old friends and acquaintances of Harry, grateful that air kisses, compliments and chit-chat distracted her a little from the concerns that teemed in her head.

'Rebecca! You look amazing! It's lovely to see you.'

'Rebecca Ryan, it *is* you. We weren't sure you'd make it.'

'Neither was I,' she admitted.

Then Paul Johnson, Harry's friend. 'Thanks so much for coming, Rebecca. Let me introduce you to our son and his beautiful bride.'

The bride was indeed beautiful. Rebecca thought of Danielle, her broken dreams, and her heart squeezed. Still, she managed to put that to one side as she laughed and chatted and glided between people, glad that she'd dressed to the hilt in her curve-skimming, cobalt blue Louise Kennedy gown. The party, with the excited buzz, the beautiful people under the ornate ceiling and the cleverly diffuse lighting, was a perfect diversion.

Not all her worries were swept away. As she mingled and sipped wine, she kept wondering how Rose was getting on at her celebrity function. It would be a taste of what was to come, a challenge for the self-effacing Rose. Slavishly loyal to her husband, Rose would never admit, even to her sister, that she was unhappy with Matthew's plans.

And then there was Juliet, throwing the equivalent of a stick of gelignite into her life, whose fallout could affect them all. No wonder Rebecca had had cross words with her just the previous Sunday.

The best man asked for some hush as they were about to show a short montage compiled by the newly married couple, a collation of photographs and video clips, charting the milestones of their lives and accompanied by the music that had formed the background to their romance. Rebecca accepted a glass of champagne and sat with a group of Harry's friends, heedless of the images rolling across the screen, seeing instead the events of the previous Sunday.

★ ★ ★

It had all been so totally unexpected.

When Rebecca dropped into Verbena View, Juliet had greeted her with a hug. 'Rebecca, it's great to see you. I want to talk to you. In fact . . . ' Juliet hesitated ' . . . I was just about to go for my power walk if you want to join me? I've been glued to the computer all day, and I could do with some fresh air.'

'Sure, I could do with some of that myself,' Rebecca said. She'd often walked the cliffs with Juliet. 'And it's gorgeous out, like summer.

Shame you were cooped up all day.'

'Busy, busy.' Juliet smiled, then nipped to her bedroom. She came back moments later, her slight figure in a navy tracksuit, smiling as she ran her fingers through her hair. 'Just caught a glimpse of my hair in the mirror. God — I didn't know my roots were that bad! I'll have to squeeze in the hairdresser before next weekend.' She ducked into the closet and reappeared wearing a pink baseball cap. 'That's better. Now, where did I leave my key?'

'Here.' Rebecca grinned, picking it up off the hall table.

They took the track that looped up around the headland. The evening breeze was light and tangy, and in the calm hiatus between the busy day and the onset of evening, sea and sky blended into a grey-blue haze. As she looked out to the shimmering horizon, Rebecca drew a deep breath and felt as though she was walking on the edge of infinity.

'First,' Juliet said, 'how's Danielle?'

'So-so, I guess. I'm afraid to go near her, and she still won't talk to me about what went wrong.'

'Poor darling. I might pop over to visit her in Rome. Phone calls and emails aren't the same.'

'Whatever about me, I know she'd love to see you.'

'I'll tell her I need to replenish my wardrobe on the Via Condotti, so she doesn't think I'm playing agony aunt.'

'She'll see through that one straight away. She's always admired the way you fly the flag for our Irish designers.'

' 'Suppose. And how are you? Oh, hell, I forgot . . . '

'Forgot what?' Rebecca asked, instinct telling her just what Juliet was about to say.

'It would have been this coming weekend, the wedding, wouldn't it?'

A silence.

Juliet went on, 'God, I feel really bad about this, but I'm tied up for most of the weekend, so I won't be around much, in case you need a shoulder to lean on.'

'I'll be fine,' Rebecca insisted stoutly, even though she'd half expected Juliet to be around for her. However, Juliet was busy, she knew, and naturally she'd be in demand on the national holiday. 'I was only going to be mother-of-the-bride,' she said. 'It's Danielle who'll want to block it out.'

'Still, I wanted to be there for you, I know it'll be rough, but I need the whole of Friday to complete some urgent paperwork, even it if takes until midnight. I'll be working from home and locking myself away in the study. I have a lunch engagement on Paddy's Day plus a couple of evening receptions. And it's all in the course of duty. Hey, why don't you come along with me to the receptions? I'm going to drinks at the university, but I'll be sticking to water as I'm going on to a charity bash where I'm the keynote speaker.'

'No, thanks. I'd only be in the way,' Rebecca said. Sometimes she found it impossible not to feel a trace of jealousy at Juliet's rather glamorous life. She was always in demand, as vice chancellor of the Institute of Dublin University, and had a string of letters after her name, various fellowships and non-executive directorships. She was also the founder and patron of the Children's Dream Holiday charity.

'It would be great to have you along,' Juliet said. 'We could have a blast.'

'It's fine. I won't be in the mood to socialise next weekend.'

'Well, if you change your mind, just text me.'

They hadn't ventured much further along the headland when Rebecca said, 'You've heard about Matthew's latest quest?'

'The presidential race? No surprises there, given his boundless ambition.'

'It's Rose I'm worried about,' Rebecca admitted. 'She says she's happy for Matthew to follow his dream, but I don't think she'd be able to cope with the kind of intrusion it would bring. She'd never survive it. And God knows what would happen if the media started to sniff too deeply.'

Juliet said nothing, and Rebecca went on, 'The last time I was talking to her, she sounded so positive that I don't know if she was trying to pretend it wasn't happening or already acting the part and practising her lines. Oh, Juliet, I don't know why they can't just be happy with what they have. Rose fell apart before, remember? Now her peace of mind could be shattered.'

Juliet was unusually quiet and Rebecca sensed that she was turning something over in her mind.

Eventually she said, 'You might as well know — I'm surprised you haven't heard the rumours by now. Approaches have been made to me from one of our main political parties about going forward as a candidate and I'm seriously considering it.'

Taken by surprise, Rebecca blurted the first thing that popped into her head. 'You're joking. You're not trying to compete with Matthew, are you?'

A cloud of annoyance darkened Juliet's face. 'Of course not. It's an honour to be asked.'

'Even though you'd be pitched against Matthew? And the last election was nothing short of a mud-slinging bloodbath?' Rebecca said, consternation rising inside her.

'I've probably a few enemies lying in wait,' Juliet said. 'I've trodden on a few toes in my time. But I'll cope with that.'

'Jesus, you do realise the enormity of what you're taking on? Have you thought this through? I'm sure you'd be brilliant in the role, but don't you think . . . God, it's bad enough that the media will be hounding Matthew and Rose, but you too? Everything you've ever done will go under the microscope.'

They strode on around the track. Down below, jagged cliffs plummeted to a silky grey sea and cawing gulls wheeled lazily on the thermals.

'Maybe that doesn't bother me too much,' Juliet said tightly. 'Maybe it's time a few things were out in the open.'

'I can't believe I'm hearing this.' Rebecca was weak with dismay. 'You can't mean that. Especially after all this time. You have a fabulous life with everything going for you. I don't

44

understand why you can't just leave things the way they are, any more than Matthew and Rose. You really can't afford to have your private life hung out to dry. God only knows what would come crawling out of the woodwork.'

'Maybe I'm willing to take my chances,' Juliet said. 'See what Fate has in store . . . '

'This is madness.' Rebecca's mind spiralled back to the time, years ago, when Juliet's world had collapsed. Rebecca had been instrumental in putting the pieces back together. It was something they never spoke about, as though it had never happened.

'Thing is, Rebecca, you don't know what it's been like to live with the deceit all these years,' Juliet said. 'It's niggled at me for a long time, but lately I've started to wake up at four in the morning, wondering if I could quietly atone for it in some way. Sometimes I wonder how on earth I could have done what I did . . . and how I could have covered it up.'

'You did it with my help, remember,' Rebecca said. 'I aided and abetted you, so to speak. Are you regretting that now?'

'Hey, no.' Juliet put a hand on her arm. 'Your support was invaluable. Any regrets are mine. You did nothing wrong. I'm the one with the stain on my conscience and the sore heart. And it's troubling me so much that maybe I'd like to have it in the open.'

'And maybe wreck your life, never mind others'?' Rebecca said.

Juliet was unusually quiet as they turned down from the summit and headed towards Verbena

View, which told Rebecca how deeply she was thinking.

'Look,' Juliet said, reaching the bungalow, 'it's probably best if you stay out of it.'

Rebecca felt stung. Danielle's refusal to talk had been a hurtful snub that lingered. Now Juliet, her best friend, was talking about pulling the pin on a hand grenade.

'How can I stay out of it? I was involved. I was there with you, all the way. Are you sorry about that now?'

What stunned Rebecca even more was the small, tight smile Juliet gave her as she said, 'Involved? My dear Rebecca, it's probably just as well you knew only half the story.'

What the hell did Juliet mean? 'Well, that puts me in my place,' Rebecca huffed, reeling with disbelief at her friend's words.

'Hey, look, I'm sorry,' Juliet said. 'I didn't mean to be short with you. I'm not myself at the minute. Too many sleepless nights.'

'Well, I'm not myself either after hearing that,' Rebecca said. 'I can't believe you're so heedless to the Pandora's box you might be opening, never mind putting yourself on a collision course with Matthew — and Rose. It's going to be great fun keeping the peace between you.'

'Then, all things considered, it's really best if you stay out of it.'

When they got back to Verbena View, Rebecca declined her friend's offer of coffee and left, barely saying goodbye, her hands shaking as she fumbled with the ignition key and accelerated out of the driveway.

Someone topped up her glass and she looked at the final scenes of the newly wed couple's photo montage. Then the lights were dimmed and the band came on. She watched the happy couple circle the floor to 'Flying Without Wings', and couldn't help recalling the Christmas table at Verbena View when James had teased Danielle and Conor about their first dance as a married couple. Life had been almost perfect. Suddenly she needed a break from the merry-making. She'd go back to her room for a while.

She left the first-floor salon, and when she reached the top of the staircase, she glanced down towards the foyer, and was flustered to see a tall man going into the bar. Liam Corrigan. Obviously back in Dublin.

He was an old-friend-turned-foe of Juliet's, someone whose toes she had totally flattened. Rebecca hadn't noticed him in the crowded reception room, but he might be there for the wedding. Liam had grown up in a modest cottage near the harbour in Howth, and had cycled to Lower Ballymalin vocational school. He'd hung around the edges of the group of friends from the Gardens, often playing football with Harry and the other lads. He'd known Juliet, too, and Rebecca had bumped into him at Verbena View over the years.

Then, during the boom time, when his construction business had taken off, he'd transformed his life, becoming one of Dublin's most flamboyant developers. Long separated from his American wife, he'd begun to live an extravagant lifestyle that gave the gossip journalists palpitations as they filed last-minute copy recounting his exploits.

Occasionally Juliet and Rebecca had been invited to champagne-fuelled parties at his County Dublin estate, just a couple of miles north of the Sea-grass Hotel. Rebecca knew about the chauffeured Bentley that had whisked him in and out of the city, and the private jet that took his inner circle to his south of France villa. Then it had all imploded and he had fled Ireland four years ago when Corrigan Holdings had gone bust, leaving his life in tatters.

And partly on account of Juliet.

7

My face feels stiff. I can't remember how it feels to be warm. The darkness is like oily black soup. The stillness is broken by the murmuring sea, and some kind of raging noise in my head. When will help arrive?

How long have I been like this? How did I end up here, like a trashed rag doll, with just the moon and the stars gleaming above me, the sheer side of the cliff looming beside me, with the murmuring sea for company. Surely my friends will notice I'm missing.

Rose and Rebecca. Rebecca and Rose.

They slide through my head, Rebecca laughing, Rose more reserved. Sometimes, if it's not a school day, they come to Verbena View with their grandmother. My mother is petite, and the hems of almost all her gowns need to be altered. Eventually the girls stop coming, and when I ask Mrs O'Malley why, she says they're at home as they're big enough to mind themselves.

Then Mrs O'Malley stops coming. My mother tells me she has passed away.

Yet Rebecca and Rose still drift on the side-lines of my life. I see them on the beach at Howth, teenagers now, with a big group of friends, too busy playing tennis or beach football to notice me walking with my father. Until Rebecca turns

49

her head and, across the distance, I see recognition, then the flash of her smile.

They pile off the bus, jostling their way towards the summit of Howth Head as I cruise by in my father's car. They're laughing and joking far too much to notice me. A couple of the guys are tall and attractive, and I can't help feeling envious of their camaraderie, but our lives are so dissimilar there may as well be a six-foot wall between us.

Rebecca and Rose might have stayed for ever on the sidelines of my early years. And everything would have been so different. But, as my grandmother said, life can turn on a sixpence.

My beloved Granny Jordan, with her baby-soft skin, lavender powder, and smiling brown eyes in her creased face, my father alarming me as he cried at her funeral: he told me later it had been the worst moment of his life.

Now I know exactly what Granny Jordan meant.

Pure chance has shaped a lot of my life. One seemingly inconsequential moment can lead you down a certain path and, before you know it, you've drifted off your track and ended up in a place you'd never imagined you'd be.

Like me, here, now . . .

Who was with me? *Was* someone with me? Did he or she join me on my walk round the cliff? All I can recall is a feeling of menace . . . my arms flapping uselessly, my body free-falling backwards, as if in slow motion . . . a scream forming but never voiced . . .

Menace? I'm surely imagining it. I've spent

too much time lying here waiting for help and I'm going crazy. And yet . . . there is something dark at the corner of my mind. But it slips away before I can grasp it.

Think, Juliet. *Think.* Who'd want me out of the way?

I see the empty wine glasses in my kitchen and —

It's possible no one has gone for help. Whoever shared my wine might have come with me for my usual evening stroll and witnessed my fall. Or even made it happen. Helpless rage bubbles at the back of my throat. Could I really be that much of a threat to anyone?

Oh, God.

I wonder if I'll be saved from an appalling fate. Anything else is unthinkable. I know, instinctively, that I've too much to sort out in my life . . . and left important things unsaid.

Help. Help. I hear the scream building, louder and louder, until my head is fit to burst, but nothing comes out of my mouth.

8

'Rose! How are you? If you don't mind me saying, you look a little frazzled around the gills. What's up?'

'I'm fine, Liz, couldn't be better! A lovely gathering, isn't it?' Rose's face felt stiff with the effort of smiling as she moved through the chattering throng only to come face to face with the one woman she'd been desperate to avoid.

But there was no escape.

Liz Monaghan detached herself from the group she'd been with and swooped on Rose, drawing her in to kiss the air near her cheeks. She stood back and Rose saw her feline eyes flick over her as the younger woman swiftly appraised her, taking in everything about her from her carefully styled dark hair to her diamanté shoes. She felt as though she'd been flayed with the thinnest scalpel.

A former model, Liz was originally from Ballymalin, but the choice, semi-detached houses on Upper Ballymalin Grove, where her doctor father had lived and practised, had been a world away from Granddad Paddy's humble abode tucked in the maze of Lower Ballymalin Gardens. Liz was in her late thirties, with a failed marriage behind her, and was now a gossip columnist renowned for her sharp tongue and outrageous comments. Her weekend diary page struck delight, fear or disappointment into the hearts of Dublin's socialites.

'Lovely?' Liz's laughter pealed. 'Only you would come out with something polite like that, Rose! I think it's a minefield.' Her voice lowered conspiratorially. 'Tons of juicy material for next week's column. Can't you sense the hostilities? Can't you smell the battle for power? I can practically see the drawn knives. Intoxicating. I love it! *Love* it.'

Rose backed away. Liz was almost feverish in her glee. Her eyes glittered with an expression that made Rose fear for anyone who got in her way.

'I can't believe we're in the thick of another pre-election skirmish,' Liz went on. 'It's the most fantastic fodder. Some of the sitting ducks are even here tonight, poor innocents!'

'Really?' Rose wondered if the woman slotted her into that category.

'Yes, I've already spotted Des Thornton, the former MEP, and Senator Colin Redmond, both pressing as much flesh as they can. And where is your eminent husband? He may be a little outside the political fold at the minute but that won't last.' Her sparkling eyes scanned the throng with a laser-like focus.

'Oh, he's around somewhere,' Rose said, waving her hand dismissively.

The room was so hot and crowded, so full of bright, shiny people, dressed to impress, that it hurt her head. Disoriented, she knew she had had too many glasses of champagne, despite her best intentions, but the silver trays revolved around her far too often for her shaky willpower.

Still, it was time to call a halt. God knew who had been counting the number of drinks she had had. She was grateful for the cache of tranquillisers in her bag: when she felt the urge to blank out her jangled nerves and detach from everything, she could disappear into the Ladies and swallow a couple.

As soon as they had set foot in the ballroom, Matthew had been whisked away by some of his cohorts. He had glanced back at her with a satisfied smile, as though to say, 'I can't help it if I'm in demand. Look happy for me, please.'

She had tried. She had drifted from group to group, wearing a forced smile, not getting drawn into any conversation until Liz had snagged her attention.

'I was sorry to hear about your father,' Rose said, relieved to have stumbled on a different topic. 'I saw the piece you wrote about him. Please accept both Matthew's and my condolences.' Liz's father had died just after Christmas, having spent his final years in a nursing home after a severe stroke had robbed him of speech and left him confined to bed.

Liz's eyes were suddenly blank. 'It was a release,' she said. 'In reality he went a long time ago. It was painful to have to visit him in that nursing home. I'm glad it's over.'

'I'd say it was difficult all right,' Rose said.

'I was in Ballymalin for the funeral services,' Liz went on, her attention once more focused on Rose. 'It was strange being back in the family home. Dad's surgery was cleared out years ago, when he retired, but the house needs to be

54

emptied before I put it on the market. I'd no idea there was so much clutter and lots of . . . ' She paused, staring into space.

'Lots of what?' Rose prompted.

'Memories,' Liz said.

Rose shivered at the stony look in her eyes. 'So you're not going to hang on to it as a second home?' She could have bitten her tongue when Liz gave her a wintry smile.

'Mine wasn't exactly a happy home,' she said. 'The memories are tarnished and rather painful. I want to be shot of it. The sooner the better.'

Rose recalled that Liz's mother had been an alcoholic and had taken her own life many years ago. It had been rumoured at the time that the then teenage Liz had found her. Her father's death had no doubt brought it all back, making the last couple of months very difficult for her, especially as she had been an only child, coming along after her parents had almost given up hope.

'Anyway, it looks like both you and Matthew are set for the big time!' Liz said, back to her normal self, her eyes flashing with naked curiosity. 'I've been following all the coverage. You could be Ireland's next First Lady. If you play your cards right, of course.'

'I'm not so sure about that. There's still a long road to go.'

Liz studied her so keenly that Rose felt like the proverbial rabbit caught in the headlights. 'And an even longer road behind you,' she said, 'if some of Matthew's more, ah . . . ambitious business ventures are to be believed. I can't wait to sit him down and have a decent in-depth interview with him. I'm keen to prove myself as a bona-fide journalist, not just a social diarist. I'm sure he'd be glad of the exposure. But do you have doubts about your husband's ability to succeed?' She had slotted in the leading question so expertly that Rose was caught off guard.

She felt herself flush. This was what she hated and feared: feeling flummoxed and anxious, having to watch every word that came out of her mouth, especially in front of someone she was no match for, like pit-bull terrier Liz, who was on top form tonight.

'I never said that,' she protested. 'You know yourself it's still early days and there are a lot of hoops to jump through. Even the best-placed person has to be careful of snakes in the long grass.'

'I hope you don't mean me,' Liz laughed. 'I presume you're talking about Juliet Jordan.'

'Juliet?' Rose looked suitably wide-eyed, she hoped.

Liz raised supercilious eyebrows. 'Didn't you hear she's been approached to stand by one of our main political parties? It's the latest gossip to hit the wires. And if anyone could give his male hotness, ahem, Matthew, a run for his money, it's Juliet. They both have connections in the right places and their Photoshopped posters would look equally attractive, hanging side by side on the lampposts of Ireland. Ah . . . ' her eyes roved over the top of Rose's head and halted, as if fastening on her next target ' . . . I see someone arriving that I want to talk to. But

56

you've no worries, Rose.' Her thin hand clutched Rose's arm, and Rose just about prevented herself from flinching. 'If it comes to pistols at dawn, or domination of the great live televised debate, I'm on your side. And I'd never be able to dig any skeletons out of your cupboard. After all, we both hail from the same little village in Dublin. So if you'd anything at all to hide, I'd have found out by now, wouldn't I?'

Rose felt faint and tried to move her rubbery mouth into the semblance of a smile while Liz studied her with hawk eyes and grinned, showing big white teeth that suddenly resembled fangs. Then she was gone, slithering through the crowd, the feel of her claw-like grip lingering on Rose's forearm.

9

Friday, 16 March, 9.00 p.m.

I'm so cold now that the inside of my head feels totally frozen. Even my terror is contained inside a solid block of ice. It's a terror like I've never known before, mixed with alarm and outrage and incredible fury, but it seems disconnected from me somehow, as though that side of my brain has become numb with overload. Or profound shock.

I stare into the dark abyss of the horror I'm in, while significant fragments of my life are stirred up around me, etched against the moon, the stars and the backdrop of the cliff.

22 May 1971
I'm making my way along the swaying railway carriage, gripping the top of a seat for balance as the floor shifts beneath me, and the Belfast to Dublin train rattles across the grey, glinting ripple of the Malahide estuary en route to Amiens Street station. Aged eighteen and I think I know it all.

I almost pass the two girls. They are undeniably sisters, with light brown wavy hair and darkly lashed blue-green eyes, but I pause and give them a second glance, and in that moment my life swerves direction, like a train rattling over points to a different track and destination.

'Hey, Rose and Rebecca? It *is* you, isn't it?'

Startled, they look up at me. They're grown-up now. Rose has a fine-boned face. She is neat and prim and beautiful. At first her eyes are suspicious, as if nervous of my intrusion.

Then Rebecca, taller and broader, slightly more relaxed, recognises me and smiles. 'Juliet! I don't believe it! We haven't seen you in years!'

'I've seen you on and off,' I tell her, 'hanging around Howth with your friends.'

The seat opposite them is empty so I slide into it. Over a few minutes we catch up with our lives. Rebecca is eighteen now, the same age as me, but whereas I'm just coming to the end of my first year at university as a law student, Rebecca has almost a year's work under her belt in the typing pool of an insurance company. Rose is a clerical assistant in the Civil Service.

'I was sorry to hear about your grandmother,' I say.

Their faces cloud.

'We're still living in Lower Ballymalin with Granddad Paddy,' Rebecca says. 'Although Rose won't be there for much longer.' She grins.

'Rose?' I prompt.

Rose finally smiles at me and extends her left hand. 'Yes, I'm engaged to be married. The wedding is at the end of July.'

I admire her ring. 'Congratulations. Anyone I know?'

'I hope not,' Rebecca jokes. 'Rose and Matthew were childhood sweethearts.'

'Matthew?'

59

'Matthew Moore. I'll soon be Mrs Rose Moore.'

I wonder why she's so keen to lose her identity, but now is not the time to debate it with her.

'We've been in Belfast, shopping for the day,' Rebecca says, with enthusiasm. 'Rose picked up a lovely going-away suit and we both got some summer outfits.' Her eyes twinkle. 'Mind you, we're wearing half the clothes under our coats to get through Customs.'

They do look a bit puffy under their belted raincoats.

'So you're not part of the movement?' I ask.

'What movement?' Rose looks at me cagily.

'The women's movement.'

Rose sniffs and twists her ring around her finger. 'Don't remind me about those women's libbers. Taking over almost two carriages. Passing out leaflets and God only knows what. We don't want to get mixed up in all that stuff, isn't that right, Rebecca?' She gives her sister a meaningful stare.

But interest flashes across Rebecca's face. She realises I may belong to the group her sister has disparaged. I wink at her, and Rebecca's face breaks into a wide grin, showing her dimples. The smile reaches her eyes, making them appear bigger and brighter.

'I dunno,' Rebecca says. 'It all depends.'

'Rebecca!'

She makes a face at her sister. 'No need to be so square. I'm not about to pull my bra off and start burning it, but they have some good things to say. Like equal pay for starters. I'd like some of that.'

'Thing is, I have a bit of a problem,' I admit. 'When we reach Amiens Street station, I need to — ah — borrow your scarf,' I tell Rose.

Rose flushes and fingers the grey scarf knotted loosely around her neck. 'My *scarf*? What for?'

'I'm not supposed to be on this train,' I tell them, with a laugh. 'I've done my best to dodge the photographers and reporters in the carriages, that was a bit of fun, but it'll be difficult to smuggle myself through the exit barriers at Amiens Street, never mind going through Customs, without running the risk of being caught on the television cameras. If I could borrow your scarf it would hide my face.'

'Oh, gosh, why do you need to hide it?' Rebecca leans across the table, alive with curiosity.

'What have you done wrong?' Rose interrupts.

'I haven't done anything wrong. I've bought some condoms but, as far as I'm concerned, I was well within my rights to do so.'

Rose draws back.

Rebecca's eyes are shining with a mixture of excitement and adoration. 'You mean you're really one of *them*? And you went up to Belfast to buy condoms today?'

'We're not a different species. A lot of the women sitting in the carriage back there are ordinary students, wives and mothers, shop assistants and typists. Unfortunately, thanks to the ridiculous laws in this country, we're treated like second-class citizens.'

'I wish I had your nerve!' Rebecca says. 'Have you got them there? Can I see one?'

'Rebecca!' Rose says. 'I can't believe I'm hearing this.'

'Why not?' Rebecca rounds on her sister. 'Don't be so stuffy. Have you never seen one before?'

Rose's cheeks are pink. 'Don't tell me you have!'

'Hey, girls,' I put in, before a row breaks out. 'Sorry to say I'm not that brave. I daren't arrive at the station with my stash or be caught with it coming through.'

'You scarcely want us to help you out there,' Rose says stiffly. 'I'm not putting my finger on one.'

'They're not for your finger.' Rebecca giggles. There is a gleam of mischief in her eyes as she says to me, 'I don't mind smuggling some through for you. I'll put them down my bra. How many would I fit?'

'I wish I'd known that,' I laugh with her. 'But I've got rid of them already. Whatever I picked up in Belfast I dumped in the bin in the toilets.'

'You didn't!'

'Look, don't get me wrong. I really believe in the movement. It's so important to shift this backward country out of the dark ages. We women have been downtrodden for far too long, and it's crazy what's going on, but I shouldn't be on this train.'

'Why not?' Rose asks. 'And why didn't you just ask one of your feminist friends to take your . . . '

'Condoms,' Rebecca prompts.

Rose grimaces.

'They're not really my friends, and they don't

know that I tagged along with them today. It was my private rebellion.'

There is a silence.

I tell them. 'If I was arrested under the Criminal Justice Act of 1935, which, in case you didn't know, forbids the import or sale of contraceptives, my life wouldn't be worth living, because my father would go nuts if he found out I was on this train, let alone in contact with some condoms. It was hard to dodge the reporters on the train, but there'll be television cameras at the station and I can't be seen. No way. My father's a judge, you see. So I'd really be in trouble.'

'That's different. Why didn't you tell us that in the first place?' Rose says, taking off her scarf and handing it straight to me.

When we get off the train the station platform is bedlam. Customs officers are out in force. Behind them, a phalanx of placard-waving sup-porters waits for the members of the Irish Women's Liberation Movement to come through. Railway officials are doing their best to block the televi-sion cameras by holding up big boards in front of them.

But the Customs men are no match for the large procession of victorious women who surge down the platform, brazenly shaking their contra-band. Condoms, packets of pills and spermicidal jelly are scattered across the ground and hurled over the heads of the officers to the waiting supporters. I find the euphoria contagious, espe-cially when I realise that the Customs people know it's going to be impossible to arrest all the militant women. And the packets of pills are ordinary aspirin, as it was impossible to get a contraceptive pill without a doctor's prescription, something the movement hadn't factored in. They eventually give up their searches and stand back to allow everyone through. Some of the more rebellious women inflate their condoms and bounce them like balloons.

Rose averts her eyes.

I want to give her a shake and tell her that these courageous women are breaking tightly controlled boundaries imposed by the Catholic Church and our male-dominated society. In years to come she'll thank them for having the guts to act on their beliefs and break through the ridiculous restrictions imposed on women. But the words stick in my chest. I feel ashamed of myself, slinking through the barrier on the coat-tails of those women instead of alongside them, hiding between Rose and Rebecca, with Rose's grey scarf swathing my cropped black hair and half covering my face.

We stand at the top of Talbot Street, unsure what to do next, and a little at a loss after the adrenalin of our march through Customs.

'Will we go for a drink?' I suggest. 'I want to thank you for getting me out of a tight spot.'

'A *drink?* I'm going home,' Rose says, clutching her shopping bags like a shield, ready to flee from any threat I may pose.

'There's no rush. You're not seeing Matthew this evening, are you?' Rebecca says.

'No, but I'd rather go home.'

'Right so. I'll go for a drink with Juliet and catch a later bus,' Rebecca says.

Rose's surprise at her sister's defection flits across her face as she weighs up leaving her to the mercy of my influence against her desire to go home. Then she says, a little grudgingly, 'Well, okay, just one.'

I'm tempted to order three pints of beer, knowing we'll be refused by the barman, but I don't want to scare away Rebecca or Rose. So, over a glass of Harp for me and Rebecca, Britvic orange for Rose, and a round of toasted-cheese sandwiches in a pub on Abbey Street, I hear all about Rose's forthcoming wedding and her fiancé. Matthew is a junior bank clerk. I might have guessed her job and her fiancé would be ultra-conservative, safe and predictable. She looks uneasily round the pub, as though someone is going to pounce on her. But, given her childhood, I don't need to look too far to see why Rose is the responsible, cautious one.

A local dressmaker is making her dress, Rebecca will be her bridesmaid, and they'll have fifty guests in total. After the wedding reception, they'll spend their first night in a Dublin hotel before catching the morning bus to Donegal.

'I wish you all the best,' I say, 'but don't you think it's unfair that you'll have to leave your job as soon as you get married?'

'No. I love Matthew and I'll enjoy making a home for him.' Rose jumps to her own defence.

'That's great if you're happy,' I say, 'but I think it's wrong that clever women are expected to give up their careers as soon as there's a wedding band on their finger. What will you do all day? Polish the brasses? Wipe specks of dust off the gleaming crystal? Iron his Y-fronts?'

Rose flushes. 'We're hoping to get the key of our new house at the end of next month, so I'll be busy with making a home for us, and we'll be starting a family soon.'

Her life is all mapped out. Safe. No surprises.

'Still, housework has its limits,' I say. 'I'd be bored out of my tree polishing and cleaning.'

'Is that why you joined the women's lib movement?' Rebecca asks.

I have to laugh. 'I'm not actually a paid-up member, much as I'd love to be. It's hard to believe how unfairly women are treated in this country. We're second-class citizens, in a country where power is held by men and the Catholic Church. So it's men all the way. And they make the rules to suit themselves . . . '

Rebecca is clearly intrigued. Even Rose is beginning to look at me with a glimmer of respect, as though I'm finally making some sense. By the time we part on the corner of Abbey Street, Rebecca has invited me to join her group of friends for drinks the following weekend and, just like that, the six-foot wall between us has fallen down and I have stepped through the gap.

10

After she moved away from Rose, Liz sidled through the crowd as best she could on her vertiginous heels. The room was too hot. When she reached the bar at the back, she sank gratefully on to a stool.

'A double vodka, please, no ice, and just a splash of soda water,' she ordered. When her drink was passed to her, she sipped it greedily.

There had been no one arriving that she'd wanted to talk to and there was no one whom she was remotely interested in right now, for all her talk to Rose.

She sipped her drink and pretended to be engrossed in her mobile, staring fixedly at her old text messages. She shouldn't have come tonight. Not after the rotten few days she'd just endured, between pacing around the empty rooms in Ballymalin, with ghosts for company, and picking through the sad debris of her parents' lives.

Then there had been the shocking documents hidden in an envelope at the back of a sideboard. No wonder she felt so cut adrift from reality. The room spun again, even though she was sitting down. She tried to take a few deep breaths, then ordered another double vodka, which she drank far too quickly. Thankfully, there was no one to lecture her if she got home pissed. Which also meant there was no one to care. She could do pretty much what she liked now that Gavin, her ex-husband, was out of her hair.

Their marriage had lasted barely a year, and had been a mistake from the very beginning. The give and take involved in marriage wasn't for her, a lesson she had learned the hard way, after many rows over silly things. It was a pattern she'd recognised, emerging from the legacy of her parents' unhappy union. She would be forty next year and more than likely still unattached, which meant she would probably never have children. And surely that was for the best.

Nonetheless, Gavin had been a great support at her father's funeral, and he'd phoned her several times afterwards, even offering to help her clear the house. She had been too caught up in herself to figure out whether he was being genuine or scenting money. Not that the sale of the house would fetch anything like it would have done a few years ago. Mind you, she'd been tempted to accept his unspoken offer to go to bed with him, and take her mind off everything. One of her colleagues swore by sex with her ex. Guilt-free, uncomplicated sex. And Gavin had seemed to be offering it on a plate. For a moment she weighed her mobile in her hand and flicked to her contacts. A quick call was all it would take. She sighed and ordered another drink instead.

After a while she felt numb enough to forget about the trauma of the last few days and the envelope she'd found. Instead she focused on Rose and the look in her eyes when she'd mentioned skeletons in the cupboard. It had been a throwaway, meaningless remark, directed to the most mousy, deferential person she knew, but it had found an unexpected target. Liz had recognised that look. It had told her that, for all her demure, ladylike airs and graces, Rose Moore was afraid of something.

Liz felt a kick of excitement in her gut as her mouth curved in a smile.

11

22 May 1971

That night, in the sitting room of the family home, Verbena View, the judge stands up and marches across to the black and white television set, snapping it off midway through the programme.

'There. I don't know what's happening to this country. Teilifís Éireann is an absolute disgrace. How can they give those immoral women any kind of air time? Before we know it they'll be demanding divorce. *Divorce!* Can you imagine it, Kitty? This country has gone to the dogs.'

Mr Justice Henry Jordan is so incensed that minuscule flecks of spray shoot from his mouth. The Saturday-evening talk show has raised the thorny subject of what is already being labelled the 'contraceptive train'. Some of the women from the train are in the audience, and naturally the judge has objected. I can see a pulse beating at the side of his face.

I meet my mother's eyes across the room, as if searching for some feminine complicity, but none is forthcoming. I think she would have preferred me to be pink-cheeked and blonde, soft and compliant, rather than awkward around the edges with unruly black hair. As though she senses the rebellious ideas boiling beneath my calm surface, she deliberately looks away and picks up her embroidery ring.

Mr Justice Henry Jordan is a tall, well-built man with a heightened complexion, a man's man, as they say, fond of his evening whiskey, the undisputed king of his home and hearth. My mother flutters obediently behind the immense bulk of his powerful persona. I sometimes wonder if she minds her own life being submerged, sacrificed and meaningless, in the shadow of his. Sometimes I see her looking at my father in admiration and helpless wonder, as though she's trying to figure out how a lowly shop girl from Mullingar landed such a magnificent specimen. Apart from visits to her sister in Dun Laoghaire, attending morning mass and the ladies' sodality in the local church, helping with the garden fête and fundraising cake sales, my mother doesn't socialise without him. An occasional Babycham at Christmas is as far as her alcohol indulgence goes.

I have sucked mints all the way home on the bus to disguise the smell of my breath. Because, for all his intransigence, and a sternness that borders on forbidding, Mr Justice Henry Jordan has an Achilles heel: his eldest child. Me.

My father loved me. Loves me. Will always love me. I could describe it by the way he looks at me, talks to me and moves around me, as though I'm a priceless gift. It is painted across his face, in the way his gaze immediately alights on me when I come into the kitchen in the mornings. As though I'm the most beautiful princess in the whole world, rather than the

71

spiky ugly sister, the only daughter ever to grace the face of this earth.

Sometimes my younger brother Robert doesn't get a look in.

Problem is, I know my father would be hugely disappointed with many of the ideas floating around in my head. Bold and dangerous ideas that would anger and shock him.

For somewhere deep inside me a different Juliet is struggling to get out. A Juliet who feels that the sky is the limit, that she is equal to any man, marriage should be on equal terms, and that a woman should be allowed access to contraception *and* divorce. The last thing I want to see is disappointment clouding my father's face and dulling the beam in his eyes as he gazes at me. Or my mother unhappy in the face of his upset. But how long can you try to be a person you're not in order to keep your parents happy?

He thinks I've spent today in the college library, poring over my books. My father has absolute trust in me. He'd never believe that I'd travelled to Belfast on the infamous contraceptive train, let alone purchased some condoms.

So is it any wonder that I find myself sitting on the edge of my seat, my heart thumping in case I look guilty?

'I'm sorry you had to hear that trash, Juliet,' my father says, as he splashes whiskey into a crystal tumbler from the decanter on the sideboard. 'I'd no idea it was going to be broadcast into the homes of Catholic Ireland. This is a new low. Decent, God-fearing people shouldn't be subject to such rubbish. It's sacrilege. Your mother

72

and I are so thankful that you have the sense to ignore all that wickedness. Isn't that right, Kitty?'

From across the room my mother sends me a tight smile.

★   ★   ★

The following weekend, I meet Rebecca in town. I can't believe how much this means to me, as I don't have many friends. I was top of the class consistently, then gained a scholarship to university, which didn't endear me to my schoolmates. And I'm still finding my feet in college, trying to strike a balance between my studies and the exciting talks and rallies that are constantly happening around the campus, nervous of taking too much interest in case word gets back to my father. But there's something genuine about Rebecca that warms me and I feel as though I've been invited to join a magic circle.

Tonight we're meeting Rose and Matthew for a meal in the grill bar beside the Gresham Hotel before going on for drinks.

I recognise Matthew immediately as one of the tall, attractive guys I've seen with Rose and Rebecca's group of friends. But we don't get off to the best of starts.

'So this is the famous, or should I say infamous, crusading Juliet!' Matthew stands up as Rebecca and I approach the table. 'I hear you're responsible for inciting all sorts of rebellious ideas in my wife-to-be.'

I'm tempted to respond with a smart

comment about our male-dominated society but manners prevail. 'I'm pleased to meet you, too, Matthew,' I say, feeling I've somehow scored a point by not rising to his bait.

He gives me a puzzled, head-to-toe sweep, as though he's trying to figure out why Rose and Rebecca have befriended a rather ordinary-looking, average-height girl, with short black hair and mischievous ideas. Up close, he's even better-looking, and I can see why Rose is staring at him with adoring eyes. Her knight in shining armour, who will whisk her out of the boring, dusty office to a new life. A new life where she will have the luxury of a Formica kitchen, a plumbed-in washing-machine and back-boiler central heating, where they will be able to have legitimate sex and he can demand his conjugal rights at any time, thanks to a ring on her finger. He wears, like a suit, the pride his parents wrapped around him when he'd landed the fabulous, permanent and pensionable bank job. He has the eager, slightly cocky air of someone who fully expects to go all the way to the top, and I sense straight away that he feels in competition with me because of my privileged background and university education.

'Rose tells me you're studying law,' he says, challenge in his eyes.

'That's right,' I say evenly, determined to stay cool.

'Isn't it a bit of a waste? What good will that do when you're married with a family?'

I'm conscious of Rose watching me. 'Who knows?' I shrug. 'Do you think I'd be better off in the bank counting other people's money instead of my own?' I smile as pleasantly as I can.

Matthew laughs. 'Fair play. I was just seeing what you're made of, Juliet. You might come in handy when I need some advice.'

'Advice?'

'I don't intend being a bank clerk for ever,' he says, with such dogged conviction that I believe him.

Rose gives me a nervous smile and I wonder how she'll keep him tethered.

July 1971

My mother invites Rose and Rebecca to lunch at Verbena View, to celebrate Rose's forthcoming wedding.

'I've never forgotten how lovely your home is,' Rebecca says, as she comes into my bedroom, admiring the bathroom off it and the walk-in wardrobe. 'Our house in Lower Ballymalin Gardens would fit into a corner of this.'

I take it for granted, the spacious, rambling, white-fronted bungalow surrounded by land-scaped grounds, with splendid views of the sea from the south- and south-west-facing rooms. It's been in the family for years. My father grew up here, and when his father died and Granny Jordan's health began to fail, he had it renovated and extended and moved back in with his wife and baby daughter — me.

The judge remembers them and has them eating out of his hands. He is full of warm old-fashioned gentlemanly courtesy when I bring them into his untidy study, a room with huge squishy armchairs set round an open fire, one wall lined with brimming bookshelves, an alcove decorated with framed certificates, including every single school certificate I've ever been awarded, and another fantastic view of the sea.

My mother has put out fresh flowers, and she fusses around, trailing after our housekeeper, ensuring the table is properly set and the lamb slow-roasted to perfection. She gives Rose a wedding present of crystal glasses and Rose turns scarlet with pleasure.

Afterwards, we go for coffee down by the harbour.

'Rose, I wish you the very best of luck,' I tell her. 'I hope they give you a good send-off from the office next week.'

'I can't believe I'm leaving,' Rose says. 'No more Monday mornings and no more gossipy coffee breaks. Even if I wanted to stay on, I can't. But I'll be married to Matthew and I'm looking forward to moving into our new home.'

We both know that the family home will belong to Matthew. If anything goes wrong, he can sell it over her head.

'I'm sure you'll be very happy, Rose,' I say to her. 'But unfair and unequal laws will change, and women will start to have choices. Clever women are speaking up at last, determined to fight for proper justice and get rid of ancient regulations.'

'And your father would agree with all of this,' Rebecca says, with a teasing glint in her eye.

'What do you think?' I hold my breath.

'That you're the apple of his eye, his golden princess, and more.' She gives me a puzzled look. 'You have so much, I don't understand why . . . '

I can see she's not quite sure how to put it. 'You're surprised I'm such a rebel. I should be happy with my lot instead of engaging in militant behaviour.'

'Well, yes. If I had what you had, I'd be pinching myself.'

I stir my coffee with a heavy hand. I hear the clink-clink of the boats bobbing about their moorings and the cries of the gulls wheeling above the rippling grey sea. The salty breeze flickers like a feather on my skin, playful and carefree.

After a while I say, 'We won't know ourselves in ten years' time. The sky will be the limit. Women will be able to have it all and do whatever they want to do. Hey, sisters, we'll be totally invincible.'

★   ★   ★

Invincible. Now, as the shadowy night presses on top of me, the memory of that long-ago day suddenly fades and my words, uttered so confidently, trail into the dark horizon. Ah, the blind, trusting innocence! I know now, only too well, that neither women nor men will ever have it all: life is full of compromise and sacrifice; rules and regulations don't matter a jot when it comes to the complexities of people, let alone the depths of the human heart.

And no one is invincible once they love somebody. That changes everything. And likewise if they are loved — even that brings burdens.

The darkness seeps into my face and slithers through my hair. Yet even in the oily black depths, there is life. I feel it all around me, as you would another presence, as though the world is taking slow breaths in tempo with the murmuring sea while it waits for the night to pass.

I wonder how injured I am, if I'll have to wait for the night to pass before I'm found. It can't end like this. It *won't* end like this. I want to walk up Grafton Street in warm summer sunshine and listen to the buskers. Pause by the flower sellers at the corner of Duke Street, and inhale the vibrant scents. Mingle with the lunchtime crowds strolling across a sun-dappled St Stephen's Green. Taste the breeze coming off the Liffey. Visit Paris again and sip hot chocolate on the Champs-Elysées. Go shopping in New York. Visit Rome and enjoy a bowl of pasta in a quaint corner of Trastevere.

Rome? That strikes a bell somewhere.

I want to have friends around for spag Bol and a few bottles of good wine, turn up the music, and sit on my patio overlooking the sea as day blends into a lingering twilight, where on calm days the sky is a vast canvas and you can see across the bay to the blue-grey ridges of the Wicklow mountains.

And I have unfinished business and important things to say.

Most of all, flashing like a beacon through the

murky grey clouds in my head, are the words I've left unsaid and the need to tell someone I love him very much, no matter what it costs.

The need that might, just might, have brought me here . . .

12

Rebecca was delayed at the top of the staircase by an old colleague of Harry's, who insisted on regaling her with funny anecdotes of Harry and himself on the golf course, telling her how wonderful her husband had been.

By the time she reached the foyer and glanced into the bar, there was no sign of Liam Corrigan, but the television screen on the wall stopped her in her tracks. The nine o'clock news was still on, and she saw Rose, caught in a blaze of flashbulbs with Matthew as they stepped out of his car and paused at the entrance to the Four Seasons Hotel, en route to their drinks reception.

Already the media were zoning in on possible contenders for the presidential race. Rose had a smile pinned to her face, but Rebecca could see that it was a little too bright. She's not as happy about this as she makes out, Rebecca thought, despite what she'd said when the sisters had met for lunch in Harvey Nichols earlier that week.

'Are you and Matthew really serious?' Rebecca had said.

'Yes, and why not?'

'Because ... Oh, come on, you know,' Rebecca said. 'I don't have to spell it out. Are you able for all the hassle this will bring?'

'That's a lovely way to talk to your sister, I don't think,' Rose said huffily.

'Anything you've done in the past, no matter

how small, will be held up for all to see. It's bad enough that Juliet's taking such a risk, but I'm surprised that Matthew . . . ' Rebecca couldn't bring herself to say any more.

Her sister looked beautiful and was elegantly dressed. But she was well able to don a pair of heels, skinny jeans and a cotton top and hang out backstage at one of The Name's gigs. Or get her casual clothes full of sticky fingers and puke when she helped out in the children's hospital.

'I'd do anything for Matthew,' Rose said. 'Years ago he made all my dreams come true. Now I want to help him have his. I hope you're giving Juliet some of this advice.'

Rebecca shook her head. 'I tried. She told me she didn't care if her life was upended. She thinks it's time a few things were out in the open. I don't know what's got into her.'

'Well, that's a first. I've never heard you criticise her before,' Rose said.

'I can't understand why you're both happy to lob ginormous sticks of dynamite into your lives. Everything's fine as it is. Why look for trouble?'

Rose stared out of the window to where Wednesday-morning shoppers strolled around the Pembroke District of Dundrum Town Centre. Then she met Rebecca's eyes, and said, 'There's no need to concern yourself with me and Matthew. We'll be fine.'

'The Moores make a nice, respectable-looking couple, don't they?' a man's voice said. 'Lambs to the slaughter, methinks. You can't afford to be nice any more. And certainly not in that battlefield.'

Rebecca swung around and stared at the man standing behind her. It *was* him. Larger than life, undeniably attractive but dangerous as hell, given his history.

'Liam!' Rebecca said, her chest tight. He was wearing a grey suit and a white shirt open at the neck. He had always been handsome, and his red hair was as thick as ever, but shot through with silver. His face was tauter than she remembered, which made his blue eyes more vibrant. Late fifties by now, she guessed, and leaner all over. His expression was easy and friendly, totally at odds with how it had seemed the last time she'd seen him. As Rebecca regarded him, the years rolled away and she saw Liam leaning over a table at the Shelbourne Hotel, where she and Juliet had been having dinner before going to the theatre.

His face had been stiff with rage, fists clenched till the knuckles showed white. From what he'd said to Juliet, in a terse voice, Rebecca had gathered that his construction empire, Corrigan Holdings, which he'd built from nothing, was imploding and he blamed her. He'd bought a pocket of land adjacent to Verbena View at an eye-watering price, but to develop it he had needed right of way along the side of her garden and to install piping beneath her property. She'd refused.

'You got yourself into this mess, Liam,' she'd said, in a perfectly calm voice. 'This time you overstretched yourself and signed on far too many dotted lines without checking the small print, including the plans for that land. It's not my fault that the property bubble has burst or that the banks are knocking down your door.'

'You were the one who stood in my way when I could have made a fortune,' he'd hissed. 'I wouldn't be in this mess today but for you. You've put the final nail in my coffin and ruined me. *Ruined* me!'

'You ruined yourself,' Juliet had said, as though she didn't really give a damn. 'Maybe if you'd spent less time strutting your stuff in the city's celebrity restaurants and clubs and more time listening to your solicitor and accountant, you wouldn't be in this mess.'

Liam had glared at her. 'You'll pay for this,' he said. Then he had picked up her glass of red wine, chucked the contents into her face and stormed out. Rebecca had been furious, and even more upset when a couple of weekend tabloids had recounted the incident in lurid detail, but Juliet had laughed it off.

'Rise above it, Rebecca,' she'd said calmly. 'Why should I let Liam Corrigan push my buttons? Obviously he's upset, and I'm sorry he's got himself into such a mess, but even if I'd allowed him right of way through part of my property, it wouldn't have made any difference. He'd already over-extended and is in deep trouble with the banks. And that's without factoring in the value of the site tumbling to rock bottom just after he bought it.'

A couple of weeks later, Rebecca had heard that Liam had fled to Spain, his legendary lifestyle in ashes at his feet. Since then, she hadn't seen or heard of him until now.

He smiled. 'Rebecca Ryan. I'm glad I haven't changed beyond all recognition.'

'It's only been a couple of years,' she said, a little haughtily.

'Four, actually.'

'So you kept count?'

'Each and every one, unfortunately,' he said, his glance full of wry humour as it rested on her, as though she'd caught him out in some misdemeanour.

'Don't tell me you're here for the wedding?' she said.

He gave her a look as though he was debating whether to take her into his confidence. 'I could say I'm supposed to be enjoying an illicit rendezvous with my secret lover, only now I see my cover is blown.'

This was accompanied by such a comical, self-deprecating smile that Rebecca was almost amused, but she recalled the last time they'd met and looked at him coldly. 'Very funny,' she said.

He recoiled. 'Nothing so torrid or interesting,' he said. 'Paul Johnson is an old friend of mine as well as Harry's — but the band's come on and it's a while since I've had the ears blown off me.'

'So Golden Boy Liam came home for a wedding?' Rebecca was surprised he'd bothered to interrupt his exile to Spain for that.

'Not just the wedding,' he said pleasantly. 'And I'm no longer a golden boy. I have some unfinished business that I need to straighten out, and the two dovetailed nicely, but it's rather a long, dull story.'

'Yeah, sure,' Rebecca laughed. 'You dull, Liam? That's a contradiction in itself.'

'You might be surprised to hear that a few things have changed since the last time we met.' He looked at her steadily and she was surprised to see honesty in his eyes. Whatever had happened to him in the intervening years, he seemed a different man from the one who had insulted her friend before hotfooting it out of Dublin with his construction business in ruins: he'd risked storm clouds in venturing back to the scene of his crimes just to be here for the wedding of an old friend's son.

'So you remember the last time we met?' she said, deciding that she was going to remind him if he'd forgotten.

He smiled ruefully. 'Of course. I was horribly rude to Juliet and I bet you haven't forgiven me.'

'No, I haven't,' she said. 'Rude, Liam?' Rebecca echoed his words. 'You were totally intimidating. See you around.' She headed for the corridor by the side of the hotel lobby, her head high.

'Rebecca — wait.'

She wheeled around. 'I've nothing to say to you, Liam.' She was wary of the way he was looking at her, as though he liked what he saw and was happy to have bumped into her, in spite of the way she was dismissing him.

'Juliet's forgiven me,' he said, his hands open in a conciliatory gesture.

'What?' It was impossible to hide her surprise.

85

'You didn't know? I thought she would have told you straight away on account of you two being such close pals.'

'No, she didn't,' Rebecca said. 'I'd have thought she was the one person you'd want to avoid.'

'Ah, you know Juliet. I couldn't stay angry with her indefinitely. Four years in Spanish exile gave me plenty of time to think. And we go back a long way, me and her.'

'That's putting it rather mildly,' Rebecca said, a little acerbically. 'So when did this great act of forgiveness happen?'

'Just today.'

'*Today?*' She couldn't keep the surprise out of her voice.

'Yeah. Juliet was part of my unfinished business. I owed her a bottle of wine and a grovelling apology, to say the least, so I dropped in to see her late this afternoon, before I came here.'

'Was she expecting you?'

'Of course. I emailed her during the week. Even I had more sense than to turn up unannounced, given our history.'

Rebecca was taken aback. Naturally, Juliet didn't tell her everything that was going on in her life, but Rebecca had witnessed their row and her friend should have mentioned that Liam was on the scene again. Then again, she and Juliet hadn't exactly been on speaking terms when they'd parted.

Liam was still talking. 'I was relieved to have the chance to put things right between us,' he said. 'I told her I was really sorry I'd lost the head with her that time. She accepted my peace offering of a rather good French reserve, and we chatted for a bit before I left. I think she was expecting someone else so it was all very short and sweet.'

'Who was it?' Rebecca asked.

I need the whole of Friday to lock myself away and complete some urgent paperwork, even if it takes until midnight . . .

'Dunno,' he said. 'I'm just glad to have squared things with her. Water under the bridge, or almost . . . I still have to make my peace with you.'

'Consider it done,' Rebecca said, edging away, glancing down the corridor to her room. She wished she was there already, away from this man. He put her on her guard.

'I'd love to buy you a drink,' he said, in such a circumspect tone that it would have been difficult to refuse without sounding churlish. 'I also owe you a glass of wine for any upset I caused. Although maybe you'd rather get back to the wedding . . . '

She hesitated. 'Liam, I've only your word that you called to Juliet and she's accepted your apology.'

There was a flicker of disappointment in his eyes. 'Do you think I'd make that up?' He didn't look as if he had. 'Give her a call if it makes you feel better. It's just a friendly drink. I promise I won't chuck it over you,' he said. 'I'd like a chance to talk, and draw a line under the past.'

There was a shriek as the bride, in swathes of

white silk, appeared in the lobby to greet some late arrivals. A pink bridesmaid appeared to join in the fanfare. She was in her bare feet, having abandoned her heels. They ran into a group hug with the newcomers, talking and laughing at the top of their voices.

Among them Rebecca saw another old golfing friend of Harry's, who threw her an interested glance. She turned back to Liam. 'I need to pop back to my room for ten minutes or so. Let's not meet in the bar,' she said. 'Somewhere away from the wedding.'

13

Above me, one of the stars gleaming in the night sky swells so that it's bigger and brighter than any other. It frees itself from the cluster and, winking brightly, cuts a brave, independent trail of its own through the heavens.

Bravo, I silently applaud, feeling a swell of recognition. I was like that, once upon a time. Just for a short while. Until my wings were clipped.

But as it comes closer, I realise it's not a freedom-fighting star after all. In the same moment that I spot tiny red lights blinking beside it, I hear the unmistakable whine of an aircraft coming in to land, the high-pitched drone that had accompanied it across the Irish Sea changing key.

From my vantage point it doesn't look much bigger than a toy, and I picture miniature people sitting in miniature seats in the brightly lit cabin, talking and chatting and wondering how quickly they'll be able to disembark, then if they'll be delayed at Baggage Reclaim or by a long queue at the taxi rank. Thoughts that usually preoccupy me whenever I approach the end of a flight.

Oh, the luxury of having that concern at the forefront of your mind.

Help. Help. Who will see me in the dark? How long must I wait before someone notices I'm missing? Why can't I feel my legs and arms?

My mind slews away from something too terrifying to contemplate. Instead I latch on to the whisper of a memory, of another time when I lay on my back and watched planes pass overhead. As the breeze stirs, cold and moist, I grasp it before it fades, and even though it was almost a lifetime ago, I'm there again, and it's as clear as though it was yesterday.

August 1971
The sun is beating down from an azure sky, and it's warm. We've picked the most comfortable spot for some sunbathing and the ground is soft with bracken and fern. I've taken off my cork-soled platform sandals and pushed up the legs of my bell-bottomed trousers as far as they'll go. At eighteen years of age, a suntan is a major fashion accessory. Rebecca's A-line skirt is tucked up around her thighs and even Rose has taken off her nylons, baring her legs. So far we have counted five planes droning into Dublin airport. I have brought along my tape recorder and we've been listening to Jimi Hendrix. Then, to satisfy Rose, we play Cat Stevens.

'Do you ever wonder where everyone's coming from?' I ask, lying between Rose and Rebecca. A welcome breeze flutters across the headland, refreshing our slowly burning limbs.

'What do you mean?' Rebecca says.

'All those people flying in from other parts of the world . . . London, Paris — I'd love to go to Paris some time, maybe even America.'

'It would be very expensive to fly to America,'

Rose points out, in her usual cagey manner. Sometimes I wonder what she would have been like had her parents not died when she was at such a critical age.

'It's very expensive to fly, full stop,' Rebecca says. 'You could become an air hostess, Juliet, and get to all those places for free. Think of the glamour and excitement! Never mind rubbing shoulders with all those good-looking pilots.'

'I've no intention of getting a job based solely on my face,' I say stubbornly.

'No, I guess that wouldn't suit a women's libber like you,' Rose says.

'And why are you assuming all the pilots are men?'

'Because they are.' Rebecca laughs.

A short silence.

Then I say cheerfully, 'When that stupid marriage bar is removed, the world will be our oyster. We can be anything we want to be. Maybe, who knows, president of Ireland?'

'President!' Rose scoffs. 'We'll never have a female president.'

'We will.' I'm full of conviction. 'If you talked to the women I meet, or heard them speak, you'd have no doubt about that. It might take twenty years but we'll get there.'

'Maybe you could become the first Irish woman pilot, Juliet, instead of an air hostess,' Rebecca says. 'They'd have to come up with a woman's uniform, though.'

'It's a bit late now,' I say. 'You need honours maths, which my school didn't think was a suitable subject for genteel ladies.'

'We had to do domestic science. It was compulsory,' Rebecca says wistfully.

'I enjoyed that,' Rose says.

'I didn't.' Rebecca snorts.

'I didn't have the option of domestic science,' I say. 'My school's view was that we'd have cooks and maids to do what had to be done while we sat back and looked pretty for our husbands.'

'I'm quite happy doing the cooking and cleaning in my home.' Rose is on the defensive. 'As soon as we start a family I'll be the happiest person on earth.'

'Yes, I'm sure you will be, but you don't actually own your home, do you?' I point out. 'It belongs to Matthew, not you. Legally, it's not even shared between you, and I bet you used your lump sum from your job when you had to leave as part of the down-payment.'

There is another silence. I didn't mean to score a point off Rose. I know it must be tough for her having to sit at home twiddling her thumbs all day and depend solely on Matthew's wages to pay the bills, the mortgage, her knickers, her sanitary pads and everything else. Sometimes I wish she wasn't so sweet-natured and reserved. She has never smoked, and rarely drinks, only when we goad her into it. But surely there's a limit to the number of Britvic oranges you can consume. And all her skirts go to her knee. A perfect model of Irish Catholic womanhood. I can imagine her baking a load of apple tarts for rosy-cheeked children and making sure they go to mass on Sundays with shiny shoes. I see her looking at Matthew the way my mother looks at my father. And Matthew, to give him his due, seems very protective towards her.

'Stop it, you two,' Rebecca says. 'We're supposed to be having a relaxing afternoon and making the most of the sunshine. I didn't bunk off work to listen to you bickering. Not much use wearing a symbol of peace, Juliet, if you're squabbling with Rose.'

I touch the pendant that hangs around my neck on its leather thong. 'I'm not squabbling,' I say. 'Rose knows how I feel by now, don't you, Rose? No hard feelings between us. I'm glad you're very happy in wedded bliss. It just wouldn't suit me. No one's going to chain me down or tie me to a kitchen sink. I'll be fancy-free, like that butterfly, flitting wherever I choose.'

'I'm fancy-free this afternoon,' Rebecca says, 'but I'll have hell to pay with Moany Mullen in the morning so you don't always get away scot-free. And yesterday I spilt a whole bottle of Tipp-Ex across the carriage of my typewriter so I'm already in the doghouse.'

'And I skipped another lecture,' I tell them. 'I'll have to beg very nicely to borrow someone else's notes. Again. Just tell Miss Mullen you were in bed with your monthlies. That'll shut her up. Here, pass over that bottle of oil so I can sizzle some more and get a tan.'

★　★　★

I can still smell the coconut scent of the suntan oil as I smeared it on my legs, but I can't remember who first brought up the subject of going to Spain the following year. I think it was Rose, boasting that Matthew was going to whisk her away on a sort of second honeymoon. Somewhere exotic, with blue skies and palm trees, like Benidorm. They hadn't even got passports and would have to save like mad.

Or was it Rebecca, talking about suntans and romantic foreign men?

Or me, talking about freedom such as we'd never tasted?

I remember thinking that anything Rose and Matthew could do, I could do better.

★　★　★

'I've already saved some money from my summer job in the solicitors' office,' I say. 'I can do the same next year, so if we plan our hols for late August I should be okay. What do you think, Rebecca?'

'Foreign men! Cheap vodka in a long glass! I can't believe it could happen to me.' Rebecca sighs. 'It's like a fabulous dream. It would be tough to save enough on seven pounds a week, though. Maybe I could take an evening job as well. I could get thirty shillings in the local fish-and-chipper on a Saturday night. Oh, I'm getting all excited just thinking about it.'

Cat Stevens finally ends so I switch to the radio and Mungo Jerry's 'In The Summertime' floats across the air.

'And what about Harry?' I ask her.

'We're just good friends,' Rebecca says, in a

nonchalant tone that reflects the way she continues to play it cool with him, unlike Rose, who clung to Matthew like a limpet.

'That's not what he'd like to hear,' I say, thinking of the way Harry Ryan's eyes follow her whenever we're out as a group.

'He wouldn't stand in my way,' Rebecca says. 'I haven't even been on a plane yet — it's so exciting! Hey, Rose, we'd get it cheaper if we went as a foursome. So long as Matthew wouldn't mind being blessed among women.'

'I don't know.' Rose is hesitant. 'I'd have to make sure we stayed away from you two as much as possible.'

'Don't worry, we wouldn't dream of butting in on you love birds. We could pretend we didn't know you,' I say. With long strokes, I slather more sun-tan oil over my legs. 'I'm a bright shade of pink already, girls.'

'Ooh, great,' Rebecca says. 'It might peel but then it'll turn a lovely golden brown. And I know it'll feel like we're waiting for ever but roll on next year. I can't wait . . .'

* * *

Darkness presses around me and I'm frozen to the bone. *Roll on next year.*

I can still see Rebecca and me sitting in that cabin, surrounded by a planeload of excited holidaymakers as we hurtle across the skies above the Irish Sea, over England and down across France on the way to Spain. Rebecca and I, our shiny new cases full of light summer

95

clothes and colourful bikinis. Our heads full of anticipation for the holiday ahead. Sun, sea, sangria, and maybe a little romance. Totally innocent of life and its vagaries.

Untried, untested. Unblemished.

14

It was late when Matthew returned to the reception, throwing smiles and greetings in all directions, as though he was already practising his walkabout. He came up to Rose and kissed her cheek.

'All good so far and thanks for being so patient,' he murmured. Then he took her hand. 'I have to introduce you to people.'

Rose made a huge effort to smile and chat, even though her head was whirling. She was still off balance after her encounter with Liz and the naked, almost feverish excitement in the woman's eyes. The fact that they were from the same small village in Dublin wouldn't cut any ice with Liz if it came to a scoop. Besides, Rose had married and moved out of Ballymalin before Liz had been born, so there would be no loyalty there. Liz would be on just one side: her own. An only child, she had always got whatever she wanted, boasting about this on her diary page as she fired warning shots at recalcitrant celebrities who refused to talk to her.

Eventually, Rose escaped up the wide staircase to the Ladies, but found no respite there. Three women were gathered in front of the mirrors: Celia Coffey, with Rachel and Megan, her cronies. And as Celia's voice floated to her, Rose hesitated in the doorway.

'It's only a matter of time before he's found

out,' Celia was saying, as she leaned in close to apply her lipstick, her loud voice carrying clearly. Celia owned a chain of beauty salons that had narrowly survived the recession, thanks to her sheer hard work and rigorous cost adjustments. She plucked a tissue from the marble container on the counter and patted her red mouth. Then she scrunched it into a ball and lobbed it into the bin.

'You don't know for sure,' Rachel said, leaning into the adjacent mirror. 'It could all be perfectly innocent.'

'Yes, and babies are born under cabbage leaves.' Celia snorted. 'Wait and see. He won't be able to keep that a secret for long, not with the spotlight turned on him, and then the shit will hit the fan.'

'It's his wife I feel sorry for,' Megan said. 'They're always the last to know.'

'Oh, *hello*, Rose,' Celia said, finally spotting her. 'Do come in and join us. Don't be shy. We were just talking about Brendan and Lorna. It seems their marriage is about to hit the rocks.'

'Dreadfully sad,' Rachel said. 'Lorna will be heartbroken.'

'And, as usual, if they break up she'll be left with the main responsibility for bringing up the kiddies.'

'While he's out gadding, wherever his fancy takes him.'

'Or wherever his mickey takes him!'

'Nothing much has changed for women, has it? We're still the main caregivers.'

'Don't let Rose's friend Juliet hear you say

that!' Celia beamed at Rose.

The trio seemed to be talking all at once and far too brightly. Rose hoped her voice didn't sound too flat. 'Sorry, I don't know who you're talking about, apart from Juliet.'

'Brendan and Lorna? Really? He's behind one of those banking scandals.' Celia flapped a hand in the air, as though everybody should be privy to that vital information. 'He's coming before some tribunal or other shortly — God knows what they'll discover. But it looks as though you'll soon have a different kind of fight on your hands, Rose!'

'What do you mean?' Even though Celia's friends had turned back to their respective mirrors and seemed absorbed in fixing their already perfect makeup, she was conscious that they were hanging on every word.

'You're going to have a hard time keeping the lines drawn between your husband and your friend!' Celia said.

'So you've heard the rumour as well?'

'Duh! As my teenage daughter would say! I think it's gone beyond the rumour stage. Everyone will know soon enough. Juliet's profile is about to go viral, to borrow my teenage son's expression.' Celia laughed as if she was extremely proud of herself for keeping up with her children. 'I'd say Professor Jordan will be a tough nut to crack, so Matthew will have his work cut out. But, Rose dear, aren't you a little concerned about the battle that lies ahead? You're far too nice for that kind of heat.'

'Why should I be worried?' Rose forced a

smile. 'I'm sure Matthew and I will be able to handle anything that's thrown at us, and if I'm that nice it shouldn't affect me at all, but thanks for your concern.'

'Well, don't say I didn't warn you. Liz Monaghan's prowling around tonight, and I've never seen her so fanatical about digging for dirt. And she's nothing compared to the big guns you'll have on your back.'

Rose composed her face as she moved past them on rubbery legs and went to the line of cubicles. She rummaged in her bag for her tablets, pressed one out of the foil, and swallowed it whole. It wouldn't take too long, she hoped, for mind-numbing relief to soothe her jangling nerves.

15

August 1972

I stare at the destination over the check-in desk.
  Benidorm.
  Rebecca's excitement dips momentarily when she meets people she knows in the queue and she's no choice but to introduce us.
  'I'm keeping away from them,' she says afterwards. 'I don't want to speak to a single Irish person for the next two weeks. Not even Rose or Matthew.'
  'We won't,' I assure her.
  Rose and Matthew are flying out to Benidorm next week, but staying in a different hotel, and we've agreed to avoid them as much as possible. Rose has said we might meet for drinks on our last night, but that's all. Rebecca has privately told me that Rose hopes the romance of it all will result in a baby.
  Rebecca's excitement mounts again when we're finally airborne. She unscrews the top of her vodka and tips the liquid into a glass. 'I can't believe we're here at last, up in the sky, looking down on puffy clouds instead of up at them! In two hours' time we'll be landing in Spain. *Spain!*'
  'Neither can I believe it,' I say. 'I was so glad to walk out of that solicitors' office for the last time.

101

They didn't think I was entitled to go on holidays, seeing as I was supposed to be covering for their staff. All I was doing was filing, answering the phone and making tea. They didn't take me seriously because I was a woman.'

'I'm sure you weren't long in demanding your rights. They didn't know who they were taking on in Juliet Jordan.'

'Too right. Let's order another drink and practise some Spanish phrases. How does 'You look very sexy' go?'

Rebecca laughs.

I want to touch the wing tip and alter the flight path, changing my destiny. But it's impossible to change the course of a life, and I see the inexorable hand of Fate playing out as the plane screeches to a halt on the foreign tarmac. Rebecca and I feel heat stifling our breath as we carry our cases out to the sun-drenched car park, where a coach, engine thrumming, waits to deliver us to our fate.

A fate in which we're captivated by clear skies and blinding sunshine, the blue sea, evenings when trellises bursting with blossom infuse the air with scent. Night-time warmth, when you need nothing more than a light lace stole over a sleeveless top and feel exotic and beautiful and far too ready to listen to sweet nothings . . .

★ ★ ★

Images of our holiday flick through my head like a series of glossy photographs: Rebecca lying on a sun lounger with the sea in the near distance,

102

me lying on a sun lounger, while past the row of oiled bodies, someone is half sitting, watching us. There is Rebecca sitting on the tiny balcony of our hotel, raising a glass of vodka and orange, wearing a garish embroidered blouse she'd bought from a market stall without haggling.

Then one photo of me, close to the camera, wearing cheap yellow sunglasses and a wide grin. (Afterwards I'd stared at the photograph for ages, heart thumping, wondering if the ephemeral reflection of the man who had taken it had been captured in my shades. But there was no sign of him.)

★   ★   ★

'You're so luscious, Juliet.'

I've never been called that before. Luscious. It makes me feel womanly, curvy and desirable. I've never in my wildest dreams thought I could be that kind of girl, but here, in the scented heat and heady romance of foreign soil, I feel different and it's all too easy.

'You've bewitched me.'

'Have I?' I ask, in a voice that isn't mine, all sexy and flirtatious. A sultry, bad-girl voice, fuelled by cheap vodka, a romantic atmosphere and a sense of breaking away from other people's expectations. I'd sensed him watching me from a distance over the last couple of days as I'd moved from the beach to the promenade restaurant, from scanty bikini to floaty kaftan.

Some Scottish guy had been eyeing up Rebecca all evening and I'd encouraged her to go to a cocktail bar with him. As soon as they were out of sight and the coast was clear, I knew he'd come looking for me.

His wife has gone to bed. She has nothing to do with the urgent need that ripples between us. It holds us in thrall, and shuts her out as though she doesn't exist. We talk for a while and then I let his hands slip beneath my kaftan to my bare breasts, teasing the nipples, sending a hot flood of want through me. Confident, assured hands that know what they're doing and how to bring me to fever-pitch excitement. Not like the hesitant fumblings of my college peers. The scent of his strong body is all around me in the warm, humid night. It's heady and musky and sharply male. I feel alive like never before.

'Have you ever . . . ?' His hand slides slowly down to the warm valley between my thighs and I gasp. My panties drop to my ankles. I step out of them.

I part my legs slightly. He knows exactly what to do with his sensitive fingers. My heart is galloping. 'No . . . not yet.'

An indrawn breath, a glitter of triumph in his eyes. Excitement crackles all around me. A sense that I am stepping out of my own skin, leaving aside the restricting ties of family love. Because I want to prove to myself that I'm not a flawless princess, but flesh and blood. Faint with giddiness, I slide down onto the night-time sand and he is kneeling over me, wrenching off his shirt. I hear the clink of his belt buckle as he opens it, and the rasp of his zip. I reach down to the hem of my kaftan and slowly bring it up as far as my waist. Then, emboldened, I sit up for a minute and pull it over my head, then lie down on the sand, part my legs and open my body to him.

Luscious . . .

The taste of forbidden fruit and the start of my private downfall. For what begins on the warm sands in Benidorm doesn't end there. One night isn't enough: it barely satiates me, never mind him, and to my shame, there is more, later, back in Dublin.

September 1972

It wasn't planned. It should never have happened. A month later, when I meet him by chance on Grafton Street in Dublin, we look so different against a light September rain and the grey afternoon that we almost pass each other by. My kaftan has been replaced by denim jeans and I'm wearing a checked jacket with a big collar turned up against the rain and hugging a briefcase to my chest. I see him first, coming towards me. He's wearing a dark trench coat and carrying a large black umbrella, and for an instant I hesitate, torn between slipping past anonymously and stopping to say hello . . .

If I could go back, would I have done it differently? Would I have scurried past on the other side of the street? But I've hesitated too long. He sees me out of the corner of his eye. And it's too late.

'Juliet!'

'Hi.'

There is a taut moment of awkwardness, both of us unsure of this new landscape, which is electrified by the desire we shared on a shadowy beach. We are aware that the right thing to do is to nod politely and go our separate ways. The moment stretches out and already we are falling into a new, forbidden space. He tilts his umbrella towards me so that we are both tucked under its shelter. We're alone together, marooned in a world of slow caresses, intertwined limbs and cries of delight, a million miles removed from the mundane reality of rain pattering on the umbrella and dripping slowly off the spokes, the legs of shoppers surging around us, and the line of cars swishing slowly up the street. Under the umbrella, the air is so heavy with possibility that it's hard to breathe and my throat closes. He lifts his hand and curves it around my face.

He smiles. 'Luscious.'

Three months. We have three months of snatched moments, time stolen from his life and mine, the lovemaking between us all the more intoxicating for its urgency. I move through lectures and reading rooms, slip into and out of anonymous country-hotel lobbies and have breakfast with my father, wondering why no one notices that all the cells in my body are glowing. I don't think about his wife as my mouth tastes the delicate hollow of his neck or my teeth nip the skin of his inner thighs, or as I move on top of him and sink down, feeling him inside me. She doesn't suspect anything, he says. She has no place in the hot, sharp current surging between us. I am amazed at my capacity to blot out everything in my need for him.

Then one Friday evening before Christmas I meet him after lectures. I haven't seen him for two weeks and he is more urgent than ever, almost rough, clinging to me with all his strength as he comes immediately. He apologises for his haste when he tears his mouth away from mine, but his wife is beginning to ask questions. Also, she thinks she might be pregnant . . .

Although he begs me to continue, and promises to be extra discreet, he knows me well enough by now to understand that, no matter how I feel about him, this will end everything between us.

But it wasn't the end of my downfall. It was only the beginning.

16

'We probably shouldn't be here,' Rebecca said, her voice lowered to a whisper.

'So? We'll wait until we're thrown out. In the meantime, everywhere is locked up, so we can't do any harm, and it's perfect.'

'How did you manage to find this spot?'

'I know the hotel because once upon a time I used to live just a couple of miles up the road.'

Rebecca sipped her wine. She didn't know what had happened to the huge mansion in the parkland setting where Liam had once held court. She was afraid to ask.

'You said to find somewhere quiet, didn't you?' Liam went on.

They were sitting in the spa reception area, on velvet-covered armchairs that backed on to a bank of leafy potted plants. Rebecca breathed in the scent of bergamot and geranium, courtesy of the adjacent spa. To one side, large picture windows faced out on to a small courtyard where spotlights illuminated water features and minia-ture shrubbery. In front of her, and behind a sheet of glass, lay the swimming-pool, and in the dim lighting, the surface of the water shimmered. The low table in front of them held their glasses and a bottle of white wine in a cooler. They were just down the corridor from the hotel lobby and through another set of sliding doors, but might as well have been in a different world.

'It's a far cry from Lower Ballymalin Gardens,' Rebecca said.

'That brings me back,' Liam said. 'Although I only went to school there.'

'I'd forgotten you hung around with Harry and the others. You were the posh one.'

'Living over a vegetable shop on the edge of Howth? You're joking. Juliet was the posh one.'

Liam had been more on the outside, looking in, Rebecca recalled. Self-possessed, tall and lean, with a hungry determination to make his mark on the world.

'They were the good old days,' he said. 'Being a teenager in the summer of sixty-nine . . . Who can forget the first time they saw *Easy Rider?* Or heard Bob Dylan? Or got drunk? We had some laughs. Harry was great. You must still miss him. How long now?'

'Six years.' She bit her lip. Sometimes it felt as though he had never been: she couldn't remember the sound of his voice and needed a photograph to conjure up his face. 'I keep busy,' she said. 'It's the only way. But it was tough. Still is, sometimes. Mostly I glide along fine, and then something happens that reminds me . . . or something goes wrong and Harry's not there to share it.'

'You kept him guessing, you know,' Liam said. 'He thought he'd never get you up the aisle. Everyone else was a little in love with Juliet.'

'Were you?'

'We all were, except Harry. Juliet was different, with that mixture of seduction and feistiness, but way off limits, living in that house on the hill. Sparky, too, when it came to cutting us down to size and letting us know who was boss. She turned into one hell of a woman. And from what I've heard she's going all the way to the top.'

'She's talked to you about . . . ?'

He lifted the bottle of wine out of the cooler and topped up their glasses. 'I knew already. It's Dublin's worst-kept secret, and it'll make for some really juicy debates. Juliet will light a fire under everyone else. I wished her the best of luck.'

'Did you?'

'I hope it goes well for her. I'd love to see her sitting in the Park — nothing against Matthew, but Juliet would be perfect.'

She watched his face as she said, 'That's a bit of an about-turn from the last time I saw you two together when you were telling her she'd ruined you.'

'I've had my epiphany,' he said, lines fanning out from his eyes as he smiled wryly. 'And a few sleepless nights. But we'd be here all night if I got started on that.'

He stared out through the darkened glass and she wondered what he was thinking. About the sleepless nights for which Juliet might have been responsible? The lifestyle he'd worked so hard for, built on a bubble? A line of creditors, baying for his blood? She felt a spike of caution. Four years ago, this man had blamed Juliet for his catastrophe. How could he have forgiven and forgotten?

Liam caught her studying him. 'Most of those

nights are behind me now. But being back in Dublin, meeting old friends . . . ' He shrugged. 'It's made me realise what a complete arsehole I used to be.'

'I can't believe I'm hearing this from one of Dublin's former hot-shots.'

'I know you might find this hard to believe, but time was, I couldn't even think of Juliet's name without feeling savage. When I'd cooled my jets a little I saw she was right.'

'I guess that could be called an epiphany.'

'I don't know how I got so carried away. When I look back now, though, I was like someone possessed. Christ, I really lost the plot. I can't believe I paid a small fortune for a tiny pocket of land adjoining her house and was arrogant enough to expect her to grant me a right of way through her property. I wasn't the only one, though, caught up a mindless gamble — but, hell,' he gave her a lopsided grin, 'it wasn't the end of the world.'

'Are you sure you weren't holed up in a Zen retreat for the last few years?'

'Not quite. After the crash, it was funny, Rebecca, but I found a strange kind of freedom in having nothing but the basics, and going back to the essentials in life.'

'Definitely a monastic retreat,' she said, a little flippantly. Where had the gilded, charge-it Liam Corrigan gone?

'Thing is, I might have had the flashy lifestyle and the big cars, but it was meaningless. It was an empty power trip. I wasn't happy. I had lots of so-called friends, but no one to love, to share my life with. And you get to know who your friends are pretty quickly when things go bust.'

'You do,' she said. It was amazing the number of 'friends' who had dropped off her radar in the couple of years following Harry's death. She took a few sips of wine.

'Harry and I had to go back to basics once or twice during the eighties,' she admitted. 'It was a struggle to pay the mortgage and raise a young family, but we had each other and were happy. And we came out the other end. What brought you back to Dublin? Apart from settling your differences with Juliet.'

'I'm home to face the music, so to speak,' he said. 'I don't want to be in exile for ever, and I need to sort out my financial affairs but I may be declared bankrupt.'

'Bankrupt? Wow.' She tried to stop the shock flashing across her face. What a tough prospect for the man with the champagne lifestyle.

'I've talked to Juliet about it,' he went on. 'I had to let her know, as there might be a problem with the land I bought behind her house. All my assets are being trawled through. But she was fine about it. It'll soon be common knowledge,' he said, 'and coming to a television screen near you. You'll probably see shots of me emerging from the law courts and trying to hide from the cameras.'

'I'm sorry to hear that. But don't try to dodge the cameras. That looks pathetic and they'll catch you anyway. Just walk tall and pretend they're not there. It's a lot more dignified. Smile at them, if you like.'

'Like this?' He put on a huge wide grin, like a child showing off his teeth, and in spite of herself and her reservations about him, she laughed.

'That's a lot better than trying to skulk behind the scenes.'

'I'll take your advice.'

Rebecca glanced at her watch. 'I'd better go back to the wedding.'

'You go on ahead,' he said. 'I'm going outside for some fresh air.'

'Thanks for the drink,' she said. 'And,' she risked saying, as she slid her feet into her shoes and got up, 'you took me away from a bad place this evening.'

He raised an eyebrow. 'Did I? I can't imagine you having any bad places.'

'You'd be surprised. There are places in my head that I don't want to go right now.'

'And there was me prattling away.'

'I was happy to listen.'

'I was glad to talk to you and maybe have you revise your opinion of me,' he said, seeming oddly vulnerable.

'Ah, but you don't know what my opinion was . . . ' she said.

'I can guess,' he said ruefully.

They left the spa area and he walked back as far as the lobby with her.

'Will I see you in the morning? At breakfast?' he said.

'Depends. I'm hoping to fit in a walk on the beach before I leave.'

'Would you mind if I tagged along with you?'

'Feel free.' She wondered why he wanted to spend time with her. And if she wanted to spend time with him.

Still, at least it would keep her bad places at bay for a little longer.

17

Saturday, 17 March, 12.30 a.m.

I wonder if I'm going to die.

The threat circles like a bird of prey in the black space over my head. What would be the language of my death? An accidental fall? Manslaughter? Murder? It seems so absurd that a prism of hope pulls me back from the brink.

I'm being melodramatic. *Of course* I'll be found. *Of course* I'll be rescued. The life of Juliet Jordan is far too precious, busy and full to end in this stupid way. I catch glimpses of myself gliding through a landscape where all is bright and warm, where I walk through open doors and people welcome me . . . where I'm full of energy and purpose.

I catch glimpses of myself with my father . . .

June 1981

Tall, strong, and puffed with pride, he smiles at me across the table.

We're dining in the restaurant of my father's club in Dublin city centre. We have done this every year, on all the occasions of my excellent academic results, my father bringing me out for a celebratory meal, carefully ushering me to the table as though I'm a piece of fragile, wickedly expensive crystal. When I sit down I allow the

115

waiter to unfold a linen napkin across my lap.

This time, it's my PhD. Next spring, I'll be going to Harvard as a research fellow in international women's rights. I'm using my law degree as a stepping stone to the area of social policy and human rights, so I'm not exactly following in my father's footsteps. Still, I'm not yet thirty and the road to further success and achievement is beckoning. Back home, my mother positively glows in the sparks of delight coming from my father.

He has, as usual, ordered a bottle of Moët. 'And here's to you, Juliet.' He beams, as he touches his glass to mine. 'Well done, darling, although I was never in any doubt as to your success. You've made your mother and me so proud.'

'Thanks, Dad.'

But as I sip my champagne, the liquid catches in my throat. It cuts an abrasive trail as it slips down to my stomach, settling in a sour pool. I should be happy. I should be on top of the world. My father is happy, therefore I am happy, I tell myself. It didn't matter that when I'd dipped my toe into the waters of rebellion, the consequences had been dire, because it is all behind me now.

December 1988

It is incomprehensible that the stalwart, indestructible Mr Justice Henry Jordan has fallen prey to, of all things, double pneumonia. Even though my mother had died three years previously, of a sudden heart attack, I had always considered my father to be immortal.

Surely the doctor is wrong about it being fatal. Surely double pneumonia is fixable, in this day and age. The 1990s are just around the corner, the new millennium just twelve short years away. The country might be in an economic slump, thanks to the recession of the eighties, but we're living in modern times and medicine has made huge advances. Besides, my father will fight this off, as he has fought against so many things in his life, with his usual determination.

I'm sitting across the table from the doctor. My hands, in the lap of my camel cashmere coat, are twisting my brown leather gloves around and around. I stare at him and wait for this charade to be over, for him to laugh and tell me it's a bad dream. I'm there, but not there.

'Your father ignored a persistent cough,' he says.

Yes, well, he's a busy man, I argue silently. He's never caught a cold in his life. He's an active, vigorous man, who had bounced back after his wife's death, pouring his energies into his work, as tireless as ever, even though he's now in his late sixties. Which, on my return from America, had made it easy for me to live in my new city-centre apartment and throw myself into my ever-expanding career.

'He hasn't been looking after himself properly,' the young doctor continues. 'The cough turned into influenza, which gave rise to a chest infection. I understand his wife has passed away?'

'Yes. Three years ago. But Dad was never sick with a cold.'

'Hmm. Sometimes it happens that the person left behind slides into a kind of depression. This can weaken the immune system.'

I've taken my eye off the ball. I, the — almost — perfect daughter, have neglected him in my headlong rush for success and achievement.

'Maybe if he'd seen the doctor in the initial stages and had adequate rest and fluids . . . '

Rest? My father had never even had a lie-in, let alone spent a day in bed. Any kind of sickness was for weak people, not strong men like him.

'But the infection that caused the pneumonia has entered the bloodstream and is now affecting other organs . . . '

'There must be something you can do . . . ' My voice trails away and I bite back my frustration. I want to dive across the table and give the doctor a good shake. Don't you understand that this is my *father?* You have to make him better. It's unthinkable that a cough has led to this.

'I'm sorry but his situation has become complicated. It's all very touch and go.' He looks embarrassed. I realise I'm sitting there with my mouth open, and close it quickly.

He's still talking: 'His lungs have swollen because the disease has filled up the air spaces and his breathing is difficult . . . ' As he continues, his words cut into the space around me: bronchioles, air sacs and alveoli. It's a foreign language, but I try to understand because this may be the absurd language of my father's death. ' . . . so at this stage we can only make every

118

effort to ensure he's comfortable . . . '

Comfortable? He couldn't be talking about the judge. For the judge didn't — correction, doesn't — do comfortable. Ever.

'I'm sorry . . . '

I stare past the poster of a chest cavity pinned to the wall and through the window, where the first snow of the winter has appeared and is dusting the top of the Dublin mountains, like icing sugar.

Only yesterday my father helped me to build a snowman in the back garden at Verbena View, his big capable hands rolling the snow with ease, the ends of his long overcoat furred with a snowy white frill, his laughter booming in the still, calm air.

Only yesterday he brought me up into the woods and forests of those same mountains in search of glossy green holly, a special trip, just the two of us, leaving my young brother at home with my mother. He turned the heat up in the car. He covered my hands with mittens to protect them from the cold and the sharp spikes of the holly.

That holly bush is probably still there, in its quiet corner of the woods, berries glowing, but today my father is thin and shrunken in the hospital bed. Like a magnificent oak felled in error. Even now I'm convinced he'll pull through. Where there's life, there's hope. Sometimes a glimpse of hope can be all that's needed to sustain us. My father's faded eyes light up when he sees me and he tries to talk through the mask, but his words are indistinct.

'Be quiet, Dad,' I say, trying not to look at the frightening jumble of tubes and monitors that are needed to support his life. 'You just have to rest and get better. We'll have you out of here by Christmas.'

Why am I saying 'we'? Robert, my younger brother, is in America, having emigrated three years ago. He's hearing it all second-hand from my regular phone calls, but he's not about to jump on a plane, not for pneumonia or, indeed, for his father. There's not much love lost there: he felt he was always a pale runner-up after me and he'll be enjoying Christmas in Florida with his new wife.

'Besides, you have to bring me out for more champagne,' I tell him.

'Another achievement?'

'More things to celebrate . . . ' I tell him I've been appointed vice-chair to the newly formed Council for Women's Political Equality. My urchin crop has gone and my hair is longer now, styled around my face in a pageboy cut. My tailored clothes, smart court shoes and expensive jewellery reflect my new status.

My father stares at me. 'I need to talk . . . to tell you . . . ' he wheezes.

'Ssh, it's fine.'

He tries to lift his head from the pillow, neck suddenly scrawny and crêpey, but the effort is too much for him and it flops down again. Even his thick, springy hair has become limp and sparse across his skull. Somehow I find this difficult to look at. It's only hair, after all, but the judge was proud of his thick, wavy hair and now its paucity seems to represent the decline in his body in the most pathetic way.

'You need to know . . . ' he begins again, crooks out a finger for me to come closer. The nurses are keeping him spotlessly clean, but there is sweat on his brow and I can smell a stale scent. I clasp his hand. It feels as soft as velvet, the bones inside disjointed. These hands once hoisted with ease a small girl on to his shoulders, but now if I squeeze them too hard I fear they might shatter. I wonder what gem of advice he's going to give me on the meaning of life.

' . . . how much I love you . . . ' he says.

'Yes, Dad, I know.' I smile at him.

'You don't.'

Even on his death bed, he is debating with me. But this cannot be his death bed, while there's the tiniest breath of life.

'You don't know how wonderful it is to have a child of your own . . . a son or a daughter . . . to see your own flesh and blood created out of nothing but love . . . ' He gathers his strength. 'You don't know the pure joy you've brought me, how perfectly you've made my life complete . . . '

Another pause.

My head is whirling. *Joy? Perfect? Oh, Dad, please don't say these things. I'm a fraud. You don't know the real me. What I've done.*

'Nothing else matters, Juliet, nothing at all . . . Success and achievement are good, and you've surpassed any expectations Kitty and I had for you, but love is far more important. Love is all that matters. In the end it's all that counts . . . I hope you relax long enough to find

121

someone to love and maybe have wonderful children of your own . . . '

He stops, exhausted, staring over my shoulder into the space beyond me, and I think he has finished until he gathers strength again and goes on, 'I want to tell you that I love you . . . I want you to know . . . the joy, the sheer wonder of it all. The circle of life is a wonderful thing . . . '

He has never spoken to me like this before, and his words gouge a painful trail through my chest. I lock them into a far corner of my mind. I cannot bear to think of the full meaning of what he is saying just yet. Later, perhaps, when I'm away from here, I know they'll crawl out of their dank hiding place and drip through my veins like poison.

Because I don't deserve his love.

'You're not going anywhere, Dad, except home with me for Christmas,' I tell him, using the brisk Ms Jordan tone that warns people I mean business and sends grown men and women rushing to do my bidding.

His eyes are suddenly childlike and contrite as they fasten on mine and wrench at my heart. 'I have to go,' he says, the once-strong voice whispery. 'Kitty's waiting for me. My life hasn't been the same without your mother . . . I miss her and I want to be with her.'

I've no answer to that. How come the woman who lived in the shadow of her husband, sublimating her own life and potential, yielded so much power that he's prepared to give up his life without a fight to be with her? Perhaps his love for her, and hers for him, which I took for granted, were far greater and more powerful than I ever realised.

A life submerged and sacrificed, I'd thought, thinking I knew it all.

How little I'd known.

'Her whole, unselfish life was all about loving me, you and Robert,' he gasps. 'Nothing more. We were her world, and she was my anchor . . . I miss her so much . . . '

Neither do I realise how much of an anchor he has been to my life, how staunchly he has formed its backbone, how much he has coloured the air I breathe, until I see him lying in his coffin, the frilly white lining almost absurd against the cold stiff marble of his patrician face. I feel something collapse inside me, as though a vital part of me has crumbled away, never to be rebuilt.

People file past me at his funeral service. I don't remember any of them or what they mouth to me. Robert struts around, basking in my father's afterglow. Rebecca and Rose are there, and I talk to them, as if through a solid wall. I watch my father's coffin lowered into the cold, muddy ground, where it will stay buried for ever on an incline overlooking the sea, and as they close the gaping hole, something closes in my heart.

He is gone. It is over. As long as I live, I will never see him again.

I am free now to be whoever I want to be. All restrictions have been loosened. All love ties cut. The person I struggled to please has gone, but I don't feel free. It's as though my right arm is missing and all I'm left with is a cold feeling that nothing much matters any more.

For my father will never know just how much I loved him because only yesterday I made the ultimate sacrifice. Only yesterday I turned my back on everything that was real and essential at the core of my life to save his pride.

18

Saturday, 17 March, 1.00 a.m.

February 1973

Rebecca runs after me.

'Juliet? Are you okay?' she asks, rapping on the cubicle door after I excuse myself from the table in the Chinese restaurant and flee for the Ladies.

It's impossible to answer her with my head stuck in a toilet bowl and everything I have eaten that day projecting itself into the mess below me. When I have a moment's respite I snatch at the loo roll. The tissue is hard and grainy against my sore lips. My stomach convulses and contracts. Then I push the hair out of my face and gingerly raise my head.

'Does it sound like I'm okay?' I ask, my voice so hoarse I scarcely recognise it. The ache in my chest is ten — no, a million times worse than any pain in my stomach.

It's Valentine's evening and I'm out for a meal in a Chinese restaurant on Dame Street with Rebecca and three of her typing-pool workmates, the unattached girls, who have no date for the evening. Rebecca is having an 'off' period with Harry and we are celebrating our date-free status in the true spirit of women's liberation. It was my idea. Why sit at home lamenting the absence of roses or Valentine cards? I'd said to Rebecca. Surely it was better to go out and enjoy ourselves.

I open the door and let her in.

'Ssh,' Rebecca says. 'You'll be fine. Here, I'll rub your back.'

I don't ask her how that's supposed to help, because once more I can't talk and turn back to the bowl just in time. All the same, the light pressure of her hand, stroking, makes me feel human again and, more importantly, brings me back from spiralling into a deep, black void.

Eventually I raise my head and look at her. She's wearing the new cheesecloth top she bought in She Gear, and blue platform shoes. She looks so young and innocent, her twenty-year-old face still showing traces of puppy fat, her skin glowing, her eyes, rimmed with sparkly green Miners eye-shadow, clear and guileless. I know that what I'm about to say is going to take every scrap of innocence out of those eyes.

'Gosh, Juliet, something didn't agree with you, to say the least . . . '

Her voice trails away in response to my immobile face, which feels so hard and flat that I can't raise even the semblance of a smile. My eyes feel like lead and perspiration prickles my forehead.

I wait. Feeling raw and vulnerable, achy and terrified, I say nothing, can't bring myself to speak, just wait for her to respond to the look on my face.

'It's not just the Chinese food, is it?' she asks.

I know she's unwilling to imagine my upset stomach is due to anything other than food, but I shake my head. I wonder if she'll still be my friend when she finds out what I've gone and

126

done. That I'm that kind of girl. That I've sinned. The unholy mess I've made, the huge shame of which I can't begin to grasp. Disgrace and dishonour. Hellfire and damnation. A living nightmare.

It's not supposed to be like this. Not standing in a messy toilet cubicle where the pungent smell of vomit mixes with cheap cleaning fluid. Not with my tummy churning painfully, my teeth chattering and my heart frozen with fear.

'Juliet! Tell me!'

Somewhere at the back of my mind I'd held a soft-focus image of myself at some future date, dressed in floaty white lace, smiling serenely at a handsome husband, who has just handed me a bouquet of flowers, while the sun shines around us and life stretches ahead, shining and bright, like a new gold coin. My parents, proud, pleased and happy for us. That's the way it's supposed to be for Juliet, née Jordan, beloved daughter of Mr Justice Henry Jordan.

My head spins. My hands tremble as I feebly clutch the top of the cistern for support.

'Juliet!' Her voice is behind me.

Then, 'You're not . . . Juliet?'

I can't bring myself to look into her eyes.

'Oh, God, you can't be . . . ' Her voice is hushed.

My silence and hunched body are answer enough. There is a long moment during which I can almost hear her thoughts, opinions and ideas about me being hurled into the air until they settle again. Then Rebecca touches my shoulder. Without a word, she begins to rub my back again.

I close my eyes and we stand like that for a long time in the grimy, smelly cubicle.

★ ★ ★

'You have to be certain,' Rebecca says. 'It could be a mistake. You might just have some kind of bug . . . '

'It's not,' I say flatly. My parents are out for the evening, my father at his club in town, my mother at a Tupperware party, and Robert at a friend's house, supposedly studying. He's studying something all right, but not his textbooks, I guess. My brother and his friend are in the middle of that awkward, pimply adolescent stage and have suddenly discovered that it's okay to talk to girls. It suits me: he's so wrapped up in himself that he wouldn't notice if I dyed my hair flaming red.

Rebecca and I are in my bedroom, able to have a decent, honest-to-God conversation without fear of being overheard. The pink and white curtains are pulled against the dull, wet February evening. I sit cross-legged on the bed, and fidget with fibres from my pink candlewick bedspread. 'I'd been hoping and praying, but I haven't had a period since early December — I've missed two now.'

Rebecca sits in my white wicker chair and fiddles with the pink flouncy material running round my dressing-table. Her face is furrowed with worry and it gives me a sense of relief that she is sharing, talking about and taking seriously the nightmare I'm hiding from everyone else. 'Still . . . you need to have it confirmed, your date and all that . . . ' she says, saying aloud what I am afraid to face.

128

I get up and go over to the long white mirror, looking at my now flat tummy. It is incomprehensible to think that it will soon fill with a baby. A *baby*!

'And have you any great ideas as to how I might do that?' I say tartly. 'I can't exactly go to the local doctor, you know. The first thing he'd do is lift the phone to my father. Then he'd call the parish priest.'

'There *is* somewhere you can have it confirmed or not . . . '

'How would you know?' I'm sharp with her in my abject fear and misery.

Rebecca sighs unhappily. 'I know from girls in the typing pool. You're not the first this has happened to and you won't be the last.'

'What did they end up doing?' I asked, curiosity getting the upper hand. I'm sure there are students in college who have fallen the same way as me, but it's been covered up so discreetly that it's impossible to find out any of the basic practical facts. And I daren't risk asking any of my peers. Word would get back to my father, like wildfire. I'm alone in this, except for Rebecca.

'There's a place in town,' she tells me. 'You hand in a sample and it's anonymous. I think it costs about twenty pounds. So it's very expensive. They give you a number and you phone them a few days later for the result.'

'And if it's positive? What then? The end of my life? Can you just imagine me telling my father?' I close my eyes against the horror of it all. 'Oh, Rebecca, this would kill him. I can't do it.' I feel a lump the size of a football in my throat. I hadn't yet cried. I still can't.

'The girls in the typing pool went to England. They got six months' leave of absence without pay for domestic reasons. I'm not sure what they told their families.'

'What's the odds their families knew and were quite happy to have them out of their hair? You couldn't keep that kind of thing a secret for long.'

'I dunno. There was another girl in the typing pool who didn't know she was pregnant until she was six months gone.'

Pregnant. Even the sound of the word on Rebecca's lips makes me feel sick. It's every Irish Catholic father's worst nightmare for his daughter. How have I allowed this to happen to bright, clever Juliet Jordan? And in the most disgraceful circumstances?

'I think she was afraid to know,' Rebecca says. 'Funny thing, none of us realised either. She didn't show much until then, and next thing she was missing at coffee break. We've been told she's gone to her aunt in Liverpool for a visit. She's still not back in the office.'

I attempt a joke: 'At least nowadays most of us are spared the horrors of the sweaty Magdalene laundries or lifelong incarceration in some mental hospital. The ferry to England will be like a holiday in comparison.'

'First things first,' Rebecca says, showing a solid practicality I cling to and am immensely grateful for. 'You need to know for sure. Only then can you decide what to do.'

*   *   *

Rebecca comes to my aid again that cold afternoon in February, by accompanying me to the second-floor office off Camden Street where my urine sample will be tested anonymously and my fate revealed.

'What if I bump into someone I know?' I hiss, as we approach the narrow doorway. I stop, terror-stricken.

'Pretend it's for me,' Rebecca says staunchly.

As we stealthily mount a worn wooden staircase to the seedy room on the second floor, where every tread squeaks and loudly announces our presence, she holds out her hand and I silently give her my small container, concealed in an envelope. It takes less than five minutes to hand it over, with the cash, to a receptionist who looks as though she's seen it all before. She glances at us disinterestedly as she passes back a small ticket with a number on it and tells us in a nasal voice to phone in a weeks time. Then we're outside again, scarpering, like frightened mice, and I draw in lungfuls of cold air.

I don't need to phone to know the answer. But in case a miracle of some sort has been granted to me, I skip a lecture the following week and go down to the public phone box on the corner of St Stephen's Green. My fingers are shaking as I push two sixpences into the slot and dial. The interval between calling out my assigned number and waiting for the reply is the longest few seconds of my life. I picture the receptionist drawing a bright red fingernail down a long list

131

of anonymous numbers, stopping at the appropriate one, then moving it across to a life-altering result in the safe security of her gloomy room. Has she any idea of the power she wields? I push more coins into the slot while I wait, and I have enough time to wonder if anyone is ever lucky enough to be told their test is negative. Or if the receptionist ever makes a mistake.

But I know it is no mistake when she comes on the line and, in a voice tinged with triumph, tells me my test is positive.

★　★　★

I fell into a deep black pit all those years ago, just as I'm doing now, when I allow my eyes to close and blot out the breathing, living, star-spangled universe around me.

Back then, an all-encompassing terror consumed me.

I thought I was doing the right thing. But I know I short-changed Mr Justice Henry Jordan. For I failed him in the most essential way of all: I didn't grant him the opportunity to be bigger than himself, a truly loving, all-forgiving, all-compassionate father. For all I know, a love far greater than his pride might have blossomed if I'd told him I was expecting his grandchild.

Now I'm gripped with a different kind of terror: the prospect of my life ending far too soon, only half lived in spite of my successes, and brimming with regret for the love and happiness that might have been, and all the love I have kept hidden from the world . . .

132

19

Rose woke with a start. The bedroom was dark, except where the closed door was framed by the landing light. She was glad of those thin lines relieving the solid blackness for she knew, from her racing heart, clammy sweat and the sickening dread swirling in her tummy, that she'd been having a nightmare. Thankfully, the details escaped her. Her mouth was dry and thick, and her head was pounding: the familiar consequences of having had too much to drink on top of a tablet or two.

Matthew's side of the bed was empty. The digital clock told her it was half past two. She'd been asleep for an hour.

She got up, pulled on her dressing-gown and thrust her feet into her slippers. Out on the landing, she paused. Slightly disoriented, she had thought for a moment she was back in their first home, where the landing was narrow and there was only one small white bathroom. Life had been straightforward then, with no room for secrets or shadows lurking in corners. Here, in Belgrave Park, the landing was spacious and elegant, with several doors opening off it, and even though the curved staircase was wide and roomy, it all pressed in on her in a suffocating way. Feeling like a stranger in her own home, she stole down to the vast, state-of-the-art kitchen, with the sandblasted glass and ergonomic Bulthaup units, complete with integrated Miele appliances. She poured a glass of chilled filtered water and helped herself to a couple of extra-strength painkillers.

She padded up the hallway to where pale light was coming through the open door of Matthew's study. He sat in his shirtsleeves in front of his computer, a single lamp burning behind him, absorbed in his task. She watched him for several moments until he sensed her presence: his head snapped up so fast that she jumped. His face was drained of colour, pale and ghostly in the light coming from the screen. 'Rose! What are you doing there? You startled me.'

'And you startled me. What are you up to?'

'Just getting some emails out of the way.' He returned to the keyboard, his fingers flying across it. After a short while he looked up again, his face alight with fervour. 'It's happening now, Rose, it's really gathering pace.'

'So I guessed from tonight.'

'Sorry if you felt abandoned, but it was important for me to touch base with some people.'

'Is this what the next few weeks will be about?'

'Hopefully. I need a dedicated website and a blog, pronto. I also need to get out there and connect with people. I hope that when they think of integrity and honesty, they'll think of me. That could be my sound bite for the campaign.'

Integrity? Honesty? 'Get real, Matthew,' she said.

He held out his hand, 'I *am* real. Rose, come here. The first thing you have to do is wipe that anxious look off your face. The world isn't about to end.'

She ignored his hand and remained in the doorway, hugging herself. 'Isn't it? You know every single part of our lives will be scrutinised.'

Her encounter with Liz Monaghan had been lightweight and fluffy, compared to what might lie in wait for them. She looked beyond him to the trappings of his hard-won success: the mulberry leather chair, the wide antique desk and book-lined walls, the thick cream curtains pulled across long, elegant windows facing out onto a landscaped back garden. For a moment it swam in front of her. She took a quantum leap in associating the earnest Matthew Moore of Ballymalin with the smooth, confident Matthew Moore sitting in front of her.

Where had their lives gone? How had everything become so complicated in the blink of an eye?

'So?' he said, rising to his feet and coming over to her. He put his arms around her waist and she caught the scent of him as he pulled her close. 'Do you think I'd go ahead with all of this if I thought I was putting us and our comfortable lives in jeopardy? Nobody is going to find any skeletons in our closet. Because there aren't any. Get it?'

She remained silent and avoided his eyes.

They never spoke of the time she'd almost lost it, just four years ago. They never discussed the days and weeks she'd spent struggling through a spiralling blackness, while strange voices had echoed in her head and she'd tried and failed to make sense of a world that had suddenly caved in on her.

It had all come to a head in Dundrum Town Centre one morning, when she'd stood frozen with panic in the House of Fraser cosmetics department, not knowing how she'd got there, unable to move or articulate anything. A kindly shop assistant had spotted her distress and had peeled Rose's clenched fingers off the straps of her bag so that she could reach in for her mobile, scroll through her contacts and call someone to come to her.

'Juliet?' she'd said, her face swimming in front of Rose. 'Will I call Juliet for you?'

'Juliet . . . ' Rose had tried to grasp the name, the fleeting image of a laughing girl flickering for a moment before that, too, slipped away from her. 'No . . . '

'Rebecca?'

'Yes, please, Rebecca . . . '

Even now, four years on, Rose was still filling in the blanks of what exactly had taken place during those lost months of her life. Panic attacks, the doctor had said. Anxiety. Depression. Words that were easy to say, but went nowhere near describing the dark pit in which she'd found herself or the months it had taken her to crawl out of its depths.

Depths that might be terrifyingly easy to plunge into once more.

She tried to banish the thought. 'What will happen to Tory Technologies, if you're taken away from it?' she asked.

'I thought you might step into the breach,' Matthew joked. Then he went on, 'I have all that worked out. My team of senior executives is more than capable of holding the fort. I wish I could convince you that everything will be fine. I'll have a good team around me to take care of the campaign details. I've already been pledged lots of support. My job is to talk persuasively to a few county councils. Yours is to go shopping and have facials and stuff with Rebecca. I'll look after the rest. You'll just smile, shake hands, and look like a future president's wife. Life is going to get busy and exciting so the best thing you can do right now is run back upstairs and get a good night's sleep.'

She was still silent, questions and concerns ricocheting in her head.

'Rose, there's no need to be anxious,' he said. He was smiling at her as though she was a child, afraid of a bump in the night. 'I want this opportunity to make my mark. It's a fantastic prospect and far bigger than anything I've ever anticipated. It's more than a dream.'

'Liz Monaghan cornered me tonight. She says you're top of her interview list.'

'That bitch? She'll have to join the queue. Anyhow, I'll be engaging a campaign manager and assistants to organise all that stuff so she might find herself off the list completely.'

'Liz thinks you're hot stuff,' she said, watching his face. ' 'His male hotness', she called you.'

Matthew laughed. 'Did she really?'

Suddenly he pulled her close and kissed her hard on the mouth. Rose found herself clinging to him for reassurance as he deepened the kiss. He pulled at the sash of her dressing-gown and thrust his hand inside her lace nightgown, clutching at her curves. Rose melted into the familiarity of him and tried to forget her fears.

After a while he drew back. 'I need you with me, Rose, every step of the way.'

'I am, but . . . ' Rose faltered. 'I want you to have your dream, Matthew, but what about Juliet?'

'What about her?'

She plucked at his shirt. 'Liz talked about your posters, hanging together on the lampposts. Juliet could take it all away from you, couldn't she?'

He flicked back her hair. 'I'll just have to work extra hard and make sure she doesn't. Trust me, I know what I'm doing.'

'Do you? Juliet said . . . ' Rose paused.

'Go on,' Matt prompted, his eyes suddenly hard. 'What did Juliet say?'

Rose swallowed, anxious that her mouth was running away with her. 'She just — asked me if you were genuinely passionate about serving our country or if it was more about . . . ' Her voice trailed away.

'More about what?'

She said, very quietly, 'More about feeling important.'

'And when was this?' he asked, equally quietly, gripping her wrists.

'A couple of days ago. I told you what she said to Rebecca,' she babbled. 'Oh, Matthew . . . ' She sighed. 'I said she had no right to speak of you like that.'

He released his hold, almost sending her off balance. 'For God's sake, I'll deal with Juliet. You just keep out of it, right?'

'I was trying to help.'

'Help?' he fumed. 'You're out of your depth. I don't think you fully grasp how big this whole thing is. From now on *I'll* do the talking. You just have to look good, hang onto my arm and keep smiling. Is that too much to ask?'

'Yes, but Juliet . . . '

He glared at her. 'I don't give a flying fuck about Juliet Jordan. Get it? There's only one thing I'm interested in right now. This is my moment, my chance to dream the biggest dream and give my life a sense of purpose.'

'*Purpose*, Matthew?' she asked, feeling suddenly cold. 'How could that be missing from your life when we have so much?'

'It's a personal validation,' he said. 'I'm as good as any of the other contenders. Why shouldn't it be me, us?'

'So is that what's really driving you?'

There was a long silence while he looked at her, exasperated. 'Go back to bed, Rose. You'll feel better after a good night's sleep. James will be home soon and has promised to lend his support,' he went on. 'He knows I'm very proud of him. I'd like to make him equally proud of me.'

'You do know the opposite could happen, if things go belly up,' she said, grasping at straws in the face of a gale-force wind.

'They won't, at least not by my doing,' he said. Then he put a finger across her lips and said quietly, 'You're hardly going to rock any boats all by yourself, are you?'

She shook her head.

She went back upstairs to their bedroom, wishing she could take some of his self-belief and wrap it around herself, like a shield. For she needed a shield against the black devils of the night that had once engulfed her, but most of all, against the unspoken treachery that had put them there.

20

Saturday, 17 March, 3.00 a.m.

I never knew the depths of the night could be so iron-hard cold and bloody lonely, or that the star-filled night sky could be so clear and vast, yet totally serene, and heedless of my terror-filled predicament.

Help. Help.

There is still no sound coming out, only gossamer threads of my life weaving through my head like glittering spider's webs. I need to piece together those threads to figure out how I've ended up here.

But can I go there, to the place I've barely touched, the memory of which has up to now been locked away for fear of the devastating pain it would unleash? Yet there can't be anything more painful than lying here, totally helpless, listening to the whispering sea and wondering if I'll ever see the people I love again . . . especially the person I love most . . .

I close my eyes and peel back the memory with a gentle hand . . .

1973

My God-fearing parents don't suspect. My mother doesn't notice that I've filled out a little around the waist. I had assumed most mothers

141

would sense such things. My father fails to notice that I'm unusually subdued and edge my way guiltily around the house. For that's how I feel: edgy and guilty. Although, to be fair to them, the idea of their darling daughter falling pregnant would never cross their minds, not in a million years.

'I'm due in September,' I tell Rebecca. I calculate the date by reference to a gynaecological book she has bought, in a bookshop at the far end of town, where she was sure of not bumping into anyone she knew.

'September? That's perfect,' she says.

'You have to be joking,' I say, stony-faced. 'How could anything about this be perfect?'

I'm like a mutinous child to her almost motherly patience.

'I'm not joking, Juliet,' she insists. 'You can complete your year in college, then tell your parents you're going to London to find work for the summer and that you'll be back in time for your next college year.'

'Yes, ha!'

'Lots of students do it.'

'Yes, but London!'

'Well, it has to be somewhere like that. If you tell your parents you're going to Cork or Galway, your father will want to visit you and expect you home at the weekends.'

I shudder. 'Yes, you're right.'

'So it has to be somewhere like London, where they'd scarcely visit, or expect you home during the summer.'

'But how — where would I stay? How could I

142

support myself? And my father . . . he's bound to ask so many questions I'd never get away with it.'

'You will. We'll work it out. I didn't say you actually had to *go* to London . . . '

I have no alternative. I lie sleepless in bed at night, turning it all over in my mind. Sometimes I look at my father's face at the breakfast table and imagine breaking my news to him. It doesn't bear thinking about. I picture my mother's reaction and visualise her world falling apart. I can't let that happen. And that is all the fright I need to plan my escape, right after my third-year exam at the end of May. It also means I have only three months at home to hide my thickening waist with larger jeans and Rebecca's borrowed cheesecloth tops.

Two of my college mates are off to London for the summer, so of course I'm madly interested in their plans. I make them my own in conversations with my parents, so that places like Oxford Street, King's Road, and offices in Marylebone begin to trip off my tongue. I even compose a letter from a supposed personnel department of a London insurance office, seal it in an envelope and address it to me, and Rebecca sends it to a cousin of hers in London to post back to me, spinning a false romantic yarn about it. I tell them I'll ring home from a local callbox every Sunday, as there is no phone in the flat I'll be sharing with three other Irish Catholic girls. And, for once, my father is distracted by two things: a course of study he will be pursuing during the normally quiet summer months, plus detailed preparation for an important case that is

143

coming up in the autumn.

Which is just as well, because I don't go to London. I spend the whole summer in Galway, hiding away from the world in fear of being found out, as I wait for my baby to be born.

★ ★ ★

The months I spend in Galway are a blur, as though there is a filmy veil between me and those lost days. The fear of being found out is so great that it threatens to overwhelm me. My belly swells and I feel the baby move and kick, but I never visualise it as a real, live baby. I never imagine it as *my* baby.

I don't think I fully accept what has happened, not because I don't understand it, but because I still can't believe it has happened to me. At one level it's easier to pretend it's not happening at all.

'What does John think of all this?' Rebecca asks, when she visits me and we talk of the baby being adopted immediately after the birth. 'Surely he has some say.'

I'd been expecting this question, but it doesn't make it any easier for me to answer. Naturally Rebecca has assumed all along that the baby is his. After all, he's my occasional college boy-friend. I find it impossible to look her in the face. 'It's not John's. I've never slept with him, so he's totally in the clear. And I finished with him as soon as I knew.'

'Then who is the father?' Her voice is tentative and she looks at me very closely for quite a long moment.

I continue with my carefully constructed lie. 'The father is a cousin of John's.'

'A cousin of John's,' she repeats.

'He was home from San Francisco for Christmas with his wife . . . '

'His *wife?*'

I force myself to look at her. 'Yes, I slept with a married man. It was a big mistake.'

She stares at me without saying anything.

'I don't blame you if you never want to talk to me again. I'm already thoroughly ashamed of myself so you don't have to lecture . . . '

'Have I said anything?' she says sharply, clearly upset at the mess I've brought on myself.

I fill in the gaps. 'We met at a family party and had a short and very stupid fling.' That part was true anyway. It had been short and stupid. And I guess I became pregnant that last time before Christmas, when he'd been so urgent that we'd taken a chance. I can't quite believe how silly I was.

'I don't remember meeting him. Did I?' She wrinkles her brow.

Oh, the innocence of my trusting friend!

I evade her question. Sometimes white lies are important. I can't burden her with the uncomfortable truth. 'He's gone back to San Francisco with his wife, and he'll never know about the baby,' I say. 'Oh, Rebecca, for all my lofty, change-the-world ideas, I'm nothing but a second-rate fraud. I've let every single woman and all my feminist friends down. Never mind my parents. And now I'm denying my baby.' I put my fist to my mouth, still unable to cry.

Rebecca stays silent, but her face shows nothing except compassion. I don't deserve it, any more than I deserve my father's love.

'You're doing what you think is best,' she said eventually. 'Best for everyone concerned. The baby, your parents, you . . . The baby will go to a loving home, and it'll never be called illegitimate. You're sparing your parents' heartbreak and disappointment, and after all this, you'll still make a great life for yourself. You're young, Juliet. This time next year you'll be getting ready for your finals and a whole new life. This will be behind you.'

I let her words trickle through the tight ball of frozen nerve endings that are lodged in my chest. It sits there as the weeks roll on, spreading to encompass my neck and head. I dutifully phone home every Sunday evening, pretending I'm calling from London, even buying English newspapers so that I can stay abreast of the news. My due date arrives, slips past, and then, four days later, I wake very early to twinges in my back. I stand by the window of an anonymous bedroom in Galway, watching the dawn unfurl across the September sky, and manage to bury the spark of awe and amazement that courses through me: I have put all my feelings on hold and this is happening to someone else, not Juliet Jordan, most perfect, beloved darling daughter of Mr Justice Henry Jordan.

This . . .

It's not me lying on the hospital bed as my body performs nature's most amazing ritual, nor is it my hands reaching for gas whenever the strong, purposeful pain threatens to overwhelm me; it's not me beginning to think my back is about to break in two and I just can't take any more, when at last they tell me to bear down; and it's not me experiencing that truly miraculous moment when the life that has been nurtured inside me for all those heart-wrenching months finally bursts forth, whole, complete and oh-so-perfect, into the waiting world, on that hushed September evening.

And it's not me who gives away that warm, white-wrapped bundle a few days later.

And arrives back in Dublin to pick up the threads of my life, as though none of it has ever happened. And fraudulently sips champagne with my proud father year on year, toasting each fresh success.

Except the one that truly matters.

21

'Liz! What the hell . . . What's been happening to you?'

The ground swayed in front of her. She caught a glimpse of her shoes before her head snapped back and her face was washed in the glare of an orange street-lamp. She clutched the railings beside her and wheeled around, crashing face first into them, hitting her lip off the cold metal. She felt something swing out and around from her shoulders and realised it was her handbag.

Gavin's anxious face appeared in her vision, blurred and indistinct. 'Liz! Jesus! I'm getting you home.'

She felt his arm anchor itself around her waist, and allowed herself to be shunted down the road. She was vaguely aware of curious glances, the tittering of passers-by, the snarl of traffic, and headlights hurting her eyes.

'Will you be okay in a taxi? Can't have you getting sick.'

Her teeth were chattering so hard she couldn't answer. She moved her head in what she thought was a nod.

'How — how did . . . you . . . ' She grappled with the words, trying to form them properly, but her mouth and teeth felt as if they were made of sponge.

Gavin knew what she was trying to say. 'Some good Samaritan called me from your mobile,' he said. 'She was concerned when she saw you slumped in a corner of the Ladies at three in the morning. You still have me down as your emergency number. I don't know what you were doing guzzling your brains out in that rip-off nightclub, but you were lucky someone was looking out for you. Otherwise you'd be in A&E right now. Or in the gutter.'

'Thanksh.'

'Can you manage?'

She felt herself being half lifted, half pushed into the back of a taxi, caught the faint smell of leather mingled with that ubiquitous taxi scent, as she relaxed into the seat, and the door closed, shutting out the cold night air. She was dimly aware of Gavin getting in beside her and asking the taxi man to drive to Harold's Cross. She closed her eyes and sank back as they swirled into the stream of traffic.

The next thing she was aware of was Gavin opening the passenger door and half pulling her out. She didn't think she was going to be able to stand on her shaky legs, but somehow she managed it. Then her handbag fell on to the pavement outside her home, scattering most of the contents. Gavin pushed her against the window ledge for support and she looked at the dark blond spikes of his hair as he bobbed around and gathered up her phone, keys and makeup. He opened the hall door, switched off the alarm, and half carried her down the narrow hall to the small kitchen. She blinked in the bright light.

'Water, lots of it,' he said, turning on the cold tap.

'I don't . . . ' Once again she tried and failed to speak coherently.

'You must. Have you any idea how drunk you are? For God's sake, Liz, how did you manage to get into this mess?' He didn't wait for her to answer. He thrust a large glass of water at her, and even pushed it against her mouth as she sipped it, her teeth clinking against the glass. It seemed to take for ever and she gagged a few times, convinced she was drowning. Then, at last, the glass was empty and he put it on the sink.

'Right. Bathroom and bed. I'm staying, but just to make sure you're okay and don't choke on something. Jesus, woman, you had me scared for a moment. I've never seen you like this before.'

He hauled her upstairs, took off some of her clothes, and pushed her into the bathroom. When she held onto the washbasin for balance and looked in the mirror, she saw two sets of red squinty eyes ringed in smudgy kohl staring back at her. Devil eyes.

Oh, God, was she going to pay for this.

Eventually she swayed out into the bedroom. Using her hands to grasp the furniture and help her unsteady legs to negotiate the room, she finally reached the bed and collapsed on to it. He pulled the duvet out from under her inert body, tucking it around her. 'Get some sleep. You'll need all your strength for the hangover you're going to have tomorrow.'

'Mmm.'

'Liz,' he asked, after a beat, 'are you really that

cracked up over your father and the house?'

'Mmm.'

'We'll talk tomorrow,' Gavin said, in a kinder voice.

Maybe someone did care about her, after all. She turned on to her side, relieved when he clicked off the lamp. She hadn't the energy to talk. Nor did she want to. How had she gone so totally off the deep end tonight? She tried to piece together what had happened earlier, wondering who might have witnessed her descent into Blotto Land. She vaguely recalled leaving the Ballsbridge Hotel with a couple of other partygoers and hitting a Leeson Street nightclub. Before that, she'd been chatting to Rose Moore.

Liz's head spun as she lay in bed, her body curved into the foetal position.

Definitely something amiss there.

22

Saturday, 17 March, 3.45 a.m.

I sense I'm reaching the deep, dark depths of the night. And I'm beginning to think I need a miracle. I haven't been one for prayer in recent years, but maybe I could do with some praying as I stare at the heavens and think of my terrible sin, my disgrace, my downfall.

It took almost four years for the reality of what I had done to hit me.

1977
Rebecca and I are having a rare evening out together as I'm home from Queen's University, Belfast, for a reading week. Rebecca has just turned to me and told me in a rush, as though she'd been holding the words pent up inside her, that she's pregnant and getting married.

Surprise catches me off guard, and sharp, black pain slices through me. It hasn't bothered me that Rose and Matthew now have James, their wonderful son. Still cocooned behind the barricade of the armour plating I built around that episode in my life as a means of saving my sanity. On the odd occasion I am in their company, I watch impassively as he grows from babyhood to toddler, and while each milestone is anticipated and feverishly applauded by his proud and loving parents, it all flows past me as though it is meaningless. Because clever clogs Juliet, expertly schooled in the rationality of law, has taught herself to be emotionally detached.

But Rebecca, my best friend, having a baby . . . It's the first time I feel a chink in my armour, and I'm not sure I can cope with the eviscerating pain.

Rebecca's eyes are appealing as they watch me. Her circumstances are different from what mine were. She is finally in a committed relationship with Harry. He works in a big accountancy firm and I was with her the night they met unexpectedly in Sloopy's disco in Fleet Street, not having seen each other for three months. He asked her to dance to Queen's 'Bohemian Rhapsody'. She melted into his arms that night and has scarcely left them since.

Even now, things are shifting a little in so-called modern-day Ireland. In the public service and semi-state bodies, women no longer have to resign on marriage — big deal — and it's possible to apply for a period of twelve weeks' maternity leave with pay.

Although Rebecca's will still be called a 'shotgun wedding', and girls are still 'getting into trouble', looking for six months' unpaid leave and quietly getting boats to England, then returning home with broken hearts.

'It'll be a small wedding,' she says, looking nervously at me.

I hug her. 'That's great, Rebecca. I'm really happy for you and Harry, and I know it will all work out.'

'Will you be my bridesmaid? I know you're going back to Queen's next week, but we're getting married at Easter . . .'

I'm improving myself further by adding a prestigious doctorate to the letters after my name. It's keeping me busy and justifying my parents' flourishing and unabated pride in me. I have given them that much, but their pride lies in tatters inside me.

'No matter. Your wedding is more important. I'll come down from Belfast anytime. And you can come up to visit me and we'll shop together for your going-away clothes.'

When sweet little Danielle is born, I've had time to prepare myself for the sight of the warm bundle in Rebecca's arms and my armour is back in place, putting a thick, hard shield between me and everything I'd felt during that traumatic time in my life. I'm relieved to feel nothing beyond the happiness you'd share with a friend. As well as that, safe behind my armour, I'm free to dote on Danielle, to hug and kiss her, to feel the warmth of her in my empty arms, and give free rein to my suppressed maternal instincts by loving her as though she's my own.

And Rebecca, in her generosity, declares I can be Danielle's honorary mother.

When Rose sees the way I dote on Danielle, as she grows from babyhood to toddler, she says I can be James's honorary aunt.

As I steadily carve out a name for myself in the area of women, gender and equality studies, the thick shield between me and that traumatic time in my life serves me well. It means I can spend the week in the cut-and-thrust of the university and business environs, but now and again indulge my maternal instincts by enjoying time with Danielle and James, taking them to the pantomime, the cinema, the beach, even Verbena View to meet my parents at Christmas, and spoiling them on their birthdays.

The best of both worlds.

Almost.

23

Saturday, 17 March, 4.00 a.m.

I know this hour like you would a familiar friend.
I've kept watch with it too often. It's the darkest
time of the night, impenetrable and still, as
though morning is a long way off and every
living person is sound asleep, except me. Not
much use calling for help, even if I could do so.
Right now, I'm totally alone in the world, and
apart from the whispering sea, it seems that even
the universe is keeping a death-like silence.

Or a vigil.

No matter what age you are, you still think it's
going to last for ever, your life. You think there's
going to be time for everything. Time to put your
world to rights. When I was younger, the years
rolled on into an infinite future that bore no
relation to how speedily they pass, and how
limited they become. Now time seems to have
flitted past on wings that beat swifter with each
successive year, just as fragmented pictures of
my life are whirling into the dark space above
me.

The acute loneliness makes me feel I have
fallen to the bottom of the void and, surprisingly,
lends me strength to watch with an eerie calm as
moments that make up my life unspool around
me. I try to make sense of what has happened,
and figure out exactly how I arrived here . . .

Who could have pushed me? Why did it happen? Could I have prevented it?

1990

'I'm moving back to Verbena View,' I tell Rebecca one afternoon, about two years after my father's death. We're having a meal in the Trocadero, St Andrew Street, before we go to see Patrick Swayze in *Ghost*, the hottest movie at the moment. By now, Danielle is a shy, smiling thirteen-year-old, on the sweet, tentative edge of adolescence. Rebecca's twin sons are nine and football mad, and she has matured into a warm, loving person whom I feel privileged to call my friend. She's beginning to get back to herself after the busy child-rearing years, and has started to tint her wavy hair with blonde highlights. It suits her.

'It's a fine house,' Rebecca says.

'It'll be perfect. It's about time I got on the property ladder and stopped renting. Robert will be only too happy if I offer to buy him out. He's never going to come back to Ireland to live. The house needs a bit of a makeover, rewiring and an upgrade to the central heating.' My father had let it go a little, which had been another symptom of his loneliness that I'd been too blind to see. 'And I'm going to knock down as many walls as I can to let in the light and fantastic views,' I continue cheerfully, 'especially in the kitchen, so it'll be something to keep me busy.'

'Keep you busy? Juliet, you're the busiest person I know. Between your career, your charity work and your travels, you don't have a spare moment.'

'I'd prefer to have no time to think. This will be something positive ... It might help me finally move on after my father ... '

'How long now?' Rebecca asked, instantly sympathetic, her hand on my arm, her gaze softened.

God bless Rebecca, one of life's nurturers. Still in mother-mode with me a lot of the time.

'Two years, and I know I should be over it by now.'

'Juliet, you never get over these things, you can only learn to adjust to them.'

'Yes, well ... ' I fall silent for a moment. 'Verbena View will be big enough for great parties and for everyone to visit. All of you. I can see us sitting on the patio sipping chilled white wine, you and Rose, with Matthew and Harry, and the kids in the TV room that I'm going to kit out. Television, stereo and a computer for games. Your children are the nearest I'll ever have to a family.'

'You don't know that.'

'I do. There's no sniff of romance in my life. I'm not interested either. Besides, I'm too old at thirty-seven to start accommodating a man in my life. And I wouldn't bring a child into the world unless I was in a committed relationship, which I'll never be.'

'You're far too young to be making announcements like that.'

I smile at my friend. 'Rebecca, you should know. I can't be truly honest with any man, therefore I'll never marry.' It was the closest I'd ever come to talking about my colourful history in all the years since I'd given up my baby. Normally it was a closed book between us. I preferred it like that, and I think Rebecca did, too.

'You're being very harsh on yourself.'

'I'm being honest and realistic. Besides, I'm married to my career. Did I tell you I've been invited to Oxford to speak to their women's studies undergraduates? They're examining a paper I wrote.'

'I'm impressed with that, but not impressed with the way you're turning your back on love and motherhood.'

'I don't deserve either, not after what I did.'

'Juliet! You can't condemn yourself like that. You were young, and maybe a little foolish. You did the best you could. That doesn't mean you have to give yourself a life sentence. Do you still have regrets?' Rebecca's blue-green eyes looked worried.

'No.' I hastened to reassure her, perhaps even to reassure myself.

But I had. Of course I had. Especially since my father had died. Two years on, I'm still finding life achingly empty without him and haunted by what I did. Rebecca has no idea how guilty I feel. Or how the ghost of my father still lurks in the corners of my life, never mind the ghost of the baby I gave away, as well as the man I loved just briefly and turned my back on.

My love for Danielle is a reflection of the love my father poured on me, and has helped me to realise that, had they known, my parents would have been far more hurt by my subterfuge and reluctance to trust them than any trouble I might have brought them. Slowly but surely, the magnitude of what I had done to my parents was crawling home to me. I had denied them a grandchild. I had denied them a chance to love me and offer me support at a time when I needed it most. And I had denied myself love. For clever, talented Juliet Jordan had thought she knew it all when she hadn't known anything about courage, or being true to herself, or the redeeming power of love.

★ ★ ★

As I lie caught between heaven and hell, neither of which I believe in, I run through the age-old prayers my father taught me. *Forgive me, Father . . .*

Then peace descends. What great wrong had I done, after all? What immoral sin had I committed? I'd brought life into the world. *Life.* Why had I carried that like a blemish for almost forty years and allowed it to colour my life so darkly? And I'd loved somebody who had badly needed my love.

So could I, please, have the chance to put things right?

Dear God, if I could have just *one* more day . . . Please? If I could wake up in the morning with a whole glorious day stretching in front of me, enough time to take care of the really important things . . .

160

24

Saturday, 17 March, 4.30 a.m.

Liam. Liam Corrigan.

Out of the dark, grinding depths of this night, the name slides through the back of my head and faint pictures twirl on the edge of my mind. Who is he? Why is the name so familiar, as though I've known it all my life? Was he with me this evening as I fell? I wait to allow the flickering images to make sense. And then they pour through me, clear and distinct and colourful, pictures of the times our lives collided . . .

1965
We are in the vegetable shop, my mother and I, and he is near the back door, weighing out bags of potatoes on big industrial scales, muffled in a brown overall brushed with potato dust. The air is pungent with the scent of citrus mingling with the deeper, earthy smell of clay.

I've noticed him before, kicking a football with the other boys in the village, and scrubbed up for church on Sundays. I've seen him trekking up and down the hills of Howth while I swished by in my father's car. Taller than the other lads, but skinny, with unruly red hair, he seemed friendly enough. But this time when he shoots glances at me between tipping hessian sacks over the lip of the scales and sending a clatter of potatoes into the bowl, his face is proud and resentful, and I wonder what I've done to deserve it. Then his eyes linger scornfully on my school uniform, the wine-coloured tunic with the crest of the private city-centre school I attend, which tells me everything.

My mother looks overdressed in her costume and pill-box hat. She's particularly choosy in placing her order, breaking off every so often to chat to May, the wife of the owner. She explains that our housekeeper is ill. I wish she'd hurry up because he's making me feel uncomfortable. I move a little closer to her and catch her light, familiar scent. Then May notices that he has slackened off a little.

'Liam, get a move on. I need them potatoes sorted by four o'clock, and you've to start making up the orders for delivery after that. Snap to it.'

He scowls at me one final time before he turns his back. His shoulders are stiff and the tips of his ears burn crimson.

May shakes her head at my mother. 'Kids nowadays. So ungrateful. He should be thankful after all I've done for him.'

'He's a bit young to be working,' I say to my mother, when we're eventually out in the clear bright air. I had put him at around twelve, my age. My mother slides her small hands into soft leather gloves and places one protectively on my arm as we cross the road to the spot where my father will collect us.

'He's lucky he has May looking after him,' she

says, when we're on the other side. 'It's only right that he should help her in the shop when he's home from school.'

'Why?'

My mother speaks softly, as though she's imparting highly sensitive information. 'He's adopted. May took him in when he was a small boy. Otherwise he would have had to go to an industrial school.'

'What's that?'

'It's a place for children who have no parents to look after them. The lucky ones are adopted. So Liam is one of the lucky ones.'

Lucky to be rescued from the grim prospect of an industrial school by being adopted. My mother's tone had seemed to imply that Liam was extra indebted to his adoptive parents, and I wonder how that makes him feel. No wonder he was scowling at me in my private-school uniform.

After that, anytime I bump into him in the village, we eye each other guardedly. When he is a little older, he begins to do the Saturday deliveries and sometimes I'm home when he drives up the hill in a battered van and calls to our house, lugging a box of vegetables and fruit into the larder off the kitchen. His face is shadowed with resentment, especially when my father's big car is slung across the driveway instead of hidden in the garage.

Occasionally I see him hanging around with the same group of friends as Rose and Rebecca. But it's not until I start college that his resentment towards me thaws a little. He works

163

for a builders' supplies company during the week, and we sometimes catch the same bus home.

May 1971
'I'm going to make my fortune by the time I'm thirty,' he boasts, one warm early-summer evening, as the bus crawls along the Howth Road.

Dublin Bay is a swathe of pearly grey silk, the outline of Howth Head at one end and the Pigeon House towers at the other seeming to drift in the heat haze. Everything in life seems possible. Still, I hear a hint of vulnerability in his tone, as though he doesn't quite believe in himself. He's trying to impress me and I'm touched.

'That's very ambitious,' I say. 'How are you going to manage it?'

In his blinkered defensiveness, he misinterprets my words. 'I knew you'd think I'm far too big for my boots,' he says wryly. 'Too presumptuous for someone who left school at sixteen and still has to help May in the greengrocer's on Saturdays. I don't even know who my real ma was. She never bothered with me, so I'm the original cocky bastard.'

'That's not what I meant,' I say evenly. 'How do you plan to make your fortune?'

He gives me a considered look. His need to impress me overcomes his pride. 'Construction. It's doing really well and I want a piece of the action. I want to send my kids to a posh school and live in a big bungalow on a hill with views of the sea, and have a big car in the garage.'

His voice is so thick with hunger that I don't know what to say. 'Will that make you happy?' I ask eventually.

'Too right it will. It'll make me very happy. I bet you're going to run the country.'

'What makes you say that?'

'You're clever and going to college,' he says. 'You could blow the present lot of politicians out of the water.'

He wouldn't be saying that to me if he knew that when the students' union was looking for volunteers to hand out contraceptives I'd balked. When feminist campaign meetings were being held off campus I didn't attend. When huge crowds attended a Women's Liberation meeting in the Mansion House I stayed away. I couldn't run the risk of word getting back to my father.

But I was going on the train to Belfast in a couple of weeks' time. I could mingle with the regular passengers and hide in the crowd, but at least I'd be part of it, if a little removed. It would be my private rebellion.

'Thanks. I'd love to rule the world, but I think you might have to adjust your expectations,' I say, trying to let him down gently.

'So I'm not good enough to aim high?'

'Of course you are. It's just — Look, we may be in an expanding construction cycle at the moment, but I don't think it'll last long enough for you to make your fortune. So don't put all your eggs in one basket.'

'Don't be such a kill-joy. The seventies is going to be a great decade.'

1985

Liam turns up at my mother's funeral, looking a little older and wiser and wearing a good suit. A far cry from the skinny, resentful adolescent with the freckled face and grubby overall. After a spell of unemployment in the late seventies, he has spent the last few years working in America.

'I know this is a bad day for you,' he says, his eyes warm, 'but can we meet for dinner? Soon? I'm home from the States for three weeks and would love to catch up.'

Funnily enough, caught in an unreal limbo after my mother's passing, there's no one else I'd rather go out with. We meet the following Wednesday night. When we have dispensed with the normal pleasantries and I've once again accepted his condolences, he fidgets with the salt cellar and says, half teasing, 'You were right with your forecast, dammit. My thirtieth birthday was a couple of years ago, and I'm far from my planned millionaire status.'

'Same here,' I say. 'I'm not ruling the world.'

He laughs and goes on to tell me about his project-management job in construction, based in Pittsburgh. 'I'm doing very well, thank you, making contacts and stashing some cash. And I'll be more prepared to jump on the bandwagon the next time the country heads into a roll. Not bad for an illegitimate brat.'

'Stop, Liam. Don't carry that kind of baggage. You're an adult and you're the only person responsible for yourself now.'

166

After a while he says, 'And what about you? Marriage? Kids?'

I manage to shake my head and smile, even though the baby I gave up lets out the plaintive cry of a newborn at the back of my mind. I give my standard reply. 'Still waiting for Mr Right.'

'I don't suppose I'd be in with a chance?' Then, almost immediately, 'Nah, don't answer that. You were always in a league of your own, Juliet, and far too good for the likes of me. All the guys were a little in love with you, back then.'

I laugh it off, hoping I don't sound too dismissive.

We order dessert and talk about the Live Aid concert that has just taken place in London and Philadelphia. We both agree that Queen and Freddie Mercury stole the show. He walks me back to Verbena View and kisses my cheek at the gate, a little tentatively, as though we're shy teenagers instead of thirty-somethings.

In the numbness of the following months, I adjust to life without my self-effacing mother, who has left a huge vacuum in her quiet wake. I tiptoe around the edge of this gaping hole with my father. Three years later, around the time that my father is dying, an invitation arrives to Liam's wedding in New York. He is to be married to a Rachel Summers. She sounds blonde and beautiful, like someone from *Charlie's Angels*, but I'm caught up in nightmarish hospital visits and ignore it.

Then years later, and out of the blue, Liam

turns up at my fortieth birthday party.

As I lie suspended between the dark void surrounding me and an even darker void that is stalking me, I close my eyes and allow myself to sink back into the embrace of that night . . .

25

Saturday, 17 March, 5.15 a.m.

1993
One minute, it seemed, we were twenty-somethings, the bright young things of the groovy generation. Then, in the next breath, we're forty, Rebecca and I, our birthdays just a couple of months apart.

'Forty! How did that happen?' Rebecca asks, sounding disgruntled.

'Don't ask me, I still feel eighteen.'

'When I was eighteen, people who were forty were old. *Old*.'

'The world's changed since then.'

'Even Ireland's come of age. You were right all along, Juliet. I didn't think we'd see a woman president.'

'The first of many, I hope. But our generation of women is still young and pushing down even more barriers. Didn't you hear that forty is now the new thirty? And by the time we get to sixty, it'll be the new forty?'

'Hmm. I might be able to live with that.'

★ ★ ★

Feeling very extravagant, we head to London for a weekend, and go shopping on Oxford Street. I buy a leather and sheepskin flying jacket, the nearest I'll ever get to a pilot's licence, I joke to Rebecca. She spends ages in Selfridges, picking out tops for Danielle, until I finally persuade her to shop for herself.

Then I throw a party at Verbena View. The renovations are complete and the house has been modernised, while holding on to some comfortable, timeless features of my grandmother's day. Out in the garden the caterers have set up a small marquee where the drink is flowing and the food is plentiful.

These are good days. Ireland has emerged from a long, grey recession and there is light at the end of the tunnel. The mood is buoyant among my friends and acquaintances from the university, as well as Rebecca and Rose, along with their friends and families. We're all glammed up. I'm clad in a Dolce & Gabbana gold dress, with black suede shoes. Rebecca goes all out in a black velvet Richard Lewis dress and a crocheted silver cardigan.

Danielle is sixteen and has turned into a beauty. She has cornflower blue eyes, blonde hair, and Rebecca's soft, warm manner. She's wearing a raspberry taffeta dress that suits her slim figure, along with the silver Tiffany pendant I'd given her. I love her to bits. She's delighted when I press a glass of champagne into her hands. 'Gosh, thanks, Aunt Juliet.'

'Hey,' I laugh, 'I've asked you before to please drop the 'Aunt'. Besides, I'm not really your aunt. That's reserved for Rose. Don't forget, I'm your honorary mum.'

She looks flustered and I could bite my

170

tongue. 'Yes — sorry — it's just, well, I've never had real champagne before.'

That I could believe, for Harry's income has been fairly average all these years, and he'd had a spell of unemployment in the eighties. Rebecca had stayed at home to raise the family, so there were no luxuries in the household. Now that the twins Kevin and Mark are twelve, Rebecca has returned to work. Just as we'd hoped all those years ago, there are opportunities for her to balance work with her home life that didn't exist for our mothers. Discrimination based on age, gender, marital status and other grounds is now illegal. This year the legislation that outlawed homosexual acts was repealed. I can't help wondering if Mr Justice Henry Jordan has turned in his grave at all these changes. Perhaps he turned in it long ago over the shadowed life of his precious, dutiful daughter.

Something that still haunts me, even at forty.

Still, he would have liked the fact that I'm living here, using his study as my own, sitting in his chair, even adding to the framed certificates on the wall. I'm sure he would have been happy, too, with the party I'm throwing, and the beautiful young people milling about, Danielle, Kevin, Mark, and Rose's son, James.

I've seen a lot of my friends' children over the years, mostly Danielle and James. They've sometimes stayed at Verbena View, in my parents' old bedroom, which I turned into a guest room with en-suite bathroom. I taught James and Danielle how to swim on the beach at Howth, I brought Danielle shopping for her first makeup kit, and I taught James to drive on the quiet roads around Howth in my trusty red Triumph, which Matthew wasn't all that pleased about. I think he wanted that milestone to be reserved for himself.

'You'll be having lots of lovely champagne in the years to come, Danielle. Your life is all ahead of you, and it'll be brilliant.' I give her a hug, and her cheeks redden with pleasure.

'Thanks, Juliet. I love coming here,' she says. 'I love the comfy feel of your house. It's so relaxing, even the study with the shelves full of books. And the big leather chair in front of a log fire on a winter's afternoon is perfect for curling up in. But the kitchen is something else. Wow.'

'Yes, isn't it?' I tuck my hand in her arm and we walk into the room that runs right across the back of the house.

I have knocked out one wall, and replaced it with glass doors that fold back on each other, and tonight they are open to the sea and sky, with friends and colleagues laughing and chatting, drifting between the kitchen, the patio and the marquee. 'You know my door is always open, don't you? And bring your friends. I've plenty of room.'

'Thanks, Juliet.'

'Where are the guys?' I ask, looking around.

'They're in the television room playing computer games. They've been holed up there most of the evening,' Danielle says. 'I think James . . .' She hesitates, colours a little. 'No, forget it,' she says, smiling in such an embarrassed way that I'm loath to question her.

It's not long, however, before I discover what was most likely bothering her. Shortly after that I walk in on Rose and Matthew having an argument about James in my bedroom. And some of my pleasure in the night evaporates. I was trying to get away from the noise and bustle of the party to touch up my makeup and have five minutes to myself, but as I open the bedroom door I catch Matthew's heated words.

'I'm not having it, do you hear me?'

'I hear you loud and clear, Matthew,' Rose says, in a tone I have rarely heard from her, a voice I scarcely recognise. Confident, authoritative. 'I'm also listening to what James has to say,' she continues, and I realise she sounds so assertive because she is defending James. Like a lioness defending her cub.

'Why don't you listen to his side of the story?' Again, a strong, direct tone, most unlike Rose. She falters when she sees me on the threshold, and Matthew, who has had his back to me so far, wheels around and glares at me.

He hates me catching him on the back foot. We are both ambitious people and have always sparked off each other, the rivalry between us thinly veiled in our debates. In front of me, Matthew likes to act as if all is perfect in his carefully controlled life, so now he is annoyed that I have seen him with his guard down.

'Sorry, Juliet,' Rose says, her face a little pale against the black lace of her dress. 'We needed a word in private and found ourselves in here.'

'No worries,' I say. I stand my ground, unwilling to back out. 'But if you want to have a row

173

about James, this party is the last place for it.'

'We have a bit of a crisis on our hands,' Matthew says, struggling to keep his voice even.

'Crisis?' I echo, and raise my eyebrows, even though I'm unwilling to be drawn into the conflict between them.

'I don't think we should be having this conversation.' Rose shakes her head.

'And when were you going to tell me?' Matthew snaps. 'Or were you going to let me find out for myself?'

I raise my hands in surrender. 'Hey, look — '

'I know, I know,' Matthew says impatiently. 'Wrong time, wrong place.'

'We're in the middle of a party. Maybe you could have this conversation tomorrow.'

'Tomorrow?' Matthew shakes his head. 'How am I supposed to wait until then to put some sense into his head?'

'Matthew! For God's sake, it's not the end of the world,' Rose says. She darts a worried glance at me and, for the first time, her composure seems ruffled.

By now I've ruled out an incurable illness, which would be the end of the world for both doting Rose *and* Matthew. Pregnant girlfriend springs to mind, or caught rolling a joint in college rooms. Neither of which is the end of the world. Nowadays.

Rose turns to me. 'Thing is, Juliet, James has decided he's dropping out of his course in college. Like now.'

For a long time, I say nothing. Then, mildly, 'Is that it?'

'Matthew's not happy with him.'

'Would you be, Juliet, if you were in my shoes?' Matthew's eyes gleam, as though he's daring me to come down on one side or the other.

It's easy to sidestep his challenge. 'I'm not in your shoes, Matthew,' I say smoothly, 'so it's none of my business. Though James could probably have picked a better time to make his announcement, rather than tonight.'

'It's all happened very suddenly.' Once again Rose jumps to defend him. 'James has been offered a place in a rock band after their bass guitarist had a car accident. But they need him immediately because they've been offered a support spot in U2's European tour. It's a fantastic opportunity, with lots of European dates, plus London and Dublin.'

'A rock band?' I try to keep the surprise out of my voice, although I should have guessed: James spent his adolescence superglued to his guitar.

Matthew interjects: 'I never heard of The Name, did you? And after everything we've — '

'Careful, Matthew,' Rose says. 'We're not having a row about this here.'

'Too right you're not,' I say. 'At this party, I want to see happy faces.'

For a moment I'm tempted to urge them to allow their son to follow his heart, not the path they'd prefer for him, but I won't challenge Matthew about it. We're interrupted by Harry putting his head round the door. He's been looking for me.

'Juliet,' he smiles in a way that tells me he

knows I've landed in the middle of a heated exchange between Rose and Matthew and that he's about to rescue me, 'there's someone at the door who wants to talk to you. I think he's a bit reluctant to come in.'

'Okay, I'll be there now,' I say to him, relieved to have an excuse to get away from Rose and Matthew.

I walk up the hallway to find Liam Corrigan standing in the porch.

If, in his heart, he still carried any remaining trace of the resentful adolescent there is no sign of it in the self-assured tilt of his chin and the ease with which he squares his shoulders in his beautifully cut suit. Confidence oozes around him, like an aura.

'Juliet, I'm here to complain about the awful racket coming from this house. You can be heard all the way down in the village.'

I laugh and, delighted to have been delivered from a rather fraught scene with my dignity intact, throw my arms around him, then invite him in rather more warmly than I otherwise might have.

He mingles easily, drawing quite a crowd. He looks at home in Verbena View as he relaxes in a patio chair, chatting with Harry and flirting unashamedly with Rebecca. It's not the first time he's flirted with her in my home, but Rebecca stays cool, and Harry curves his arm around her shoulders, marking his territory. Danielle blushes crimson when Liam tells her she's a fabulous young woman, beautiful enough to rival any New York model.

Rose and Matthew have effected some kind of truce: they stroll back out on to the patio, holding hands, as if they've stepped out for a photo call. I wonder how often they have posed like that for the sake of appearances and it bothers me. Even though they haven't met in years, Matthew and Liam still don't quite hit it off, both of them eyeing the other, like circling dogs trying to establish which is superior. And when James stalks out of the TV room, sensing the storm has abated, it is clear that Matthew is the winner.

If Danielle, at sixteen, is dazzling enough to outshine a New York model, then James, at twenty, might have stepped out of a Hollywood movie. Tall and lean, with messy dark hair, he's not conventionally handsome, but he has a sensitive, caring face and the kind of smiling, darkly lashed blue eyes that could hold an audience. I manage to wink at him and give him a thumbs-up out of Matthew's view, then follow it with a grin as I strum an air guitar. He flashes me an answering smile.

'Your son, all grown-up?' Liam asks, in a voice tinged with envy.

Matthew positively swells, any grievance with James swiftly smoothed over in the interests of impressing Liam. 'Yes,' he says.

'Lucky man,' Liam concedes. 'I don't have family.'

He looks at me as he says this and I wonder what has happened to his marriage.

* * *

'I can't believe I've hit the grand old age of forty and still haven't made my fortune,' Liam says later, as we sit at the kitchen table after everyone has left.

'Life doesn't always turn out the way we expect it to,' I say, marvelling at my understatement as I crumple a pile of discarded paper napkins together.

'I'll give you a hand clearing up,' he says, half rising to his feet.

'No need. The caterers are sending people tomorrow to put the place to rights. Here.' I hand him a bottle of wine. 'Pour some more and tell me what happened with your wife.'

Liam refills our glasses and gives me a sad summary of his failed marriage. 'Unfortunately Rachel and I have irreconcilable differences,' he says. 'We rushed into things far too soon and I'm filing for divorce.'

'Sorry to hear that.'

'It's fine. She doesn't mean anything to me any more.'

'Hmm. I thought I saw you giving Rebecca a few interested glances tonight. What's that about?'

'Ah, you were the sparkling unattainable one we drooled over, Juliet,' he grins, 'up there, in a league of your own. But Rebecca's the warm, reliable girl next door. She's turned into a very attractive lady and Harry's a lucky man. Then again, it was always Rebecca for him. I think he was the only one of us who didn't lust secretly after you in the days of our youth.'

'You're making me out to be a right

schoolboy's crush, and if you say it once more, I'll make you clean up.' I laugh, lobbing a tinfoil tray at him. 'When are you heading back to the States?'

'Next week, but just to tie up the red tape on the divorce, and then, well, I have some big plans.'

'I'm glad your dreams haven't been crushed.'

'Anything but,' he says, sitting up a little straighter. 'I'm coming back to Dublin permanently, and setting up my own construction business. This little country of ours is ripe for economic expansion and I want to get in at the start. I have some investors lined up, and I'm about to launch Corrigan Holdings.'

'Corrigan Holdings? Sounds impressive.'

'Doesn't it? I'm getting there at last, Juliet. My time is finally coming. When we hit the new millennium, I reckon I'll have a few million turned over and then some. Not bad for someone whose ma didn't want to know him.'

★ ★ ★

This time Liam is right. Corrigan Holdings rides the wave of the building boom. Then, years later, it judders to a halt before plummeting in spectacular free-fall.

Just as I have, now. Although I don't believe in karma.

Let's get going before the light fades too much. Otherwise we could walk off the edge of the cliff . . . I hear laughter in my voice as I pick up my key. Then, nothing.

Liam? Didn't he threaten to make me pay for ruining him?

I've a feeling he's not the only one who would sleep better in his bed at night if I weren't around. Have I really that many enemies? But whatever happened earlier this evening, and whatever transpired at the top of the cliff, is still a blank. I know that shock can partially wipe out memory for a short while. So can concussion.

Still, other fractured images of my life drift through my mind's eye, and while cold rage at my helplessness burns inside me, I watch them slide past, wondering if there will be any clues, any pointers, as to how I ended up here . . .

New Year's Eve, 1999

'Is Liam not coming tonight?' Rebecca asks. 'I thought he might have dropped in for the great occasion. It's not every New Year's Eve we turn a century.'

She pops the cork on yet more Veuve Clicquot in the kitchen at Verbena View. The room is decorated with swirling streamers and drifting balloons bearing the legend of the new century. Rebecca and I are wearing matching silver tiaras in the shape of '2000' and sipping champagne from similarly emblazoned glasses. I don't know what we're expecting at the dawn of a new century, and neither of us has bothered to dress up for the occasion — I'm wearing my grey silk shirt over black Zara jeans bought in Madrid — but we're having a small party anyway, a girly night, as Rose and Rebecca's husbands are caught in their respective offices. Chilling in the fridge, I have a vintage Bollinger someone gave me, ready for the midnight chime.

'I haven't seen Liam in a couple of years,' I say. 'I expect he's celebrating in Barbados or somewhere exotic like that. Or else he's buying up half the Maldives. From what I'm reading in the papers and hearing on the grapevine, his empire's growing by the day and shows no sign of letting up.'

'Same with Matthew.'

Rebecca tops up my champagne, judging it perfectly, as though she's been pouring it all her life. 'One last blast,' she says, 'before everything goes belly-up on the stroke of midnight. Although I hope, for Harry's sake, it doesn't. I'm sorry he's stuck in the office tonight, in case the dreaded millennium bug strikes and the accounts files fall through the cracks.'

'And what about Matthew?' I ask her, with a teasing glint in my eye. 'He's on call tonight as well. God forbid his business goes down the tubes.'

Rebecca glances around. 'What's taking Rose so long? Did she lose her way back from the bathroom?'

'She went into my study to phone James and wish him a happy millennium.'

'Between you and me,' Rebecca eyes are dancing, 'I'd love to tell the millennium bug to jump up and take a lump out of Matthew's arse.'

'Ah, Rebecca! You don't mean that!'

'Bloody sure I do. I can't forget all that carry-on about him being the first of us to get a

181

mobile phone and an email address. It did my head in. Fair play to him that his business has taken off like a rocket, but I'm sick of hearing about his personal tailor. And all that name-dropping! So what if he's in with a few politicians? And suddenly he's an expert on fine wines and food. It's far from Leinster House or duck confit he was reared.'

'Careful you don't sound jealous. Matthew is doing his very best to make up for his humble beginnings. Still, who'd have thought he had the balls, never mind the vision, to expand his business so successfully? Fair dues to him. And, like Liam, there's no sign of him resting on his laurels.'

'He was always very ambitious, but he seems almost, I dunno, blinkered in his quest to be bigger and better. God knows where it will end.' Rebecca sighs. 'I get the feeling he's still dissatisfied and always searching for fulfilment of some kind.'

I help myself to some nibbles on cocktail sticks and ask, 'Do you think he's making up for something missing in his life?'

'Could be.' Rebecca shrugs. 'Still, Rose is doing well out of it, between her beautiful jewellery, designer clothes and gorgeous home. And now Matthew's talking about having a Dublin 4 address, so I reckon they'll be on the move again to even bigger and better in a year or two. She told me one night after a glass of wine too many that if Matthew floated his company they could live off the fortune for the rest of their lives. But I don't always think she's happy.'

'I never thought I'd see the day when Rose would have a glass of wine too many, and a couple of charge accounts, never mind getting glammed up to the hilt.'

'Same here. I get the feeling she's doing her best to keep up with Matthew and be the kind of wife he needs. She loves him, warts and all.'

'What do you think is making her unhappy?'

'She's never come right out and said it . . . ' Rebecca paused ' . . . but, between you and me, I think she suspects that Matthew has played away now and then.'

Then Rose walks into the room, preventing me from responding. I don't think she heard what Rebecca said as she's all talk about James and his band's sell-out tour of west-coast America. Unlike us, Rose has dressed up for the night in her Vivienne Westwood olive green dress. We forgot to tell her we were staying strictly casual. 'He won't be back in Dublin until February,' she says.

Rebecca thrusts a glass of champagne at her sister. 'Drink up, Rose, before the millennium bug bites!'

I know, from her slightly shadowed face, that she's missing her son a lot, even though he moved out of home soon after he joined the rock band. I wonder what it's like rattling around in her house with just Matthew for company, wondering if he's playing away. For the first time ever I feel as though I'm getting into her shoes.

And they're not very comfortable.

26

Saturday, 17 March, 5.45 a.m.

More of my life is speeding past me, like a movie on double fast-forward. My rage at my helplessness has been overtaken by a blank weariness. It steals across me slowly, and all the fight and feistiness I ever had is beginning to drain away. It's easy to drop into the slipstream of images and wonder if it will jog a more recent memory . . . tonight, for example, and who might have pushed me off the cliff . . .

2003
Then we are fifty.

Rebecca and I celebrate our half-century with a luxury break at the Mandarin Oriental in Barcelona.

'I'm being spoiled,' Rebecca says, as we sit on sunny Las Ramblas, sipping expensively hiked-up cocktails, our senses filling with the heat and noise of the colourful city as it parades by.

'It's about time you did some self-spoiling. You always seem to run after everyone else.'

Rebecca slips her feet out of her jewelled sandals and stretches out her sun-tinted legs. 'Life definitely gets better.'

'So, you enjoyed your Caribbean cruise?'

'Harry and I had a ball. I could easily get used

to this way of life. Here's to the next fifty years. We'll make a pact to celebrate together, even if we're on Zimmer frames and have lost all our teeth.'

'Hey, it'll be more like face-lifts and titanium hips, thank you. Still, I can't imagine us growing old,' I say. 'Even now I get a terrible shock when I look in the mirror some mornings. In a funny way I still expect to see my nineteen-year-old reflection.'

'It'll be fun.' She laughs. 'We'll only be interested in enjoying ourselves and it'll be to hell with everything else. I can't wait to get to the stage when I can tell people exactly what I think and not worry about the consequences.'

I don't think she realises quite what she's said until I tell her, 'You can do that any time. You don't have to wait until you're old.'

She's silent for a while, then forces a short, careless laugh. 'That depends on what I'm telling them.'

I take off my sunglasses, lean forward, and ask, 'What exactly are you afraid to say? And to whom?'

Once again, Rebecca is silent and I sense she's chasing around in her head to form the right context for her words. I wonder if it has anything to do with me.

Then she says, 'I'd like to be able to tell Rose to relax. She's too — anxious, I guess, a lot of the time. She worries about every little thing. What has happened, what's going to happen and what may happen in the future.'

Her eyes are hidden behind her glasses so I

can't see their expression, but her voice is sombre.

'Has this anything to do with Matthew?'

Rebecca sighs. 'Let's just say I'd kill anybody who hurts her. Even Matthew. Anyway, forget it, we're on holidays.' She straightens and summons the waiter from the nearby bar, her cheap bracelets jangling and glinting in the sunlight as she raises her arm.

Afterwards I wonder if it was just Matthew that both of us meant, or if we were speaking a silent language of our own.

2006

There is another funeral.

This time it's Harry's. Rebecca, Danielle and the twins are inconsolable. It's a mournful day, freezing January rain sleeting down, all of us garbed in black, clustered beneath the undertakers' giant umbrellas as the remorseless rituals of death and burial are carried out. Now I know how it feels to be helpless in the face of your friend's distress. I wonder if this is how Rebecca sometimes feels when she's faced with Rose's insecurities: powerless, useless, nothing to say but trite, meaningless words. At the graveyard, Rose is huddled between Matthew and James.

James flew back that morning from a tour in Germany, and squealed to a halt outside the church in a car a lot flashier than his father's, jumping out in full leather regalia and causing an excited wave of interest to ripple around the mourners gathered at the gate. They parted like the Red Sea to watch him stalk up the steps into the church. Matthew, standing by the door, waiting to escort Rose and Rebecca inside, had witnessed it. Now he catches me looking at the three of them, and we stare at each other for a long moment before he looks away.

★ ★ ★

Matthew!

Then, 'You're not just trying to compete with Matthew, are you?'

My mind slews forwards again. Yesterday? Last week? Rebecca is talking to me with a worried frown. Snatches of our conversation come back to me against a backdrop of charcoal grey cliffs and a murmuring sea. 'The last election was nothing short of a mud-slinging bloodbath,' she is saying, her voice distorted by the breeze and the white noise in my head. 'It's bad enough that the media will be hounding Matthew and Rose, but you, too? You know that everything you've ever done will be put under the microscope?'

And me, dismissive of her worries: 'Maybe I'm willing to take my chances . . . '

Matthew is someone else who may not sleep too easily from time to time, thanks to me. He may well be responsible for where I am now. Then, again, so may Rose.

Or even, for that matter, Rebecca.

Rebecca. My true friend. Loyal. Always there when I need her. But always there for Rose. A loyal sister. *I would kill anybody who hurts her.*

Blood, they say, is thicker than water. Family

187

will always come first with Rebecca.

Let's get going before the light fades too much. Otherwise we could walk off the edge of the cliff . . .

Oh, God, how have I ended up here? When will help arrive? There is so much I still want to do and see that I could weep from frustration and aching loss. Will I ever again marvel at a tree in summer or a winter sunset? I couldn't bear not to see Danielle having a baby . . . or his face ever again . . .

I'm suddenly saved from falling into the blackest pit of despair when memories of my golden holiday in Australia hang suspended above me like a jewelled ball, spiralling around like an ornament on a Christmas tree.

2010

'The sun shines almost every day, Juliet, you won't believe it,' Danielle twists around from the front passenger seat to talk to me as we leave the airport terminal behind and Conor takes the slip-road for the motorway into the city. The car roof is down and her blonde hair whips in the breeze. I haven't seen her for nine months, except for photographs she's emailed, and now her eyes are sparkling. She's beautiful. 'And the beaches,' she rolls her eyes, 'wait till you see them! Gosh, I love it here!'

'How long is left on your visa?'

She pulls a face. 'Just three months. I don't know where the time's gone.'

'You're only allowed to use that expression

when you get to my age,' I tell her.

'Age? It's just a number with you, Juliet. Anyway, I've arranged to take some time off work to show you around. James will be here later this week and has emailed to say he'll be free some days. We're all going to his concert in the ANZ Stadium. So you planned it well.'

'Didn't I just — thanks to you!'

Rebecca had already been to visit Danielle and Conor, and urged me to go. It was almost the only country in the world I hadn't yet been to. Then we heard that James and the band would be on tour for a couple of months, including Australia and New Zealand, so Danielle suggested I time my visit to Sydney to coincide with him. Both Rose and Rebecca said they'd love to be in my shoes. I had asked Rose if she wanted to come with me, but she'd refused. I wondered if she was afraid to leave Matthew alone for a couple of weeks. It would have done her the world of good after the way she'd been 'under the weather' the year before last. That had been Rebecca's way of describing the sudden panic attacks and depression that had gripped Rose, and the months it had taken her to recover.

This holiday would have restored Rose's faith and hope, I decide, looking out of my hotel-room window. I had seen it plenty of times, in the movies and on postcards, but the real-life tableau of the opera house, the iconic bridge and the wide, majestic harbour is one of incredible, uplifting beauty.

'Fantastic!' I say.

189

Danielle has been waiting for my reaction, holding her breath. She smiles with almost childish delight. 'You like?'

'I love, love, love!' I sweep her into my arms and catch her light, clean scent as excitement lifts me. 'Thank you so much for dragging me over to this side of the world.' Then I hold her at arm's length. 'Do you feel you were right to give up your job and follow Conor out here?'

Conor is the latest in her long line of boyfriends, but she seems serious about him. They've been together for four years, and when he was transferred out here by his software firm to manage a twelve-month project, Danielle handed in her notice and came with him.

'I know it was a big step to chuck it in, when jobs are so thin on the ground,' Danielle says, 'but I needed to see what Conor and I would be like together, away from family and friends. Just the two of us.'

'And? Are you happy?'

'So far, so good,' Danielle says. 'We're still together. Besides, Juliet, I was sick of what I was doing. Marketing and research have become hugely competitive and such a painful treadmill that I was beginning to stress out.'

Time flows by, no matter how hard I try to hold it back: a blur of days spent on long golden strands, Danielle running through the surf, blonde hair flying, seawater glistening on her tanned, slim body. She is a more confident version of her mother. Her youthful bloom is palpable and intoxicating to be around. She laughs a lot, as does Conor, when we get

190

together for barbecues in the evenings, sometimes sitting long into the twilight on the small balcony outside their apartment. I listen to their laughter and look up at a sky crowded with stars. I bring them to a restaurant overlooking the harbour, where we watch the ripple and swell of the water as the ferries and boats cut across the expanse.

James arrives, with the juggernaut of the band, fresh from sell-out dates in Melbourne. The Name cause a major sensation when they walk in to join Danielle, Conor and me for a meal in a restaurant overlooking Darling Harbour. It's fun, and Danielle glows.

One afternoon when James is free, he arranges a car and driver to take Danielle, me and him to the Blue Mountains. It's a special afternoon and every moment is ingrained on my memory. I know that Rose and Rebecca would give anything to swap places with me as we explore the spine-tingling, hand-of-God terrain on the sunny afternoon and have our photographs taken against the blue-haze backdrop of the Three Sisters in Katoomba.

I have always thought that the sunsets off the west of Ireland are among the most spectacular in the world, until we are coming home along the motorway, all of us quiet and reflective after the day we've just had, and Danielle tells me to look behind. She is sitting in the back seat with James and, rather than twist in the front passenger seat, I lower the sun visor and look in the mirror, where the view through the back window is reflected.

For long minutes I soak it up. The car radio is on low, an Alicia Keys ballad. Danielle and James, the family I never had, are silhouetted against the back window and a sky that defies description, such is the bold luminosity of the yellows and tangerines shooting through a violet haze. I feel a rush of contentment and know that this is a moment of perfect happiness. I fix it in my mind, like a freeze frame, so that I can take it out and relive these moments whenever I need to.

We are VIP guests, naturally, in the ANZ Stadium, for The Name concert. The pure energy and excitement of the night make me feel young again. Then, barely giving themselves time to come down after a sensational night, James and the band are gone, off to another sell-out gig in Perth, and the days I have left begin to slip through my fingers like grains of sand, and there is nothing I can do to slow them.

Then I'm down to counting the precious hours. We're out in Watsons Bay, Danielle and I, eating melt-in-the-mouth fish and chips from paper containers, and on the horizon the gap-toothed skyline of Sydney's steel and glass skyscrapers is like a misty mirage, floating across the bay.

Later Danielle and I climb to the top of the hill behind us. We lean against a wall and stare out to sea. There's something in the atmosphere of that golden, sunshiny afternoon that saddens me. I look at the blue swell of the Pacific Ocean below us, feel the gentle heat caressing our limbs, and the knowledge hits me that I'm off tomorrow and this won't ever come again — although, when I see the glint of tiny planes in the sky above us, I can't picture myself leaving.

'Have you had a good time?' Danielle is a little subdued, as though she senses my mood.

'It was magic,' I tell her. 'The best. And you're magic,' I say, 'both you and Conor.'

'Do you think so, Juliet?' She looks uncertain.

I want to squeeze her tight and tell her how beautiful she is. I want to pour the best of my good wishes for her directly into her veins so that she'll never doubt herself for a single moment. 'Danielle, of course you are. You're special. You're beautiful, intelligent and talented. Never underrate yourself. And I'm sorry if this sounds like a lecture, but I mean every word. Never sell yourself short. Make every minute of your precious life count. And always . . . '

'Always what?' She smiles at me.

'Above all else, no matter what kind of storm is raging about you, listen to your heart.'

I feel choked as I utter those words. It's far too late for me to take my own advice, and sometimes when I wake at four in the morning I can't help wondering where I'd be today if I'd had the guts to listen to my heart.

Danielle puts her hand on my arm and kisses my cheek. 'Is that what you did, Juliet?' she asks. 'Mum always said you were a trail-blazer and she found it hard to follow in your slipstream in those stuffy, olden days. And you're still blazing a trail. But me and my friends, we take all that hard-won equality and freedom for granted.'

'Which is exactly how it should be. Things

193

were . . . a lot different in Ireland not so long ago. It's still hard to think how repressed we all were.'

She looks at my face for a long time with her observant blue eyes. Can she see through the shutter over my guilt to the sadness that is normally hidden?

I blink and the connection is broken. I talk to her about the importance of being her real self, rather than fitting in to please others. 'I keep telling Rebecca she should be busy blazing a trail of her own and not bothering about me. And, Danielle, unfortunately I didn't have the courage to listen to my heart at one very important time in my life. I took the easy option instead of standing my ground, and it's something I've lived to regret.'

'I can't imagine you having any regrets, Juliet.'

'Oh, believe me, I do. And I know they're a pure waste of time, and I can't change anything in the past, but it doesn't stop me having them. There's someone . . . Well, I love someone very much but, thanks to the situation I'm in, I can't speak of it. So take heed of my words and always listen to your heart. Sometimes we have to adjust our sails, but whatever you do, don't compromise the essence of who you are.'

I turn away in case she sees my loneliness in my eyes. She puts her arm around me, rather awkwardly, but I don't shrug it off. I let it rest there peacefully and we stand like that for a while, looking out across the sparkling Pacific Ocean.

27

Even though Rose had slept fitfully, and had been disturbed by Matthew coming to bed at an unearthly hour of the morning, she still woke up just before six. She eased herself above the warmth of the duvet, feeling a slight chill on her bare shoulders. She was far too wound up to settle back to sleep.

She went downstairs, pausing outside Matthew's study. Once again she stood in the doorway and looked into the shadowy room, at the mounds of papers on his desk, and wondered if there was anything she could do to stop this dangerous circus invading their lives. All was quiet, the room itself and his desk cloaked in semi-darkness, looking perfectly peaceful and friendly in the shadowy pre-dawn. She went across and pulled back the curtains.

It was only when she turned that she saw Matthew's mobile on the desk. She jumped as though she'd come face to face with a dangerous animal. Her head told her to keep on walking, go out into the kitchen and make some coffee. Forget it was there.

But the mobile was difficult to ignore. It seemed to pulsate as though it had a life of its own. She drew level with the desk and tried to move on.

Impossible.

Feeling as though she was putting her hand into a blazing fire, she reached out and touched it with her finger. Nothing happened. The house alarm didn't shriek. Neither did the roof cave in. She reached out again, but this time she lifted it and felt the weight of it in her palm. Then she put it back on the desk and told herself to move away before she was tempted to do anything silly.

She was about to leave his office when, on impulse, she snatched it up again and feverishly keyed in his password, wondering as she entered the final digit if he had changed it.

He hadn't.

She didn't know what she had expected to find: the screen sprang to life, she brought up his text messages and, sure enough, there was a line of new ones, messages she dare not allow her finger to linger on lest they open. She scrolled down, very carefully, very lightly, past the unopened messages, but there was nothing very alarming until she came to his recently sent and received messages. A name jumped out at her.

Juliet.

Juliet? What had Matthew got to say to Juliet? Or she to him? She could already see the first few words of the message, which danced in front of her eyes until she took a deep breath and steadied her vision: *We need to talk asap. Your place. Call me. M.*

Her hands shook as she switched off the phone and, very carefully, placed it back on the table, struggling to recall the exact position she had found it in. Had they met? And, if so, when? And what was so secret about it that he hadn't told her?

Something heavy thudded into her stomach.

28

I'm feeling very tired. Funny, really, to feel tired when I'm lying stuck like this. And there's a strange kind of calm stealing over me. It wouldn't bother me to close my eyes and drift off in an instant. Just let go of everything and float quietly away. Rise out of my broken body to be carried away on a magic carpet, as though I'm as light as fairy dust.

It must be close to dawn because the sky has lightened against the dark shape of the cliff and the stars have faded. There's no sign of the moon, which has sailed away from my line of vision. Morning will soon be breaking, and I've been here all night so no wonder I'm having silly delusions about who might or might not have pushed me.

'Your laugh. It hasn't changed at all. Neither has your sense of humour,' Rebecca says. Her face is floating in front of me, mouth curved in a half-smile, hair tossed in the breeze. Far below her, the sea boils against the cliffs, and ahead, the track veers around a corner of the headland where, for several metres, the grass verge has crumbled away.

The image fades. When was that? Last night? Did I stumble and fall where it's all too easy to slip and slide down the steep embankment? Or was I pushed?

Not Rebecca, surely. Giver of life and love?

I can't think much more. White noise is filling my head. My eyes are now half closed. The sheer effort of keeping them open is too much. Even so, I see that the sky is lightening further: bands of night-time inky blackness are separating. There is a rift in the darkness, a soft chink, where a thin pink streak is outlining the rim of the billowing clouds. Pink. Danielle's favourite colour. When she was a young girl.

There's something about Danielle . . .

We're together around the table at Verbena View. It's Christmas because I have red berries decorating the table in memory of my father. I glance out of the patio door at the purple twilight and, for a nanosecond, I catch her reflection in the glass. The look on her face before she senses my eyes on her stills my heart.

Ah. I'm glad I remember that.

There are sounds of a new day burgeoning all about me. I never realised how musical it is, the early-morning call of the birds against the dawn hush. Close to me, the sea is a gentle, rhythmic whisper, as though it is breathing deeply, slowly, in and out. I know that at this hour it resembles crumpled dark grey silk. Soon the sun will rise and I could paint it from memory, from the first band of fiery red on the horizon, until the rift in the clouds stretches and widens, the sky turning orange and gold. The sea will run a trail of scarlet, until the crumpled silk reflects the apricot sky. Then it will fall into the palest duck-egg blue. The whole show will remind me of an artist having fun with a palette.

I'd love to see it, really see it, and soak it up just one more time.

The start of a new day can be impossibly beautiful, especially along the Dublin coastline. No matter where you are, and no matter your circumstances, the sight of it can seep into every cell in your body — if you let it — and fill you with hope.

It's a pity so many people are still asleep and miss this daily miracle. What could I do if I had the gift of today ahead of me? If I was waking up as usual in my bed, putting my feet to the floor and going into the bathroom to look at my face in the mirror before I shower. If I was living and breathing, like the sea, and able to do things.

What would I do if I had so much precious time? I'd love to see his face once more. I wouldn't waste a single minute in telling him I love him very much. Then I realise that that, too, doesn't matter. I only want to see him and voice my love from the selfish point of view.

Sometimes love means letting go. Maybe, if I slip away on that magic carpet, some truths will come out into the open. If so, it will have been worth it, and how I got here will be totally irrelevant in the grand scheme of things. It doesn't matter if I can't say goodbye. I have lived, I have loved and been loved. He is also loved, and that comforts me. In the end, when life is distilled to the crucial essence, that's all that matters.

It is there now, the beginning of the sunrise, a single brilliant speck so low on the horizon that I can see it through my half-closed eyes. But it is a glimmer of a morning sunrise, so bright and warm and beautiful that I just want to float into it and let it flood through me, like breath itself.

Part Two

Danielle

29

Rome, Saturday, 17 March

The loud blare of a scooter horn caught me by surprise and caused me to jump back from the kerb, almost tripping over it in my haste.

'*Scusi* — ' I began.

The young motorcyclist gave me a black scowl and shook his fist before he buzzed off into the traffic.

I shook my fist back even though I'd deserved it. I'd stepped out on to the road without paying attention. I'd been too occupied with looking ahead and spotting that the Campo de' Fiori was already clogged with a slow-moving mass of early-morning people, inhabitants of Rome as well as tourists. I was also too occupied with asking myself if this had been such a good idea after all. When I was almost dragged under the scooter's wheel, I was tempted to take it as a sign to turn back the way I'd come, forget about the day ahead and the prospect of drowning my sorrows in the company of friends.

Still, it was far better than sitting at home, where I'd spent more than enough time staring at the walls of my rented apartment, feeling sorry for myself and closing my ears to the shouts of carefree children playing in the courtyard below.

So, I stepped out of the cool, shadowy side-street into the riot of colour, noise and the scents of coffee, fruit and vegetables, the fragrance drifting from the flower sellers that typified this piazza in Rome on a spring Saturday morning. I moved through the rise and fall of conversation and laughter, the shouts of stall-holders plying their trade. Up through the cobblestoned square, past the fountain, the medley of open-air markets, the restaurants and cafés, where staff had already opened shutters, set out tables and chairs and unfurled awnings as they got ready for the first of their Saturday customers, the coffee-and-croissants brigade.

I reached the Irish bar, sidled past people sitting at pavement tables, and went inside. Naturally it was open. Today, of all days, it would be open all hours to help the bemused tourists and dedicated Irish expats celebrate our national feast day in style. I had to press through shouts of 'Viva Irlanda' and 'Buona festa', a wall of noisy, green-clad bodies, and a forest of shamrock-shaped balloons and shamrock-decorated banners. A huge television screen to the side of the bar was showing the opening credits of *The Quiet Man*. Then, in a corner, I saw Erin waving, then Gemma, and the stool camouflaged under their coats.

A small rush of gratitude that they were here, waiting for me, even at this early hour on a Saturday. It brought a little warmth fluttering across the empty space where my heart had once glowed.

'Hi, Danielle! Thought you'd changed your mind,' Erin said. She was wearing a hairband decorated with a row of spring-loaded plastic shamrocks that bobbed wildly on their moorings every time she moved her head. Matching earrings danced at each side of her face. The effect was ridiculous but engaging. She gave me a big bright smile that told me she was glad I'd come. It gave me another little lift.

'I didn't think you'd pass up the chance to drown the shamrock,' Gemma said. 'Even if we are a little early, we're not the only ones. I think the Irish celebrations will go on the whole day and well into the night. We'd awful trouble hanging on to this stool. So lucky you,' she said, swiping off the coats and tossing them behind her on to the back of the banquette. 'Give me yours.'

I sat down and handed my jacket to Gemma. I waved at a bar girl, who smiled and shrugged to indicate she had no chance of making it across to us through the throng. 'Thanks. I felt so lazy this morning I almost had second thoughts,' I said.

Second thoughts. It was one way to describe the near panic attack that had momentarily convulsed me. The feeling that everything was pressing down on me, fluttery sparks of anxiety mixed with a sense of desolation. On impulse I'd called home, even though it was an hour earlier in Dublin, for my mother, Rebecca Ryan, could be relied upon to chat away about family gossip or the goings-on back home for long enough to give me something solid to latch on to.

But the call had gone to voicemail. And then I remembered she was at the afters of a wedding in a north County Dublin hotel.

My voice had felt strained as I left a message

on the landline, and I didn't bother calling her mobile: the small act of speaking out loud, in response to the greeting of my mother's voicemail, had broken the worst of my panic. I felt calm enough to catch my hair back in a scrunchie, put on my Hilfiger jeans and canvas jacket, then move beyond the four walls of the apartment, where I'd been holed up since leaving work the previous evening, and meet my friends.

In that Irish bar, on the fringe of the Campo de' Fiori, the national party was kicking off with a special breakfast screening of *The Quiet Man*, followed by the RBS Six Nations rugby live from the Stadio Olimpico in Rome, where Scotland were taking on Italy, and the crowd were wasting no time in getting revved up.

'I hope he was worth it,' Gemma said. She dunked her spoon in her cappuccino, breaking up the foam, and looked at me, raising her eyebrows coquettishly.

'He?' I asked, feigning a casualness I didn't feel. In the last couple of weeks Gemma had seemed to be on a mission to discover the finer points of my love life or, more to the point, the lack thereof, almost as though she sensed there was a story to be told.

Which there was, and I wondered what kind of radioactive vibe I was sending out. The woman who had loved and lost? Who had given it all away? Although that wasn't quite true. More like the woman who had loved unwisely . . . and still lived to regret it.

It would always be there, running through my

veins. It would always have the power to come back and bite me at any given moment. Even in a noisy, crowded Irish bar on a Saturday morning. Especially in a noisy bar: there was nothing like feeling raw and isolated in the midst of jollity. But I was expecting far too much of myself, I thought, this weekend of all weekends. I needed to cut myself some slack. Be kind to myself. Be my own best friend instead of my own worst enemy.

'I assume it was a man who encouraged those second thoughts,' Gemma said, her voice questioning.

I couldn't blame her for being curious. I'd been in Rome for two months, working alongside her, partying most weekends with her, listening to her mojito-fuelled, full-on confessions, yet I hadn't shared with her so much as a titbit of my rather sad and inglorious history. Given that I would be thirty-five next birthday, I knew it must be obvious to Gemma that I'd been around the block more than once. And by now she was surely a little aggrieved that she had been so forthcoming in the face of my reticence.

'I wish,' I said, putting on my usual nonchalant act. The one I sensed Gemma was beginning to see through. 'If only I could conjure up a hot-blooded, well-packed, sexy alpha male, who's brilliant and generous in bed. I'm beginning to think it's a contradiction in itself. But I promise you'll be the first to know as soon as I have any action between the sheets.'

My eyes met Erin's. She gave me a brief sympathetic smile, picked up her bag and rummaged for her purse. 'Danielle, let's get you a coffee. They're doing Irish breakfasts as well, if you're peckish. Or how about a Buck's Fizz? I know it's early but we need to wet the shamrock properly.' With a rush of gratitude I saw she was smiling casually, as though she didn't know anything about my messed-up life, as though a Buck's Fizz at just after nine o'clock on a Saturday morning was compulsory because it was a regular St Patrick's celebration, and not because she knew, as Gemma didn't, that I might feel the need to lose myself behind a fog of alcohol that day.

But even Erin, good friend as she was, only knew the half of it.

I watched two plates of the traditional full Irish breakfast being passed across the counter and knew I had no appetite. 'Just coffee for now,' I told her. 'And maybe a muffin. I couldn't manage anything more.'

'Gemma?'

'Nothing yet, thanks. I'll have a Buck's Fizz soon, if you insist,' Gemma said, in the kind of voice that suggested she was allowing herself to be persuaded against her better judgement.

'I'll go,' Erin said. 'I need a coffee refill.'

'No, let me,' I insisted, knowing it would be much easier to brave the crowded throng and return with the drinks than be left to fend off Gemma's unbridled curiosity.

'Will you manage?' Erin asked, frowning. 'I think I stand a better chance than you of getting through that crowd.'

I stood up and straightened my shoulders. 'I'm

not as delicate as I look.'

Erin flashed me a smile that said, 'Good for you.'

I was glad that by the time I returned with the coffees they had increased the volume on the sound system and the three of us began to watch the film. It was the sort of distraction I welcomed.

'I never imagined myself watching this in an early-morning Irish bar on a Paddy's Day in Rome,' Erin laughed.

I felt like saying I'd never imagined lots of things happening, things that filled me with the greatest joy at the same time as the greatest fear and trembling. Things, also, that filled me with heartbreak and left me with an empty space where my heart should have been.

But right now, this minute, I was among friends, doing nothing more demanding than sipping coffee, nibbling a chocolate muffin and watching a film in which a horse and cart trundled across the magnificent sweep of the Irish countryside. As I relaxed a little on the stool, Erin met my eye. 'Hope you're up for the rest of today, Ryan!' She winked at me and gave my hand a quick squeeze.

'I'll try.' I smiled.

'Try? Not good enough.'

We had the whole day planned. Erin had already generously offered to forgo a precious Saturday at home with her Italian husband and little daughter to keep me company. When Gemma had heard us making tentative plans, during lunch break in the office, and assumed we were merely celebrating the feast day of the patron saint of Ireland, she came up with an idea from when she'd been at home last, not knowing I had a hidden agenda. 'We should do the twelve pubs of Christmas,' she'd said.

'The what?'

'I went out with my cousins one night before Christmas, and we dropped into a total of twelve pubs. It was a mad dash around the city centre but great fun.'

'And all the funnier as it went along because you must have been getting more and more maggoty.' Erin had gazed at her sceptically.

'And what's that got to do with Paddy's Day?' I'd asked. I'd already planned to erase the date from my calendar, but Erin wasn't having that. Better to face up to it, but keep myself extra busy — she had volunteered to make sure I did just that. And now Gemma wanted to join in.

'We could do the twelve pubs of Paddy's Day on Paddy's Day,' Gemma had suggested. 'That's if we find enough pubs in Rome, although we could always call back to some of them twice.'

'Gosh. Sounds like you'd need some stomach.'

'I'm sure the day doesn't have to revolve completely around alcohol consumption,' Erin said. 'I'm not in my twenties and able for those mad days any more. We could go for food in between, have plenty of water, and take in some of the sights. Maybe fit in a beauty parlour. A girls' day out.'

And so it was agreed. I went along with it because of the effort Erin was putting in on my behalf but mostly because it promised to stop me thinking too much.

From thinking about anything at all.

Especially what I should have been doing that day.

Getting married.

★   ★   ★

Erin had met me at the airport when I arrived in Rome in January, broken and bloodied, too exhausted to cry. She was waiting in Arrivals, a welcoming smile plastered to her face, her right hand on a buggy in which her small, pink-cheeked daughter sat.

She let go of it long enough to throw both arms around my neck and give me a hug. 'Danielle! Lovely to see you.' She held me at arm's length and studied me critically in the manner of a true friend. 'You look good,' she said. 'Considering.' She was trying her best to be positive and upbeat.

She was the only one allowed to speak to me like that. I hadn't talked to my mother, beyond giving her the bare facts — my engagement was off, my wedding cancelled, and I didn't want to discuss it. I knew I'd hurt her with my refusal to confide but I just couldn't take that on board right then. I was far too raw and couldn't bear to sift through the burning embers of my life, even for Mum.

'Do you reckon?' I said to Erin, with a faint smile.

I knew I didn't look so good. I'd popped into the Ladies en route to Baggage Reclaim and had been shocked at the sight of myself in the mirror. I looked exactly how I felt on the inside:

211

wretched, raw, my eyes flat, expressionless and ringed with shadows.

'Has it been desperate?' Erin asked.

I nodded.

'Sorry I had to bring Aimee,' she said, giving the buggy a push. 'I couldn't arrange for anyone to mind her . . . '

I could have finished the sentence for her: ' . . . at this short notice.'

Following a long phone call with Erin — who'd sent me a lifeline to help me get away from Dublin and my imploded love life — I'd applied for the English-speaking temporary job covering maternity leave in the sales and marketing division of the computer software company where she worked, starting in mid-January. Early in the new year, I'd emailed my CV across to their human resources division and they'd conducted a phone interview with me.

My escape to Rome had been confirmed just two nights ago, and I was starting next week. Luckily, I'd had no notice to serve in my Dublin job as, thanks to the economic downturn, I'd only managed to secure employment on a six-month contract after my stint in Australia; the last had expired at the end of December.

I got down on my hunkers and smiled at nine-month-old Aimee. 'It's lovely to see her — she's fab.' Her blue eyes were solemn as she looked back at me. I stroked her cheek gently and she gave me a wide smile, showing tiny pearly teeth, followed by a heart-warming gurgle. It made me feel I was good for something, if only for making a baby smile. And at least Aimee had no idea of the sad basket case I'd become. She was totally neutral.

Erin pushed the buggy and I wheeled my case across the concourse and out into the raw afternoon, feeling almost as though I was sleepwalking through an unfamiliar landscape. I watched as she strapped Aimee into her car seat and stowed the buggy in the boot, along with my case.

We'd been friends since our first day in college, meeting in the lecture hall when my papers had slewed out of my hand, across the tiled floor. Erin had immediately bent down to help me pick them up. We were from opposite sides of the city centre, and neither of us knew anyone else in our business-science year, but as soon as we went for coffee something clicked between us, a warmth, a friendship. I wondered if this was the kind of female kinship that my mother often banged on about, the kind she shared with Juliet and her sister Rose, so close for so long that they almost talked in shorthand.

'Your friends are so important, Danielle,' she'd said to me, more than once. 'Always make time for them, no matter what. Good friendships can last a lifetime if they're nurtured properly.'

Like me, Erin had no sisters. During our summer vacations as students, we'd gone to America together on J1 visas. Then we'd taken a year out to travel the world, and started our careers in the same marketing company, where we'd worked together until our lives had diverged. While I was still based in Dublin, between jobs right now and with a jettisoned romance weighing heavily on my shoulders, Erin had married an Italian pilot and settled in Rome.

'Lorenzo is away for the next couple of nights so it'll just be us,' she said, as she navigated the airport environs and headed out on to the motorway.

Although he was lovely, and I knew he wouldn't pry, his absence meant I didn't have to put up any kind of a front for those first two nights. 'Great,' I said.

'You can stay with us as long as you like,' she said.

'Thanks, but I'll get a place of my own as soon as I can. I presume it's easy enough to rent for six months?'

'Yes, there are plenty of places within easy commute of the job. It'll be fine, Danielle. You'll fit in well and I'll introduce you to Gemma and Paola, a couple of friends of mine who are single and fancy free, and have a far better social life than I have.'

'Once they don't know why I'm here . . . '

She shot me a glance, as though to say, 'Who do you think I am?'

★　★　★

Now, just over two months later, nothing much had changed since I'd arrived in Rome. There were times when I still felt as though I was moving mechanically in a strange vacuum. At others I allowed the mental shutter I'd brought down across the mess of my life to lift a little, but the turmoil in my head still raged so intensely that I quickly closed it again.

Erin, the one person in Rome in whom I'd confided, didn't yet know the details, and hadn't dared ask me. And I was still maintaining radio silence with Conor Kennedy, the man I had known for almost six years, had lived with for two, and should have been marrying later today in the south of France.

30

Rebecca half opened one eye to the opaque, early-morning light. Snatches of the night before floated back to her and all of a sudden she was wide awake. Without allowing herself any more time to think, she got out of bed and went into the shower.

She was putting on her grey Nike tracksuit when she remembered that Liam had talked of joining her for breakfast and debated whether to slink off to the beach first or brave the dining room. Chances were, he was still sleeping off the indulgence of his mini-bar.

But when she reached the lobby, he was there already, sitting on a sofa, reading the morning paper. A ridiculous wave of uncertainty washed over her, but she strolled across to him with as much nonchalance as she could muster.

'You came prepared,' she said, noting he was wearing the same clothes as the night before.

'Unfortunately I don't keep a sports bag, never mind gym clothes, in the boot of the car,' he said, eyeing her tracksuit. 'Where to first? Breakfast or the beach?'

'Breakfast,' she said, 'while the restaurant's quiet.'

'Agreed. Better than coming back from a bracing walk to find it overrun with hung-over wedding guests.'

'I guess you passed on joining them in the

residents' bar?' she said, as he fell into step beside her.

'Didn't you hear us partying all night long?' he joked.

'So that's why you're still wearing yesterday's clothes . . . '

There was a moment's confusion when the breakfast manager assumed they were sharing the same room, and Rebecca felt embarrassed. The dining room was on the first floor, facing the beach, and she gazed out of the big plate-glass windows to the long, sandy dunes, and beyond to the pale grey sea. On the horizon, the sky was tranquil and swathes of blue were overlaid with streaks of thin grey cloud. It was all incredibly calm.

Liam broke a bread roll with his long fingers and opened a small, foil-covered container of butter. Then he gave her an interested glance. 'I did all the talking last night. Now it's your turn. How are your family?'

She gave him a wry smile. 'My daughter, Danielle, should have been getting married this weekend.' The words came out of her mouth before she could stop them. 'Today, in fact, in the south of France. But just after Christmas everything went belly-up and now she's in Rome. She had to get away for a while.'

'Sorry to hear that. Was she . . . or did . . . Sorry, I don't mean to pry.'

'It's okay. You mean was she dumped or did she call off the wedding herself? That's the thing. I don't know,' Rebecca said. She sipped more orange juice, finding relief in unburdening

217

herself. 'Danielle won't talk about it and I won't force her. If she did call it off, I could take crumbs of comfort from the fact that she should know her own mind by now — she's almost thirty-five. Then I reason that if Conor called it off, and was capable of inflicting that much hurt, she's better off without him.'

'Either way, it's difficult. It must make you feel helpless.'

'It does.' She flashed him a grateful smile.

'Yet you had the guts to turn up at another wedding yesterday evening, looking extremely glamorous and in party mode.'

'It's how I cope,' she said smoothly. 'Keep busy. What would have been the point in sitting at home alone?'

'That takes some spirit.'

'Spirit?' She laughed. 'It's more about not giving yourself time to think. Because deep down you're afraid of wallowing in black thoughts. Especially when there's nothing you can do to change things. Same after Harry died.'

He gave her a thoughtful look. 'Yes, you weren't long widowed when you arrived at one of my mad parties along with Juliet. Both of you were half cut and looked like you'd been having a good night. It must have been difficult for you.'

'Again, better than sitting at home moping. If you're going through hell, keep going — isn't that what they say? My parents died when I was seven. It was a shock, and Rose did enough crying for both of us. I blocked it out because it was too horrific to contemplate. I learned to keep going even then.'

'I see.' He smiled at her as though she was still seven.

'And with Danielle,' she went on, trying to ignore that smile, 'it's out of my hands, even though I'd do anything I could to make it better for her.'

'I know you would, if you're still the soft-hearted woman I remember under that practical shell.'

She stared at him and his gaze held hers. Then she broke the connection. She forced a laugh. '*Soft*-hearted? I don't believe in mollycoddling myself, but my family mean everything to me and I'd do whatever was in my power to ensure their happiness.'

'Like a lioness with her cubs?'

'Exactly.'

'And your sons?'

'Kevin is working in Japan, and Mark is in Dubai with his girlfriend, so I don't see much of them.' She began to spear some of the fruit in her bowl, paying a lot of attention to it rather than to the little ache she felt whenever she thought of her scattered family.

'So they're all around the world.'

'Yep. Gone to the corners of the globe. They're healthy, solvent and working,' she said, counting her blessings.

'So how do you keep busy, Rebecca?'

'Hill walking, Pilates, a book club with Rose, and my job.'

'Is the village bijou boutique still going strong?'

Rebecca hadn't expected him to remember.

After Harry had died, she'd decided life was too short to spend any more time in her boring office job. She'd heard about a new boutique opening nearby and knew it was the perfect solution to get her out of the house.

'Olivia Jayne? Yes, I'm still there, doing three or four days a week.'

'Good. Although with your get-up-and-go, you could have opened a string of boutiques.'

'So I've been told,' Rebecca said. 'But I'm quite happy working for Amanda. I help to manage the day-to-day stuff, but I don't have any other headaches. Amanda might have a few glam trips here and there to fashion shows, but she has all the business end to look after and the tough decisions to make. All I have to do is turn up looking my usual fabulous self, and I get to spend the day around beautiful clothes, fabulous bags and killer heels, as well as friendly, chatty customers, who are dressing up for parties or weddings. The important thing is, I enjoy it, and I'm quite happy not to have the ultimate responsibility. There are fewer sleepless nights that way.'

'There's a lot to be said for that,' he agreed. 'Far too many people are scrambling up the wrong ladder against the wrong wall in search of the wrong kind of satisfaction. Like me, once upon a time. I've had more than enough dark nights of the soul to last me a lifetime.'

Rebecca felt a sharp jolt. She'd forgotten about his crashed dreams. 'And how are you managing now?'

'I'm not destitute. I have enough to get by.

And some of my friends have been great — one's given me the key of a small apartment near the canal in Rathmines that's between lettings, and another has lent me his son's car as he's away in Australia for a while.' He caught her looking at him. 'It's okay, I'm fine with it. I had too much time to think about things when I was living in Spain on a shoestring but I've come through to the other end.'

★ ★ ★

Twenty minutes later they were out on the beach, picking their way through tracts of briny seaweed to the hard, compact strand where it was easy to walk. The sea hissed back and forth, like a flirtatious dance, furling and unfurling a creamy lace foam with the pull of the tide, leaving wet slicked sand in its wake. Other people were dotted about, strolling, jogging or walking a dog.

'I don't think we realise how lucky we are that this is on our doorstep,' she said, needing to break the silence, suddenly conscious of him matching her strides as they walked along. Liam Corrigan, the almost boy next door and an old history that had connected them at intervals.

'That's what I love about Dublin,' he said. 'Ten or fifteen minutes in either direction and you're by the sea. Or the mountains.'

Rebecca was enjoying the spread of the bay, shimmering in the pale morning sun, when they heard the whine of a helicopter in the far distance, shattering the calm of the morning.

'Some guest arriving in style,' she said.

'It's not, actually,' Liam said. The dot in the sky grew bigger until Rebecca saw that it was red and white. 'Search and rescue,' Liam added, shaking his head. 'Some poor bugger . . . ' He left the rest of his sentence unsaid.

They stalled for a moment, watching as the helicopter veered out to sea, before banking and returning towards land. Then it hugged the coastline as it travelled south, the noise gradually receding. Rebecca shivered. The beautiful sea had its dark underbelly as well, and the crisp morning air seemed suddenly chilly. 'Someone's in trouble, God help them.'

They walked in silence for a while, and as they turned back towards the hotel, Liam said, 'Do you suppose, if I called you, you might come out for a drink some time? Just to chat?' His voice was ultra-casual and she knew he was afraid he might be treading on thin ice.

'I dunno. I haven't really . . . since . . . ' Her voice trailed away.

She hadn't been out with a man since Harry had died. Liam was an old friend, and he looked so attractive when he smiled, his face relaxed and his eyes kind, that she wondered what he'd be like if she got to know him better. Still, she didn't need an added complication in her life right now.

'I can't compete with tycoons or toyboys, so the odds are stacked against me,' he said. 'I can only offer a fish-and-chips supper and a bottle of supermarket wine. Maybe stretch to an Indian takeout and the odd movie.'

'It's not that . . . '

'So I'm not totally ruled out,' he said, giving her a long, appreciative look that surprised her.

'Look, Liam, I think it's too late for me,' she said.

He insisted on walking her down the corridor to her room, even though she told him there was no need. He was leaving shortly to spend the day sorting through his accounts.

'Maybe you should give yourself permission to unblock stuff and wallow in the darkness for a while,' he said, as he leaned against her door. 'When you come out the other end, the light may surprise you.' He took out his mobile. 'Can I at least have your phone number?'

She gave it to him, wondering how she might react if her phone rang and he was at the other end.

'We'll talk soon,' he said. 'And mind that soft heart of yours.' Then he gave her a quick hug before he loped back down the corridor.

31

His voice came from very far away.

'Liz, are you okay?' Then, 'Liz, wake up and let me know you're still alive . . . You need more water . . . Here, open your mouth.'

She didn't want to wake up, to face the day. She wanted to stay as she was, disconnected from everything, thanks to her shattering hangover. But she felt her head being lifted off the pillow, causing fresh aches to ricochet around her shaking body. Her teeth clinked against the glass, as cool water seeped into her parched throat and dribbled down her chin. If hell was every cell in your body racked with pain, and a heart scalded to unbearable torment, then this was it.

The acute throbbing behind her eyes stopped her opening them. Turned inwards, her gaze flicked back jerkily over the last twenty-four hours, until she was there again, sitting on the floor in Ballymalin, picking through the wreck-age of her parents' lives. Oh, to have everything back to the way it used to be before her life had slipped off its axis, to have those hours wiped away and her heart scoured clean of everything so that it was blank and untroubled. Then again, her heart had never been untroubled.

Her sore head was lowered to the yielding softness of her pillow and the duvet tucked around her limbs.

'You didn't have to stay,' her voice came out hoarse and croaky, 'but thanks anyway.'

'There was no way I could have left you on your own, the state you were in,' Gavin said. 'And still are. I've never seen you as bad as this, Liz. And your face . . . Jesus . . . hold on a mo . . .'

The bed shifted as he got up, and shortly afterwards she felt her hair being smoothed back and the refreshing sweep of a warm flannel across her forehead and cheeks. A soft towel was gently pressed to her damp skin.

'Why are you doing this?' she asked, her throat hurting with the effort.

'Never mind.'

'I thought you never wanted to see me again.'

'Stop asking questions and just relax.'

'We're supposed to be separated.'

'We still are. But even you would put your differences to one side to rescue a drowning kitten.'

'A drowning kitten?' she squeaked.

She heard him give a long sigh. 'Well, you weren't far off it. Drowning in alcohol. Like a helpless kitten.'

'Thanks a bunch.'

He was silent for a while, but it was a relaxed kind of silence, and she was oddly grateful for his calming presence. The small house in Harold's Cross had resounded with emptiness after he'd gone: he'd stormed out after a particularly bad row, during which he'd blamed her for pushing him away. She couldn't remember what the row had been about, something silly about food or a

225

bottle of wine, like many of their rows had been. She had instigated them, as though she was testing him to the limit, deliberately provoking him to see how far she could push him. Childish and irrational, she knew, and Liz had been horrified, more than once, to hear herself arguing over trivialities.

'It's as if you don't want to be married to me,' Gavin had snapped. 'In which case you've got your wish, for our marriage is over, *finito, kaput*. I've tried, really I have, but I'm beginning to think nothing will make you happy, Liz.'

She'd been beginning to think that her marriage had been a battlefield of her own making, and at first it was a relief that he was gone and she didn't have to accommodate him in her life. Neither did she have to question his love for her, as though she didn't quite believe somebody could value her enough to want her to be such an intimate part of his life.

After all, Annie Monaghan hadn't wanted to be part of her life, showing her in the worst possible way that Liz had meant nothing to her and that she couldn't bear to live, not even for her daughter.

'Just because we've separated, it doesn't mean I've switched off all my feelings for you,' Gavin said. 'They're still there.'

She didn't believe what she was hearing — he couldn't mean it — but she was too drained to rebuff him with a smart comment. Instead she allowed his words to trickle into her sore head.

And then, 'I still care for you, Liz,' he said.

'What?' she croaked.

226

'You drive me mad. You test every ounce of my patience. You're the most awkward, belligerent and vulnerable woman I know, but — '

'Vulnerable?'

'You hide it well,' he said, 'with those razor-sharp eyes and that caustic tongue. But I've seen it in your face when you look at me . . . that little-girl-lost look.'

'Stop.' She couldn't bear to hear any more. She couldn't bear him to be nice to her. And she couldn't figure out how they were having this conversation in the first place, the kind that was normally reserved for late-night, wine-induced honesty, when this was the morning after the wretched night before, with the light of day pressing against the bedroom curtains.

And she couldn't bear his kindness now, especially, when nothing mattered any more. Neither secrets nor stories.

'Well, you do, and I have . . . ' he said.

He had to be joking. Still, though, he hadn't gone too far away. He hadn't slipped off or disappeared out of her life when she'd least expected it. The kind of behaviour she had learned to deal with. He was still there. And now she hadn't the energy to push him away.

'You look at me . . . sometimes . . . with your big, innocent eyes as though you're lost,' he said. Then he gave a soft laugh. 'I always thought I'd save you, Liz, but I think you need to save yourself. And whatever you did last night, mixing your drinks or going on a bender, isn't going to help.'

'Save me from what?'

'Sometimes you're your own worst enemy. It's as though you scuppered our marriage with silly rows because you feel you don't deserve any happiness — not because you're so spoiled that nothing will make you happy. Big difference.'

'Since when did you come up with that fantastic notion?'

'Over the last few months, while I've had space away from you and time to think.'

At last she opened her eyes, painful though it was. He was sitting by the bed, still wearing his clothes from the night before. He looked tense, as though he hadn't slept very well, and he needed a shave, but his hazel eyes were gentle and concerned. For a moment she wanted to reach up and pull his face down to hers, to hold him tight and lose herself in their warm lovemaking. The echo of many, many nights when they'd made love into the small hours came back to her. It seemed like a life belonging to someone else, not the altered existence that had stared Liz Monaghan in the face less than twenty-four hours ago.

She summoned words, knowing that what she was going to say would drive him away from her, but it had to be done. Deep inside, she felt so wretched that she couldn't bear anyone's tenderness. Least of all Gavin's.

'You could be wrong,' she said tiredly. 'They might have been silly rows to you, but perhaps they were important to me. Look, Gavin,' she went on, 'you've been more than kind, and thanks again for coming to get me last night, but I'd rather you left me in peace for now.'

He sat up straighter. 'You're sure this is what you want?'

'Perfectly sure. I just want to be on my own.'

She saw the hurt in his eyes as he got to his feet and, to her shame, it gave her a vicarious thrill.

She might be weak and defenceless now, but Liz Monaghan, social diarist, hadn't gone away. As soon as she got rid of this crippling hangover, and put the previous twenty-four hours behind her, she'd be back.

She had lots of secrets to uncover . . .

32

'Smile, ladies!' Gemma ordered.

Sitting on the low wall surrounding the Trevi fountain, I did as I was told and smiled for the camera as Erin put her head close to mine and Gemma pointed her mobile at us. Beside us, young children scampered about under the watchful eyes of their parents, and my ears rang with their excited shrieks above the splash of the water.

I had a sudden memory of Juliet trying to take photos of us all on the beach at Howth. Mum had been there, and James. The twins were still quite young. Juliet had had a very elaborate camera, and as she fiddled with its buttons, Kevin grew impatient and began to run in and out of the water, splashing at the spray. Mum had got cross with him, but Juliet just smiled.

It would have been one of our earlier summers there, when I still saw life as an exciting adventure.

'That's one for Facebook,' Gemma said, coming back to join us at the edge of the fountain. 'We'll show them how we celebrate Paddy's Day in Rome.'

'Don't tag me,' I asked, forgetting to be discreet. Not that I imagined for one minute that Conor would be checking my Facebook page: he had a horror of it as a form of social media and thought it ridiculously intrusive, but his sisters or

230

some of our mutual friends — if they were still my friends — might see it and tell him. I didn't want to look as though I was having the time of my life on the day we should have been getting married. I hadn't gone near Facebook since Christmas. Not even to update my status. Every part of my life in Dublin had been locked away in cold storage.

I could see Gemma was bursting with curiosity. 'I've had my account hacked,' I fibbed, 'and I'm not updating anything for now.'

'Fine by me,' she said, sounding unconvinced.

'Are we making a wish?' Erin asked, her hand delving into her bag.

'I thought you could only wish to return to Rome,' I said, immediately regretting my cynical words. Erin had been trying to distract Gemma's attention.

'You can make any kind of wish,' Erin said evenly, handing me some coins.

For me, the Trevi fountain symbolises the heart of Rome. No matter when you visit, the area around it is always teeming with life, from babies to lovestruck teenagers to great-grandparents, as well as foraging sparrows, and you have to angle for space on the seating.

Rome was crazy, with its higgledy-piggledy energy, nightmare traffic, narrow streets, ancient build- ings and historic monuments almost subsumed by the modern city springing up willy-nilly around its ancient heritage. You never knew what jewel you were going to discover when you turned a corner, a monument, church or fountain. The fact that an ancient church was often cheek by

231

jowl with a graffiti-covered wall didn't lessen the city's quirky charm. Even the wonderful Trevi fountain was surrounded on three sides by drab-looking apartment blocks.

I viewed the jumble from the safety of my dislocated status, the chaos and disorder somehow blending with my mood, mirroring the chaos and disorder boiling in my head behind the shutters.

'Just don't tell us what you wish for,' Erin said, as I lifted my hand.

'There's no fear of that,' I said.

I flung the coins into the air, one by one, and watched them glint in the sunlight before they plopped on to the surface of the enclosed basin in front of the fountain to disappear beneath the pale green water. I had just the one wish.

That I could set my heart free from loving the man I couldn't have.

*   *   *

It was late in the afternoon when Rebecca swung her BMW into the driveway of her south Dublin home. She'd driven from the Seagrass Hotel via the M50, but instead of taking her usual exit, she'd stayed on the motorway and headed for Dundrum Town Centre.

She'd gone shopping, splurging a little on cosmetics and shoes in House of Fraser, then picking up two dresses in Harvey Nichols. She was able to buy a lot of her clothes at cost in Olivia Jayne, but now and again she liked to shop elsewhere. Today it had been more to delay her return to the empty house. She'd even stopped for lunch in Harvey Nichols.

But when she stepped on to the parquet floor in the hall, she felt suddenly relieved to be in her own familiar surroundings, the family home she and Harry, Danielle and the twins had moved into fifteen years ago. Tucked into the far end of a quiet cul-de-sac, it was spacious and comfortable, rather than elegant, decorated in cool, neutral tones, with a bay window in the sitting room, looking out over a well-kept front garden, and a conservatory giving on to the good-sized mature garden that was her pride and joy.

She was up in her bedroom at the front of the house, unwrapping a cashmere jumper from soft tissue paper when she glanced out of the window. A police car cruised down the road. It slowed to a crawl as though it was picking off house numbers. And then it stopped. Right outside her garden.

Her scalp prickled and her heart flew into her throat. Don't panic, she ordered herself. She blinked, steadied herself, and watched a man and a woman get out. The man was looking at her door and talking into a mobile, as though he was checking he had the right house. He opened the gate, and bent his head to confer with his female colleague. As though to check who was going to say what.

The pressure in her throat was so tight she could barely breathe.

If she could just stay like this, in her bedroom, her hand clutching pink tissue paper, if she

233

didn't go down to answer the door, didn't listen to their words, she'd be safe from knowing whatever disaster had obviously happened.

The doorbell shattered the peace, like a signal dividing her old, familiar life and the new knowledge she wanted to avoid. There was the Rebecca in her bedroom, staring at her new outfits, who wanted to know nothing. Then there was the Rebecca who walked stiffly downstairs, to the hallway she'd recently passed through, the familiarity that had wrapped round her now part of a different life.

For a moment she felt a pang of sympathy for the people visible through the opaque glass of the door, waiting to deliver their news. She felt a pang of sympathy for the Rebecca she'd left in the bedroom, clutching the filmy tissue paper that had been wrapped around a dress. But that vanished when she opened the door to their sombre faces.

'Mrs Ryan?' the man said, very deferentially.

It was bad.

Even though her head felt stiff with tension and pain, she made what must have seemed like a nod, because his female colleague gave her a look of sympathy. They introduced themselves, and she understood that they were part of the police force but their names and rankings floated over her head. They produced identity badges that swam in front of her and asked if they could come in.

Wordlessly, she stood back and let them invade her home. Not the conservatory, though. Whatever she was to hear, whatever she was about to bear, it would begin in her front room, not the oasis of the conservatory.

The young policewoman fiddled with her notebook.

'Sorry to disturb your evening,' the policeman began, 'but we've been asked to contact you by a Robert Jordan.'

She couldn't think who he was. 'Who?'

The policewoman said, 'Robert Jordan, from Florida, has asked us to contact you. It's about his sister, Juliet.'

'Juliet?'

Rebecca stared into the policewoman's eyes and felt chilled by her expression. Her heart dropped like a stone, down and down, as though there was a cavity all the way through her body from her chest to her toes. She fell forward, the centre of her gravity shifting. The policewoman caught her before she fell too far, easing her on to the sofa. She sat down beside her, and told her to breathe slowly. Rebecca didn't think she'd be able to get oxygen into her lungs as her chest was so tight, but after a minute she inhaled a thin stream of air, and then took a stronger breath. The policewoman began to talk to her, words that Rebecca at first found impossible to follow.

She shook her head. 'Sorry, you're not making sense. Could you start again?'

The policewoman spoke very slowly: 'Earlier this morning, a woman was found close to the bottom of the cliffs at Howth. Initially there were signs of a faint pulse, but she was pronounced dead on arrival at the hospital. We've reason to

235

believe it's the body of Juliet Jordan . . . '

Rebecca shook her head. 'It can't be.'

'A member of the Coastguard team involved in the rescue believes the body to be that of Juliet.'

'You don't understand. Juliet told me she wasn't going out anywhere last night.' What silly words, but she clung to them, as if to deny this new, shocking reality.

'The member of the rescue team wouldn't have volunteered the information unless he was fairly certain. We've checked her house and she's not there. Her car is in the garage and there's no reply from her mobile, but the last signal was traced to the cliffs, late yesterday evening.'

Rebecca shook her head, which felt heavy. 'Sorry, I just think — no, this can't be. Not Juliet.'

The policewoman checked her notebook, as discreetly as possible. 'The woman is average height and was wearing a navy tracksuit.'

A navy tracksuit.

'Her hair might have been dark originally, but it appears to have blonde highlights and pink tones . . . '

Rebecca stared at her. 'Please tell me this is some kind of a joke.'

'I'm afraid it's not, Mrs Ryan.'

The room spun. Shock made her light-headed. 'You said she was . . . unconscious. Had she been . . . like that for long?'

In other words, had she known what was happening? Had she felt lonely and terrified? Or in some dreadful pain?

'We don't know the full circumstances yet. We traced Ms Jordan's brother in Florida, and he asked us to talk to you. He said you were very close to Ms Jordan, that you knew her very well, and he hoped . . . ' She hesitated.

'He hoped what?' Rebecca balled her fists, so tightly that they hurt, but it was impossible to stop herself trembling.

'He hoped you might be able to help,' the policewoman said gently, 'in giving a formal identification. Of the body. Just to be sure. He said he'd really appreciate it. He's on stand-by for a flight home. I have his number if you'd like to talk to him.'

The body. Not Juliet any more, her funny, laughing, clever, beautiful friend. This wasn't happening. A terrible mistake had been made.

She stood up, feeling she was being sucked into a long, dark tunnel from which there was no escape.

33

When I was growing up I remember my mother and Juliet saying more than once that they'd never forget where they were the night they heard the news about John F. Kennedy being assassinated. Childishly, and thinking I sounded very clever, I had once said their lives must have been very boring, and both of them rushed to explain what an unprecedented shock it had been, as though all the pillars that present-day society rested upon had been breached and nothing would ever be the same. I wondered what it must have been like to witness such a defining moment in history.

I witnessed my own when the Twin Towers in New York were attacked, another unprecedented atrocity, which had me gasping with disbelief and sadness. I had been working in London for the summer, and wanted to hop on a plane and come home to see my family and friends, reassure myself that everyone was alive and well. Of course, the airports were in chaos and flights were all over the place, so a quick trip home was out of the question.

Then there was the shock of my father's death, still too raw to remember at times.

And now it seemed that history was repeating itself.

Because, for the rest of my life, I'll never forget where I was when I heard that Juliet was dead.

For most of Saturday my mobile had remained switched off at the bottom of my bag, as Erin, Gemma and I had continued our eating and drinking fest all around Rome. That night I had fallen into a deep, alcohol-induced sleep, when I should have been bedding down with Conor Kennedy as his wife, instead of sleeping alone in my small Rome apartment. It was late the following morning when I woke up and switched it on.

It beeped straight away, and my mother's text, which she'd sent a couple of hours earlier, didn't alarm me: *Give me a call when u get a chance and can talk*, she'd said. She wanted to find out how I was after yesterday, I thought. Knowing Mum, she'd been tying herself in knots, reliving every moment as it should have happened, maybe shedding a few silent tears. That was another reason my phone had stayed at the bottom of my bag. I'd wanted no sympathy texts. However, from the timing of this one, she'd waited until she'd thought the worst of the proverbial storm had passed. It sounded as though there was no particular rush so I had a long, lazy shower with my favourite L'Occitane shower gel and sipped a big mug of milky coffee while I relaxed on the sofa, flicking through a three-day-old magazine. When I felt more alive, I called her.

What she had to say didn't make sense. She might as well have been speaking to me in a foreign language. I felt as though I had been sliced into two halves, the slightly hung-over me who'd faffed about in the shower, wasting time, and the me who knew that something truly terrible had happened, the full enormity of which my mind couldn't absorb just yet.

'Are you talking about *our* Juliet?' I said, my voice somehow continuing to function, even though the rest of me felt freeze-framed, stalled, stuck in limbo. I was convinced I was talking about a person who was still alive, not someone who, according to my mother, seemed to have lost her footing and stumbled down the treacherous cliff face, close to where she lived.

'Yes, darling, I'm afraid so.' My mother's voice was hoarse and sympathetic, her concern at that moment for me, not for herself, even though she'd just lost her lifelong friend. Typical Mum. Always looking out for someone else. Especially me. Sometimes I felt like giving her a shake and telling her to be more selfish.

'But I was only talking to her on Thursday night,' I said, foolishly thinking she might say she'd made a terrible mistake.

'*Last* Thursday night?'

'Yes. She called to say she might be over in Rome soon and we ended up having a great chat. Are you *sure* it's Juliet?'

'I am. I saw her myself.'

'*What?* When?'

Then she told me, in brief, about the police calling to the house the previous evening, and escorting her to a hospital morgue, and, yes, she went on in a small voice, so hard to believe, *impossible* to believe, and a terrible shock, but it was Juliet all right. She'd waited until this morning to tell me: she hadn't seen the point in

240

phoning me last night to deliver such bad news, especially when I was on my own in Rome. 'I thought you might as well get your night's sleep,' she said.

My mind slewed away from the terrible image of Juliet lying dead in a hospital morgue. 'Were you on your own when all this happened? Didn't Rose or someone go with you?'

My mother sighed. 'I couldn't get Rose on her mobile until afterwards — she and Matthew were at a St Patrick's Day dinner. The guards had contacted Juliet's brother in Florida and he was waiting to know if . . . and he asked if I'd . . . '

There was a silence.

I could guess the rest. Robert Jordan probably hadn't wanted to come all the way home from Florida unless he was sure it was his sister. From the little I'd known of him, there wasn't much love lost between him and Juliet. Then again, it would have been harrowing to make that journey home without knowing for sure.

'And why you?' I asked. I couldn't imagine how desperate it must have been for her. I thought my mother had been remarkably brave and my heart swelled with love and pride. I wanted to give her a big hug. She'd been through so much, holding us all together after my father had died, more concerned about our grief than hers.

'They don't have much family,' Mum said. 'Some cousins, I think, on Juliet's mother's side, but no one that Juliet keeps in close contact with. And she has plenty of colleagues and acquaintances, and some good friends in that circle, but I suppose I'm the closest to her.'

She was talking as though her friend was still alive. 'There's something about it in the newspapers this morning, but they're not releasing the name until Robert is home and has notified all the relatives. He's expected this evening.'

As she spoke, I stared around the rented apartment at the yellow walls, the small spindle table with the jug of dried lavender, the thin-cushioned sofa, and hated it. I hated it for not being home, for not being my space, the Dundrum apartment with the view of the mountains where I'd lived before moving in with Conor. Most of all, though, I hated it for being the strange place where I'd heard that Juliet had died.

'I don't suppose there'll be any word on the funeral arrangements for another day or two,' Mum said. 'It will depend on when they release the body. There has to be a post-mortem.'

Her words thudded into my head and I badly needed to breathe fresh air. I went across the living area, phone in one hand, opened a glass door and stepped outside to a tiny balcony that could barely hold one person standing. Down below me in a small cobbled courtyard, children were playing, their voices echoing. Beyond the terracotta roofs on the opposite side, I could make out the grey sprawl of the city stretching into the distance. Above that, puffy clouds floated serenely in a pristine blue sky. From the near distance came the muted roar of traffic and the chime of a church bell. The scent of a spicy

242

tomato sauce drifted out of an open courtyard window along with the staccato Italian of someone having a row. Life going on as normal. As though nothing dreadful had happened. I wanted to scream at everyone to shut up. I wanted to be back in my normal life. Whatever that was. I didn't bother reminding myself that life hadn't been normal for a long time.

'It's just unthinkable,' I said. 'I can't believe we're having this conversation.'

'Neither can I, love. It hasn't sunk in yet.'

She sounded so incredibly sad that I wanted to be there with her, right now.

'I'll be home as soon as I can,' I said.

'And, darling, how are you, after yesterday?'

'I went out for the day with friends. We did a sort of pub crawl around Rome.'

'One way of passing a few hours.'

'Did you say Juliet was found yesterday morning? So that all the time I was out, she was already . . . ' I couldn't say the word. It didn't belong in the same sentence as my mother's warm, sparkling friend.

'Danielle, don't let that get to you. What could you have done differently? And you weren't the only one who was busy living your life. We were all getting on with things. I was even — ' She broke off and gave a short, harsh laugh.

'You were even what?'

'I was drinking wine and going for walk with an old enemy of Juliet's.'

'Oh, gosh.'

'Yes. Liam Corrigan. Do you remember him? Supposedly he's turned over a new leaf. We were even talking about Juliet' — another harsh laugh — 'and I can't contact him because although I gave him my mobile number he didn't give me his.'

There was the sound of my mother choking back tears and once again I longed to be with her.

'I'll be home tomorrow evening,' I said. 'Can I stay with you?'

I had nowhere else to go.

'Of course, darling. I'd love that. I'll have your old room ready.'

'I'll have to go into the office in the morning and do a quick handover. Then it'll be straight to the airport for the next available flight.'

'I suppose you mean you're just coming home for the funeral? Not for good?'

'Yeah, I'm not ready for that just yet, Mum.'

'Okay, love, just asking.'

She still didn't know why my wedding had been cancelled, and she was puzzled by that. But I couldn't take her into my confidence. I just hoped I could cope with the emotional ghosts of being back in Dublin, as well as the funeral of the woman who had been a second mother to me. The beautiful, kind woman, whose unconditional love had always burned brightly in my life and whose advice I'd eventually followed: she'd told me to listen to my heart.

I can see her still: Watsons Bay, Sydney, the sun in her eyes when she turns towards me — and she shades them with her hand while she reaches for her sunglasses.

'Let go of who you think you should be,' she

said. 'Just be who you are in this world, your real self.' Something passed between us, I dunno, a message from woman to woman.

Surely if anyone had been their real self, it was Juliet.

There was more.

'Make every minute of your precious life count, Danielle,' she'd said. For a long, charged moment, her eyes were sad, and her message was that she didn't want me to have similar regrets. I wondered what had happened to make her feel sad, in a life so full of achievement and success. I hadn't asked Mum — I couldn't bring myself to pose the question — if Juliet had died instantly, or if she'd been lying there on the rocks, thinking of her regrets as her life ebbed away.

It didn't bear thinking about.

After I'd ended the call, I stood for ages on that tiny balcony, feeling icy cold inside, unable to work out what had to be done next, recalling the similar shock that had numbed me when I'd heard about my father's death. That time, I'd thought my broken heart would never repair itself. Now, it was as though a particularly bright light had been extinguished so everything seemed drab and grey.

And I had to return to Dublin, quite possibly face the man I loved but couldn't have.

34

'Do you want some coffee?' Matthew asked.

'Coffee?' Rose said, heedless of her scathing tone, which implied he'd suggested a trip to the moon. 'I don't feel like anything. I don't even know why I got up and I'm sitting at the table.'

He busied himself with the cafetière and took a mug out of the press. 'You have to have something. You need to keep your energy up. It'll be a long week. And a busy one.'

'Oh, yes, I should have known that's exactly what you'd think,' she snapped. 'A long week with more public appearances, but now it's a funeral instead of a drinks reception. And there'll be people there, important people, wanting a piece of Juliet. Politicians, scholars and dignitaries. People to impress. Never mind the television cameras. I bet you've already planned your wardrobe. I bet you began to work that out as soon as Rebecca phoned yesterday evening,' she ended savagely.

'Rose! For Christ's sake! I think you do need that coffee.'

'I don't want coffee,' she shouted.

'Jesus, what's wrong with you?'

'This is!' She stabbed at the newspaper. 'Look! Look at that picture and tell me you feel like coffee.' She pushed the page in his direction. The page with the short article about the body of a woman found at the base of the cliffs. She knew it by heart already, the short, terse sentences sickening her, so ridiculously had they summed up Juliet's end.

According to the article, the body had been spotted by a young man out for an early-morning jog. The coastguards had been called but rescue from the top of the cliffs had had to be aborted. A search-and-rescue helicopter had gone in. There was even a photograph of a winch man steadying a stretcher suspended in mid-air. The name of the deceased was being withheld until close relatives had been informed. The Gardaí weren't looking for anyone else in connection with the incident, but they were appealing for witnesses, and anyone who might have seen anything unusual along the cliff path, from Friday evening onwards, was advised to contact them immediately.

She watched Matthew's face pale as he glanced at the newspaper before averting his eyes. He turned away and gazed out of the window at the back garden, where the morning breeze was riffling through clumps of daffodils that were artfully grouped around the lawn, made to look as though they had sprung up naturally.

'See?' Rose said, her voice shrill. 'Now tell me you can think of coffee.'

'I've already seen it, thank you. On the Internet. Long before you were even awake,' he said tiredly. 'I know you're extremely upset but — '

'I'll have to get a grip.'

'I didn't say that.'

'What do you think happened? How did she

have such a stupid accident?'

'How should I know? I'm also finding it hard to believe. And I'm as saddened as you are.'

'Really, Matthew?'

'She was my friend, too, you know.'

'Was she, though?'

'Of course.'

'But she's no threat to you now, is she?' The words flew out of her mouth and quivered in the air between them.

Matthew became very still. Like an animal waiting to spring, as he stared out of the window, his head tilted slightly, as if checking for danger. He stayed like that for so long that something cold slithered down Rose's back.

'Matthew? Matthew, turn around and say something.'

'I might say something I'll regret.' His voice was tight.

'Like what?'

He wheeled around, his jaw clenched, his blue eyes full of anger. 'How could you think like that? How could you . . . ' his voice broke ' . . . at a time like this? Christ, Rose, what's got into you?'

'I don't know,' she cried, as she put her head into her hands. 'I don't want this to be real. I don't want Juliet to be dead. I can't bear it. I keep seeing her face, over and over. When she was young. I keep seeing her smile and hearing her laugh. But I can't help thinking this will change everything for you. She's out of your way now. And I wonder if I'm going mad again.' She burst into tears. She didn't know how she had any tears left. She'd already cried herself to sleep the night before, when they'd come home from Rebecca's, having called over to her after she'd eventually managed to contact them to break the shocking news.

'Juliet was never in my way,' Matthew insisted, in a quietly furious voice. 'Do you understand that? She was never a threat to me. Or to us.'

'What I can't believe is that my friend is dead and awful thoughts are going through my mind. I must be a horrible person. I *am* a horrible person. Or else I'm going mad all over again.' More sobs shuddered through her and she fished in the pocket of her dressing-gown for a non-existent tissue.

Matthew silently tore off a few sheets of kitchen roll and handed them to her. 'You're far too upset to think straight. You've had a bad shock. Go back to bed and sleep some of it off. There's nothing you can do right now. Everything's on hold until Robert Jordan gets here.'

'What about James?' Rose asked, her throat sore. 'Are you going to tell him about Juliet? Rebecca's phoning Danielle this morning. He has to know but I can't bear to tell him.'

'I'll call him.'

'Do you think he'll come home for the funeral? He was very fond of Juliet. Oh, God, this is awful. I can't believe I'm actually talking about Juliet as though she's dead.'

She felt herself being lifted out of the chair, which prevented her from falling into a fresh storm of crying. 'Back to bed with you,' Matthew said, guiding her out of the room and towards the staircase. 'It might be best to stay there until Rebecca comes over this evening.'

'Rebecca's coming here?'

'You asked her for dinner.'

'Did I? I can't remember. I don't know why I asked her for dinner. How can we eat when Juliet is dead? None of us will have any appetite.'

'You might have by this evening. We can order in whatever you feel like.'

She stopped at the bottom of the stairs, under the Waterford crystal chandelier, and stared at him. 'Do you think Juliet fell on purpose or was it just a crazy accident?'

'Look, love . . . ' Matthew sighed and shook his head. Wearing a plain grey jumper with black jeans, he looked more like the Matthew she'd known years ago and was comfortable with. She wanted to rewind time and go back to the start of their marriage when life had been innocent and full of promise. When they'd had no stair carpet for two years, and armchairs instead of a sofa. When they'd had to walk two miles to the nearest shop for bread and milk.

'It must have been an accident,' Matthew said. 'How else could it have happened? And Rebecca says the police aren't looking for anyone. So don't start imagining all sorts of things.'

'I can't stop thinking . . . ' She stared at him, unable to move. It seemed as though her head had been hurting ever since Rebecca had broken the news to them. It had been hurting before that, since Matthew had told her he was interested in becoming a candidate in the presidential race. Nothing had been right since then. And now, with Juliet gone, it would never feel right again.

'This all started when you got ambitious ideas about yourself.'

'What all started?'

'My head. Feeling sore.'

Matthew looked as though his patience had been exhausted. She didn't care. At least he was paying as much attention to her as he did to his computer screen.

'Stop thinking,' he said. 'Just get some rest.'

'I don't know if I'll ever rest properly again.' She didn't wait for his reply. She walked up the thickly carpeted stairs, along the corridor and into the bedroom. She lay in the big wide bed with the Egyptian cotton sheets and Chantilly-lace-edged duvet and stared at the same spot on the Farrow & Ball-painted ceiling where Juliet's laughing face superimposed itself.

The face of the young girl whose sparkling eyes and big, rebellious ideas had made her feel uncomfortable in her tightly ordered world, until she'd eventually found a grudging respect. It had been a respect tinged with envy, for Rose had never possessed a scrap of the careless insouciance that had been Juliet's trademark. She'd even been nervous about introducing her to Matthew, when they'd met for a meal all those years ago, terrified in case Matthew would find the bright, vivacious Juliet a more attractive proposition than the staid, rather safe Rose.

'Do you like her?' she'd asked Matthew afterwards, as they'd left the grill bar and strolled up O'Connell Street, the night somehow flat and colourless once they'd left Juliet and Rebecca behind. The girls were heading into a pub to meet friends for a drink, Juliet checking for her mints so her father wouldn't smell beer on her breath.

'Like her? Yeah, she's a bit of craic.'

'Am I a bit of craic?'

'Not in that way, thank God.' He'd tightened his grip on her hand. 'I'd hate you to turn into one of those women's libbers, always yelling for their rights. What's the betting she can't even boil an egg? Or iron a shirt? You're sweet and gentle, Rose, and that's why I love you.'

Later, he'd tried to go further with her than ever before, his kisses longer and deeper, his hands more forceful as he squeezed the swell of her breasts. She'd let him slip his fingers inside her bra, and he'd pressed her hand against the rather alarmingly long, hard bulge at his crotch. She couldn't imagine how it might feel, pushing all the way inside her on their wedding night.

Juliet, she'd thought, wouldn't be nervous of that. She'd welcome and enjoy it. And as soon as the ring was on her finger, and she was Matthew's wife, she couldn't afford to be nervous of it either. She'd have to welcome it.

Rose closed her eyes and waited for the pills to work. Sweet and gentle, Matthew had said, that long-ago night. He'd only been partly right, she thought, as she drifted into drug-induced sleep, for there were times when Rose Moore felt quite, quite savage.

35

Stretched out on her sofa in front of the television, Liz tugged the soft velour rug closer around her. She had spent most of Sunday relaxing and watching her favourite feel-good DVDs, in which love, romance and happiness reigned. She'd originally planned to write up her diary column full of juicy gossip and sharply drawn innuendoes about Friday night's gala reception, but all of Saturday had been spent in the throes of hangover hell. Today, even though she felt marginally better, she hadn't got as far as checking Facebook or Twitter, never mind opening her laptop.

People would be wondering why she was off the radar, but she hadn't the energy to care.

Gavin hadn't contacted her since he'd marched out at lunchtime yesterday. It would be a while before she'd hear from him, if ever. He had looked totally pissed off with her, and she didn't blame him. Even she was pissed off with herself for rejecting his kindness and concern.

The closing credits of *Love, Actually* rolled up the screen, with everyone finding their happy-ever-after, something she sensed would always be elusive to her. She picked up the remote and flicked desultorily through the channels. She left on the main evening news because the newscaster's jacket was similar to one she'd recently tried on but rejected during a shopping trip to London. Now she studied it critically, trying to judge if it would look cool and sexy on her.

Only for that, she might have missed the item about Juliet Jordan.

Professor Juliet Jordan had died suddenly at the weekend, the newscaster was saying. 'Vice chancellor of the Institute of Dublin University, Professor Jordan was renowned for her ground-breaking work as chairwoman of the European Equality Legislative Agency, her many publications and media appearances, and for her tireless contribution as founder and CEO of the Children's Dream Holiday charity. The professor died as a result of an accident near her home.'

As she spoke, file photos of Juliet flashed up on the screen: receiving a crystal bowl at an award ceremony in the Mansion House, being handed a bouquet of flowers at a dinner in Dublin Castle, and last, in Dublin airport, looking ridiculously young in jeans and a T-shirt, surrounded by an assortment of sick children, some wired up to portable drips.

'It is expected that Professor Jordan's funeral arrangements will be announced in the next couple of days,' the newscaster finished, before continuing with an item on the St Patrick's Day celebrations in New York.

Liz sat motionless, practically unblinking, and let the rest of the bulletin wash over her. After a while she lowered the volume, reached for her mobile, and called one of her news correspondent colleagues. 'Dave, hi.'

'Liz, what's up? Or should I ask who's going down this week under your sharp scalpel?'

254

'It could be you.'

'All my secrets are well out in the public domain, so there's nothing left for you to pillage. Although, knowing you, you'd find a needle in a haystack. Or a stray pubic hair on the wrong person's pillow.'

'Not always,' she said soberly. 'I've just been watching the news. Have you the inside track on Juliet Jordan?'

'What's it worth? And what are you doing sitting in on a Sunday, watching the news? You must be really ill if you're not out on the prowl.'

'It's worth a double tequila on the rocks, and I'm busy writing my copy.'

'Yeah, what's the betting you're recovering from an industrial-sized hangover?'

'Well, what's the news on Juliet?'

'Why are you interested?'

'I was hoping to feature her in my diary.'

'You were hardly putting Juliet Jordan under your dissecting knife?'

'None of your business. So, come on, what's the goss?'

'Very little, actually. She had some sort of accident off the cliffs at Howth on Friday night, I think, but her name was held back until her brother got home and informed the relatives. There will be a post-mortem tomorrow, but it's thought she missed her footing and fell. That's it. Seems an awful stupid tragedy for such a wonderful woman. And so bloody final. You won't be talking to her now. Maybe that's just as well. I wouldn't like to see you doing a hatchet job on her.'

'Thanks for your faith in me.'

'Unfortunately I have every faith in you, Liz, as well as your scandalous pen. Hey, how about meeting me for some hair of the dog? Or maybe some off-the-record scandalous sex? I enjoyed our last romp.'

'Shut up, Dave,' Liz said. She'd known him for a few years and had fallen into his bed on a couple of occasions, the last time after she'd split with Gavin. They'd had a fun, no-strings night, prancing between his bed and his bath, but right now she didn't want a repeat.

They chatted some more, and when she ended the call, Liz went into the kitchen and put the kettle on to boil. She felt shaky and outside herself, funnily devoid of feeling, and she wondered if those were the final effects of her mega-binge. She took a mug out of the press and then, on second thoughts, replaced it and got out a glass instead. She switched off the kettle and picked up the bottle of vodka, splashed a generous amount into the glass, then topped it with cranberry juice. She took her drink into the sitting room and settled herself once more on the sofa.

One drink would be okay, maybe two, just to get over this weekend. It didn't mean she was going to end up like her mother, who had been an alcoholic for years. Her parents might have had plenty of money and lived in Upper Ballymalin Grove, but Liz would have swapped it all to have been born into a large, rough-and-tumble family with a more modest home in Lower Ballymalin Gardens. There, children sometimes slept three to a bed. She shivered in spite of the central heating. Growing up, she'd always felt cold. It had been a house that had echoed with bitter rows and icy silences between her parents, and where Liz had sometimes stolen through the rooms trying to avoid them and their angry words.

'If I'd given you sons, would it have made any difference?' she'd heard her mother cry. 'I know you desperately wanted a son to carry on your name.'

'Sometimes I feel like a failure, and not a real woman,' was another favourite lament.

'I've let you down, I know I have.' Over and over again.

The hard crack of a hand connecting with soft flesh. A muffled thump.

Then, sometimes, 'I hate myself. I hate you. Only for Elizabeth, I'd be long gone . . . '

'And where would you go, woman?' her father had growled.

'That's the problem, isn't it? I'm stuck here. Because of Elizabeth. There's nowhere for women like me to go.'

Annie Monaghan had finally found her way out when she'd overdosed on vodka and pills just after Liz's sixteenth birthday.

The following year, as soon as she'd left school, Liz had fled to southside Dublin, a damp and noisy bedsit in Rathmines. She'd never looked back, leaving her father to his own sad devices much of the time. But her modelling career hadn't been the success she'd craved, even though she'd had the looks and the height, the deep blue eyes and the silky dark hair.

'You need to have more empathy with the camera,' they said. 'You need to mix a little vulnerability with that cool, calculating streak of yours.'

A load of crap, she'd thought. She was invulnerable. But when the modelling had led to a job helping on the fashion pages of a fortnightly magazine, she knew she'd found her niche. Her talent with words, combined with her stored-up anger and resentment, gave her a sometimes black but always pithy voice that got her noticed. Determined to make a go of it, she went on to study media and communications in her spare time, honing her craft, and shortened Elizabeth to Liz: it looked far punchier on a byline. And it had worked.

But love, marriage and the happiness thing had eluded her. Still, having witnessed her mother's misery in her marriage, Liz congratulated herself on cleverly avoiding that fate by ridding herself of Gavin at the first sign of trouble.

But she hadn't known the truth behind her mother's sense of failure until she'd emptied the house in Ballymalin and stumbled across documents that had changed everything. Liz took another gulp of her vodka and tried to stop shivering. In her shock, she'd left them behind, scattered on the floor. She needed to look at them again to make sense of what they had told her.

The truth might have made a difference.

Who was she kidding? It would have made all the difference in the world.

She went out to the kitchen to refill her glass.

Even though her life had been pulled from under her, she wasn't going to follow her mother down the alcoholic trail, she told herself. Liz Monaghan was a voice to be reckoned with, every weekend in the society pages. Juliet Jordan might be beyond her reach now, but there were other people she could talk to. There were still some secrets to be unveiled no matter how deep their hiding place.

And, come hell or high water, Liz would find them . . .

36

'Rebecca?'

Liam. At last. Rebecca excused herself to take the call. She took a deep breath to steady herself. 'Hi, Liam, I'm in my sister's.' Her voice echoed around the vast, clinical space and she wished she was somewhere other than Rose's mammoth kitchen while she had this difficult conversation with Liam.

'You've seen the news? About Juliet?' he said, his voice strangled.

'I haven't watched it, but I'd been hoping you'd call,' she said. 'I wanted to avoid you getting a shock.'

'How long have you known?' It was almost an accusation.

'Since yesterday evening.'

There was a choking noise. 'God almighty.'

Her heart went out to him. 'Liam, I'm sorry you had to hear it on the news, but I'd no way of contacting you.'

'Of course. I know. Sorry, I'm just upset.'

'Juliet's brother arrived home this afternoon and, between us, we reached as many people as we could before the news was broadcast. If I'd had your number, I would have called you straight away.'

It had been an exhausting couple of hours. Robert had called her from his hotel room as soon as he'd arrived, and she'd begun contacting people who needed to know as soon as he was satisfied that immediate relatives had been informed. Thankfully, some of Juliet's colleagues had offered to pass on the sad news to their own circle of friends, thus sharing the burden with Rebecca.

'Dear God, I don't believe this.' There was another muffled sob, as though he was crying.

'Look . . . ' She paused to gather her scattered thoughts. 'Do you want to come over? Rose wouldn't mind — she's so distressed that the whole army could march through her house and she wouldn't notice. Although . . . ' she hesitated ' . . . it might be best if you called over to my house. I can be home soon.'

'Yes, please.'

Rebecca gave him her address. 'Are you okay to drive?' she asked, conscious that he was in shock.

'Of course,' he said.

She made her excuses to Matthew and an inconsolable Rose, who hadn't touched a morsel of the beef dish Matthew had ordered in. 'We'll talk tomorrow,' she said, hugging her sister. Rose clung to her, and it was difficult to prise her away, until Matthew took his wife into his arms.

'She'll be fine,' he said to Rebecca, over Rose's head. 'I'll keep an eye on her.'

'Make sure you do,' Rebecca said, her tone light but meaningful. 'No starting down that campaign trail tonight or tomorrow. Rose needs you. What about James? Is he coming home?'

'In a couple of days.'

'God, it's an awful mess, isn't it?'

'Death is messy and rather awful at times,' Matthew said, looking at her steadily.

Just as Rebecca reached the door, Rose stirred in his arms and raised her tear-blotched face. 'At least Matthew has nothing to worry about any more where Juliet is concerned,' she said, in a slurred voice.

Rebecca threw her brother-in-law a startled glance. In the time she had been there Rose hadn't been drinking. She could only guess that her sister had taken one too many Xanax. 'Rose? Are you feeling all right?'

Matthew looked grim. 'Rose is . . . too upset to think straight,' he said, his arms wrapped securely around her.

'I *am* thinking straight,' Rose protested. 'It's all very clear to me. At least Juliet's out of Matthew's hair now.'

Matthew looked at Rebecca, his expression unreadable. 'Rose has this idea that Juliet was some kind of threat.'

'And you were the one who said we'd nothing to worry about,' Rose said, stepping back and staring up at him.

She was keeping well out of this, Rebecca decided. 'Stay where you are,' she said. 'I'll see myself out and, Rose, I'll call you tomorrow.'

★ ★ ★

Shortly after Rebecca got home, Liam arrived in a taxi. He stood in her hall, looking like a haunted child.

'Did I say I was going to drive? I couldn't put

the key into the ignition, let alone turn it,' he said.

A wave of dizziness washed over Rebecca. On impulse, she held out her arms and he went into them. They held each other for long moments. She found it strange to be in another man's arms, but needed some comfort and wanted to comfort him, and the heat of his body to warm her. Just for that moment it was good to be alive, breathing in and out, her heart pumping so that all her cells hummed, able to hold someone else and be held in return.

She brought him through to her plant-filled conservatory, with the bright, cheerful furnishings. The evening had fallen into night, and outside, garden lighting dispelled the darkness. She lit a white jasmine-scented candle, one that Juliet had given her and she'd been saving for a special occasion, and opened a bottle of Shiraz that Juliet had brought her from Stellenbosch. Then she sat beside him on the cane sofa and filled him in on everything that had happened since the police had called to her door.

She felt as though she was going through the motions on automatic pilot, that some weird adrenalin had kicked in to help her cope with the trauma of the next few days. Her grieving had to be carefully laid aside for now. People needed her: she had to talk to Robert about the funeral arrangements, possibly help with them, be there for mega-distressed Rose, prepare her spare room for Danielle tomorrow evening and comfort her, and now deal with Liam's shock.

But he had some inkling of how she must be

feeling. 'If I feel as though I've been landed a sucker punch in the gut, how did you go through all that on your own?' he asked. 'Never mind the mortuary.'

'I did it for Juliet's sake,' she said, his concern warming her. 'Someone had to. No sense in Robert getting a heart-in-the-mouth flight home unless it was definitely his sister.'

'How did Juliet look?' He squeezed her hand.

She managed to smile. 'Rose didn't ask me that but, in fairness to her, she's very upset. It was okay, I suppose, as far as these things can be okay. I didn't know what to expect, and I was quaking. Juliet . . . ' She faltered as the image of her friend, pale and lifeless under the garish hospital lights, came back to her. Unreal. Surreal. Like Harry all over again: the searing pain was waiting behind a thin sheet of glass until the rituals were over, until weeks and months had passed and she missed Juliet more and more, the longer it was since she'd seen or talked to her. She lifted her chin a little, looked at the flickering candle flame and went on, 'Juliet looked like she was in a very deep sleep. She'd suffered internal traumas, and injuries to her legs and the back of her head. Still, I kept expecting her to wake up and laugh, and call out, 'Gotcha!' or something silly like that.'

Liam's eyes were warm and they lifted her heart. 'You're a very courageous lady,' he said. 'I can see why Juliet is — was, God — proud to have you as a friend.'

Rebecca shook her head, tears gathering behind her eyes. She blinked several times. 'Don't talk

264

like that, please. I can't bear it. Anyway, she was the trail-blazing lady of courage, not me. And my biggest regret, which will never go away, is that we had cross words the last time we were together.'

Liam put his arm around her shoulders. She was surprised by how good it felt. 'Hey, what are a few words compared to a lifetime's friendship? She forgave me for a lot worse. She would have forgiven you anything.'

'I still can't understand how it happened,' Rebecca went on, a little comforted by his words. She poured more wine, slipped off her shoes, swung her feet under her on the sofa and allowed herself to relax into the curve of his arm. 'Juliet told me she was going to spend the whole of Friday in her study because she had to put her head down and clear her reports.' She paused. 'God, Liam, you must have been one of the last to see her alive . . . '

His face blanched. 'Don't say that.'

'What time were you there?'

'Around five o'clock. I didn't stay long.'

'You've no idea who else she was expecting?'

'No, she wouldn't say. She was joking about it. I started teasing her about her hair . . . It was kind of blonde with . . . um — I'm not sure what colour you'd call it. Oh, Christ, I can't believe I'm talking about the colour of her hair. This is awful.'

'It was a pink wash,' Rebecca said bleakly. 'She told me once she hated going grey — her hair was her one vanity.' She shivered, and Liam tightened his hold. 'I'll never get used to talking about her in the past tense. It feels so strange that it's like I'm sleepwalking.'

'Same here. Talk to me about her . . . Fill me in on the last couple of years . . . if you feel like it.'

She tilted her head so that she could look at him properly. He seemed genuinely interested and she gave him a grateful smile. 'That's exactly what I'd like to do. I could talk all night about her.'

He stretched out his legs. 'I'd love to listen.'

It grew late, and another bottle of wine was opened as they shared memories of Juliet, chatting about funny times and good times, Rebecca alternating between laughter and tears, as it passed midnight, and then one o'clock. Liam talked of calling a taxi. Rebecca worked out that almost two whole days had passed since Juliet was alive, so it was already days rather than hours since her friend had slipped from the world, and it was so sad that she didn't want to be alone in the darkened house. She knew the icy echo of dead silence in empty rooms, and she didn't want it tonight, while her warm, bubbly friend lay cold and stiff in a hospital mortuary.

'Rather than turf you out, I can put you up, if you like,' she suggested. 'I've three spare bedrooms and it means I won't be afraid if I hear a bump in the night. I even have a couple of spare toothbrushes.'

He looked pleased, and she felt unexpected warmth in her chest. 'Thanks, Rebecca. I'd like that. So long as you don't mind my rough face in the morning. If there's anything at all I can do, just ask, no matter what it is.'

266

'Rough faces are fine in the mornings,' she said, automatically glancing at his lean jaw line and lingering on his nice mouth. She slid her gaze away from it. 'I'll even stand you a cup of coffee.'

'How did you get through last night?' he asked, searching her face. 'It must have been torture. I can't believe we were joking and laughing about Juliet only yesterday morning.'

'Neither can I. I zoned out with the help of double-strength sleeping pills, but I was so befuddled this morning that I don't want to repeat that. Tomorrow will be busy, between talking to Robert about the funeral and Danielle coming home.'

She was comforted by his presence in the adjoining bedroom as she chased sleep, her mind on a constant loop from the moment the police car had driven slowly up the cul-de-sac to when she'd asked Liam to stay. What had happened to Juliet continued to haunt her. She tried not to see it re-enacting in front of her: Juliet setting out along the track in her usual jaunty manner, then the heart-stopping moment when she stumbled and pitched forward into the space between sea and sky . . .

How much had she been aware of? Had she lain unconscious all night? Or had she waited in vain for rescue, her body broken and battered, terror gripping her, and rescue, when it came, far too late?

They would never know.

Had anyone seen her out for her walk? Lots of people would have been walking along the headland. Had someone somewhere an idea of what had happened to her friend? She felt a howl of anguish building up inside her and tried to bite it back, but Liam must have heard a noise, a whimper, because he stood in the doorway against the landing light, still dressed.

'Are you okay?'

She sat up in bed, hugging herself. 'Yes. No. Oh, God, this is a nightmare.'

'Isn't it just? I still can't believe it.'

'Come here, Liam. Hold my hand, please,' she said. 'I can't bear lying awake in the dark.'

'Neither can I.'

Liam lay on top of the bed and held her hand, and she was glad he was there as the night darkened and deepened around them.

37

Sleep was elusive.

Friday night, it had been okay, the same for Saturday. But tonight the ghost started to appear. The ghost of Juliet. She could have been another presence pulsating in the room, her shimmering outline twisting and writhing, moving forwards and backwards, only now her eyes were as black as coal, her teeth yellow like fangs, her nails long and blood red.

It had been too easy.

Juliet had suggested the headland stroll. As they walked and talked in the gathering evening shadows, she had been defensive and on her guard, but still maintaining a calm kind of assurance that was infuriating. Then the angry words flowing into the air had become more barbed and heated, but Juliet had held on to that maddening composure, refusing to be rattled.

A glance along the temporarily deserted headland track, and the perfect solution presented itself. It hadn't taken a minute. Juliet hadn't even had time to cry out as she slipped over the edge and dropped like a stone, disturbing a flock of gulls that rose on beating wings circling and cawing into the calm evening air.

Now the room was pulsing with a giant image

of Juliet's blanched face and terror-stricken eyes in the split second she'd realised what was about to happen.

It would never go away.

38

Rebecca found it almost impossible to face the new morning when the reality of Juliet scored itself freshly on her heart the minute she woke up. Weird, also, to see Liam Corrigan asleep on top of the duvet. No one had lain on that side of the bed since Harry. Rebecca picked up a throw and tucked it around him. She felt she was almost sleepwalking as she showered and dressed, then went downstairs to make coffee.

Liam joined her just as the doorbell rang.

It was the police. The same pair who had called to tell her of Juliet's death. Nausea rushed to her throat.

'May we come in?'

Wordlessly, she stepped back to allow them to enter. 'Liam, this is . . . ' Her mind flailed as she tried in vain to recall their names. They stood awkwardly in the hall.

'Detective Inspector Callaghan and Detective Woods,' the policeman said.

Detectives! She hadn't realised. Their rank reinforced the gravity of it all.

'Liam Corrigan. I'm an old friend of Juliet's.'

'We need to have a few words with you about Juliet, if that's okay, Mrs Ryan,' Detective Woods began, in a sympathetic voice.

'Of course,' Rebecca said, leading the way into her front room.

For a moment the atmosphere was charged,

Rebecca's mind whirling helplessly, the detectives looking as though they didn't know where to begin.

'Would anyone like coffee?' Liam asked.

The detectives shook their heads.

'We're trying to piece together what might have happened on Friday night, Mrs Ryan,' Detective Woods said.

Something cold slithered around Rebecca's gut. She was glad that Liam was sitting on the sofa beside her.

'We're keeping an open mind on everything,' Detective Inspector Callaghan said, 'but we need to conduct a fuller investigation into the circumstances around Ms Jordan's death and her movements on Friday evening.'

He was young, Rebecca realised. For all that, his eyes were sharp and keen, and slightly world weary, as though he'd seen it all before. She might have found him attractive had she been watching him on some detective programme. Juliet would have given him ten out of ten for those eyes.

They'd never watch television together again. Or go to the movies. Or out for a drink and a meal. Deep inside, she felt a huge reservoir of tears ready to burst through a dam. But not yet, please, not just yet.

'How can I help you?' she asked.

Detective Woods flipped open her notebook. 'According to Robert Jordan, you were Juliet's closest friend. Is that right?'

'Yes. We've been friends for a long time.'

'Since?'

'A lifetime ago.'

'So you'd know if anything had been bothering Ms Jordan?'

Rebecca felt the blood drain from her face. 'You don't think — you can't mean — '

'We don't think anything at the moment,' Detective Inspector Callaghan said. 'We're just trying to get as full a picture as possible of Ms Jordan prior to Friday night. These are routine enquiries.'

'She was much the same as ever,' Rebecca said. 'Busy in her life, quite busy, actually. I know she intended to spend Friday catching up on her paperwork . . . '

'When was the last time you spoke to her?'

Rebecca gulped.

Maybe it's time a few things were out in the open . . . Maybe I'm willing to take my chances . . . See what Fate has in store . . .

'What is it, Mrs Ryan?' Detective Woods leaned forward. She wasn't just a pretty face. She was as quietly alert as a cat waiting for a mouse to come out of its hidey-hole.

'Nothing. I was just remembering something she said, the last time I saw her.'

'Which was?'

Her mind sheered away from Juliet's words. 'I saw her last Sunday, when we went for a walk around the headland.'

Detective Woods consulted her notes. 'We've obtained Ms Jordan's spare set of keys from Mrs Breen, the elderly lady who lives in the adjacent property. Mrs Breen says she has known Juliet for most of her life. She was very surprised that

Juliet might have slipped and fallen. She said Ms Jordan knew the cliff walk like the back of her hand. Would you agree with that?'

'Yes. She walked those cliffs most evenings. Sometimes when I called in for a chat she dragged me along with her. She often did that when friends or colleagues popped in.'

'It had rained earlier on Friday, so part of the track could have been damp and slippery,' Detective Woods said. 'But Mrs Breen says that Juliet was used to going out in all kinds of weather.'

'Had Ms Jordan any adversaries that you know of? Sorry we're intruding like this, but we have to eliminate all we can.' This was from Detective Inspector Callaghan.

Rebecca stared at him. 'Like what? What are you trying to eliminate?'

'Let's put it like this, Mrs Ryan,' Detective Woods said, 'We need to satisfy ourselves that Ms Jordan died by misadventure, accident or — or — '

'Whether we should be looking for someone else in connection with the incident,' Detective Inspector Callaghan said, his tone deferential but firm.

'Someone else?' Rebecca's voice shook. She was grateful that Liam immediately took her hand.

'All avenues have to be examined before they're excluded from our enquiries,' the detective continued.

'But who — ' Rebecca couldn't continue.

'Ms Jordan was well known, with a very high

profile. She could have been a target for someone she might have known or perhaps not. We have to consider everything.'

'Have you witnesses?' Rebecca asked. 'Did anybody see Juliet out on Friday evening?'

'We've nothing definite yet.'

'You might want to talk to me,' Liam said. 'I think I was one of the last to see Juliet alive.'

Both detectives sat up straighter, and Rebecca's stomach lurched as they began to question Liam in a manner of brisk efficiency that made her feel sick, jotting down his account of Friday night in their notebooks.

'You said you think she was expecting someone else, Mr Corrigan?' Detective Woods asked.

'Yes, we were in her kitchen and she threw an eye to the clock a couple of times. I joked and asked her if she had a hot date lined up.'

'And what was her reply?'

'She said it wouldn't be Friday night without a flaming hot date and I'd have to make myself scarce.'

'She didn't mention any names?'

'No, but it could have been anybody or nobody. That was the way Juliet went on.'

'Mrs Ryan, to your knowledge, was Ms Jordan in a relationship with anyone?'

'No,' Rebecca said immediately.

'And yet you were of the opinion that she intended to spend Friday catching up on her paperwork.'

'Yes, I was,' she said.

'So you weren't aware that Mr Corrigan

would be calling to her.'

'No. I wouldn't always know the daily incidentals of Juliet's life,' Rebecca explained, 'but I'm positively sure she wasn't in a relationship.'

A small seed of doubt burst open in her head. Juliet could be very discreet, when the occasion demanded it. She saw her face on the cliff-top . . . *just as well you knew only half the story.* How much had she kept from Rebecca, then and now?

'Can you confirm that you met Mr Corrigan in the Seagrass Hotel afterwards?'

'Yes,' she said. 'I saw Liam in the lobby . . . it was after nine o'clock that evening, wasn't it, Liam? The news was still on the television. You hardly think — '

'We don't think anything at this stage,' Detective Woods said. 'As I said, we're keeping an open mind while we get a fuller picture. As you saw her on Friday evening, Mr Corrigan, we'll need you to come to the station in the next day or two to sign a statement. Could we have your contact details, please?'

'Fine by me,' Liam said, and gave them his mobile number.

'And, Mrs Ryan, we'll need your help with one further matter,' the policewoman said, her face full of empathy. 'Robert Jordan considers you're the best person to throw your eye around Juliet's home in case there's anything amiss.'

'Like what?' Rebecca asked, feeling chilled right through to her bones.

'Anything at all out of the ordinary. Any kind

of disturbance. We still have the house sealed off, so we'd like to bring you across as soon as is convenient. Is that okay?'

'I can go with you now, if you'll give me a few minutes to have some coffee,' Rebecca said.

'I'll come too, if you like,' Liam said, squeezing her hand.

She shook her head. If she had to do this, she wanted to be alone, apart from the police.

'We just need Mrs Ryan,' Detective Woods said. 'If there's anything amiss, or evidence, we don't want to compromise it more than we have to.'

Evidence of what? Rebecca felt desolate. Still, she was the only person who could do this, for she was the one to whom Juliet had entrusted all her details in case of an accident: 'Someone has to know where I keep the keys to my safe and where I store all my important paperwork, my will and insurance and all those tiresome details we can't live without,' she'd said to Rebecca, soon after they'd both turned fifty. 'You're the person I'd trust the most to look after the pernickety stuff, should I get lost on a Himalayan adventure or in the South American jungle.'

'Don't talk like that.'

'I have to be practical. I don't have a spouse or partner, and Robert's in America. And it's much easier to sort out these matters while I'm still in rude health.'

'Knowing you, Juliet, you'll see us all down,' Rebecca had joked, and Juliet had gone on to tell her what kind of commemoration service she'd like.

There was no end, she thought. No end to the tunnel into which she'd pitched on Saturday evening.

★ ★ ★

She braced herself as they neared Verbena View, filled with sickening dread as she saw the police tape across the driveway flicking in the breeze and the officer standing in the porch. Rebecca's heart was in her mouth as she stepped across the threshold. She moved down the hallway and into the empty rooms, waiting to be assaulted with images of her friend, wondering if there would be any clues as to what had happened on Friday evening. Funnily enough, the house seemed peaceful and at ease. It was just as though Juliet had popped out to the shops and would be back at any moment.

Rebecca went into the study, half expecting Juliet to jump out of the deep leather armchair drawn up in front of the fireplace. She saw that the computer was logged off and the desk had been tidied, as though she'd completed her work before she'd left for her walk. She had a quick look through the papers on the desk, and in the drawer, but there was no sign of anything untoward. It was painful, however, to look at the framed certificates in the corner alcove and impossible to think that Juliet would never set foot in there again and sit at her desk with the glorious view of the sea.

'Nothing out of the ordinary here,' she said to Detective Woods.

The detective must have signalled something, for two officers moved in and began disconnecting the hard drive of the computer. Rebecca wanted to ask them to leave the room exactly as it was: she didn't want to see familiar parts of Juliet's life being fragmented.

Silly, really, when her life itself had been destroyed.

Into her bedroom, and Rebecca's heart squeezed, but all was neat and tidy, save for a pair of jeans and a pink cashmere sweater thrown on top of the laundry basket in the en-suite. The clothes she must have been wearing on Friday before she'd put on her tracksuit. She wanted to pick up the sweater and bury her face in it, to see if she could catch a lingering fragrance of her friend. She checked the walk-in wardrobe and Juliet's clothes were neatly arranged, along with her bags and shoes. The concealed door to her wall safe, which contained her jewellery and important papers, was still securely locked.

'This is fine also,' she said to Detective Woods.

Then Rebecca went into the kitchen, which had always been the beating heart of Juliet's home. She strangled a sob as she looked around the warm familiarity of it all and memories surged. Juliet popping the cork on yet another bottle of champagne: 'Just one more. Life is too short not to drink all the bubbly.'

Juliet in a funny Naked Chef apron, brandishing a wooden spoon coated in tomato sauce. 'Which brave soul wants to try some of my home-made lasagne?'

Juliet folding back the patio doors and

opening the kitchen to the outdoors. 'What a totally fabulous evening. Look at that ginormous sky. I could sit here and gaze at it all night . . . '

Juliet would never set foot in her kitchen again. A pulsebeat of pain ricocheted in Rebecca's head. She balled her hand into a fist and pressed it against her mouth. She felt Detective Woods place a hand on her arm.

'I know this is difficult,' the detective said, 'and you're doing great. Take your time, there's no rush. We just need to know if anything strikes you as odd.'

'Juliet — ' Rebecca swallowed hard. 'She often wrote appointments into her calendar on the wall. Danielle gave it to her last Christmas, to help her plan ahead, as she was inclined to get so involved in her work that she forgot what was coming up.' She went over to the corkboard beside the fridge unit, but there were no entries in the box for the previous Friday.

And then: 'She must have left in a hurry,' Rebecca said, voicing her thoughts as she turned back and her eyes roved around the kitchen.

'Why is that?'

'Just . . . the only odd thing — the glasses on the counter . . . Normally Juliet would stick them into the dishwasher or at least rinse them. I can only guess that she was in a hurry to get going . . . '

'Did she always clear up before she went out?'

'Yes. She might have been a bit absent-minded now and again, but she was a tidy person and never left food, dirty dishes or glasses lying around, especially if she was going out.' Rebecca

280

stared at the glasses.

Liam, with his bottle of wine? Whoever had visited after Liam? 'And there are two glasses,' she said, 'so Juliet had company before she left, although that doesn't mean anyone went with her. She usually invited you to tag along, you know, if she was heading out for her walk.'

Another nod from Detective Woods, and the glasses were photographed, then sealed in plastic bags and borne away.

'You're taking this very seriously,' Rebecca said. 'Do you think whoever was here — ' She couldn't continue.

'It might mean nothing at all,' Detective Woods said. 'There could be a perfectly innocent explanation. But, in the circumstances, we're leaving no stone unturned.'

Rebecca's glance rested on the kitchen table, where the group of them had sat at Christmas before everything had gone crazy. Before Juliet had decided that a few things should come out into the open. Had she started down this road? Had she upset anyone? And something else had been nibbling at her subconscious since Sunday evening: *At least Matthew has nothing to worry about anymore where Juliet is concerned.* Just what had Rose meant by that? It seemed that Juliet's death was sending her sister spiralling back into the black void.

'We can leave now, Rebecca,' the policewoman said gently.

She didn't want to go. She wanted to sit in Juliet's kitchen and wait, in the hope that this was all a crazy mistake and any minute now Juliet might breeze through the door. Funnily enough, it was much harder walking back up the hall and out of the door than it had been to come in.

39

Funerals shouldn't be allowed to take place on warm, spring days, I decided. Especially the funeral of someone like Juliet.

All the way home from Rome I had been dreading this moment, and Mum, bless her, must have sensed it for she squeezed my hand and smiled at me as we drew up outside St Patrick's Cathedral for Juliet's commemoration service. I couldn't believe the size of the crowd gathered outside, although I hadn't expected anything less.

Earlier that morning, Juliet's coffin had been quietly brought to the cathedral directly from the funeral home, where her body had lain since it had been released on Monday evening. I didn't go to see her in the funeral parlour: I wanted to remember Juliet as she had been, full of laughter, full of love and full of life. I couldn't yet think of her as a body.

Rose and Matthew had accompanied us in the mourning car, and there was a flurry of interest as we stepped out, some photographers elbowing through the throng, cameras at the ready, anxious to get to us. Rose was dressed in designer black, from head to toe, oversized dark glasses hiding her eyes. Matthew was wearing charcoal grey and I felt he was more protective than usual of her. I couldn't help noticing, though, that rather than trying to avoid the reporters, as Mum and I did, my media-savvy uncle guided her in the general direction of the television crew, who were busy picking off the beautiful and important people.

Mum was wearing an elegant royal blue Joanne Hynes dress and coat, topped off with a jaunty hat. 'You look like you're off to a wedding,' I'd said to her, before we'd left our house, immediately sorry that I'd brought up the W-word. My abandoned wedding still hadn't been mentioned between us. We'd had little chance to talk alone: since I'd come home we'd been busy with endless phone calls and cups of tea, and people coming and going, including Robert Jordan, to arrange the service with Mum's help, and Liam Corrigan, who'd been hanging around like he didn't know what to do for the best. A far more subdued, reflective Liam compared to the flash poster-boy I'd remembered from the Celtic Tiger days. Then Rose had phoned, twice or three times, and I knew my aunt was crying from the way Mum tried to soothe her, and my cousin James had arrived home from the States and called over as well. So it was full on.

'A wedding?' She'd smiled easily, as though the word had no nasty connotations. 'That's exactly what Juliet would have wanted. And you look perfect yourself, darling. Juliet would have approved.'

'I hope so,' I said, smiling back. Our tacit understanding was that there would be no tears today: we would see Juliet off in the style she deserved. I was wearing a champagne knee-length dress embellished with black lace, and a matching tight black-lace jacket. I'd bought it in a boutique on the Via del Corso in Rome before I'd travelled to the airport, hardly able to believe I was buying an outfit for Juliet's commemoration service. My hair was swept to the side and secured with a diamanté clasp Juliet had given me.

We slipped through the throng of academics, politicians, television and radio personalities, and went into the cathedral. In contrast to the sunny morning, the interior was cool and dim, and filling up quickly. My eyes flew straight to the top of the main aisle, and my heart fluttered at the sight of Juliet's coffin, with the single spray of lilies on top. I told myself that the Juliet I knew and loved wasn't really there, in that shiny wooden box. Yet neither was she here with me and Mum, taking the piss with sharp comments about some of the jumped-up crowd milling around outside. The part of my life that she'd inhabited seemed cold and silent for now.

Mum and I went up the aisle and sat in the second row, leaving the front pew for Robert Jordan, his wife and sons. Behind us, I heard increased activity, as more and more of the crowd streamed in and took their places. Robert and his family arrived, shaking hands with Mum and me.

And then I sensed the person I loved most in the world arriving. My senses prickled and hummed, like stretched electric cable, but I kept my eyes focused on the stained-glass window over the altar.

Oh, Juliet, I cried silently, I've listened to my heart, but it's breaking in two and I've never been unhappier. Is this what you meant? And how could I even be indulging in thoughts like these when you're dead and gone from us all, and I'm alive and well, apart from my shattered love life? But no matter how hard I listened, in case some Juliet-type words of wisdom were floating in the sanctified air, I heard nothing but a resounding silence. If only I had entrusted her with my feelings, maybe called to see her at Verbena View, she might have been able to offer advice. Instead I'd hotfooted it out of Dublin, leaving Mum to pass on the news of my broken engagement to family and friends, and had only exchanged emails and an occasional phone call with Juliet. I thought back to our call last Thursday night, less than a week ago, when I'd put on my best happy voice and laughed along with her as though life was great. If she'd had time to come out to Rome, would I have confided in her? Hard to say, and all the wondering in the world was futile for I'd never know now.

The service started with the allegro from Bach's Brandenburg Concerto No. 1, and as the pure, joyous sound soared around the cathedral, I couldn't have thought of a more fitting tribute to Juliet's effervescent spirit. The service went by in a haze. Robert said a few words about his sister and her huge, unselfish capacity for striving to make the world a better place, her endless charity work, and thanked the large crowd for being there to celebrate her life. The chancellor of the university spoke about the pleasure of working alongside Juliet, the high regard in which she was held by the hundreds of students who

286

had passed through her hands over the years, and he commended her absolute dedication to her job. There were more speakers, and finally Mum stood up and took the microphone. She stared at the congregation for a long moment, and then she spoke simply, in her husky voice, from the heart about the enriching value of friendship and love in all its forms, a lot of which she'd learned from Juliet. 'We go back a long way, Juliet and I, and I was privileged to share so much of my life with her . . . '

She finished by asking for a minute's silence. 'I want everyone to remember, just for one minute, something happy that you enjoyed about Juliet, perhaps it was something that made you laugh, smile or just want to be around her . . . and let us give thanks for our dear friend and send her off with a lift in our hearts.' She stood, for a full minute, alone at the front of the altar, with Juliet's coffin a few feet away, and then she led the packed cathedral in a burst of applause, during which everyone rose to their feet.

I swallowed tears and thought my mum had never seemed braver or more beautiful. I know she annoyed me from time to time, in the way she fussed around us all with no regard to herself, but that was my mum. She was made of far more gracious stuff than I was, and quite perfect in every way.

Then it was all over. We followed Robert and his family behind the coffin up the aisle, as the music broke into Vivaldi's 'Spring' from *The Four Seasons*. Out of the corner of my eye, I saw my cousin James standing at the edge of a pew several rows up the aisle. He gave me an encouraging wink as I passed, and then we were spilling outside into the spring sunshine as the coffin was placed in the hearse.

A queue of people had lined up to talk to Mum, more so than to Robert, most of whom I didn't know, from elderly statesmen to young college students. I stood quite close to her in support, as they expressed their sadness. Some of the college students clung to her and cried, and Mum took it all in her stride. I realised belatedly that she didn't really need me. She was more than able to take care of herself.

Except for one, who was pushing her way forward now to the head of the queue.

I knew by Mum's face and the slight recoil of her body that she didn't want to talk to Liz Monaghan, the jumped-up pseudo-journalist who'd made herself a household name because she had the bitchiest voice in tabloid newsprint.

'Have you any comment to make, Rebecca?' she asked, in strident tones. 'We know the police investigation is still wide open.'

'I have no comment,' my mother said calmly, moving slightly away from her. Just as well she had filled me in on the whole rotten story and the questions the police had been asking. At least I'd been forewarned, but other mourners close by were startled.

'But you must have a theory of your own. You knew Juliet so well,' Liz cooed.

Mum refused to be drawn. 'I have nothing to say, if you'll excuse me,' she said, politely but dismissively.

Liz pressed closer to her, her eyes wide and calculating, 'Do you think Juliet had any secrets up her sleeve?'

Mum seemed a little alarmed but, to my surprise, Matthew came to the rescue. Standing close by, he had observed what was happening. Now he stared at Liz with a glint in his eye. 'Liz, we know your dedication to your job is paramount,' he said, in a silky voice, and drew her away from my mother. 'But surely you'll agree that there's an appropriate time and place for everything.'

'Well, hello, Mr Moore, it was worth it to get this close to you,' Liz said, in an equally silky voice, looking him up and down slowly and deliberately. 'You're on my hot list, you know. I've been hoping to do a no-holds-barred interview with you, and perhaps your lovely wife, but you keep ignoring my Twitter messages. I appreciate you're very busy at the moment.'

'Contact my PA,' he said. 'I'm sure you'll be able to ferret out her details. Or look up my new website.'

'So, is that a date?' She raised her eyebrows archly.

'Hardly, Ms Monaghan,' Matthew said. 'I usually do the running. It's never the other way around.'

'Can I quote you?'

'Feel free.'

'Your wife won't mind?'

'Why should she? The lovely Rose is the only woman I run after. And you can quote that too.' He turned away.

Good on you, Matthew. That put Liz in her place quite neatly. Although Liz wasn't one to let that bother her. I heard her shrill tones as she addressed no one in particular, confident that everyone within hearing distance was attuned to her. 'Oh, my God, is that Liam Corrigan? I'd heard he'd returned from exile but I'd never thought he'd have the neck to turn up here.' I hoped fervently that he was able to make himself scarce. I wasn't quite sure what to make of him, and was a little bemused by how friendly he was with my mother, but he didn't deserve to have Liz on his back.

Mum was talking now to a learned-looking gentlemen and his elegant wife. I was making my way across to her when a pair of arms came around me from behind.

'Hey, little cuz, how are you today?'

James.

I turned to face him. 'I'm good, considering. How are you?'

'Okay. Sort of. Mum's still in bits and Dad's doing his best to keep her upright, but I didn't realise how much I adore Rebecca until I saw her in action today. She played a blinder.'

'Yeah, she did. I'm very proud of her.'

The good thing about Ireland is that, by and large, famous people get to do their own thing, without too much interference or hassle. James Moore might have played a sell-out concert in Madison Square Garden a few nights ago, but today he was simply a mourner at the funeral of a dear family friend. Although we attracted lots of sidelong glances as we chatted, people gave him space and no one came rushing over to annoy him. Even Liz was busy chasing Liam.

'I didn't get a chance to ask you last night, but how are you now, after everything? And I don't mean Juliet.'

'So-so,' I said.

James was one of the few people I'd emailed about my crashed wedding in the immediate aftermath, conscious that The Name planned tour dates well in advance, so he'd have to know the band didn't need to be in the south of France on St Patrick's Day, after all. He'd called me immediately and had accepted that I didn't want to discuss it.

'Although . . . ' I paused.

'Although what?' He tilted his head to one side and waited. 'Come on, spit it out, cuz.'

I decided it was safe enough to reveal the monster that had stalked my thoughts since Mum's horrific phone call. 'If things had gone ahead,' I said, 'Juliet would have been at my wedding and this wouldn't have happened.'

He bundled me against the front of his long navy overcoat. My head was stuck somewhere in his chest when he said, 'Danielle Ryan has managed to find a lovely stick to beat herself with. What time were you supposed to be getting married?'

'Five o'clock in the evening,' I said, my voice muffled.

'Right. Chances are, given how busy she was, Juliet would have planned to fly out that morning. And of all the conspiracy theories I've heard, that's pretty much the worst. Don't ever let me hear you repeat that, little cuz.'

He knew all about the police and the investigations from chatting to me and Mum last night and was just as bewildered as we were at the inexplicable circumstances surrounding Juliet's death.

'Right, big cuz.' We'd fallen into our nicknames for each other easily enough.

'Are you going with your mother to the crematorium?' he asked.

I shuddered at the thought of seeing Juliet's plain wooden coffin sliding through the velvet curtains to what lay beyond. She'd told Mum, years ago, that she wanted her ashes scattered off the cliffs by Howth, and Mum was following her wish, even though we agreed how sadly absurd it seemed, given how she'd died. 'Yeah, I guess I'll have to go with her for company, although I don't think she needs me, and your parents are in the mourning car as well. How did you get out of that?'

'I'm staying in my apartment in the city centre and travelled from there.'

'Duh. Silly me, I'm not thinking straight.'

'How could you be? And I came in a specially borrowed car. I think Juliet would have approved.'

'I might have to approve it as well,' I said. 'If Mum doesn't mind, I'll take a lift with you.'

James tensed and looked over my head at someone beyond me.

'Somebody looks like he's anxious to talk to you. If you still want to come with me, I'll be waiting for you outside the side door.' He took his arms from around me and gave me a little push. Then I was face to face with Conor.

I'd hoped he'd leave quietly without talking to me, but he was too well mannered for that. A hysterical bubble rose in my throat — we should have been on our honeymoon. More poignantly, all the intimacy between us might as well have been sucked into a black hole, and I was like an awkward, self-conscious teenager.

I'd met Conor at Erin's thirtieth birthday party in the Odessa. I'd had a succession of unsatisfactory boyfriends and equally unsatisfactory relationships, and as soon as I was introduced to the software whiz, with the soft brown eyes, I'd thought it was the real thing. He seemed to feel the same about me.

Now his eyes were guarded. 'Danielle,' he said, taking my hand as you would a strangers, 'I'm so sorry about Juliet, I can't imagine how difficult this is for you but I know how much you loved her. I was very fond of her myself.' As his warm, familiar voice washed over me I thought I was going to cry. It wasn't quite three months since we had split up, and I had a sudden urge to throw myself into his arms and make it all right again, all the love and the laughter we'd shared. But nothing would ever make it right again.

'Thanks for coming,' I said, through the ocean of tears at the back of my throat.

'I couldn't not. How's your mother?'

'She's okay. It was a terrible shock, of course.'

'And not all that long after your father, either.'

'Six years,' I said softly, holding his gaze, recalling how he had comforted me during those terrible dark days.

'Wow, that long?'

It had been just before my father's death that we'd started going out, and all of a sudden I'd needed him so much it had cemented our relationship: the hospital dash that had been in vain, the funeral on a freezing cold and wet January day, the nights I couldn't sleep when he'd held me in his arms.

We both spoke at once.

'Time flies,' I said, so banal.

'You still have things left in — '

'I know.'

'They're safe, for whenever you want to collect.'

'Thanks.'

And just like that, we had exhausted the polite chit-chat suitable for funerals and there was nothing else to say. Nothing and everything, for it was all waiting to be thrashed out between us. What had gone wrong, how it had gone wrong, as well as the mundane details of breaking up our relationship and shared home, and on the other side of the huge chasm between us, there was a mountain of hurt and anger, but this wasn't the time or the place.

'We will have to talk, you know,' he said.

'Yes.'

'We can't just leave it in limbo.' He gave me a worried look.

'No.' I began to walk away, my legs trembling.

'Danielle?'

'Yes?' I half turned to glance back at him.

'Look after yourself, won't you?'

'I will, and you.'

I went in search of my mother, who had almost finished accepting condolences. People had started to drift away, and the hearse, the spray of lilies on the coffin, was ready to bring Juliet on her final journey. I told Mum I was getting a lift to the crematorium with James.

'That's fine,' she said. 'Did you see Conor?'

'I did.' I managed to keep my face neutral, though I could feel my mouth trembling.

'Good girl. See you later.' She gave me a warm smile — I'd held it together. She was thinking of me, instead of her own heartbreak. How had I ever felt irritable with her?

I slipped through the dispersing crowds back into the cathedral and out of the side door to where James was waiting, a gaggle of girls standing nearby laughing far too loudly and drawing as much attention to themselves as they could. When he saw me, he put on his shades and took my hand. Together we hurried around the side-streets to where his car was parked.

'Hey, little cuz, I thought we'd see Juliet off in style.'

It was a vintage soft-topped Triumph in classic red. He opened the passenger door with a flourish.

'Where did you get this?' I asked, amazed.

'I borrowed it from a friend just for today. Remind you of anything?'

'Of course,' I said, a lump in my throat. My earliest childhood memories of Juliet were of her coming to visit in her red Triumph, squealing to a halt outside the house, appearing very daring and glamorous as she hopped out of the car, with her short dark hair and leather trousers. She had sometimes brought me and James out for the day, to the sea, or the mountains, occasionally to Verbena View where I'd met her quiet, ladylike mother and tall, proud father, who had always slipped me and James crisp five-pound notes. Juliet used to pretend she'd kidnapped us and might never return us to our parents, and we had great fun going along with her game. She brought us to McDonald's, telling us it was a brilliant excuse for her to scoff their delicious stringy chips and cheeseburgers, and to pantomimes at Christmas, laughing as loudly as we did.

The engine roared, and James grinned as we pulled out on to the main road and joined the stream of cars behind the hearse. I began to cry then, silent tears that slipped down my cheeks and slid into my mouth. I heard myself sniff and rummaged furiously for my tissues. James said nothing, merely shoving his hand into the side compartment of the door and pulling out some Kleenex, which he handed to me. I was grateful for his silence and was composed when we reached the crematorium, as Juliet's coffin was lifted out of the hearse, the polished wood gleaming mockingly in the sunlight.

Then, after a short ceremony in a rather airless room, and to the sound of The Beatles' 'Here Comes The Sun', my beautiful Juliet was gone for ever and it was all over.

On the way back out through the porch, the final cadences of the music were echoing in my ears, and the mourners were discussing the best way to get to the Merrion Hotel, where Robert Jordan had organised lunch. Something cold clutched my insides: we were leaving Juliet behind. Already life was moving on without her. On impulse I picked up the spray of lilies, which had been left in the porch. The final, flimsy link to my honorary mum.

'Are you hungry?' I asked James, carrying the flowers to the car, thinking how odd it was to be talking about food on a day like this.

'Not particularly, but I'm going to the Merrion anyway,' he said.

'Fancy making a detour?' I felt a little shaky as I said this, barely acknowledging to myself what I wanted to do.

James looked at the flowers in my hands, and his gaze travelled over my face, finally breaking into a smile. 'I think that's a great idea,' he said.

We drove back through the city centre, over the quays, then out to the north side and Howth Road. We swept up the hill close to Verbena View, where police tape still fluttered outside her house. James parked the car and opened the passenger door for me. I stepped out, the sea breeze so fresh and invigorating after the crematorium that it almost took my breath away. He held my hand as we walked, the spray of flowers tucked into my other arm.

Then the sparkling sea came into view.

I didn't know the spot where Juliet had fallen, and I was glad. I didn't know how long she'd lain injured, waiting for help, how much she'd known, how angry and terrified she might have been, but none of that mattered now, for it was over and

297

she was beyond all pain. I took deep gulps of air, and felt strands of my hair escape from its clasp, whipping around my face as we absorbed the panorama. This was where I wanted to remember her for this was where her spirit danced and soared. This was all hers, the sea and the sky, the track around the headland. Her spiritual home, which she'd loved with every fibre of her being. When we were part of the way around, I buried my face in the spray of delicate flowers, inhaling the fragrance. Then I silently handed it to James. He reached out a long arm and sent it whirling as far as he could, so that it seemed to dance in the space between the sea and sky. I turned away as it began to fall. Then we held hands and walked back to the car.

40

'Rebecca? How have you been?'

'I've seen better days,' Rebecca said, her hands tightening on her mobile as she stared out at the rain-washed garden. She had decided it was safe not to pretend with Liam. 'Danielle went back to Rome this morning and I dropped her out to the airport. It was good of her to stay on for a couple of days, but I miss her now.'

'Of course you do,' he said. 'It was lovely to see her. She's turned into a beautiful woman. You must feel very proud of her.'

'Yes, she is, and I do. That's why I was so gutted about her cancelled wedding. She deserves the best and I hate to see her upset. Not that we spoke about it.' She gave a half-laugh. 'It didn't get a look in because all our conversations revolved around Juliet.'

'Now that I've met her, Rebecca, I have to agree with what you said. If her fiancé broke it off with her, he doesn't deserve her and she's better off without him. If she cancelled her plans, she knew exactly what she was doing.'

'That's what's keeping me going. Why don't you come over for lunch?' she asked him. She hadn't seen him since the day of the funeral and it would be good to chat to him and reminisce about the day. By now, Sunday midday, it was already more than a week since Juliet had died. Rebecca knew, from Harry, how swiftly the weeks would fly by, how easily a loved one could slide into your past and their lives close over, unless you brought up happy memories of them with friends and family.

Rose had invited her to Belgrave Park that evening, as Matthew was hosting a drinks party for some of his inner circle, but it was the last place she wanted to be. Matthew would be trying to impress, and Rose . . . Rose had had such a look of desperation on her face on the day of the funeral, and she had sounded so edgy on the phone since then that, for once, Rebecca wanted to avoid her instead of jumping to the rescue. A case of healthy self-preservation.

'Thanks for the invite, but I don't think you'll want to see me for lunch,' Liam said ruefully.

'Why not? You're very welcome.'

'You haven't seen the tabloids this morning.'

'So?'

'Somebody thought it their duty to remind everyone about the heated exchange I had with Juliet before I legged it to Spain.' Liam sounded as if he was doing his best not to take it too seriously but his voice was tinged with annoyance.

'The heated exchange?' Rebecca was puzzled for a moment. Then, 'You're joking.'

'I'm not. Oh, it's all very carefully worded, not even a hint of libel, but the row we had has become a blazing quarrel, and it's also mentioned that I've just arrived back in Ireland, and the person with whom I had the altercation has had a most unfortunate accident.'

'Don't tell me, Liz fecking Monaghan,'

Rebecca said, bile rising in her throat. 'What a perfectly horrible insinuation, with no regard to how you must be feeling about Juliet, never mind dishonouring her memory.'

'I don't care what she writes about me, I'm used to it, but I can't forgive her for dragging Juliet's name across her sordid page.'

In those halcyon days when Liam had been living the high life, he'd sometimes featured on Liz's society page as she regaled the nation with details of his lavish lifestyle.

'Liz Monaghan was always a bloody cow, but this is a new low,' Rebecca fumed. 'I don't know why she's decided to stick the knife into you. And I can't believe she featured Juliet like that. What the hell is she thinking of? She has no respect for Juliet, never mind her family or friends. No one with any decency will take any notice of what she's written.'

'How any editor had the gall to send it to print is beyond me.'

'Probably afraid of her tongue as well. She has no conscience.'

'About Juliet — have you heard anything from the police?'

'I haven't spoken to them since the day before the funeral.'

'So you don't know if there have been any further developments?'

'No, and I don't know how they operate, or what they do in these circumstances,' she said, feeling sad. 'There'll be an inquest, I expect.' There was a brief silence. Then Rebecca said, with forced cheer, 'Just relax, Liam, forget about

Liz, and I insist you come for lunch. Better still, we should go out somewhere busy and public and be seen together. We'll stick our fingers up at Liz's grubby gossip.'

Liam laughed. 'Are you sure you want to be seen with me?'

'Don't you start believing the drivel that that poisonous pen wrote. Let's meet in the Shelbourne. The scene of the crime.'

'Are you serious?'

'Yes, I am. It'll show Liz we don't give a damn about her rubbishy column. I'll be there for two thirty. Meet you in the bar. Right? No excuses. I hope it's mad busy, that lots of people see us together and word gets back to that scheming bitch.'

Rebecca went upstairs to change out of her jeans into something a little smarter. Even though Danielle had stayed for less than a week, the house felt thick with the silence of empty rooms in which nothing but the light patter of rain on the windows disturbed the quiet. She felt a cold shiver as she went into her bedroom. All week, she'd been too busy and preoccupied to contemplate the huge gap that Juliet's death would leave in her life.

Far, far better to be meeting Liam than sitting here alone. That was the only reason she was meeting him for lunch, she told her reflection in the mirror. And if she had a sudden need to be around him, to relax in his company, to watch the warmth in his eyes as they talked, it had everything to do with staving off the emptiness of the day and the overwhelming sadness of loss.

'You look great, Rebecca,' Liam said, when she arrived in the bar. He was sitting at a high table close to the window. He kissed her cheek, then pulled out a stool for her. 'Is three thirty okay for food?'

'It's perfect,' she said. The bar was humming with laughter and conversation, the iconic murals a splash of energy on the walls. Hard to believe life was still going on when Juliet was no longer around. She glanced outside. A constant stream of people passed the windows and taxis pulled in and out of the rank. Across the road on St Stephen's Green, the trees lining the perimeter of the park were frilled with baby green fuzz.

Spring. The renewal of life, whose cycle was fundamental and steadfast, no matter what else was happening in the world. She looked at Liam, took a deep breath and sank into the moment, feeling the tension that had gripped her all week dissolve. She was glad she was there: she was going to enjoy the afternoon, with this man as an antidote to the difficult week they'd had and the painful moments that lay ahead.

'However, Liam, I don't want a repeat of the last time I saw you in that restaurant,' she joked.

He looked startled, and then he smiled. 'Relax. I've ordered a bottle of champagne in honour of Juliet and I'm not going to waste a drop. Besides,' his voice softened a fraction, 'I'm not an angry bastard any more and I wouldn't dream of hurting you.'

'And, by the way, I asked you out,' Rebecca said, suddenly mindful of his financial constraints.

He shook his head. 'This is my treat, and please allow me.'

'In that case I will,' she said. 'I'll get you another time.'

'You'll probably have to. How've you been, really?'

'Too busy to think,' she told him. 'It hasn't hit me yet. I'm still numb and slightly stupefied by what's happened. I keep thinking of something I have to tell Juliet. Even today, when I was in the taxi coming here, I was about to text her to say I was meeting you . . . ' Her voice trailed away.

'And what do you think she would have said?'

'If it was a text she would have replied either WTF or LOL. Or perhaps TAB.'

'What's TAB?'

'Totes Amazeballs.'

'Typical Juliet. I think it's safer to stick with LOL.' Liam laughed, an attractive and engaging sound, and she stared at him for a millisecond too long.

Liam looked at her with interest, as though he could read her thoughts. 'At the risk of putting my feet in it, I used to be jealous of your husband,' he said. 'Anytime I met you in Juliet's it was obvious you were still in love and very close to each other. You always seemed to be a warm, loving person and I wanted some of that.'

'Funny — I thought all the guys fancied Juliet.'

'She was my teenage crush, an exciting but

empty kind of attraction. You, on the other hand — '

'Come off it, Liam.' Rebecca flapped her hand and ignored her quickening heartbeat. 'You were married yourself,' she pointed out.

'I was,' he admitted, 'and it was a mistake almost from the word go. I panicked, because I felt it was time I settled down with a wife and family. It's ancient history now. Then when Harry died . . . I didn't want to intrude at first, and later my head was somewhere else. Up my arse, to be precise.'

She burst out laughing. And then she recalled other times when Liam Corrigan had looked at her with interest, even years ago, when Harry was still alive and they'd met at Verbena View. Harry had been extra vigilant around her, but Liam had never overstepped the invisible boundary that Harry had silently marked out.

She wondered what Harry would say if he could see her now. They'd talked, of course, about what to do if the other went first, but just lightly, as though it was something that might happen in another century or two.

'If I go first, don't sit around moping,' Harry had said. 'You're allowed to grieve for a little while, and have a good cry, but after that, live your life, Rebecca. Go out there and live every day. Fill your life with good things and go on dates with men.'

'Dates with men? You mean sunbathing on the Riviera with my French lover, or yachting with my Greek tycoon? Or what about touring South Africa with my toyboy?'

Harry had smiled. 'Of course, but only if they're good and kind.'

'Only if they're sexy and well hung, you mean,' she'd said, laughing. 'Like you.'

Little had they known how swiftly he'd be taken from her.

The champagne arrived and she touched her flute to his. 'To Juliet,' she said.

'Juliet,' Liam echoed. 'And to Harry.'

'Harry.' She smiled.

★   ★   ★

'I know you don't feel up to it, but for my sake, can't you just pretend to be happy?' Matthew hissed, as they met in the hallway.

'Sometimes I feel I've been pretending most of my life,' Rose hissed back, momentarily shaken out of her usual restraint and gratified by his startled glance.

'This evening is important to me,' he said, his voice low and tight, mindful of the caterers taking over the kitchen and moving around with refreshments. 'You don't have to *do* anything, except smile. It's all being looked after.'

The doorbell chimed and he straightened his tie along with his shoulders as he went to open it. Rose saw him switch on a megawatt smile for the benefit of yet another political activist, who stood in the porch accompanied by his wife. A taxi was drawing away from the kerb. Rose wanted to ask the driver to take her somewhere. As the couple stepped inside, bearing flowers and wine, one of the hired waitresses moved forward with her tray of drinks, as composed as if she was the hostess. She looked barely twenty, and her slim figure was poured into a tight black dress. She had a beautiful Nordic face and a cascade of blonde hair. Another waitress, coming out of the kitchen, had short dark hair and red-glossed, pouty lips. She wondered if Matthew had hired them deliberately to sex up his campaign.

An informal evening, he'd said, when he'd suggested it just before Juliet's death. At home with the Moores. Drinks and nibbles for a few influential business friends. He'd hire caterers, and arrange for cleaners to do the necessary afterwards. Rose wouldn't have to lift a finger.

She had expected him to cancel the evening on account of Juliet's funeral earlier that week, but only yesterday he'd confirmed that it was going ahead. 'It's too late now to call it off,' he'd insisted.

'I just assumed . . . ' She'd floundered.

Matthew had sighed impatiently. 'I understand you're still upset, but Juliet is the very person who'd tell us to go ahead with whatever plans we'd already made.'

'I feel as though my home and my life are being invaded when I least want it.'

'I don't have the luxury of time,' he'd snapped, looking distinctly hassled. 'Every day counts from now on. Every hour has to work for me. I'll make it up to you, Rose. I need you with me in this. I can't do it without you.' His blue eyes had been steadfast as they fastened on her.

She'd put on her Paul Costelloe silver sheath

307

dress and white gold jewellery, then slid her feet into sparkly high heels and stared at herself in the mirror. She'd remembered for a fleeting moment a tartan A-line skirt she'd bought in Roches Stores that had once been her pride and joy and had cost the guts of two weeks' wages, never dreaming in those innocent days that, in time to come, she'd have an account at Brown Thomas, and a wardrobe chock full of designer clothes, courtesy of her successful husband.

Never dreamed, either, of the complex way their life together would become so entangled that she was being slowly suffocated.

She thought she'd looked the part as she greeted Matthew's guests, but some strain had shown in her face as she circulated around, hence Matthew's terse words.

Matthew escorted the political activist and his wife into the party, where more beautiful waitresses were gliding around with trays of canapés and sushi, and stuff Rose didn't recognise on cocktail sticks. The long, elegant room — they'd opened the interconnecting doors between drawing room and dining room — was filling with influential luminaries from business and political circles, milling about under the Waterford crystal chandeliers, against a backdrop of silk wallpaper and Irish paintings. Some were there because Matthew was keen to impress them, and others wanted to align themselves to his rising star, sensing the power struggle that was about to play out and hungry to be part of it.

After a while Rose slipped upstairs to cool her

flushed cheeks, only to encounter a guest wandering along the landing. She tensed.

'Can I help you?' she said. 'There's a bathroom downstairs, if that's what you're looking for.'

The woman wheeled around, looking guilty, and Rose recognised her as Emma Brady, the wife of a prominent barrister.

'Rose! I've been caught trespassing. I'm terribly sorry,' she said sheepishly. 'I'm afraid my curiosity got the better of me. I was just sneaking a peek around the house of James Moore's parents. Sophie, my daughter, is a massive fan. She and I went to see The Name the last time they were in Croke Park.'

Rose felt dizzy with relief. She could manage this. 'Don't worry about it. Unfortunately James isn't here tonight. He went back to the States on Thursday after a flying visit. It was such a busy few days that I hardly saw him.'

He'd arrived and left in the space of three days, had disappeared with Danielle on the day of the funeral, both of them arriving in the Merrion Hotel just as people were starting to disperse. He'd been too busy with other engagements the following day to come over for lunch or dinner, merely calling in on the Thursday morning for coffee before his after-noon flight to New York. It had been just as well she hadn't seen very much of him, considering her dark frame of mind. All she could remember from Juliet's funeral service was the heart-rending image of James blinking back tears as he'd put his hand on the coffin.

'James never actually lived in this house,' she continued. 'He left home long before Matthew and I moved here.' The house had never resonated to the sound of his guitar in the way their earlier, more modest, homes had. Maybe that was partly why Belgrave Park felt so lonely and empty.

Delayed empty-nest syndrome had been one of the reasons trotted out for her breakdown. She'd nodded and watched the counsellor take note of it on her file, even though she knew it wasn't true. It was far preferable to having the counsellor probe deeper and deeper, no matter how non-threatening she had seemed in encouraging Rose to face a truth, for it was a truth Rose had no intention of confronting, even though it played havoc with her peace of mind.

Emma was talking. 'Of course, I don't know what I was thinking,' she said. 'I knew he was back in Dublin for Juliet Jordan's funeral. A terrible tragedy,' she went on. 'And you were a good friend of hers. It was incredibly sad.'

'Yes. Absolutely.'

Emma began to move back down the curved staircase towards the ground floor. 'And bitchy Liz Monaghan in that rag of a newspaper this morning didn't help matters.'

'I must have missed it,' Rose said, her pulse accelerating.

'A load of rubbish. She dragged up the row Juliet had with the property tycoon Liam Corrigan, or was it the other way around? She passed some cleverly worded but lethal comments about him arriving back in Ireland just as

310

Juliet met with an accident.'

'But that's — ' Rose stopped, her heart hammering, the staircase seeming to rise and fall in front of her eyes.

'Yes, verging on libel.' Emma paused on the stairs and looked up, her face a white blur to Rose. 'And from what I've heard on the grapevine, Liam Corrigan is a changed man. I think Liz would want to watch her step very closely indeed . . . ' Emma's voice receded as she moved down the stairs so Rose missed her last words in the cadences of laughter and conversation floating up from the party.

On the landing, she gripped the mahogany banister and slowly let out her breath. She'd been about to speak when luckily Emma had interrupted her. She'd been about to blurt out something along the lines that it was silly to assume Liam had had anything to do with Juliet's accident when someone else had a far better reason for wanting her out of the way.

Someone like Matthew.

Or maybe even someone like Rose.

41

Sometimes, during those first few days back in Rome, it was easy to forget I'd been home to Ireland for Juliet's funeral. The office was busy, we were now officially in summertime and the evenings had lengthened. At odd moments, dream-like snippets of it all would catch me off guard, sending the blood pounding through my head so that I felt dizzy. All the emotive images of those strange days were packed between Mum waiting in Arrivals on the Monday evening, with a brave smile, then pulling up outside Departures the following Sunday morning and jumping out of the car to give me a hug.

She'd dropped me at the airport many a time, and I'd usually said a hasty goodbye, my mind on the journey ahead, but for the first time, my concern was all for her as I steadied my case on the pavement and turned to say goodbye. All about us, cars were pulling in and disgorging travellers, and an Aer Lingus jet passed over our heads, engines screaming.

'Are you sure you'll be okay?' I searched her face and pictured her going back to the empty house, learning to live without her friend just as she'd learned to live without Dad all those years ago. Mum has a friendly face and a ready smile, and sometimes I thought she looked too soft and considerate, as though you might take advantage of her, but now I knew that her demeanour masked a core of steel.

'Of course, darling. I'll be fine. I'm going back to work on Monday, so that will keep me busy.'

'Let me know if you have any news about . . . '

I couldn't bring myself to say 'about the cause of Juliet's death', but Mum knew what I meant.

'I will, straight away.'

'And wish Rose and Matthew the best of luck from me. Do you think it will actually happen? That he'll secure a nomination? James said — '

'What did James say?'

I knew my words wouldn't go any further. 'He said he's fully behind his father, but thinks he's being overly ambitious. He has the impression that, in spite of all his success, his father is still trying very hard to prove himself. Which he can't understand.'

'Very often, Danielle, we don't know what's truly going on behind the scenes. We can only accept people as they are and run with that.'

Once upon a time, in the days when I thought I knew everything, I would have commented that Mum was being her usual, ultra-tolerant self, but after the last few months I found myself in total agreement with her. Not even Mum knew what was going on behind the scenes in my life, and maybe this was her way of acknowledging that that was okay for both of us.

'Do you think you'll be seeing Liam now and then?'

'I don't know. Maybe. He's a friend from years back, and he's a link to both Harry and Juliet.'

'I won't feel too bad about going off if he's there to keep an eye on you. I don't think you can count on Rose for much support at the minute. All her energy will be going into Matthew's campaign.'

'And that's only right,' Mum said. We gave each other a final hug and she wished me safe travel. I wheeled my case across the pedestrian crossing, turning for a last wave before Mum drove away and I went inside the steel and glass monolith of Terminal Two.

Back in Rome, Erin was great. She didn't flutter around me with twenty questions. She seemed to know I was feeling subdued and had lots on my mind. She gave me time to settle back into the routine and find my own level. Even Gemma was more careful and considerate around me. But I couldn't slide back into the closed, defensive, uptight person I'd been when I'd first arrived in Rome. I don't know if it was because time had healed a little, or if a chink had opened in my shield after my trip back to Dublin. Or if the cold finality of Juliet's death had put things into perspective for me.

Things like, my heart wasn't going to break in two if I had to live without the man I loved. It could be done, on the physical and the emotional level. Things like, it was far more important that he was alive and well, laughing and talking and going about his normal day, and I could learn to accept that I would not feature as I wanted to in his life. My love for him didn't need to be spoken of, acknowledged or even acted upon to be legitimate. The reality that I loved him enough to let him go was validation in itself.

These were the lofty ideas that streamed through me as I sat at my desk inputting data on a spreadsheet, went for lunch with Erin and Gemma in quirky little restaurants, and dodged the traffic on the Piazza Venezia on the way home from work. I wasn't sure what had prompted them, beyond a changed perspective. And, despite my sadness over Juliet, I knew I would survive.

At least, I thought I would until I had an unexpected visitor.

42

'Well, Dave, it's spill-the-beans time. What have you got for me on the Jordan case?' Liz asked. In Dave's bed, she propped herself on her elbow and scraped a red fingernail down his bare chest.

Dave grinned at her and looped an arm around her shoulders. 'I should have known you had an ulterior motive when you turned up here. You're not still banging on about our friend Juliet?'

She traced circles with her nail on his taut belly. 'I never said she was my friend and you should know if there have been any developments. Come on, dish the dirt.'

'You're hoping I'll say Liam Corrigan has been hauled in for questioning, especially after your hatchet job.'

Liz widened her eyes in mock-innocence. 'Why should I hope that? Liam is a friend of mine.' Her lips curved in a smile.

'He won't be after the way you kicked him in the bollocks last Sunday.'

'I never!' She slid her hand lower and cupped him.

'You as good as . . . '

She squeezed, until he gasped. 'For fear that I might meet similar treatment,' he said, lifting her hand and placing it outside the duvet, 'I can tell you that, according to my source, Liam had already called to the police station to give a

316

statement. Even before Juliet's funeral. Apparently he'd dropped in to see her late that afternoon and left after a short while. So that's that.'

'So he's guilty as hell.'

It was his turn to sit up and fix a pillow behind his head. 'Guilty of what? Sorry, Liz, it was all perfectly innocent, and I hope I won't regret giving you that snippet of information.'

She lay back and cuddled into the duvet. 'So do I — hope you won't regret it, I mean.'

'You're dangerous, you know that?'

'So I've been told.' She giggled. 'But only by people who have something to hide.'

'What makes you think there's anything to hide in this case? Is that the only reason you came over and hopped on me? You think I have some insider knowledge?'

'I know you have your sources, and I have a suspicion that Juliet Jordan wasn't all she was cracked up to be.'

Dave threw her a puzzled look, alerted no doubt by her bitter tone. Liz reminded herself that she needed to stay in control.

It had been one thing to lose herself in Dave's arms. She'd been glad when he'd answered her call and told her he'd be happy to see her. Both of them had known without saying where it would lead. And she'd wasted no time. After a glass of wine, she'd sat on the sofa and begun to kiss him. She'd enjoyed their romp in bed — at the very least it had given her a physical release and obliterated the memory of the cruel way she rejected Gavin. It had been easy to close her eyes and pretend, just for a moment, that it was Gavin who was touching and stroking and bringing her to the brink before tipping her over the edge. For that moment it had felt so good, so right, so brilliant that she had revelled in it, only crashing back to earth when she opened her eyes and saw Dave's face above hers, his glazed look telling her he was about to come. She'd felt a shard of regret when she'd thought of what she could have had with Gavin, if things had been different.

If *she* had been different. If her life had been different, and she'd known a few truths.

Dave stroked her hair away from her face. 'I'm not sure what your agenda is, Liz,' he said, 'but, speaking as a friend, I think you should tread very carefully. Juliet was very highly thought of by most people, and now that she's met with an unfortunate accident, she'll be even more revered. Joe Public is very upset over her untimely death.'

'So the police are happy that it was an accident?'

'I didn't say that. Their investigation is still open. But if you start throwing mud in her direction it could boomerang and stick all over you. You barely escaped with it last Sunday. You were so close to the bone that even I almost choked on my breakfast.'

She fastened her eyes on him in what she hoped was a suitably seductive fashion. 'Oooh, we can't have that,' she murmured. She pushed the duvet off him, and gazed down at his naked body. 'I'll have to make that up to you,' she said,

318

reaching out for him as she kicked the duvet off herself and straddled him.

'This is just for you, Dave,' she said, guiding him into her and moving down on him very slowly. She savoured the moment, clenched herself around him, and began to rock back and forth. 'Just for you,' she murmured. 'No strings whatsoever.'

'You're a witch, Liz,' he said, pulling her face to his.

'Believe me, I've been called far worse.'

★   ★   ★

It was later than she'd realised when Liz left Dave's inner-city apartment. Although pale blue light lingered in the western sky, banks of pewter clouds were gathering in the east. When she reached the traffic lights at Christchurch, she felt like going home and shutting the door on the world, but there were things to do and papers to check, so she took the turn for the north side of the city and soon she was sweeping into Upper Ballymalin Grove.

She parked her car on the gravel driveway and opened the complicated lock on the front door. The hall smelt musty and the chill hit her as soon as she stepped inside. Her footsteps echoed as she walked around, switching on lights and the central heating. Then she stood outside the living room and steeled herself before she went in.

It was almost two weeks since she'd sat on the floor of this room, sifting through the papers and documents that had turned her life upside-down. In that time she'd begun to wonder if she had misinterpreted what she'd seen, but everything was scattered across the carpet exactly as she'd left it in her haste to escape the brutal facts that were staring her in the face.

The same name leaped out at her now: *Juliet Jordan*.

She'd never be able to confirm the truth with Juliet. She got down on her knees, and her hands trembled as she gathered everything together and replaced the papers in the faded envelope she'd found at the back of the bureau, stuck between old photo albums she'd been emptying. Annie Monaghan had meant her to find this, Liz realised. She'd wanted her to know. This envelope had lain untouched since before she'd died, more than twenty-three years ago. But across that space and time, she had suddenly reached out to Liz.

Liz shivered uncontrollably and took several deep breaths. She tried to cry, but the tears wouldn't come through the wall of anger and confusion that wrapped around her. After a short while she got to her feet and picked up the crystal-framed photographs that had sat on top of the bureau for years of Liz on her Communion and Confirmation days, taken with her parents.

Her loving parents and their happy family. Not.

She picked up the Communion photograph and bashed the frame against the side of the bureau until the glass broke into smithereens and fell to the carpet in a hail of glitter. She pulled out the photograph and stared at it, Tom Monaghan, tall and dark, very good-looking in his day, his arm curled around Annie, his blonde, petite wife. Liz ripped it up, let the pieces fall to the carpet and ground them into the crystal shards. Then she did the same to her Confirmation photograph.

In the kitchen, she searched until she found an unopened bottle of whiskey. She rinsed a glass and sloshed some into it, topping it up with water. Her teeth chattered against the glass as she drank. When it was finished, she helped herself to more, knowing she couldn't drive home now. Then she poured enough whiskey down her throat to make sure she'd sleep. Later she turned off the central heating, but left all the lights on as she went into her childhood bedroom. She lay on the bed and fell into a deep sleep.

The following morning she locked the house, securing everything. This time she had with her the faded envelope as she went to her car. The morning was so grey and overcast that the shrubbery, lining the boundary of the garden, was a startling green against the drab background.

She pulled into the first service station she came to, and sat on a stool inside the plate-glass window sipping scalding coffee out of a cardboard cup and making an effort to nibble at a blueberry muffin. She stared out at the traffic surging by and wondered how she could get to the bottom of everything now that Juliet was gone.

Her mind flew back to the funeral service, just

over a week ago. Outside the cathedral she'd spoken briefly to Matthew Moore, his aura of smooth confidence getting up her nose. His wife, Rose, however, was the opposite. Her eyes had darted nervously about and Liz wondered yet again what secrets she might be hiding. Someone with such a successful lifestyle and rich, handsome husband ought to be happy and contented. A thought struck her, like a blinding light: was Rose edgy around her because she knew something she thought Liz was unaware of? Something that perhaps her sister had told her?

There had been another person at the funeral, who surely knew all there was to know about Juliet. She'd spoken eloquently about friendship, and the importance of female kinship, her love for her friend apparent in her moving words.

'We go back a long way, Juliet and I . . . '

Surely if Juliet had confided in anyone it would have been her closest friend. The friend who was also a connection between Juliet and the Monaghans. Liz squeezed the cardboard cup of coffee so tightly that some of the hot liquid spilled on to her hand. She didn't notice it.

Rebecca.

43

'Why didn't I do this before?' Liam said, as they crested the hill and the breadth and sweep of the Dublin mountains unrolled before them, a panorama of flinty grey granite and yellow gorse running through folds of green, indigo and purple. Springtime had cast a fuzz over the pockets of trees and shrubs that dotted the route, and sunshine licked the tender green shoots so that they were almost iridescent. Behind them, and far below the curve of the terrain, the city unfurled.

Rebecca paused beside him. 'I love coming up here at this time of the year. It's wonderful to see everything coming alive again after the long grey winter.' More importantly, it was a pilgrimage of renewal after the dark, upsetting days they'd just been through. She didn't need to say that: she knew from Liam's smile that he understood.

'Do you go hill walking often?'

'Once a month. I joined the group after Harry died. It's a great way of forgetting your worries and shifting your perspective, and this is my favourite time of year for it. Occasionally I brought Juliet up here, but mostly she dragged me around her cliffs,' Rebecca said easily. She hoped that, wherever Juliet was, she was as peaceful and serene as she herself felt.

It had been Rebecca's idea to go out for the afternoon. She'd returned to her job at Olivia

Jayne the previous Monday but, much as she loved it, it had suddenly seemed so pointless. By midweek she'd been feeling hemmed in and even jittery, and the call from Detective Woods on Tuesday evening hadn't raised her low spirits.

'We've no further leads,' Detective Woods had said. 'If you think of anything, no matter how small or insignificant it may seem, please contact me straight away.'

'So there have been no developments at all?'

'No. We've had a big response from people who were out walking that evening but nothing we can pin down and no definite sighting of Juliet,' Detective Woods had said. 'The glasses we found in the house are being checked for DNA and fingerprints but I think they were too partial to be viable. We've examined the lie of the land above where Juliet was found and it's quite possible she could have slipped, particularly if the track was damp.'

'What's going to happen now?'

'In the absence of anything suspicious or questionable, the case will be wound down.'

It would be filed away, Rebecca had thought bleakly. Her friend's death would just be another statistic, a dusty file on a shelf. Juliet didn't deserve that.

Liam had called her later that evening, and she'd filled him in on what the detective had said. He was spending the week equally cooped up, but in his case it was with his accountants and solicitors, as he sifted through the financial wreckage he'd left behind.

'Any chance you could be free tomorrow

afternoon?' she'd asked him.

'If it's for you, I am.'

Then she'd suggested hill walking. 'Nothing too strenuous,' she'd said. 'I'll go easy on you the first time. I really need to get away from it all, even for one afternoon.'

'Count me in. I'd love that, thanks,' he'd said.

She'd picked him up outside his Rathmines apartment and driven up into the mountains, where she'd parked the car and taken one of the many walking trails that criss-crossed them. The afternoon was cool, but the morning's rain had died away and a pale sun peeped out occasionally from behind thin cloud.

'If you'd asked me to go hill walking a couple of years ago, I would have laughed,' Liam said. 'If it didn't include champagne, involve a flashy car or cost a fortune, I didn't want to know. Sometimes I can't help thinking what a fool I was.'

To Rebecca's surprise, she found herself stepping forward impulsively and putting a finger across his lips. 'Shush. You're not allowed to talk like that. What's done is done and it's in the past. And it doesn't suit you, Liam, to put yourself down.'

His mouth felt soft beneath her fingers. All of a sudden she could imagine kissing those lips. Kissing Liam Corrigan. Making up for some of his hurts. Letting him make up for some of hers. Time froze as they stared at each other, and then she dropped her hand as though it stung and took a quick step backwards.

'Don't tell me you preferred the old arrogant

me?' he said, with a gleam in his eye.

'I'm not saying that,' she told him, a little waspishly, 'but I'd rather see you with some of your original spirit instead of this — this crappy self-disparagement. It doesn't solve anything. And I planned today as a day out, just for us, away from everything. Time out that we both need. It wasn't to have you beat yourself up because a while ago you couldn't see what was under your nose.'

He caught her hand and brought it to his lips again. Then he turned it over and watched her face as he kissed the palm. She felt as though he was kissing her on the mouth and her heart leaped.

'I like that, Rebecca,' he said. 'A day out, just for us. And I love the way you're not afraid to give me a boot in the right place, if I'm being self-indulgent. You look gorgeous when you're indignant.'

'Right then.' She grinned, ignoring the somersault in her chest. 'We've a bit of a way to go yet before we stop for food.'

'So there's food. All this and heaven too.'

'I was hardly going to starve you. Or myself. I have a lovely pub in mind where they do fabulous chowder and smoked salmon on brown bread.'

They fell into step once more, cresting the brow of another hill, where blue-green folds merged into one another, then took a path through the woods where the breeze whispered among the trees, and above their heads, patches of blue sky peeked down between the shifting canopy of branches. Rebecca let the healing power of her surroundings seep into her bones.

★   ★   ★

The whitewashed pub boasted an aromatic turf fire and a vaulted timber ceiling. Trade was brisk, but they managed to nab a small table, with a view across the valley, just as some customers were leaving. They sat side by side and ordered seafood chowder and Dublin Bay prawn salad with homemade brown bread.

'I could sit here for ever,' Liam said afterwards, sipping his coffee.

'So could I,' Rebecca said.

'I feel like I'm playing truant from school. Rebecca, I . . . ' He paused.

'Yes?'

He reached for her hand and held it gently. 'I know things won't be great with me for a while, and it's going to take time, especially for you, to come to terms with Juliet's death, but I meant what I said when we met in the hotel, about seeing each other. That's if you want to. On the other hand,' he grinned, 'you might just want to tell me to sling my hook and get out of your hair.'

'If I hear any more negative talk like that, I certainly will,' Rebecca said, with feeling. 'Look, Liam,' she went on gently, 'we both have history and complications in our lives, and at the moment things are topsy-turvy for both of us, but let's take it a day at a time. And let's make a pact.'

327

'Okay . . . '

'No matter what kind of crappy day we're having, you and I will try to be as positive as we can. Think happy thoughts. Even if we have to make an effort to turn something around, we'll do it.'

'And can we do happy things as well?'

'Of course. There are lots of days out around Dublin and activities that won't bore a hole your pocket . . . ' As she met his eyes, her throat dried.

'Because I wish I could kiss you, Rebecca,' he said, his grip tightening on her hand. 'That would be a happy thing for me. I wanted to kiss you when I heard you speak at Juliet's funeral service and you asked everyone to remember something funny about her. It was perfect and you melted my heart. I wanted to kiss you the night we first met in the hotel, and you listened to me prattling on, even though you had worries of your own. I wanted to wrap you in my arms and kiss you when you told me about having to go and identify Juliet's body, and make up for such an ordeal. Harry was a very lucky man. Granted, his life was cut short, but the time he had was surely blessed. So, in the muddle all around me, you're the one honest, attractive and beautiful thing.'

Rebecca's face was hot. Sensations she'd long forgotten were chasing each other around her body. Her skin felt alive with anticipation. She stared out at the landscape, shimmering in the spring. She wondered what Juliet would say if she saw her now. *Go for it . . .*

And Harry? *Live your life* . . .

Liam was still talking: 'You must know I'm very fond of you, Rebecca. I love the way your face glows when you talk about your family. I'd love your face to glow like that when you talk about me. But I don't want to rush you and, as I said, I'm not exactly — '

'Hush.' She forestalled him. 'What did I just say? Only happy thoughts. Right?'

'Oh, I have some very happy thoughts,' he said, a smile playing on his lips. 'I just wish I wasn't sitting here now, in a busy bar.'

Something light-hearted freed itself from the dark tunnel of recent days and rose up inside Rebecca. She had the sense of being alive to something new, and not only revelling in the anticipation darting around her body but being grateful for it. 'I think it's perfect that we're sitting here. I hope some of Liz Monaghan's friends are around, if she has any left. This will tell her what I think of her nasty innuendoes.'

Then she moved into him and kissed him on the lips. It was brief, but it was warm and enticing enough to make her feel that everything about it was right.

★   ★   ★

Later, she drove him back to Rathmines.

'I daren't ask you in just yet,' he said. 'The apartment is upside-down. Everywhere I look there's a sea of paper and forms that I'm still trying to organise.'

'No worries. I'm going home for a long soak in

329

the bath,' she said, glad to be putting space between them: she wanted to get her head around the way he made her feel alive again to the endless possibilities of life.

'Don't be saying those suggestive things to me,' he said in a husky voice.

An unexpected wave of desire flashed through her. 'Just as well I'm going home,' she said.

'You might never talk to me again if you knew what I was thinking.'

A tiny pause, and he smiled at her, murmured her name and took her into his arms. This time they kissed tenderly and slowly. Her face was hot by the time they moved apart and she swayed against him.

'You're lovely, Rebecca, but far too tempting. I'd better get going while we're still friends,' he said, opening the door and climbing out.

She watched him as he mounted the steps, his long legs taking them two at a time. She was about to drive off, her foot poised on the accelerator, but something made her pause: a speck of glimmering sunlight peeping below a silvery rift in the clouds, the sound of birdsong flowing across the calm evening, the way Liam had looked at her as he told her she was beautiful? The feeling of his mouth on hers? Hope and expectation coursed through her veins. Life was precious and, oh, so transient. It was not only right but necessary to make the most of everything and to appreciate whatever gifts the universe saw fit to send your way.

44

By four o'clock on Friday I was in countdown mode for the weekend, dying to get away from the office and the endless spreadsheets. It was a bright afternoon in Rome, a thick band of sunlight streaming across the ochre-stone buildings opposite, reminding me of what spring looked like. It didn't seem right that the sun should be shining now that Juliet wasn't around to see it, that she was gone and we didn't know why or exactly how. I was staring at my screen but wondering how I was going to fill the hours until Monday. Everything seemed meaningless, especially on a Friday night.

Even Gemma was shooting me worried glances. She was chattering on about a new club she'd discovered in picturesque Trastevere, trying to round up a crowd to go there and telling me it might do me good to get out for the night, but I was sunk in a quagmire of sadness and anger.

More worryingly, all the noble ideas I'd had about the man I loved, which had helped keep me sane in the immediate aftermath of Juliet's death and my return to Rome, seemed irrelevant now that real life was rumbling on around me. It was one thing to acknowledge that I'd never be part of his life in the way I wanted, but as shock gave way to sadness, I just wanted to cry on his shoulder and be entwined in his arms.

I had just decided I was going to get pissed

enough to blank out the whole weekend when my mobile bleeped with a new message. It was from James, short and to the point: **Hey lil cuz what time r u off at? J**

I texted back that I'd be in the office for another hour. I guessed he wanted to call me when I was free. We hadn't talked since Juliet's funeral: he'd returned to America almost straight away and was busy with tour dates in Boston, Chicago and Pittsburgh.

> **They're working u 2 hard!** ☹
> Some of us have to earn a living
> **And some of us are sipping G+T . . .**
> Jealous.com
> **. . . in the St Michel**

It took a minute for that to sink in. Then I was all fingers.

> What??? Here?
> **Call over as soon as yur thru** ☺

I took a deep breath, then another, as everything crashed through my head and the empty Friday night altered completely. James here in Rome? In the St Michel? I was gripped by a sudden wave of euphoria, until I reminded myself that I was stuck in the office until five. Not only that but I was in my office clothes of slim black trousers and a grey shirt. Hardly suitable to darken the illustrious door of that glitzy hotel, let alone cross the foyer.

332

Not glammed up enuf
Who cares? Lining up a cocktail 4 u

From across the work-station, Gemma had watched it all. 'Is everything okay, Danielle?'

'Yes, fine.'

It was and it wasn't. It was brilliant and fantastic and crap all at once. I didn't know why James was in Rome, or for how long, and wonderful as it would be to see him, if we were talking for any length of time, he was one person it would be difficult to fob off about my cancelled wedding. I'd got away with not talking about it in Dublin because we'd been wrapped up in Juliet and her funeral.

And it would be hard too, given our shared history with Juliet, to paper over the cracks of her absence.

'My cousin has arrived in Rome,' I said, 'so I'll be meeting him after work and won't be able to go clubbing after all.'

'Why don't you bring him too?'

'I don't know what his plans are,' I said, smothering a hysterical giggle.

Thankfully, she didn't know that James was an international star, fresh from a sell-out tour of the States, and would cause a major security incident if he happened to step into a nightclub in Rome. Erin knew of him, of course, and had met him in Dublin several times over the years, but she wasn't around so I didn't feel the need to explain anything to anybody.

At half past four, I went out to the Ladies and refreshed my makeup. Then on the dot of five, I left the office and headed for the St Michel. The pavements were crowded with workers streaming out of offices and the ever-present tourists, but the hotel was less than two miles from work and it was far quicker to walk than take a taxi through the congested traffic.

I hadn't realised quite how lonely I was in Rome, despite Erin, until James uncoiled himself from a deep armchair at the far end of the hotel foyer and stood up. He was wearing black jeans and a black shirt, and his wide mouth was curved in a big smile. He opened his arms and I flew into them, choked up at the warm familiarity of him, and the link he represented to home and Juliet. He ruffled my hair as I clung to him, the top of my head barely reaching his shoulder. I knew all the staff were watching covertly, even though they were keeping a respectful distance and pretending to be engrossed in their jobs, but at that moment I needed his hug so much that I didn't care.

'Hey, Dani — are you okay?'

I made a monumental effort to pull myself together, stepped away and sat down, balancing on the edge of one of the sofas. 'I'm fine.' I gave a shaky grin. 'It's just so lovely to see you. I've been feeling a bit upside-down.'

'Thought you might.' He sat down beside me, sinking right into the sofa and stretching out his legs. For a moment I thought he was a mirage.

'How come you're here?'

'We finished in the States on Tuesday night, and this weekend it's Croatia to shoot a video before we wind up the tour with a couple of East

European dates. The rest of the guys are in Croatia now, but I got them to drop me off in Rome so that I could see for myself that my little cuz was okay after everything. Now I'm glad I came.' He put his head to one side and smiled.

'So, what's the plan? You're just in Rome for the evening? Nothing like having a private jet at your disposal.'

'It's handy for getting around, all right. I fly out in the morning. Here, I ordered this for you,' he said, handing me a Bellini. 'You look like you need it.'

I took a long slug of the cocktail. 'This is lovely, ta.'

'We could have a couple of drinks here and go for food. Or else, if I put on a big pair of shades, do you think we could go out and mingle with the crowds? I flew in earlier today and crashed out for a couple of hours, but I'd love to stretch my legs. And I haven't seen much more of Rome since we gigged here than the inside of the stadium.'

I looked around the ornate, high-ceilinged foyer, at the gilt and marble décor, the sumptuous sofas. The elegant five-star hotel was shiny and beautiful, and then I thought of the sunlit evening outside, the lively, cheerful city.

'Let's go out as soon as I've finished this,' I said. 'But I can't guarantee you won't be papped.'

'I'll take that risk.'

'I'll probably be camouflage of some kind. I look far too mousy to be in the presence of greatness.' I said it lightly, tongue-in-cheek, and

335

James gave me a sharp glance.

'I've a good mind to ground you for that crappy remark,' he said.

'Come on, I'm in my work clothes, and they're not exactly glam, are they? And grounding me would be a bit difficult,' I said, 'considering my apartment is on the other side of town.'

'You always were contrary, little cuz.'

'Ah, thanks,' I said. 'I'm the naughty little sister you never had.'

'So it seems,' he said, his face unreadable.

★   ★   ★

When we'd finished our drinks, he brought me upstairs to his enormous, deluxe room and I nosed around, teasing him about the sumptuousness while he checked his email.

'I only get to see the inside of a five-star luxury suite when I bump into you on a tour somewhere,' I said, 'but this is the most decadent yet.'

'Is it?' He gave it a casual glance.

'Yes, you chump.'

'One hotel room looks like another to me.'

'What a waste.'

'Why? What do you think I could use it for, besides sleep?'

'Never mind.'

I helped myself to some of the freebie toiletries in the enormous bathroom.

'Are you that hard up?' he asked, picking up his jacket.

'No, but these are irresistible,' I said, showing

him my hoard of designer soap and bath oil, comb and paper tissues before I threw them into my bag. 'Don't worry, there were three of everything so I've left some for you.'

I felt several pairs of eyes boring into my back as we crossed the foyer and walked out of the hotel. As we stepped into the sunny evening, the atmosphere at the heart of old-town Rome surrounded us: hectic, warm, almost carnival, the air redolent with the scent of olives under the traffic fumes; ancient palaces and dusty old churches side by side with dazzling graffiti. James whipped out a pair of wraparound sunglasses from the pocket of his leather jacket, but there was no disguising his wavy dark hair, which he had always worn shaggy. It stopped an inch or two above his shoulders. I knew that, as a teenager, he had grown it long to annoy his father, and when The Name had begun to establish themselves, his hair had stuck as one of their hallmarks.

We were a few streets away from Piazza Navona, where I thought it would be good to sit over some food and a drink, and we strolled along without attracting too much attention. I sensed the ripple of is-it-really-him interest coming from an occasional group of tourists, who stopped in their tracks and raised their cameras, some more discreetly than others, but we weren't unduly bothered. I don't think they quite believed that James Moore of The Name was wandering through the back-streets of Rome with an ordinary girl in very ordinary clothes.

Even though James had been famous for years,

I still found it funny that the cousin I'd grown up with and seen falling off his bike and crying over an injured kitten was now making heads turn and causing grown women to giggle and simper. That the guy I'd watched kangaroo-hopping Juliet's Triumph around the quiet roads of Howth as he learned to drive could impel an audience of eighty thousand to remain on their feet, waving lit mobile phones, in a dark stadium for three encores, right until the last notes of his guitar resonated into the night. Rob might be the lead singer, Gary the drummer, and Steve played lead guitar, but at six feet two James, with his long legs and lean hips, was the most striking figure on stage. It was no wonder I felt extra tiny as we walked to Piazza Navona, where we sat down at a table on the canvas-covered terrace of a restaurant.

By now, the shadows were lengthening, candlelight flickered on the table, and above us, tiny jewelled fairy lights threw a warm glow over our heads. There was a buzz in the atmosphere, the scents of herbs and spices mingling with perfume, laughter and chat rising above the chink of glasses and cutlery. Rome on a Friday evening.

James ordered a bottle of champagne without checking the drinks menu.

'So, how've you been, Dani?' he asked, leaning across the table towards me as soon as the wait-ress had hurried off in a ferment of excitement.

I knew he was in serious mode when he called me Dani. 'Really? It's crap,' I said, fiddling with the strap of my bag.

'I know.'

'I'm just finding everything so surreal,' I told him, over the lump in my throat. 'I can't believe I won't be visiting Juliet at Verbena View again.'

'Same here,' he admitted. 'I've never lost anyone I loved so much before, not that I wasn't fond of your dad.'

'You don't have to explain. Juliet was out on her own.'

'Holy shit.' He was staring into space. 'It's a bummer.'

'After losing Dad I know what to expect, not that it makes it any easier.'

'And what can I expect? You might as well tell me.'

'You really want to know?'

'Yes, little cuz, I do.'

I paused for a minute, arranging my thoughts. With my index finger I traced invisible doodles on the tablecloth as I spoke, giving me something else to focus on instead of his eyes. 'There's disbelief, such as now, mixed with a kind of unreality. Then there's anger, that she's gone and you're totally helpless to change it, gut-wrenching sadness that can take you by surprise when you least expect it, and there are moments,' I went on softly, my fingers running in circles and figures of eight, 'when you might feel you're going absolutely mad, crazy, but that's normal.'

I could have gone on — I can't sleep, I'm not eating properly, I'm drinking too much — but I wasn't going to admit to being such a total gibbering mess, especially when it wasn't only on account of Juliet.

For I wasn't only talking about Juliet. Or Dad. I was talking about the horrible sense of loss I felt, the howling anger and sadness, the utter helplessness that the love I wanted to share with all my heart, mind and body was impossible.

Our champagne arrived, and James poured it with a flourish, then handed me a fizzing glass. We waited until the waitress had left the table — she'd spent longer than necessary fixing a white cloth over the ice bucket.

'Sorry I wasn't around much when you were going through that after your dad,' James said.

'You were there when it mattered. I went back to work too, you know. It does get easier, in time. But you never stop missing them. Other people come and go in your life but there's always a space where they used to be. It's hard and jagged around the edges at first, then it begins to soften, but it never goes away.'

He picked up my left hand and looked at my ringless finger. 'Speaking of spaces, is there a big one in your life now that Conor's out of it? And I don't want the stock answer, Dani. We've never pretended to each other, have we?'

'No,' I lied, swallowing hard.

'You never got to tell me what really happened. Although I didn't help in that I was a few hundred miles away at the time.'

'I hardly spoke to anyone about it, James. Not even Mum.'

'Too sore?'

'Exactly.'

'So Conor hurt you badly?'

'Not exactly.'

340

'Hmm.' He gave me a long, searching look. 'I'd like to know if you need big cuz to go and beat the crap out of him, because if he hurt you, that's what I'd want to do.'

'You don't have to do that.'

'So if he didn't exactly hurt you badly, what did he do that there's no wedding? Last time I saw you guys together you were talking about your hen and stag parties, and we were working out the play list for the post-ceremony knees-up.'

'I know,' I said, remembering it all too well. Christmas, at Verbena View, the group of us gathered around the kitchen table, when all the tumblers had clicked into place in my head.

'Conor didn't do anything,' I said. I'd known I'd have to face this with James sooner or later, that he wouldn't rest until he got to the bald, honest truth, but it was even more difficult than I'd thought it would be.

James raised an eyebrow. 'No other woman? No deciding he suddenly had cold feet? All those reasons, by the way, are traitorous in my book if committed against you and they need to be punished.'

I gave a half-smile that somehow went wrong when my mouth trembled.

He spotted it immediately. His hand gripped mine. 'Hey, Dani — sorry if I'm upsetting you, big plonker that I am.'

'You're not a plonker,' I said. 'But there's no need to go dragging Conor down a back alley in search of retribution.' I took a deep breath and went on, 'You're the first person I've said this to, so, hey, you're privileged, but it was me.' I gulped. 'I'm the one who called off the wedding and gave Conor back his ring.'

His brows drew together in disbelief. 'You?'

'Yes, it was all my doing. I called off the wedding and broke up with Conor.' In spite of my sadness, I felt giddy and light-headed after this admission.

He looked at me for a long time. Then he picked up the bottle of champagne and topped up our glasses. He sat back, as though he was perfectly relaxed, and asked calmly, 'Well, little cuz, you must have had good reason. What went wrong?'

No way could I tell him the truth. No way could I be honest and up front. And no way could I spill my heart out and tell him what was keeping me tossing and turning night after night, over-shadowing my whole life.

I stared at him. My cousin James. The man I loved but could not have. I'm not sure what the legalities were, with first cousins, but conventional wisdom went against us having a relationship, never mind that he saw me purely as his little cuz, his honorary sister. I couldn't bear to think of his shock were I to admit my feelings, or how it would spoil our friendship for ever, never mind reverberate across our families.

It was a love that had crystallised inside me in the kitchen at Verbena View in the instant that I'd looked at him across the Christmassy table when we'd laughed about songs The Name could perform for the traditional first dance, the special moment when Conor Kennedy led me out on the floor as his wife. Something inside me had rebelled at the thought of James witnessing that significant moment. At the thought of having that significant dance with Conor. What did it mean for me and Conor? I'd laughed to cover my nerves, and said we'd really need to think about that one. Then, after the moment had passed, I couldn't look directly at James because a whirlwind of emotions sent everything I'd ever known up into the air, only to settle back again into a completely different pattern. Afraid in case he saw what was in my eyes, I looked to where he was reflected in the glass doors instead, and allowed my gaze to linger on him.

Then I caught Juliet watching me watching James.

Listen to your heart, Juliet had said, on an iridescent evening in Watsons Bay, her eyes imploring me not to have the kind of regrets she seemed to have.

I *had* listened to my heart. Later that night, in the quiet of the bedroom, long after Conor was asleep, I had paused the endless chatter of everyday life, where hundreds of impressions, assumptions and obligations, big and small, fudged together to constitute life's purpose and meaning. I had taken a deep breath and dived until I reached the very source of my heartbeat. And when I arrived there, all was light and clear and calm, and in the perfect stillness, the truth shone so blindingly that there was no denying it. My love for James had been there always, as much part of me as breath itself, privately unacknowledged and painfully ignored.

45

Somewhere in the vicinity a church bell chimed, the sound resonating across the air, bringing me back to the Eternal City, where evening shadows settled a mauve cloak over the terrace and gave a deeper glow to the fairy lights twinkling above our heads.

And bringing me back to where James sat opposite me.

'Well?' he repeated. 'What went wrong?'

'Nothing went wrong. I just fell out of love with him.' It was partly the truth. 'The spark was gone. I think it had been happening for a while, but I ignored it, what with all the wedding plans. I thought that maybe I was nervous, but when the wedding was weeks away rather than months, and panic set in, as opposed to happy anticipation, I knew I had to do something. I knew I didn't really love him.'

'So you called the whole thing off.'

'Yep.' I forced myself to meet his gaze. His eyes were kind.

'That took guts. It must have been difficult.'

'It wasn't,' I said, and this time I was speaking honestly. 'The hardest thing was facing the truth.' My voice cracked a little, but I continued: 'Once I'd accepted that, I was, like, God, I couldn't wait to get away from everything to do with the wedding, including Conor. It was hard telling him. We spent a whole weekend arguing and thrashing it out. It was a nightmare and I'll never forget his face, but it was like something inside me had closed down and I was outside myself?' I ended on a questioning note. 'Does that make sense? It was as though I'd gone through so much of it in my head beforehand that I was full of a numbed resolve that stayed with me and almost sheltered me while I turned my back on it all.'

'And you came to Rome.'

'Yeah, typical flight syndrome. After I'd called the reception venue and the wedding planner, I had to get away. I'm not very proud of letting Conor down, or the way I left Dublin, and all that crap is running through me at another level, waiting for me to make some kind of resolution.' I gave a mirthless laugh. 'I mean, how do I even start to make it up to Conor? Sometimes I can't believe I actually did what I did. It's surreal. Between that and losing Juliet, I guess you could say I'm a right mess. I just feel totally adrift. I don't know where my life is going to go after this.' I stopped babbling, picked up my glass and drained my champagne.

'Ah, Dani,' he said, so softly I had to lean closer to hear him. 'If only . . . '

'If only what?' I asked, my voice suddenly thin.

We looked at each other for ages. My eyes roved over his face, his blue eyes, under dark brows, long nose and wide mouth. I knew that face as well as I knew my own. I would know it blindfolded. It had been there, laughing, teasing, sometimes sad, at all the stepping stones of my life.

He gave me a rueful grin. 'Nothing . . . More champagne?'

I put my finger on the bottom of my glass and slid it across the table. 'Yes, please.'

He ordered another bottle — the waitress almost swooned with delight at being called back to our table.

'I'll be pissed,' I said, the idea very attractive.

'You'll be fine. We'll get some soakage,' he said, passing me a menu, 'and then I'll see you home.'

And tomorrow morning you'll be going to the airport and heading off to your busy video shoot with the guys from the band, the crew of stylists and makeup people and creative directors, and it'll be a great laugh and a huge success, and I'll be alone in Rome with the whole of Saturday and Sunday to fill.

Self-pity will get you nowhere, Danielle Ryan.

Erin had said to call her any time, and that I was always welcome to drop in, but weekends were her precious time with Lorenzo and Aimee, and I wasn't going to hijack any of that. Neither did I want her feeling sorry for me — I'd rather spend the weekend alone than appear needy.

I didn't want to think about going home or to look any further than that minute, here and now: James sitting opposite me, his long, tapering fingers curled around the stem of his glass, chatter going on all around us. Except for the surreptitious glances of people sitting nearby, stabbing furiously at their mobile phones and looking as though they were having the time of their lives for James's benefit, we seemed to be marooned in a capsule of our own.

It was wonderful and crap all at once.

Then James sat back and said, 'Tell me about Conor. How did you know that the spark was gone? How could you put your finger on it? In what way were you sure enough to call off a wedding? I'm not trying to be picky here or delve into your intimate life, Dani, but just in general. Love changes as it grows and evolves. How did you know it wasn't just the first flush of passion settling into a different phase?'

'Why do you want to know?' I fielded the question.

'I'm curious.'

'They're rubbish questions,' I said, unwilling to answer. 'Hey, what's the betting you're trying to figure out if you're finally in love?' I said, darting him a glance. 'Who is she?'

It was a shot in the dark.

James had had a succession of girlfriends down the years, but he'd never hooked up with anyone for any length of time. He was too busy working and enjoying his life to be tied down, he'd said to me, when I'd pressed him on his lack of commitment. He had never met the right woman, had been another excuse. Some of his ex-girlfriends had gone running to the tabloids after their brief liaison crumbled, and there had been lurid headlines rating his performance as a lover, based primarily on the decibel levels emanating from a hotel bedroom and the number of times he was purported to have done it in one night. I think the record stood at nine. When I'd teased him about it, James had said it was made up. 'Anyway, it's quality, not quantity, that counts.' He'd laughed.

Now, for the first time, when the subject of his love life came out for an airing, James Moore looked embarrassed. Whatever I'd said had struck home, and my heart plummeted.

'Come on, there's someone, isn't there?' My voice was brittle and I hoped he wouldn't pick up on it.

'She's . . . I — ' He slumped in his seat. 'I can't tell you.'

From James, this was totally out of character.

'Then you're not in love,' I said acerbically. 'For if you were, you'd be shouting it from the rooftops and telling me how wonderful she is.'

'I could tell you all that, and more. She's beautiful, talented and charming, but . . . '

'But?' I could hardly breathe.

'Never mind, Dani.' He rubbed his face, looking suddenly tired, as though he hadn't slept enough recently. 'Sorry I started this conversation.'

'Hey, you can't leave it like that,' I said, picking up a coaster and scrunching it between my fingers.

'I'm not trying to figure out if I'm in love. I know I am,' he said quietly. 'I'm trying to figure out if it will go away of its own accord. If the spark will burn out.'

'What? James Moore, you really are the biggest commitment-phobe,' I said, lobbing the balled-up coaster at him.

'Yeah, well, maybe so.' He shrugged, his expression inscrutable. 'Time for food, I think.' He waved the menu in front of me. By now

348

we were halfway through the second bottle of champagne and, to judge by the way the night-time piazza was becoming blurred and indistinct, coloured lights merging into a rainbow whirl, soakage was definitely called for.

'I'm not hungry,' I said.

'You have to eat.'

'No, I don't.'

'Come on, little cuz . . . What will Rebecca say if I don't look after you properly?'

'Rebecca?' I asked, seizing on this for necessary distraction. 'Is that why you're here? My mum sent you? To keep an eye on me?'

'No, hang on, you've got it wrong . . . '

'So she doesn't know you're here.'

'Well, she does, but I'm not here because of her.'

'Oh, yeah?' I felt icy cold inside and ready for a fight. I had tried to keep my emotions in check but it was impossible. Hurt and misery had been building inside me since James had started to talk about love, and described some other woman as wonderful, talented and beautiful. 'I thought you'd stopped off in Rome out of the goodness of your heart,' I said, my voice thick with childish resentment and hurt. 'I didn't know my mum had anything to do with it.'

'She didn't. I called her to see how she was and happened to mention I was planning on dropping in on you.'

'Well, when you report back to her tell her I'm fine, I'm great, I've never been better.'

I rose to my feet.

'Where are you going?'

'Home.'

'Dani, don't be like this.'

'I told you, I'm fine,' I said, pain shooting through me as I hooked my bag over my shoulder. A little devil inside me urged me to pick up the half-full bottle of champagne. 'No sense in leaving a hundred euro worth of bubbly behind.'

'You always were contrary, but this is as bold as it gets,' James said, taking out his wallet and flicking through some notes. 'Wait for me.'

I ignored him and marched away, barely conscious of him following me and the wave of interest that rippled after us, heads swaying like a field of wheat in a light breeze.

He caught up with me just as I passed the fountain. 'Where are you going?'

'I told you, I'm going home.'

'I said I'd see you home, didn't I?'

'Was that another of my mother's instructions?'

'Christ, Dani, you sound like a sulky teenager.'

'Maybe that's how I feel right now.'

We walked in silence through the night-time streets, me feeling secretly ridiculous as I grimly held the slippery bottle of champagne while we wove through the strolling crowds, my route home taking me along the Corso Vittorio Emanuele until we reached the Piazza Venezia.

Of all the squares in Rome, this, to me, was the most notorious for chaotic traffic and one of the most striking, with the lavishly decorated monument to King Vittorio Emanuele II, commanding a position right at the top of the Via del Corso.

'Holy shit, what's that?' James was looking

across the piazza to the massive white marble structure that dominated the skyline. 'A wedding cake gone wrong?'

I couldn't help but laugh, which eased the tension between us. 'That's what a lot of the Romans call it,' I said. 'But it can be distracting, and this road is busy, so wait until we get across to the other side. Then you can gaze at it all you want.'

It took us a while to negotiate the careering cars and scooters, most of which took absolutely no notice of a red traffic light. James looked at the extravagant edifice in disbelief as we walked past it and turned down the side, coming alongside the Forum, with the Colosseum ahead.

'Some walk,' James said, whistling in appreciation. 'You get to see all the historic sights.'

'Cross here,' I said, leading the way across another junction, and marching up the street until I came to a McDonald's.

'You can't mean it . . . the sublime to the ridiculous.'

'I do, and I don't care. The walk made me peckish,' I said, forced to climb down off my high horse because I was weak with hunger. 'I'm getting a takeout as my apartment's not far from here. So if you want to hop into a taxi to bring you back to your posh hotel, that's fine.'

'You are joking?' He looked at me with a mixture of exasperation, impatience and a tinge of sadness. 'Look, Dani, I don't know how it all went wrong between us this evening, but this wasn't what I envisaged when I landed in Rome this morning.'

I knew the precise moment when things had gone wrong. I could pinpoint it exactly: when he'd told me about the girl who was beautiful, talented and charming, his talk of loving another woman twisting a knife inside me. Which was stupid. I had, in the depths of the nights before and after I had called off my wedding, reminded myself that I could never have James. I should have expected he'd fall in love with some wonderful woman. For, no matter how I felt about him, to James I would never be anything more than a contrary cousin, a sort of sister. I had a sudden memory of us sitting together on the floor of someone's house, and he was telling me I would be four years old the next day.

'And how old are you?' I'd asked.

'I'm eight,' he said. 'So I'm twice your age. I'm four years older than you. So, no matter what age you are, you'll always be my little cousin. You can be my sort of sister as well because I have none.'

Now, on the side-street in Rome, heartsick and forlorn, I said, 'This wasn't what I envisaged when I met you in the St Michel.'

'Hey, Dani, come here,' he said, clutching me to his jacket as he gave me a hug. 'It's silly for us to fall out. We both know that life's too short. And Juliet would kill us,' he finished, a smile in his voice.

When I moved away from him, I asked if he'd like some food. 'We went to McDonald's together for the first time with Juliet, remember?'

'Right, little cuz, you win. Let's get some fat-laden chips and quarter-pounders.'

352

★ ★ ★

I'd thought I'd be afraid of James's presence in my small, claustrophobic space. That he'd be overpowering, almost too much for me to handle, but instead I found it soothing, despite the stomach-churning knowledge that his heart was wrapped up with someone else. Having him there, in my space, was like a blessing, and he rid the apartment of all the bad vibes that had filled it since the day I'd heard about Juliet. So I soaked up the sight of him moving around my tiny kitchen and living area, his hands deft as he found plates and dished out the food. I hooked up my iPhone to speakers and tuned in to a radio station playing the hits of the eighties and nineties, including Duran Duran, Human League, Madonna, U2; all the music that had once formed the backdrop to our lives.

'I'm glad I brought this home,' I said, producing two glass tumblers and tipping the contents of the bottle of champagne into them.

'So am I, you bold thing,' he said, giving me a quirky grin.

And so we ended up in my tiny apartment, at my minuscule table, washing down chips and burgers with the last of a bottle of champagne, in the glow of a bargain-basement apricot-shaded lamp. Afterwards we stood for a while on my little balcony, listening to the thrum of the city as the cool, clear night settled around us. When we stepped back inside I opened a bottle of wine. We sipped it slowly and chatted about music and tour dates, carefully skirting any topic that might

353

prove explosive, both of us knowing it might be a while before we saw each other again, and neither wanting to part on a bad note.

It was two o'clock in the morning and he was just about to leave when he said, 'You never answered my question earlier tonight.'

'Didn't I?'

'Do you know which one I mean?'

I gave a half-laugh. I knew full well. 'Remind me.'

'How did you know it wasn't for keeps with Conor? Was it really just a missing spark?'

'That's a different question.'

'Okay, then, how did you know it was missing?'

I glanced round the apartment, wondering how to answer. 'James. It's late . . . '

'Come on, cuz, this is me, remember? I'm probably one of your best friends.'

'I can't really explain. I just knew it was the wrong thing for me, marrying Conor. Juliet said — '

'Juliet said what?'

'Oh, hell. We were talking . . . that time in Australia . . . and she let slip that she had regrets in her life. I think it was because she didn't want me to have any. To learn from her mistakes. She said always to listen to my heart. And when I stopped long enough to ignore all the frivolous, meaningless crap and really listen to it, it told me not to go through with the wedding. I didn't love Conor enough. Does that answer your question?'

He smiled at me. 'I guess it'll do.'

I watched him move towards the door, wishing

354

I could make him stay, knowing it was impossible. I wanted to squeeze my eyes shut so that I wouldn't see him leave. He gave me a hug and kissed my forehead, and then there was just a space where he'd been.

46

When her landline pealed on Saturday morning, Rebecca snatched it up without checking caller identity.

'Could I speak to Rebecca, please?' It was a woman's voice, which she didn't immediately recognise.

'This is Rebecca. How can I help you?' she asked, wondering if it was the new part-time assistant at Olivia Jayne. Only friends and family had this number, and Amanda, her boss.

'You can help me lots, I hope.'

And just before she announced herself, Rebecca knew, for now there was no mistaking the strident tones: Liz Monaghan.

'It's Liz here, Liz Monaghan, and — '

'I've nothing to say to you,' Rebecca interrupted, outraged at the gall of the woman. 'I'm not sure how you got this number, but I'm ending the call now.'

'Afraid, are you? Of what I might be looking for?'

Rebecca shook with anger. 'I'm not afraid of you, Ms Monaghan, or your vituperative pen. But I'd rather not have anything to do with you.'

'We'll see about that. You were a good friend of Juliet's, weren't you?'

'That's got nothing to do with you,' Rebecca said sharply. 'And I'd be very careful, if I were you, of whatever scurrilous stories you intend to concoct in future.'

'I don't intend to concoct anything, Rebecca,' Liz said, in a smooth tone that grated on her. 'I'm putting together an article at the moment and I just wanted you to know that I might need your help. You may like the opportunity to confirm some of the facts before they go to print.'

'I've already said I'd rather not have anything to do with you.'

'You might change your mind. The facts are rather . . . ah, compromising. Have a think about it, and I'll contact you again early next week. And, by the way, I don't take kindly to my work being labelled scurrilous or vituperative. What I'll be writing about Ms Jordan will be nothing but the unvarnished truth.'

There was a soft click. She had hung up.

Rebecca stood staring into space, wondering what the hell that had been about. Once Liz Monaghan was involved, it could scarcely be good. She checked her phone but the number had been withheld, so there was no way she could call her back.

She went down to the kitchen and was sitting at the table with a cup of coffee when her mobile rang. She stared at it for long moments, not putting it past the woman to call her again on her mobile, just to throw her off balance. She snatched it up, ready to give her a piece of her mind.

But it wasn't Liz. It was the police, Detective Woods to be precise, and Rebecca had to ask her to repeat her words, because she couldn't grasp them at first.

'There's been a small development,' Detective Woods said. 'We've found Juliet's house key. Can you confirm where she usually put it on her person when she went walking?'

The room swayed around Rebecca. She saw Juliet laughing as she walked up the hall, tucking her mobile phone into her tracksuit pocket. Her key would be shoved into the other pocket as soon as she had double-locked the door. It was a ritual Rebecca had seen many a time. She took a few deep breaths.

'Rebecca — Mrs Ryan, are you there?'

'Yes,' Rebecca said, her voice faint. 'I just — sorry — lost it for a minute. Juliet usually tucked her key into her tracksuit pocket. Where did you find it?'

'That's the thing,' Detective Woods said. 'It was found on the cliff top, near to the spot where she must have fallen. It was hidden in some undergrowth so it wasn't found before now. It appears to have dropped out of her pocket before she fell.'

'*Before* she fell? What does that mean, exactly?'

'That it's possible there was an altercation on the cliff, which caused her key to be knocked out of her pocket and kicked into the undergrowth beside the track. If the key had slipped out as she was falling, more than likely it would never have been found.'

She closed her eyes. 'You're joking. Are you saying — do you think someone pushed her?'

'It's not at all clear what happened. As we said, Mrs Ryan, the inquiry is very much open and our investigation is continuing. So far we haven't located her mobile. We'll contact you and Ms Jordan's brother if there's anything else to report.'

After the call, Rebecca put her head into her hands. She was back there again, in the horrific spot she'd inhabited just after Juliet's death, only now the shock was wearing off and the pain was ready to attack her in large, unrelenting waves. How had this happened to Juliet? Had someone really been with her on the cliff top?

God, no. Who could have wanted to cause her darling Juliet any harm?

Rebecca felt a swell of sadness building inside her and clutched at her stomach, as if to contain it. Eventually she picked up her phone and called Amanda. She was due at Olivia Jayne at midday, but no way could she be there today, smiling and greeting customers.

'No problem, Rebecca,' Amanda said. 'Take care of yourself, and I'll get someone to cover.'

Liam was next.

With her phone pressed to her ear, Rebecca stood up and went across to the conservatory window as she told him what had happened. It was a bright morning, with patches of blue sky visible above the shredded clouds, the trees glowing with feathery green tips that danced with careless grace in the light breeze.

Juliet had danced with careless grace, laughing as she twirled her body with such ease that Rebecca had always felt clumsy beside her. She

359

took a few shallow breaths, trying to ignore the knife slicing into her heart.

'I don't believe it,' Liam said. 'No wonder you're so upset. Will I come over?'

'I'd rather just chill, Liam,' she said, feeling the urge to be alone in her familiar surroundings, like an animal hiding in its cave as it licked its wounds.

'Of course,' he said. 'Just look after yourself. And make sure you eat. We'll talk soon.'

When she called Rose, her sister was silent for so long that Rebecca decided she must have dropped the phone in her consternation.

Then she took her landline off the hook in case Liz Monaghan happened to call back. She was tempted to power off her mobile as she didn't want to talk to anyone else that day, but she left it on in case Danielle happened to call. She went out into the garden and tidied the straggling daffodil stalks. She mowed the grass, steadied a trellis under some ivy, and pulled weeds out of the flowerbed. Later, she took out her laptop and checked her emails, forgetting about the last email Juliet had sent until she saw it in her folder. As she stared at her friend's name and the opening line of her email, written in Juliet's usual enthusiastic tone, something cracked inside her. The tears finally came, falling swiftly, running down her face, trickling around her nose and dripping into her mouth. Her breath came in gasps as she struggled to fill her lungs. She heard a wail and realised it was her own.

It wasn't just Juliet, it was Harry, and the shock, long ago, of her parents. The loss of loved ones and the sheer transience of life.

Wallow in it, Liam had said. Don't block it. She fetched a box of tissues and blew her nose again and again, but made no attempt to stop the tears, and she put the television on purely to have some sound in the house besides her own sniffing and crying.

By early evening she was all cried out and the worst of the storm had passed. For now. There would be other moments, she knew, when raw grief would catch her unawares before she learned to adjust to it.

Later, when Liam arrived, juggling a bottle of wine, flowers and a takeaway meal, she was able to smile.

'I took a chance on you being home and maybe feeling a bit peckish. You can send me away, if you like . . . '

'Come in,' she said, glad that he didn't give her red-rimmed eyes a second glance. 'I wouldn't have opened the door to anyone else.'

★ ★ ★

'I can't believe we're going out for a meal with Celia Coffey and her husband of all people,' Rose said, as she sprayed herself with Chanel perfume and looked at Matthew's reflection in the bedroom mirror.

Matthew was too busy fixing his platinum cuff links to meet her eyes. 'Don't you know how influential Michael Coffey is? He's a respected economist who has contributed to the Forum, and his brother is a head honcho on the county council. It's unfortunate he was away in Marbella when we had our evening at home, because we really need the likes of him in our corner. And you don't normally get a table in Patrick Guilbaud's at short notice. I was lucky.'

Lucky? Celia Coffey was someone Rose usually tried to avoid. The other woman always grated on her, with her constant bitching and those supercilious eyebrows. You'd think she was the only mother who was trying to be hip with her teenage children. Oh, she smiled to your face, but you never knew what she was about to say behind your back. She always seemed to know what was going down, and the thought of an evening spent in her company was anathema to Rose. The meal in the restaurant with two Michelin stars would be wasted on her.

She tried to imagine what it would be like if it was just her and Matthew going out for a cosy Saturday-night dinner, a normal couple with a normal life, no talk of elections, campaigns or canvassing, or the infernal need to influence people, issues that had consumed their lives so much recently that she was beginning to wonder what they'd talked about before.

Some of their best nights out had been years ago, when they had gone to a local restaurant to save on the taxi fare home. Then Matthew had talked of his dreams, his vision carrying them away as he painted a picture of a lifestyle that both of them would enjoy. In time, his dreams had become their reality, but somewhere along the way Rose had got lost.

Or else, she thought, in a sudden moment of

clarity, she had got real.

Real to the fact that their lives were built on secrets and bound by lies.

She stared at her reflection in the mirror, at the startled eyes of the elegant, mature woman about to put on her diamond necklace, and knew it was the dark corners of their life together, not her inability to cope with the pressure of Matthew's success, that had pushed her into a downward spiral. The dark corners that had become more frightening with Juliet's death, but couldn't be spoken of, even between them, because they weren't supposed to exist. Throwing a light on them would bring their lives crashing down around them.

'Darling, you look wonderful,' Matthew went on, his tone determinedly cheerful and upbeat. He stood behind her and squeezed her shoulders. 'Whatever you had done to your hair, it's fabulous. I know it's hard for you, going through the motions after Juliet and all of that. I know how devastated you must feel, but it's best to keep busy.'

'Busy,' she said. 'That's always been your solution, Matthew, your panacea to whatever problem you faced. Bury yourself in work, and make sure you're too busy to think.'

'Well, it got us where we are today, didn't it?'

She thought she caught the faintest glimmer of uncertainty beneath his smile and was tempted to speak. Instead she looked at the reflection of Matthew and Rose Moore in the mirror and felt like flinging her crystal perfume bottle at the glass so that the image would splinter and crack.

Rose air-kissed Michael and Celia Coffey when they met in the Merrion Hotel, and Matthew ordered champagne to begin with, then insisted the Coffeys chose the wine to accompany the meal. Conversation was relaxed and friendly, the only sad note being the mention of Juliet's death, with Celia ferreting for details.

'We missed the whole thing because we were in Marbella,' Celia said, her eyes huge with drama. 'We flew out on the Sunday morning, and we heard the shocking news when we were having a drink in the Marbella Club. I kept thinking of you, Rose, and how we were only chatting about Juliet on the Friday night at the reception. I can't imagine how you must have felt. I had to have several brandies and I'll never be able to go to Marbs again without thinking of Juliet.'

To Rose's relief, Matthew steered the conversation towards holidays, and before long, Celia was in full swing, having moved on from there to boast about the varied exploits and accomplishments of their teenage children.

'They couldn't believe we were going for a meal with James Moore's parents tonight,' Michael said, as if conscious that his wife was dominating the conversation. 'All of a sudden it upped our currency. Big-time. It must be a good feeling to have a son who's followed his dream and worked hard enough to achieve such global success. We're still at the stage where we're at war with ours over their science homework.'

'I've worn that T-shirt,' Matthew said, with a good-natured, empathetic smile. 'But I think I lost that particular battle.'

'Just as well,' Michael said. 'It could have been a huge loss to us all if James had become a white-coated scientist.'

Rose heard herself laugh with Celia as though she hadn't a care in the world.

Before their dessert, Michael said he was going to stretch his legs in the garden outside the restaurant.

Celia laughed. 'Don't pretend, Michael, it doesn't suit you,' she said. 'He's off out for a sneaky cigar.'

'I'll come with you,' Matthew said. He grinned at Celia. 'And I'm only stretching my legs, honest.'

She flapped her hand. 'Oh, go on with you! It'll give me a chance to talk to Rose. We need some girly talk, don't we, Rose?' She turned to Rose, her eyes sparking with meaning.

Rose felt weak.

It didn't take Celia too long to produce her trump card: 'Tell me, Rose, how are you really coping with Juliet's death? It must have been terrible to lose such a good friend.'

'It was, of course, and it's hit Rebecca particularly hard. They were very close.'

'So maybe you should know . . . ' Celia lowered her voice conspiratorially and her gaze swept around the restaurant as if she was making sure she wasn't being overheard.

'Know what?'

'Oh dear, it's all very dreadful, and I don't like to speak ill of the dead . . . '

'Celia, you must want to tell me or you'd scarcely have raised the subject,' Rose said, with unusual spirit.

'I'm afraid you may be sorry to hear the rumour circulating about Juliet.'

Rose kept her face straight, although her heart was hammering. 'I think I'd rather know.'

'Well, then . . . ' Celia moved in so close that Rose caught the scent of her perfume. She looked delighted to be imparting the information. 'You see, Rose, being a good friend of Juliet's you ought to know that there's a whisper going around, just a tiny whisper, mind you, that she might have been embroiled in an affair. With a married man.'

She sat back, her sharp eyes observing Rose.

'That's ridiculous. Where did you hear this?' Rose's voice was thin.

'I think it was mentioned in my flagship salon on Wicklow Street. It's a mine of information, you know, all the stories that are revealed between Brazilian waxes and spray tans. Nothing like being stripped of your clothes and your dignity to loosen your tongue. Can you imagine if that got into the tabloids? Even if it's all totally innocent, Juliet's reputation would be tarnished for ever. Not to mention the man's.'

★ ★ ★

For the remainder of the night, Rose kept up a front with Michael and Celia, forcing herself to chat and smile, only lapsing into silence when she and Matthew were in a taxi on the way

366

home. But as she sat in the television room, having a nightcap with him, she could contain it no longer.

'That was a very productive evening,' Matthew said. 'I had a good brainstorm with Michael in the garden and we're going golfing next week.'

'There's a rumour going around that Juliet had an affair with a married man,' Rose blurted. She watched him carefully, remembering that she'd wondered if Matthew had found Juliet irresistible, thinking of how they'd sparked off each other. But Matthew's hand was perfectly steady as he handed her a glass of wine and poured himself a whiskey from the decanter.

'Is that all? I was wondering why you were so quiet all the way home,' he said calmly. 'Don't let it worry you. I'm surprised something like that hasn't come up before now. Or that Juliet had lesbian sex, or seduced a couple of schoolboys behind the bike shed. Or that she was snorting coke. No matter how much of a humanitarian she was, Juliet lived a lot in the public eye and there's always going to be someone intent on stirring up mindless shite.'

'Which is exactly why I'd prefer it if we stayed as we are. I don't want to live the next few years in a goldfish bowl with the tabloids taking pot-shots. And supposing . . . ' her hand shook so badly that wine slopped over the rim of her glass ' . . . just supposing someone decides to dig a little deeper. What then, Matthew?'

He sighed. 'I've told you before, and I'll say it again. We've nothing whatsoever to worry about.' He sat down beside her and squeezed her arm.

367

'I've no intention of letting any silly little rumour stand in my way. Not now I've come this far.'

She wanted to ask him what he proposed to do if a silly little rumour took on legs of its own and spread into their lives. She wanted to ask him how exactly he might stop things getting in his way. She thought of Juliet's key being found in the undergrowth, pointing to the possibility of a struggle at the top of the cliff, and wondered how soon the police might decide to investigate Juliet's friends for any possible motives.

After all, both she and Matthew had come home late that Friday night.

47

It's getting worse. More and more difficult to pretend it never happened, and harder and harder to keep up a front.

Sometimes in the night Juliet stares down from the bedroom ceiling, her huge eyes reflecting that split second of terror, mouth wide open in a scream that never comes.

Sometimes she crawls out from under the bed, first her waving hands, clawlike and clutching, searching for a grip on the carpet, then her arms, pulling her broken torso behind her, and then her fractured legs, breaking away from her body so that they're severed at the hips.

Other times she steps through the wardrobe and floats about the room, sitting on the dressing-table or hanging off the curtain rail, her pale face glimmering with a ghostly sheen, coal black circles smudging her eyes.

She's even in the bed. Lying there cold and stiff, except for her eyelids, which snap open and closed on empty sockets. On those nights, sleep is impossible.

And she's starting to appear at the breakfast table, pale grey from head to toe, her eyes sad, her hair matted with dried blood.

It should never have happened. It had been a mistake, borne of a single flash of fury and resentment, like an electrical trip-switch hitting overload.

And horrifying to think what a split second of madness has done . . .

48

'Mrs Ryan, may we come in?'

Rebecca blinked. It was Sunday morning and the radio was blaring in the kitchen, her toast browning nicely and eggs on the boil. She'd actually been singing along to Adele, a sudden burst of light-heartedness lifting her spirits and telling her that somehow she'd get through this dark tunnel and come out the other side.

The previous night, Liam had stayed until after midnight before getting a taxi home, and it had helped. She hadn't suggested he stay over in any of her spare beds or held her hand during the night. Much as she felt like having his arms around her, she knew it wasn't the right time. He seemed to sense that, taking her face in his hands and kissing her slowly and deeply before he left, stopping before they went further.

'Hey,' he'd said, their foreheads touching. 'Whatever that was about it was lovely.'

'Yes,' she'd said, drawing back so that their faces were inches apart.

'I'd better go.'

'Yes.'

Then he'd given her a quick hug and told her to look after herself.

Now Detective Inspector Callaghan and Detective Woods were standing in the porch once more, but his time, as she showed them into the front room, they seemed more distant and purposeful.

Detective Woods was without her usual empathetic manner, as though the business of the day was more important than how Rebecca might be feeling.

'I presume this is about Juliet?' she said, fighting unease.

'Yes,' Detective Inspector Callaghan said. 'Our enquiries are still continuing, but we need to ask you a few questions.'

The pang of unease flexed and pulsed inside her. She sat on the edge of the sofa and tried to contain it. 'Sure,' she said, bracing herself for whatever might come.

'Mrs Ryan, how well do you know Liam Corrigan?'

Her face flushed. Well enough to want to go to bed with him, a little voice whispered. 'Has this anything to do with last Sunday's putrid article in — '

Detective Woods was shaking her head. 'Nothing whatsoever.'

'I've known Liam for a long time. He and my husband went to the same school. I ran into him several times over the years, in a purely social context, before he went to Spain,' Rebecca said. She tried not to think of how he'd been just before he went to Spain.

'And recently?'

'I hadn't seen him for quite a while until I bumped into him at a wedding in the Seagrass Hotel.'

'Were you at the wedding yourself, Mrs Ryan?'

'Yes. I'd been invited to the evening reception by the father of the groom who had known my late husband.'

'We need to verify some details. What time did you get to the hotel?'

Rebecca forced herself to sound patient as she recounted her movements, right up to the time she had seen Liam going into the hotel bar.

'Can you remember exactly what time this was?'

Rebecca shrugged. 'Around nine, I guess. I bumped into him later in the lobby as the television news was coming to an end.'

'And you were with him for the rest of the evening?'

'I went back to my room around half past nine and joined Liam for a drink soon after that. We were chatting for an hour, an hour and a half, I'd say. Why? What is this?'

'Did Liam Corrigan actually tell you he was at the wedding?'

She felt confused and tried to remember his exact words. 'From what he said, I understood he was. He's already been in to sign a statement, hasn't he? I'm sure he's told you all this. He dropped in to see Juliet before coming to the Seagrass, and he might have been the last person to see her alive.'

Detective Inspector Callaghan gave her a sharp, alert look. 'He might indeed, Mrs Ryan.'

'You see, Rebecca,' Detective Woods changed tack, 'we've intensified our enquiries in the light of recent developments. We've confirmed that Liam wasn't actually attending that wedding. He wasn't on the guest list, and he only made his hotel reservation at around . . . ' she consulted her notebook ' . . . half past nine that evening.'

'Oh, gosh.' Rebecca felt all the air being sucked out of her.

'So if you've anything to add, or anything different to say, we'd like to hear it.'

She tried to breathe evenly. 'Hang on — sorry, what exactly are you getting at? I told you all I know. Have you talked to Liam?'

'Yes,' Detective Woods said. 'He has now stated that he didn't attend the wedding, but that's all he's prepared to say at the moment. We're putting out another appeal for information and will be checking CCTV in the area. Unfortunately Ms Jordan's system was malfunctioning, which is a pity, as it could have told us a lot.'

'Are you aware of the contents of Ms Jordan's will?' Detective Inspector Callaghan asked.

'Yes, I'm the executor of her estate,' Rebecca said, dread making her scalp prickle. 'I haven't even thought that far ahead yet. I'm still trying to get used to the idea that Juliet's . . . no longer around. I know I'll have to contact her solicitor soon. And then talk to the beneficiaries and advise them of the contents.' That would be another day's work entirely.

Detective Inspector Callaghan studied his notebook. 'We've already been in touch with Ms Jordan's solicitor. You know she changed the terms of her will earlier this year?'

'Yes, I'm aware of that.' Rebecca felt faint, knowing what was coming next. There was no point in ducking it. 'Originally my sister Rose and I were her chief beneficiaries and there are some charitable bequests also.'

'What about her brother?'

'Juliet bought out his share of Verbena View years ago, but if there are paintings or furniture he'd like, he's to have them. Juliet hardly ever saw Robert,' Rebecca babbled. 'She didn't feel he was part of her life in the way we were. And he'd already made it clear to Juliet that he regarded Florida as his home.' She took a deep breath. 'But in February she drew up a new will, naming my daughter Danielle and Rose's son James as her chief beneficiaries instead of Rose and me.'

'Do you think Ms Jordan had any particular reason for changing her will in favour of them? Did she talk to you about it?'

'She told me she'd done it, but she didn't mention any reason in particular. She was very close to Danielle and James and always regarded them as the family she never had.'

'And had you any problems with this?'

'None whatsoever. And neither had my sister. Naturally enough we assumed this would all be happening at some distant time in the future. Even before she changed her will, we expected that Juliet's legacy would inevitably pass to Danielle and James through us.'

'Thanks, Mrs Ryan, that's all for now,' Detective Inspector Callaghan said, rising to his feet, and shoving his notebook into his jacket pocket.

'You've been very helpful.' Detective Woods's mask slipped as they went out into the hall and she gave Rebecca a sympathetic look.

As though what? Rebecca asked herself, as she

stood in the hall and watched their figures recede into the distance until there was no sign of them through the glass door. As though Rebecca was someone to be pitied? Having been taken in by a bunch of lies?

What kind of a fool had she been to fall for Liam's sweet talk? And a bigger fool to have responded to his kisses. Humiliation scalded her at the way she'd been tempted to take him to bed, needing the comfort of his kisses and caresses.

And what else had Liam Corrigan lied about? Maybe there had been no reconciliation with Juliet. Maybe there had been no caller after him at Verbena View. She recalled his angry face in the dining room of the Shelbourne before he'd fled to Spain, and the way he'd admitted to once feeling savage towards Juliet. Could he have been angry enough to do something in the heat of the moment?

When her mobile rang and she saw his name, she snatched it up.

'Thanks, Liam,' she began, anger flaring inside her. 'How *dare* you lie to me like that? Have you any idea — '

'The police have talked to you.'

'Oh, yes,' she said, trembling. 'You weren't even invited to the wedding the night Juliet died. More fool me. How dare you lie to me? What kind of a fool do you think I am?'

'Rebecca, just hear me out,' he said, sounding so desperate that she was forced to listen. 'I would have come clean, but after Juliet died everything went belly-up — '

'Don't you dare use Juliet as an excuse. What else did you lie to me about?' Her voice was ragged. 'How do I know you made it up with her, you arrogant bastard?'

'I did,' he said quietly. 'You have my word. As soon as Juliet accepted my apology, I told her I wanted to talk to you. She told me you weren't around that evening as you'd be in the Seagrass. She suggested I drop into the hotel on the off-chance of seeing you, as it was less than thirty minutes' drive up the coast road. And she even told me — '

'What? Come on, I'm waiting.'

'She told me to say she'd sent you.'

'I don't believe you.'

'It's exactly what happened. Honestly, Rebecca. I was hesitant until Juliet laughed and she said she knew I'd always been attracted to you. She told me to go for it or I'd have her to answer to.'

'Keep talking,' Rebecca said, her heart sinking further and further. 'This is all very interesting.'

'When I saw you in the lobby, looking so lovely, I was afraid to scare you away,' he said. 'It was much easier to let on I was there for the wedding. When you went back to your room, I decided to book into the hotel for the night so that I could relax properly over drinks with you.'

'That sounds very romantic, but it's a heap of shit.'

He sighed. 'It's not, believe me.'

'It has to be,' Rebecca said wretchedly, feeling sick to her bones. 'You see, Juliet didn't know I was going anywhere, let alone to the Seagrass. I hadn't spoken to her all week. I can't believe you have the nerve to spin me a story that I can't even check with her.' Her voice wobbled. 'I don't know what your game is, but don't dare contact me again.'

She was hoarse with anger and fear by the time she ended the call. Anger that she'd allowed herself to be duped, and fear because she couldn't help wondering what exactly Liam had been doing at Verbena View or, to be precise, with Juliet.

After all, it was only a few short years ago that he'd threatened she'd pay for ruining him.

49

After a weekend with nothing but her sore heart for company, there was something very soothing, Rebecca decided, about coming to work. The daily routine was almost calming in its pure normality, giving her something else to focus on besides the pain in her chest. It helped that she was spending that quiet Monday morning refreshing the spring-summer stock in the window of Olivia Jayne. She blanked her mind to everything except colour co-ordinating the display in shades of cobalt blue and lily white, smoothing materials over the mannequins, tucking and pinning, the drift of gossamer satin quite different but just as beautiful as the whispering silks and the frilly texture of lace.

She was alone in the shop except for Maria, one of the part-time assistants who lived locally. Then, at half past ten, Amanda bustled in with a selection of croissants. Although it was just a flying visit, she invited Rebecca into the tiny office at the back for a cup of coffee and a chat. 'How are you feeling?' she asked.

'I'm okay.' Their relationship was warm and friendly but business-like, which suited Rebecca. No matter how much she might be tempted to unburden herself, she couldn't take Amanda into her confidence about the unsettling police visits or the devastating fall-out with Liam. She hadn't even told Rose yet. Funnily enough, during a low moment on Sunday she'd found herself lifting her mobile to call Juliet — until the painful knowledge that she was gone hit Rebecca like a ton of bricks thudding into her chest.

'You don't look okay, Rebecca. You look as though you haven't slept all weekend. Losing your friend like that must have been a deep shock and it'll take time to adjust. If you need any more time off, it's no problem. I'll get cover for you.'

'Thanks, Amanda. I need a couple of days to pop over and see Danielle in Rome, whenever it suits you,' Rebecca said. Over the weekend, it had become very clear to her that she needed to talk to Danielle about Juliet's will and what it would mean for her. She had to be told before word leaked out from somewhere else. James needed to know as well. He was somewhere in eastern Europe at the moment so she'd let Rose and Matthew look after that.

Danielle had called her on Sunday evening, sounding lost and lonely, obviously missing Juliet. She'd try to persuade her to come home: hanging about in Rome wouldn't solve anything.

'Rebecca, go whenever you like,' Amanda said. 'Just look after yourself and take off whatever time you need. Once I have some advance notice it's fine by me.'

'Thanks, Amanda.'

Amanda arranged croissants and tiny pots of jam on a plate. 'It's the least I can do and no thanks are owed, except from me to you. I wouldn't be where I am today but for you. Don't even think about the shop. Just be good to yourself for a while. Starting with this,' Amanda said, proffering the plate.

Rebecca helped herself to a croissant, her eyes blurring. She'd thought she'd been good to herself by letting Liam into her life, and allowing herself to hope that love could come around once more. She'd even considered opening doorways to warm desires that had vanished with Harry. She remembered the way Liam's mouth had felt beneath her fingers, and the way she'd kissed him back on Saturday night, melting into his arms. Even, her throat swelled, the way she'd imagined going to bed with him.

What kind of a fool had she been? She had trusted him instinctively, but maybe she'd just clung to him because her heart had been frozen in those sad days after Juliet's death. Not that it mattered any more. He'd been spinning a very tall tale, and she still didn't know what the ending was going to be.

Rebecca spread jam on a croissant, and then she smiled at Amanda, trying to ignore the appalling image of Juliet and Liam quarrelling on the cliff. Of Liam's anger getting the better of him, then of him jumping into his car afterwards, blind rage causing him to flee up north County Dublin lanes towards the mansion he'd once lived in, only to realise he didn't live there any more and stop off in a nearby hotel.

Where he'd met Rebecca . . .

She told herself it sounded so appalling that it couldn't have happened. But why had he lied to her?

After lunch, she was in the shop window

arranging a drift of scarves, classy shoes and soft leather bags when she felt a shadow falling across her, blocking out the light. She glanced up and started, almost stabbed herself with the thin stiletto heel of a glittering sandal.

Liz Monaghan was standing in front of the window, her face pressed to the glass as she stared in at Rebecca. Rebecca stepped back on to the shop floor. Thankfully, Maria was busy with a customer who was deciding between outfits for a wedding, so she didn't pay undue attention when Liz strolled in, looking as though she owned the boutique.

She'd forgotten how tall she was, Rebecca realised, bracing herself.

'Thought I might find you here,' Liz said.

'How can I help you?' Rebecca asked smoothly.

'You'd love to help me, I'm sure.'

'Liz, I'm sure you appreciate that I'm in work and busy. Why don't you just say what you've come to say and let me get on with my job?'

Liz smiled, cat-like. 'I'm getting on with my job as well. I want to know if you have any comment to make about the rumours that Juliet Jordan was having an affair with a married man.'

'That's a load of horse shit,' Rebecca said, in the pleasantest voice she could muster. 'And if you try to concoct anything false or defamatory about Juliet, you'll regret it because I'll be straight on to her solicitor.'

'Oh, it might well be scandalous, but it won't be false, I can assure you. I might run the piece by you later this week as I'm still trying to fill in some gaps. Then again, I might not. If you won't help me, I'll keep digging until I find what I'm looking for.'

'I don't know what's driving you, but I'm beginning to think you're one hell of a vindictive bitch,' Rebecca said, immediately sorry she'd allowed the woman to rattle her.

Liz paled. She stared at Rebecca for a long moment, then leaned in close to her and hissed, 'You'll regret those words when I blow Saint Juliet Jordan out of the water.'

Next minute she was gone, and when Rebecca looked out of the window, her hand still clenched around the stiletto heel, there was no sign of Liz's tall figure weaving through the afternoon shoppers. She had disappeared into the ether. Rebecca shivered and wondered for a moment if she'd imagined it. But she hadn't: even the air around her seemed to vibrate with Liz's naked venom.

50

In the days following James's visit to Rome, I went around on auto-pilot. Seeing him on the Friday night and having his presence seep into all the corners of my tiny apartment had me brimming over with so much quiet joy that it lingered in my heart long after he'd gone. I sat in the chair he'd sat in, and stood on my balcony in the same spot he had, as though it possessed a magic aura. However, as the days slipped past, I began to feel lonelier than ever before. I tried as hard as I could, but it was difficult to recapture those unselfish, high-flying ideas I'd had that at least the man I loved was alive and enjoying his life, when I wanted so much to be part of it.

But it wasn't going to happen, not in a million years.

And no matter how often I thought of the tender smile James had given me, or the way he'd looked at my face when he'd wished that if only — if only what? My mind flew off in a million different tangents. I told myself I was colouring everything like a woman possessed, that I was reading all sorts of fantastic things into ordinary moments and imbuing them with a meaning that didn't and couldn't exist. For he was in love with someone else.

I decided it was best to avoid James as much as I could. Even if it meant going to live far away from Ireland. My heart was battered every time I saw him.

If his visit had taught me one thing, though, it was that I needed to talk to Conor, to try in some way to make up for my disgraceful behaviour. I finally plucked up the courage to send him a long email, apologising once more from the bottom of my heart for all the upset I'd caused, and asking him how he'd been.

There was nearly a row in the office when Gemma found out the identity of my cousin. Erin let it slip when she joined us for coffee on Tuesday morning and asked about our weekend. The fantastic nightclub Gemma had discovered hadn't been so great after all, but few of the girls in the office had gone with her so her reputation as a raver was still intact.

'Did you go, Danielle?' Erin asked.

Gemma jumped in before I had a chance to answer: 'No, Danielle was too busy with her cousin. I thought she might have brought him along, but we weren't good enough,' she joked, in a half-mocking way.

'I don't blame her,' Erin laughed. 'Could you imagine James Moore let loose in a Rome nightclub? You'd have to call the *carabinieri*.'

Gemma's face went red. 'James *Moore*? You're joking. Not *the* James Moore? He's not your cousin, is he?' She looked at me almost furiously, as though I'd no right to have any claim to such celebrity.

Erin shot me a funny, questioning glance, then asked Gemma, 'Didn't she tell you?'

'I had a headache on Friday evening,' I said. It

385

was partly the truth. My head had been swimming with thoughts of James. 'I wasn't much in the mood for talk.'

'Was he here for long?' Erin asked.

'Just Friday night. He was on his way to a video shoot in Croatia.'

'Jeez, Danielle, I can't believe you kept it to yourself,' Gemma said reproachfully. 'All that time you were texting him you never said a word. I'm a great fan of The Name. I've been following them for years and I'd've loved to meet James. Maybe I'd be the one to mend his broken heart. Maybe he's waiting for me to come into his life.'

'What broken heart?' I asked.

'It's obvious, isn't it? He's never married, despite all the gorgeous women who throw themselves at him. He's never been in a long-term relationship. Somewhere along the line he must have had his heart turned over.'

'Nonsense. He's too busy having fun,' I said, ignoring the pain in my chest.

I'd asked him before about his love life, and that had always been his stock answer.

'Yeah,' said Gemma, 'having fun while he's waiting for the right woman to come along and have his babies.'

My chest contracted at the thought of another woman having babies for James. I was a sad case. 'That's nonsense,' I said.

Gemma looked at me sharply. 'It's written all over his face, Danielle. I've watched him on stage and I have two of their concerts on DVD. Sometimes in the music he has this lost look in his eyes as though he's looking for love. Even

386

in the extra material, where they show The Name relaxing with their families, James is playing with the other band members' kids. I'd say he's dying to be a dad when the right woman comes along.'

'I never heard anything more ridiculous,' I said, conscious that my voice was thick with resentment.

For the rest of the day, Gemma was offhand with me, as though I'd personally snubbed her by not introducing her to James. It was all I needed on top of my sore heart. And then, into that whirlpool of emotions, my mother called to say she'd decided to visit me. This coming weekend.

Perfect timing, I don't think.

I loved my mother. I was bursting with pride when I saw how she managed herself at Juliet's funeral. I just felt too raw and vulnerable right now to cope with having her attention focused on me. And I didn't know how long I could avoid talking about the reasons behind my busted wedding, especially when there would be no other distractions to hide behind.

'You can stay with me.' I felt obliged to offer when she began to make booking-a-hotel noises and the likelihood of there being one handy to my apartment.

'I don't want to disturb you,' she said, so lovingly that I was appalled by my reluctance to see her. 'But . . . well, it'll be just the two nights if you have room.'

'I have, of course,' I said, not bothering to explain that I'd have to sleep on the sofa and give her my bedroom, and that my bed was bigger than a single bed but smaller than a double.

The following day, Gemma relented enough to be pleasant and polite to me. I guess she figured that there was no point in scuppering her one and only minuscule chance of getting close to James Moore and The Name.

She asked me if I thought he'd be dropping in to Rome when his video shoot was over, and I felt a surge of power when I wafted a hand in a superior way and said nonchalantly that I hadn't a clue what part of the world the private jet was taking him to next.

51

Rose and Matthew joined the stream of theatre-goers spilling out of the heat of the auditorium into the wet Thursday night. As they moved away from the portico of the Gaiety, Rose looked up at the slanting rain in the light of a streetlamp and drew her scarf closer around her. She blinked, briefly unsure of where she was.

The opera was still swirling in her head, the purity of sound swooping into hidden corners and dark secrets, blowing away the dust with its true, shimmering notes, tugging at everything that was soft and vulnerable in her heart, and wrenching it into a fragile maelstrom.

A mistake, she thought, to have come tonight when she was already an emotional wreck, for now all the complicated layers of her life seemed to have been laid bare by the music.

'Rose.' Matthew's voice was close to her ear, as he put a hand on her arm.

She looked at his familiar profile, saw him smiling down at her it and whirled back in time to when he was the earnest young man she'd started dating all those years ago.

'Will we make a run for it?' he said.

'Yes, why not?' She grinned.

Together they hurried up the street to the taxi rank at the corner of St Stephen's Green, Matthew's arm around her shoulders. She gulped the fresh night air, felt the rain veiling her face and, in the energy of the moment, could have been nineteen again on her first date with him.

All the way home to Belgrave Park, as night-time Dublin flowed by the window, her head was filled with the music they had left behind. She felt raw and exposed. The odd sensation persisted as Matthew ushered her up the garden path and into the house, locking the door behind them. When she saw their reflections in the hall mirror she was even more disconcerted for it was a long, long time since she had been nineteen and innocent of what life would bring.

In the hallway Matthew looked at her. 'Rose, you're shattered. Straight to bed with you.'

'I don't think I can sleep,' she said.

'Didn't you like the opera?' He took off his coat and hung it in the hall closet. He began to slide hers off her shoulders, with her cream cashmere scarf. 'I thought you'd enjoy it. And the opening night is always special.'

She was tempted to ask if he'd brought her simply to secure more column inches — she could already see it in the newspaper: 'Matthew Moore and his elegant wife, Rose, were there, blah blah blah . . . ' But she let that go, allowing him to remove her coat and scarf and hang them up. She said, 'It was beautiful, so beautiful it made me cry and think of Juliet, and everything else . . . ' There was a lump in her throat.

He drew her close. 'Ah, Rose.'

She leaned against him, needing the solidity of his body to centre her. Then she moved back and gazed at his face. 'Matthew,' she said gently, 'we need to talk.'

His arms were still clasped round her. 'About what?'

'You know . . . Juliet's will — and James.'

'There's nothing to talk about.'

'Matthew, you might be the cleverest and most shrewd businessman, but we have to stop burying our heads in the sand.'

'My head isn't buried in any sand.'

'Yes, it is. Not once have we spoken of James or what Juliet's death means.'

His eyes were guarded. 'You're upset. Now is not the time. It'll all seem better in the morning.'

'I can't.' She felt as though she was going to shatter into tiny pieces.

'Can't what?' he asked, putting a finger under her chin.

'Can't stop the pictures going through my head . . . Juliet . . . everything . . . '

He sighed. 'Look, you'll have to take it easy and give yourself time . . . We've all had a shock.'

She continued as though he hadn't spoken, the words rushing out of their hiding place, the dark place in her heart that the wonderful music had reached: 'I can't stop seeing Juliet's coffin — ' she halted for a moment and dropped her head into her hands, overcome with emotion, then forced herself to look into his eyes and make sure he understood where she was coming from ' — and James coming up the cathedral and putting his hand on it.' Her voice broke.

A muscle jerked in Matthew's cheek. She thought she saw the glimmer of uncertainty in

391

his eyes. 'If you're that upset about it, we'll talk in the morning.'

'You mean that? Promise?'

'Promise.'

Later, when he joined her in bed, they made love, almost feverishly, clinging to each other as though they needed to escape into a world where they were united, where there were no shadows and secrets, nothing but the physical closeness of deep, warm kisses, soft caresses and the long, hot moment of release.

Afterwards, when Matthew was asleep, Rose lay next to him, her mind still racing with the image of James putting his hand on Juliet's coffin, and all the dark corners of her life were illuminated, so that the memory pulsed, fresh and strong, the memory of when everything had changed for ever . . .

1973

That day, in the middle of March, was freezing cold, with heavy grey clouds that darkened the afternoon sky and promised snow. A cold wind whipped around the deserted roads of the housing estate. It wasn't the kind of day you expected your life to take on a whole new meaning or all your dreams to be handed to you on a plate.

Her housework had been finished by eleven o'clock. The Formica kitchen presses were shining, the net curtains starched whiter than white, the floor in the small front room gleaming with lavender polish. All the ironing was done.

She'd even smoothed clean white sheets over the bed she shared with Matthew. The good sheets, edged with pink embroidery, had been a wedding present.

Matthew seemed happy with their love life, reaching for her three or four times a week. She hoped it was enough for him and that she was doing everything right. Sometimes she even reached for him, well used by now to the feel of him inside her and the ache it satisfied.

But the ache in her heart that longed for a baby of her own still hadn't been satisfied.

Rose put on the radio and listened to Gay Byrne's morning programme to break the silence of the house and the empty hours that stretched boringly ahead until Rebecca's visit. Her sister had written to say she was taking a half-day off work and would be on the two o'clock bus out from town. Rose and Matthew had no phone. Nobody on the estate had one, as there was a three-year wait for a line to be installed.

Into this spotlessly clean house Rebecca arrived, full of vitality, the noise, chatter and gossip of the bustling typing pool still clinging to her. Rose made tea and set out her wedding-present tea service of cups, saucers and plates, as well as a glass stand with biscuits and small cakes.

Then Rebecca began to talk and Rose's heart swelled with the enormity of what she was saying.

★   ★   ★

'What do you think, Matthew?' Rose asked, later that evening, her nerves stretched taut as she told him everything in a shaky voice. About Juliet falling pregnant. About her having a short fling with a married man. Naturally Juliet was weighed down with remorse and guilt, but she was also terrified of her father finding out. And she didn't want her baby to end up in some kind of industrial school or, if the baby was lucky enough to be adopted, to feel beholden to adoptive parents. She'd seen the chip it had placed on Liam Corrigan's shoulders. She was going to give the baby away and Rebecca had suggested Rose and Matthew, two people who would be the most loving parents, people she could trust to bring the baby up as their own in a safe and secure home.

'Rebecca knows I'm very unhappy because we've no baby of our own yet,' Rose said. 'And it has been nearly two years. But I blame myself for that,' she went on hurriedly, in case Matthew thought she was questioning his virility. 'I'm probably over-anxious about it, which doesn't help.'

Matthew's face was set as he considered what she'd said. Then, after a while, he smiled. 'Yes, I think it could work out,' he said slowly. 'If it makes you happy, then I'm happy. I know how much you've dreamed of becoming a mother, and I'm sorry it doesn't seem to be happening for us.'

'I'm just afraid it might go wrong later,' she said, surprised by his acquiescence — she'd been expecting him to put up more of an argument.

'How could it? With Juliet's plan, we'd be the registered parents. We're not doing anything morally wrong, just circumventing some red tape.'

'According to Rebecca, Juliet said it's the one sure way she can guarantee we'll have the child, and it means the little one won't grow up with the knowledge that it was adopted.'

'If she goes ahead with it, she can't change her mind later, ever,' Matthew said. 'Neither can she tell this married man, whoever he is, that she's had his baby. Ever.'

'She knows that,' Rose said. 'She says it's all over between them and she's already forgotten about it. And if she's afraid of her father finding out, she's never going to admit to having an illegitimate baby, let alone arranging to give it away outside the legal channels.'

At first Rose had lain awake at night, her mind whirling with the joy of having a child to call her own after so many long, barren months. Mixed with this was her surprise at Matthew's ready agreement to raise another man's child as his own. Occasionally, at night, she caught herself wondering if the baby was indeed another man's child, or if Matthew had finally been unable to resist the vivacious Juliet, something she'd privately feared might happen since the night they'd first met.

But as the weeks went on, it slotted into place so easily, as though it was meant to be.

She even didn't have to *do* anything beyond wait for the baby to arrive.

She and Matthew sold the first home on

which she'd lavished such care and moved to the outskirts of Galway, where they lived very quietly with Juliet in the three months preceding the birth of her baby. Matthew found it easy enough to get a transfer to a Galway City branch of the bank. It was Juliet who had to be brave, wearing a wedding ring and passing herself off as Mrs Rose Moore when she visited a busy doctor's practice and got a referral to the equally busy maternity hospital in Galway.

Beyond Matthew going to work and Juliet to the hospital, the three barely ventured out, Rebecca coming down some weekends to see how things were, and bringing messages of love from Granddad Paddy who, with their friends and extended family, not to mention Matthew's ageing parents, thought Rose was having a difficult pregnancy and needed lots of bed rest.

When Juliet arrived home from the hospital and baby James was placed in Rose's arms, her aching heart flooded with love, and the joy of holding him outweighed all her fears. Juliet went home to Dublin, while Rose and Matthew settled into life in Galway with their brand new baby. By the time Matthew got a transfer back to Dublin, and they moved to another new house in a sprawling estate further out from the city centre, teeming with young families and stay-at-home mothers, James Moore was six months old and Rose, with her son, blended in easily.

From time to time, she looked at her baby's face, wondering if there was any resemblance to Matthew. Like her husband, he had dark hair and blue eyes, but his eyes were a far deeper blue than Matthew's and, unlike Matthew, he was a quiet, sensitive child.

From time to time she wondered at the strained atmosphere between her friend and her husband. Eventually she plucked up the courage to raise it with Matthew. 'How come you and Juliet can't have a civil conversation without sparking off each other?' she'd asked.

He'd laughed. 'Our heated debates, you mean? They're just a bit of craic. Women like Juliet get on my nerves with all their equality shite. Thinking they're better than men. Thinking they can rule the country, never mind the world.'

In a sense they do, she'd felt like saying, for they give life to another human being, and what could be more brilliant, powerful or amazing than that? Something she hadn't been able to accomplish . . .

By tacit agreement, she and Matthew never spoke of the circumstances of James's birth. Neither did Juliet. It was a silent intrigue that lurked between them and a subject they all avoided, as though it had never happened.

But Rose had never anticipated that what she and Matthew had brought about or, more importantly, how they had deceived James, as well as the stark terror of being found out, would explode in her consciousness now and again. It had nibbled away at her peace of mind, culminating years later in her breakdown. Still, she managed to paper over the cracks and glide along with the help of her pills.

It might have been okay if Matthew hadn't decided to blow the fragile peace apart with his plan to run for the presidency. Rose thought he was tempting Fate. As far as Matthew was concerned, there were no skeletons in their cupboard because they simply didn't exist.

And then Juliet had told Rebecca that she was having regrets, and didn't care if some secrets came out into the open. Naturally, Rebecca had told Rose, who had told Matthew, who had thought that Juliet was being her old rebellious self and simply trying to rattle him.

Juliet had plummeted down a cliff face less than a week later.

And after that it was never going to be okay.

52

'Don't forget I'll be late tonight,' Matthew said.

'You told me all about your busy day. I'm not to call you unless the house is on fire.'

'Too right.'

Rose lay in bed and watched him moving around the bedroom. It was barely seven o'clock on Friday morning and he'd already spent twenty minutes on the cross trainer in his den before he'd showered and dressed. Now he was off to Tory Technologies to put in a full day of wheeling and dealing, starting with a stand-up breakfast meeting. She imagined harried executives gulping coffee as they listened to his instructions, then scattering to do his will. He would have a working lunch, followed by an afternoon conference call with New York, and later, an exploratory meeting with his trusted advisers to begin mapping out the strategy for his presidential campaign. A day in the life of Matthew Moore.

'A hectic day with important people to meet,' he said, a lift of excitement in his voice, as though he couldn't wait to get started. 'I don't know how late I'll be so don't wait up.' She watched as he chose a tie, then looked at himself in the mirror and expertly knotted it so that it sat perfectly with his expensive grey suit. Then, with a flourish, he fastened his white-gold cuff links.

'Aren't you forgetting something?'

He paused by the door to his dressing room, alerted by the tone of her voice.

'You said we'd talk, Matthew. Last night? Remember? You promised.'

He came over to the bed and kissed her cheek, smelling of expensive cologne, looking handsome, trustworthy, the embodiment of honesty and integrity. 'Of course. We'll talk later. As soon as I'm home.'

'You told me not to wait up, that you might be late.'

'I know how you fret, darling, but just remember, you've nothing whatsoever to worry about. Everything is perfectly fine.'

He walked across to the door, his impatience to be gone flowing from every line in his body. He couldn't wait to get his teeth into the important challenges of his day, leaving her to her own frivolous devices.

Mrs Barry wasn't coming in that morning, and Rose had no appointments, no lunch dates, no charity work or anything else significant to do. It would be another long day when her fears and anxieties hung heavy in her head, when she took cat naps trying to make up for her sleepless nights.

All of a sudden, she couldn't stand it any more. She couldn't stand the thick silence between her and Matthew, the ease with which the day ahead had already absorbed his energy. Most of all she couldn't stand his naive conviction that everything was fine when, in reality, it was far from it. Especially now that Juliet was gone and everything had changed.

Suddenly she could remain silent no longer. For someone who hadn't a rebellious bone in her body, she was surprised by the strength of the mutiny that bubbled up inside her. It broke free in her head, sparking around her temples, and she felt a moment's dizziness as she said, in a loud and determined voice, 'No, Matthew, it's not perfectly fine.'

Her husband froze. He turned very slowly and looked at her. 'What is it? You know I've a busy day ahead.'

'I don't care how busy it's going to be,' she said. 'We have to talk.'

'Now?'

'Yes, now.'

Something resolute in her face must have got through to him for he took his hand off the door handle and stood there, looking, she thought, unusually awkward.

'James . . . ' She gulped. 'He didn't *know*, Matthew. He didn't know his real mother was dead. It's an image that's haunting me. I've been trying to ignore it, hoping it would go away, but it's getting worse and now I can't ignore it any longer. I can't get away from the image of James putting his hand on Juliet's coffin, not knowing she was his mother.' She gripped the duvet between her clenched hands and willed herself not to break down.

'Are you suggesting we tell him the truth?' Matthew asked, in a steely voice.

'How can we?' Rose said, her heart thumping. 'I looked at James standing there and knew he must never know, now that it had come this far.

401

He'd hate us, and never talk to us again. Oh, Matthew, I feel overwhelmed because it's all so horribly sad.' She stared at him, dry-eyed.

Matthew glanced at his watch and walked over to sit on the bed. 'Look, I know you're upset, but think about it logically for a moment,' he said, taking her hand in his. 'Lots of adopted children never get to know who their birth mother is. And in the Ireland before the eighties, and God knows for how long afterwards, hundreds, if not thousands, of births were compromised in some way,' he continued, 'so there are hundreds, if not thousands, of grown men and women who are probably walking around quite happily unaware of their true birth circumstances. And that's without adding donor sperm or any modern interventions into the mix. The main thing is, they're walking around happily.'

'And does that make it right?' she countered.

'What is right?' Matthew gazed at her appealingly. She couldn't help wondering if he'd practised that look for the television cameras. 'We raised James as our son,' he said, in his warm, assured voice. 'Our names are on his birth certificate. We're the parents who loved him and took care of him from when he was a few days old.'

'Yes — but surely he has a right to know his true origins?'

'Why? What difference would it make? James has a fantastic and successful life. Why upset everything? Is it right to pull the rug from under him?'

'My head is telling me all this, and I know we daren't tell him the truth, but my heart is saying that it's different now that Juliet is dead.'

'Why is it different? If you feel so strongly that he should know his birth mother, surely it was more important when she was alive.'

'I couldn't think about it then. I was too afraid to. I didn't want James to hate me for what we did. Now if he finds out somehow, he'll hate me even more. Besides, while Juliet was alive I always thought in the back of my mind there would be time to put it right. Maybe when you'd retired . . . There was always the possibility that we'd find some way to resolve what we did.'

'And supposing it was all out in the open? Can you imagine how that might hurt James? How devastated he might be?' Matthew, the great debater, knowing what to target. 'I don't want James to hate me either. And I'm poised in front of the most challenging test of my life, Rose. We don't need this complication in our lives. And, believe me, neither does James. It would ruin everything.'

'I know what you're saying. It's everything I've said to myself, but I'm finding it impossible to live with at the moment. And whatever about James accidentally discovering the truth when Juliet was alive, it would be ten times worse now that she's gone.'

'I agree,' Matthew said. 'Apart from that, you must remember that what we did was illegal and unconstitutional. It might be similar to what went on in some Irish families, and it's a rather ordinary, everyday scandal compared to what passes for scandal nowadays, but because of who we are, including James, it would make front-page news and destroy our family, never mind every atom of my credibility. Neither of us can afford that to happen.'

'Don't remind me.' Rose buried her head in her hands. 'But just supposing someone got wind of it? I told you there are rumours flying around that Juliet had an affair.' She raised her head and looked at him closely, old insecurities rising to the surface, but nothing flickered across Matthew's composed face.

'Absolutely no one will find out, Rose. The only people who know about Juliet's link to James are you, me and Rebecca. There's no one else involved. Right? So unless one of us talks, which we won't, James is our son. Don't ever think anything otherwise. Don't let your fears get the better of you and we'll all be fine.'

He stood up and kissed her forehead. He was putting a useless sticking plaster on a raw, gaping wound, Rose thought.

★   ★   ★

Rose watched Rebecca weave through the tables and across the restaurant to where she was seated in a booth at the back, looking so purposeful and vital that Rose was envious for a moment. It wasn't until her sister shrugged out of her leather jacket, and sat opposite, that she saw her face was pale and drawn.

'I'm glad you could meet me,' Rebecca said, putting her mobile on the table and her bag on the banquette beside her.

The hours since Matthew had left for the

404

office had hung heavily on Rose's hands and she had felt a warm rush of gratitude when Rebecca had called, suggesting lunch in a city-centre hotel.

They ordered a fish starter, then lemon chicken, and a bottle of San Pellegrino.

'I wanted to see you before I headed off to Rome this evening,' Rebecca said quietly, fiddling with her napkin. 'You know I'll be telling Danielle about Juliet's will?'

'Yes.'

'And James needs to be told, too, sooner rather than later, before it gets splashed across the tabloids and he and Danielle are named as prime suspects in causing her death.'

Rose put down her glass of water. 'Don't joke about things like that.'

'Well, be warned. I had Liz Monaghan in the shop earlier this week. She's concocting some piece on Juliet and I shudder to think what's in it. She's already asked me if I knew Juliet was having an affair. I don't know what she's trying to get at.'

'Not Liz as well?'

Rebecca looked at her sharply. 'Why? Did you hear it too?'

'Matthew and I were out with the Coffeys on Saturday night, and when Celia got me to herself she said much the same thing. Apparently it was going around the beauty salon.'

'And what did you say?'

'What do you think? Should I have said Juliet had loads of affairs? Or left a trail of broken hearts behind her? I told her it was a ridiculous idea. Problem is, once something like that starts circulating, it's hard to rein it in. Oh, Rebecca, where is all this going to end?'

'I don't know,' Rebecca said soberly. 'It's a nightmare that Juliet's gone in such a mindless way, and we're left with whispers and rumours, and my gut feeling that her death couldn't have been an accident.'

Rose's heartbeat accelerated. 'You scarcely think that Juliet herself . . . '

'No, definitely not,' Rebecca said stoutly. 'But something happened, something went wrong. And whether it was a person she knew or whatever . . . ' She let out a slow breath and looked totally dejected. 'And I still have to tell you about Liam Corrigan.'

Rose listened silently as Rebecca filled her in. 'No wonder you look so cut up.'

'Do I? Thanks,' Rebecca said drily. 'I don't understand all the lies. God knows what he's covering up, and I can't help remembering that time in the Shelbourne when he threatened to make Juliet pay.'

'Don't laugh, but if anyone needed Juliet out of the way it was Matthew. And me. If anyone starts digging too deeply, we'll both be in trouble.'

'Rose!'

It was a relief to unburden herself to some degree. 'That's how spooked I'm getting,' Rose said. 'I'm just . . . feeling as though things are slowly falling apart. As though I'm falling apart. You see, Matthew was home later than me that Friday night, even though we had an important reception. He barely had enough time to get ready. And he was very agitated. Later on, I had a look at his mobile and he'd been texting Juliet, wanting to see her. And, let's face it, he has a huge motive because Juliet was an obstacle to his dreams in more ways than one.'

Rebecca leaned across the table. 'Rose, hang on. You're talking about your *husband*, for God's sake. No matter how ambitious Matthew is, you hardly think he's capable of cold-blooded murder?'

'No, I don't, any more than anyone else is. But supposing . . . supposing he didn't mean it? That it was an accident that just happened. Juliet used to get up his nose sometimes. Supposing he got very angry with her . . . '

Rebecca smiled sympathetically. 'You've really worried about this, haven't you?'

'Supposing they went for a walk along the cliff,' Rose said, unable to contain herself. She twisted her wedding ring around and around as she spoke, her voice low. 'She often invited her friends to do that. And if they had a quarrel halfway around? I know Juliet could be maddening at times. What if she riled Matthew so much that he became incensed and hit out at her?'

Rebecca shook her head. 'I know Matthew gets fired up at times, but I can't see him being angry enough to strike any woman.'

'Yes, but supposing Juliet totally enraged him and he had a mad, senseless moment? She could have destroyed his credibility along with his dream if she'd lived long enough to take the skeletons out of her cupboard. We don't know what people are capable of, when pushed to the

407

limit, do we? God, Rebecca, I know all this sounds awful but my brain feels so scrambled at the moment that I can't think straight.'

'Neither can I. Once or twice I had ridiculous images of Liam doing much the same.'

'Oh, God, what are we like?' Rose felt the prick of tears at the back of her eyes.

'We're both gutted over Juliet,' Rebecca said, clasping her hand. 'We're both crazy with grief, underneath it all. Sometimes I forget she's not around any more, and then it overwhelms me like a black tide.'

'Same here. Matthew and I had a talk this morning,' Rose said. 'What's really upsetting me is James . . . '

Rebecca gave her a sharp look. 'James? As in . . . '

Rose toyed with her chicken. 'I was very upset last night after we'd got home from the opera. I can't believe I didn't realise how badly I'd feel about him not knowing . . . anything. It's tearing me apart. And now it's impossible to tell him the truth.'

Rebecca's eyes were wide with alarm. 'In all these years, that's the first time you've ever brought it up. You must be very badly shaken. I'm really sorry and wish there was some way I could help you and make it better.'

'It's not your problem. It's mine and Matthew's.'

'Yes, but I can't help feeling partly responsible.'

'It was me and Matthew who made the decision to raise James as our son,' Rose said. 'You weren't responsible for our actions. We were. Sometimes, Rebecca, you assume too much.'

'What do you mean?'

'I know you like to be helpful, but sometimes you forget that other people are grown adults, in charge of their own lives. There's a fine line between . . . God.' She stared at Rebecca's set face. 'I know this is coming out wrong.'

'It's not. I think I get the picture. Keep your nose out of our business, Rebecca. Get a life of your own. You only know the half of it.'

Rose was mystified. 'Did I say that?'

'No. Juliet did,' Rebecca said, looking haunted. 'I'm still trying to figure out what she meant. I'll probably never know now.'

'I'm sorry,' Rose said. 'I wouldn't hurt you for the world.'

'I butt in too much, don't I? I just want the people I love to be happy.'

Rose bit her lip. 'I know you do, but I wish you weren't so naïve at times. Sometimes that just isn't possible. People have to make their own mistakes, then live with them as best they can. There's no such thing as happy ever after.'

Rebecca stayed silent until the waiter had cleared their plates. Then she laughed a mirthless laugh. 'Well, if the last two weeks have taught me anything it's that. Do you think you made a mistake all those years ago?'

Rose stared into space for a moment. 'No, I don't, and at the time we had to go by Juliet's wishes, but looking at the nightmare situation we're in now, I think I would have handled it differently.'

Their coffees arrived. Rose stared at hers, feeling she'd had enough coffee over the last fortnight to last her a lifetime.

'James has to know about her will,' Rebecca said.

'I know.' She sighed heavily. 'He'll be back in Dublin early next week.'

'I'll see how I get on with Danielle,' Rebecca said, 'and we'll talk some more. But whatever you do, keep away from Liz Monaghan while you're feeling upset,' she cautioned. 'I don't know where she's coming from, or what her problem is, but with the mood she's in at the moment, her tongue would tear you to pieces.'

53

It was late on Friday evening when Mum arrived. She called my mobile as soon as she was outside the apartment building, having got a taxi from the airport. I went down to let her in and bring her up to my second-floor apartment. As soon as I saw her, I realised how selfish and wrong my assumptions had been.

For this wasn't about me: Mum hadn't come over to Rome just to lavish love and undivided attention on her only daughter, or to offer consolation in the aftermath of my busted wedding and mend the cracks in my shattered life. She was tired and sad, with military-sized shadows under her eyes, and I could have kicked myself for losing sight of the fact that she was grieving for her best friend, a sad journey she was only beginning. Maybe, I thought soberly, as I hugged her and picked up her weekend case, it was my turn to lavish a little attention on her.

But some things hadn't changed. Because it was mine, she thought my dog box of an apartment was fabulously chic, even down to the mismatched cushions and fake lavender in the blue jug. It wasn't, by any stretch of the imagination. She was nonplussed when she noticed there was only one bedroom.

'You're in here, Mum,' I said to her, putting her case on the floor.

'And where are you?' Her eyes cast about as

though another room was going to manifest itself. 'Ah, no, Danielle, I can't let you do that.'

'Do what?'

'Give me your lovely bedroom. Where will you sleep?'

'I've a perfectly good sofa, with a soft, patchwork quilt, and it's only two nights. No arguments, right?' I said, in a jokey voice.

To my surprise, she acquiesced a lot more readily than I would have thought. Another sign that she wasn't herself.

'Do you want a rest after your journey, Mum?' I asked solicitously. 'If you don't feel up to going out, we could have a drink here.'

'A rest? I'm not decrepit yet,' she said, a little smartly. 'I wouldn't say no to going out and having a few decent glasses of chilled Sauvignon Blanc.'

'There's a bar on the corner, and if they like the look of you they'll put out nibbles on the house,' I said. 'Or we can hit the town,' I continued, trying to sound cheery.

'Hit the town,' said Mum. 'It's a while since I lived it up in Rome.'

I knew from the faraway look in her eyes that the last time she'd been here she was with Juliet.

Mum had a quick shower, emerging in a waft of Jo Malone and declaring she was fresh and ready for action. She wasn't, not really, for her face was strained and pinched. When I suggested we start with the bar on the corner she sounded relieved. It was very modern and cosmopolitan, and we sat side by side in a booth by the window, watching the swirl of cars, scooters and people going by outside while we lashed back chilled white wine and chomped at a large bowl of crisps.

Another Friday night in Rome. The first three months I'd been here, I'd seen no one. And now, for the second week in a row, I had a visitor. The background music was coming from a pop station playing English love ballads, and my heart ached with a mixture of homesickness, unrequited love, empathy for my mother and the loss of Juliet. I wished that, for one moment, I could transport us back to Juliet's kitchen at Verbena View with the warm welcome, the big table and the doors folded back to the sea and sky. I wanted one more chance to hug Juliet really tightly and tell her how much I loved her, the way I'd meant to time and time again; the way I should have before she was gone and it was too late.

I still couldn't believe I'd never see her again. Ever.

After a while we'd exhausted safe topics such as the weather, my job, Rome traffic, her flight, and there was no mention of moving on to another bar. I knew something was seriously wrong when Mum said, 'I don't know where to start.'

'I thought we'd already started,' I said inanely, unease prickling under my skin.

'Ah, Danielle, if only . . . '

'If only what?' I asked, my heart contracting: the same words had been spoken to me just last weekend.

'If only I was just here for a social visit.'

413

'What is it, Mum? What are you trying to tell me?'

She stared out of the window for so long that I grew alarmed. Then she gave me a piercingly sad look and said, 'It's about Juliet. And I'd prefer to get the unsavoury news out of the way first.'

She told me then, in a voice drained of emotion. I listened in growing disbelief and dismay about the police call to the house, the ongoing investigation and the possibility that Juliet had been involved in a struggle at the top of the cliff. 'We still don't know what happened,' Mum said. 'I don't know if we ever will for sure. I feel as though my head is going to burst with the craziness of it all. Rose and I are at our wits' end. Rose, even,' she gave a harsh laugh, 'was wondering if Matthew pushed her in a fit of anger.'

'*Matthew?*' I couldn't keep the shock out of my voice. 'Why would Rose think that?'

I remembered then that Rose had had some kind of a breakdown a few years ago. The stress of Juliet's death must have unhinged her slightly.

Mum blinked, then looked at me as though she was coming back from somewhere far away. 'That's how mad it's all becoming,' she said, her voice a little shaky. 'I was even imagining Liam Corrigan having a fight with Juliet and maybe . . .'

'That's a turnaround. I thought you guys were getting on,' I said, sad that something had gone pear-shaped with her and Liam, just when she could have done with a big, strong shoulder to lean on.

'We were.' Mum gave another gruff laugh and, to my horror, a tear slid down her cheek.

I'd seen her cry before, when Dad had died, but that didn't make it any easier to see her struggle to hold back tears now, as all about us the bar was filling with laughing people and Friday night revved up a gear.

I let her pull herself together. Then I said, very gently, 'What happened with Liam?'

'I found out he wasn't to be trusted,' she said, and told me about yet another police visit to the house.

No wonder they were all finding it difficult to cope back in Dublin. My head was spinning with supersized images of Detective Woods and Detective Inspector Callaghan taking up all the space in our front room and upsetting my mother not once but twice and then again. On top of which her best friend had died. In fact, my head was spinning so much that I missed some of the details, the gist eventually trickling through to me.

'Hang on a minute, Mum,' I said. 'You think Liam didn't know you were going to be in the Seagrass? That he was telling lies about wanting to see you?'

'How could he have known I was there? He said Juliet told him, but I hadn't spoken to her all week.'

I found it surprising that Mum hadn't talked to Juliet all week, but I ignored that for now. Something else was flowing through the synapses of my brain, like a crystal stream: the knowledge that I could, with a few words, make up for some of Mum's desperate unhappiness.

'Actually, she did know,' I said softly.

Mum frowned at me. 'Please don't talk in riddles, Danielle. I can't take any more.'

'I'm not. I was talking to Juliet on Thursday evening, remember? The night before she . . . the accident . . . She was talking about coming to see me in Rome. And,' I smiled, 'she said she was sorry she wasn't going to be around for you that weekend on account of her commitments, and I told her you'd just decided . . . ' I was unable to stop the smile spreading across my face as I watched her grappling with the meaning of my words.

'You told her I was going to the wedding in the Seagrass,' Mum said flatly. 'And when Liam called to see Juliet, she told him.'

'There you are,' I said. 'He wasn't making it up.'

'God.' She closed her eyes and sat back against the banquette. She stayed silent for ages, as though she was trying to absorb it all. Then she opened her eyes and looked at me in consternation. 'What have I done? I bawled him out of it, Danielle.'

'Yes, Mum,' I grinned, not believing her for a minute. 'I'd love to see you bawling someone out of it.'

'I did. I was so angry. You should have heard me. I told him he was never to contact me again.'

'So? Think how delighted he'll be when you call him. If he has any sense, he'll know you were under terrible strain. And if he doesn't understand, he's not worth bothering with.'

Mum gave me a tiny smile. 'You wouldn't find it a problem if I was seeing him?'

I flashed her a stern glance. 'What have I said to you time and time again? Get a life for yourself. Look, Mum, who knows what will happen tomorrow? If you have a chance of happiness you seize it with both hands.'

'That has come home to me more than ever over the past couple of weeks.'

'And the other thing is,' I went on, amazed that I was meting out advice to Mum, 'whatever did happen to Juliet, you can't change things now, nor could you have prevented it. Juliet would disown you if you didn't live your life and make the most of it.'

'I hope to God I had no hand in what happened to her,' she said, mystifying me completely.

'Of course you didn't,' I said stoutly. 'Any more than you could have prevented what happened to Dad. Unfortunately, Mum, you don't have a magic wand to prevent all bad things from happening. Neither do you rule the world.'

Once more she stared out of the window, deep in thought, for so long that I had to wave my hand in front of her. 'Are you there?'

She seemed to snap back to attention, as though she was throwing a mental switch inside her head. Whatever was flickering in her eyes disappeared behind a shutter as she put on a smile, and said, 'I'm here, Danielle, and now I want to get fresh drinks and talk to you about the good news.'

'So there's good news?'

'Yes,' she said, smiling as she summoned the barman, who promptly refreshed our drinks and gave us a dish of assorted nuts, as well as refilling the bowl of crisps. When he had left our table, she twirled the stem of her glass, and said, 'You know I'm the executor of Juliet's estate?'

'Yes?'

'Well, darling, I have some rather surprising news for you. Juliet changed her will in February and she named you as one of her chief beneficiaries.'

She sat back, clearly waiting for me to react with some level of enthusiasm, but I couldn't. Shock mingled with foreboding snagged my breath. 'What does that mean exactly?' I asked, as though there were jagged boulders in my mouth.

'Juliet's will includes some charitable bequests, and Robert Jordan can have whatever furniture or paintings he wants. After that, Juliet had savings and investments, and those, with Verbena View, make up the bulk of her estate, which she has willed equally to both you and James.'

Something punched me in the solar plexus and I gasped. All the fragmented pieces that had made up my life in the last few months exploded in front of me: the Christmas table at Verbena View, me catching Juliet watching me in the reflection of us all in the darkened window, me calling off my wedding, and Juliet changing her will soon after. Fast forward a few weeks and she'd wanted to come out to Rome to see me, to talk to me, but before she'd had a chance she'd had a fatal accident.

James's eyes when he'd said, 'If only . . . '

The unconnected pieces twirled in front of me, making me giddy and nauseous.

'Danielle?'

I made a huge effort to anchor myself in the present. My mother was waiting patiently, a smile on her face, anticipating my joy at the life-altering news.

'You're not serious,' I said.

'I am, darling.' Mum gave my shoulder a squeeze. 'It means you won't have any money worries for a long time, if ever.'

When I fell back into silence, she went on, 'Now I'm going to give you some of your own advice. I know it's a little bittersweet, that you're receiving Juliet's legacy because she's gone, but . . .'

I put up my hand. 'Please don't say it.' Don't tell me to enjoy the benefit and live my life to the fullest.

'I can see it's upset you.' Mum was stroking my arm. 'And that's the last thing Juliet would want. She'd want you to be happy, Danielle.'

Poor Mum! She hadn't a clue why I was so upset, and thought it was because I was distressed at benefiting from Juliet's death. That, too, was going on in the background. The prospect of owning the wonderful Verbena View was something I couldn't quite grasp. But most devastating of all was that Juliet had bequeathed the bulk of her estate to me and James.

James! The person I most needed to avoid. Now we would be thrown together. No way would I emerge unscathed.

'Why me and James?' I managed to ask, my

419

voice reduced to a high-pitched squeak.

'She always regarded you two as the family she never had,' Mum said.

I'd known that much because Juliet had told me several times that I was her honorary daughter. It had made me feel special.

'And did she give you any reason for changing her will?' The million-dollar question. Had she seen something in my eyes? If so, how did she think that throwing us together as we sorted out the legalities, never mind the emotional trauma of going through her effects, would solve anything? It would scald my heart.

'No, Danielle, she didn't. She only told me when it was done and dusted. Originally Rose and I were her beneficiaries, so chances were, her legacy would have filtered through to you and James anyway.'

'This is why you came to Rome, isn't it? To tell me.'

Mum nodded.

'Does James know?'

'Not yet,' she said. 'If Rose won't talk to him I guess I'll have to.'

I focused on this because it was easier than imagining James's reaction to the news. 'Why wouldn't Rose tell him?

'No particular reason. She's still gutted about Juliet.'

'So are you,' I said, emerging from my shell shock for long enough to touch her arm. 'You're obviously made of sterner stuff. And now I know why Rose thought Matthew might have had a motive for fighting with Juliet.'

My mother spluttered as her wine went down the wrong way. It took her several moments to recover her breath. 'Like what?' she asked me, in a strangled voice.

'Matthew was probably raging that he'd lost the chance for him and Rose to get a claim on Verbena View.'

'Danielle! No way. They're so comfortable it wouldn't make much of a difference to them.'

'Yes, but it was Juliet's house, and Matthew's always been a little jealous of her. He'd love the idea of lording it in her home and sitting at her antique desk. He'd probably take great pleasure in dumping all her certificates in the bin,' I added, in a fit of petulance, still overwhelmed by the twist of fate that would throw me head to head with James.

'Darling, you don't mean that.'

'Come on, Mum, you know he was always defensive around her. You've heard him trying to outdo her at dinner-table debates and dishing out faint praise on her successes. Maybe she made him feel a little inferior, with her education and background, because he could never compete with that, and life, to him, is a competition.'

'I don't know . . . I suppose that's one way of looking at it.' Mum's brow furrowed. Then she brightened, in typical Mum fashion, looking for the best in something, trying to make me happy. 'What's done is done, Danielle, and I'm glad you'll have the comfort of that financial cushion, even though it's hard to accept the hows and whys of it, and it'll be difficult sorting through the red tape. But Rose and I will help with the house and Juliet's personal effects. Robert Jordan has already asked me for help as he wouldn't have a clue.'

'Yes,' I said, still feeling faint, knowing that I had the hardest struggle in my life ahead of me. And there was absolutely nothing Mum or anyone else could do to ease the pain of it.

54

Rose smiled and remembered to put her weight on one foot as Juliet had advised when she posed to have her photo taken for the diary pages in a glossy magazine. She looked the part in her softly draping jersey sheath and L.K. Bennett peep-toe shoes, with her hair freshly blow-dried. But she shouldn't have had that second glass of wine. Not mixed with her little white pill. And not in the middle of Saturday afternoon, at the fundraising fashion show in the D4 Berkeley Hotel. Especially when there were so many press around. She'd seen Liz Monaghan slithering through the crowd at the back of the hall earlier and prayed she'd manage to avoid her.

She shouldn't even be here in her fraught frame of mind, but Matthew had insisted.

'I think I'll give it a miss,' she'd said to him, during breakfast that morning, when he'd asked her what time she was leaving. 'I don't feel up to all that happy socialising.'

'You have to be there, Rose,' he'd said, pouring more coffee. 'That fundraiser is going to get a lot of media coverage and it'll be valuable exposure for you.'

'Exposure!' She'd laughed. 'That's exactly what I'm afraid of. We're frauds, Matthew, you and I, pretending to be above reproach, people of honour and integrity. Supposing our little secret got into the wrong hands? What then?'

'It had better not,' he said curtly. 'And I wish you'd stop obsessing about it. You have to pull yourself together and forget it ever happened. Maybe we ignored some red tape, but we did what we thought was best. That's all you have to remember. Forget the rest. If word leaked out now, it would be explosive.'

'Do you feel at all relieved that the threat of Juliet letting the cat out of the bag is gone?' she asked, watching him closely.

'What kind of a question is that?' He rose from the table and picked up his mug of coffee. She could see him moving into work mode, his mind ticking off what had to be done, like a well-oiled machine. 'I've calls to make,' he said, 'and I've meetings with potential advisers later this morning. It's going to be another busy day. Let me know what time you're leaving and I'll call a taxi for you. And, darling,' he paused by the door and smiled reassuringly at her, 'just relax about everything. The sky is not about to fall in.'

Oh yes it was, Rose decided, remembering his words as she gripped the stem of her wine glass and watched Liz Monaghan plunge through the crowds, homing in on her like a shark having scented its prey.

'Rose! I thought you might be here! Great to see so many people turning out to support the charity, isn't it? And amazing that so many A-list models and celebs are giving their time. Still, it's a great cause. Juliet would have been thrilled.' Liz fixed her with a laser-like stare. 'She was one of the patrons of this charity, wasn't she,' Liz went on, 'along with her own foundation? She was a busy lady on the fundraising circuit. I wonder what will happen to that now?'

Rose found her voice. 'I've no idea. If you'll excuse me . . . ' She darted a look towards the exit, which Liz intercepted. There was a swathe of designer-clad people milling around between her and the double doors to the hotel lobby and her ultimate escape. She wished there was someone to come to her rescue. She couldn't handle Liz by herself. Not today.

Liz put a hand on her arm and Rose flinched.

'Before you go,' the gossip columnist said, 'did you hear the rumour going around about Juliet? That she had an affair? If anyone should know the truth it's you and your sister. But Rebecca won't talk to me. I went by that little boutique she hangs out in yesterday and again this morning but she wasn't there. Do you think she's trying to avoid me? She told me she thinks I'm a vindictive bitch. What do you think, Rose?'

'Whatever Juliet did or didn't do, it had nothing to do with my family or Rebecca,' Rose said, her voice tight.

'Your *family*? What happened in your family?' Liz asked, her eyes alight with curiosity as she pounced on Rose's words.

'Nothing,' Rose said, hot colour sweeping across her face.

'Nothing?' The twin arches of Liz's eyebrows lifted in perfect unison. 'I was only asking if you knew about Juliet's affair with a married man. Seeing as you were such good friends with her, I thought you'd know. I certainly wasn't asking about your family. Or your drop-dead gorgeous husband. There's hardly any connection, is there?' she asked silkily.

'You'll have to excuse me,' Rose said, sidling away.

As Rose put her glass down on a table and moved in the direction of the door, Liz followed her. 'Oh, gosh, you are edgy, aren't you?' she said. 'What could you have to hide, Rose?'

Rose passed Celia Coffey chatting to her cronies, Rachel and Megan. Feeling ridiculous, and hotly embarrassed, she smiled brightly as though nothing was amiss, even though it was obvious that Liz was stalking her.

Never again, she decided grimly. No matter what Matthew said, she was never again attending any function on her own.

'Rose? Did I hit a nerve? I can see you're upset.'

Then, 'Rose! What's up? Why won't you stop and talk to me?'

When they reached the doorway, with the lobby ahead and the taxis lined up outside the entrance, waiting to whisk her away, Rose finally turned to face her.

'I've nothing to say to you, Liz. Nothing at all.'

'What are you afraid of?'

'I'm not afraid of anything.'

'Like hell you're not.' Liz's mouth curved in an empty smile. 'And why won't your husband reply to my emails? What's going on there? Or is he afraid of something too?'

'Rebecca was right. You are vindictive.' Rose grabbed at the words and flung them out like daggers, trying to stop Liz in her tracks.

'You may be sorry you said that,' Liz said, 'when I get to the bottom of whatever is going on between you, Rebecca and Juliet.'

'Why don't you fuck off?' Rose said, her legs shaking. She hurried towards the lobby and the safety of the waiting taxis beyond. She gave the driver her address, sank back into the soft leather, and wondered how much longer she'd be able to stop her life totally unravelling. Her tenuous hold on her emotions was slipping.

55

I watched Mum close her eyes behind her shades as she tilted her head to the sun, and the contours of her face relaxed, as though she was finally unwinding and grateful to be here. We were sitting with what seemed like a million chattering tourists by the fountain at the bottom of the Spanish Steps. Saturday afternoon was sunny, but cool enough to wear a jacket. Ahead of us stretched the Via Condotti, and the narrow street of designer shops was heaving with weekend shoppers.

Even though she'd visited years ago, I'd spent the morning bringing Mum on a whistle-stop tour of the main sights in the historic centre of Rome, which, thankfully, allowed us little time to talk. We'd had toasted panini for lunch in a small café on a narrow street near the Trevi fountain. Then we'd strolled to the church at the top of the Spanish Steps, where we'd stood and looked at the vista of the city, the elegant buildings washed in pale apricot and yellow, the green-grey domes and steeples of the churches and, hugging the horizon, the undulating green of the hills. It had seemed so peaceful from that perspective, and it had obviously relaxed Mum, but I'd felt detached from reality since she had dropped her bombshell about Juliet's legacy.

'Are you feeling any better about things today, Danielle?' she asked, as we sat by the fountain, raising the topic we'd avoided all morning.

'Sort of,' I said lamely.

She took off her sunglasses. 'I wish you'd come home,' she said.

'Is that another reason why you came out to see me?'

'Yes,' she said. 'If you were here for the pleasure of it, I could live with that. But you're not. You came here to run away from a bad situation and that's fine for a while, sometimes we need a hidey-hole, but it's not going to fix anything. The longer you leave things unresolved between you and Conor, the more difficult it's going to get.'

'Who said anything was unresolved?'

'Danielle, I can see by your face that you're deeply unhappy, and something is eating you up. You've lost weight as well. I don't want to interfere, but I don't like seeing people I love unhappy.' Then Mum gave an embarrassed laugh. 'There I go again. You can tell me to take a hike and get my own life, but I'm concerned about you.'

'It's okay, Mum, I know you are, and it's nice,' I said, feeling so rotten inside that for once I welcomed her attention.

Mum positively beamed.

'And while we're on the subject,' I continued, watching a small dark-haired girl skip happily around the fountain, 'I emailed Conor earlier this week and he replied the other night. So we're talking now, and we've a lot of stuff to work through but it's well and truly over. And, Mum,' I took a quick breath, 'I was the one who

429

cancelled the wedding, not Conor. I decided I couldn't go through with it as I didn't love him enough.'

I waited for remonstrations: Conor was wonderful; I wasn't getting any younger; how about our lovely home, that fabulous wedding dress and the honeymoon? But those were the arguments that I'd imagined in those fraught nights before I'd called the whole thing off. I hadn't given enough credit to my mother.

'Oh, darling,' she said, her face soft with affection, 'I'm sorry to hear that, but you were very brave to do what you did and perfectly right. The world would be a much happier place if people stopped doing what they felt they should do, and just listened to their own instincts, no matter how difficult it seems at the time.'

'In other words, listen to your heart,' I said, loving her and feeling a little choked because what she was saying was so similar to what Juliet had told me. I had a sense of them forging a path through life from their teenage years, learning from their knocks along the way, and swapping gossip as well as advice.

'Exactly' Mum smiled, as she patted my knee. 'It won't lead you astray.'

But it already has, I felt like weeping. It's made me fall in love with my cousin. I held back my urge to throw myself into her arms and suggested we take the Via Condotti by storm. Mum laughed and stood up. She hoisted her canvas shoulder bag and, perching her sunglasses on the top of her head, she asked which I'd like

430

to hit first: YSL, Prada or Hermès.

'Let's pick up a few Armani bags,' I joked.

Neither Mum nor I had any truck with designer labels for the sake of it. Okay, if you wanted to look groomed, a little splurge was sometimes necessary, more so at Mum's age than mine. But I couldn't understand women who joined waiting lists to pay the guts of a king's ransom for a bag. Surely you'd get tired of it after a few seasons.

I pretended to enjoy running in and out of the horribly expensive shops, nosing around the opulent accessories departments, comparing hugely expensive shoes and bags we'd no intention of buying. Mum seemed to enjoy it, and was a lot more relaxed than when she'd first arrived. She was clearly relieved to hear I'd called off the wedding and she was also buoyed up by the realisation that Liam hadn't been telling her a load of fibs after all. He *had* been interested in seeing her; furthermore, he'd been sent to her with Juliet's blessing. I just didn't know what kind of blessing Juliet had been invoking when she'd changed her will and set me up against James.

And afterwards, most unfortunately for me and my mother's sensitive ears, it all came flooding out.

★   ★   ★

Later that evening, we sat in a restaurant off the Via del Corso sipping Prosecco and nibbling pan-fried sea bass. The restaurant was chic, with

431

whitewashed walls, wooden ceilings and flickering candlelight in coloured glasses dotted around the tables. A few hardy souls were sitting outside on the terrace, watching the world go by, but we had opted for a table inside.

'I'm so glad we had this weekend together,' Mum said.

'Yeah, it was good,' I said, realising too late that I sounded totally pissed off.

'But, Danielle, I don't understand.' My mother looked at me shrewdly. 'How come you still look so — I dunno — woebegone, three months down the line, if it was you who called off the wedding? And why couldn't you tell me at the time? Am I that much of a monster? Or are you having big regrets?'

I sighed and bit my lip. 'No regrets, Mum, but it's a long story.'

It wasn't that I looked woebegone, not literally. It was more that my state of mind was at an all-time low. The hopelessness of my situation had been running through my veins, faster and faster, building up inside me ever since I'd seen James in the St Michel. That weekend had been the first occasion I'd spent any length of time with him since I'd realised how I felt. I didn't count the day of Juliet's funeral — that had been a fragment of time out of step with everything else. And I was beginning to realise that it wasn't just a case of learning to live with unrequited love, or unfulfilled desires: it went deeper than that, as though everything that defined me, both physically and spiritually, had utterly changed.

No matter how hard I tried to reach back to

the me who had been chugging along, putting down a growing dissatisfaction with my life and impending wedding to pre-nuptial jitters, or to the me who'd been putting up a false front for Erin and Gemma, that Danielle was gone for ever. The new me's nerve endings were exposed like frayed threads, and even my heart felt raw and tender, as though all the protective layers had been removed. How I was going to stay sane as I went through the ordeal of talking about Verbena View with James, I did not know.

And now that Mum was feeling a lot more on top of things than she'd been when she'd first arrived in Rome, her problem-seeking antennae had zoned in on that. She was obviously scared of putting her feet in it because she merely said, 'I'm glad you have no regrets, and I won't probe, darling. I'm sorry if I've upset you.'

'No worries,' I said, attempting to eat some lettuce that tasted like rubber as depression settled like a heavy cloak on my shoulders.

'Well, this is nice, isn't it?' Mum said, with forced cheer, as she glanced around the restaurant, determined to look on the bright side. Her mouth curved in a wide smile, but it was totally at odds with the pained look in her eyes as she glanced tentatively at me.

That look tipped me over the edge. My face collapsed and I burst into tears.

I don't know who was more horrified, me or Mum. I stared at her wildly and caught my breath, but instead of managing to compose myself, it was as though something had been breached inside me and the floodgates opened. I picked up my bag and dashed for the Ladies.

I thought I was never going to stop crying. Even my stomach was heaving. I pictured Mum sitting alone outside, agonising about her choice of words as she tried to figure out what she'd said to send me into a meltdown. After a short while the outer door opened and I heard her voice.

'Danielle, I'm outside,' she said calmly. 'Take your time, darling, and whenever you're ready we'll head off, okay?'

'Okay,' I said thickly.

It was another full five minutes before I was composed enough to open the door of the cubicle and go to the washbasins. Mum was sitting on a chair. She jumped to her feet and wordlessly gave me a hug. I fixed my face as best I could, tidied up the mascara running down my cheeks and patted my hot, damp skin.

'I think I'm ready now,' I said, giving her a watery grin.

She smiled. 'Right so.' Head high, she led the way out of the restaurant, as though she was shepherding the Queen on a walkabout. I followed her, bravely ignoring the curious glances. Outside, I drew in gulps of the chilly night air. It slid across my hot face, cooling and soothing. I had a peculiar blank feeling, as though I was totally drained inside. We said very little as we walked home, along the same route I'd taken with James just over a week before.

Then I found my voice. 'The reason I broke up with Conor . . . ' I began.

'Danielle — honestly, love, you don't have to

tell me if you don't want to.'

I ignored her. 'It was because I knew I didn't love him, not properly, because, you see, I realised I loved someone else.'

'Oh, God. Then of course you'd no choice but to call off the wedding.'

'I know.'

We reached the big intersection in front of the monument to Vittorio Emanuele II. I felt dizzy, remembering the feel of James's hand on my arm last week as we crossed the busy road. I could almost pretend he was there now, could feel his tall frame moving alongside me, that I just had to tilt my face to see him silhouetted against the street-light.

I blinked. Of course he wasn't there. And I missed him so much that the ache swelled inside me, like a cold, sharp wave.

'This other man. The one you love, is he here in Rome?' Mum asked, as we waited for a safe moment to cross.

'No, Mum. He doesn't even know how I feel about him and he can't find out. So it's a hopeless situation.'

She digested this in silence as we concentrated on getting across the intersection. There was a slight break in the traffic and we ventured into the road, Mum doing her best impression of a traffic warden as she raised a forbidding hand against a motorcyclist, lest he dare pass within a few feet of me and harm a hair of my head.

When we got to the other side and headed in the direction of my apartment, she said, 'That's too bad, Danielle. I'd imagine any man would be

435

delighted to know you love him.'

Ahead of us lay the Forum. The remnants of temples and basilicas lay eerily still in the night air, a lot of the magnificence now reduced to rubble, tumbled walls and redundant columns rising a ghostly grey into the sky. On the road, scooters buzzed and cars honked.

'Look at that landscape,' Mum said, pausing in her stride. 'The heart and soul of ancient, civilised Rome. So many historic ruins. It makes you think, doesn't it?'

'Think what?' I asked, a little annoyed that she'd changed the subject so easily, when I'd just revealed what was in my innermost heart.

'About all the thousands of spirits that have passed through here for generations, living and loving. Our ancestors. All gone now and most of them forgotten.'

'Yeah, we're just insignificant dots in the great scheme of the universe, aren't we?' I guessed where she was coming from: it was typical Mum-speak for putting your problems into perspective.

'That's not what I was trying to say, Danielle,' she said, turning to face me. 'I guess I'm a bit emotional right now, thinking of Juliet, your dad too, but the gift of your life, *your* life, is very significant and beyond price. It's worth everything. You're very precious to me, to your family and your friends. And the love you have for someone, even if it can't be reciprocated, is a very special gift. Juliet loved you, and that's still there, in your heart, even though she's not around. Don't ever think love is hopeless or put

436

yourself down for feeling it. Love is never, ever wasted and it's always positive.'

'Yes, but supposing . . . supposing you love the person so much that you want to be with them and you can't, and it makes you sad?'

'Ah, that happens,' she said, smiling at me. 'I didn't say loving someone was easy. It brings its own costs, like anything else worthwhile. I was in great pain after Harry died and he was gone from my life. Now I'm grateful for what we had, and it's still in my heart. Have you even tried telling him you love him? Or, better again, something more important, have you shown him by your actions that he means so much to you? Just in case?'

'No way,' I said. 'That would cause all sorts of problems. Even your best magic wand, Mum, can't sort this out for me.'

'Of course not, Danielle. I know that. I can't make everyone happy, much as I'd like to. I'm just giving you something to think about. Imagine for one moment if Juliet was in your situation, what do you think she'd do? Would she take a chance? Risk all for love?'

I started to cry again. For a moment I felt Juliet putting her arms around me, full of warmth and love, then smiling at me in that jokey way she had. I heard her telling me to listen to my heart. I saw her watching my face in the reflection of the glass at Verbena View and intercepting the way I was gazing at James.

Mum didn't know what to make of me as, once more, I sniffed and choked and bawled into a wad of tissues.

'I'm sorry, I shouldn't have mentioned Juliet,' she said, her hand creeping around my shoulders. 'It's still so raw and sore.'

And then the words gushed out of me, as though a plug had become undone.

'I think Juliet knew,' I gasped through my tears.

Mum was puzzled. 'Knew what?'

'Knew that I was in love . . . '

'What makes you say that?'

'She saw. She saw me looking at him,' I babbled, my whole body shaking. 'In Verbena View. At Christmas. And then she went and complicated everything. And now she's gone I can't even ask her what the hell she was thinking . . . '

'Danielle, calm down. Just breathe slowly. In and out. Who did Juliet see you looking at?' Even though her face looked swimmy through my tears I saw that her eyes were huge with apprehension and I think she knew what I was going to say before the words shot out of my mouth.

'James. My cousin. See?' I glared at her. 'And it's all a big fat crappy mess.' I promptly leaned into her and burst into more tears.

56

There was a lot to be said, Rebecca decided, for being enclosed in a capsule speeding thousands of feet above the ground, looking down at fuzzy cotton-wool clouds and, between the gaps, the sugar-dusted slate grey peaks of the Alps. Detached like this from ordinary life, with a stranger sitting beside you, there wasn't much you could do and no one was able to contact or expect anything of you. A welcome respite between the trauma of Danielle in Rome and whatever difficulties lay ahead when she got back to Dublin.

If only she could stay like this for a little longer. Because, for once in her life, Rebecca knew that there was no easy way out of this dilemma. No matter what she did or didn't do, she was caught between her daughter and her sister, and one of them was going to be hurt. The hardest part of love, she decided, was standing back while others got hurt, and all you could do was to pick up the pieces.

'Don't tell a single soul, Mum,' Danielle had urged, the previous night, when they were back in her apartment and she was a little calmer. 'Whatever I said, please keep it to yourself.'

'I will, if that's what you want,' Rebecca had answered, her heart heavy. 'Whatever happens, I love you, Danielle. I just want you to be happy.'

Long after she'd gone to bed in Danielle's tiny

439

bedroom, Rebecca had lain awake, tossing and turning. How could she tell Danielle the truth about James? If she remained silent, was there any chance Danielle might patch up her sore heart and get on with life as best she could? If she told her the truth, all hell would break loose. Danielle couldn't be expected to keep something so shattering to herself. James would find out sooner rather than later. Rose would never speak to her again. And she hadn't even started to think of Matthew, hell bent on his latest challenge.

They couldn't even keep it within the family, because if Danielle and James did get together, the news and gossip would explode across the media stratosphere and the likes of Liz Monaghan would have a field day.

If they got together.

For, as Danielle had told her when they had chatted late into the night, even with all conventions laid aside, James still regarded her as a sort of sister. Yet, Rebecca told herself, Juliet, in changing her will, had set them up for some kind of showdown. And she'd spoken of setting the past to rights just before she'd died. She might have retained some of her youthful rebellious streak, but no way would she have set out to hurt either Danielle or James.

It had been almost light by the time Rebecca had nodded off, managing to snatch a couple of hours' sleep before she had to get up, grab a quick breakfast and head to the airport. Once she'd been through security checks and Passport Control, she'd sat down with a large cappuccino and an apple croissant, taken a deep breath and texted Liam, apologising for the misunderstanding.

Liam had replied just before she boarded her flight:

Would love to c u right now to clear this up in person x
Difficult! I'm in Rome about to board a flight home xx
Hope to c u later xxx

All too soon, they landed in Dublin airport, and Rebecca's heart was heavy as she disembarked, thinking of the difficult predicament she faced.

To her pleasure, Liam was waiting for her when she came through Arrivals. He was looking elsewhere, his attention caught by three small children hurling themselves at their waiting grandparents, and it gave her time to study him unobserved. He was smiling at them, his eyes kind, his face soft. He looked like the sort of man she'd want to spend time with and get to know a whole lot better. And maybe have him at her back if things got too crazy.

The kind of man Harry would have approved of.

The man Juliet had nudged in her direction.

Her heart lifted a little. She moved towards him, feeling a little giddy. Then he looked at her and his face changed as something like gratitude broke across it. They came together in the middle of the hall, and she inhaled his lime scent as his arms went around her.

'Thank you,' she said, her voice muffled against the curve of his neck. She leaned back to look at his face.

'I haven't done anything yet,' he said.

'You're here. You've forgiven me for being so horrible to you.'

'Oh, have I?' His eyes teased. 'I could be working out an appropriate, equally horrible revenge.'

'Like what?'

'Let me see . . . ' He linked his hands around the small of her back, holding her securely. 'This for starters,' he said, bending his head so that his mouth was inches from hers. She waited, leaned into him more and gave a little sigh. At last he began to kiss her, very thoroughly, heedless of everyone else. She clung to him and kissed him back, equally heedless because, she reasoned, the airport was one place you could kiss in front of crowds of people and get away with it.

★   ★   ★

She'd never liked Sunday afternoons. They reminded her of tedious Sunday afternoons in Ballymalin when the stale air permeating the house seemed weighted with her mother's abject unhappiness. Not to mention the Sunday afternoon when Annie Monaghan had decided that enough was enough and taken leave of a life that had brought her heartbreak, heedless of the fact that her sixteen-year-old daughter would find her.

Now the walls of her house in Harold's Cross were crowding in on Liz, the solitude crushing

442

her spirits, and she couldn't rest easy. On impulse, she put on some mascara and lip gloss, tied her hair back in a ponytail, fetched her Polaroid sunglasses and a jacket, and left the house. She hailed a passing taxi and went to Grafton Street. Better to mingle with the cheery noise and life of city-centre crowds on a Sunday afternoon than sit moping alone at home.

The street was thrumming with life and colour, thanks to the mêlée of flower sellers, buskers, tourists and shoppers, but as she drifted through it all, observing the vitality around her, she felt eerily detached from everything. She stood outside Brown Thomas, staring in at the busy cosmetics counters, but couldn't bring herself to venture in. She was barely able even to recognise her reflection, thrown back at her from the large mirrors inside.

As luck would have it, on the one day she was hoping not to run into anyone she knew, she bumped into Gavin as she turned away dejectedly from the window. He was marching purposefully down Wicklow Street. At the last minute he saw her and stopped abruptly.

'Liz! What happened to you?'

She stared at him, her heart sinking. 'What do you mean?'

He was clearly flummoxed. 'It's just . . . you look different . . . '

She took off her sunglasses and narrowed her eyes, meeting his gaze. 'You mean I'm not all glammed up.'

'That's probably it, yeah, right,' he said. He seemed embarrassed, yet he went on to ask her solicitously, 'You're a bit pale. Are you feeling all right?'

'Why wouldn't I be?'

'Everything okay?'

'Yes, of course.'

'I didn't see your diary slot this weekend.'

She shrugged. 'Just taking a break.' She was unwilling to admit that she'd been too low and depressed to summon any enthusiasm for her usual outrageous commentary.

There was another silence between them and, to her horror, he put out a hand and smoothed back tendrils of her hair that had escaped from her hasty ponytail.

'I still think we could have made a go of it, you and I.'

She felt sudden tears at the back of her eyes and ordered them to stay there. He was right. He'd been right all along when he'd sussed out the problems in their relationship. She knew that now. And if she'd known earlier that she hadn't, after all, been responsible for her mother's unhappiness, she might have had the guts to make a go of her own marriage.

But it had come too late to rescue her.

'We might have, once upon a time,' she said, 'but too much has gone wrong.'

'Has it really, Liz?' He looked at her intently, and her heart leaped with the hope she saw in his face. And then it crashed back to earth.

'It's too late for us, Gavin. Too late for me.' She laughed dismissively. 'But thanks anyway.'

She swung through the door into the big department store, trying to get away from him, conscious of him staring at her through the window as she went through the cosmetics department until she was satisfied she was out of his sight. Then she headed for another exit.

Back home, she sat at the kitchen table and poured herself a vodka. She opened the envelope she'd brought up from Ballymalin and spread the documents across the table, examining them closely: the bills from a psychiatric hospital, where her mother had been a patient not once but *three* times. One of those times had been soon after her parents' wedding. Two receipts from a hotel, just one night each, so faded they were almost indecipherable; she made out that one was dated several months before she was born. Then, tying the whole lot together, the small, square, borderless photograph with the name 'Juliet Jordan' written in pencil on the back. She wouldn't have recognised the girl with the short black hair wearing the yellow-rimmed sunglasses but for that. The photograph, also, was faded. She knew from its condition that it had been taken many years ago.

Separately, they could have meant anything. Her mother ill, yeah, right. Thanks to her alcoholism, she'd been ill throughout Liz's life. That was no secret. Hotel bills? Her father might have been on a business trip. But a photo of someone she hardly knew, with all of these, was another matter. Especially when they had been carefully placed together in an envelope for her to find.

Together they spelled out the sordid little secret behind her mother's ill health and alcoholism. She wanted to cry for that bewildered child, and even more devastated teenager, who'd felt somehow responsible for her mother's unhappy life, never mind her tragic death. But she couldn't allow herself the luxury of tears just yet.

Rose and Rebecca, Juliet's friends, must have known something. Coming from Ballymalin, they were the only obvious link between Juliet and Liz's father. Without them, it was very doubtful that their paths would have crossed. She'd enjoyed spooking Rebecca who, naturally enough, wasn't going to admit that her friend had had an affair, but the anxiety sparking in her eyes had told Liz that she was on the right track. She'd enjoyed spooking the terrified Rose even more: she had looked so full of guilt and for some reason seemed to think her whole family was under threat.

There was another story there, she sensed. Something deep and dark was troubling Rose. But that was for another day. Right now it was time to find out which of those bitches had been responsible for bringing Juliet and Tom Monaghan together. Because it was perfectly clear to her that his affair with Juliet had caused her mother heartbreak, destroyed her marriage and led her down the road to a psychiatric hospital, followed by alcoholism and a tragic death.

And ultimately ruined Liz's life too.

57

'I'm incredibly nervous,' Rebecca said.

'Me too.' Liam smiled at her.

'I haven't . . . since . . . '

'And I've waited a long time for this.'

'Really?'

'You look beautiful when you blush like that.'

'Do I?'

His hand reached out and curved around her hot cheek. 'Yes, Rebecca, you do.'

She'd known this was about to happen since she'd seen him waiting for her in the airport. She wanted it to happen. She wanted to forget, for an afternoon, her dilemma: she had to choose between the happiness of her sister and that of her daughter.

Although it was no real dilemma: Danielle would always come first.

But, no matter what happened, this was her life too, and she wanted to live the rest of it to the max, to feel desire fulfilled and the heat of a lover's caress, as well as the warm comfort of a cuddle. She wasn't going to waste a single moment, or pass up any capacity she had to give or receive love.

Liam had driven her home after he'd collected her at the airport, and she'd felt full of edgy anticipation as she'd hurried upstairs and changed out of her travel clothes. Her hands had been shaking as she'd riffled through her wardrobe, picking out a scarlet shirt, black trousers and thin stiletto heels. They went for a late Sunday lunch in Dawson Street. Now it was the early evening and they were sharing a bottle of wine in his apartment. It was basic but modern, and had everything a person could need. Outside the window, the evening sky was serrated with herringbone clouds, and the muted rumble of passing traffic mingled with the cries of the seagulls along the nearby canal.

Sitting on the sofa, she said, 'Seeing as you've waited a long time, and I'm so nervous that I'm trembling, I think we should get this over with as quickly as possible.'

His eyebrows shot up. 'Get it over with? My dear Rebecca, I want to take my time and enjoy every inch of you. Slowly and leisurely.'

Her face flooded with more heat. 'I meant the, um, undressing part. I'm not exactly in my prime. The quicker I get between the sheets . . . '

'I've no intention of hiding you under the sheets,' he said gently, 'and you are fabulously beautiful, every part of you. But, yes, the sooner we get started the better.'

Before she knew it, Liam had lowered the blind on the window, and swung her around so that she was lying along the sofa. Her heart tripped alarmingly as he took off her shoes and kissed her feet. Her throat tightened as he began to undo the buttons of her shirt, his eyes widening as he took in the scarlet lacy bra she was wearing underneath.

'Wow,' he said, smiling at her, the spark in his eyes melting away all her fears.

She didn't tell him that Harry had bought it for her, on holiday in Spain one year, but he had passed away before she'd had the chance to wear it for him, and she'd stored it in its tissue paper. Until now. She didn't tell him that under her black trousers she was wearing matching scarlet briefs. She'd let him find that out for himself. Which he did, flashing her another look: it was thick with desire and melted her insides.

Soon the room was filled with the sounds of love: laughter and long, deep sighs, of Rebecca's sharp intake of breath and low moans, of helpless giggles when one side of the sofa suddenly jerked backwards so that they had to abandon it for the accommodating width of the bed, pattering hurriedly across the wooden floor in bare feet, their giggles quietening down once more to soft murmurs and cries of pleasure.

And finally, long afterwards, the sound of sleep as night fell and they cuddled under the duvet.

★   ★   ★

Rebecca waited until Monday evening before she made the difficult call to Rose: she wanted to prolong the lovely glow that surrounded her after her night with Liam. She clung to it like a safety net, letting it warm her as she speed-dialled her sister.

'How were Rome and Danielle?' Rose asked.

'So-so,' Rebecca said, and chatted about her flights, shopping and Danielle's apartment before she came to the point. 'Danielle was very surprised when I told her about Juliet's will. I don't think it really sank in. Have you given any thought to what you might say to James?'

'No . . . ' Rose sounded hesitant. 'I was half hoping you might talk to him, you being the executor of the will.'

'Yes, but he'd think it strange that his own parents hadn't mentioned it to him.'

There was a short silence and then Rose admitted, 'I'm terrified of somehow saying the wrong thing. Even Liz Monaghan — '

'What about her?' Rebecca asked, feeling her hackles rise.

'She was chasing me for a comment on Saturday at the charity fundraiser. I didn't want to go but Matthew insisted, and she managed to snare me. Anyway, I lost the plot and told her — God, Rebecca, I went and told her to fuck off.'

'*You?*'

'Yes. I was so shaken by her. She says she's determined to get to the bottom of whatever's going on between us. Oh, Christ, I'm falling apart. I don't know what else might come shooting out of my mouth.'

'You're not falling apart. But I was thinking of what you said about everything changing now that Juliet is gone. And maybe,' Rebecca went on ultra-carefully, 'just supposing you were to tell James the truth, in a quiet way?'

'Are you *mad?* I can't do that.'

'You said it yourself, Rose, that you felt badly about James not knowing his mother was dead. And supposing Liz does manage to stumble on something . . . or if you let something slip . . . It

450

could be a whole lot worse.'

'I wish you wouldn't scare me like this.'

'I'm not trying to scare you. I'm just suggesting that if somehow James was to discover the truth, it would be far better coming from you than for him to find it headlined in Liz Monaghan's tabloid column. Think about it.'

'It's totally and unbelievably out of the question,' Rose said, her voice shaking.

'Is it? I'm sure it could be sorted out quietly, somehow, without getting blasted across the national press. Where is James now?'

'He's home since this morning. So, please, would you talk to him? And forget all this other nonsense.'

'God knows what I might say to him.'

'Don't be like that, please, Rebecca. You know I trust you.'

And so does Danielle, Rebecca thought bleakly.

After the call, Rebecca went into the conservatory and tried to recapture the magic of the previous night with Liam. She'd be seeing him tomorrow evening and, all of a sudden, it couldn't come quickly enough. Yet her head was filled with Rose and Danielle and she kept coming back to the moment on the cliff when Juliet had talked about the truth coming out, telling Rebecca she didn't know the half of it. What had she meant? Had Juliet known something about James that had made her feel it was time to come clean? Changing her will didn't mean all that much: chances were, Juliet had expected to live a long and happy life. It might have been another thirty years before

Danielle and James were thrown together in the melting pot of her legacy.

Unless it had been just the start of Juliet allowing things to come out into the open.

It was all so terribly messy. Rebecca was caught between her daughter's happiness and her sister's peace of mind, and for someone who liked everyone to be content, it was an impossible place to be.

58

'Rose? What's the matter?' Matthew asked, stepping into the kitchen where she was sitting at the table with a glass of wine. He was in his shirtsleeves as he took a glass from the press and filled it with filtered water and ice.

In other words, he was still working, even if she was relaxing to the point of getting quietly drunk.

'Oh, nothing,' Rose said. 'As if Liz Monaghan wasn't bad enough in her mission to dig up some dirt, now Rebecca's trying to scare me half to death.'

'What is it?' He looked impatient. Impatient, but resigned to the prospect of talking his wife through yet another mini-meltdown.

'Nothing you need worry about,' she said. 'I daren't keep you from your busy mobile or your all-important blog.'

'Right so,' he said. 'I won't ask you what you're doing drinking in here on your own.' He walked back to the kitchen door.

'You might be free of Juliet's threat,' she said, halting him in his tracks, 'but you could have a problem with Rebecca.'

He wheeled around. 'Don't tell me we're back to this again! I told you, Juliet was no threat.'

'I always wondered why you were so sure of that,' she said. 'You know, Matthew, you never told me you were texting Juliet. The day she died.'

'What are you on about now?'

453

'I know you sent Juliet a text that day.'

'So? I would have sent her a few texts. We sometimes compared notes and I checked points of business law with her.'

'Wanting to meet up at her place doesn't sound like a business call to me. 'We have to talk. Your place.'' The words that had imprinted themselves on her brain flowed all too easily, considering how choked up she felt.

There was a tiny pause. Then, 'For God's sake, Rose, okay, maybe I wanted to talk to her to make sure she wasn't going to do anything stupid, anything that might hurt you or me, but she never replied.'

'So you weren't having an affair?'

She hated the way he looked at her, as though she was stark, raving mad.

'I don't know what's got into you tonight,' he said evenly, 'but I've work to be getting on with.'

'You didn't answer my question. So. You. Weren't. Having. An. Affair. With. Juliet?'

'Of course not. What's brought this on?'

'But you were concerned about the can of worms she might have opened after all, even though you told me not to worry.'

He gave a small shrug. 'It doesn't matter now, does it? I didn't get a chance to talk to her.'

'Didn't you? I've had nightmares, Matthew. I've been having them for years, but they've got much worse since Juliet died. I even had a nightmare that you could have been with her on that cliff just before she fell. Because she could have pulled the plug on your ultimate dream.'

He looked disbelieving. 'For God's sake, Rose,

how many bottles of wine have you drunk?'

'It doesn't matter. It's not the wine. I just can't hold it together any more,' Rose said, trying to make sense of the formless panic that had swept through her during Rebecca's phone call and stayed. 'I've had the feeling that my life was about to unravel and I think this is it. I've lost the plot. So I'm just getting some stuff off my chest, stuff I was afraid to say before. But now I don't give a damn. Nothing matters.'

'You'd better pull yourself together in time for tomorrow night,' Matthew said. 'We've a reception to go to. And I don't know where you got the crazy notion that I was having an affair with Juliet.' He seemed mildly insulted as he headed for the door.

And once more Rose stopped him: all her pent-up insecurities and fears were finally getting the better of her. 'You see, I sometimes wondered if James was actually yours,' she said. 'I even thought you might have been the married man Juliet had the affair with. I was amazed you agreed to take him on as your son.'

'I wanted to make you happy, Rose. I knew how desperate you were for a family. And it was the least I could do.'

In the distance, from his study, there came the tinny sound of his mobile.

'What do you mean, the least you could do?' she asked.

Matthew went to the door. 'I have to get that.'

She got up and followed him along the corridor, the mobile increasing in volume. 'You didn't answer me, Matthew. The least you could do for Juliet, having made her pregnant?'

Just as Matthew reached his desk, his mobile stopped ringing. He picked it up and checked the caller display, exasperation darkening his face. 'I don't know who that was,' he fumed. 'And I'm expecting an important call.' He tossed his mobile on to the desk and gripped the back of his chair. 'I told you I wasn't having an affair, God damn it.' His voice was raised. 'Neither did I push Juliet off a cliff. And I wish you'd pull yourself together. I did it for you, Rose, to give you the baby you desperately wanted.'

She stared at him, something astounding shimmering at the edge of her mind. When her voice came out it didn't sound like hers. 'Did you not think, Matthew, that we might have had one of our own?'

His easy confidence faltered. 'Well, we weren't, were we?'

She felt a coldness crawling up her spine. In spite of the fuzz of the wine, she saw a guarded apprehension in her husband's face that alerted her. 'You seem very sure of that, Matthew,' she said, her voice soft. 'Did you know for definite we weren't having any ourselves?' Then she raised her voice: 'Did you?'

'It scarcely matters now, in the overall scheme of things,' he said, his eyes flickering to his laptop screen. 'It was another lifetime ago.'

'What scarcely matters? Why did you accept Juliet's baby so readily?' she pressed.

'I told you, I was only too happy to make sure you had your dream of motherhood.'

'Because you couldn't give it to me,' she said,

456

taking a wild leap into the very worst of her dark corners. 'You couldn't give me a baby.'

'Well . . . I didn't know for sure . . .' He stared at his mobile, as though he was willing it to ring.

Her head felt light. For a minute she couldn't breathe. Her voice, when she managed to speak, was thin and whispery. 'Is this — are you telling me — What do you mean, Matthew?' She found it impossible to grasp what he was saying.

'Look,' he snapped, 'if you really have to know, I'll spell it out, will I? There was no affair with Juliet, and James is not my biological son. I had a rather bad case of mumps the year before we married.'

She shook her head. 'I don't remember that.'

'I told you it was tonsillitis.'

'*What?* Why did you lie to me, Matthew?'

'Because I had to. Because I was told there was a good possibility that I couldn't father a child. But it worked out all right, didn't it? You had your baby.'

Unable to believe what she was hearing, she scrabbled for words. 'You mean you knew, when you married me, that there was a good chance we'd never have a family?'

'Not for definite. But when nothing happened after we'd been trying for more than a year, I — um — guessed it was my fault.'

She was sinking into icy water. It was closing around her, so cold she could hardly breathe. 'But how — how could you have married me, knowing that? Knowing how much I wanted children?'

'I told you, I didn't know for certain. I thought you loved me for myself and not for my capacity to give you kids.'

'Yes, but we talked about having a family.' Her breathing was laboured. 'You knew how I felt about that and you said *nothing*?'

'Rose, it was years ago,' he entreated. 'Look how far we've come. I took you away from that crappy job and working-class Ballymalin. I gave you everything you could wish for. Stop looking at me as though I'm the devil himself. It scarcely matters any more, does it?'

She felt faint. 'I can't believe this. I gave up my job . . . my *life* . . . to marry you and have your children.'

'I'm sorry if it's a shock,' Matthew said, uncertainty in his eyes, 'but everything turned out fine, didn't it? We have our son, even if it wasn't quite how we expected to. I've spent my life making up for it, giving you everything I could.'

'I can't believe your arrogance. Why did you marry me? *Why*?'

'I loved you. I still do.'

Something snapped inside Rose. She was still trapped in that freezing water, but now she struggled to free herself instead of allowing it to overpower her. 'No, you don't. You didn't,' she said, her voice quivering. 'If you'd really loved me, you'd have told me the truth. You married me because you thought I'd be a good, placid wife, happy to cook and clean and iron your shirts, there in the background of your life, nothing better than an unpaid skivvy and an unpaid

458

prostitute. Someone who thought it was *her* fault when no children arrived . . . someone who wouldn't dare question the virility of ambitious, egotistical, fucking brilliant Mr Matthew Moore.'

'Jesus, Rose, that's a bit over the top.'

'I haven't even started,' she stormed. Trembling with shock and rage, she continued, her voice hoarse, 'I used to wonder, Matthew, what was driving you onwards and upwards. Why you weren't content with your lot. I used to wonder why you clashed with Juliet at times. I thought it was some kind of unfulfilled passion running between you. Now I know it was envy on your part. Because she did something you could never do. She'd had a child of her own. You owed her big-time for getting you out of a stinking big hole, and you resented that because you didn't like being beholden to her. It all makes perfect sense to me now.'

'You're talking rubbish.'

His mobile rang.

'Leave it,' she barked.

His hand reached out, but she was too quick for him. She grabbed his shrieking phone and lifted her arm.

'Rose. Don't.'

'Don't what?' For someone who'd been drowning a moment ago, she felt an amazing surge of power.

'Put that down.'

'It's payback time, Matthew.'

'For what? I gave you what you wanted.'

'No. You gave me what suited *you*. You deceived me. You married me under false pretences. You

459

lied to me by omission.' She brought down his mobile with such force that it crashed against the keys of his laptop and was instantly silenced. 'And that's just for starters.'

'For fuck's sake, Rose, are you mad?'

'Yes, I am, I'm as mad as hell — and do you know something? It feels bloody great! It feels brilliant!' The words tumbled out, like a volcano spewing lava. 'All these years I felt guilty for not giving you a family. I thought *I* was to blame. That I was doing something wrong, or wasn't good enough to have a child of my own. All these years I've lived with the fear of being found out over James. Sometimes it made me feel savage inside. And it got much worse in the last few weeks. But guess what, Matthew? I feel liberated at last. I'm not afraid of anything any more.' Her eyes darted about his desk and she picked up his laptop so swiftly that the power cord was yanked out. Then she hurled it across the room so that it hit the glass doors of the antique bookcase, shattering them.

He stared at her, his face pale. 'You've gone too far this time.'

'You're the one who went too far, Matthew. You've forgotten who you are — that's if you were ever anyone to begin with. And don't let me get started on your integrity bullshit, or God knows what damage I might do to that monstrosity of a kitchen.'

She knew from the shock in his eyes that he had finally grasped the depth of her rage.

'You have to calm down,' he urged. 'We can talk about this, work it out.'

'Don't you get it? It's too late,' she cried. 'I've been living on a fault line for years. Now I've finally fallen through the crack, right to the bottom, and guess what, I'm still alive. At last I'm making sense of me. Nothing worse can happen.'

'Yes, it can,' he said, his jaw tight.

'Oh? And what might that be?'

'You'd want to be very careful.' He spoke to her as though he was dealing with a particularly fractious child. He started to move around the table towards her. 'You'd want to calm down, chill out, maybe go away for a few days to a relaxing spa. You'd like that, wouldn't you? If you don't cool down you might say something you regret and, who knows, word might get back to James.'

'Ah, yes.' She smiled, standing her ground. 'James. I was wondering when we'd get around to him.'

59

'It's fine, honestly,' Rebecca said to Maria. 'You go ahead and I'll lock up.'

Tuesday afternoon at Olivia Jayne had been quiet, and it was just coming up to a quarter to six when Rebecca told Maria to go home.

'Are you sure?' said Maria. 'You know Amanda likes two of us to be here at a time.'

'Yes, but it's not as if we're going to be deluged with last-minute customers,' Rebecca said. 'I'll be after you shortly.'

After Maria had left, Rebecca refreshed the Mimosa fragrance diffuser and checked the bargain rail. The occasional customer had the happy knack of placing a full-priced dress or shirt on it, then looking for a discount. Outside, the skies were low and grey and the car park in the small shopping complex was slowly emptying. The bookshop next door had already closed for the evening and the chemist would be next. The wine shop on the corner would be open until ten o'clock, and as soon as she locked up the boutique, Rebecca was going to pop in to pick up a couple of bottles of her favourite rioja reserve and some nibbles.

Liam was calling over at seven, and bringing an Indian takeaway. They both knew he would be staying the night, in one of the spare rooms, with Rebecca. She wasn't quite ready yet to take him into the bed she'd shared with Harry, but she couldn't wait to spend the night with him and feel his arms around her.

She'd had the weird feeling all day that she was moving about in the eye of a storm. There had been silence from Rose after her call the previous evening. Funnily enough, she'd half expected to hear from Matthew, angry with her for upsetting his wife. And she hadn't dared to contact Danielle, beyond a couple of texts, afraid of what she might be tempted into saying over the phone.

A few short weeks ago, she would have asked herself what right she had to find happiness in Liam's arms, given the mess that her sister and daughter were caught up in. Now, as she fastened buttons on silk shirts and hung dresses tidily in size order, she felt curiously disengaged from their problems, as though she and Liam existed in their own private bubble, away from whatever was going on around them.

Sometimes she'd felt like this with Harry, that they drew strength from each other against the world.

At five to six, she checked that the back of the shop was locked up, the cash and receipts secured in the safe. She went out into the blustery evening and pulled the shutter across the window, locking it in place. Then she pulled the door shutter halfway down and ducked back inside to fetch her bag, switch on the alarm and turn off the lights.

She was turning off the lights in the small storeroom when she heard the shutter over the door being pushed up, then yanked down again.

'I'm sorry, we're just . . . ' The rest of the sentence dried in her mouth as she turned around and came face to face with Liz Monaghan.

'Liz?' she said. 'Are you okay?'

★ ★ ★

Rose stepped out of the taxi at Spencer Dock and shivered in the blustery wind blowing off the Liffey. For once she didn't have to put on a false mask in front of a camera lens or pretend to be someone she wasn't. The river was running at full tide, the choppy surface mirroring the slate grey sky, against which the arches of the Samuel Beckett Bridge gleamed like bleached bones. She took a deep breath of the salt-laden breeze.

She was amazingly calm as she straightened her shoulders and wove through the oncoming pedestrians, guessing from the high-spirited groups of jeans-clad twenty-somethings making their way down the quays that there was a gig on tonight in the O_2.

Oh, to be young, carefree and heading off to a pop concert. She'd never had that freedom. She'd never travelled the world, or even backpacked around Europe. She'd never watched the sun rise in Paris or the sun set off a Greek island. She'd never spent a gap year in Australia, gone up in a hot-air balloon or risked a parachute jump. At sixteen, she'd gone straight from school into the civil service, and a few years later into marriage with Matthew. Another form of servitude. There had been no such thing as the luxury of finding herself. She'd thought her marriage had been

464

bound by lies, little realising she'd been oblivious to the biggest lie of all: Matthew's false promises.

'You're not going to do anything foolish, are you, Rose?' Matthew had said, the previous night, as she'd marched out of his study and up to their bedroom. She'd ignored him, taking her small travel case out of her dressing room, her hands remarkably steady as she'd folded in clothes and underwear.

'We're in this together,' he'd said. 'You don't want James to hate you, do you?' He was moving around the bedroom, towards her. If he put his arms around her she'd scream.

'All of a sudden that doesn't matter,' she'd said, surprised by how free she felt, how clear it all was, so simple and yet so right. 'The most important thing is that I'll never stop loving him. That won't change, no matter what happens. But now I love him enough to tell him the truth, whatever it costs me.'

She'd walked out of the gilded bedroom and he'd followed her down the stairs.

'This has gone far enough,' he'd said, standing between her and the door, but not laying a finger on her, as though he knew she'd explode. 'Come on, Rose, cut the crap.'

She'd smiled at him. 'That's exactly what I'm doing, Matthew. I'm cutting the crap out of my life. If there's one thing I've realised, with Juliet gone, it's that life is far too short. It only happens once and there are no second chances. For me, this is it.'

As she'd walked out of the door at Belgrave Park, Matthew had stood in the porch, looking as though he expected her to turn tail and come back, but she didn't. Legs shaking, she'd walked up to the junction and hailed a taxi, asking the driver to take her to a business hotel on the outskirts of the city where it was unlikely she'd be recognised.

Without Matthew, nobody had given her a second glance. The receptionist had barely looked at her as she'd asked if Rose had a reservation.

'I don't,' Rose had said.

The receptionist had checked her computer terminal as she ran her fingers over her keyboard. 'We have availability.' She'd smiled a polite smile. 'What's the name?'

'Rose O'Malley.'

It was a long time since she'd been Rose O'Malley and it would take a while to find her again, get to know her. As she'd stood by the desk, something had shimmered in front of her eyes.

The rest of her life.

Now she hurried towards the entrance to the apartment block on Spencer Dock, where James's luxury penthouse took up the top floor.

★ ★ ★

'Hey, lil cuz.'

My heart warmed at the sound of James's voice on the phone. 'Hey, yourself. And what fabulous hotel room in what fabulous part of the world are you calling from now?'

'Would you believe I'm holed up in some

466

crummy flat in Dublin, down by the Liffey?' He laughed.

'You're back,' I said, a wave of homesickness sweeping over me.

'Yeah, I got home yesterday morning, and it's good,' he said.

'I think I'd call a five-star signature penthouse pretty good. You'd have to bolt down your toiletries if I happened to visit.'

'I'd give them to you for free if you happened to visit.'

His words echoed in my heart and I told myself not to make too much of them. It was just James talking to his sort-of little sister.

'I think it'll be a while before I'm home,' I said lightly.

'Pity. I could do with having you around.'

'What for?' My voice cracked.

There was a beat of silence, and then he said, 'It feels weird this time. No Juliet to laugh with, and I don't think I've any idea yet how much I'm going to miss her.'

'I know.'

'You didn't hear any more from your mum, I suppose, about how Juliet died?'

'The investigation's still going on,' I said. 'The last I heard from Mum is that the police are still not sure if she fell or was pushed.'

'Jesus. Pretty rough for Rebecca and my mum. Never mind Juliet. Who the hell would — Christ, if I thought anyone had touched a hair on her head, I'd strangle them myself with my bare hands. Mum's calling over to see me this evening so I'll get the latest from her.'

Suddenly my heart was hammering.

'She said she needs to talk to me,' he went on. 'I'll ask her if The Name can keep up the promo for Juliet's children's charity. It's the least we can do. What's happening to that, do you know?'

'I'm not sure,' I said slowly. 'It'll be a while before her affairs are sorted.'

'Seems a shame to let that slide. There's a job for you, if you ever come home. You could put your marketing skills to work. Anyway, my door buzzer's going so Mum's here. Earlier than I'd expected. I'll catch you later, lil cuz.'

'Thanks, James.'

I looked at his name disappearing off my mobile display as the call ended and something like desolation swept over me.

★ ★ ★

'I'm sorry, Liz, we're closed,' Rebecca said, as the other woman advanced into the boutique, her feline eyes darting about.

'I'm not interested in any of your crappy clothes,' she sneered.

'What do you want?' Rebecca asked, suddenly alert, her skin prickling.

'I want to find out which bitch introduced Juliet Jordan to my father. You or Rose?'

'Your *father*?' Rebecca was perplexed. 'Tom Monaghan?' An image of the tall, attractive doctor who'd lived on the affluent side of Ballymalin popped into her head. He'd been a few years older than her and she'd hardly known him because their paths had rarely crossed. She

468

did remember, though, the hushed gossip when he'd married Annie: people were astonished that kind-hearted Tom had lumbered himself with such a troublesome, vexatious woman.

'Yes, my father. The great Tom Monaghan. Only he wasn't so great after all when he went and had a dirty little affair with that slut Juliet, ruining my mother's life. *And* mine.'

'I don't know what you're talking about.'

'Yes, you do. You must have introduced them. Either you or your sister. How else would they have met?'

'Sorry, Liz, I haven't a clue what you're on about.' Rebecca wondered how quickly she could get rid of her.

'Like hell you don't. I know for a fact that Juliet had an affair with my father. The stress of it landed my mother in a psychiatric hospital.'

'Your mother? But she passed away years ago. Besides . . . ' Rebecca fell silent, deciding it was best not to say that Liz's mother had been well known in Ballymalin for having so-called delicate nerves long before she'd married Tom.

'I *am* talking about years ago,' Liz said. 'I knew my mother was unhappy with her life, and I thought I was somehow to blame. Because of me she was stuck fast in a marriage she couldn't escape from. See?'

She didn't see at all, but Rebecca nodded. Maybe Liz just needed to get something off her chest.

'All along I thought I'd done something wrong by being born.' Suddenly she poked at Rebecca's shoulder with her index finger and Rebecca backed away. 'But when I was emptying the house I found it.'

'Found what?'

'An old photograph of Juliet in an envelope.'

'That doesn't mean anything,' Rebecca said, her head whirling as she tried to make sense of this.

'Not by itself, no,' Liz said, her hand now clenched around the bargain rail so that the knuckles were white. 'But it was in an envelope, hidden in a press, with old hotel bills and bills from a psychiatric hospital . . . It all adds up. Juliet had an affair with my father. And it broke my mother's heart.'

'I don't know anything about this,' Rebecca said, feeling faint. 'And if the photograph is old, how do you know it's Juliet?'

'What about this?' With a flourish, Liz pulled a small photograph out of her jacket pocket and held it so that Rebecca could see the name pencilled on the back. She turned it around, and Rebecca saw her friend smiling at her against a background of a bright blue sky. The way she'd smiled at her years ago. On the beach in Benidorm. She even recalled Juliet haggling over the cheap yellow sunglasses in a local souvenir shop. How the hell had a picture of her in Benidorm ended up in Liz Monaghan's parents' house?

'Where did you get that?' she asked Liz.

'I told you, it was hidden away by my mother. She knew I'd find it in years to come, when I'd be clearing out the house. She must have discovered it in my father's office some time before she died.'

470

Then everything clicked into place.

They'd met at the airport. In the long check-in queue. He'd been in a group of four, all people Rebecca knew, all on the same flight, heading for the same resort.

'I didn't think half of Ballymalin would be on our flight,' she'd grumbled.

'He's a bit of all right,' Juliet had said, eyeing a tall, attractive man.

'Yes, he's lovely,' Rebecca had said, 'but he's married and his wife is very odd. I hope they're not going to the same resort as us.'

'You might as well introduce us.'

'Okay, but after that I'm keeping away from them as I don't want to speak to a single Irish person for the next two weeks . . . '

You knew only half the story, Juliet had said. It had been an affair with a married man, all right, but not a far-flung anonymous cousin of her old boyfriend — Rebecca couldn't even recall his name. It had been someone far closer to home. It had been the unhappily married, good-natured, attractive Tom Monaghan, who had died soon after Christmas, after a long spell in a nursing home.

And all those years ago Rebecca had introduced them. She could easily see how Tom had fallen for the bright, effervescent Juliet and vice versa. She could imagine the sparks flying between them. No wonder Juliet had withheld the truth from her. She'd known her friend would have felt partly responsible for Juliet's predicament in having introduced them, and it would have made the arrangements for the baby a lot more difficult.

James! Was Liz his half-sister? Rebecca couldn't even begin to work out what it meant for him. 'Holy shite.' The words escaped her lips.

'So you did know.' Liz's eyes glittered.

'I didn't,' Rebecca said. 'I don't know anything about this at all.'

Liz leaned in close to her, her eyes blazing. 'You're just as infuriating as she was.'

'What do you mean?' Rebecca asked, a sliver of foreboding creeping up her spine.

'Juliet. When I asked her.'

'When did you talk to her?'

Was this why Juliet had talked of regrets? Had Liz snagged at her uneasy conscience? Rebecca fervently hoped it was, rather than the terrifying thought that hovered in the air. She was aware of how defenceless she was against the height and strength of an angry Liz, almost as defenceless as Juliet would have been on the cliff. She was alone in the shop with her, and no one could see in through the shutters. Her bag, with her mobile tucked away, was down by the far side of the counter. Liz was standing rather threateningly between her and the doorway.

'When were you talking to Juliet?' Rebecca asked once more, blood turning to ice in her veins.

Liz's eyes were suddenly guarded, and Rebecca realised she was doing this all wrong. 'Why don't we go out for a coffee, or a glass of wine, and have a proper chat about it?' she suggested, in the pleasantest voice she could muster. 'I can see how this must have been upsetting for you, Liz. I'm sure there's a rational explanation.'

'That's exactly what she said,' Liz replied, leaning towards her. 'She got the surprise of her life. But she still wouldn't admit anything.'

'When was this? Tell me about it, Liz,' she asked softly, quietly amazed at herself.

'I called her and told her I wanted to do a profile of her, seeing that there was talk of her running for the presidency. She said she was busy and I should make an appointment. Then I said I was keen to prove myself as a serious journalist. I told her I'd love to publicise her charity efforts. Just five minutes? That was clever of me, because she said she hoped to go out for her walk later that evening, so if I could join her then, it was the only free time she had to chat. But when I called to the house I was too early so she even poured me a glass of wine . . . ' Liz's eyes had a faraway look in them that chilled Rebecca to the bone. 'I insisted that she have one as well, and I said a walk would be lovely — I could get to know the real Juliet that way. But that was only a ruse, of course. We hadn't gone too far around the cliff top when I told her I knew about her and my father. But she wouldn't admit it. She wouldn't admit *anything*. She even got cross with me for pretending I wanted an interview. How was I supposed to feel?' Once again, Liz poked Rebecca's shoulder, and continued until she was pinned against the wall.

'I don't think Juliet meant to get cross with you,' Rebecca said, willing herself to remain calm.

'Yes, she did. The slut! She didn't care about my mother, or the crappy childhood I'd had.'

Rebecca found herself rising to her friend's defence: 'Your mother was sick, Liz, even before she married your father. Everyone in Ballymalin knew it. I think your father thought he'd cure her but he couldn't. It wasn't Juliet's fault she landed in a psychiatric hospital. Look, let's go somewhere and talk properly about this.'

'That's exactly what *she* said, about my mother being sick. But it's a lie. I got so angry that I shouted at her. But she still didn't say she was sorry.'

Rebecca's throat almost closed with fear. Every cell in her body turned to water. 'I can understand how angry you must have felt,' she said.

'My mother was a very angry person. Do you know what she used to do to my father? And sometimes me?'

Rebecca shook her head.

'This,' said Liz, drawing back her arm and striking Rebecca hard across the face. 'She hated being stuck in her marriage,' she shouted. She swung her arm the other way and struck her again, harder this time.

'You're a fucked-up bitch,' Rebecca said, through gritted teeth.

'And guess who caused it,' Liz roared, lunging at her.

All of a sudden Rebecca was fighting for her life. She tried to get away from Liz, but she was no match for the taller woman. Liz caught hold of her from behind, one hand gripping her hair, the other her shoulder, and pushed her hard against the end of the bargain rail so her neck was squeezed against the chrome. Rebecca was winded and dazed. Her arms flailed uselessly into the row of clothes, the hangers jangling. She aimed feeble kicks at Liz's shins. Liz pulled her back, almost lifting her off her feet, handling her as though she was a rag doll.

'See? You can't even cry, can you? Juliet had no time to cry out. I don't think she even knew what was happening.' Once again, she shoved Rebecca's neck hard against the chrome rail. Rebecca was so dazed she might have collapsed, except that Liz was holding her. Once again she dragged her back from the brink of unconsciousness. Rebecca dimly noticed she was pulling her further back to propel her even harder against the end of the chrome rail. Through half-closed eyes, she watched the hazy jumble of chrome and clothes rushing towards her, but this time she burrowed her arms into the clothes, clawing at them, her fingers working furiously and instinctively until she'd freed a hanger. As she slumped against the rail, she slid the hanger down between the clothes until she was grasping it with both hands. The minute she felt Liz draw her back again, she lifted the hanger and pushed it back as hard as she could over her head, in the direction of Liz's face, until she felt it connect.

Liz let go of her, which gave Rebecca one split second. One second to make a dash to the doorway, half running, half crawling, to push up the shutter enough to crawl out, feeling Liz's hand snaking around her ankle. Supporting herself on her hands, she aimed a kick with her free leg, and then she was gulping cold, fresh air, her heart thumping as she crawled on to the pavement, lurched to her feet and staggered to the safety of the chemist.

The girls in the shop sat her down and phoned the police. But when they went up to the boutique, all three of them, to fetch Rebecca's bag and her mobile so she could call Amanda and Liam, the shop was empty.

60

Liz took another slug of neat vodka. It burned her throat and helped another layer of comforting fuzz to settle around her. She was in the front room of the house in Ballymalin, half sitting, half slumped on the sofa. Outside, the bushes were rattling in the breeze and it was getting dark. Inside, the house was full of shadows and silence. She hadn't bothered to switch on the lamps, the light slanting in from the hall more than enough for her. She had plenty of tablets and plenty of vodka. She wondered if she'd pass out from too much drink before she managed to complete the job.

There was no point in anything any more.

She couldn't sleep and she couldn't eat. Every time she closed her eyes she saw Juliet in the moment before she fell. The look in the other woman's eyes haunted her. She hadn't meant to push her. She certainly hadn't meant to kill her. Afterwards, she'd tried to blank it out, convince herself it hadn't happened. But Juliet's eyes hadn't allowed for that.

That was why she'd made sure Rebecca Ryan was facing away from her as she'd bashed her against the clothes rail. Somehow that had gone wrong, too. She hadn't meant to hurt Rebecca any more than she'd intended to hurt Juliet, but they'd fired up her temper so much that she'd lost control.

Who did they think she was that they couldn't just admit the truth? Why had they been so dismissive of her? What had they been afraid of?

Juliet had ended up plunging down a cliff, making things messier than ever, and Rebecca had almost broken Liz's nose. After Rebecca had escaped and run for help, Liz had rushed out to her car and driven on instinct to Ballymalin.

She wondered how long it would take the police to figure out she wasn't in Harold's Cross. She hoped she'd be unconscious before they arrived here. She'd never realised she'd feel quite so sad and lonely near the end. Had her mother felt like this before she'd lost consciousness? Had Juliet? Then again, she'd had good friends, friends who clearly loved her.

Her father must have loved Juliet to risk an affair with her, given how angry her mother could be.

Her father. He'd never got over her mother's death and Liz had turned her back on him in the aftermath, as if blaming him in some odd way.

But there was someone who would have loved her, Liz realised, if she'd allowed him to. If things had been different. Her mobile sat on the table in front of her. It would take a minute to press a couple of buttons and bring up her emergency contact number. But she couldn't do it. How could she drag Gavin into all this? It was far, far too late, now that she had murder on her conscience, no matter how much he said he loved her.

And no one would believe she hadn't meant it to happen.

478

She took another tablet and lifted the vodka to her lips, tilting her head to take a decent long slug. One more should do the trick. Maybe two.

And then she saw it, shimmering against the dark shadows in the corner of the room. It was the figure of a woman, not grey or frightening, not bloodied or terrifying. She looked ethereally beautiful. And her eyes were smiling.

Liz froze. She was still sitting there, the bottle poised against her mouth, when from outside the flash of revolving blue lights lit up the room, scattering the shadows and anything within them. She waited quietly, ignoring the lone tear that trickled down her face.

61

As luck would have it, the Friday-evening flight from Rome to Dublin was delayed and I had to sit, my irritation rising, with at least a hundred impatient travellers in the holding area beside the boarding gates for more than half an hour. Mum's call had been mystifying, and I was dying to get home to find out what was really going on.

'I'll pay for your flight,' she'd said hoarsely, when she'd called me on Wednesday evening. 'I know it'll be expensive as you're booking it at the last minute, but just get home this weekend. I have to see you.'

She'd sounded as if she'd spent at least three weeks crying.

'I'm not that hard up,' I'd said. 'Aren't you going to tell me what's wrong?'

Mum gave a heavy sigh. 'There's a lot going on, Danielle, and I have bad news that I'd rather tell you face to face than have you come across it online.' She paused.

'What is it?'

'It seems Juliet *was* pushed off that cliff,' she said. 'For some reason Liz Monaghan, the gossip-column woman, was with Juliet that evening. She was hoping to write a piece about her but freaked out when they were walking around the headland. Next thing . . . '

The hairs rose on the back of my neck. '*What?* I don't believe you.'

Mum was silent. After a while she said, 'It's a long story, and I want to see you and talk to you about it. So far it hasn't got into the papers as the police have a lid on it while they investigate further, but it's only a matter of time before it reaches the networks. Has . . . has James been on to you?'

'No, he was supposed to call me back the other evening but he didn't.' I'd sounded defensive — I was nervous of her mentioning his name, knowing what she knew.

'I see.' Another silence.

'Does he know what happened?'

'Look, Danielle, I'll see you on Friday night.'

The minute Mum had ended the call I'd tried James's mobile, but he seemed to have disconnected it as it didn't even go to voicemail. Now I felt even more uneasy. I'd tried to call him again on Thursday and the same thing happened. When I'd texted Mum my flight details, I made myself ask if he was okay. She texted back that he was fine. At least he was alive and well, but something big was definitely amiss. My impatience was spilling over as I joined the queue shuffling down the grey tunnel to the plane.

And I knew for sure something was wrong when Liam Corrigan was waiting for me in the arrivals hall at Dublin airport. Without Mum.

'What's going on, Liam? Where's Mum?' I asked, alarm mounting inside me when he picked up my weekend case and led the way not to the car park but to the coffee shops and sitting area.

'She's fine. Take a seat and I'll explain in a minute.' He smiled at me and went to the counter to order two coffees. I had no choice but to wait until he returned.

'Your mother is taking it easy at home for a few days,' he said. 'She asked me to collect you, just to put you in the picture. She doesn't want you to get too much of a shock when you see her. You see, Danielle, she was attacked in the shop by Liz Monaghan on Tuesday evening, but she's fine now.'

'*What?*' I spluttered into my coffee and pushed the cup away.

He told me then, glossing over the details, about the attack, then Mum managing to break free and running to the chemist. The assistants had called the police, and when they went to Olivia Jayne, no one was there and nothing had been disturbed. Then Mum had called Liam and Amanda, both of whom rushed over. As far as Amanda and the girls in the chemist were concerned, an intruder had broken in as Mum was closing up. But Mum had told the police about Liz, and what she'd said to her, and they had called the detectives involved in Juliet's case. Mum had had her injuries checked out, and afterwards had given a full statement to the detectives.

I was numb with shock, but I knew my questions would have to wait, for right then my main concern was Mum.

'Rebecca has bruising to her neck, and a black eye, but she'll make a perfect recovery,' Liam said.

I could see anxiety flickering in his eyes. 'I hope you've been taking good care of her,' I said.

'I have, and I'm going to keep on taking care

of her, if she lets me. I hope you don't have a problem with that?'

I met his gaze head on. 'I'll only have a problem if you don't look after her properly. I want Mum to be happy.'

'You're your mother's daughter.' He smiled.

A few weeks ago I would have dissed that remark. Now I glowed with it. 'She's very special,' I said, 'and I love her to bits.'

'So do I.'

'Make sure you tell her that,' I said.

★　★　★

Even though I'd been prepared, it was hard to hide my shock when I saw my beautiful mum with so many bruises discolouring her jaw and neck, never mind the black eye. I flew into her arms, careful not to hurt her.

'You should see the other guy,' she joked, sitting on the sofa in the conservatory, surrounded by a forest of flowers and magazines.

'Where's Liz?' I asked.

'She's still in hospital. In the psychiatric unit. She tried to . . . to take her own life, but they caught her in time.'

'What a pity,' I fumed. 'I can't believe what she did, Mum. She must have been crazy. I hope she'll be locked up for life. I presume she's been arrested?'

'She will be. And now, Liam,' she gave him a meaningful look, 'thanks a million for collecting Danielle, but I'll let you head off and see you tomorrow.'

Liam gave her a kiss and a hug, and he hugged me, too, before he left, then gave me a warm smile that put me on guard. He knew whatever there was to know, I guessed. And I was going to find out pretty soon.

I braced myself when Mum asked me to get a bottle of wine and two glasses, then patted the sofa beside her and asked me to sit down. 'I need to tell you exactly why Liz Monaghan did what she did.'

'I always knew she had a screw loose,' I said flippantly — the grave look in Mum's eyes had told me I was going to be well and truly shocked.

'She has big problems, all right,' Mum said. 'She's had an unhappy life and she lost her own mother tragically when she was only sixteen.'

'As if that makes it okay.'

'Anyway, Danielle, I need to start at the beginning, so you'll understand everything. All this goes back years . . . back to the time, I guess, when Rose and I met Juliet on the train and we picked up the threads of our friendship.'

'Are we back to that story?'

'Yes,' Mum said gently. 'But this time I want to tell you the other side of it. And, please, don't hate any of us for what we did.'

I laughed. 'Of course not. How could I?'

It was the last time I laughed. It was after midnight before Mum got to the end of the story, about Juliet, James, Liz, and what had happened between Rose and Matthew, then Rose calling over to James's apartment to tell him the truth after her row with Matthew.

James had gone ballistic. It was just after he'd

484

been talking to me. And I knew then why I hadn't been able to reach him on his mobile.

That was the moment I put my head in my hands and begged Mum not to tell me any more.

I don't know how my legs carried me up the stairs to my bedroom. I felt so fragile I thought I was going to disappear. My hands seemed transparent and my legs felt like water. I only knew I was still alive by the breath coming in and out of me, and the thump of my heart. It was mad, I thought, how the physical body continued to exist after the rest of you was smashed up. I was still awake at three o'clock in the morning, trying to make sense of the way every single part of my life had been torn asunder and flattened into microscopic dust.

I must have slept eventually because when I woke up and reached for my mobile, it was eleven o'clock the following day. I got out of bed automatically. This is how a robot must feel, I decided, as I showered and dressed. Then I saw how ridiculous that idea was: robots had no feelings because they were mechanical objects. I wondered if I'd go through the rest of my life like an unfeeling machine.

But when I caught the scent of coffee coming from the kitchen, my mouth watered. I went downstairs to find Mum at the table with a light scarf wrapped around her neck, and her black eye all the colours of the rainbow.

She gave me a tentative smile. 'I'm glad you're still here,' she said.

'I am, just about,' I said, unable to return her smile. I poured a mug of coffee and sat down opposite her. 'I don't hate you, Mum,' I said, 'but I'm all over the place and I need to get my head straight.'

'Of course.'

'Where's Rose now?' I asked, still piecing stuff together.

'She's staying in a hotel while she decides what do to. She called over on Wednesday and we had a long chat.'

I took a few sips of coffee. 'I can't believe she's walked out on Matthew, never mind had the guts to come clean with James.'

'She says she found the courage from somewhere inside her. She said that James deserved to know the truth and she loved him enough to risk his anger.'

I sipped more coffee and silently applauded my aunt.

'She's upset, of course, that he went mad, but she's still glad she told him,' Mum continued. 'She's not going to rush into anything, and for the first time in years she feels free of the burden that was eating her up inside.'

'Do you think she'll go back to Matthew?' I asked, helping myself to a croissant.

'I honestly don't know, Danielle. If she does, it'll be on her terms.'

'I suppose his campaign has gone down the tubes.'

'I'm not sure about that either, but it hadn't really started. I haven't been talking to him, but I gather from Rose that he's devastated she's walked out and he's more concerned with saving his marriage, if there's anything left to save.'

'Good. I guess he does love her, then.'

'I don't know what kind of media fallout we can expect, but none of us will be talking to the press.'

'No.'

We fell silent, while I finished the croissant and toyed with the burning questions I was terrified of asking. And, full credit to my mum, she guessed what I needed to know but was afraid to voice.

'James is over at Verbena View,' she said.

'Oh?'

'Yes. He called in to see me on Thursday for a chat. He wanted to hear the story again from my point of view. Unfortunately I had more shocks in store for him as he didn't know I'd been hurt. Neither did he know about Liz Monaghan and that connection . . . I didn't breathe a word of our conversation, Danielle. He's . . . ' She paused.

'He's what, Mum?'

'He's very upset and confused. In shock, I suppose. He told me he's never talking to Rose or Matthew again. He understands what they did, years ago, even if they did ignore the law, but he can't believe that they hadn't the guts to tell him the truth before now. He's even more broken-hearted now that Juliet's gone.'

'In that case,' I asked, my voice shaking a little, 'what's he doing at Verbena View?'

'I gave him the spare keys,' Mum said. 'The police finished with the house on Wednesday and handed them back to me. It's still as Juliet left it, full of her presence. I suggested he spend a

487

couple of days there, among her things, remembering the good times he had with her. I thought it might help him to feel close to her and come to terms with her in this new light, to cherish her memory and appreciate her love. It may give him some kind of consolation, if that's possible.'

I was crying by the time she'd finished talking. 'I have to see him,' I said, my voice thin and jittery.

Mum's hand came across the table and covered mine. 'Of course you do,' she said. 'Take my key in case he won't answer the door.'

We sat in silence for a while as her hand rested on mine, all the energy and warmth of her love flowing into me.

I wondered if I could do the same for James.

62

A torn remnant of police tape, still caught in the gates to Juliet's house, fluttered in the breeze. I parked in a corner of the driveway beside James's car. The front windows of the house glinted with pale sunshine, the sky was a faint blue, scored with jet trails, and the air tasted fresh and tangy.

I'd already texted James to say I was on the way, but I didn't know if he was checking his mobile. I wasn't surprised when he didn't answer the door, but I pressed the bell and called through the letterbox to warn him that I was there. Then my shaky fingers fitted the key into the lock and I went in, my blood pounding in my ears.

Mum was right. The house echoed with Juliet's spirit, and it was as warm and inviting as ever, not in the least bit spooky. I wouldn't have been afraid to be there on my own. I passed down the hall, echoes of her laughter wrapping around me, and in the kitchen her smiling face was everywhere.

My throat closed when I saw the calendar pinned to the corkboard, the one I'd given her last Christmas. It still displayed the month of March, and the picture was one James had taken of Juliet and me against a backdrop of the Blue Mountains in Sydney. I'd even had my wedding printed in the box for 17 March.

Beyond the table, the patio doors were folded back, and I could see the top of James's head as he sat in one of Juliet's patio chairs, facing the back garden and the crystalline light of the sea beyond.

Something was knocking on the wall of my chest. After a minute I realised it was my heart.

'James, it's me,' I said.

He remained motionless. I walked out on to the patio. He was slumped in the chair, legs stretched out, eyes fastened on the blue-grey infinity, while a muscle flexed in his unshaven jaw. He ignored me as I pulled out a seat and sat alongside him.

'James, your little cuz wants to talk to you,' I said, not knowing how I managed to speak.

No reaction whatsoever.

'I know you're shocked and upset. I understand.'

Still a stony silence.

'I'm here to help.'

I waited. He continued to ignore me. I tried a different approach. 'James? What kind of crap is this? You can't just pretend I'm not here.' I was hoping to jolt him out of his silence.

It didn't work. I racked my brains, wondering how to get through to him.

'Juliet loved you very much,' I began, stumbling over my words. 'Remember we were talking, when you visited me in Rome, about the long conversation I had with Juliet in Sydney? When she said she had big regrets? She told me there was someone she loved very much but she wasn't in a position to tell him. I thought at the

490

time she might have been involved with a man, but looking back on our conversation now, I realise she was talking about you.'

I stole a look at him. Nothing about his face had changed. I stared beyond the light of the sea to the folds of the Dublin mountains, shimmering on the far-off horizon, and wondered what to say for the best.

'Juliet told me she didn't have the courage to listen to her heart at an important time in her life,' I went on. 'And in case you were too shocked to take on board anything my mum said to you on Thursday, Juliet was talking to her in the week before she died about putting the past to some kind of rights. Unfortunately,' my voice softened, 'she ran out of time. I'm glad to say I've plenty of time. I have the whole evening just to sit here talking to you.'

There was still no response from the man sitting beside me and my courage was faltering.

'I know you're very angry with Rose and Matthew,' I said. 'I don't know what to say except they loved you as best they could. No way would Juliet have given you to them, to love and cherish and take care of, unless she was pretty sure she could trust them to do a damn good job. Which they did.'

He was still silent.

'As time went on it must have seemed impossible to tell you the truth. I'm not surprised Rose ended up having a nervous breakdown. This is exactly the kind of situation that she and Matthew were terrified of. You, their cherished son, refusing to talk to them, ever again.'

491

My heart quickened when James ran a hand over his stubbly chin and closed his eyes. I didn't know what kind of pictures he was seeing. I wondered about the girl in his life, the beautiful, talented and charming girl he'd told me about in Rome. The spark he'd hoped would burn out. But I was going to tell him what Juliet hadn't had time for. I was going to risk all for love. And it was easier to speak when he had his eyes closed.

'It was my fault that Juliet changed her will in favour of us,' I began tentatively. 'She saw me, at Christmas, when . . . ' The rest of the sentence died in my throat, because he finally opened his eyes. My heart lurched when I saw the tenderness in them.

'How could it have been your fault?' he asked.

I took a deep breath. 'Juliet caught me looking at you, just after we were joking about the wedding music.'

'So?'

I wasn't sure how to do this. I heard the echo of Juliet telling me to make every moment of my life count, and this, surely, was as important as it would get. 'It was the way she saw me looking at you. Like this . . . ' Suddenly I had the courage to face him head on, and I gazed at him, my eyes roving slowly across every contour in his face as though it meant the world to me. I absorbed every part of it, the slight grooves in his wide forehead, and his suddenly guarded deep blue eyes. I let my gaze linger on his soft mouth, then down to his square chin, my own eyes full of longing, full of desire, and then at last I spoke the words that Juliet had never been able to, the words I had thought I could never voice.

'I want you to know that I love you, James,' I said. 'You're the reason I called off my wedding. I knew here, at Christmas, that I couldn't marry Conor because of how I felt about you. And I love you enough to risk making the biggest fool of myself. I don't care if you think I'm mad, or speaking out of turn, but I'm not going to have the same kind of regrets that Juliet had. I know you just think of me as your honorary sister, your nuisance of a cousin, but — '

'I don't,' he said, looking at me.

My eyes locked with his. There was a moment of silence when nothing else existed, not even the running of the sea, because of the way James was looking at me. As though I was beautiful, talented and charming. As though he loved and desired me. As the world slowly moved again, I scented the salty breeze riffling through the bushes, I felt the light coming off the sea on my face and I blinked. I heard two gulls call as they wheeled into the air. And all my raw, spiky nerve endings healed so that they glowed and sparked, and my heart rose into my throat.

'When . . . when did this happen?' I asked.

'I've always loved you, Dani,' he said. 'Didn't you know? You mean the world to me. You always have. I think Juliet guessed how I felt because she would have caught me looking at you. But from the time you were sixteen, there was always some guy in your life. You had a right procession of them, all dancing attendance on you, and then you went and hooked up with Conor . . . and,

493

anyway, it would have been a little messy between us, to say the least.'

'Those guys? James, you've come between me and every man I've ever known. I tried really hard to make a go of it with Conor because I thought I couldn't have you. Then I realised that marrying him would be wrong. But it's not messy any more,' I said, rising to my feet and going across to where he was sitting.

Juliet's tall and beautiful son.

Mr Justice Henry Jordan's beautiful grandson.

The man I loved.

I put my arms around his shoulders and kissed the side of his face, my heartbeat thrumming in my ears.

He put his hand up, caught my arm and said, 'I've wanted you for ever, but I'm not in a good place right now, Dani. I feel too dark and down to impose myself on you. You deserve better than this.'

'Better than this?' I asked, moving around in front of him, putting my cheek close to his, feeling his breath on my face, his skin against mine. 'I'm in the most perfect spot in the world with the man I love. What more could I want? Juliet can't tell you she loves you, but I will, over and over. Every day, for the rest of my life.'

I drew back slightly, touched his mouth with my fingertips, and something rippled across his face. His eyes filled with tears. Then he turned his head so that his face was cradled in my hand and the tears slipped through my fingers.

'Whatever place you're in, I'm with you,' I said, just before I kissed his mouth.

KT-441-214

THE RECOVERY OF EUROPE

From Devastation to Unity

RICHARD MAYNE

THE RECOVERY OF EUROPE

From Devastation to Unity

WEIDENFELD AND NICOLSON

5 WINSLEY STREET LONDON W I

To my Father
and
the memory of my Mother

Stockton - Billingham
LIBRARY
Technical College

20572
940

© Richard Mayne 1970

All rights reserved. No part of this publication may be reproduced,
stored in a retrieval system, or transmitted, in any form or by any
means, electronic, mechanical, photocopying, recording or otherwise, without the prior permission of the Copyright owner.

SBN 297 00156 6

Printed in Great Britain by Willmer Brothers Limited, Birkenhead

CONTENTS

A Generation of Change

Ask nothing of history except the past itself. *Ernest Renan*[1]

Man is incredibly forgetful of his ancestors' living conditions and incredibly ungrateful for technological progress.
Jean Fourastié[2]

To most men, experience is like the stern lights of a ship, which illumine only the track it has passed. *S. T. Coleridge*[3]

If it works, it's obsolete.   *Anon., c. 1950*[4]

IN the world of today, we are all apprentices. Once, when change was less rapid, the only true novices were the young; for their elders, 'experience' was the consolation-prize for sheer survival into middle age. Now, old and young start level, because a single generation has transformed our universe. The fact is so familiar that we tend to overlook it. Like drivers on an express highway, we forget how fast we are moving: our reflexes were trained at lower speeds. Time and again, statesmen whose formative years were the nineteen-thirties have found that 'experience' can be a fallible guide. Yet just because the men who built the postwar world were survivors from its predecessor, any contemporary historian has a preliminary duty to look backwards—not to seek analogies or lessons in the past, but to make clear how profoundly it differs from the present.

The task seems simple; yet its very simplicity is baffling. Those old enough to remember even the end of the nineteen-thirties may find it hard to realize vividly how remote that decade has become. Old fashion plates and family photographs reveal archaic strangers who were once our parents—or ourselves. Newsreels reanimate a restless Neville Chamberlain, with umbrella, wing collar, and moustache. Newspaper files preserve the moment's fears and crises, mummified in the language of thirty years ago. 'I used a lot of my favourite words,' wrote a well-known 'thirties' novelist some time later, recalling a conversation from 1934: '*Gauleiter*, solidarity, *démarche*, dialectic, *Gleichschaltung*, infiltration, *Anschluss*, realism, *tranche*, *cadre*.'[5] In a later generation, he might have written 'apparatchik, confrontation, détente, credibility, charisma, massive, polycentrism, software, option, crunch'. Reading today's newspapers, a Rip van Winkle awaking from thirty years' sleep would be bewildered by a whole new alphabet of technological, economic and political change:

apartheid	JFK	Sputnik
Benelux	Kinshasa	Terylene
Comecon	laser	UNESCO
Dounreay	Mach 2	Vietcong
Eurocrat	NATO	WEU
FAO	overkill	Xerox
GATT	Pakistan	Yalta
Hiroshima	Quisling	Zimbabwe
Iron Curtain	Rapacki Plan	

With a new vocabulary, he would also face new surroundings. To restore even everyday life to what it was thirty years ago, a number of familiar objects would have to be subtracted from the present: nylon stockings, after-shave lotion, selective weed-killers, automatic gear-shifts, motels, credit cards, supermarkets, frozen foods, tape-recorders, long-playing records. Some are relative newcomers. The mixed blessing of the transistor may be said to date from 1948, when Brattain and Bardeen produced the pioneer study that baptized it. Jet aircraft, atomic energy, rockets and missiles, artificial satellites, masers and lasers, DDT, various antibiotics—all are partly the product of wartime or postwar research. But just as the transistor has an earlier origin in the work on semi-conductors published by A. H. Wilson in 1931, so the best known of today's seeming novelties already existed in embryo at least a generation ago. What is really new is their sudden efflorescence.

Washing-machines, for instance, were first patented as long ago as 1780, and first began to be built in the mid-nineteenth century. It was a hundred years before they came into household use in Europe; but within two decades there were some twenty-five million in Britain, France, Germany, Italy, Belgium, the Netherlands and Luxembourg.[6] The beginnings of television go back to the nineteen-twenties: in London, the Baird company first put out experimental programmes as early as 1929 from a studio in Long Acre and a transmitter in Oxford Street; and the BBC began a regular service from 1936 to 1939. Within twenty years of World War II, there were 13 million television sets in Britain, over 40 million in Western Europe, nearly 70 million in the United States, and 160 million in the world.[7] Plastics, likewise, had a lengthy history before their recent dizzy growth. The term first came to be used in the nineteen-twenties to describe such veteran man-made substances as celluloid and bakelite. Accustomed to these, some people were surprised or sceptical when experts in the early nineteen-forties predicted a 'Plastic Age', complete with plastic tiles, toys and table-tops, mugs, spoons and toilet articles, glues, flooring, pipes, clothes, shoes, book-covers, and even plastic sailboats. Fifteen years later, the experts were vindicated. 'It is astonishing,' wrote two of them, 'to find how far our prophecies have been fulfilled.'[8]

Similar astonishment has been caused in more spectacular fields. In 1938, even Ernest Lawrence, the inventor of the cyclotron, remained very sceptical about the practical possibilities of 'subatomic energy'. 'We are aware,' he said, 'of no greater prospect of destroying nuclear matter for power, than of cooling the ocean . . . and extracting the heat.' Yet in the following winter, nuclear fission was achieved and proved; 1945 saw the first atomic explosions; and by 1951 experimental quantities of electricity were being produced by nuclear means. Within a further fifteen years, despite delays and disappointments, the world's output was already $16\frac{1}{2}$ million kilowatt-hours, more than half of it in Western Europe.[9]

Space research, however, is the subject whose prophets have been most notably overtaken by events. In 1955 Sir George Thomson, the winner of the Nobel Prize for physics, wrote that 'there are many difficulties to inter-planetary travel besides the obvious one of getting off the earth, but there seems to be nothing that is really fundamental and one cannot help feeling confident that in the next fifty to a hundred years the ingenuity of engineers will have overcome them'. Only two years later, the Soviet Union put into orbit the first man-made satellite, Sputnik. This had been predicted, accurately, by another expert writing in 1955; but the latter's further forecasts were too cautious by several years. The year 1957, not 1960, saw the first animal sent into space; in 1961, not 1965, the first human cosmonaut circled the earth; in 1962, three years ahead of expectation, the first television relay satellite came into service. By 4 October 1967, the tenth anniversary of Sputnik, nearly 600 satellites had been launched by the United States, the Soviet Union, France, Britain and Canada. One rocket had reached Venus; a dozen had landed on the moon, and samples of its soil were soon to be collected by human visitors for examination on earth. The lunar landscape had been photographed as if it were the Sahara, and the planet earth as if it were the moon. Over a thousand man-made objects and fragments were in orbit, including nearly 300 artificial satellites, a third of them still transmitting signals. By the nineteen-seventies the total was to reach

3

7000. In all, about 150 tons of miscellaneous hardware were rotating in the skies.[10]

But even the headlong rapidity of the space race is only the most dramatic instance of what has happened in almost all fields of technology. For centuries, by comparison with our own day, many of life's material foundations scarcely seemed to alter. Empires rose and fell, dynasties succeeded each other, administrative groupings and methods changed, and frontiers were moved back and forth, often at great human cost. Within this shifting framework progress was discernable. Architecture, dress, weapons, tools, foodstuffs, language and thought all evolved. Agriculture improved, towns were built, commerce spread, prosperity grew, knowledge increased: yet the pace of change was relatively slow. Men invented few new substances and discovered few new sources of energy. The fastest means of travel remained a galloping horse. Then, with steel and the steam engine, came the first industrial revolution. The curve of technological change revealed itself as exponential: its imperceptible gradient began to rise quite sharply. Today, with plastics and electronics, we are learning to live on its vertiginous upward leap. Two centuries elapsed between the age of Copernicus and that of James Watt; one century between Watt and Michael Faraday; half a century between Faraday and the Wright brothers; a quarter of a century between the Wright brothers and Einstein. Since then, the intervals between major landmarks have grown ever shorter. New inventions snowball, themselves providing high-speed instruments that hasten further research. Even the milli-second is now no symbol of rapidity. Thirty years ago, the fastest computer took one hundredth of a second to process a single elementary datum. Its present-day counterpart takes one thousand-millionth of a second.[11] 'A new sense of time,' it is said, 'was one of the outstanding psychological features of the industrial revolution.'[12] One product of today's technological revolution is a new sense of speed.

In the lives of statesmen and citizens, speed makes its greatest impact through travel by air. In a single generation, this has become so commonplace that an effort is needed to recall its comparative novelty. The first British statesman to use an aircraft was Andrew Bonar Law, who flew on his rare visits to the Versailles peace conference after World War I.[13] Neville Chamberlain first travelled by air when he went to Munich to meet Adolf Hitler on 15 September 1938.[14] Cordell Hull, US Secretary of State during World War II, made his first short journey by air in 1943.[15] The first transatlantic passenger service—by flying-boat—was inaugurated in 1939; but six years later, when President Harry S. Truman wanted to fly home from Europe after the Potsdam

4

conference, his advisers vociferously forbade it: 'They all yell their heads off,' he complained.[16] In America, the traditional whistle-stop rail tour, rather than a series of flying visits, was still a feature of the presidential election campaign in 1952. When Dwight D. Eisenhower became president, his personal aircraft was the piston-driven *Columbine*. Not until 1959 did he travel by jet—'an exhilarating experience', he characteristically recorded.[17]

Exhilarating or not, the experience is now widely shared. The world's commercial airlines at present operate more than a thousand jet aircraft. In these and others, they annually carry some 240 million people, a total of 275,000 million 'passenger-kilometres', about a fifth of them in Western Europe. Since 1958, more travellers have crossed the Atlantic each year by air than by sea. In Britain alone, the number of air passengers has grown by over four thousand per cent in the past thirty years.[18]

Over the same period, moreover, the maximum speed of piloted engines has increased at almost the same rate. In orbit, a manned space capsule travels at about 18,000 miles an hour—some forty times as fast as any prewar aircraft. Even the ordinary passenger flights between London and Paris can break the 1939 world speed record: in a rocket-powered Bell X-15 it has been multiplied by ten. The 1939 land record is not far short of being doubled; and when Donald Campbell was killed on Coniston Water in January, 1967, his Bluebird speedboat was travelling more than twice as fast as his father's had when it set the record for 1939. Meanwhile, as if accelerated by the pace of his own mechanical creations, man himself has attained running speeds once thought quite impossible. On 6 May 1954, Roger Bannister ran the first four-minute mile. Since then, his record has been broken more than fifty times.[19]

But not in every respect has man proved able to respond even so modestly to the pace of change. With dizzy speed, science and technology have provided new tools, new toys and new weapons. Economic life has changed more slowly; and the world's political organization lags further behind still. Most of men's present ills and dangers derive from the fact that their achievements in different fields are out of phase. Only latterly and painfully, that is, has man begun to find ways of using in economics and business the type of intelligence he displays in the laboratory; still less has he yet learned how to apply it to the political relations between states.

One result of scientific progress in the last thirty years has been a further marked improvement in health and sanitation. Even in countries already industrialized, this has made possible a much greater expectation of life. Between 1930 and 1958, the average life-span in England and Wales rose from 58·7 to 67·5 years for men, and from 62·9 to 74 years for women. In Western Europe as a whole the death rate per thousand fell from 13·7 in 1938 to 10·2 in 1958.[20] In Britain, as in other European countries, far fewer people now die of tuberculosis, diphtheria, whooping cough, poliomyelitis and measles, and far more from cancer and the typical afflictions of age—circulatory and respiratory diseases, and vascular lesions of the central nervous system, or 'strokes'. The proportion of older people in our society is therefore on the increase; but while this has led to loneliness and hardship in the midst of a sometimes uncaring society, the economic and political framework has not been disrupted by the benefits of modern medicine, except in so far as the medical services themselves—and their financing—have been put under strain.[21]

Quite different is the situation in the so-called 'developing countries' of Africa, Asia and Latin America. Here, too, better medical care—and even simple hygiene—have helped to reduce the death rate, but far more drastically. As late as 1946, the average expectation of life in India was only 32 years; today it is more like 50. In neighbouring countries, infant mortality has been cut by fifty per cent in fifteen years. The consequence, as in nineteenth-century Britain, has been a startling increase in the total population. In 1939 there were just over 2,000 million people in the world. Thirty years later there were nearly 3,500 million. In a single generation, the rapidity of the change has outstripped the boldest forecasts: it has even overtaken some that have been made since World War II. Over the ages, the time taken for the world's population to double has shrunk from about a thousand years around the time of Christ to about a hundred years in the past century. Current estimates suggest that in the next three decades the population will double again. Even now, two-thirds of humanity are underfed—and it is they, broadly speaking, whose numbers are growing the fastest.[22]

To produce and distribute enough food for the world's present population ought to be technically feasible: few purely scientific obstacles stand in the way. During the past generation, in Europe and the United States, agricultural machinery and chemical fertilizers have greatly increased farm productivity per man and per acre respectively, in many cases by well over 100 per cent. But in the poorer countries, for obvious reasons, both have grown far more slowly: in places, they have actually diminished. Even in Europe, the rise in food production has done little more than parallel the growth of population; and what is true of Europe is true of the world. At this rate, the proportion of those who go hungry may remain constant: but their numbers will undoubtedly grow. If the problem were scientific or technical, it might be solved

relatively quickly—but it is not. It requires a vast and concerted programme of material and financial aid, industrialization, instruction and
birth control; and this in turn requires changes in habits and attitudes
on the part of the rich countries as well as the poor. In short, because
the organization of the world's economy has failed to keep pace with
its technological progress, the plight of the world's poor is almost certain to get worse before it grows better. The term 'developing countries'
is in many cases not merely a euphemism, but a lie. And because politics, finally, lags even further behind economics, the resultant conflicts
could endanger the whole globe.[23]

In the face of existing misery and prospective famine, there is much
that seems repellent in the richer countries' pursuit of their own wealth.
With some exceptions, we tend to behave as if two-thirds of our fellow
human beings were scarcely real to us, although none is more than a
few hours' flying time away. Shall we ourselves appear to future his-
torians as callous and short-sighted as the nobles of the *ancien régime?*
Good intentions, and private or public charity, are surely suspect unless
they lead to adequate large-scale action—but so, on the other hand,
would misdirected guilt be. In fact, no 'developing country' would be
better off if the industrialized nations gave up their apparently selfish
struggle for faster economic growth. Their increasing wealth may widen
the gap between them and the poor: but the attack on world poverty
can only be really effective if the impetus of the rich countries' growth
is maintained. To believe otherwise is to bring the mental habits of the
past to an age of potential abundance. Thirty years ago, it was still just
possible to feel that mankind's essential problem was the sharing out of
resources that were ultimately limited: if the richer nations were not
already robbing the poor, they were robbing posterity by stripping the
earth of fuel and metal. Today, by contrast, the technological revolution
offers a prospect of virtually limitless energy and countless new materials—as well as the future products of processes yet unknown. In this
unprecedented situation, what is really remarkable is the double paradox of how little our most recent technology has so far affected the
economy, and how great are the problems of adjusting to even this
degree of change.

In thirty years, while man's technical knowledge has increased perhaps a thousand-fold, the world's wealth has doubled. Today, men produce and use more than twice as much energy and three times as much
steel as in 1939. Industrial production has nearly tripled, and the value
of world trade has been multiplied by seven. Revenue per head has

increased in all the industrialized countries: in some, real wages are twice as high as before World War II. In all of Europe, the total output of goods and services is more than fifty per cent greater, and production per head of population has risen by one-third. Unemployment has receded—in one case to less than a thirtieth of the prewar level. The amount per person spent on social security is four times as much as in 1930. Twice as many people as in 1939 now enter higher education. In general, Western Europeans work shorter hours with the aid of more machinery in larger productive units, more of which they now own either as stockholders or through nationalization. They invest fifty per cent more than in the nineteen-thirties; they employ more civil servants; they reserve fewer jobs exclusively for men. They eat more fruit, sugar, meat and eggs, but fewer potatoes and grain products. They live in larger cities; they communicate more; they take more and longer holidays; they travel further and faster. Together they now own—or are paying for by instalments—seven times as many motor-cars and motor-cycles as were already crowding the roads a generation ago. In 1939 there were six million cars in Western Europe; twenty years later, there were sixteen million; today, after a further decade, there are forty-two million. If the process continued at this rate, the total would reach a hundred million within the next five years.[24]

The industrialized countries, in other words, are near the threshold of an age of plenty—the so-called 'society of leisure'. Their movement towards it is slower than technology theoretically warrants; but already it seems too fast for adjustment to be painless. Some have even claimed that we retard our own progress through unconscious fear of growing idle: we see to it, under 'Parkinson's Law', that 'work expands so as to fill the time available for its completion'; and while industrial working hours shorten, administrators multiply the unfinished paperwork they feel obliged to take home.[25] At all events, in Europe as elsewhere, men are discovering with some surprise the side-effects of affluence. Air-pollution, diesel fumes, smog, road congestion and accidents, automobile cemeteries, oil contamination of the beaches, chemical poisoning of rivers, rusting metal refuse and undecaying plastic litter—all are material proof of our inveterate improvidence. Sonic booms, the scream of jets, the roar of traffic, and the snarl of speedboats are some of the audible penalties of living in a machine age; standardized entertainment and preserved foods are equivocal examples of its benefits. Into cities appropriate for nineteenth-century numbers we crowd a vastly expanded population: the suburbs creep outwards to meet each other on the ruins of fields and woods. Telephones, teleprinters, tape-recorders, digital computers, and closed-circuit television might already make it possible to disperse and decentralize offices, if not to dispense with them; but competitive rivalry keeps them in the city centres, and a huge unhappy tide of commuters wells back and forth daily, in conditions reminiscent of the salt mines. Even the day itself is curiously organized. Work claims the better part of it: private life is squeezed into its margins. Most shops are closed when wage-earners are free to use them, and armies of housewives collect their families' requirements in small quantities several times a week. At night, as at the weekends, the business sections of any large city become expensive deserts of brick and concrete, and the roads into the dwindling countryside are choked with lines of cars.

In such an environment, man's nature seems almost to be transformed. Violence explodes out of boredom and alienation: the roadhog and the tearaway enact similar mute rebellions at the cost of human lives. Small wonder that students rebel, alert to tensions, contradictions, and futilities that their elders accept out of habit rather than choice. Stress diseases multiply, and some fail to be diagnosed; research discovers that smoking may cause lung cancer, but the complex causes of smoking remain obscure. Other drugs acquire new and younger addicts, seeking the spice of danger which they feel modern life denies. More sensible if no less sensitive, others find an outlet in deliberate, unnecessary physical effort: sport, camping, do-it-yourself and gardening—apart from their practical value—are occupational therapy for a sickness the middle-aged share with the young. To palliate it, more and more people join the self-defeating quest for 'unspoiled' holiday resorts, usually in the less-developed regions. Evoking the biblical simplicity of age-old fishing villages complete with water-skiing, the travel brochures echo and debase an understandable nostalgia—for societies in which, we tell ourselves, man still felt at home. And yet, bronzed and slightly disappointed, we often return with some relief from these excursions, glad to be back with the challenge and stimulus of our own strenuous civilization. Its blemishes, after all, are merely a reminder that 'the price of pace is peace'.

If this is a painful truth for private individuals, statesmen and politicians confront it in sharper form. A generation ago, it was a commonplace that motor cars, telephones, radio and aircraft were reducing distances and bringing nations into closer contact, while men still organized their political affairs as if nothing had changed. Today, this assertion has as much a period air as nineteen-thirties roadsters, pedestal telephones, crystal wireless-sets and fixed-undercarriage biplanes; yet how much, even now, have we heeded its warning? Jet travel, artificial satellites, universal television and nuclear explosives have made the traditional forms of international relations still more obsolete and

9

dangerous: but recent political history shows how halting are men's efforts to behave as if they realized the fact.

In a generation, that is, the scale of the world has altered. Already, at an early stage of the technological revolution, size became important: it was often a decisive advantage in the competition between private firms. Now it is even more so. The possibilities and needs of mass production, and the cost of research and development in the so-called 'science-based industries', have led to mergers and take-overs, culminating in huge international corporations whose horizons are broader than even the largest nation state. At the same time, and increasingly during the past thirty years, the state itself has become more and more concerned in the economy—either as owner or part-owner of specific industries, or by accepting responsibility for welfare and for the stimulus and guidance of economic growth. Even in the least socialist of societies, government contracts and some degree of indicative planning have forced the administration into economic territory that once was alien; elsewhere, the conventional frontiers between the private and the public sector have become still more blurred. Large-scale business and industry have acquired some of the tone and features of national or international civil services; public authorities have assumed some of the functions of old-style private enterprise. Within the nation, this double process has raised political problems. Unnerved by monolithic institutions whose similar size may give them convergent interests, smaller concerns, workpeople, and individual citizens feel the need for some impartial 'Ombudsman' to defend private rights.[26]

No less striking, however, are the international repercussions of modern welfare capitalism. By taking responsibility for national economies which are now so closely interlocking, governments once 'sovereign' have become more involved with each other, notably in trade, investments and monetary affairs. World trade, in particular, has expanded so much faster than gold production that its financing now depends on a complex network of credit, mutual confidence, and collective fear. This has severely limited national freedom of action—a fact most explicitly acknowledged in 1944, when the Bretton Woods conference sought to codify international economic behaviour, laying the foundations of what were to be the International Monetary Fund and the World Bank. But despite these preliminary efforts, governments have proved reluctant to allow the world's supply of money to be regulated by equitable international decision-making: rather than control their destinies jointly by pooling their sovereignty, they prefer to cling to its appearance while its reality leaks away. The international monetary system, such as it is, continues to be based on the so-called 'key currencies' of the United States and Britain. Since neither now has adequate reserves, the one-time 'gold-exchange standard', whereby holders of dollars or sterling could convert them freely into gold metal, has had to be virtually abolished, largely by gentlemen's agreements which have been well described as 'threateningly precarious and short-term'.[27] The outcome is general uneasiness, occasional danger, and—beginning in Britain but not confined to any one country—intermittent stagnation. Through attempts to evade the implications of interdependence, economic freedom has actually been reduced.

In politics, likewise, interdependence has proved to be inescapable. Statesmen now travel between continents in the time it once took to cross a single country. Heads of government converse directly on the scrambler telephone or, more slowly, via the teleprinters of the 'hot line'. One incidental result has been to devalue diplomatists and their dispatches—an unusual instance of the truism that our culture is now more oral and less literary than a generation ago. Radio and television, largely responsible for this last shift of emphasis, are themselves further elements in the growth of interdependence. Every night, the citizens of the richer countries have the chance to see from their own armchairs a little of other nations' lives. Very gradually, foreign affairs are being domesticated: once distant countries and peoples—'aliens'—are becoming real. Soon, with the aid of relay satellites, multiple polyglot versions of a single television broadcast may be addressed to the whole world, ignoring distances, the earth's curvature and national or political barriers: jamming, in this case, would be extremely difficult. The effects of such universal television can only be guessed at: much will depend on the honesty and skill with which it is used. But whatever the motives of those who exploit it, its political significance is incalculable. In this respect at least, for good or evil, the world is now potentially one.

Here once more, however, the organization of human affairs lags far behind human technology. Telecommunications may have shrunk our planet; yet the numbers of its separate nations have greatly swelled. The past generation has fostered more than fifty new sovereign states, with a total population of 800 million. Essentially, this is the outcome of postwar decolonization. The Italian colonies in North and East Africa, like the Japanese empire in the Far East, were dismantled at the close of hostilities. Armed rebellion spurred the ending of Dutch rule in Indonesia, and of French rule in North Africa and Indochina. Denmark granted independence to Iceland, France to Syria and the Lebanon, the

United States to the Philippines, and Britain to a score of countries in-cluding India, Pakistan, Ceylon, Burma, Malaysia, the West Indies, Guyana, Cyprus and Malta, while the Belgians, the French and the British have relinquished the greater part of Africa. Here, in particular, frontiers are more often the relics of colonial map-making than the expression of ecological boundaries. In some of the new nations this has led to regional tension and bitter conflict; elsewhere, economic logic calls for the integration or federation of adjacent territories, but natural pride, fear and sometimes jealousy stand in the way. With the large exceptions of India, Pakistan, Indonesia and Nigeria, none of the newly independent states has a population of more than thirty-five million people; the majority of them have less than ten million, and a number of these have less than one million each. As a first step towards justice and equality, decolonization was long overdue; but allied with nation-alism it has proved to be a splintering process—a grim paradox in a world of increasing interdependence, where technology puts a premium on size.

The growth of new giants, indeed, is a further decisive feature of the past thirty years. Its beginnings were discernible well over a century ago when Alexis de Tocqueville observed that 'there are, at the present time, two great nations in the world which seem to tend towards the same end, although they started from different points: I allude to the Rus-sians and the Americans.' 'Each of them,' he added, 'seems to be marked out by the will of Heaven to sway the destinies of half the globe.'[28] In 1835, such prescience was visionary; but so familiar has the vision grown that we forget how little it was credited even a generation ago. In the 'thirties, America was still isolationist; only reluctantly and briefly had she entered the world scene. To many ordinary Europeans, 'the typical American' was either a stereotype from the cinema or a stage 'Yankee' with horn-rimmed spectacles, a name like 'Hiram J. Rickenbacker', and a poorly imitated drawl. Viewed from Europe, the United States still seemed a distant land of hustle and skyscrapers, if not of cowboys and Indians. Yet by 1939 it was producing a third of the world's most widely-used metals, a third of its coal and electrical energy, two-thirds of its oil, and three-quarters of its automobiles.[29] Today, al-though the percentages have dropped, the absolute figures are greater. America's standard of living, by any economic indicator, is twice as high as that of her closest competitors; and her total output of goods and services amounts to $756,000 million—nearly seven times as much as any other country for which there are comparable figures.[30]

The missing exception, of course, is the Soviet Union. This too seemed very distant in the 'thirties, even if to some it appeared a precarious experiment in socialism or, as André Gide put it, 'the land where the future is being born'.[31] What astonished Western observers at that time was less the scale of Russia's industrial production than the speed of her growth. In 1929, the United States accounted for 42·2 per cent of the world's industrial output. By 1938 this had fallen to 32·2 per cent —not because American production was declining, but because the Soviet percentage had leapt from 4·3 to 18·3 in less than ten years. Since World War II, especially, Russia has begun to enjoy the fruits of her progress. She now produces two-thirds as much steel and energy as the United States; and although America remains predominant in many fields, the Soviet Union's achievements in space are symbol enough of her new status as the world's second giant.[32]

Beyond America and Russia, moreover, other giant powers are beginning to flex their muscles. Physically the biggest is Communist China. Before World War II, the Republic of China was ruled from Nanking by Chiang Kai-shek's Kuomintang. Today, the People's Republic has its capital in Peking; it has exchanged the Kuomintang for the Community Party, and the dictatorship of Chiang for that of Mao Tse-tung and Chou En-lai. But the essential difference is more fundamental. In 1939, with the disputed territories of Manchuria, Mongolia, Sinkiang and Tibet, China comprised over four million square miles and 458 million people. Huge, undeveloped, largely uncolonized, and attractive to outside capital and commerce, it seemed fated to be a pawn in other countries' games of power. Thirty years later, with much the same area, China has a population not far short of 700 million, and increasing at the rate of 20 million a year. Cleared of invaders if not of civil strife, it has embarked on a ruthless programme of modernization and mass education. The 'Great Leap Forward' in agricultural production made in 1958 may well have been exaggerated, but it evidently took place; and similar if steadier progress has been made in industry. China's crude steel production has now reached twelve million metric tons—more than Italy's; its installed electrical energy capacity is in the region of fifteen million kilowatts—more than Sweden's; and its annual output of science and engineering graduates is well over sixty thousand—more than that of any other country except America and Russia. The most spectacular result of these endeavours has been China's development of nuclear weapons and ballistic missile systems—and, more recently, her first venture into space.[33] By comparison with the 'thirties, this is already an extraordinary change. Equally significant, although perhaps not surprising, is the fact that after some years of seeming to follow in the wake of the Soviet Union, Communist China is now beginning to steer a course of her own. This redoubles the contrast with the backward and passive Republic of a generation ago.

But while China's progress is the more obvious, no less remarkable is the growth of that smaller giant, Japan. This is no new phenomenon. It began towards the end of the nineteenth century, with a largely un-assisted 'great leap forward' from medieval feudalism to western tech-nology in the space of some forty years. By 1938, Japan was supplying 3·5 per cent of the world's manufacturing output—more than Belgium, Canada, Italy, or Sweden.[34] Since World War II, the country's economic expansion has broken all comparable records. Even in 1964, when the brakes were applied to the economy, total production rose by nearly 14 per cent, and exports by 22 per cent. On average, Japan has main-tained an annual growth rate of some 10 per cent for more than a decade —enough to quadruple her output within fifteen years. With 100 mil-lion people in an area more densely populated than Britain, she now produces more energy than France and more steel than Germany; her output of trucks is second only to that of the United States. She is the world's biggest shipbuilder, and by 1965 she was producing nearly half the gross tonnage launched. One day, by their sheer numbers, China and even India may eclipse her; but China is still very far from achieving her full potential, and India incalculably further. Meanwhile, Japan is already what *The Economist* has called 'the greatest practical research laboratory of economic growth in our time'.[35]

The past thirty years, then, have witnessed crucial changes. Techno-logy has transformed men's everyday environment, given new meaning to notions of speed and distance, unlocked the power of the atom, and opened the way into space. Economic progress, although remarkable, has been less rapid: the world's growing millions remain undernour-ished, while the industrialized countries develop more quickly than is comfortable, but more slowly than they could. Men's political beha-viour, at the same time, adapts itself more sluggishly still. Most nation states have yet to accept the implications of their increasing involve-ment with the economy and with each other; and while the world grows smaller and its economic units larger, minute new nations proliferate alongside existing and emerging giants.

Amid this unprecedented turmoil and upheaval, Europe is responsible for the biggest change of all. It is not merely that today's technology, economics and political organization are largely of European origin. What most sharply divides the present from past generations is still the grim landmark of the second—European—world war.

In the six years from 1939 to 1945, war itself changed its nature. In previous conflicts, the state's defences had been its frontiers or its front line: its armies acted as a carapace which might be dented or even fatally pierced, but which short of disaster sheltered the civilians—and many of the generals—in its rear. With air raids and conscription, this concept had to be modified. The civil population, as the phrase went, 'was now in the front line'. In the days of trench warfare, the metaphor still seemed valid; but it was certainly inappropriate by the time of World War II. Even before Hitler's armies invaded Belgium to turn the flank of the Maginot Line, *Blitzkrieg* tactics had made static linear defence anachronistic. Mobility was the keynote of this new kind of warfare: parachute troops, commando raids, guerrilla skirmishing and sabotage by resistance circuits behind the lines were as typical of it as the lightning thrusts of the Panzer divisions. Mass air attack, flying bombs and rockets made the carapace concept even more obsolete by virtually abolishing the distinction between military targets and civilian victims—a process carried to the ultimate in the extermination camps and, on a smaller scale, in the aerial massacres of Dresden, Hiroshima and elsewhere. When the last of the ashes had settled on Nagasaki, the carapace and its contents were one.

Immense, impersonal and indiscriminate, today's destructive weapons have dwarfed even those of World War II. The biggest bomb dropped on Germany in 1945 contained ten tons of TNT; the biggest since tested by the Soviet Union is the equivalent of ninety-seven million tons. The total explosive power now in existence is ten million times as great as in 1943. Intercontinental missiles, thermonuclear weapons and radioactive fall-out have robbed front lines and frontiers of most of their military meaning: such notions as 'fortress America' are now doubly out of date. True, the carapace concept lingers. Perhaps its last vestige is the hope that anti-ballistic missiles might one day make nations invulnerable—a costly and precarious form of carapace in the sky. At present, no industrialized and densely populated country could hope to 'win' a nuclear war, and all have an interest in preventing it. In 1969 the existing nuclear powers spent nearly £150,000 million on 'defence'; but unless they are willing to find still greater sums for an anti-ballistic missile race, their military strategy is in fact not defensive, but deterrent. They eye each other like poker players or stock-market speculators, acting on hypotheses about each other's future behaviour rather than on their own plans. The survival of civilization must remain uncertain so long as it depends on such gambler's dexterity—especially if the number of nuclear powers continues to grow. Contrary to some expectations, however, even the 'balance of terror' has not put an end to armed conflict. As Jean Cocteau once remarked: 'If men offer to get rid of nuclear weapons, it is not to make war impossible, but to make it possible'; and under the virtual ban on nuclear and germ warfare imposed by men's fear of the consequences, 'conventional' struggles continue, sometimes threatening the whole world. War has dramatized the interdependence of nations. Already brought closer in so many other ways, since 1945 they have been handcuffed together by military technology.[36]

Their response to this situation makes a further contrast with the world of thirty years ago. The shock of war released political as well as technical inventiveness, quickened by the knowledge of what a third world war would mean. By 1939, the diplomatic nationalism of the past had revealed its antiquated bankruptcy: six years of war demolished its last pretensions: now was the chance for statesmen to start afresh. For once, they were impatient to do so. Within five years, in an extraordinary burst of creative energy, they endowed the world with almost all its present network of global institutions. The year 1945 saw the establishment of the United Nations Organization (UNO), the Food and Agriculture Organization (FAO), the International Monetary Fund (IMF) and the International Bank for Reconstruction and Development (the (IBRD or World Bank). In 1946 came the United Nations Educational, Scientific and Cultural Organization (UNESCO), the United Nations International Children's Emergency Fund (UNICEF) and the International Court of Justice; in 1947, the General Agreement on Tariffs and Trade (GATT); in 1948, the International Refugee Organization (IRO) and the World Health Organization (WHO); in 1949, the United Nations Relief and Works Agency (UNRWA) and the International Confederation of Free Trade Unions (ICFTU).

The supreme aim of such co-operation was to build a world-wide system of what had once been known as 'collective security', although its old embodiment, the League of Nations, had already proved disappointing when Maxim Litvinoff popularized the phrase in 1935. The practical outcome now was UNO, which despite its weaknesses has been stronger and more comprehensive than the League. But almost equally significant was a psychological change that accompanied postwar reconstruction; and this had its origins in World War II. Unlike most of its predecessors, the war had been ideological, concerned as much with principles as with power. Fascism and Nazism at one extreme, Soviet Communism at the other, each claiming a universal mission; and a similar universalism marked more moderate thinking about the future peace. It was hard, after what had happened, to go on regarding the nation state as more than a stage in the slow evolution of human society: still less did it now seem sacrosanct, a proud eternal solitary with no permanent friends or allies, but only permanent interests. If the 1914–18 struggle had been 'the war to end war', the victors of World War II spoke more insistently of the need to 'build a better world'. The generation that now came to maturity found it natural to see that world as a unit, as if from an aircraft or a satellite, rather than from the arrow-slits or gun-turrets of separate national positions. Equally natural was the conclusion that international anarchy must soon be replaced by the rule of law.

Sometimes, this feeling was superficial and unpractical; sometimes it was Messianic; sometimes it reflected one or another great power's conviction that it alone knew best. In retrospect, the hope of world-wide law and order may seem premature or even Utopian—especially to those for whom nations are the sole political 'realities' in a fundamentally unchanging world. But 'realist', egotist or nationalist prognoses are often self-fulfilling prophecies, spells which summon the devils that they claim are already here. And however imperfect or tainted the ideals of the postwar generation, there was so much to be done when the war ended that to think in world terms was a practical necessity. It was also a significant break with previous mental habits; and it left its mark. So ingrained, now, is the notion of 'building a better world' that many are unduly puzzled by the policies of statesmen who ignore it. A measure of its strength is that even out-and-out nationalists, in this sense deeply pessimistic, sugar their doctrines with hopeful universalist words.

But if the beginnings of peace aroused high expectations, these were quickly dashed by a partial legacy from the war. Instead of uniting, the world became polarized, split by the growing tension between America and Russia. The origins of this 'cold war' have been variously interpreted: there was perhaps as much misunderstanding on both sides as there was malevolence on either. Nor is there a consensus about whether the 'cold war' has ended. Fear, greater wealth, restiveness in Eastern Europe, and growing rivalry from Communist China have certainly been nudging the Soviet Union into a new relationship with the United States. In the 1962 Cuban missile crisis, Moscow overruled Havana in order to preserve peace; in 1963 came the nuclear test ban treaty, followed later by a draft agreement against the spread of nuclear weapons; in 1967, both Moscow and Washington stood aside from the Israeli-Arab war, and the meeting of President Johnson with Mr Kosygin in Glassboro, New Jersey, seemed to confirm the bilateral link already established by the 'hot line'. Yet if the change is dramatic, it remains none the less gradual, as was dramatically shown when Russian tanks invaded Prague in 1968. The 'cold war' may indeed be moving into the Far East, leaving a wary, uneasy complicity to grow between America and Russia: but in the meantime one of the essential differences between our world and that of the nineteen-thirties is still the twenty-year confrontation of these two giants across the former battlefields of Europe.[37]

Down the middle of Europe, in fact, runs this particular division of the world. In a typical atlas of the 'thirties, the European map spanned two pages: it stretched from Reykjavik, 21° 20′ West, almost to Obdorsk, 66° 50′ East. This was still the traditional 'Europe from the Atlantic to the Urals'. Thirty years later, the map on the right-hand page has changed completely. With the growing industrialization of parts of Siberia, the Urals have lost their old significance as a boundary; to the West of them, the cartographer's expression 'Russia in Europe' has acquired new, ironic overtones. Estonia, Latvia and Lithuania have become Republics of the Soviet Union, whose borders now also include what were formerly parts of Finland, East Prussia, Poland, Czechoslovakia and Rumania. 'People's democracies' of varying shades have been established in the eastern zone of Germany, in Poland, Czechoslovakia, Hungary, Rumania, Bulgaria, Albania and—*mutatis mutandis*—in Jugoslavia. The so-called 'Iron Curtain' may no longer be impenetrable, but it still marks the borderline between rival forms of society. In political terms, the fold in the pre-war atlas has become real.

On the left-hand page, the map shows fewer changes. The biggest and most serious is the division of Germany, crucial to the division of Europe and of the world. Nearly half its prewar area is now sealed off in the east. Of this, rather less than half, with a population of some sixteen million, is ruled by the so-called 'German Democratic Republic'; the rest has been split between Poland and the Soviet Union. Berlin, the former capital, is divided by an ugly makeshift wall of breeze blocks, and its western sector forms an extensive but claustrophobic enclave within Eastern territory. In the 95,737 square miles which now make up the western half of Germany—the Federal Republic—there are sixty million people, the ninth largest nation in the world, and almost as many as lived in the whole German *Reich* before World War II. Their provisional capital is the small, unpretentious university city of Bonn, remote and a little sleepy in the muggy climate of the Rhineland. Despite the big new office blocks on the Koblenzerstrasse leading south to Bad Godesberg, Bonn has scarcely even modernized its railways: four level crossings still hold up the traffic in the middle of the town. Like so much else in today's divided Germany, Bonn maintains a mute insistence that its present situation cannot last.

Compared with the division of Germany, the other changes in the map of Western Europe are small. Italy's northern frontiers have been adjusted; the Saar has passed back and forth between France and Germany; the Dutch have reclaimed more of the North Sea. But no major differences meet the eye of the map-reader, and few can be seen by a traveller looking down at Europe from the air. In places, the scars of World War II still show. Berlin, in particular, has made monuments of its ruins, like the broken spire of the Kaiser-Wilhelm-Gedächtniskirche, deliberately left unrepaired. Yet even such wounds as these seem less deep than the angular imprint of the World War I trenches, still just visible from the air like a palimpsest in Flanders fields reploughed and planted for the past fifty years. Even the military graves of World War II, row upon row of standardized crosses, are far outnumbered—in western Europe—by those of 1914–18.

A little more obvious to the airborne traveller are the signs of peace. The clustered lights of the cities are brighter and more widespread; more cars move faster along broader ribboning highways. Airfields are crowded; new towns have sprung up, anonymously modern; the steel-framed windows of ferro-concrete buildings flash in the sun. Europe's outward appearance has altered dramatically: but the biggest change of all can be seen only by looking at statistics.

In less than a generation, interrupted by six years of war, Western Europe has nearly tripled its wealth. Its total output, measured at constant prices, is almost three times as great as in 1939: so is its purely industrial production. Imports have tripled, exports quadrupled. Energy consumption has doubled. Hydro-electric power production has tripled; the output of crude oil has been multiplied by thirteen, and that of natural gas by 300. True, the population has increased also: but just as striking as the rise in output has been that of output per head. Since World War II, the average increase in productivity has been in the region of 3·5 per cent a year, compared with less than half that figure before 1939. The postwar economic expansion, moreover, although still uneven, has so far been spared the severe crises and depressions that recurred so regularly in the past; and although there have also been variations from country to country, even the laggards have shared, less spectacularly, in Western Europe's general, unprecedented and unusually self-conscious pursuit of growth.[38]

Paradoxically, however, these figures partly mask a relative decline. While Western Europe's industrial production has risen by more than 130 per cent, that of the United States has increased by 234 per cent.

While Europe's trade has expanded, its share of world trade has diminished: its imports from 47 per cent to 42 per cent of the total, its exports from 57 per cent to 43 per cent. Its gold and currency reserves, which a generation ago covered 77 per cent of its annual imports, now cover only 48 per cent; and whereas Europe once met more than 90 per cent of its own energy needs, it now supplies only 70 per cent, depending on imports for the rest. Greater dependence is thus the obverse of Europe's new prosperity; and in some respects its growth has lagged behind that of the rest of the world.[39]

Europe's relative decline has been greatest, moreover, in some of the most crucial fields. At present, Western European countries pay some 200 million dollars a year more than they earn for technological knowledge, patents and licences, while the United States has a comparable surplus on such earnings of more than 500 million dollars a year. Not for nothing has it become fashionable in Europe to speak of 'the technological gap'. In pure science the gap is just as evident. During the thirty-nine years from 1901 to 1939, Europe produced 109 Nobel prize-winners in physics, chemistry, physiology and medicine, compared with thirteen from the United States. In the twenty-three years 1943–65, Europe's score of fifty-six was almost equalled by the United States with fifty-four, while other countries—which before World War II had had only two laureates—now had thirteen, seven of them from the USSR.[40]

If Western Europe as a whole has thus lost ground over the past thirty years, its individual countries have done so even more. Even the largest of them is now dwarfed by the Soviet Union and the United States. A country that was in the same proportion to America as America is to, say, France would be gigantic—a nation of 800 million people in a territory of 60 million square miles. Each of its inhabitants would produce one-and-a-half times as much as the average American, and its standard of living would be twice as high. The sales of its biggest firm would be seventeen times those of General Motors. Its scientists might be experimenting with intergalactic travel, with the total prevention of ageing, with custom-made newspapers electronically printed in every home. Nor would the disparity be confined to economics and technology. To pursue the comparison further, this hypothetical giant power would have 12 million men in its armed forces and an annual defence budget of more than 500 million dollars.

The psychological and political effects of such disproportion are very evident. Thirty years ago, Western Europe was still the bright and tragic stage on which the world's dramas were enacted. Its nations, in those days, could still see themselves as protagonists and arbiters. Today, this is no longer possible. Pageantry has replaced power in the chancelleries of Europe: the drama is now dominated by non-European giants.

In the past thirty years, then, Europe has gradually been forced to face a challenge of scale. But even more fundamental is the challenge to political maturity. Just because Europe thirty years ago was the world's cockpit, it was Europeans who paid most dearly for man's failure to match political wisdom to technological skill. The Fascist and Nazi regimes used the resources of civilization for ends that were plainly barbarous; the democracies, in self-defence, committed themselves to 'total war', to the demand for unconditional surrender, to the bombing of Dresden, Hiroshima and Nagasaki. The agony of the old Europe cost the lives of fifteen million of its citizens, half of them in extermination camps. Many had fought and died for a world and a Europe where such things could no longer happen. The task of the survivors was to make that hope a reality, and to honour their debt to the dead

CHAPTER TWO

The Waste Land

Though we had Peace, yet 'twill be a great while e'er things be settled. Though the Wind lie, yet after a Storm the Sea will work a great while.   *John Selden*[1]

War is no longer declared,
but continued.   *Ingeborg Bachmann*[2]

I preferred the war to that 'sickness' which, after the Liberation, had soiled, corrupted, and humiliated us all.
                    Curzio Malaparte[3]

THE nightmare ended prosaically, in the small hours of a Monday morning, inside a red-brick building not far from the railway station of Rheims. This was the Boys' Technical High School, taken over by General Eisenhower for Supreme Headquarters, Allied Expeditionary Force. In the war room, formerly used for recreation, a small crowd was gathered—staff officers, journalists, newsreel cameramen. 'The damned war room,' said Eisenhower, 'looked like a Hollywood setting.' Chairs were arranged at a long whitewood table; at each place there was a clean ashtray and a freshly sharpened pencil. Around the table stood senior Allied officers: a Russian general and two companions; a French *commandant*; an admiral, a general, and an air chief marshal from Britain; and the Commander of the US Strategic Air Forces in Europe. Of Eisenhower himself there was no sign.

The door opened; in came the Supreme Commander's Chief of Staff, General Walter Bedell Smith. He was followed a moment later by two German officers, looking strained and uneasy, holding themselves stiffly erect. One was *Generaladmiral* Hans-Georg von Friedeburg: the other, set-faced, with precise lips and cold, heavy eyes, was *Generaloberst* Alfred Jodl. The principals took their places. Documents were set before them; aides came forward with pens. In the bright glare of the newsreel floodlights, they signed. It was 2·41 a.m. on 7 May 1945. Those present had just witnessed the unconditional surrender of Nazi Germany.

It is often hard to live up to great occasions. Perhaps the participants feel, in the words of a perceptive novelist, 'somewhat insincere, as any intelligent person is likely to feel who performs a symbolic action'.[4] Perhaps, too, blunders are inevitable at the only performance of an un-rehearsed drama. At all events, in the agony and exultance of those swift spring days, not much could be well stage-managed; and the early-morning ceremony in Rheims was followed by considerable confusion. As one of Eisenhower's aides commented: 'I've learned the hard way that it is much easier to start a war than to stop one.'[5]

There was uncertainty, first, about the time when hostilities were due to cease. *Grossadmiral* Karl Dönitz, Hitler's official heir as *Reichspräsident*, now established with his short-lived government in the quasi-exile of Mürwik-bei-Flensburg on the Danish frontier, had done his best to delay the capitulation, hoping that as many as possible of his troops would give themselves up to the Western allies and avoid captivity in the East. The Rheims documents called for a cease-fire at one minute after midnight on 8–9 May DBST; the message received by Dönitz, how-ever, gave the time as Central European Time—i.e. one hour later. According to German records, this was due to a mistake in transmission, and was quickly rectified. Whether it might have led to needless slaughter is problematical: isolated battles in fact continued for several days.[6]

Greater confusion marred the public announcement of the surrender. For some time, the Soviet Union had feared that the Nazis might make a separate peace with the West. This they had indeed attempted: but Eisenhower had been firm. Although he had allowed their armies in north-eastern Germany, Holland and Denmark to surrender to Field-Marshal Montgomery at Lüneburg Heath on the previous Friday, 4 May, he insisted that this was a tactical, purely military proceeding, like the surrender of the German forces in Italy at Caserta two days before. The capitulation at Rheims, however, marked the end of the war in Europe; and the Allies had agreed to announce this simultaneously on Tuesday 8 May, at 9·00 a.m. Washington time, or 3·00 p.m. in Western Europe and 4·00 p.m. in Moscow. To respect the deadline, the press had been asked to hold the story for a day and a half. It was a long embargo for such momentous news; and in the event it was broken. At 12·45 p.m. on Monday 7 May, 'to anticipate the enemy announcement and thereby maintain order', Dönitz's Foreign Minister read a proclamation over Flensburg radio: his speech was monitored by the BBC and re-broadcast in English that same afternoon. By 3·35 p.m. the story was on the news-agency wires. In London, excited crowds began to gather. Everyone now knew that the war in the West was over; but because of their prior agreement, the Allies were not due to admit the fact for nearly twenty-four hours.[7]

This seemed to Winston Churchill 'an idiotic position'. Within half an hour he was on the secret telephone to the Pentagon, arguing with Admiral Leahy, President Truman's Chief of Staff. Earlier that day he had already badgered Eisenhower with repeated attempts to have the embargo lifted; now, as Truman put it, 'he was mad as a wet hen'. 'What is the use,' he exclaimed, 'of me and of the President looking to be the only two people in the world who don't know what is going on? The whole of this thing is leaking out in England and America ... I feel it absolutely necessary to go off at 6·00 p.m., and I will telegraph to Stalin the very message that I am sending you ... in view of the fact that the Germans have blasted it all over the world.'[8]

Left to himself, Truman might have accepted this argument. Stalin, however, was still not convinced that the Germans on the eastern front would in fact surrender; and he was anxious to avoid an announcement that might be premature. Leahy sent an urgent teleprinter message to General Deane at the US Military Mission in Moscow; but although he waited at the Pentagon in the hope of a quick reaction from Stalin, none came. Within the hour, Churchill was once more on the telephone: he too had had no reply from the Russians. In view of public feeling, he could delay no longer. 'The Moscow people,' he complained, 'have no public opinion — but you cannot control your press, nor can I control mine — that's the difficulty of living in a free country!' Reluctantly, he postponed his own broadcast to the nation until the official deadline; but 'the thing must go forward'. That evening, the British Ministry of Information made the announcement: the next forty-eight hours would be a public holiday, and V-E Day (for 'Victory in Europe') would be tomorrow, Tuesday 8 May. That day had already dawned in Europe, and was already a few minutes old in Washington, when at last an answer came from Moscow. The Russians would not yet celebrate victory. Stalin wanted more time to examine the surrender terms.[9]

These, indeed, were the third source of that week's manifold confusion. In Rheims, at General Eisenhower's headquarters, they had already caused commotion during the previous night. Shortly after the surrender ceremony, the American career diplomat Robert Murphy, who was acting as the Supreme Commander's political adviser on German affairs, cast a routine glance at the document that had just been signed. To his astonishment, he found that it contained the wrong text. Two months earlier, he had sent to Eisenhower's Chief of Staff, General Bedell Smith, the surrender terms laboriously approved by the three Allied governments. Where were they now? Bedell Smith had by this time gone to bed. Roused by a telephone call from Murphy, he hastily dressed again and hurried back to the office. There, locked in his top-secret filing cabinet, was the big blue folder which Murphy had sent him. Had he simply forgotten it, as Murphy afterwards claimed?

In fact, the explanation was more complex. Supreme Headquarters in Rheims had received several printed copies of the agreed surrender terms, and its representatives had discussed in some detail with the State Department the arrangements for their translation and signature. Apart from the fact that this text officially committed all the Allied governments, including the Russians, to the rudiments of an agreed policy, it was also the only legal basis for the exercise of Allied authority in Germany after the war. But military headquarters believed that to present so elaborate a document to the Germans would risk protracted argument with them; and while argument continued, so would fighting and loss of life. Two years earlier, in 1943, the military had unwillingly ceded to their civilian colleagues' insistence on elaborate surrender terms for Italy. This time, as one participant put it, they were determined to have their revenge. The document signed that morning, therefore, had been an improvization, concocted on the basis of reference material as soon as capitulation had begun to seem likely; the Russian liasion officer who had certified and counter-signed it had clearly not realized that it was unofficial. Not until the evening of the previous Saturday, 5 May, had news of the Rheims document reached the US Ambassador in London, John G. Winant, who had helped draft the official terms. Only by strenuous efforts, including a talk with Churchill and an urgent telephone call to Bedell Smith, had Winant managed to secure the insertion in the Rheims document of an enabling clause providing for the Allies' later assumption of political authority in Germany. Even so, the military surrender terms just signed had still not been cleared at governmental level, except in London. While Murphy and Bedell Smith were comparing the two texts and wondering how to proceed, a priority cable arrived from Washington: Moscow had noticed the discrepancy too. Early that same Monday morning, Supreme Headquarters made a rueful announcement. The Rheims document had merely 'formalized the surrender': 'the official surrender' would take place in Berlin, as the Russians had requested, on Wednesday 9 May.[10]

At last, it might have seemed, the chapter of accidents was finished; but the Berlin ceremony itself was no model of order. First, the Western allies had to wait five hours for Marshal Georgi Zhukov: when he arrived, they still had to wait for Andrei Vyshinsky, the Deputy Foreign Minister. As at Rheims, Eisenhower preferred not to participate: his place was taken by Air Chief Marshal Sir Arthur Tedder. As Deputy

Supreme Commander, Tedder was to sign for all the Western allies; but General de Gaulle insisted that General Jean de Lattre de Tassigny sign for France. It was therefore agreed with Zhukov that Tedder should act on behalf of Britain only, while General Carl Spaatz represented the United States. When Vyshinsky arrived, however, he would have none of it. Since Tedder was Eisenhower's deputy, he argued, there was no need for Spaatz. If so, Spaatz answered, there was no need for de Lattre. For two hours the problem looked insoluble; then Vyshinsky at last conceded that both could sign as witnesses lower down the page. Meanwhile, de Lattre had discovered that Red Army headquarters possessed no tricolour to hang with the other Allied flags behind the conference table; and when he had one made up by Russian seamstresses, they at first sewed the stripes horizontally, producing a Dutch flag. Even when they put right this mistake, the makeshift banner was still rather small. Finally, at the solemn moment of signature, a fist-fight broke out among the reporters and cameramen. The ceremony began at 11·30 p.m., and ended at sixteen minutes past midnight. By the time it was over, the first arrivals had been waiting about for more than fourteen hours.[11]

Nor, even now, was the confusion at an end. The double surrender had been negotiated with the representatives of *Grossadmiral* Dönitz — at Rheims with Friedeburg and Jodl, in Berlin with Friedeburg, *Generalfeldmarschall* Wilhelm Keitel, and *Generaloberst* Hans Jürgen Stumpff. But Dönitz's status was, to say the least, ambiguous. Appointed by order of Adolf Hitler, he had set up the apparatus of government at his headquarters in the Flensburg Naval College, complete with guards of honour and civilian personnel. He had not received the full list of ministers nominated in Hitler's 'political testament'; but he had rejected those whose names Josef Goebbels had sent him in the telegram announcing Hitler's death. On Saturday 5 May he had appointed what he called 'a purely caretaker cabinet', with the avowed aim of 'winding up as well as possible the practical problems arising at the end of the war, and thereby laying the basis on which to build anew'. For some days the cabinet debated whether or not to stay in office. Although it went through the motions of governing, even bureaucratic routine could not quite sustain the illusion. 'We do not even know,' complained the ministers, 'how far the German people outside the limited area of Flensburg even knows about or recognizes the Dönitz government.'[12]

For understandable reasons, the attitude of the Allies was equally uncertain. Dönitz had been a faithful follower of Hitler. When first appointed *Reichspräsident*, and still unaware that the *Führer* was dead, he had cabled back: 'My loyalty to you will be unconditional.' Earlier, he had been willing to serve under Heinrich Himmler; and although he soon dismissed the *Reichsführer SS* and other notorious party members, he and his ministers continued to exercise what was indisputably a Nazi mandate. Among those he dismissed was Josef Goebbels, whose suicide in Berlin was still unknown in Flensburg; but the policy he now appeared to advocate might have been dictated by Goebbels himself. The coming danger, Dönitz argued, was the Bolshevization of Europe: against it, Germany and the Western Allies must stand firm together. This, it was true, had been urged by some members of the German Resistance against Hitler; but by now it was the watchword of Himmler and Hermann Göring, most memorably voiced in the last doomed broadcasts made from Hamburg by the English-speaking Nazi propagandist, William Joyce. To Eisenhower, the stratagem seemed obvious. Dönitz, he concluded, 'was trying to make trouble between SHAEF and the Russians', and he sent Robert Murphy and a senior staff officer to Flensburg to investigate. When they arrived, Dönitz repeated his anti-Bolshevik arguments. 'He seemed totally unaware,' wrote Murphy later, 'that the entire continent hated and feared Germany more than Russia.' Dönitz, in turn, was astonished by 'the complete lack of understanding of this problem on the part of the Anglo-Americans': their 'short-sighted, colonialist treatment of the German people further serves to throw us into the arms of the Russians'. He was more astonished still on Wednesday 23 May, when he and his cabinet were taken into custody by military police. Both sides could plead some justification. Perhaps the aptest comment was the German war diarist's grim bureaucratic footnote on the Rheims surrender: 'Overall impression after thorough reflection and discussion: *"Es ging nicht anders".*' There was indeed no other way.[13]

The multiple confusion of these anxious weeks contained much future history in embryo. The chaos itself was revealing; and so was each of its components. The Germans' anxiety to avoid capture by the Russians was a measure both of Nazi atrocities in Eastern Europe, and of the savagery with which they were being avenged. Churchill's vain attempt to persuade Truman to override Stalin foreshadowed the ever clearer contrast between Britain's declining greatness and America's growing strength. Stalin's suspicion that the West might make a separate peace with the Nazis typified the insecurity of a nation with no natural western frontier, prone to what has been well called 'defensive expansion', and hence a ready participant in the 'cold war'. General de Gaulle's characteristic concern for protocol was a similar presage of friction. Finally, the makeshift arrangements for the surrender reflected the sketchiness of the Allies' preparations for peace. For several years, the essential task of winning the war had had first claim on their attention. When Nazi resistance collapsed, they were like men bearing a battering-ram, carried headlong into the castle by the very impetus that had smashed down its doors. Few had realized the long-term implications of their call for 'unconditional surrender'. Natural and inevitable as it was in response to the nihilism of Hitler's 'total war', it was bound to prolong the conflict; but this was not all. Interpreted as the surrender not just of a regime, but of a nation, it helped to create a divisive political void in the wasteland that was now the heart of Europe.[14]

The continent that now lay open to its liberators had once been the richest in the world. This implied no special virtue in Europeans; nor was it necessarily due to an uniquely favourable providence. Just as the windings of a river across flat country may be the cumulative effects of once minute irregularities, so Europe's wealth may well have derived from a series of fortunate accidents, each favouring the next. Fertile, densely populated, with a temperate climate and many waterways, the continent was bounded to the north, south and east by an unusually long coastline, dotted with islands and fretted with creeks and harbours; only to the east were there few natural barriers, merely the plains and steppes so often crossed by hordes from the vast Eurasian land-mass. From Europe's rocky backbone of the Pyrenees, the Massif Central, and the Alps, flowed the tributaries of its great rivers—the Garonne, the Ebro, the Rhone, the Rhine, the Po, the Danube, the Elbe. Some divided the nations; others linked them together. The Alps and the Rhine, in particular, separated three broad regions, each of which in turn had been the main focus of Europe's wealth. To the south were the lands of the Mediterranean, source of ancient civilizations, home of hardy, long-rooted plants and trees—lemons, olives, vines, figs, almonds—which conserve their secret moisture through the hot dry summers when the 'trade winds' blow offshore. To the north of the Alps, in cooler regions, the westerly 'anti-trade winds' brought rain to nourish the forests of oak, elm, beech and birch that once covered the continent, interspersed with dark conifers on the heaths and uplands. Gradually, men had cut back the forest to make way for fields and pastures: west of the Rhine, the land had grown especially green and lush. 'France is just a plate of salad,' cried the eight-year-old son of the King of Afghanistan when he saw it for the first time from the air.[15] In the east and north-east, some of the soil was poorer; but the earth below was rich. Here lay the mineral deposits—the coal and iron ore—that helped to forge the first industrial revolution. Here, spread diagonally across Europe, was the powerhouse of its prosperity from the nineteenth century onwards, a huge populous workshop straddling the frontier between Romance and Germanic languages which stretched from the North Sea to the Alps.

Now, as so often in recent history, Europe's workshop had become its battleground; nor had other areas been spared. One after another, with the exception of the neutrals, most countries in continental Europe had been invaded or occupied: Austria, Czechoslovakia, Albania, Poland, Finland, Denmark, Norway, Belgium, Holland, Luxembourg, France, Latvia, Lithuania, Estonia, Rumania, Bulgaria, Hungary, Greece, Jugoslavia, Russia; then, when the tide turned, Italy and Germany. Many had been fought over twice in the same war.

No one who saw the results is likely to forget them. By 1945, beyond the joy and frenzy of liberation, beyond the panic of defeat and conquest, much of the continent shared a grim uniformity. Europe, and above all central and eastern Europe, was a land laid waste. In the cities, the skyline was jagged with destruction: amid the ruins and craters, rubble and wreckage blocked the streets. The spires of churches stood truncated, broken; machinery rusted in the bombed-out factories; doors hung askew on torn hinges; window-glass crunched and crackled underfoot. Roads were pitted with shell-holes; the abutments and piers of demolished bridges were left like the stumps of giant teeth. Railway tracks jutted over empty space, or reared in stiff contortions; skeletons of wagons, stripped for firewood, lay with their wheels in the air. Tunnels were flooded; in canals and rivers there were swollen corpses, drifting half-waterlogged, occasionally catching on submerged tugs and barges, whose wheelhouses broke the surface like huts in a swamp. Harbours were full of listing sunken ships.

Much of the countryside was charred and blackened. Mutilated trees, burned bushes, and fields ploughed by tank tracks marked the site of battles; here and there, nothing was left of a village but crumbled walls, ashes and wisps of straw. Nature, once tamed, now retaliated. Grass grew between the paving-stones; rats multiplied; in some areas, unchecked by peasant bows and arrows, herds of wild pigs roamed the land for forage.

Yet amid the desolation there were people. Smoke curled from tin chimneys poking through boarded roofs and windows. Sheds on weekend vegetable plots became houses; cellars and caves were turned into homes. Now and then, there was a sudden crash of masonry and a choking explosion of dust. Peace had silenced the thud of bombs and mortars, the whistle of shells, the rattle of small-arms fire. Instead of the roar and shrill clatter of tanks, there came the more humdrum sound of army lorries, jeeps and motor-cycles; as well as the steady tramp of marching men, there was now the endless shuffle of the defeated, the captive, the homeless. To many of the troops who first encountered them, the people in parts of Europe seemed a population of cripples, of women and children and the very old. Some were starving; some were sick with typhus or dysentery; in the concentration camps, millions had already died. The survivors, grey-faced ghosts in parodies of clothing, trundled their salvaged belongings in home-made handcarts—rugs, threadbare overcoats, a kettle, an alarm-clock, a battered toy. They waited at standpipes for a dribble of brown water; they queued for bread and potatoes; they rummaged for sticks and scraps. For them, this wasteland of rubble, rags and hunger was a prison without privacy or dignity; and like all prisons, it smelled. It smelled of dust, oil, gunpowder and greasy metal; of drains and vermin; of sweat and vomit, dirty socks and excrement; of decay and burning and the unburied dead.

In all of Europe, not including the Soviet Union, at least five million houses had been destroyed, and very many more were badly damaged. In the Soviet Union, twenty-five million people had lost their homes. Out of ten million houses in France, the number destroyed was over half a million; those severely damaged were a million and a half. In Holland, the respective totals were 92,000 and 400,000; in overcrowded Italy, where losses were counted by rooms rather than houses, they were two million and four-and-a-half million. In Britain, the combined total was four million. In Germany it was ten million.[16]

Of Europe's capitals outside the neutral countries, only Brussels, Paris, Prague and Rome had escaped large-scale destruction. Many cities, like London, Coventry, St-Nazaire, Toulon, Vienna, Trieste or Lübeck, had whole sections gouged out of them. Others—Warsaw, Budapest, Rotterdam, Le Havre, Cologne, Frankfurt, Essen, Rostock—were largely in ruins. Some had been consumed by fire-storms: among the victims of these mass cremations were Hamburg, Wuppertal, Kassel, Stuttgart, Darmstadt and Dresden. A few—Jülich, Düren, Nuremberg, Hanover, Düsseldorf—had been almost totally destroyed. The condition of Berlin, in particular, horrified those who came to it from the west. 'I never saw such destruction,' declared Truman; for General Lucius Clay, 'it was like a city of the dead'. Ninety-five per cent of its urban area lay in ruins. There were three thousand broken water mains, and only twenty fire stations out of more than eighty were in operation. 149 of the city's schools had been demolished, and not one of its 187 Evangelical churches was untouched. In the streets were over 400 million cubic metres of rubble: one estimate reckoned that if ten trains a day with fifty wagons each were used to remove it, the process would take sixteen years.[17]

Between the devastated cities, communications had become difficult and slow. Many roads were closed to traffic. In the western regions of Germany, 740 out of 958 major river bridges were impassable. Many of the Seine and Loire bridges, and all those across the Rhine, had been demolished. When the war ended in Sicily, no permanent bridges had been left on the road from Catania to Palermo, and even a short journey of ten miles on the map could entail a drive of more than twice that distance across country. Vast numbers of vehicles had been destroyed or requisitioned. Nine-tenths of the trucks in France were out of action, and of the ten thousand needed to bring food to Paris, only two-and-a-half thousand were in use. Petrol, oil and spare parts were at a premium: early in 1945, most of the trucks produced by the French Renault company remained useless for want of tyres.[18]

The railways were in a worse state than the roads. Long stretches of track were out of commission—4,000 kilometres in France, 12,000 kilometres in north-west Germany, two-thirds of the entire system in Jugoslavia and Greece. Many viaducts were down—more than two-thirds of those in Poland, and 2,395 in Germany. In Berlin, rowing-boats had to be used in the flooded subway. One-quarter of the railway tunnels in Czechoslovakia were blocked. Few locomotives were in working order—fifty per cent in Germany, forty per cent in Belgium and Poland, twenty-five per cent in Holland, 3,000 out of 17,000 in France. Rolling stock was scarce, and scattered all over Europe. In north-west Germany, only 5,000 out of 12,000 wagons were usable, and in France only 115,000 of 475,000.[19]

Europe's waterways, once so vital to its prosperity, were now equally paralysed. Out of the 8,460 kilometres of French canals and rivers normally bearing traffic, only 509 kilometres were navigable at the time of the Liberation. Ninety per cent of the Oder barge fleet, and thirty-five per cent of the Rhine fleet, were destroyed. Many locks were badly damaged. Traffic on the Rhine was at a standstill. In its upper stretches, 754 barges had been sunk; to the north, the debris of 540 bridges was waiting to be removed from the canals. Antwerp and Bordeaux were the only large continental ports still functioning almost normally. In Hamburg harbour, fifty merchantmen, nineteen floating docks, and various other craft had foundered; the port of Toulon was encumbered with the scuttled grey wrecks of the French fleet. Most European countries, finally, had lost a large proportion of their merchant marine—Holland forty per cent, Britain and Norway fifty per cent, Belgium sixty per cent, France seventy per cent, and Italy ninety per cent.[20]

The paralysis of transport in Europe was partly matched by that of industry. Everywhere, there were shortages—of machinery, of raw materials, and especially of fuel and power. European coal production outside the Soviet Union was down to two-fifths of its prewar level. The Ruhr, which had once produced 400,000 tons a day, was now producing 25,000. In Italy, the total output of electricity stood at less than sixty-five per cent of the 1941 figure, and less still in the centre and south. Some items were particularly scarce: in France, coal production was held back by the shortage of pit-props, while the output of textiles had been greatly reduced by damage to the mills in the north-east. In southern Germany, with ninety per cent of the factories and eighty-five per cent of their plant out of action, industrial output was down to only five per cent of normal capacity. Production in Italy had fallen to less than one-quarter of what it had been in peace-time; in Belgium, France, Greece, Holland, Jugoslavia and Poland, it had fallen to one-fifth.[21]

In money terms, World War II had cost more than the combined total of all European wars since the Middle Ages. In France, the expenditure was estimated at 36,000 million dollars, or nearly three times the country's prewar annual income. Italy's national resources were reckoned to have been reduced by one-third. Even in Great Britain, which had been spared invasion, ten per cent of the national wealth had been destroyed by bombing and by the running down of capital assets. Britain's biggest loss, however, was invisible. Government expenditure had risen during the war to five times its previous level, while the exports with which to pay for it had been reduced by sixty per cent. To try to fill the gap, Britain had been obliged to liquidate £1,118 million's worth of overseas investments and other resources: but this still left an external debt of more than £3,000 million. Within six years the world's biggest creditor nation had become the biggest debtor. Much of continental Europe likewise, had also been living on credit and aid. By October 1945, the United States had granted 46,040 million dollars' worth of supplies on the 'Lend-Lease' basis of permanently deferred payment. Of this, some 30,000 million went to the British Empire, and 11,000 million to the Soviet Union. The other main beneficiaries included France, the Netherlands, Greece, Belgium, Norway, Turkey and Jugoslavia. When the war and Lend-Lease ended, Britain, France, the Netherlands and Belgium found it necessary to raise American loans. In Germany, the public debt had increased from 40,000 million marks to 357,000 million; in Italy, the budget deficit for 1945–6 was 300,000 million lire. Inflation plagued most European countries, although in varying degrees. Relatively mild in Britain, Denmark, Sweden and Switzerland, it was worse in Belgium, Bulgaria, Czechoslovakia, Finland, France, the Netherlands, Norway, Spain and Turkey; in Italy, prices rose to thirty-five times their prewar level. In Greece and Hungary, the currency collapsed completely.

In November 1944, the Greek government devalued the drachma at the rate of 50,000 million to one; and by the time that Hungary introduced a new monetary unit, the final quotation for the old one had reached the rate of 11,000,000,000,000,000,000,000,000,000,000 pengoes to the United States dollar.[22]

'Butter, chocolate, meat!' ran a front-page headline in the *Amsterdamsch Dagblad* on 8 May 1945.[23] Inflation might be an ominous symptom of Europe's longer-term problems; it might swallow up private savings and further demoralize an already shaken society: but even more immediate for most Europeans that summer was the search for food.

Throughout the continent, immense tracts of arable land had been laid waste. Nearly forty per cent of Europe's livestock was gone, and countless farm buildings had been destroyed or damaged. The Ukraine had twice suffered from 'scorched earth' devastation. In Italy, nearly two million acres of farmland south of the Apennines had been flooded, mined, or used for airfields; in the Netherlands, 540,000 acres had been flooded, 190,000 of them with salt water. In the whole of Europe, the area under wheat and rye had been reduced by twenty-three per cent; and when the war ended, it was too late for further sowing.[24]

The land still cultivated was in poor condition. Farming, like other industries, was subject to serious shortages—of seeds, pesticides, machinery, draught animals, manure. There was even a shortage of twine. Fertilizer output had fallen to one-fifth of its prewar level: this, coupled with severe drought, reduced yields per acre in 1945 by about twenty-five per cent. The wheat crop was forty per cent below normal, and the total harvest of bread grains in continental Europe outside the Soviet Union was only thirty-one million tons, compared with an average of fifty-nine million before the war. The total, moreover, concealed wide variations. If Denmark's 1945–6 crops were ninety-three per cent of the prewar average, those in France, Belgium, Germany and Italy were only a little above fifty per cent, and those in the Netherlands and Austria even lower.[25]

Hunger became commonplace in Europe. Even where agriculture had traditionally flourished, many remained underfed; and because the lack of transport made distribution difficult, there were notorious contrasts between the countryside and the towns. In France at the Liberation, while food in the provinces was adequate though meagre, the average Parisian had lost nearly three stone in weight. The official daily ration of bread, when available, was 275 grams or 500 grams for workpeople; the daily fats ration was ten grams; the meat ration, bones included, was 400 grams—less than a pound—to last for a month. On the Paris black market, bread was six times, butter ten times, and meat nearly three times the official price. For many Europeans, indeed, the black market had become a grudgingly accepted necessity; but for those unable to pay its prices, it was a bitterly resented privilege of the rich. At one black-market restaurant in Rome in 1945, old women and children crowded round the open-air enclosure to snatch food from the table; elsewhere in Italy at that time, bread was being sold by the slice.[26]

A man leading a sedentary life normally consumes between 2,400 and 2,800 calories a day, while a physically active man needs 3,200 to 5,500, depending on the nature of his work. Long after the war was over, United Nations experts reported that 140 million Europeans were still receiving fewer than 2,000 daily, and 100 million of them fewer than 1,500—less than the average inhabitant of India, and less than the normal ration for a seven-year-old child. In the last year of the war, many people in Holland had been subsisting on only 900 calories a day.[27]

But war had not only pauperized Europe; it had also taken unprecedented toll of human life. To the previous generation, World War I had seemed the ultimate Armageddon: it had left twenty-one million wounded and eight and a half million dead. World War II had killed thirty-two million, twenty-three million of them on the battlefield: of the total dead, more than fifteen million were Europeans. World War I had been the first to claim more victims among conscripts than among regular servicemen; World War II was the first in which so many civilians had lost their lives. Of all the belligerents, the Soviet Union had lost the most servicemen—seven and a half million; the next largest loss was that of Germany, with three and a half million men missing or killed. When the war ended, twenty-four per cent of the Germans born in 1924 were either dead or missing, and thirty-one per cent were more or less severely mutilated. In the western regions of Germany there were two million cripples. In the whole country, out of a population of nearly seventy million, there were now 7,279,000 more women than men.[28]

Yet however grim the fate of so many civilian and service victims of the actual war machine, the worst treatment of all was reserved for those who died—and those, perhaps less fortunate, who nearly died—in the concentration and extermination camps. Their story has been told so many times that anyone who was not an inmate may well question his own credentials, and perhaps the quality of his own motives, for returning to it. Needless repetition would be doubly obscene. Nevertheless, the stripe-clad scarecrows condemned to the 'bone-mills' of Auschwitz, Bełżec, Sobibór. Chełmno, Treblinka and the rest have their place in any account of postwar Europe—no less than Stalin's forced labourers, the bombed victims of Coventry or Dresden, the women and children massacred in the church of Oradour-sur-Glane, the German plotters against Hitler, hanged on meat-hooks—and, indeed, the degraded, brutalized, sometimes frightened men who devised and ran the apparatus of extermination, and whose minds must surely be numbered among its victims. Altogether, at least six million people died in the camps before the war was over. When the Allied forces entered them, behind the look-out towers and the double barbed-wire fencing they found a total of some 670,000 survivors—befouled apathetic skeletons of men and women, huddled five to a shelf on multi-tier bunks, or lying, sitting and dragging themselves about amid the reeking, fly-covered litter of corpses outside their huts. To their liberators, many seemed half-human, reduced by cruelty to the very condition of *Untermenschen* that their captors' ideology prescribed for them—the most appalling circular argument in the history of mankind.[29]

The death camps set an absolute for human suffering: beside the long shadow they cast on history, few comparisons are valid. But among the ruins of Europe in 1945, suffering was not rare; and alongside the dead and the half-alive there were many more for whom sheer existence had come close to misery.

Between 1939 and the end of 1945, at least sixty million Europeans—not counting servicemen and prisoners of war—had been uprooted from their homes. Twenty-seven million of them had left their own countries, or been driven out by force. Four and a half million had been deported by the Nazis for forced labour; many thousands more had been sent to Siberia by the Russians. When the war ended, two and a half million Poles and Czechs were transferred to the Soviet Union, and more than twelve million Germans fled or were expelled from Eastern Europe. At one period in 1945, 40,000 refugees a week were streaming into north-west Germany. All told, the shifts of population involved fifty-five ethnic groups from twenty-seven countries. Some had been displaced more than once: one group—420,000 Karelians from between the Gulf of Finland and the White Sea—was shuttled to and fro no less than three times. By the summer of 1945, moreover, in addition to such refugees and 'displaced persons', there were seven million prisoners of war in Allied hands in Western Europe, and more than eight million Allied troops.[30]

Statistics may indicate, but can hardly convey, the realities of such mass removals: the trains and cattle trucks crammed with human beings; the straggling processions with their prams and cardboard suit-cases; the women and children staggering under knapsacks; the road-

side deaths; the weary fugitives limping across border zones in the darkness, their boots clogged with heavy mud. Several million died in the
process; the impossibility of knowing how many is a rough measure of
their ordeal. Of those who survived it, many were destitute. Germans
expelled from Hungary were allowed to take 100 kilograms of personal
belongings; from Czechoslovakia, 70 kilograms; from Poland, what they
could carry: none was permitted more than a small quota of already inflated Reichsmarks. Europeans deported as forced labourers had naturally had even less; so had many of those who had fled from the advancing armies or escaped with only their lives from the air-raids that had
destroyed their cities. All were desperate for food and shelter—and for
news of their families. At the centre set up in Germany to trace missing
persons, a staff of 240, using twenty-four languages, dealt with a thousand enquiries a day. With millions to be collected and cared for, lodged
in converted factories, equipped with soap and blankets, fed on bread,
thick soup and coffee substitute, humanitarian efforts were bound to
seem dehumanized. Alongside the refugees' own languages, alongside
'Lagerdeutsch' and the polyglot scapegrace slang of postwar Europe—
'comme ci comme ça', 'Alles kaputt', 'finito', 'nix OK'—there grew up a
new bureaucratic jargon: 'DP' (for 'displaced person'), 'post-hostility
refugees', 'internal displacement', 'infiltrees', 'non-repatriables', 'uncovered children', 'unaccompanied children'. It was a verbal device for
facing the intolerable; but to some compassionate and sensitive observers it inevitably seemed cold. Others, at first, found equally disconcerting the unattractiveness of the unfortunate, at once aggressive and
feckless, clinging to a few symbolic possessions; conspiring and often
fighting to gain small material advantages; sometimes apathetic, often
touchy and ungrateful, resenting the overworked helpers who were
saving their lives.[31]

Such symptoms were part of the plight of the homeless and uprooted;
and they were very widespread in the Europe of 1945. The destructive
force of war had been more than physical. When peace came, many
Europeans were deeply weary and demoralized. Inflation, rationing, the
black market, the wealth and power of the occupying forces—all added
to the disruption of normal ethics; looting, armed robbery, pimping, corruption and subterfuge were the result. And beneath the obvious signs
of social disturbance there remained a legacy from dictatorship and
defeat—a profound sense of impotence before alien authorities that
was often taken for inherent submissiveness or cynicism. 'Der kleine
Mann, was kann er doch machen?' was a question continually asked me
by prisoners of war. Nor was the feeling confined to Germany. Depicting
the moral anarchy of postwar Naples, the novelist Curzio Malaparte

added, 'All of us in Europe ... are more or less Neapolitan'; and a young French writer from the Paris suburbs, René Fallet, described with something of Malaparte's florid bitterness the world in which he and his contemporaries grew up:

We are the children of the occupation. In 1940 we were twelve, thirteen or fourteen. We began our life in an atmosphere of defeat, pillage and theft. We begged cigarettes from the Germans. on the roads of a country in ruins. We stuffed ourselves with swedes when what we wanted was bars of chocolate. We got in on the rackets. ... For us, 'before the war' was a faded memory. Our years of discretion were years of utter absurdity, utter misery. ... The older generation dropped us flat, although it was they who produced us! All they can do is keep on at us: 'In my day, we didn't answer our mothers back like that. ... Young people today don't like work any more. ... I don't know what's become of morality and honesty. ...' So what? To hell with all the virtues that that lot couldn't preserve![32]

The tone was authentic and familiar: more radically than the celebrated 'disillusion' of the nineteen-twenties, it expressed a general postwar mood. The writings of Jean-Paul Sartre, Max Frisch, Cesare Pavese, Graham Greene, George Orwell; the films of Henri-Georges Clouzot, Marcel Carné, Wolfgang Staudte, Vittorio de Sica; the plays of Jean Anouilh; the verses of Jacques Prévert; the paintings of Francis Bacon— all on their different levels, whatever their affirmations, seemed to imply that happiness and hope were incompatible with intelligence or sensibility. Looking at the world in which they were welcomed, it was hard to disagree.

During the past six years, even in the democracies, a number of the civilized virtues had indeed had to be suspended 'for the duration', like non-essential adjuncts to civilian life. For all the belligerents, violence, hatred and killing had become legitimate, patriotic, heroic; for resistance workers in the occupied countries, law-breaking, sabotage and occasional necessary murders had become the norm. The skill of professional criminals had been recruited to combat crimes against humanity. Peaceable, kindly men and women had been taught cruel trades. To survive in such a moral climate, the sensitive had had to steel themselves; others had had to exploit, yet hold within limits, a natural aggressiveness that served their cause. Not everyone succeeded. When the great convulsion ended, when the Fascist and Nazi empires crumbled and the dictators went to their squalid deaths, some of the weapons that had defended freedom, peace and civilization proved to be double-edged. Nothing was more natural, more to be expected even by its victims, than the orgy of vengeance that broke out in Europe. Nothing was more inevitable: but it was an ugly sight.

At the elemental level, it took the form of what one writer bleakly called 'the good old standbys of murder, torture, robbery, and rape'. 'There is a sad monotony,' he commented, 'about what one can do to a human being.' For a time, there was lawlessness in most of the conquered and liberated countries. In Berlin and elsewhere the Red Army, its depleted ranks replenished from distant, primitive regions, earned a grim reputation for drunken violence, plunder and indiscriminate sexual assault. In many parts of Germany, forced labourers and prisoners, suddenly freed, ran riot; and ordinary thieves and other criminals seized their chance, amid the general anarchy, to enrich themselves or pay off old scores. In the liberated countries, Nazi collaborators were rounded up and punished, sometimes summarily. The one-time conquerors' girl friends—what the Dutch called the *'moffenmeiden'*—were subjected to treatment in which long-pent anger, prurience and puritanism seem to have had equal shares; but even they, paraded with shaven heads and sometimes shaven bodies, were better off than some male collaborators, reviled and bloodily beaten amid the smiles of peaceful-looking crowds. Many were executed on the spot. In France at the Liberation, at least 5,000 men and women were killed by their compatriots, and many more were imprisoned without proper trial. By no means all of the victims had been collaborators; by no means all of those responsible were members of the Resistance. In some areas, the Communist underground *Francs-tireurs et partisans* used force to try to eliminate their rivals: but many cases of murder and torture—some rivalling those of the Nazi Gestapo —were simply the work of rapacious armed thugs. True, the picture was not entirely black. Many deserved their fate, and a number of others showed restraint and courage. Just as, at the Ebensee concentration camp, two German Luftwaffe pilots turned guns on the guards and saved the inmates from last-minute massacre, so in the pillage of Berlin some Russian soldiers defended German women from their own drunken comrades. Even in that darkness there were points of light; and when some of the survivors in the death camps rounded on their SS captors, it could hardly be said that darkness was greatly deepened.[33]

'Revenge,' wrote Francis Bacon the essayist, 'is a kind of wild justice.' At the end of World War II, certainly, much rough justice was done. But retribution, however deserved, is a questionable aim in international policy; and if it assumes judicial status, it may cause justice to be mistaken for a kind of pedantic revenge.

This, at least, is what happened when the victors of World War II set out to judge some of the vanquished, most notably in the first Nuremberg trial. In the dock were twenty-one defendants. A few of the Nazi ringleaders were absent: Hitler, Himmler and the labour organizer Robert Ley had already committed suicide; Goebbels had had himself shot by an SS orderly; and Martin Bormann was missing, perhaps dead. The star defendant was the once plump Hermann Göring, also later to kill himself before he could be hanged. With him were some of the pillars of the Third Reich—Rudolf Hess, dazed and vacant, staring and fidgeting; Joachim von Ribbentrop, no longer the icy diplomat, but cowed and pallid; Karl Dönitz, looking to one observer 'for all the world like a shoe clerk';[34] Wilhelm Keitel and Alfred Jodl, sitting sternly upright; Julius Streicher, angry and insolent; Ernst Kaltenbrunner, nervously chewing. They and their colleagues now seemed dim and unimpressive in their rankless uniforms and crumpled suits. For 216 days they sat in the big wooden enclosure, flanked by US military police. From November 1945 to October 1946 the trial continued, with five million words of testimony and ten million words of printed record. The documents processed weighed several tons, and the published proceedings filled forty-two volumes. At the end of it all, three of the accused were acquitted; Hess, Dönitz, and five others were sentenced to varying terms of imprisonment; and the remaining twelve—including Göring, Ribbentrop, Keitel, Jodl, Streicher, Kaltenbrunner and the absent Bormann—were condemned to death.

The verdicts, like the volume of evidence, were proof of the tribunal's anxiety to be fair. It attempted to blend British, American and continental European procedure. Its president was Lord Justice Lawrence; each of the four main victorious powers supplied one distinguished judge and one alternate. The prosecution was conducted by eminent Allied counsel, and the accused were defended by lawyers of their own nationality, all but one of whom wore legal robes, as did all but one of the judges. Simultaneous interpretation, with adjustable headphones, ensured that all the testimony was instantly understandable. In the dock, the defendants were allowed to talk together; and Göring, at least, spoke so long when giving evidence that the chief American prosecuting attorney appealed to the president of the court to silence him—in vain. The records of the trial were of unique documentary importance: in the words of one scholar, they 'threw valuable light upon the history of the war from the former enemy side'.[35] More than this, they provided conclusive proof of Nazi barbarity: some of the atrocities they revealed would have earned the maximum penalty in any civilized court of law.

In this respect, the trial succeeded. It was no longer possible to deny with any honesty the nature of Adolf Hitler's 'new order'—or the mediocrity of those who served it: Julius Streicher, for instance, who had so

39

long preached 'Jewish inferiority', proved to have the modest intelligence quotient of 106.[36] Nevertheless, if justice must not only be done, but also be seen to be done, the Nuremberg trial was a partial failure. It was perhaps too soon to be judicial about those who had caused unimaginable suffering; it was certainly too soon to appear so.

Despite the tribunal's fairness, in fact, it could hardly avoid the appearance of being both prosecutor and judge. The principle that men are innocent until proved guilty was understandably difficult to apply to the Nazi leaders. Before the trial, the Soviet judge had argued that they already stood convicted by proclamation of the Allies; and according to Sir David Maxwell Fyfe, British representative at the meetings preparing the trial, 'Our work is to see these top-notch Nazis tried, condemned, and many of them executed.' To enable all the prisoners to be kept in solitary confinement—forbidden to officers by the Geneva Convention—the defendants from the services were stripped of military rank. For reasons of security, none of the accused was allowed to speak alone with counsel, and all at first shared a small consulting-room a dozen at a time. In court, the prosecuting lawyers, unlike the defence, wore plain clothes or military uniform; also in uniform was the Russian judge. Finally, the gladiatorial nature of British and American court procedure, which predominated, was unfamiliar to the defendants' lawyers, for whom normal judicial proceedings were at least theoretically biased towards collective truth-seeking rather than attack and riposte. In the subsequent trial of the munitions manufacturer Alfried Krupp, arraigned in lieu of his senile father Gustav, there were serious clashes between the judges and defending counsel, who once walked out in protest and were briefly imprisoned for contempt of court.[37]

One argument before the Krupp tribunal, in particular, raised more clearly than most a question that was implicit in all the trials. 'Much can be understood,' the defence pleaded,

... only by him who experienced it himself: the extraordinary mixture of genuine love of one's country and unhealthy nationalism, of justified consciousness of one's self and [a sense of] racial superiority; the harmony between voluntary readiness for sacrifice and terroristic force, the intermingling of faith, self-deception, and betrayal.[38]

Such words could not bring back the dead, nor mitigate the enormities they helped explain; but they applied to many. There was and remains, in fact, a deep enigma in apportioning guilt and responsibility. When death and torture are inflicted on so many millions, it becomes more difficult than ever to draw a reasonable line between the obvious culprits and those whose co-operation, acquiescence, forced obedience, indifference or voluntary ignorance helped make such things possible. Those who blame only the ringleaders may dishonour the active resistance—for whose members the concentration camps were partly intended—by tacitly grouping it with the inactive mass. Those, chiefly foreigners, who tend to depict Hitler as in some ways a normal statesman, thereby implicitly blaming a whole nation, seem not only to discount the Führer's long-avowed intentions, but also to have no logical grounds for totally absolving themselves: their countries too could have acted from outside to check the Nazis sooner—even if then it was still impossible to forestall them by establishing law and order on an international scale.[39]

In one respect, therefore, the Allied tribunals had an insuperable task. Inevitably, there were inequities if not injustices: some slipped through the net in which others, with similar records, were caught. To many, for instance, it seemed unfair that military men should be hanged for obeying orders, however iniquitous: a soldier's obedience, they claimed, should be unconditional. This dubious doctrine was convincingly answered by those who pointed out that every man, soldier or not, has an ultimate duty of his conscience, and that blind obedience was one of the evils against which the war had been fought. Their case would have seemed stronger, however, if Allied propaganda had analyzed less superficially the causes of World War II. As it was, 'Prussian militarism' had been denounced alongside 'Nazi tyranny'—despite the fact that a number of the plotters against Hitler had been 'Prussian militarists' themselves.

Confusion of this sort was compounded by the double nature of the Nuremberg indictment. On the one hand it accused the defendants of war crimes and crimes against humanity, of which most of them were manifestly guilty, and were proved so; but on the other it made the much more general charge of 'waging aggressive warfare'.

'Aggression' was a word from the political vocabulary of the 'thirties; perhaps because it was so familiar, it was never adequately defined. The impulse behind its use was a groping towards some system that would make war illegal, as Henry L. Stimson—later, ironically, to be US Secretary of War—had declared it to be as early as 1932. In 1939, Russia had been expelled from the League of Nations for violating the Kellogg-Briand Pact by attacking Finland; 'aggression' of this kind was now 'a crime'. At Nuremberg, at least, this became a prosecution thesis. Robert Jackson, the American prosecutor, claimed that 'no political, military or other considerations justify going to war ... The law ... requires that the *status quo* be not attacked by violent means.' Sir Hartley Shawcross, for the British, was only a little less categorical: 'It is a fundamental part of these proceedings,' he declared, 'to establish for all time that international law has the power ... to declare that a war is criminal ...' But however well-meaning, arguments such as these were juridically and morally precarious. In the opinion of the French delegate at the preparation of the tribunal, 'If we declare war a criminal act of individuals, we are going further than the actual law.' On this count, moreover, the Allies themselves—including the Russians—were by no means immune from reproach.[40]

At the safe and comfortable vantage-point of more than twenty years' distance, therefore, the Nuremberg trials reveal many imperfections. To condemn these now would simply be to echo them; it has to be recalled how very different, to most people, the whole question looked at the time. In their context, the trials were a marvel of impartiality; then, perhaps only the saintly—or the insensitive—could be truly detached. Yet, in historical perspective, the mood of those concerned seems fatally tainted by the moral climate of war. Hatred and cruelty had called forth hatred, even on the part of the innocent; in some cases, elsewhere, they had called forth further cruelty as well. Writing in the shadow of Europe's collective tragedy, the American critic Edmund Wilson drew the stark conclusion: 'Our whole world is poisoned now, and we must recognize that outlawing the enemy makes it easy to dislike one's allies.'[41]

CHAPTER THREE

The New Frontier

This war is not as in the past; whoever occupies a territory
also imposes on it his own social system. Everyone imposes
his own system as far as his army has power to do so. It
cannot be otherwise.
                                        Joseph Stalin[1]

Stalin was always asking for as much as he could get.
                                        Harry S. Truman[2]

The King was evidently very uncomfortable at having to
sit down between the two giant creatures: but there was
no other place for him.   *Lewis Carroll*[3]

THE East-West confrontation had begun on Wednesday, 25 April 1945,
when Russian and American troops had met on the Elbe. At least three
separate advance parties from the American side pushed forward
across the last strip of enemy territory between them and their allies;
recollections and dramatic reconstructions differ about who met whom
first and where. Was it at Torgau or at Strehla? Was it a rowing-boat or
a sail boat that the Americans paddled across the river with their
rifle-butts? Did the meeting take place at 12·05, 1·30, 4·40 or 4·45?
In fact, a man in a fur hat riding on a pony seems to have been the first
Russian sighted, in the village of Leckwitz, a mile from the Elbe; he was
hailed from a jeep by Lieutenant Albert Kotzebue of the 69th Division
of the V Corps. The time was about 11·30 a.m. Shortly afterwards came
the first encounter on the river itself. There, photographs were taken;
a public relations officer appeared as if from nowhere, to have them
posed and retaken with officers of higher rank. There was laughter,
friendly babel, handshaking and gesturing with the flags that hung limp
in the still air. Toasts were drunk; little speeches were made for posterity.
Then the war continued. In Europe, it was almost over: but for anyone
who sought them, that day's thin sunshine was already casting new
shadows. At Torgau, an American patrol had come under Russian fire
before it could establish its identity; later, to the Americans' surprise,
the Russians dug themselves into further defensive positions—facing
west.[4]

Both these incidents arose from routine battle drill; but they symbolized the fact that the world's two giants now confronted each other, warily, across a prostrate continent. The sequel, although neither may have consciously intended it, was the partition of Europe.

To impute 'inevitability' to historical processes can be a tempting substitute for investigation and thought. But now and then comes a moment in history when circumstances conspire against men's efforts to change them; and one such moment was the last winter of the war. By that time, all the belligerents were weary. All three of the statesmen then supremely responsible in the struggle against Hitler had reached what in many less demanding professions would have been the retiring age. Joseph Stalin was 65, and long tainted by what his opponents later called 'the cult of personality'. Winston Churchill, at 70, was 'very tired'[5] by the crushing burdens he had borne for more than four years, and he had recently been shaken by two attacks of pneumonia, one of them extremely severe. Franklin Roosevelt, although only 62, was a haggard semi-invalid already close to death. Weighed down by the day-to-day tasks of war, obliged to deal pell-mell with problems as they presented themselves, they were even less able than statesmen ever are to transform the basic situation from which the problems arose. In many respects, therefore, their efforts for the future peace were bound to fit into a predetermined pattern. It was unfortunate, and ironical, that the pattern should largely have been set by Adolf Hitler.

All three of the leading Allied powers had originally been 'insular'. Britain was an island in the literal sense; her traditional aspiration had been non-involvement in continental Europe, whose peace she had sought to ensure by using a casting-vote to maintain successive balances of power. The United States, more decisively protected by a broader ocean patrolled by the British navy, had tended to regard non-involvement as not merely prudent, but virtuous: Europe was an Old World from which many Americans' fathers and grandfathers had been glad to escape. Russia's historical situation had been different. Lacking the natural protection of a western coastline, it had fought to establish on its European borders a defensive ring of cowed or conquered territory; internally, it had developed a siege mentality, becoming autocratic in order to survive. But while in these respects it had been the opposite of America, at a deeper level its experience had been similar. It too had lived alone. Communism, with its revolutionary mission, had modified Russia's traditional solitude; but defensiveness ran deep. It was even intensified by the Communists' belief—or their claim—that they alone were building the good society. In their various ways, in fact, all three Allies had been 'right little, tight little islands', with the typical islander's sense of superiority, shared, for slightly different reasons, by the fourth Ally, France.

Hitler, by destroying the old Europe, had destroyed the Allies' isolation and had brought them face to face. The crippling of France and the impoverishment of Great Britain ensured that the confrontation was now essentially between America and the Soviet Union. America, which had distrusted the balance of power in Europe, was forced into similar balance on the world scale. For a while, she seemed to grope for the role of arbiter which had once been played by Britain: Roosevelt, in particular, sometimes saw himself as a mediator between Russian Communism and Churchillian 'imperialism'. But the British Commonwealth could be no real counterweight to the Soviet Union; and in the end America entered and almost filled one side of the global balance. The other, as in the past, was occupied by the strongest power on the continent of Europe. Until very recently, that power had been Germany; but now, Hitler's 'total war' and its corollary of 'unconditional surrender' had brought Germany to the brink of destruction; and the Soviet Union took its place. Even before the war ended, distance, language, history, ideology and conflicting conceptions of their interests had already helped to divide America and Russia. Once they were deprived of a common enemy, their new proximity divided them even more.[6]

Between the two giants and partly under their occupation, Europe faced an uncertain future. Only by making a separate peace could either America or Russia disengage herself. This was barely conceivable, although each suspected the other of toying with the idea. It was equally unlikely that both, when the war ended, would return to their former isolation—if only because so much remained to be settled; and unless both did so, neither could afford to retire. Of the two, the United States was the more inclined to withdraw from Europe; but for the Soviet Union this had become unthinkable. Stalin, although fighting for his life and that of Russia, had always made it clear that the prize he expected for his indispensable aid against the Axis powers was a free hand in Eastern Europe. As soon as this demand was even tacitly accepted by the Western Allies, the partition of Europe—at least into spheres of influence—became virtually certain. What was still undecided was the position of the new frontier, its effectiveness as a barrier, and its consequences for those on either side.

The question had arisen as early as December 1941, when enemy tanks had reached the outskirts of Moscow. There, Stalin had urged Anthony Eden, the British Foreign Secretary, to recognize Russian possession of Estonia, Latvia and Lithuania; he had also pressed his claim to those areas of Poland east of the so-called 'Curzon Line', which had remained Russian when the Polish republic had been recreated at Versailles in 1919, but which it had invaded and conquered in the following year. Backed by American prompting, Eden had resisted: when Britain signed a treaty of alliance with Russia six months later, the territorial clauses that Moscow had wanted were left out of the agreement. The result, unforeseen at the time, was that the claims made by Russia in a position of weakness were later restated and augmented in a position of strength.[7]

By the autumn of 1944, the tide of war had turned and the Red Army was sweeping westward. In January it had entered Poland, and begun absorbing or disbanding the national resistance forces; throughout August and September, unable or unwilling to come to the rescue, it had allowed the Warsaw rising to be crushed by the Nazis. In August, Rumania had ended its war against Russia; in September, Soviet troops had entered Belgrade, and were soon to enter Hungary; at about the same time, Marshal Tito of Jugoslavia had quietly slipped off to Moscow for talks with Stalin, and the Communist-dominated EAM (the *Ethnikon Apeleftherotikon Metopon* or National Liberation Front) was gaining control in Greece. Hopes that an effective world organization—the United Nations—might replace power politics had been dimmed by the disputes over voting rights within it when the United States, the Soviet Union, China and Great Britain had met to discuss it that autumn at Dumbarton Oaks, near Washington. Churchill, already sceptical, agreed with the South African Prime Minister Field-Marshal Smuts that with Eastern Europe and the Balkans falling under Russian influence, 'our position in the Mediterranean and in Western Europe must be strengthened rather than weakened'. He therefore 'felt acutely the need to see Stalin, with whom I always considered one could talk as one human being to another.'[8]

Flying into Moscow with Anthony Eden on the afternoon of Monday, 9 October 1944, he quickly made himself at home in the small but unusually comfortable house that the Russians had provided. The prospect of direct action was exhilarating. 'How are you going to begin with Uncle Joe?' asked Eden when he arrived for dinner. 'I shall say that the President and I have been like brothers,' said Churchill, 'but I don't want the USSR to feel it is just an Anglo-Saxon affair. I want them to know it's the three of us. We can settle everything, we three, if we come together.'[9]

At ten o'clock that night, Churchill and Eden went round to the Kremlin. Within an hour or two they had concluded with Stalin what in the words of a French writer 'can only euphemistically be called a "gentlemen's agreement" '. It was Churchill who proposed it. 'Let us settle about our affairs in the Balkans,' he said. 'Your armies are in Rumania and Bulgaria. We have interests, missions and agents there. Don't let us get at cross-purposes in small ways. So far as Britain and Russia are concerned, how would it do for you to have ninety per cent predominance in Rumania, for us to have ninety per cent of the say in Greece, and go fifty-fifty about Jugoslavia?' While this was being interpreted, Churchill took a half-sheet of paper and wrote out the percentages, adding further figures for Hungary ('50-50 per cent') and Bulgaria ('Russia 75 per cent, the others 25 per cent). Stalin looked at it for a moment; then he made a large blue-pencil tick on it and passed it back. There was a long silence. Churchill hesitated. 'Might it not be thought rather cynical,' he said, 'if it seemed we had disposed of these issues, so fateful to millions of people, in such an offhand manner? Let us burn the paper.' Stalin had fewer scruples. Perhaps he was pleased to involve Churchill in unholy complicity. 'No—you keep it,' he replied.[10]

So began the partition of Europe. The bargain indeed seemed cynical in its very rapidity; but it might have seemed no less so if disguised by diplomatic niceties, when in fact it was a recognition of the reality of power. The fate of Poland in 1939, crushed by the Nazis despite the Allied declaration of war against Hitler, had already shown the virtual impossibility of Western intervention to defend Eastern Europe; and if the Balkans now suffered for the same reason, Poland herself was about to do so a second time.

Historically, relations between Poles and Russians had never been happy; now, despite the common struggle against Hitler, they remained tense. The dispute over Poland's eastern territories was still not settled; and the atmosphere was hardly improved by the growing suspicion that Stalin, not Hitler, had been responsible for the slaughter of several thousand Polish officers in the forest of Katyn, near Smolensk. Nevertheless, in February 1944, under pressure from Churchill, the exiled Polish government in London agreed to discuss possible changes in the eastern frontier, and to envisage compensation with further territory in the West. It was the Soviet Union which remained adamant. Not only did Stalin insist on retaining all those regions of eastern Poland which he had recovered in 1939 under the Nazi-Soviet pact; he also set about ensuring a firm Russian grip on the postwar Polish government.[11]

In July, 1944, Stanislaw Mikolajczyk, the Peasant Party leader who had succeeded General Wladyslaw Sikorski as head of the London government-in-exile, visited Moscow to discuss the territorial question; but instead of being able to negotiate with Stalin, he found himself obliged to haggle with the Polish Committee of National Liberation, the 'provisional executive authority' set up in Lublin, the temporary capital. As Churchill wrote after meeting the Committee's representatives: 'It was soon plain that the Lublin Poles were mere pawns of Russia. They had learned and rehearsed their part so carefully that even their masters evidently felt they were overdoing it.' Mikolajczyk had the same impression. The Lublin Committee was already planning to dominate the postwar government: its Communist leader, Boleslaw Bierut, hoped to be President. True, he was prepared to offer Mikolajczyk the post of Prime Minister, but with only three other 'London' Poles in a cabinet of eighteen. Meanwhile, Warsaw had risen against the Nazis; yet both Bierut and Stalin seemed deaf to appeals for help. Returning to London, Mikolajczyk even now induced his colleagues to propose a further compromise on the frontier question and the shape of the postwar government; but he can hardly have been surprised when Stalin paid no heed.[12]

For a further six weeks the deadlock continued. Then, rather peremptorily, Churchill summoned the leader of the 'London' Poles to Moscow. On Friday, 13 October 1944, Mikolajczyk and his colleagues met Churchill, Eden, Stalin and the Soviet Foreign Minister V. M. Molotov; the American Ambassador, William Averell Harriman, was present as an observer. To Mikolajczyk's dismay, Stalin and Molotov announced that at their Teheran meeting a year before the three Allies had already decided to return Poland's eastern territories to Russia. This was stretching the truth: but Churchill was acquiescent and Harriman, true to his observer's status, said nothing—rather as Roosevelt had done at Teheran. Molotov and Churchill then described how Poland could be compensated by the extension of its western boundaries as far as the Oder. Finally, Churchill put strong pressure on Mikolajczyk to come to an agreement with the Lublin Committee. It seemed to be a case of *force majeure*.[13]

Looking from one calm, stubborn face to another, Mikolajczyk could do nothing—feel nothing but impotent rage and pain. Churchill, despite appearances, was equally powerless. The frontiers that he was proposing seemed to him reasonable: they would nullify the results of Polish aggression against Russia in 1920, yet offer compensation at the expense of the common enemy who had attacked Poland in 1939. As for the postwar government, the very unattractiveness of the Lublin

Committee seemed likely to tell against it once free elections were held. Above all, Stalin had shown that he would accept no other solution; and against Soviet intransigence there was little that Churchill alone could do. The London Poles weighed on his conscience; but like all the exiled governments, precariously embodying the ideal of their countries' freedom, they were bound at times to seem needlessly touchy, pretentious poor relations in permanent residence, with no real power to endorse or justify their theoretical claims. Alternately exasperated and conciliatory, he argued for several days in the hope of reaching a compromise. At one bitter moment, Mikolajczyk asked leave to be parachuted into Poland, saying that he preferred to die now 'rather than be hanged later by the Russians in full view of your British Ambassador'. But the dispute, if acrimonious, was inconclusive: Mikolajczyk returned to his indignant cabinet in London and Churchill to a restive House of Commons. America, meanwhile, was deep in a presidential election, and Polish appeals to Roosevelt produced only tardy and partial assurances. Finally, Mikolajczyk and his Peasant Party colleagues resigned, leaving the government-in-exile in the hands of anti-Soviet Socialists.[14]

Thereupon, preparations began to be made in Poland for the Lublin Committee to become a provisional government; and in January, 1945, this was formed. The Soviet Union instantly accorded it diplomatic recognition. A fortnight later, the Red Army entered the ruins of Warsaw, and the Provisional Government was set in place. At the Yalta Conference in February, the United States, the Soviet Union and Britain made small adjustments to the Polish frontiers proposed by Stalin and Churchill, and agreed that 'the Provisional Government which is now functioning in Poland should ... be reorganized on a broader democratic basis, with the inclusion of democratic leaders from Poland itself and from Poles abroad'.[15]

This formula bore every trace of its conflicting origins. Much of the Yalta meeting, as one French diplomat has remarked, turned into a verbal exercise. 'The march of events creates difficulties. These take the form of documents. It is necessary to reach agreements, i.e. texts. This is what happens at nearly all such conferences. Never really prepared, they degenerate into drafting committees. Men who are responsible for the destinies of the world get entangled in a mesh of words and phrases, like giants sent back to school.'[16] Applied to the 'Lublin' government, the word 'reorganized' made agreement possible only at the cost of ambiguity. For the Western powers, it meant something like 'replaced': for the Soviet Union, it implied minor modifications to a largely puppet government. In the long run, the latter interpretation prevailed.

In all essentials, therefore, the fate of Eastern Europe had been decided in Moscow in the crisp October days of 1944. In Greece, Stalin
kept his bargain with Churchill: that winter, the Communist-run
EAM's military arm, ELAS (*Ethnikos Laikos Apeleftherotikos Stratos* or
National People's Liberation Army), was defeated in its attempt to seize
power. In Jugoslavia, Marshal Tito captured his Serbian rival Draža
Mihailović and had him executed for allowing his Cetnici to join forces
with Germans and Italians against the Communist partisans. Tito's independence of character kept Jugoslavia's status ambiguous; but elsewhere—in Bulgaria, Rumania, Hungary and Czechoslovakia, as in
Poland—non-Communists were finally eliminated from office by various
combinations of threats, propaganda, faked elections, purges, deporta-
tion, judicial murder and armed coups. The details differed, but the
broad pattern of Soviet policy was everywhere the same. Its purpose
was simple and very evident. As Stalin remarked at Yalta, Poland had
been throughout history 'the corridor through which the enemy has
passed into Russia'. His aim was to turn that corridor into a barrier,
alongside similar barriers in the rest of Eastern Europe. The results,
however, were further-reaching. By annexing part of Poland and establishing a defensive ring of satellites on its own western borders, the
Soviet Union merely shifted its problems westward with itself.[17]

In part, this reflected the new world balance. On the world stage,
Western Europe now found itself between the United States and the
Soviet Union in a position similar to that once occupied by Poland
between Germany and Imperial Russia. On the European stage, Poland's
traditional role of buffer state was now assumed by Germany, with all
the risk of partition which that implied. But whereas Poland had been
small and weak, and its people very various, Germany even now was
potentially the second greatest power on the continent, with a strong
sense of national identity. To divide Germany would be to cut deep
into the heart of Europe, inflicting a wound that might dangerously
fester if it were left unhealed.[18]

Already during the war this danger had been tacitly acknowledged. In
July 1943, for example, the British Foreign Office had suggested to
America and Russia a joint organization to administer the future armistice, with a local Allied Commission in each ex-enemy country. At the
end of August, Stalin himself proposed a single organization to negotiate
with Hitler's allies; and at the Moscow Foreign Ministers' Conference
that October, Anthony Eden had put forward a resolution on Allied
responsibility in postwar Europe, repudiating separate spheres of influence.[19]

Yet behind this apparent harmony, the realities were more conflicting and confused. Stalin's proposal of August 1943, in particular, had been a response to the current armistice negotiations with Italy, which were concluded on 3 September and announced five days later. As elaborated by Molotov at the Moscow Conference, it would have given the joint Allied organization in Italy control over both the civil and the military activities of the Commander-in-Chief, General Alexander; and this, the Western Allies feared, might hamstring their armies without in return ensuring joint control over Eastern Europe. They therefore successfully insisted that the Allied organization be merely advisory. In practice, this by no means excluded all Russian influence: within six months, the Soviet Union had accredited an independent representative to the Italian government, and Palmiro Togliatti had returned from Moscow to lead the Italian Communist Party. But although such tolerance contrasted sharply with Soviet absolutism in Eastern Europe, the Allies' agreement on Italy further confirmed the emergence of separate spheres of influence, which the Western Allies officially opposed.[20]

In the case of Germany, the question of spheres of influence, or partition, was entangled with that of 'dismemberment'. If postwar Germany were to have a unified government, partition would be unlikely; if it were to be 'dismembered' into separate states or regions, partition might be difficult to avoid. On this subject, each of the three principal Allies had differing opinions; and each shifted its viewpoint during the later stages of the war.

The idea of partition had been broached by Stalin at the end of 1941. Then, he had envisaged independence for Austria, the Rhineland, and perhaps Bavaria, and the transfer of East Prussia to Poland and of the Sudetenland to Czechoslovakia. He felt, as he said two years later at the Teheran Conference, that 'if Germany was to be dismembered it should really be dismembered'. When his ambitions in Eastern Europe began to be satisfied, however, Stalin seemed ready to listen to other proposals: in February 1945 at Yalta, he asked if dismemberment was still accepted, and whether the whole of Germany should have a single government. By the time of the armistice, on 9 May 1945, he appeared to have swung round completely. 'The Soviet Union,' he announced in his Proclamation to the Peoples, 'celebrates victory but it does not intend to dismember or destroy Germany'—a view he confirmed at the Potsdam Conference in July. To Harry Hopkins, Roosevelt's friend and adviser, Stalin explained this apparent *volte-face* as a concession to British and American feelings; more probably, it was a bid to have some say in administering the Ruhr, from which he hoped for reparations.[21]

British policy was equally changeable and equally consistent. Shifting with events, it yet remained true to diplomatic reflexes conditioned by the balance of power. In 1941, when Germany was in the ascendant, British diplomatists had assured sceptical Americans that postwar collaboration with Russia would 'recreate some reasonable balance of power in Europe, destroyed by the collapse of France, against the possibility of revived Germany'. After the Nazi defeat at the battle of Stalingrad two years later, however, Churchill became more cautious. 'The prospect of having no strong country on the map between England and Russia,' he said, 'was not attractive': it was therefore important 'to recreate a strong France'. He also reverted to his favourite plan for a south German confederation that might include Bavaria, Württemberg, Baden, and even Austria and Hungary. At Teheran, although he repeated that he was 'all for' dismemberment, its most important purpose in his eyes was to remove Prussia, 'the evil core of German militarism'.[22]

American views, finally, were marked by conflict as well as change. Temperamentally, Roosevelt had been inclined towards dismemberment: he had thought of dividing postwar Germany into three or more sovereign states, only economically linked. Sumner Welles, the Under-Secretary of State, had actually drawn up a plan for this purpose when he resigned in September 1943 over policy disputes with the Secretary of State, Cordell Hull. The Welles plan envisaged transferring East Prussia to Poland and splitting the rest of the country into three states, one in the north-west, one in the south-west, and one in the north-east. At Teheran, Roosevelt went even further, suggesting five self-governing entities: Hanover and north-west Germany; Saxony and the Leipzig area; Hesse-Darmstadt, Hesse-Kassel, and the region south of the Rhine; Bavaria, Baden and Württemberg; and Prussia, 'to be rendered as small and as weak as possible'. He also proposed internationalizing the Ruhr, the Saar, Hamburg and the Kiel Canal. Allen Dulles and the State Department, on the other hand, were more in favour of a centralized Germany, provided it were democratically run; and as the war continued, Roosevelt himself grew more reluctant to take decisions in advance. As he wrote to Cordell Hull on 20 October 1944, 'In view of the fact that we have not occupied Germany, I cannot agree at this moment as to what kind of a Germany we want in every detail.'[23]

At Teheran, Yalta and Potsdam, the Allies held long, sometimes desultory debates on the subject; but all the time, like a slow fuse unobtrusively burning, the force of events was bringing partition nearer. Any one of a number of circumstances might have prevented it. Had a German government survived the collapse of the Nazis, the country might not have been ruled by the Allies. If 'unconditional surrender' ensured that it was, it might yet have been governed as a single unit; failing that, in each zone of occupation a mixed contingent might have exerted joint control. If this in turn were out of the question, the zones might have been designed to converge on Berlin, making it easier for a joint Allied council to supervise their separate administration. Finally, if none of this proved feasible, the Allies might still have gradually lowered the inter-zonal barriers, and free elections might ultimately have been held throughout Germany. At each moment of decision, the issue still seemed open; but one by one the possibilities narrowed. The fuse burned steadily on.

The process began in 1943. In January, the idea of 'unconditional surrender' was publicly launched by Roosevelt at the press conference following his Casablanca meeting with Churchill. In the spring it began to take diplomatic form when the British Foreign Office, preparing a visit to Washington by Anthony Eden, proposed that no German government be recognized in the period after the armistice. This same suggestion, still not yet adopted as an Allied policy, was tacitly put to the Russians at the Foreign Ministers' Conference in Moscow that October. There, towards the end of the proceedings, Cordell Hull went up to Molotov and slipped a document into his pocket. It was unofficial, he explained. Molotov showed it to Stalin. Next day he came back beaming. 'This text,' he said, 'expresses Russian ideas about Germany just as we should have expressed them ourselves.'[24]

Cordell Hull's document had been drafted in Moscow on 23 October 1943, by two members of the US delegation. It was based partly on State Department position papers, but partly also on a private study made by the New York Council on Foreign Relations. As such, it reflected the conflicts and uncertainties in American policy, and tried to suggest a suitable compromise. It was divided into three sections. The first dealt with 'unconditional surrender', the third with the final peace. The latter raised the possibility of dismemberment, but it also envisaged eventual free elections in Germany as a whole. It was the document's second section, however, that was to prove decisive. Covering the period between the armistice and the peace treaty, it called for disarmament, reparations and the total occupation of Germany by the three main Allies, ruling through a tripartite commission. It thus implied, without actually stipulating, the absence of any central German government until the peace treaty was signed.[25]

Stalin's delight at these proposals is hardly surprising. They made it clear that Germany, unlike Italy, would be a political vacuum; and by confirming the implications of 'unconditional surrender', they set the scene for division into zones. The first line of defence against partition had fallen. The second was to follow within a few weeks.

The principle of zoning in Germany had already been put forward that summer. In London, a special Cabinet Committee under the chair-manship of Clement Attlee, then Deputy Prime Minister, had recom-mended that after the armistice there should be three separate zones of occupation, with only Berlin under joint Allied control. This plan, worked out in agreement with the British Chiefs of Staff, had been transmitted to Washington; but in view of Churchill's changing attitude, it might have remained a dead letter had it not been revived at the Moscow Foreign Ministers' Conference that October and at the Nov-ember meeting of Allied leaders in Teheran. There, Churchill, Roosevelt and Stalin agreed 'in principle' to a three-zone system, with a fourth inter-Allied zone in Berlin. The details they left to a new tripartite body of senior officials, the European Advisory Commission, set up by the Moscow Conference of Foreign Ministers, and due to meet in London at the end of the year.[26]

The Commission convened, informally, on 15 December 1943, and held its first formal session on the afternoon of 14 January 1944. The setting was Lancaster House, an opulent early nineteenth-century build-ing with giant Corinthian porticoes and a vast marble staircase, over-looking St James's Park and Green Park at the west end of The Mall, near Buckingham Palace. Before the war it had housed the London Museum; now, it was newly redecorated in white and gold, with red and green fabrics on the walls. The host, as representative of the British govern-ment, was Sir William Strang, very much the professional diplomatist, extremely able, sensitive, conscientious, and a little donnish. The Soviet Union and United States had delegated their respective ambassadors —Fedor T. Gusev, whom Strang later described as 'a grim and rather wooden person, with, as a saving grace, a touch of sardonic humour and, as a virtue, a somewhat blunt straightforwardness', and John G. Winant, 'a self-tortured soul, noble and passionate, inarticulate, decep-tively simple, the pattern of honour'. Later they were joined by the French Ambassador, René Massigli. Altogether, the negotiations lasted nineteen months, ending in August, 1945: in the course of twenty formal and ninety-seven informal meetings, the Commission produced twelve separate agreements for government approval. Except for the allocation of the two western zones between the United States and Britain, the occupation plans for Germany were settled by mid-Sept-ember, 1944. Seldom can such crucial decisions have been reached in so short a time.[27]

Despite some American second thoughts on the subject, it was too late to contest the principle of zoning. The next possibility—that of mixed Allied contingents in each zone—had already been proposed in Wash-ington by a British Foreign Office official in December 1943. Then the

United States had rejected it, chiefly on military advice and for technical reasons rather than because the State Department feared Russian interference in the West. British military opinion shared American misgivings: mixed-manning of the occupation zones, it was said, would be 'administratively impracticable'. Even so, in the summer of 1944, Strang was instructed to repeat the same suggestion. In his own words, it 'was opposed—and I think rightly—by the Americans and soon dropped'.[28]

With the zonal division of Germany hardening, the next most important question became the actual demarcation of the zones. On this subject, astonishingly enough, there was, as Strang put it, 'little discussion and early agreement': the greatest difficulty was not between the West and the Soviet Union, but between the United States and the United Kingdom, each anxious to secure the industrialized north-west area that at length became the British Zone. It was on 15 January 1944, that Strang officially proposed zonal boundaries on the broad lines recommended by Attlee's Cabinet Committee; and at the next formal meeting, on 18 February, Gusev indicated Russian assent. Such rapid compliance may seem unusual, and it certainly caused euphoria at the time. Yet if Gusev took even as long as five weeks to accept the offer, perhaps it was because he could hardly believe his ears. The proposed Soviet one consisted of Mecklenburg-Pomerania, Brandenburg, Saxony-Anhalt, Thüringia, and areas to the east; it included forty per cent of Germany's 1937 territory, thirty-six per cent of her population, and thirty-three per cent of her productive resources. Berlin lay deep within it, and it brought the Soviet occupation forces to within a hundred miles of the Rhine.[29]

Defending what in retrospect looked like ill-considered generosity, Strang pointed out that some of the eastern zone was likely to go to Poland. The Western zones were more fully industrialized, and the military authorities already feared that the administration of a large and populous area might overstretch their manpower. When the zones were delineated, moreover, the Western Allies were still very uncertain how far and how rapidly their armies would advance. A related worry was whether the Soviet armies might not halt on Germany's eastern frontier, leaving Britain and the United States to finish off the war—although this contrasted oddly with the American War Department's prediction that Russia might occupy all of Germany as far as the Rhine. Was the Western offer a bribe to coax the Russians forward, or a sop to keep them at bay? The two explanations were mutually incompatible; but at times of great uncertainty, conflicting hypotheses can often seem to point to the same practical conclusion. A smaller offer, Strang feared,

T 022393

would have caused a deadlock; and although delay might have enabled the Western Allies to claim a larger area once they had reached the Elbe, no one at the time could be sure that they would do so. Even then, there would be no certainty of taking Berlin, and if the Russians reached it first without having signed a zoning agreement, they would no doubt refuse joint control of the capital, and take it over entirely themselves.[30]

Mistaken or not, these arguments seemed plausible; but there was a further question that they failed to answer. Could the Eastern and Western Zones not have met in the German capital, thereby making it easier to govern the country as a single whole? Such a suggestion had in fact been made by Roosevelt. In November 1943, on board USS *Iowa* on the way to Cairo and Teheran, he had pencilled across a *National Geographic* map of Germany an East-West boundary running through Berlin. Handed to the US Chief of Staff, General George C. Marshall, and by him to Major-General Thomas T. Handy, Chief of the US War Department's Operations Division, this map had been filed away in the Pentagon and was never officially communicated to the State Department. It seems, however, to have inspired a superficially similar proposal made by the US Joint Chiefs of Staff in Cairo two weeks later. The crucial difference was that in this revised version the suggested zonal boundary carefully skirted the German capital, leaving it firmly in the east. A third, more radical variant of Roosevelt's project, mooted informally by some State Department officials, was to re-draw the three zones so that they would converge on Berlin like 'slices of pie'; and yet a fourth suggestion was circulated later by General Eisenhower, who proposed to ignore the claims of Berlin for the time being and establish what he called 'a cantonment capital' in Southern Germany at the *de facto* junction of the American, British and Soviet ones.[31]

None of these ingenious plans, in fact, was feasible. Eisenhower's, in particular, would have weakened still further the occupation authorities' hold on German loyalties, as well as virtually abandoning Berlin to the East. The other three proposals, apart from greatly complicating the work of military government by cutting across German administrative boundaries, would have stood little chance of acceptance by the Soviet Union. Only one of the projects in question was ever transmitted to Winant at the European Advisory Commission in London; this was the memorandum by the Joint Chiefs of Staff. Although drawn up on 4 December 1943, it was not shown to the State Department until late in the following February, through the 'Working Security Committee' in which representatives of the Navy, State and War Departments were responsible for drafting Winant's instructions. After having, at first, re-fused to take part in the Committee, and then maintained that the

European Advisory Commission had no right to deal with zoning, the Civil Affairs Division of the War Department now suddenly produced the Joint Chiefs of Staff proposal, insisting that it be sent to London, but declining to supply any explanation of its principles or aims. The result was what George Kennan, then Winant's assistant, called 'a most curious communication'. Even the accompanying map, on which the proposed boundary between the British and Russian Zones stopped short of Germany's eastern border, 'made no sense at all'. Kennan's military colleague in London, a former lawyer, was prepared to be belligerent. 'We have to fight for it, my boy,' he said; 'We have to fight for it.' 'How does one fight,' asked Kennan, 'for something which makes no sense and which one does not understand oneself?' After what another official in the State Department described as 'frantic queries' from London, Kennan flew to Washington to raise the question with the President. When Roosevelt saw the War Department's bizarre map he laughed. 'Why, that's just something I once drew on the back of an envelope,' he answered. Shortly afterwards, the project was formally abandoned, and the United States accepted the East-West zonal boundary already provisionally agreed on by Britain and the USSR.[32]

There was, however, one further device that might at least have ensured that the Western Allies had land access to Berlin. This had been put forward as early as December 1943 by Professor Philip E. Mosely, then in the State Department's Division of Political Studies and later to replace Kennan in London. Mosely had proposed 'that a corridor should be established connecting the prospective Western areas of occupation with Berlin, this to be accomplished by joining certain intervening districts of Saxony-Anhalt and Brandenburg to the Western Zones.' 'I realized,' he said later, 'that such a proposal by the United States would probably meet with Soviet objections, but I believed that if it could be presented first, with impressive firmness, it might be taken into account by the Soviet government in framing its own proposals.' Mosely's suggestion was incorporated in a State Department memorandum; but when this was put to the Working Security Committee, it was blocked by the War Department's Civil Affairs Division. After some time, Mosely went to see the colonel in charge to make sure that he had received the proposal. 'It's right there,' said the colonel, opening the bottom drawer of his desk. Then, leaning back, he propped his feet on the open drawer and added: 'It's damned well going to stay there, too.' The delineation of the future zones, it appeared, was a 'military matter' which would be decided 'at the proper time' and 'at the military level': it was no concern of the European Advisory Commission in London. When the Working Security Committee finally accepted a revised version of the State

Department's memorandum, all mention of zoning—and of Mosely's proposal—had been dropped. The question of a land corridor was never officially put to the European Advisory Commission; and although Winant later raised it verbally with the War Department, he was rebuffed. By late June, 1944, when Mosely himself was transferred to London, the issue was already closed.[33]

So it came about that the European Advisory Commission abandoned, one by one, the lines of defence against the partition of Germany. Amid uncertainties and illusions, each step seemed logical enough when it was taken. But at least one of the illusions was a little difficult to justify. By the summer of 1944, in view of the Allies' plans to dispense with a German government, it was unrealistic to assume, as at least one member of the Commission did, 'that there would be a central German authority competent to sign the terms of surrender and to exercise a measure of jurisdiction over the whole country, subject to the overriding control of the Commander-in-Chief'.[34] Roosevelt himself remarked at Yalta that 'the permanent treatment of Germany might grow out of the question of the zones of occupation.' Nor, as Mosely's suggestion showed, was everyone still optimistic about Soviet intentions. Yet for most of those involved on the Western side, the whole zoning exercise was an interim expedient to be followed by a peace treaty and the formation of a democratic all-German government. It was hard to imagine that the Soviet Union would so soon seal off the Eastern zone, that a 'cold war' would develop so quickly, and that free elections for the whole of Germany would be delayed so long.[35]

To blame the European Advisory Commission for the division of Germany, however, would be to condemn the machinery for the failings of the men at the controls—Edward R. Stettinius, Jr., Under-Secretary of State; the tired, ageing Cordell Hull; the State Department officials hamstrung by the military, who, in the words of one participant, 'saw the war as a football game you just won and then went home'. Moreover, while in practice the European Advisory Commission acted only on government instructions, its decisions were by no means necessarily final. In October 1944, Roosevelt wrote to Cordell Hull: 'We must emphasize the fact that the European Advisory Commission is "advisory", and that you and I are not bound by its advice. This is something which is sometimes overlooked, and if they do not remember that word "advisory" they may go ahead and execute some of the advice which, when the time comes, we may not like at all.' Churchill felt equally independent. 'The proposals of the European Advisory Council [*sic*]—were not thought sufficiently pressing or practical,' he wrote, 'to be brought before the War Cabinet. Like many praiseworthy efforts to make plans for the future, they lay upon the shelves while the war crashed on.'[36]

By the spring of 1945, indeed, peace in Europe seemed likely to be shaped as much by the Allies' armies as by their diplomatists. By ousting the Rumanian government and failing to allow free elections in Poland, Stalin had at least twice strained his Yalta pledges, if he had not technically broken them; and Churchill in particular thought that, whatever zoning agreements might have been drafted for Germany, it was vital to 'shake hands with the Russians as far to the east as possible.' The question in his mind was whether or not the Western armies could be the first to reach Berlin.[37]

All the Allies agreed that it was important to seize the German capital; but the United States and Britain differed fundamentally as to how important it was, and why. American distrust of the balance-of-power system in Europe, and their hopes for the nascent United Nations Organization, reinforced Roosevelt's 'tough' line on Nazi Germany and his faith in the Soviet Union; all discouraged the idea of a united postwar Germany as a counterweight to Russian strength. True, the President's views were changing: on Saturday 24 March 1945, when he learned from Harriman in Moscow what was happening to Poland, he exploded with anger, pounding the arms of his wheelchair and exclaiming, 'Averell is right! We can't do business with Stalin!' But by now he was too near death to reshape United States policy; and in the last month of his life matters tended to drift on the tide of a public opinion understandably reluctant to suspect a valiant ally. With a 'policy vacuum' in Washington, it was all the more natural for the American Supreme Commander in Europe, General Eisenhower, not to look beyond his strictly military task of winning the war. Churchill, on the other hand, had the statesman's duty to look further; and his conservative patriotism, together with Britain's balance-of-power psychology, made him privately sceptical of the United Nations Organization and alert to the designs of that rather different nationalist, Joseph Stalin. For Eisenhower, whether or not to capture Berlin was a question of wartime strategy *vis-à-vis* the Nazis: for Churchill, it was one of postwar foreign policy *vis-à-vis* the Soviet Union. Agreement was hardly likely on the price to be paid or the risks taken for an objective they saw so differently. In the last few months of the war in Europe, in fact, this led

C

to sharp friction between the Western Allies, and to mutual recrimina-
tions that have sputtered intermittently for the past twenty years.[38]

The dispute first arose between Eisenhower and Field-Marshal Montgomery, the gaunt British hero of El Alamein, now commanding
Eisenhower's 21 Army Group. Montgomery was a difficult though loyal
subordinate: his flamboyant austerity mixed badly with his Supreme
Commander's sometimes irascible doggedness. Their personal relations
were made no easier by the fact that Montgomery's position under
Eisenhower's order reflected Britain's diminished role in an Alliance increasingly upheld by American money and men. Each at times suspected
the other of stealing—and mismanaging—the show.

From August 1944 onwards, Montgomery pressed for what he called
'one really powerful and full-blooded thrust towards Berlin.' This, he
thought, 'would not only have shortened the war; it would also have
held out possibilities of bringing it to an end in Europe with a political
balance very much more favourable to an early and stable peace.' But
Eisenhower feared the strength of enemy reserves, the difficulty of getting supplies across the Rhine, and the danger of borrowing transport
from the rest of his armies; he saw Montgomery's project as 'a knife-
like thrust' or 'a pencil-like thrust' doomed to 'certain destruction'.
When after more than a fortnight's delay he at length modified his attitude, it was too late: at Arnhem in Holland, bad luck and bad weather
had forced Montgomery's airborne assault troops into a costly withdrawal.[39]

Six months later, Montgomery tried a second time. On Tuesday 27
March 1945, when he had just crossed the formidable barrier of the
Rhine near Wesel, he telegraphed to Field-Marshal Sir Alan Brooke,
Chief of the Imperial General Staff: 'My tactical HQ moves will be
Wesel-Münster-Herford-Hanover—thence via the *autobahn* to Berlin, I
hope.' Several times he urged Eisenhower to authorize and aid a spearhead drive towards Berlin; but the Supreme Commander was puzzled by
the contrast between Montgomery's present eagerness and what he regarded as his previous over-caution; he even suspected, as he told an
interviewer many years later, that Montgomery's aim was to 'make sure
that the Americans—and me, in particular—got no credit'. As before,
he feared that so long a spearhead would deplete and immobilize the
armies on other parts of the front. Instead, he proposed that Montgomery should push towards the lower Elbe, cutting off the Nazis in the
north. In the south, by advancing through Regensburg to Linz, Eisenhower hoped to breach the so-called 'National Redoubt' in southern
Bavaria, western Austria and northern Italy, where the SS, the Gestapo
and other hard-core Nazis were said to be preparing for a suicidal last

resistance. In the centre, meanwhile, Eisenhower planned to make a major attack through Erfurt, Leipzig and Dresden to meet the Red Army and cut Germany in two. For this purpose, he proposed for the time being to withdraw the American Ninth Army from Montgomery's command, assigning it to the northern flank of the central advance. Berlin, he wrote later, 'was politically and psychologically important as the symbol of remaining German power. I decided, however, that it was not the logical or the most desirable objective for the forces of the Western Allies.' As he told Montgomery, 'that place has become, so far as I am concerned, nothing but a geographical location, and I have never been interested in these. My purpose is to destroy the enemy's forces and his powers to resist.'[40]

Montgomery had to acquiesce in this decision; but a tactical error by Eisenhower now gave Churchill one last hope of reversing it. On Wednesday 28 March 1945, without previously informing either his British Deputy, Air Chief Marshal Sir Arthur Tedder, or the Combined Chiefs of Staff, the Supreme Commander telegraphed his plans to Stalin. This, he thought, was justified by the communication arrangements that the Combined Chiefs of Staff had approved earlier, as well as by the fact that Stalin was Commander-in-Chief of the Red Army; but the British Chiefs of Staff were instantly, and understandably, incensed. When Tedder tried to placate them by suggesting that Eisenhower had acted to forestall a contrary directive issued by Montgomery, Brooke retorted that he was 'astonished Ike found it necessary to call on Stalin in order to control Monty'. For several days, sizzling telegrams were exchanged between London, Washington and Eisenhower's and Montgomery's respective headquarters. 'Please explain,' snapped Churchill in a note to his Chief of Staff, General Sir Hastings Ismay. Brooke complained in his diary of 'the nationalistic outlook of allies', and sent his American colleagues a long, barbed enquiry from the British Chiefs of Staff. The US Chiefs of Staff returned what seemed to Brooke a 'rather rude message'; but General George Marshall tartly telegraphed Eisenhower: 'Your comments are requested as a matter of urgency.' Montgomery, meanwhile, was warning Brooke that 'we are about to make a terrible mistake'; Brooke sympathized but told him, 'You should take no further action.' Churchill pointed out to Eisenhower that 'I should greatly prefer persistence in the plan on which we crossed the Rhine'; and in a message to Roosevelt he repeated: 'I say quite frankly that Berlin remains of high strategic importance.' But Roosevelt was by now too ill to answer, and Marshall backed Eisenhower. To Churchill, the Supreme Commander replied: 'I think you still have some misunderstanding of what I intend to do ... I have not changed any plan ... The only difference between your suggestions and my plan is one of timing.' With that, Churchill had to be content. He once more stressed 'the importance of entering Berlin', but added: 'I regard all this business as smoothing itself down quite satisfactorily'; and he told Roosevelt, 'I regard the matter as closed.'[41]

The final irony of the whole incident was that Stalin could not believe Eisenhower's original telegram to be anything but an attempt to deceive him: he now became convinced that the Western Allies planned to race to Berlin. Determined to meet bluff with bluff, he answered that Eisenhower's proposal 'entirely coincides with the plan of the Soviet High Command'. 'Berlin,' he said, 'has lost its former strategic importance. The Soviet High Command therefore plans to allot secondary forces in the direction of Berlin.' Before sending this answer, he had already made clear to Marshals Koniev and Zhukov that they were to speed up and strengthen their advance on the German capital.[42]

But the Western Allies were to have yet a third opportunity to reach Berlin, if not to capture it. On Wednesday 11 April 1945, the armoured vanguard of the US Ninth Army crossed the Elbe near Magdeburg. When General Bradley reported the news by telephone, Eisenhower asked him what the cost would be of breaking through to Berlin. Bradley answered: 'I estimate that it might cost us 100,000 men.' For the moment, Eisenhower said nothing; but on the night of Saturday 14 April when US patrols were within forty-eight miles of the German capital, he cabled to Washington that although 'it would also be most desirable to make a thrust to Berlin', this 'must take a low priority in point of time unless operations to clear our flanks proceed with unexpected rapidity'. If the Ninth Army pressed on, its long supply lines would make it highly vulnerable to the strong-points it by-passed: nor was he sure what reception a precarious vanguard might meet at its destination—either from a desperate enemy or from a triumphant Red Army. Next morning, therefore, the word came down through Bradley: the Ninth Army was to stop at the Elbe. Once again, Churchill protested to Washington; but Franklin Roosevelt had died on the eve of victory, on Thursday 12 April 1945, and the new President, Harry S. Truman, gave the stock answer that 'the question of tactical deployment of American troops is a military one'.[43]

The decision was certainly prudent, and it may have been wise. As Truman reminded Churchill, the occupation zones had been 'the subject of long and careful study and negotiation', and 'a demand by our governments for modifications of agreed zone boundaries ... might have serious consequences. The Russians could certainly consider such a bargaining position as a repudiation of our formal agreement.' Nevertheless, as Churchill wrote later,

... I never suggested going back on our word over the agreed zones provided other agreements were also respected. I became convinced however that before we halted, or still more withdrew, our troops we ought to seek a meeting with Stalin face to face and make sure that an agreement was reached about the whole front. It would indeed be a disaster if we kept all our agreements in strict good faith while the Soviets laid their hands upon all they could get without the slightest regard for the obligations into which they had entered.

In retrospect, in fact, it is hard to avoid the impression that in these weeks the Western Allies lost the last chance to stave off the partition of Germany—although only the last of many.[44]

Retrospective judgements, however, must be treated with caution. Perhaps the British government was to blame for so blithely proposing the zoning arrangements; perhaps Roosevelt, for placing such faith in Stalin; perhaps Eisenhower, for dispersing his military effort; perhaps Montgomery, for exacerbating national jealousies. Yet all of them acted honestly, thoughtfully, and reasonably at the time. Even Stalin no doubt believed that he was serving the cause of future stability and peace. In the last resort, indeed, the partition of Germany was perhaps truly 'inevitable' once Adolf Hitler had started the process that brought it about. Whether Hitler and the Nazi regime were inevitable is a separate question; but human history knows no such thing as a 'first cause'.

Whatever the causes, the results came quickly. By Wednesday 25 April 1945, the day on which American and Russian troops met at the Elbe, the Red Army had encircled Berlin. It was only a matter of days before the war in Europe was over. Despite more last-minute protests from Churchill, the Western Allies were obliged to withdraw to their zonal boundaries, contenting themselves with four-power control in the capital only, and that imperfect and short-lived. So, in the heart of Germany, Europe's new frontier was established. Not the least of its dangers was that it cut off two-thirds of the German people from their food-growing lands in the east.

CHAPTER FOUR

Self-Help

Salvation lies in taking one step forward. Then another. It
is always the same step that one begins again.
Antoine de Saint-Exupéry[1]

To learn to command is easy: what is hard is learning to
govern.
Johann Wolfgang Goethe[2]

The spirit of self-help is the root of all genuine growth.
Samuel Smiles[3]

RUINED and divided, Europe in 1945 was soon in some respects to find
herself also alone. Some of the generous aid planned by the wartime
Allies failed to reach its intended beneficiaries; some was cut off when
the fighting ceased. For a time, several European countries were thrown
on their own depleted resources. Britain's overseas debts forced her into
austerity. Reparations, and the limits at first imposed on industry,
helped retard Germany's initial growth. The demands of the Far Eastern
war, and the desire to return to normal, hastened the departure of the
US armies; America's attention, also, tended to shift elsewhere. Europe's
postwar rulers, whether military governments or civil administrations,
all faced tasks that were essentially similar: all had to bury the dead,
tend the sick and wounded, feed the hungry, house the homeless, clear
away rubble and ashes, rebuild, repair and reform. Politically and economically, each of them had what Dwight D. Eisenhower later called a
'mandate for change'. For two years, each did his best to fulfil it, largely
in isolation. Each brought order out of chaos with astonishing speed.
But beyond the material damage lay very much deeper problems; and it
soon became clear that national self-help, although essential, was not
enough.

Early in the war, Winston Churchill had pledged his government's aid
in the future relief of continental Europe. On 21 August 1940, at the
height of the Battle of Britain, he had told the House of Commons: 'We

shall do our best to encourage the building up of reserves of food all over the world, so that there will always be held up before the eyes of the peoples of Europe, including—I say it deliberately—the German and Austrian peoples, the certainty that the shattering of the Nazi power will bring to them all immediately food, freedom and peace.' This was the seed that three years later produced UNRRA, the United Nations Relief and Rehabilitation Administration, aptly if fulsomely described by one historian as 'tantamount to a declaration of the moral solidarity of the whole human race'.[4]

In all, UNRRA distributed some 3,700 million dollars' worth of food, clothing, medical supplies, manufactures, raw materials, farm equipment, and machinery. In many places, it prevented widespread famine. Food accounted for half of its deliveries to Italy, nearly half of those to Poland, and sixty per cent of those to Greece. It was equally vital in China, where in the words of its official history, 'two to three million destitute people were rescued from starvation'; while Austria, according to the head of its Mission there, 'owes its survival to UNRRA aid'. Of the organization's operating funds, ninety-four per cent were provided by America, Britain and Canada. Nearly three-quarters came from the United States, including gifts by private citizens amounting to almost one dollar per head of the population. Canada supplied over seventeen million dollars' worth of private gifts of clothing, Australia nearly five million, New Zealand nearly one and a half million. At its peak, UNRRA employed some 25,000 people; but its administrative expenses were only 1·18 per cent of its total costs. Its aid was offered without discrimination by race, religion or political allegiance: its multi-national field staff, isolated, overworked, short of supplies and often inexperienced, trod precarious tightropes between rival factions. Some UNRRA employees were ineffectual; a few were extravagant; one or two may have been corrupt. But the vast majority, courageous lonely figures in khaki battledress with special distinctive shoulder-flashes, distributing dried milk and chemical fertilizer, teaching new methods to doctors or to peasants, organizing construction gangs, or trying to turn barracks into something like home for smudge-eyed orphan children, well earned their charges' frequent tribute, 'Oonra—OK'.[5]

Really effective altruism is seldom wholly unselfish; and this was true, in 1940, of Churchill's promise of aid. It had accompanied the announcement that Britain was extending her blockade of Germany to all the occupied countries. One of its aims had been to quell the misgivings of exiled European governments and servicemen—especially Norwegian seamen—unwilling to penalize their countrymen; another had been to offer future outlets for any overseas food surpluses caused by the blockade. Equally hard-headed, later, were the long negotiations which preceded and followed the formal establishment of UNRRA on 9 November 1943. To provide 'relief' was indispensable and urgent; but United States negotiators, in particular, feared that Congress might frown on 'rehabilitation' if this were to include long-term assistance to future industrial competitors. UNRRA's scope was therefore limited to immediate reconstruction. The range of its beneficiaries, moreover, was restricted in two ways.[6]

Under the UNRRA Agreement of 1943, aid was to go to 'the population of any area liberated by the armed forces of the United Nations', the wartime Allies; but despite Churchill's original promise, this was held to exclude ex-enemy countries. In practice, Austria and Italy came to be admitted, as, to a lesser degree, were Hungary and Finland; but UNRRA's work in Germany had to be confined to the relief and rehabilitation of refugees. Secondly, moreover, UNRRA's governing Council curtailed its freedom further by imposing a 'means test' on the recipients of aid. To avoid the vicious circle of war debts that had paralyzed international finance after World War I, it had been agreed that 'acceptance of relief should not result in a burden of indebtedness'. As a reasonable counterpart of this enlightened generosity, aid was debarred to any area 'the government of which is in a position to pay with suitable means of foreign exchange'. The unforeseen practical result of these two restrictions was to exclude from UNRRA assistance the greater part of Western Europe.[7]

The largest sum spent by UNRRA in any one country—nearly 518 million dollars—went to China. Next came Poland, with 478 million; then Italy, with 418 million; then Jugoslavia, with 416 million; then Greece, with 347 million. The next biggest beneficiaries, in order, were Czechoslovakia, the Ukraine, Austria, Byelorussia, Albania, the Philippines, Hungary, the Dodecanese, Finland, Korea, Ethiopia and San Marino —and that was all. In other words, except for Italy, Austria, and Greece, the bulk of UNRRA funds in Europe went not to the Western European recipients originally envisaged, but to the countries of Eastern Europe that were already becoming known as 'satellites' of the Soviet Union.[8]

Britain, which might have sought UNRRA relief, if only for air-raid victims, had already decided not to do so. The former occupied countries of Western Europe had a still more obvious claim to assistance; but the 'means test' discouraged them from pressing it. All of them still had overseas assets that had been 'frozen' during the war to prevent their exploitation by the Nazis: all might technically be held capable of paying 'with suitable means of foreign exchange'. For the most part, the assets in question would have proved too small to pay for all the imports needed; but their owners were reluctant to have them scrutinized by UNRRA, and very unwilling to sell them in order to qualify for aid. It has always made better sense to borrow than to liquidate sound investments—even in the hope of future gifts. So it came about that France, Belgium, the Netherlands, Luxembourg, Norway and Denmark followed the British example and made no claims on UNRRA; all they received were small liaison missions to advise on health and welfare and on the problems of 'displaced persons'. Their overseas imports they paid for, dealing directly and unilaterally with the Combined Boards that had handled the Allies' wartime supplies.[9]

Receiving no aid from UNRRA, these countries naturally turned to other forms of overseas assistance, and in particular to the existing machinery of 'Lend-Lease'. This, like UNRRA, had been conceived early on in the war. On 8 December 1940, Churchill had written to Roosevelt asking whether American ships might not be allowed to carry some of Britain's vital imports; he had added that before long it would become impossible to pay for the armaments ordered from the United States. Roosevelt's response was the press conference of 17 December 1940, in which he explained the situation with the homely metaphor of the garden hose. If a neighbour's house caught fire, he argued, a man who owned a hose would not demand payment for the use of it, but would lend the hose, help put the fire out, and then take the hose back. In a radio 'fireside chat' a few days later, Roosevelt announced that America was to become the 'great arsenal of democracy'; and on 7 January 1941, he proposed the 'Lend-Lease' bill to Congress. Two months later, on 11 March, it went on the Statute Book under the memorable designation of HR 1776.[10]

Essentially, the 'Lend-Lease' Act empowered the President to authorize the production or procurement of any defence article for the government of any country whose defence he deemed vital to that of the United States. It enabled him to test, inspect, prove, repair, outfit, recondition or otherwise place in good order any such article, to exchange information about it, and to 'sell, transfer title to, exchange, lease, lend, or otherwise dispose of' it on whatever terms and conditions he thought fit. 'The benefit to the United States' might be 'payment or repayment in kind or property, or any other direct or indirect benefit which the President deems satisfactory.' No cash was to be transferred to the beneficiaries; but in practice no cash was demanded in return: the only requirement, beyond that of fighting the Nazis, was the promise made by Britain in the 'Lend-Lease' Mutual Aid Agreement of 23 February 1942, to reduce trade barriers and eliminate trade discrimination after the war. Between March 1941 and October 1945, 'Lend-Lease' cost the United States more than 46,000 million dollars. As President Truman remarked later, 'We may never get the money back, but the lives we saved are right here in America.'[11]

In Roosevelt's eyes, the possible uses of 'Lend-Lease' procedure were not confined to the supply of materials for war. On 11 December 1942, in his Seventh Lend-Lease Report, he told Congress: 'Where commercial channels of supply have been cut off, lend-lease can be the instrument for renewing them. Where relief distribution is necessary, lend-lease can supply the materials of relief.' Whether or not such aid should cease at the end of hostilities was another question. 'Success in restoring the countries we free,' Roosevelt's message continued, 'will be a powerful factor in shortening the war and giving the liberated peoples their chance to share in the victory.' But could Lend-Lease be continued long enough to give them a reasonable share in the peace?[12]

The question was partly juridical. Some of the President's advisers believed that Lend-Lease would still be legal when the war was over; but Roosevelt himself was uncertain. His Chief of Staff, Admiral Leahy, told him quite bluntly: 'Mr President, I know almost nothing about lend-lease and I don't want to go to jail when they begin, after the war is over, to investigate what has been done with the money.' Roosevelt smiled. 'If you go to jail,' he answered, 'I'll be going along too, and we will have good company.' Many others, however, including the American Joint Chiefs of Staff, were convinced that Lend-Lease could only be used for war.[13]

Behind the legal dispute, moreover, there were political issues. A vociferous minority had always opposed Lend-Lease on principle. Others wished to keep it within strict limits; some were unhappy about its going to Communist Russia; and a further group, including the Secretary of State, Cordell Hull, was anxious to use it as a 'bait' to secure from the British something 'they were trying to run away from'—a diminution of Commonwealth preference. All this amounted to a sizeable opposition, which reinforced the natural tendency of Treasury officials to hold the purse-strings tight.[14]

Such was already the climate when the future of Lend-Lease came up for discussion at the second Quebec Conference between Churchill and Roosevelt in September 1944. Churchill asked for an assurance that Lend-Lease would at least continue beyond the end of the war in Europe. Roosevelt was about to give in, when Henry Morgenthau, US Secretary of the Treasury, interposed. The problems involved were complex, he argued; they required further study. At his suggestion, Churchill and Roosevelt agreed to refer the future of Lend-Lease to an American Committee consisting of Morgenthau himself, the Under-Secretary of State Edward Stettinius, and the Irish-American Leo Crowley, head of the Foreign Economic Administration. They were to consult with a corresponding British Treasury team led by Lord Keynes and Sir Robert Sinclair.[15]

After several months of hard discussion with the British, the Morgenthau committee reached what seemed reasonable compromise arrangements: it then considered itself dissolved. But the problem itself did not dissolve so easily. On Tuesday 8 May 1945, the day after the Nazi surrender in Rheims and the day before the formal armistice in Berlin, Leo Crowley and the Acting Secretary of State Joseph C. Grew came into the office of Harry S. Truman, who had been President for less than a month. With them they brought a draft order cutting back Lend-Lease supplies, which Roosevelt, they explained, had approved but not signed. Would Truman sign it? Without reading the document, he reached for his pen, and it was done.[16]

In Truman's own words, 'The storm broke almost at once.' Crowley put an immediate embargo on all shipments to Europe, and even had some of the ships turned round and brought back to be unloaded. Instantly, protests began flooding into Washington, and they continued for some weeks. On Sunday 27 May, in Moscow, Stalin expressed bitter indignation to Harry Hopkins about the unloading of ships bound for Russia; and on the next day, Churchill sent a personal telegram to Truman complaining that the US War Department was trying to cut down on the supply arrangements made after Quebec.[17]

Truman quickly rescinded the order of 8 May, and in a press and radio conference on 23 May he explained that his intention had been to honour existing commitments, and not to cancel shipments but to make, as he put it, 'a gradual readjustment to conditions following the collapse of Germany'. The studied vagueness of these words reflected his embarrassing position, immobilized under crossfire from several directions at once. When he had been Vice-President, presiding over the Senate, he had given a personal promise that Lend-Lease would lapse at the end of the war. He was convinced, as he wrote on 15 June to five complaining Congressmen, 'that the Lend-Lease Act does not authorize aid for the purposes of postwar relief, postwar rehabilitation, or postwar reconstruction.' But this left open the question of how far it could continue to apply in Europe during the remainder of the war in the Far East. The American Joint Chiefs of Staff had told the British on 7 June that 'there was no legal authority for further assignment of any

Lend-Lease materials except for use in the war against Japan.' Leo Crowley agreed with them, and wanted Truman to give an order to this effect; but the State Department and the Army wanted to continue giving Lend-Lease aid to Europe, especially for use by the French occupation forces in Germany. Truman continued to hesitate; but when the British asked point-blank at the Potsdam Conference for Lend-Lease aid to be used in the occupation of Germany and Austria, he told Churchill that in his opinion this was 'very definitely a part of the war'. 'After all,' he added, 'we technically still are at war with them.'[18]

Here matters might have rested, had the war against Japan not been brought so rapidly to its bitter end. Thereupon, quite suddenly, the whole issue of Lend-Lease was re-opened. The Far Eastern war ended on Thursday 14 August 1945. Five days later, on Sunday 19 August, the radio made an unexpected announcement. Lend-Lease had been cancelled: henceforth all overseas supplies would have to be paid for—including those already ordered and on their way.[19]

Will Clayton, the Assistant Secretary of State, was in England when the news came. Hurrying back to the American Embassy, he exploded with rage over the transatlantic telephone. 'It was good,' noted one observer, 'to see the whole six-foot-six of him reinforcing the vehemence of his rebukes.' All he could secure, however, was a promise that the question of payment for goods already in transit would be held over for negotiation; and in the end, even so, 650 million dollars had to be paid. On the following Tuesday, Washington made the formal announcement: 'The President has directed the Foreign Economic Administrator to take steps immediately to discontinue all Lend-Lease operations and to notify foreign governments receiving Lend-Lease of this action. The President directs that all outstanding contracts for Lend-Lease are cancelled.'[20]

The burly and pugnacious Hugh Dalton, Chancellor of the Exchequer in Britain's 1945 Labour government, believed that the decision was chiefly the work of Leo Crowley, whom he accused of showing 'no sign of either hesitation or regret'. In London, it was tempting to look for scapegoats and alternatives. If only Roosevelt had still been living —if Truman had been longer in office—if Dean Acheson, the new Secretary of State, had not been on holiday in Canada—if Clayton had not been away in England—if Fred Vinson had not so recently succeeded Morgenthau at the US Treasury ... then, surely Britain might have had a reprieve. As it was, wrote Dalton, 'this heavy blow was struck at us without warning and without discussion. We had expected at least some tapering off of Lend-Lease over the first few years of peace. But now we faced, not war any more, only total economic ruin.'[21]

In reality, speculation was largely beside the point. The legal and political pressure to stop Lend-Lease when the war ended was nothing new. Truman himself had already made his views clear; and it was the collapse of Japan, rather than anti-British malice in Washington, that was responsible for the shock. Even tapering Lend-Lease off, moreover, would hardly have changed the basic situation: the end could not have been postponed for long. Although Truman subsequently authorized further shipments to China 'on the grounds of that country's grave economic and political difficulties'—galloping inflation, famine and the threat of renewed civil war—all Lend-Lease operations virtually ceased on 1 October 1945.[22]

With characteristic restraint, Clement Attlee told the House of Commons on Friday 24 August 1945, that the termination of Lend-Lease placed Great Britain in 'a very serious financial position'. Before the passing of the Lend-Lease Act in March, 1941, the country had undertaken a determined export drive to earn foreign exchange; but since American exporters would have objected to being undercut by an economy that their own government was subsidizing, this had had to be abandoned. By the end of the war, there was in any case little to export, and Britain was overspending her income by about £2,100 million a year. With strict control of imports, a successful export drive, drastic cuts in overseas expenditure, and a great deal of luck, Treasury experts believed that it might be just possible for Britain to pay her way by 1949; but by then, even on the most optimistic reckoning, she would have incurred an additional deficit of at least £1,700 million. Her gold and dollar reserves at the end of 1945 were expected to stand at about £500 million; but they could not, it was thought, be run down below half that sum. £200 million might be raised in loans from the sterling area, finally, leaving an overall deficit of £1,250 million, or 5,000 million dollars.[23]

Such was the stark prospect that faced Attlee's government in the summer of 1945. There was clearly no alternative but to seek further help from America; and Lord Keynes was sent to Washington to begin talks on Tuesday 11 September. Before he left, he was optimistic; he hoped, indeed, to secure a free gift or 'grant in aid' of £1,500 million or 6,000 million dollars. But when he reached Washington he found the atmosphere very different from that of wartime. The Americans, he reported were now interested in the future, not the past; and an old soldier showing his medals was not a persuasive advocate. Gradually, Keynes had to retreat from the idea of a gift to that of an interest-free loan, then to a loan bearing interest; from a larger sum to a smaller; from the prospect of credit with few strings attached, to that of precise conditions. The contrast between Keynes's Old Etonian urbanity and Fred Vinson's frontier manners only served to emphasize Britain's reduced status in the world.[24]

But Britain's was only an extreme example of a general European plight. In the early years of the peace, many countries of Western Europe were seeking North American credit. France borrowed 550 million dollars from the US Export-Import Bank in December 1945, and 650 million five months later; the Netherlands obtained 300 million, the Netherlands East Indies 100 million; and a further 100 million went to Belgium. France was lent a further 720 million dollars to buy up remaining Lend-Lease and other American equipment, while the Soviet Union received 360 million, and other countries smaller amounts. Canada, likewise, not only loaned 1,250 million dollars to Britain, but also advanced 100 million to Belgium, 140 million to the Netherlands East Indies, and 240 million to France.[25]

By comparison with most of these arrangements, the terms that Keynes finally secured for Britain on Thursday 6 December 1945, were fairly favourable—a loan of 3,750 million dollars repayable from December 1951 onwards in fifty annual instalments, at an interest rate of two per cent, to be waived in any year when Britain earned insufficient foreign exchange. At the same time, she was to receive all the Lend-Lease material ordered or about to be ordered when the war with Japan ended, together with stocks of American goods in the United Kingdom and Colonies. The wartime costs of Lend-Lease were written off; and to pay for postwar deliveries of goods 'in the pipeline', Britain received an additional credit of 650 million dollars on the same terms as the larger loan.[26]

Two major drawbacks, however, marred the American credit agreement. One was the United States' insistence that sterling be made convertible against the dollar within fifteen months. This was in line with the 'non-discrimination' principles that the Allies had accepted at the Bretton Woods Conference and that were now to be embodied in the International Monetary Fund and the World Bank; but the deadline for applying it soon proved to be absurdly unrealistic. The agreement's other weakness was its failure to solve the problem of the sterling balances—Britain's largely wartime debts to other members of the sterling area, and particularly at that time to India. For a while, Keynes envisaged joint Anglo-American pressure to persuade Britain's sterling creditors to write off some of their claims. Politically, this might have been unwise as well as rather unreasonable; and the American loan agreement merely recorded Britain's intention to approach each of her creditors herself. Friendly persuasion in fact produced gifts of £10 million from New Zealand and £20 million from Australia; but with these 'shining exceptions', as Dalton said, 'no creditor was willing to write off a cent'. Worse still, the American agreement forbade Britain to use any part of the dollar loan to reduce her sterling area debts. In both these ways, trouble was laid up for the future. The problem of the sterling balances, in particular, was to remain unsolved for more than twenty years. In this respect, if other European countries were physically devastated in the struggle against Hitler, the economic wounds that Britain suffered were no less deep and enduring.[27]

More immediately, the British were dismayed to find that life in the early years of peace was in some ways more austere than in wartime. This led to anomalies. UNRRA clothing standards, for example, had been based on the 1944 British ration; but when they came to be applied, the British ration had dropped to below the UNRRA minimum. One regular item in Britain's wartime diet had been imported dried egg; in February 1946, while the American loan agreement was still before Congress, supplies abruptly vanished from the shops. When they were restored in response to public protests, there began to be a shortage of bread. For a time, campaigns were waged against waste; then, in April, the Ministry of Food reduced the weight of standard loaves. The bakers had advised putting more air in the dough, so that the bread would look no smaller; but the Ministry preferred a reduction in size. The result was easily predictable: housewives bought more loaves, and bread consumption remained the same. Three months later the government announced that bread was to be rationed, something that had never happened during the war.[28]

Most of Britain's postwar privations were due to her shortage of dollars; but bread was rationed on account of the world shortage of food. At the beginning of 1946, Attlee had held a long telegraphed correspondence on the subject with Truman, and had sent the British Minister of Food, Sir Ben Smith, to Washington to discuss it with the American administration. At that time, world food production was twelve per cent below normal, and European production twenty-five per cent down. North America had just brought in a record wheat crop; but war damage and severe drought had greatly reduced output in Europe and North Africa, and wheat supplies in the first half of the year threatened to be seven million tons short of what the importing countries had already asked for. In Asia, moreover, the rice crop was fifteen per cent below normal; and if famine was to be prevented, one to two million tons of wheat would have to be diverted to India and the Far East. As Truman wrote later, 'More people faced starvation and even death for want of food during the year following the war than during all the war years combined.'[29]

Spurred by Attlee's urgings, Truman appointed a Famine Emergency Committee under ex-President Herbert Hoover, to recommend a detailed programme of relief. In conjunction with most of the producing countries, steps were taken to save wheat, to increase acreage, to speed and regularize distribution, to co-ordinate buying and to conserve food. The United States and Britain both raised their flour extraction rate, to eighty per cent and eight-five per cent respectively—thereby incidentally narrowing the residue used as feed grain and reducing the supply of pigmeat, poultry and eggs. By these measures the worst was avoided; but the danger of famine came very close. Even the United States suffered twice from meat shortages; and in Europe, as elsewhere, many people still went hungry.[30]

At the heart of Europe's problem, as so often, was Germany, the origin, exemplar and principal victim of the general distress. 'Germany,' said Attlee in a conversation years later, 'was down to her last potato almost.' At the time he wrote, more formally, to Truman: 'The ration there is already very low and substantial further cuts will bring starvation and unrest, which, apart altogether from humanitarian considerations, will increase our military commitments and retard Europe's economic recovery by reducing the export of essential supplies from Germany, particularly the coal which is so urgently needed.'[31]

Germany's plight, moreover, was worsened by East-West divisions. Poland now held what had once been part of the country's food-growing area, and much of the rest was under Soviet control. As Churchill had written to Truman on 18 April 1945, 'The Russian occupational zone has the smallest proportion of people and grows by far the largest proportion of food, the Americans have a not very satisfactory proportion of food to conquered population, and we poor British are to take over all the ruined Ruhr and large manufacturing districts, which are, like ourselves, in normal times large importers of food.' For this reason it had seemed essential to pool all German food resources and divide them equitably between the zones; but when the question was raised with Stalin at the Potsdam Conference it was without success. Now, the population of the Western zones was swollen by at least four million refugees. In the spring of 1946, rations in the American zone had to be cut to 1,275 calories, and in the British zone to 1,040. In April, Herbert Hoover was told that even these meagre allowances might have to be reduced, perhaps to 915 calories a day. It was little wonder, despite the unpopularity of austerity measures in Britain, that Attlee felt obliged

74

to furnish no less than 400,000 tons of foodstuffs to the British zone.[32]

This was a far cry from some of the ideas about Germany's future that had been current in Britain and America during the war. In August 1944, Roosevelt had written in an angry mood to Cordell Hull:

> ...It is of the utmost importance that every person in Germany should realize that this time Germany is a defeated nation. I do not want them to starve to death, but, as an example, if they need food to keep body and soul together beyond what they have, they should be fed three times a day with soup from Army soup kitchens.

'If I had my way,' he was further reported as saying, 'I would keep Germany on a breadline for the next twenty-five years.'[33]

It was in this frame of mind that Roosevelt had accepted the 'Morgenthau Plan' drawn up by the US Secretary of the Treasury, Henry Morgenthau, and by his assistant Harry Dexter White, who was later accused of being an under-cover Communist — 'not Dexter White,' as someone remarked, 'but sinister Red.' Gleefully exploited by Goebbels's Nazi propagandists, the Morgenthau Plan became notorious as a handbook of repression; but its basic premise, paradoxically, was that the rebirth of nationalism could not be prevented by repressive measures such as those applied by the Allies after World War I, however sternly they were imposed. Reparations in kind, as favoured by the British, would strengthen German industry, Morgenthau argued, at the expense of its competitors. The destruction of existing armaments, merchant ships and industrial plant would merely remove what would soon become obsolete, leaving room for brand-new replacements. The distinction between wartime and peacetime industries was in any case hazy: the latter could quickly be converted in time of war. The suppression of Nazism would simply drive it into hiding; forced re-education would prove impossible; and Allied occupation, however permanent in theory, would in practice sooner or later come to an end.

Much of this was sensible; but instead of concluding that repression was self-defeating, Morgenthau wished to carry it to extremes. Germany, he said, should be dismembered, its large estates broken up, and all but its lightest industries dismantled. Even perfume factories should be eliminated, since they could be converted for the production of poison gas. At first, Morgenthau suggested the closure of the Ruhr's mines and industries: later he proposed their internationalization. Himself an enthusiastic agronomist and owner of a model farm near New York, he intended that Germany be 'pastoralized'. The resultant mass unemployment, he said, would provide labour battalions to rebuild the rest of Europe.[34]

Looking back, it is hard to see the Morgenthau Plan as anything but an index of the insane atmosphere of war. Its proposals, however, were contested even at the time. Henry Stimson, US Secretary of War, was particularly outspoken: 'The question,' he told Roosevelt, 'is whether over the years a group of seventy million educated, efficient, and imaginative people can be kept within bounds on such a low level of subsistence as the Treasury proposals contemplate ... It would be just such a crime as the Germans themselves hoped to perpetuate upon their victims—it would be a crime against civilization itself.' When Roosevelt put the project to the British at the second Quebec Conference, in September 1944, Churchill was equally hostile. At a men's dinner party for the Allied leaders on 13 September, Morgenthau argued that the closure of the Ruhr would help British steel exports; but Churchill answered, 'England would be chained to a dead body.' 'I'm all for disarming Germany,' he said, 'but we ought not to prevent her living decently. There are bonds between the working classes of all countries, and the English people will not stand for the policy you are advocating.' He paused, and added: 'I agree with Burke. You cannot indict a whole nation.'[35]

Unfortunately, the matter did not end there. It was well known that Churchill could sometimes be influenced through his friend Lord Cherwell, formerly F. A. Lindemann, commonly nicknamed 'the Prof'. Harry Dexter White therefore approached Cherwell, and hinted that acceptance of the Morgenthau Plan might make it easier for Britain to obtain postwar American aid. 'The Prof' went to Churchill. 'I explained to Winston,' he said later, 'that the plan would save Britain from bankruptcy by eliminating a dangerous competitor. Somebody must suffer for the war, and it was surely right that Germany and not Britain should foot the bill.' Within forty-eight hours, Churchill had swung round to supporting the project. When someone suggested that it might not work—'why shouldn't it?' he demanded. 'I've no patience with people who are always raising difficulties.' So, on 15 September 1944, Roosevelt and Churchill both initialled a memorandum embodying Morgenthau's proposals for the 'metallurgical, chemical and electric industries in Germany'. 'The industries referred to in the Ruhr and in the Saar would ... be put out of action and closed down,' it stated. 'This program for eliminating the war-making industries in the Ruhr and in the Saar is looking forward to converting Germany into a country primarily agricultural and pastoral in its character ...'[36]

Churchill soon returned to the more generous principle embodied in the epigraph of his war memoirs—'In Victory: Magnanimity.' He acknowledged, however, that the tide of feeling was strong. In January 1945 he wrote to the Foreign Secretary, Anthony Eden:

I have been struck at every point where I have sounded opinion at the depth of the feeling that would be aroused by a policy of 'putting Germany on her legs again'. I am also well aware of the arguments about 'not having a poisoned community in the heart of Europe'. I do suggest that, with all the work we have on our hands at the present moment, we should not anticipate these very grievous discussions and schisms, as they may become. ...

It is a mistake to try to write out on little pieces of paper what the vast emotions of an outraged and quivering world will be either immediately after the struggle is over or when the inevitable cold fit follows the hot.[37]

In Washington, likewise, cooler counsel prevailed. Widespread opposition, especially from Stimson, Cordell Hull and James Forrestal, induced Roosevelt to abandon the Morgenthau Plan, at least as public policy. But its influence lingered; and it strongly marked the directive JCS/1067 drawn up by the US Joint Chiefs of Staff to guide their occupation authorities. When President Truman issued it on 14 May 1945, Stimson thought this a 'fairly good paper'; later, more accurately, he called it 'a painfully negative document'. In the words of General Lucius D. Clay, Eisenhower's Deputy Military Governor in charge of the American zone, it prescribed that:

Germany was to be occupied as a defeated nation under a just, firm, and aloof administration which would discourage any fraternization. ... It specifically prohibited us from taking any steps to rehabilitate or maintain the German economy except to maximize agricultural production. ... Patents and trade processes were declared subject to seizure. Production in war plants was to be stopped and plants equipped for such production were to be removed without awaiting action by the Allied Control Council. Until agreement was reached in the Council, there was to be no production of iron, steel, chemicals, machine tools, radio and electrical equipment, automobiles or heavy machinery. Only the production of light consumer goods and the mining of coal were to be encouraged.

A broadly similar policy was to be followed in the whole of western Germany, including the French zone established after the Yalta Conference. As a plan, it was almost entirely arbitrary. Before Clay left the United States to take up his appointment in Germany, no one suggested that he pay a call on the State Department; future long-term peace arrangements still seemed very far away. One consequence was that when the occupation forces came to apply official Allied policy, they found that for the most part it denied their genuine needs and ignored their practical problems. If Berlin had looked remote from Washington,

Washington seemed even more remote when looked at from Berlin. In this way, at a time when US troops were withdrawing from other countries in Western Europe, the military government in Germany found itself likewise on its own.[38]

Initially, the occupation involved severe restraint of German industry. At Yalta, Stalin had demanded that Germany pay 20,000 million dollars' worth of reparations in the form of plant, goods, and labour—half of this sum to go to the Soviet Union. This had been accepted as 'a basis for discussion'. At Potsdam, the Allies agreed on a formula allowing reparations from resources 'unnecessary to the German peace economy'; later, with some difficulty, they fixed on a 'level of industry' as the basis for pooling the spoils they hoped to divide. This assumed that the economy of all Germany would be treated as a single whole; but in practice it was not. Without even waiting for the inter-Allied Reparations Commission to report to the Potsdam Conference, the Russians had begun removing a large variety of goods and capital equipment from the Soviet zone. An observer in Berlin described some of their exotic booty—a truck containing 'a mountain of brass: tubas, trumpets and trombones, covered by heavy Bokhara rugs', and another filled with 'thousands of naked typewriters'. More systematically, they collected miles of rail track and stripped a number of steelworks, plywood factories and hydrogen processing installations. At the same time, however, while the British were blowing up the Blohm and Voss shipyard in Hamburg and finding it hard to get even half their target output from hungry and exhausted steelworkers in the Ruhr, the Russians successfully boosted industrial production in the East. By 1946 it had reached seventy per cent of its prewar level, the highest figure for any of the Allied zones. Since the Soviet authorities refused to account for either the equipment they removed or the manufactures they received without payment, it began to look as if the Western Allies, by handing over material from their own zones, into which they were pouring food and money, were paying much of the reparations bill themselves. To many, this was reminiscent of the economic absurdities that had followed World War I. At length, in the spring of 1946, Clay stopped reparations deliveries from the American zone, thereby formally acknowledging the economic cleavage between east and west Germany, and paving the way for the later amalgamation of the Western zones that led to the formation of the German Federal Republic.[39]

As it turned out, the effect of reparations was paradoxical. In all, about 500 million dollars' worth of equipment and machinery was dismantled. This caused much resentment among the Germans; but its benefit to the Allies and its harm to the German economy were both much less than had been expected. The Russians, in particular, failed to profit from much of their plunder. It took time and skill to reconstruct dismantled material: intelligence reports and photographs revealed many sidings in eastern Germany and the Soviet Union crowded with freight cars full of machine tools uselessly rusting. Moreover, as Morgenthau had predicted, the removal of existing plant made way for later innovations, and when the time came helped put Germany ahead in the competitive race.[40]

A more serious handicap for Germany's immediate recovery was the inflation and demoralization that most of all affected the Western zones. Anyone who went there in the first two years after the war had the strange, unnerving experience of entering a barter economy. The basic and very simple reason was that, amid so much destruction, war financing had increased the supply of money by more than 400 per cent. The results, although predictable, were grim. Cigarettes, and in a lesser degree coffee and chocolate, had almost replaced normal currency. Such business as there was had to be conducted by composite bilateral exchanges of goods. Nominal incomes were largely meaningless. The usual incentives to work were lacking; so were health and strength. Everyone was poor and shabby, and almost everyone was hungry. The mood was one of tired exasperation and bewilderment; only those who were exceptionally determined, or lucky, or agile managed to resist.[41]

In a world so much awry, the occupation authorities performed wonders; but since their power was virtually absolute, mistakes and lapses were inevitable. The most celebrated blunder was that of the unfortunate Brigadier Barraclough, who on 6 October 1945, dismissed Konrad Adenauer as *Oberbürgermeister* of Cologne and forbade him 'to indulge either directly or indirectly in any political activity whatever' for his lack of 'proper supervision and energy' in 'the general task of preparing for the coming winter', 'the repair of buildings and the clearance of the streets'. At a lower level, temptations abounded. The official historian of the American zone admitted that 'looting was all too frequent'; and black-market trading of PX and NAAFI supplies was notoriously common. In July 1945 US troops sent home a million dollars more than they received in pay; one man sent back a complete motor-cycle, in three separate shipments. In these ways, as in others, the occupation proved the difficulty of applying in practice stern and high-minded precepts worked out so far away. Of all of them, however, the earliest casualty was the ban on fraternization. On 12 June 1945, Field-Marshal Montgomery relaxed it to allow British soldiers to speak to, and play with, German children. 'They were, of course, doing it already,' he said. Soon, the ban was lifted entirely—a necessary concession to human nature in a situation where hunger, desire and compassion were often quite literally bedfellows.[42]

In a grey universe of shortages, undernourishment, corruption and disorder, the occupation authorities faced the same twin tasks as all Europe's postwar governments. One was the indispensable mundane duty of administration; this was headache enough. The other was more inspiring, but also far more challenging—the overriding need to build society anew.

'Denazification' was to Germany what '*épuration*' had been to France, southern Belgium and Luxembourg, '*epurazione*' to Italy, and '*zuivering*' to Flanders and the Netherlands: the attempt to identify, expel from office, punish and perhaps reform or re-educate those who had willingly served the dictators. As elsewhere, it made for very rough justice, and it created as much resentment as it appeased. More constructive were the Allies' positive efforts to reintroduce democracy, fostering free speech and discussion, spreading information, counteracting the years of lies and half-truths, using authority to fight the long habit of yielding to it, and gradually building up, with the aid of the liberated Germans, new political institutions that would make occupation unnecessary. It was an uphill struggle against conditioning and prejudice—on both sides. Rightly or not, some Allied officers could not but believe that the German people was subservient by nature; even anti-Nazi-Germans, for their part, grew tired of being lectured on their nation's collective guilt, although many were prepared to acknowledge it. A few on both sides had unshakeable faith in the rightness of their own methods and institutions, from newspaper layout to proportional representation: often it took close personal contact between occupied and occupier, working together on the same job, to reveal that what was unfamiliar in either Anglo-American or pre-Nazi German tradition was not necessarily inferior, but in most cases merely different.[43]

Slowly and imperfectly, the task was accomplished. The press, the radio, the cinema, publishing, education and political life were gradually overhauled. Nazi newspapers were at first replaced by Allied bulletins; then, on 31 July 1945, the Americans licensed a new German paper, the *Frankfurter Rundschau*, to be followed by forty-four others during the next two years. The British were slower to begin, with the *Braunschweiger Zeitung*, inaugurated on 8 January 1946; but by midsummer they had licensed thirty-four others. Parallel with them, to provide competitive stimulus and a standard of comparison, the Allies maintained their own semi-official argans—*Die Neue Zeitung* in the American zone,

Die Welt in the British. In both zones, the occupation authorities did their best to lighten the traditionally heavy make-up of German newspapers and to remodel their contents; in particular, they sought to establish a clear distinction between comment and news. Radio was handled separately. In Berlin, the Russians had taken over both the transmitter and the studios, although all were located in the western sectors of the city. The British and Americans therefore set up regional networks in their own zones. At first, unlike most of the newspapers, these were staffed by the Allies; gradually, later, they were transferred to German control. Cinemas, which had initially been closed altogether, were re-opened to show purely escapist productions from the Nazi epoch and dubbed or subtitled versions of British and American films. The old UFA studios in Neu-Babelsberg were now in the Soviet zone: under a new company, DEFA, they re-opened in 1946 to produce Wolfgang Staudte's powerful, guilty, slightly evasive *Die Mörder sind unter uns*— a first attempt to scrutinize 'the murderers in our midst'. In the western zones, film production revived a little later, and the shortage of capital, stock and equipment ensured the predominance of foreign films for several years. A similar pattern at first emerged in publishing, where translations of authors long forbidden by the Nazis—from H. G. Wells and Upton Sinclair to Proust and Emile Zola—were quickly released for eager German readers, sometimes under special copyright arrangements. Meanwhile, in the summer of 1945, universities began to re-open, followed by elementary schools in October, and by secondary schools in the spring. Finally, German public life began to be liberalized on the lines laid down at the Potsdam Conference, which had called for 'the decentralization of the political structure and the development of local responsibility.' The Americans allowed parties to be formed on a district basis in August 1945, on a *Land* basis in November, and on a zonal basis in February 1946; the British sanctioned party activity from September 1945 onwards. But already, in fact, the trade unions had begun to turn their own gatherings into political rallies. As one British official put it,

Each meeting had the same pattern: after a few words of thanks for their liberation (we were still liberators in those days) the speakers launched a tirade against their former bosses, many of whom had been Nazis and had by then disappeared. They were not, however, after their blood, nor did they even want to see them sent to prison. They merely wanted to see them take their coats and collars off and do some real work by which they apparently meant manual labour. I always knew when a speech was veering round to an attack on the bosses, as the passage invariably started with the words: 'Let them take a pick and shovel....' and the rest was usually drowned in applause.[44]

Crudely, this expressed a feeling that was general in Germany and in Europe—the urge to transform the old political, economic and social structure, which many believed had been largely responsible for Europe's present ills. 'From Resistance to Revolution' was the masthead motto of *Combat*, the underground newspaper founded by Albert Camus and his friends in January 1941, which first appeared openly just after the liberation of France in 1944. 'Politics is no longer something remote from the individual,' wrote Camus at the beginning of September; 'it is now a matter of man speaking to man.' Many of those who had fought against Hitler, including the German Resistance, had fought not only for their countries but for a new kind of democratic comradeship, something of which they had experienced either as rankers in the services, as colleagues in the underground, or as victims of the air-raids. In time of danger, it had been easy to feel that all men were fundamentally equal, differentiated only by their courage or their skill. Now, it seemed, was the time to take in hand the old structure of society, to make it and the state no longer hierarchical and alien, but a true and direct expression of human kinship.[45]

In Italy, at the end of March 1944, the political committee of the Action Party partisans in one section of Cuneo province issued a characteristic circular. They were far from being Communists; but they wrote in rousing terms:

The soldiers of this army are not so much, or at least are not only, the champions of a general patriotism, aiming simply at 'driving the foreigner off the sacred soil of the mother country', but rather the armed force and the resolute advance-guard of a movement of renewal, of a revolutionary process that is at work on the country's whole political and social structure, to give to Italy, disgraced and degraded by the Fascist tyranny that was backed and upheld by well-known accomplices, the new aspect of a free, democratic, and civic nation.

In Holland, the Christian-inspired *Volksbeweging* or People's Movement similarly called for help in 'the common task: the necessary radical renovation of our people's life—economically, socially, politically, spiritually'. It was a cry that was echoed by the many Christian-Democrat parties that now came into prominence, seeking to apply firm moral standards to political and social life. Its eloquence was perhaps greatest in Germany. In Berlin, in June 1945, the Christian Democratic Union issued a resounding appeal:

From the chaos of guilt and shame into which the idolization of a criminal adventurer threw us, an order of democratic freedom can grow only if we return to the cultural, moral and intellectual forces of Christianity and open up this source of strength more and more for our people....

Great is the guilt of wide circles of our people who lowered themselves all too willingly to being the tools and help-mates of Hitler. All guilt calls for atonement.... Fighters of truly democratic faith, Protestant and Catholic Christians, countless Jewish fellow-citizens, men and women from all classes of the people suffered and died. In the spirit of their legacy, united by the same love of our people, we recognize our duty of going with this people the way of atonement, the way of rebirth.

From all parties, but especially from the left and centre, the call was similar. In Britain, when the Labour party won its sweeping 1945 victory, one of its ministers wrote:

That first sensation, tingling and triumphant, was of a new society to be built; and we had the power to build it. There was exhilaration among us, joy and hope, determination and confidence. We felt exalted, dedicated, walking on air, walking with destiny.

It was in Britain, indeed, that inept slogan-makers called the new world they wanted 'the century of the common man'. For many, the phrase conjured up visions of caricatured proletarians in cloth caps and mufflers, following each other sheeplike through the turnstiles of a giant bureaucracy. But for its originators it signified a vision, and one they were determined to fulfil.[46]

In France and Britain, in particular, this new impulse led to a broad extension of public welfare and public ownership. General de Gaulle's first postwar government introduced a fairly comprehensive system of social security; Britain inaugurated the National Health Service to provide medical care free. In both countries, the railways, gas and electricity, and cables and wireless were nationalized; in France, government ownership or control was extended in the oil industry, to air transport, to the Renault motor works, and to several important banks, while Britain nationalized coal and steel and long-range road transport. Similar movements took place on a lesser scale elsewhere. In Austria, government control ranged over large segments of heavy industry; in Italy, the *Istituto di Ricostruzione Industriale* extended and strengthened its already firm grip. In these ways, the state was directly involved in many of Europe's first postwar measures of reconstruction, whether through new nationalization, through existing corporate holding companies, or through the cognate controls established by the Allies in Germany.[47]

For a while, such efforts succeeded remarkably. Transport was rapidly re-established: by the end of 1946, ninety per cent of all France's railway bridges had been rebuilt, and 300,000 tons of shipping had been salvaged. Despite war damage and reparations, Germany emerged from the war with increased industrial capacity; soon, it was to be brought back more and more in to production. Belgium successfully fought off inflation with a new note issue; Norway, later, did the same. For roughly eighteen months, in fact, European governments struggled to return to normal; and it seemed as if their self-help would suffice. Yet all the time, new dangers were looming, and old weaknesses were about to be revealed. By 1947, the immediate hopes of the postwar period had begun to dim again; politically and economically, the countries of Europe were now abruptly reminded that war, among other things, had cut them down to size.[48]

CHAPTER FIVE

The Reluctant St George

If 1946 was *Annus Mirabilis*, 1947 was *Annus Horrendus*.
Hugh Dalton[1]

The best public measures are... *seldom adopted from previous wisdom, but forced by the occasion.*
Benjamin Franklin[2]

America was thus clearly top nation, and History came to a .
W. C. Sellar and R. J. Yeatman[3]

IN the grey late afternoon of Friday 21 February 1947, the US State Department took an urgent telephone call from the private secretary to the British Ambassador in Washington, Lord Inverchapel. Could the Ambassador come round at once to see General George C. Marshall, the newly appointed Secretary of State? As it happened, Marshall was already on his way to Princeton, New Jersey, to attend the University's bicentennial celebrations, make a speech and receive an honorary degree. An appointment was arranged for the following Monday; but Dean Acheson, the Under-Secretary, asked whether the notes that Lord Inverchapel wished to deliver could be brought round unofficially and studied over the weekend. It was a wise precaution, for their message was momentous. Britain was serving notice that from the end of March 1947, in less than six weeks' time, she could no longer be responsible for economic aid to Greece and Turkey. As Joseph Harsch, the American broadcaster, put it a few days later, 'London might just as well have dropped an atomic bomb on Washington; the impact could have been no more startling.'[4]

The immediate implications of the British move were serious enough. Although the largely Communist EAM had failed in its bid for power in Athens, its guerrilla fighters were still active in the Pindus Mountains and the Peloponnese; only British aid, and the presence of a British division, enabled the Greek army to hold them in check. Sir Clifford Norton, Britain's astute and affable ambassador, had warned the Foreign Office that the Greek government would fall if there were 'even a whisper' of British withdrawal. The country's economy was near collapse: with only 14 million dollars of free foreign exchange in the Treasury, it would need a further 240 to 280 million dollars during 1947 alone. Turkey's economic situation was less alarming; but her strategic position was extremely vulnerable, and she had been continually subject to political pressure from the Soviet Union. If Britain were now to leave the Balkans and if nothing were done to fill the resultant power vacuum, the outcome would at best be further instability in an area traditionally dangerous, at worst the extension of Soviet control to the shores and harbours of the Aegean and a direct threat, from a new direction, to the oilfields of the Middle East.[5]

Rumours that Britain was about to reduce her Balkan commitments had long been circulating, and urgent warnings had reached the State Department by early February 1947. Few in Washington, however, had expected so drastic a cut-back to be announced so soon. What had happened was that Hugh Dalton, the British Chancellor of the Exchequer, had finally and abruptly won the running battle for economy that he had been fighting all winter against the Foreign Secretary, Ernest Bevin.[6]

It had been a hard winter in more senses than one. Several British Ministers were ill, including the bulky and energetic Bevin, whose heart was showing signs of strain. The Prime Minister, Clement Attlee, was thought by his colleagues to be in need of a holiday; both Herbert Morrison, the Deputy Premier, and James Chuter Ede, the Home Secretary, were suffering from thrombosis; Ellen Wilkinson, the Minister of Education, was near to death. To make matters worse, the weather suddenly became Siberian. For three days at the end of January 1947, Britain suffered her biggest blizzard since 1894. Snow fell continuously almost everywhere: in places it was twenty feet deep, burying trees and hedgerows in an undulating white waste. Even in the densely populated industrial Midlands, many villages were isolated, and food supplies had to be dropped to them by parachute. When the thaw came, it lasted twenty-four hours. Then the thermometer fell again, and the partly melted snowdrifts turned to ice. Roads were blocked, railways immobilized, dock gates frozen solid, helping to cause a fuel shortage that aggravated the cold. Coal could still be produced wherever miners could dig their way to the pits; but some pithead machinery was frozen, and many stocks could not be moved. Overloaded power stations were forced to reduce their output; industry in London, the South-East, the Midlands, and the North-West was largely paralyzed. Eighty per cent of the country, it was estimated, was once more plunged into the gloom of the wartime blackout. Severe restrictions were placed on electric heating, and domestic supplies were cut off altogether from 9 a.m. to noon and from 2 to 4 p.m. every day.[7]

The fuel crisis dramatized and helped decide the Chancellor's battle with the Foreign Secretary. As Dalton confided to his diary,

> Bevin, very short of breath because he had had to walk up two flights of stairs to a Committee in Great George Street [the site of the Treasury] since, with electricity cut off, the lifts were not working ... wanted me to come round to the Foreign Office and pore over a lot of papers. I said that I did not think I need trouble him with all this detail. I wanted firm instructions sent both to Norton and to Inverchapel, but I was quite prepared to do a deal and was willing that Norton should be allowed to hold his hand, provided we sent Inverchapel into action at Washington. Bevin said, not perhaps quite realizing what he was agreeing to, 'Well, that's quite fair.'

With that, Dalton acted, and 'a stiff Treasury draft' was sent off.[8]

The real dispute, however, went far deeper than the clash of personalities or government departments. In fact, it was the beginning of a struggle between Britain's traditional world responsibilities and her newly reduced economic resources; and it was to continue for the next twenty years.

In December 1945, Britain had met her early postwar difficulties by negotiating the 3,750-million-dollar United States loan. Since then, American wholesale prices had risen by more than forty per cent, reducing the loan's effective value by nearly one-third. The first credits became available in July 1946; by the end of the year, 600 million dollars had already been spent. At that rate, the British Treasury reckoned, the loan would be exhausted by September 1949. In the New Year, however, the rate of expenditure rose alarmingly; now, it was feared, the money might run out as early as February 1948. Still worse was to come. On 15 July 1947, in accordance with the loan agreement, the pound was declared convertible: holders of sterling were now at liberty to change it into dollars. The result was a flight of capital from London—and the still more rapid exhaustion of the loan. In July, the drain on Britain's reserves was 115 million dollars a week; in August it increased to 150 million dollars, and it rose to 237 million dollars in the third week of the month. On Wednesday 6 August, the Prime Minister estimated that the American loan would all be drawn by the end of 1947. The next day, Dalton corrected this to October, just two months ahead. Finally, on Wednesday 20 August 1947 convertibility was suspended, five weeks after it had begun.[9]

Living on rapidly dwindling credit, Britain was at the same time bearing heavy overseas burdens. Not only Greece and Turkey, but a number of other countries, were dependent on her aid. In 1946, she had spent 60 million dollars on feeding the German people, however inadequately; in the first quarter of 1947 she was to spend 60 million dollars more. Around the globe, moreoever, rightly or wrongly, British soldiers were still acting as policemen—against Communists in Greece, against the Zionist *Irgun Zvei Leumi* in Palestine, between Hindus and Muslims in India. Nearly two years after the end of World War II there were still a million-and-a-half men in the Services, while at home the available manpower was 630,000 short of Britain's needs.[10]

In this situation, clearly, something had to give. The question of Palestine was referred to the United Nations in February 1947; but Britain's inglorious involvement was to continue until the State of Israel was proclaimed on Friday 14 May 1948. The withdrawal from India was more precipitate. In May 1946 a Cabinet mission had proposed a federal union of the Indian provinces, which had been accepted both by the mainly Hindu Congress Party and by Mohammed Ali Jinnah's Muslim League. But mistrust and hostility between the two was soon redoubled by a tactless press conference given by the Congress President, Jawaharlal Nehru; and when Lord Wavell, the British Viceroy, invited Nehru to form a government, Jinnah refused to join it, calling for 'Direct Action'—which led to a four-day riot in Calcutta, with 5,000 dead and 15,000 wounded. Only the personal intervention of Mahatma Gandhi prevented violence spreading throughout the country. Although the Muslim League joined Nehru's Executive Council in October 1946, this was only, in practice, to hinder its work. With civil war once more threatening, the British government called Nehru, Jinnah and the Sikh leader Sardar Baldev Singh to a conference in London. When this, too, proved inconclusive, Attlee decided to replace the long-suffering Wavell by Lord Mountbatten; but Mountbatten insisted that if he became Viceroy it could only be 'to wind up the show'. On Thursday 20 February, therefore—on the day before the withdrawal from Greece was announced in Washington—Attlee told the House of Commons that Britain would leave India 'by a date not later than 1948'. In the event, she was to quit by the middle of August, 1947.[11]

Thus, within the span of a few months and by a few crucial decisions, the British government tacitly acknowledged the closing of an epoch. *Pax Britannica* was coming to an end. Harried by economic necessity, Britain was embarking on a long, painful and halting process of readjustment: very gradually, she was becoming one European country among many, each no longer strong enough to play a decisive world role by herself.

The reality of the change was not always dramatic. In many places, British garrisons were to linger for two more decades. Elsewhere, despite the military withdrawl, administrators and technicians remained behind —as did, in some cases, a sprinkling of Service personnel. When British troops withdrew from Cairo early in 1947, for example, they at first fell back only to Suez and the Canal Zone; and the British Embassy's powerful radio continued to be serviced, *sub rosa*, by army signalmen in civilian clothes, driven to and from the Egyptian capital in disguised military trucks.[12] At home, moreover, the significance of the British withdrawal was masked by the very emergencies that prompted it. Undefeated and uninvaded, Britain still felt undiminished. Her economic plight was so acute as to seem temporary, not structural; and the dismantling of the Empire, although permanent, was camouflaged by its metamorphosis into the Commonwealth.

From across the Atlantic, however, the situation looked very different. As one State Department official put it,

Each day's cables, each day's newspapers and broadcasts, brought the story: From the Mediterranean eastward to the Sea of Japan nationalism was successfully asserting itself. In the very heart of the British Empire six independent states were emerging: India, Pakistan, Burma, Ceylon, Nepal and Afghanistan. Revolutionary movements were challenging French and Dutch control in Indochina and Indonesia, with good prospects of success. The Philippines had achieved independence; Thailand had thrown off British influence. Victorious China had freed herself of Western controls. In the Middle East, colonies were moving toward self-government, mandated countries toward independence, all toward nationalistic self-assertion that weakened alliances.... What was clearly happening was the sudden disappearance of the imperial system and the rise of independent, weak, nationalist states. This had happened in Europe hundreds of years earlier – and had led to centuries of bloody, nationalistic strife.[18]

In this context, Britain's announcement that she was to end her aid to Greece and Turkey became a symbol and a portent: it triggered off a process of rethinking in Washington that was all the more radical for being so long overdue.

Already for eighteen months, in fact, America had manifestly been the greatest power on earth. During World War II, her total production had doubled, from 90,000 million to 180,000 million dollars. Less spectacularly in the face of wartime restrictions, her standard of living had also risen: her annual meat consumption, for instance, had increased from 125 to 163 pounds a head. But most striking of all was her new preponderance in the military field, where she now enjoyed the equivocal privilege of seemingly absolute power. If one precise moment may be quoted as a turning-point, it was shortly before noon on Monday 6 August 1945. Sailing home after Potsdam Conference, in the USS *Augusta*, President Truman was eating lunch with the crew when Captain Frank H. Graham, watch officer of the White House Map Room, hurried in with a top-priority signal: 'Big bomb dropped on Hiroshima.' Truman, in the laconic words of Admiral Leahy, 'was excited over the news'. As he himself put it, 'I was greatly moved.' Shaking Captain Graham by the hand, he said: 'This is the greatest thing in history.'[14]

It would have been understandable if, from that moment onwards, *hubris* had begun to dominate American policy. Reared in optimism, conditioned to feel that most things are possible if given a big enough effort, Americans might have been expected to want to start running the world. 'Dominance' might have been far from their intentions, but 'leadership' has always been a seductive euphemism. Yet during the months that followed Hiroshima, the United States in some respects retreated from world responsibilities. The termination of Lend-Lease, the resumption of business-as-usual, the concern to bring the troops home—all seemed to echo the universal tendency to model the future on the past. The Republican party, traditionally isolationist, in November 1946 won a majority in both Houses of Congress for the first time in fourteen years; quickly calling for cuts in taxes and military expenditure, it sought to reduce by half the sums requested for food and emergency relief in ex-enemy countries. For a while, some Americans seemed to have forgotten that whereas once— until the battle of Midway—they had sheltered behind the British navy, Britain and other countries now had to rely on the military and economic strength of the United States. Perhaps America's nuclear monopoly encouraged comfortable unconcern. At all events, Britain, in those early days, was still counted on for a leading contribution to world order. Typical of the climate of opinion was the title of a thoughtful essay published by the Yale University Press in 1945—*The Big Three*. Two of the three, quite naturally, were the United States and the Soviet Union. Twenty years later, the third might well have been China, or—just possibly—Europe; at that time, it was Great Britain. Not until the cruel Spring of 1947 was it fully obvious how anachronistic this notion had become. Then, over the cold weekend of 22-3 February 1947, the 'big three' were revealed as only two. Britain's postwar weakness was suddenly made manifest; America had to take her place. If not a reluctant dragon, the United States now had to become a reluctant St George.[15]

By comparison with prewar American attitudes, the change was profound; and subsequent publicity made it spectacular. But most such political turning-points are somewhat fictitious; and President Truman's response to Britain's impending withdrawal from the Balkans was certainly no exception. On several occasions since the end of World War II the Administration had affirmed, as the then Secretary of State James Byrnes had put it in a crucial speech in Stuttgart on 6 September 1945, America's intention 'to continue our interest in the affairs of Europe and of the world'. On 28 February 1946, in particular, Byrnes had told the New York Overseas Press Club that while 'there is no reason for war between any of the great powers', 'we will not and we cannot stand aloof if force or threat of force is used contrary to the purposes and principles of the [United Nations] Charter.' Exactly one year later, in February 1947, Truman was given the chance to dramatize and make concrete this conception of America's role. 'This was the time,' he wrote in retrospect, 'to align the United States of America clearly on the side, and at the head, of the free world.' It was an ambition that he had cherished ever since succeeding to the presidency on Franklin Roosevelt's death. In private letters —later published—he played, as in a Frank Capra movie, the small-town hero catapulted into power; but in fact he had long held firm and downright views on foreign as well as domestic policy. On Thursday 19 April 1945, just a week after taking office, he had told Averell Harriman, US Ambassador to the Soviet Union, that in negotiating with the Russians, whom Harriman saw as bent on a 'barbarian invasion of Europe', 'I would not expect one hundred per cent of what we proposed. But I felt we should be able to get eighty-five per cent.' When he saw the Soviet Foreign Minister, V. M. Molotov, a few days later, Truman spoke so 'sharply'— his own adverb—that Molotov protested: 'I have never been talked to like that in my life.' 'I told him,' Truman wrote afterwards, ' "Carry out your agreements and you won't get talked to like that." ' This was the same truculent Middle-Westerner who later claimed to have told James Byrnes, 'I'm tired of babying the Soviets'—although Byrnes denied that the letter containing these words was ever sent or read to him. Now, as a Democratic president facing a Republican Congress, Truman saw in the British Notes of February 1947 an opportunity to assert America's newly realized world role.[16]

If Truman was eager to seize this opportunity, the same was true of the State Department. For years, its officials had suffered from continual frustration. Under Roosevelt American foreign policy had been constantly and often capriciously remade in the White House; of successive Secretaries of State, Cordell Hull had been tired and had seemed uninterested in the future, while Edward R. Stettinius was crisply described by one of his former colleagues as 'a disaster'.[17] During the early months of Truman's Administration, Byrnes had conducted a somewhat personal foreign policy, and relations with the White House had become severely strained, culminating in the Secretary's resignation. Now, under General Marshall, the atmosphere changed. One of his first decisions as Secretary of State was to move the Department from its old Washington headquarters at Seventeenth Street and Pennsylvania Avenue into a new and bigger air-conditioned building at Twenty-First Street and Virginia Avenue—a

D

material symbol of its altered status. In headily modern surroundings, its officials found themselves once more in effective teamwork with the White House, although physically further away from it. With a new sense of power and purpose, they reacted swiftly to the two British Notes they received on Friday 21 February 1947.[18]

That same afternoon, Under-Secretary of State Dean Acheson called for an urgent study of the Greek and Turkish problems, and arranged for close consultation with the War and Navy Departments in Washington. In the evening, a senior staff meeting discussed practical proposals for aid; one of those present went home late that night 'with the stimulating impression of having participated prominently in a historic decision of American foreign policy'. Drafting and further discussion continued throughout the weekend. On Monday morning, 24 February at 10.00 a.m., Marshall officially received Lord Inverchapel, bearing the British government's formal message; he at once conferred with the President, as well as with James V. Forrestal, Secretary of the Navy, and Robert P. Patterson, Secretary of War. On Tuesday, after a further staff meeting, State Department officials worked late to produce a final version of their detailed 'Position and Recommendations', proposing loan legislation, military supplies, administrative aid, consultation with Britain and a programme of public information. On Wednesday 26 February, Forrestal and Patterson endorsed this document, and at 3·00 p.m. Marshall and Acheson presented it to the President. At 10·00 a.m. next morning. Truman received Congressional leaders in his office, together with Marshall and Acheson, who in turn explained the situation and, despite initial suspicion, convinced their audience of the need to act. The Republican Senator Arthur H. Vandenberg, who had previously been isolationist, admitted that he was 'greatly impressed' by Acheson's presentation in particular, and urged that any presidential request for funds be accompanied by a similar message to Congress and to the American people. That night, Acheson gave a first background briefing to selected newspapermen; and on the following morning, Friday 28 February, a full information campaign was roughed out. At the same time, with the aid of officials from the War and Navy Departments, and in liaison with Clark Clifford at the White House, the State Department began drafting what later came to be known as 'the Truman Doctrine'.[19]

During most of the week that followed, Truman himself was absent, on a state visit to Mexico. He was not on hand, therefore, to receive the formal request for aid that the Greek government submitted on Monday 3 March 1947; but this hardly mattered, since its text was a State Department draft. Returning to Washington late on Thursday 6 March, Truman held a full Cabinet meeting on the following day; and on Monday 10 March he again saw a Congressional delegation, this time including the formidable Republican Senator Robert A. Taft. Finally, after last-minute drafting changes, the message to Congress was ready. At 1·00 p.m. on Wednesday 12 March 1947, in a House of Representatives crowded to overflowing for this joint session with the Senate, the President spoke to the nation and to the world. 'His voice,' as one of the audience noted, 'was flat and not impressive, but this day he spoke with a newly acquired forcefulness.' He was asking Congress for 400 million dollars in aid to Greece and Turkey because, in his own words, 'it must be the policy of the United States to support free peoples who are resisting attempted subjugation by armed minorities or by outside pressures.' He himself had insisted on the world 'must' in place of his speech-writers' 'should'. This was 'the Truman Doctrine'. It was the beginning of America's systematic contribution to the recovery of Europe.[20]

Applause greeted Truman's words that sunny March afternoon on Capitol Hill; but the audience was subdued and, to one participant, it seemed bewildered. One reason was the gravity of the President's message; another was the scale of the proposed expenditure. But the Truman Doctrine was also criticized more fundamentally, on the one hand because it seemed to ignore the United Nations, and on the other because it made an issue of principle out of two not identical cases.

On the subject of the UN, Truman's message to Congress was pungently brief. 'We have considered how the United Nations might assist in this crisis. But the situation is an urgent one requiring immediate action, and the United Nations and its related organizations are not in a position to extend help of the kind that is required.' A further paragraph, proposing the study of means whereby the UN 'might undertake financial and economic responsibilities in such areas', had been inserted in the original draft at the suggestion of Dean Rusk, then Director of the State Department's Office of Special Political Affairs; but it had been dropped by the White House, and at least one member of the drafting committee had not even noticed. This, it seemed, was no time for pious aspirations. Experience had shown how the UN could be paralysed by the veto in the Security Council, which by December 1946 had already been used so often that the General Assembly had called for the voting rules to be changed.[21]

More serious, however, was the objection that the Truman Doctrine linked two dissimilar cases under a general principle that was debatable and ill-defined. On the afternoon of Thursday 6 March 1947, a late draft of Truman's message to Congress had been handed to George Kennan, who was soon to inaugurate the Sate Department's Policy Planning Staff. Reading it, he became 'extremely unhappy'. Economic aid for Greece was one thing; military aid for Turkey was quite another. 'I suspected,' he wrote later, 'that what was intended primarily was military aid, and that what had really happened was that the Pentagon had exploited a favorable set of circumstances in order to infiltrate a military aid program for Turkey into what was supposed to be primarily a political and economic program for Greece.' Whether or not the Pentagon was responsible, Kennan was probably right. Even the State Department's semi-official historian, himself involved in shaping the Truman Doctrine, admitted that 'there was a grain of truth' in the Washington gibe that 'when the new dish was being prepared for American consumption, Turkey was slipped into the oven with Greece because that seemed to be the surest way to cook a tough bird'.[22]

Kennan's uneasiness had also a more general cause. 'On many occasions, both before and after this Greek-Turkish episode, I have been struck by the congenital aversion of Americans to taking specific decisions on specific problems, and by their persistent urge to seek universal formulae or doctrines in which to clothe and justify particular actions.' The 'sweeping language' of Truman's message, he thought, 'might be subject to misinterpretation': 'it implied that what we had decided to do in the case of Greece was something we would be prepared to do in the case of any other country.'[23]

Kennan was not alone in scenting danger. On Monday 24 March 1947, Dean Acheson was careful to assure the Senate Committee on Foreign Relations that 'any requests of foreign countries for aid will have to be considered according to the circumstances in each individual case'. It was perhaps as well, at that moment, that Congress had not yet been called upon to authorize economic aid to the whole of Western Europe.[24]

Yet this was precisely what Truman's advisers were soon to propose. The problems of Greece and Turkey, they now saw, were not exceptions but symptoms. It was Britain's economic weakness that had thrust them on America's attention; but although Britain's plight had some unique features, most European countries were in similar or worse distress. Its underlying reasons had the cruel logic of a trap.

Before World War II, Western Europe had imported much of its food and raw materials, and had paid for them largely by exporting industrial goods. Now, the terms of this rough equation were drastically altered.

Crippled by war and by under-investment between the wars, Europe's industrial production in 1947 was still only a fraction of the peacetime norm—less than two-thirds in Austria, Greece and Italy, less than one-third in Western Germany. Output per man-hour was even lower, partly on account of undernourishment. The population had increased by twenty million, but it now had only four-fifths the prewar supply of food. Farm yields had fallen, and traditional supplies of food and raw materials were no longer coming from Eastern Europe and the Far East. The only alternative was to buy them from America, together with urgently needed capital goods and manufactures; but this required vast sums of money that European countries were no longer able to pay. Their currencies were often monstrously inflated; their overseas assets were shrunken or rapidly shrinking. With exchange rates unstable, and without multilateral clearing arrangements, even their trade with each other had to be mainly bilateral—reduced to a quasi-barter system that in turn stifled production. Both France and Italy, for instance, had un-used capacity for making ball-bearings; but in 1947 it remained idle be-cause neither had kronor to buy enough chrome steel from Sweden. In trade with the rest of the world, Europe was equally handicapped. Its annual exports to non-European countries were now worth only 5,400 million dollars as compared with 8,000 million dollars in 1938; its cur-rent-account deficit with the dollar area—seven-tenths of it with the United States—was 7,000 million dollars.[25]

Even the elements seemed to conspire against Europe. Britain's hard winter of 1946–7 was no less severe on the Continent. Coal production was partly paralyzed, and when the snow at last melted, many pits were flooded. Already in 1946 Western Europe had had to import seven-teen million tons of coal from America at eleven dollars a ton—twice the domestic price; now it needed even more. In Western Germany, with steel plants starved for energy, coal output in 1947 reached only 144 million tons as compared with 221 million before the war; steel production stood at less than four million tons, not even a quarter of the prewar figure. France's coal production, it was true, had risen above the 1938 level; but her output of crude steel and pig-iron was well below it. In Norway, the production of finished steel had dropped from 82,000 to 53,000 tons.[26]

The winter, moreover, was preceded and followed by two torrid sum-mers. In January, Europeans shivered in flats, offices, farms and fac-tories, or trundled through a white landscape in unheated trains with ill-fitting boards for windows; in August, for two years in succession, they saw drought shrivel the crops. In France, the 1947 harvest turned out to be only fifty per cent of what it had been a year earlier, and the bread ration had to be cut below its wartime level to only 200 grams a day. In Norway, the daily food ration fell from 2,500 calories to 2,200; for a time in Germany it was little more than 1,000. Finally, to add to Europe's difficulties, the cycle of hardship, unemployment and inflation helped to touch off widespread disruptive strikes.[27]

With gloomy reports and forecasts beginning to pile up in Washington, it gradually became obvious that Europe's postwar problems had been seriously misjudged. As Dean Acheson admitted to a later interviewer, 'We had operated on a theory of dealing with hunger, disease, and unrest until one or two good crops could come in. But the problems were more far-reaching, and it grew upon us toward the end of 1946 that we were heading for very bad trouble.' Partly through self-help, partly through emergency assistance, Europe had survived for two years since the end of hostilities. Now, with the blood-transfusion ending, radical action was needed to prevent a relapse.[28]

That action, when it came, marked America's decisive assumption of world responsibilities. The form it took was the European Recovery Program, better known as the Marshall Plan. Not surprisingly, its pedigree was more complex than its name.

Fundamentally, it sprang from American generosity; but this was spiced with a saving grain of self-interest. The United States had long been pressing for the reduction of trade barriers, and in December 1945 had made formal 'Proposals for Expansion of World Trade and Employment', calling for a liberal, non-discriminatory and multilateral trading system, with an International Trade Organization (ITO) as an offshoot of the UN. Many of these ideas were to re-appear in the Havana Charter agreed by fifty-four nations during the winter of 1947–8; and although the US Congress at length refused to ratify the Charter, some of its content was salvaged by perpetuating the General Agreement on Tariffs and Trade (GATT), a looser interim arrangement made in the previous summer. America's sponsorships of these efforts reflected her new economic role. Since the war, she had become more deeply involved in international commerce: in 1946 her total exports of goods and services were nearly four times the prewar average of 4,000 million dollars a year. Early in 1947, the President's Council of Economic Advisers was expecting a slight domestic recession; and if this coincided with a fall in exports, the results at home could be serious. Here was a subsidiary reason—and a useful political argument—for helping to save Europe from economic collapse. More pertinent still, as time went by, was the fear of further Soviet expansion. A poverty-stricken Western Europe looked a likely breeding-ground for Communism and a prey too tempting for Stalin to ignore. In this respect, the Truman Doctrine and the

Marshall Plan, as Truman himself put it, were 'two halves of the same walnut'.[29]

Motifs and motives intertwined as the US Administration laboured at the double task of planning aid for Europe and persuading Congress to support it. In doing so, the planners gradually arrived at two basic principles, both apparently simple. The first was that recipient nations should be dealt with *en bloc* as a collective entity; the second, that Europeans themselves should take the initiative and be encouraged to stand on their own feet. In the circumstances, both notions seemed natural; but in fact they were very novel. Together, they were the negation of the maxim 'Divide and conquer' that previous world powers had taken as their watchword; together, they contained in embryo the twin concepts of European unity and equal transatlantic partnership. In this way, almost without realizing it, a handful of officials in Washington helped to make possible a gradual revolution in international affairs.

The question of further aid to Europe had already been informally discussed in the later months of 1946; but it was in the following Spring that a number of separate and little-publicized efforts, overlapping and sometimes contrasting, began to dovetail into a coherent plan. The first step was taken on Tuesday 11 March 1947, when at Dean Acheson's suggestion the State, War and Navy Departments' Co-ordinating Committee set up joint machinery to study foreign aid requirements. To prepare its formal position in these inter-departmental palavers, the State Department appointed its own Foreign Aid Committee. This included in particular three young officials from the staff of Will Clayton, Under-Secretary for Economic Affairs: the acute economist Charles Kindleberger, fresh from active service in Germany with the G-2 Section of 12th Army Group; Harold van Buren Cleveland, distinguished member of a well-known political and civil-service family; and the shrewd, burly, gravel-voiced Ben T. Moore. All three had long been concerned at the plight of Europe; and in the early meetings of the Foreign Aid Committee they strongly urged that it be tackled not on a national basis, but as a coherent whole. Later, dismayed by the slow workings of the administrative labyrinth, they produced a crisp and authoritative paper of their own. Its final version was not completed until 12 June 1947; but preliminary drafts were circulating early in May. America, they argued, should if possible induce the Soviet Union to negotiate a global settlement in Europe restoring the former pattern of intracontinental trade. 'Europe's three hundred and fifty million people must be allowed to play a positive international role by helping to blunt the sharpness of the antithesis between the United States and the Soviet Union.' For this purpose, aid should ideally be channelled through the Economic Commission for Europe (ECE) recently set up by the United Nations. However, in case the East European members of ECE should refuse to co-operate, the United States must show that it was able and willing 'to go ahead with a consistent and adequate recovery program for non-Communist Europe with or without the USSR'. This part of their recommendations they summarized in one half-sentence: 'Solidarity for ever if at all possible, but a well-protected flank if not.'[30]

The case for a global approach, meanwhile, was being put more publicly. On Thursday 20 March 1947, Walter Lippmann wrote one of a series of articles on the need for foreign aid, urging that it go to Europe as a whole rather than to individual European nations. His argument was reinforced on the following Sunday, 23 March, when the veteran engineer, businessman, statesman and former American President Herbert Hoover released a report on economic conditions in Germany and Austria that he had recently completed for President Truman. In the previous year, as honorary chairman of Truman's Famine Emergency Committee, Hoover had made a country-by-country report on the food needs of twenty-two nations. Now he insisted that Europe—including Germany—be treated as a single economic unit:

There is only one path to recovery in Europe. That is production. The whole economy of Europe is interlinked with the German economy through the exchange of raw materials and manufactured goods. The productivity of Europe cannot be restored without the restoration of Germany as a contributor to that productivity.[31]

This was partly what the US Secretary of State, George C. Marshall, was just then trying to negotiate in Moscow. The meeting was a crucial instalment in the series of Foreign Ministers' Conferences—in Paris, London, and Moscow—which have been aptly called a 'constitutional struggle' over the future of Europe and of Germany.[32] Resisting British and American calls for German economic unity, as well as French appeals for the internationalization of the Ruhr, Stalin's Foreign Minister V. M. Molotov had long since taught Western diplomatists and newspaper readers at least one word of Russian—his harsh and monotonous *nyet*. Now, in Moscow, as the wrangle continued evening after evening, often into the small hours, hopes of a settlement grew more and more distant. Stalin's terms for a unified German economy were a strong central government—especially unacceptable to France—and a further 10,000 million dollars in reparations. He refused either to account for previous pickings or to allow the Western zones of Germany to resume their prewar imports from the East. Even if the Soviet Union no longer hoped to conquer the whole of Germany, it clearly planned to exploit her, virtually siphoning off the aid with which its wartime allies were keeping the Western Germans just above starvation. By the time that Marshall returned to Washington on Saturday 26 April 1947, he was deeply disillusioned. Was Stalin's aim to delay a German settlement while awaiting Western Europe's economic ruin? At all events, there was no more time to be wasted. As Marshall said in a broadcast on the following Monday, 28 April, Europeans were crying out 'for help, for coal, for food, for most of the necessities of life . . . The patient is sinking while the doctors deliberate.'[33]

Next morning, he summoned George Kennan to his office. The State Department's Policy Planning Staff, which Kennan was to head, must be recruited and must start work without delay. Its top priority would be aid to Europe. 'Avoid trivia' was Marshall's final, characteristic advice.[34]

Within a week, by Monday 5 May 1947, Kennan had gathered round him a small, close-knit team. He himself at that time was still acting as 'deputy for foreign affairs' at the recently established National War College; and it was here that on the following day, Tuesday 6 May, he set out in a lecture some of his ideas on Europe. The Soviet Union, he said, thought that America would not 'be able to muster, as a nation, the leadership, the imagination, the political skill, the material resources, and above all the national self-discipline necessary to bring material stability, confidence, and hope for the future to those areas of Western Europe which have been brought low by the effects of the war.' Yet 'it may be fairly stated, as a working rule for dealing with the Russians, that only those people are able to get along with them who have proven their ability to get along without them.' 'Today,' he concluded, 'we find ourselves before the recognition that the economic rehabilitation of Western Europe is of urgent and primary importance. The restoration of German productivity, if only in a part of Germany, is essential to that rehabilitation. We cannot wait for Russian agreement to achieve that restoration.'[35]

While Kennan and his staff were working out what this conclusion implied in practice, other officials were looking at the problem in its broader context. A month earlier, Truman had asked Dean Acheson to take over a speaking engagement that he himself had had to cancel, a talk to be given to the Delta Council in Cleveland, Mississippi, on Thursday 8 May 1947. One of the officials called in to prepare a draft text suggested that he base it on preliminary papers from the State Department's Foreign Aid Committee. Acheson agreed. The result, as the speechwriter put it, was to 'elaborate the economic intent of the Truman Doctrine into a comprehensive statement of our foreign reconstruction policy'. After recalling the extent of wartime devastation in Europe and Asia, the postwar restraints imposed on German and Japanese production, and the 'acts of God' that had destroyed most of Europe's food and fuel supplies, Acheson pointed out that 'the accumulation of these grim developments has produced a disparity between production in the United States and production in the rest of the world that is staggering in its proportions'. America had already done something to redress the balance:

We have contributed nearly 3 billion dollars to foreign relief. We have taken the lead in the organization of the International Bank for Reconstruction and Development and the International Monetary Fund, and have subscribed to these two institutions to the extent of almost 6 billion dollars. We have increased the capacity of the Export-Import Bank to make loans abroad by almost 3 billion dollars. We have made a direct loan of $3\frac{3}{4}$ billion dollars to Great Britain. We are proposing this year to contribute a half billion dollars for relief and reconstruction in the Philippines, and a billion dollars to relief in occupied areas. The President's recommendations for aid to Greece and Turkey to the extent of 400 million dollars and for post-UNRRA relief to the extent of 350 million dollars are still under consideration by Congress. And there are a few other smaller items....

[But] great as is our supply of commodities and services to the world during the current year, it is still far short of what people of the world need....

What do these facts of international life mean for the United States and for United States foreign policy?

They mean first that we in the United States must take as large a volume of imports as possible from abroad in order that the financial gap between what the world needs and what it can pay for can be narrowed....

[They] also mean that the United States is going to have to undertake further emergency financing of foreign purchases....

Since world demand exceeds our ability to supply, we are going to have to concentrate our emergency assistance in areas where it will be most effective in building world political and economic stability, in promoting human freedom and democratic institutions, in fostering liberal trading policies, and in strengthening the authority of the United Nations....

The fourth thing we must do in the present situation is to push ahead with the reconstruction of those two great workshops of Europe and Asia – Germany and Japan – upon which the ultimate recovery of the two continents so largely depends....

Quoting Marshall's broadcast, Acheson added:

European recovery cannot be complete until the various parts of Europe's economy are working together in a harmonious whole. And the achievement of a co-ordinated European economy remains a fundamental objective of our foreign policy.[36]

Two weeks later, on Friday 23 May 1947, George Kennan's Policy Planning Staff produced a thirteen-page paper of recommendations to this end. 'The ideas by which it was inspired,' wrote Kennan later, 'came from many sources; the drafting was largely my own.' To sharpen its impact, the memorandum distinguished between the present emergency, which called for immediate action to raise Europe's coal output, and the need for a longer-term aid programme, 'directed not to the combatting of Communism as such but to the restoration of the economic health and vigor of European society'.

It would be neither fitting nor efficacious for this government to undertake to draw up unilaterally and to promulgate formally on its own initiative a program designed to place Western Europe on its feet economically. This is the business of the Europeans. The formal initiative must come from Europe; and Europeans must bear the basic responsibility for it. The role of this country should consist of friendly aid in the drafting of a European program and of later support of such a program, by financial and other means, at European request....

The program which this country is asked to support must be a joint one, agreed to by several European nations.... It must, for psychological and political, as well as economic reasons, be an internationally agreed program. The request for our support must come as a joint request from a group of friendly nations, not as a series of isolated and individual appeals....

This European program must envisage bringing Western Europe to a point where it will be able to maintain a tolerable standard of living on a financially self-supporting basis. It must give promise of doing the whole job....

It was no accident that the Policy Planning Staff's memorandum twice spoke of 'Western Europe' rather than just 'Europe', although in one instance the Marshall Plan's semi-official historian later omitted the adjective. Kennan and his colleagues agreed with the State Department Foreign Aid Committee that the forum for action should ideally be the Europe-wide ECE. However, forewarned by hearing of Soviet tactics at the ECE's first meeting, they added a sharper proviso: the United States, they suggested, should ensure that the Eastern European countries 'either exclude themselves by an unwillingness to accept the proposed conditions or agree to abandon the exclusive orientation of their economies'. Finally, the Planning Staff proposed 'the despatch of instructions to certain European missions designed to obtain a uniform digest of the views of the respective chiefs. It is also proposed that secret discussions with the British be undertaken at once ...'[37]

By now, the essentials of what was to be the Marshall Plan had taken shape in Washington. But the final impulse had still to be given; and it came just four days after the Policy Planning Staff memorandum. For the past week Will Clayton, Under-Secretary of State for Economic Affairs, had been back in Washington from a six weeks' tour in Europe. He had cut it short chiefly to advise the President to veto a Congressional attempt to raise the wool tariff—a question that kept him busy for several days. No sooner was it settled than he fell ill with a heavy cold; and not until Tuesday 27 May 1947, was he able to send to Marshall, via Dean Acheson, his urgent report on the situation in Europe. Clayton's first-hand impressions revealed more vividly than bare statistics just what Europe was suffering; but even more forceful than what he wrote was what he said. In a voice still not quite recovered from fever, he described with homely logic

... the peasant who would not produce more than he and his family and his cattle could eat because with the money he might get from selling his surplus produce in the market he could not buy buttons or thread or cloth or farm tools; the manufacturer of buttons and thread and cloth who could not produce for want of materials and fuel and because workers, being unable to satisfy their wants with money, were refusing to work; the middleman, and everyone else for that matter, who was hoarding supplies because of mounting inflation.

In the present crisis, Clayton's paper concluded, it would be 'necessary for the President and Secretary of State to make a strong spiritual appeal to the American people to sacrifice a little themselves, to draw in their own belts just a little in order to save Europe from starvation and chaos (not from the Russians) and, at the same time, to preserve for ourselves and our children the glorious heritage of a free America.'[38]

On the morning after receiving Clayton's memorandum, Marshall called a meeting in his office. One by one, at his request, the officials present gave their views on aid to Europe: Acheson, Clayton, Kennan, Charles Bohlen, Benjamin Cohen. Marshall listened gravely, thanked the group, and dismissed it. As usual, it was hard to tell exactly what he himself thought. Late that afternoon, one of his senior assistants brought in a pile of documents for signature. While there, he asked whether the Secretary could now confirm his tentative acceptance of an invitation to the Harvard Commencement Exercises in a week's time. Marshall thought that he would; presumably, he added, his hosts would expect him to make a speech. His assistant remarked that this might be a good opportunity to launch the appeal for aid to Europe that had been discussed that morning. When Marshall put this idea to Acheson, he advised against it for fear of inadequate news coverage; but next day, after further thought and consultation, Marshall sent a telegram agreeing to speak at Harvard, and he asked Charles Bohlen to draft him a text. Working chiefly on the basis of Clayton's and Kennan's memoranda,

Bohlen produced his draft early in the following week. When Clayton and Acheson had gone over it, Marshall himself made some alterations, the last of them on the flight to Boston, Massachusetts on the afternoon of Wednesday 4 June. He stayed the night with the Harvard President, James B. Conant; and on Thursday 5 June, in company which included General Omar Bradley, T. S. Eliot, and J. Robert Oppenheimer, he duly received an honorary degree. Then, after luncheon, he addressed the Harvard Alumni—and the Marshall Plan was launched.[39]

What Europeans faced, Marshall told his Harvard audience, was nothing less than 'the dislocation of the entire fabric of European economy': 'the modern system of division of labor upon which the exchange of products is based is in danger of breaking down.'

The truth of the matter is that Europe's requirements for the next three or four years of foreign food and other essential products – principally from America – are so much greater than her present ability to pay that she must have substantial additional help or face economic, social, and political deterioration of a very grave character.

The remedy lies in breaking the vicious circle and restoring the confidence of the European people in the economic future of their own countries and of Europe as a whole. The manufacturer and the farmer throughout wide areas must be able and willing to exchange their product for currencies the continuing value of which is not open to question. . . .

It is logical that the United States should do whatever it is able to do to assist in the return of normal economic health in the world, without which there can be no political stability and no assured peace. Our policy is directed not against any country or doctrine but against hunger, poverty, desperation and chaos. Its purpose should be the revival of a working economy in the world so as to permit the emergence of political and social conditions in which free institutions can exist. Such assistance, I am convinced, must not be on a piecemeal basis as various crises develop. Any assistance that this Government may render in the future should provide a cure rather than a mere palliative. Any government that is willing to assist in the task of recovery will find full co-operation, I am sure, on the part of the United States Government. Any government which maneuvers to block the recovery of other countries cannot expect help from us. Furthermore, governments, political parties, or groups which seek to perpetuate human misery in order to profit therefrom politically or otherwise will encounter the opposition of the United States.

It is already evident that, before the United States Government can proceed much further in its efforts to alleviate the situation and help start the European world on its way to recovery, there must be some agreement among the countries of Europe as to the requirements of the situation and the part those countries themselves will take in order to give proper effect to whatever action might be undertaken by this Government. It would be neither fitting nor efficacious for this Government to undertake to draw up unilaterally a program designed to place *Europe* on its feet economically. This is the business of the Europeans. *The initiative*, I think, must come *from Europe*. The role of this country should consist of friendly aid in the drafting of a European program and of later support of such a program *so far as it may be practical for us to do so*. The program should be a joint one, agreed to by *a number, if not all*, European nations.[40]

It was this paragraph that Marshall had still been revising on the way up to Harvard. Although closely modelled on Kennan's Policy Planning Staff memorandum, it revealed one important change and one shift of emphasis, italicized above. Where Kennan had written 'Western Europe', Marshall's text read 'Europe', and it replaced 'several European nations' with the awkward but comprehensive 'a number, if not all'. Marshall, in other words, was anxious to keep the offer open to the East. At the same time, he qualified American 'aid in the drafting' and 'later support' with the proviso 'so far as it may be practical for us to do so'; and he stressed more firmly the 'initiative from Europe' that Kennan had described as merely 'formal'.

This point, indeed, was crucial. 'I have always wondered,' said a British official afterwards, 'if Mr Marshall expected the reaction that his speech received.' His apparently casual approach to it seemed to suggest that he did not; but he himself, in retrospect or hindsight, claimed that he had wanted it to break with 'explosive force'—and without premature leakage; his nonchalance may have been a smoke-screen. Good luck, good timing and some degree of conspiracy or subterfuge are usually needed to make the march of history change step. 'It is easy to propose a great plan,' wrote Marshall, 'but exceedingly difficult to manage the form and procedure so that it has a fair chance of political survival.' And whatever his intentions, his Harvard speech might have been no more than a further persuasive argument if Dean Acheson had not helped to engineer a response.[41]

Already, before making his Delta Council speech a month earlier, Acheson had had a private lunch with three British reporters: Stewart McCall of the *News Chronicle*, Leonard Miall of the BBC, and Malcolm Muggeridge, then of the *Daily Express*. Now, on Wednesday 4 June 1947, while Marshall was leaving for Harvard, they lunched together again. During the meal, Acheson explained the importance of the next day's speech, and the need for a swift and decisive European reaction. As a result, Miall made an eloquent broadcast on the following afternoon, while McCall and Muggeridge, at Acheson's request, telephoned their editors to urge that the full text of Marshall's remarks be sent round at once to Ernest Bevin, the British Foreign Secretary.[42]

Bevin was at home in bed when the private message reached him. The rumour ran that to save cable costs the British Embassy in Washington had delayed the official version by entrusting it to the diplomatic bag. If so, Bevin scarcely waited for it: that same night he sent out an urgent call to his senior advisers. 'It was astonishing,' said one of them, 'the way in which he, with his elephantine frame, sprang into action.' Sir William Strang, his Permanent Under-Secretary, suggested that a query be sent to the Embassy asking if Marshall's speech really meant what it seemed to imply. 'No,' said Bevin, 'I don't want to ask Marshall that question. I don't want to take any chances that it wasn't meant. I want to go on the assumption that it was fully meant, and give an answer myself.' As he afterwards told the House of Commons, 'When the Marshall proposals were announced, I grabbed them with both hands.'[43]

As it happened, the first quasi-official reaction to Marshall's speech was a communiqué issued on Saturday 7 June 1947, by Agence France Presse. This, while recalling previous French actions and proposals, welcomed 'an appeal to the peoples of Europe that will be heard in France with especial sympathy because it corresponds to a concern for international organization and economic recovery that France has always shared.' A week later, on Friday 13 June, Bevin made the first public and official response in a talk to the Foreign Press Association; and on the same day the French Foreign Minister Georges Bidault invited him to discuss the Marshall proposals in Paris. There, on Tuesday 17 June, they agreed to suggest a 'European Economic Commission' to study the needs of Europe; and on the following day they issued a communiqué expressing 'the greatest satisfaction' at Marshall's statement and inviting Molotov to a three-power meeting during the week of 23 June. Less than two weeks after its launching, the Marshall Plan was already under way.[44]

CHAPTER SIX

Europe of the States

So we grew together...
But yet an union in partition.
William Shakespeare[1]

To quicken the Memory of past Kindness thou hast done
to any one, is a very nice Point to manage.
Thomas Fuller[2]

When great revolutions are successful, they eradicate the
causes that produced them; their very achievements make
them inexplicable. *Alexis de Tocqueville*[3]

Welcome, Mr Marshall (*¡Bien venido, Mister Marshall!*) was a film made
in 1952 by the Spanish director Luis Berlanga, then thirty-one years old.
Its title was paradoxical, since American aid to Spain was not included
in the Marshall Plan; but this is immaterial to the plot. The setting is a
small Castilian village due for a visit from fund-distributing officials.
The mayor, already gloating over the prospect of riches, plans to impress
the visitors with a display of local colour; but the village, unfortunately,
is far from picturesque. All it can offer are priests, ruined aristocrats
and rascally peasants. So the mayor hires an impresario to supply some
instant tradition, complete with shawls, mantillas, castanets and inept
toreros. At last, when rehearsals are more or less over, the officials appear
—and drive straight through without stopping. The only American who
finally lingers is a nuclear physicist who would rather make fireworks
than bombs.

Written by its director and his friend Juan Antonio Bardem, who later
made *Death of a Cyclist* and *Calle Mayor*, this mild, ironic, rather in-
gratiating fable hinged on the uneasiness felt in transatlantic relations
between individual European countries and the American giant. The
mayor was a characteristic figure. For him, Americans were wealthy
innocents hungry for 'folklore', easy prey for the ruthless, sad-eyed
Europe of Machiavelli and Talleyrand. His scorn was a poor disguise for
the indignity of his own position, part huckster, part sutler, part beggar;

106

and it misjudged the seriousness of the visitors, too briskly altruistic to notice local antics, although no doubt willing to pay for any spectacle they enjoyed. The physicist, finally, embodied the hope that not all Americans were happy with their nuclear-backed omnipotence, and that old-world picturesquerie, however corrupted, still expressed something important in human life.

Uneasiness of this sort, born of inequality, has haunted and somewhat muffled discussion of the Marshall Plan. Initially, some Americans may have felt that their generosity and idealism entitled them to give more commanding advice than was always welcome; later, they may well have resented some Europeans' grandiloquent ingratitude. In Europe, while knowing and even stating that Marshall Aid was a precondition of all later 'affluence' and 'economic miracles', as well as of moves toward European unity, some have tended to take it for granted, like a successful man making light of the legacy that set him up in business. Orthodoxies, moreover, usually provoke reactions; and attempts to correct—or over-correct—the excesses of 'cold war' rhetoric have sometimes unjustly impugned the Marshall Plan's origins or one-sidedly critized its results. Impatience, propaganda, clichés, gratitude, guilt, boredom, resentment and counter-propaganda have all in turn combined to confuse a central episode in Europe's postwar history.

At the vantage-point of twenty years' distance, it seems fair to say that the Marshall Plan was Europe's 'great leap forward', marred by one big and two smaller steps back. With food and raw materials, it saved Europeans from imminent economic ruin. With investment aid, fertilizers, machines and machine tools, productivity programmes and planned growth, it laid the real foundations of later prosperity. With America's insistence on a co-ordinated approach to European recovery, it supplied the incentive and the institutional machinery for permanent mutual consultation; and it led to the gradual reduction of quantitative and monetary barriers to intra-European trade. But it suffered from three weaknesses. In the first place, most obviously and crucially, it was rejected and later opposed by the Soviet Union and the other countries of Eastern Europe. Secondly, it failed to involve America in a fully reciprocal economic 'dialogue'; and thirdly, its European participants, while agreeing to co-operate, refused at this stage the degree of economic unity that such a dialogue would have required.

The restriction of Marshall Aid to Western Europe was by no means a foregone conclusion. Most Washington officials, certainly, had divided minds on the subject; but Marshall, in the final text of his Harvard speech, had been careful to extend the American offer to the whole of Europe—a point he repeated formally a week later, on Thursday 12 June 1947. The next day, Ernest Bevin told the Foreign Press Association in London that 'when the United States throws a bridge to link east and west, it would be disastrous for ideological or other reasons to frustrate the United States in this great endeavour'. At their meeting in Paris on Tuesday and Wednesday 17 and 18 June, Bevin and Georges Bidault were quick to invite their Soviet colleague V. M. Molotov to join them during the following week. True, on Thursday 19 June, Bevin warned the House of Commons that Britain would go ahead with or without the Soviet Union; but twenty-four hours later, in a speech to the French National Assembly. Bidault stressed that the invitation to Molotov was genuine, not merely formal: it had empha- sized, in fact, that Marshall had not officially approached the French and British Governments, and that the aim of the three-power meeting would be to begin working out a joint European programme in close liasion with the United Nations. Two days later, on Sunday 22 June, came a Note from the Soviet Union accepting the invitation and propos- ing to meet on the following Friday.[4]

Bevin and Bidault agreed; and at 4·00 p.m. on Friday 27 June 1947, the three Foreign Ministers met at the Quai d'Orsay. All were accompanied by advisers and assistants, but Molotov had brought with him no fewer than eighty-nine—a fact that to some Western observers seemed encouraging. As representative of the host Government, Bidault opened the proceedings with a long statement that was to prove crucial in the subsequent debate:

The Government and Congress of the United States must quickly be given a document as precise and complete as possible explaining the effort made by Europe itself, its needs and the conditions that would result from a more marked deterioration of its economy. On this basis the American authorities will be able to take their decisions.

This document, which must be our first objective, should be completed by the beginning of September.

What is meant by Europe? In our view, it should include all countries of Europe, allies, ex-enemies, or neutrals, with the provisional exception of Spain.

All these European countries, in different degrees, are suffering from the same ills. . . .

At a European level, every country faces the same task.

In essential economic fields, European states must make a balance-sheet of the efforts that each is undertaking and the results that they promise. They will find that they lack large quantities of supplies and equipment. As far as possible, this deficit should be made up by inter-European action, and only for the remainder should we seek outside help....

To call a vast conference to evaluate Europe's needs and resources does not seem an efficacious method. A good way to proceed would be to arrange as quickly as possible to set up a number of *ad hoc* committees, each for a different branch of economic activity, with a steering committee to co-ordinate their work.

These committees might be composed solely of representatives of the three powers [France, Great Britain and the Soviet Union] or, preferably, of their representatives assisted by those of the European States most concerned in the activities under consideration....

Two sorts of studies should be made:

(a) A study of ways of increasing production in essential sectors of the economy, i.e. agriculture (fertilizers, farm machinery, seeds); energy (equipment for mines, refineries and hydro-electric power stations); transport (equipment for railways, sea and river transport, and ports); and the iron and steel industry.

(b) The steering committee and *ad hoc* committees, taking account of the result they expect from this development of Europe's means of production, would draw up the balance-sheet of Europe's resources. In this way it would be possible to work out the tonnage of food (grains, fats) and essential raw materials (coal, steel, textiles, petroleum, etc.) that Europe lacks....

Six *ad hoc* sub-committees should be set up: (a) agriculture; (b) energy; (c) transport; (d) iron and steel; (e) raw materials; and (f) balance of payments.

But if we wish to get the job done quickly, we must ask them to concentrate their efforts on a few products only, those that I have enumerated and that are indispensable in national life. What is more, it will be advisable to be very precise about the questions – which should be kept as simple as possible – to be submitted by the steering committee to each of the nations concerned. To this end, each country should present to the steering committee a balance-sheet of its own situation, its production targets, and its needs, on a uniform model; the *ad hoc* sub-committees would discuss the particular programmes on the basis of the overall programme thus drawn up by each country.

The Europeon countries must be able to make known their observations and to say whether or not they accept the methods suggested.

The simplest procedure would be to submit joint proposals to the Economic Commission for Europe, which will be meeting in Geneva on 5 July. The Economic Commission for Europe could not draw up these documents because it so far scarcely exists, because its statutes are not yet complete, and because questions about voting and about the composition of its various constituent bodies are still under discussion. This does not mean that we should exclude the Economic Commission for Europe: it will make its observations on the machinery as a whole. The closest contacts will be maintained with the ECE Secretariat-General; finally, when it is definitively established, we must study how to transfer to it the whole of this heavy task.

Clearly, it is impossible to imagine an overall European programme not including Germany. It may be objected that the reconstruction of Germany raises all those questions on which agreement has yet to be reached in the Council of Foreign Ministers—the level of German industry, reparations, the Ruhr, etc., This is undeniably a difficulty. But the first 'European report' to be drawn up should not prejudice future decisions about the ultimate status of Germany. On the one hand, because it would essentially be a study of how to increase certain types of production that everyone agrees should be developed in Germany – agriculture and coal. On the other hand, because as regards other types of production, such as iron and steel and the electrical industry, the projects are not required to cover more than one or two years. German production is still far below the levels set by the Control Council on 15 March 1946. Whatever efforts are made over one year or two, these levels will not be exceeded. If, in the meantime, it is agreed to increase the figures fixed by the Control Council's decision of 15 March 1946, account will be taken of this in drawing up the European report.[5]

Bevin seconded these proposals; but Molotov, from the start, was more reserved. Already, ten days earlier, *Pravda* had attacked the Marshall offer as a further installment of Truman's 'plan for political pressures with dollars and a programme for interference in the internal affairs of other states', and on 25 June had alleged that its real aim was to prolong America's postwar boom. Now, on Saturday 28 June, the second day of the three-power conference, the *Tass* news agency in Moscow carried a message from its Paris correspondent denouncing the Franco-British proposals as 'foreign interference'. 'Obviously,' it said, 'the internal economic problems of a State are a matter of its own sovereignty, and no other country can concern itself with them.' At that day's meeting, Molotov made the same point:

Hitherto [he declared] it was established that every country should decide for itself what were the best means of reinstating and developing its economy. It seemed perfectly clear that questions of internal economy were a matter concerning the sovereignty of the peoples themselves, and that other countries should not interfere in such questions. Only on this basis can relations between countries develop normally, Attempts made from without to intervene in the economic life of various countries have not had nor can they have any positive results. If this is the case the attempts made to force the Conference to draw up a general economic programme for the European nations – which would inevitably involve the intervention of certain States – could not serve as a basis for collaboration between the countries of Europe.[6]

He proposed instead that each country submit its own list of requirements to the United States: he added that a distinction must be made between allied, neutral and ex-enemy countries, and that Germany must be dealt with only by the four-power Conference of Foreign Ministers.[7]

Bevin pointed out at once that 'it has never been our intention that anything in connexion with this work which we have to undertake should interfere with the sovereignty of participating Governments, and if it were to do such a thing I should not wish to be a party to it ... It is, however, necessary that we should undertake work in collaboration with each other and that our demands should be co-ordinated.' For this purpose, the British delegation formally proposed that 'a steering Committee should be set up forthwith to draft, for the consideration of the Governments of Europe, a programme of reconstruction co-ordinating the needs of European countries over the next four years for presentation to the United States.'[8]

But Molotov remained unconvinced. When the Conference met again on Monday 30 June, he made a counter-proposal re-stating his previous objections. 'The Conference believes,' his draft read, 'that it is not its function to draw up an all-embracing programme for the European countries, since the drawing up of such an economic programme for the whole of Europe, even with the participation of certain other countries, would inevitably result in the imposition of the will of strong European Powers upon other European countries, and would constitute intervention in the domestic affairs of those States and a violation of their sovereignty.'[9]

To Bidault, these fears seemed quite unjustified; and at the next day's meeting, on Tuesday 1 July, he set out his arguments in detail:

The idea of co-operation embodied in the French proposal, I must state, not only with firmness but with the greatest insistence, does not imply any interference in the internal affairs of the European States, nor any infringement of their sovereignty. The aim of our proposal is to collect and to coordinate the statistics, the economic data which will be provided voluntarily by those European States which declare themselves ready to associate themselves with our action. On the one hand we are not dreaming of constraining anyone to join in against his will; and on the other hand, we impose no sort of modification on national economic policies, no change in existing economic plans, which can only be modified in the exercise of national sovereignty. We do wish, naturally, to harmonize the efforts of everyone, with a view to obtaining the maximum development of production, but this can only be accomplished by the consent, freely given, of all the interested parties, who are at all times in a position to refuse it.

I would like, to make myself clearer, to recall the example of the co-operation which was obtained during and after the war, in a certain number of international bodies, whose existence has never been considered as being an infringement of the independence of the member States. Now this is a

III

kind of war which we have to win, not war against the invader, fascism, and criminal violence, but against poverty and penury, and ruin. This war must be won by the same means as the other, that is, by the co-operation of the nations. During the war there existed what were called 'combined boards', organisms whose duty it was to distribute raw materials. More recently, in important European bodies like E.C.O. [the European Coal Organization], which distributes coal, a useful collaboration has been established. We have never considered, either yesterday or to-day, that the sovereignty of the States could be involved in this way. It is this same spirit which the French delegation wishes to see presiding over the working out of the common programme for Europe which we have in mind.

At the end of this statement, Bidault read a revised version of the French proposal, which now explicitly stressed that its aim was to collect and collate information, not to interfere in national affairs.[10]

By this time, however, there was little hope of avoiding a breach. At the next day's meeting, on Wednesday 2 July, as if he had not heard or understood Bidault's explanation, Molotov once more attacked the idea of 'a new organization standing over and above the countries of Europe and interfering in their internal affairs down to determining the line of development to be followed by the main branches of industry in these countries'. If the French and British proposals were adopted, he said, 'the European countries would find themselves placed under control and would lose their former economic and national independence because it so pleases certain strong powers.' Poland, for example, might be pressed into producing more coal while neglecting other industries; Czechoslovakia might be required 'to increase her agricultural production and to reduce her engineering industry'. In this way, 'American credits would serve not to facilitate the economic rehabilitation of Europe, but to make use of some European countries against other European countries in whatever way certain strong powers seeking to establish their domi nion should find it profitable to do so.'[11]

Bidault answered that he was disappointed, but he added:

France solemnly declines all responsibility for the consequences that may arise from a decision that she has done all in her power to prevent... France is determined, and the French Government feels obliged, to continue studying the prospects opened up by Mr Marshall's suggestions. This task will be undertaken with all those who would like to co-operate in it. I express the hope here and now that no refusal is definitive and that, as a result, the labours ahead of us will not be the work of only a part of Europe.

Thereupon, Molotov and his huge delegation withdrew.[12]

On the following day, Thursday 3 July, after a further meeting between Bevin and Bidault, the French Foreign Ministry issued a brief communiqué:

The French and British Governments have reached the following decision with a view to giving rapid effect to the suggestion made by Mr Marshall in his speech on 5 June at Harvard University, according to which Europe should take the initiative in the work of reconstruction.

It is essential to draw up as rapidly as possible a programme covering Europe's resources as well as her needs. A temporary organization must be set up to collect the data on which such a programme will be based.

The French and British Governments have therefore decided to invite all European States, with the provisional exception of Spain, that wish to take part in working out a response to Mr Marshall's suggestions, to collaborate with them in order to establish this organization. The task to be undertaken will be to draw up a European reconstruction programme in which the resources and the needs of each State will be co-ordinated as each of the European countries freely decides.

This invitation to take part in the organization will remain open to all European countries.[13]

In the event, only one East European country accepted the invitation to the forthcoming conference, which began in Paris on 12 July 1947. This was Czechoslovakia, But her acceptance was short-lived. On 9 July, the Czech Premier Klement Gottwald and his Foreign Minister Jan Masaryk visited Moscow. By the time that they returned to Prague they had changed their minds. The Marshall Plan was to be confined to Western Europe.[14]

Challenging the pieties of much official history, some recent writers have questioned whether Bidault and, especially, Bevin were sincere in discussing the Marshall Plan with Molotov.[15] 'Bevin and the British Foreign Office,' it has been said, 'were fearful that Stalin would agree and took no pains to create a hospitable atmosphere at Paris.'[15] Certainly, they went there with mixed feelings, and they may well have feared that Soviet acceptance might alienate the US Congress. Chilled by recent experience, moreover, they may have been privately relieved to escape the delays, exhaustion and exasperation of trying to collaborate with Stalin. But there is no proof that they or Bidault deliberately alienated Molotov, and little likelihood that diplomatic cordiality could reverse a Soviet decision.

It is just conceivable, as some have suggested, that Molotov had instructions to accept or at least explore the Marshall proposal, and that he misplayed his hand. But although a few Soviet officials—including, perhaps, Anastas Mikoyan—may have favoured the Marshall Plan, *Pravda* had already condemned it as early as 16 June; and at least one Western observer was convinced that the final decision came from Moscow. 'It seems,' he told an interviewer, 'that Molotov has a bump on his forehead which swells when he is under emotional strain. The matter was being debated, and Molotov had raised relatively minor questions or objections at various points, when a telegram was handed to him. He turned pale and the bump on his forehead swelled. After that, his attitude suddenly changed and he became much more harsh.' During the last twelve hours of the conference, moreover, he had a telephone line through to Moscow all the time.[16]

In Soviet terms, indeed, the decision to withdraw was understandable. The Marshall proposal, although partly distinct from the Truman Doctrine, looked from a distance like an extension of it. Impressed by the fighting speeches made by all and sundry since Churchill's denunciation of the 'Iron Curtain' at Fulton, Missouri on 5 March 1946, officials in Moscow were not to know how scrupulously their counterparts in Washington—not least Marshall himself—had kept open the door to the East. To the men in the Kremlin, the mere idea of having Soviet needs, resources and production targets discussed internationally was highly suspicious. Conditioned by 'realism' as much as by Marxist mistrust of capitalist imperialism, they could hardly imagine that America, if not France or Britain, would refrain from interfering in the economic plans she was invited to see. Equally extraordinary, in their eyes, was the proposal to stop penalizing ex-enemy countries. Most fundamentally of all, perhaps, they suspected that the programme described by Bidault and Bevin would encourage East European countries to turn their economies westward, expanding farm production to feed Western Europe in exchange for imported manufactures—a form of 'economic colonialism' well understood in Moscow.

Was the East-West clash over the Marshall proposals, then, merely another decisive instance of mutual incomprehension, for which both sides were equally responsible? The conclusion looks temptingly impartial: but in fact it shirks a necessary judgement. To assess Soviet behaviour on its own terms would be to accept as normative Moscow's habits of proselytism, *Realpolitik* and secretive suspiciousness: and the Western proposals, however mixed their motives, were undoubtedly more intelligent, humane and adult than the Soviet reaction. To that extent, the main responsibility for deepening the division of Europe in 1947 must surely rest with Joseph Stalin.

The Soviet withdrawal from the Marshall Plan deferred all hope of restoring prewar trade between Eastern and Western Europe. At the same time, however, it cleared a path for action in the West. As one official put it, 'When the cat was away the mice could work.'[17] Thrown together by common necessity, freed for the moment from haggling with the stone-faced Molotov, and fired by the prospect of being able at last to get things done, Western statesmen and civil servants rediscovered a wartime vigour and adaptability.

Responding to Bevin's and Bidault's invitation, representatives of sixteen countries—Austria, Belgium, Denmark, France, Greece, Iceland, Ireland, Italy, Luxembourg, the Netherlands, Norway, Portugal, Sweden, Switzerland, Turkey and the United Kingdom—met in Paris on Saturday 12 July 1947. On Wednesday 16 June they set up a Committee of European Economic Co-operation (CEEC) under the chairmanship of the British delegate Sir Oliver Franks, to produce a rough four-year recovery programme. By 22 September—in less than ten weeks—it was completed. Only two months later, on 18 November, France, Italy and the Benelux countries made the first halting move towards multilateral payments clearance, followed at some distance by a number of their colleagues. In Washington, meanwhile, President Truman had already endorsed Marshall's proposals on 11 June; eleven days later, he called for three separate reports on Europe's needs and America's potential assistance. Shortly afterwards, he and Marshall began a series of consultations with Congressional leaders from both political parties. On 29 July, the House of Representatives set up a nineteen-man study committee, whose members toured Europe in August and September under the leadership of Christian Herter. They returned in the same ship that was taking Franks and a group from the CEEC to help the United States Government present the European case to Congress. Now, at short intervals, successive reports arrived to back it: on 25 September, the Anderson report on world food problems; on 19 October, the Krug report on 'National Resources and Foreign Aid'; on 28 October, the Nourse report on 'The Impact of Foreign Aid upon the Domestic Economy'; on 7 November, the highly influential Harriman report on 'European Recovery and American Aid'. But on 23 October, long before the scheduled hearings, Truman called a special session of Congress to propose emergency measures: the result was interim aid of 522 million dollars for France, Italy and Austria, raised to 577 million dollars by a further grant on 31 March 1948. By this time, on 19 December 1947, Truman had submitted to Congress 'A Program for United States Support to European Recovery'; and on 8 January 1948, the Senate Foreign Relations Committee and the House Committee on Foreign Affairs had begun their public hearings. Altogether, they took oral or written testimony from 350-odd witnesses, filling five volumes and 3,735 pages; the documentation available, it was estimated, would have taken four or five months to read.[18]

At last, worked over day and night in committee, the Economic Co-operation Act drafted by a Democratic Administration was ready for presentation to a predominantly Republican Congress. Supporting it before the Senate, in a speech that he had himself rewritten half a dozen times, the white-haired Arthur H. Vandenberg, once known as an isolationist, admitted that:

It would be a far happier circumstance if we could close our eyes to reality, comfortably retire within our bastions, and dream of an isolated and prosperous peace. But that which was once our luxury would now become our folly. This is too plain to be persuasively denied in a foreshortened, atomic world. We must take things as they are....

Within the purview of this plan are 270,000,000 people of the stock which has largely made America. These are 26 percent of all the literate of the earth. Before the war they operated 68 percent of all the ships that sailed the sea. They grew 27 percent of all the world's cereals. They produced 37 percent of the world's steel. They sold 24 percent of the world's exports and bought 39 percent of the world's imports. They are struggling, against great and ominous odds, to regain their feet. They must not be allowed to fail.[19]

On Saturday 3 April 1948, after large majority votes in both the House and the Senate, the Economic Co-operation Act became law. One week later, its initials changed their meaning, adding a new ingredient to Washington's alphabet soup, when the Economic Co-operation Administration (ECA) came into being to direct the European Recovery Program (ERP).[20]

Like most creative ventures, the ECA had few precedents to smooth its path. Truman initially thought of appointing Dean Acheson to run it. Both Acheson and Senator Vandenberg, however, advised him that the fifty-six-year-old Paul Hoffman, President of the Studebaker Corporation, would be more congenial to Congress. Truman took the point. 'It seems,' said Hoffman in private afterwards, 'that I was the least obnoxious of the Republicans.' Even so, although he had helped to prepare the Harriman report, he was reluctant to take the ECA post; and he only agreed, finally, when Truman had forced his hand with a purposely premature rumour of his acceptance. He was sworn in on Friday 9 April 1948; but at first he had no proper Washington headquarters, and the ECA began its official existence in Room W-900 of the Hotel Statler. Within two weeks, the freighter *John H. Quick* was sailing from Galveston, Texas, with 9,000 tons of wheat for Europe, although Hoffman himself had originally opposed large food shipments. 'I had not myself been up against the kind of situation in which chronic under-nourishment cut down people's working energy,' he confessed.[21]

If the ECA's policy had to be flexible, so did its staffing arrangements. For the first two weeks, all appointments were provisional; and most of the 400 people ultimately engaged—many of them from outside public administration—were handpicked by co-optation rather than selected from lists of applicants. When Averell Harriman was persuaded to head the ECA's Office of the Special Representative (OSR) in Europe, this was thought of as a roving embassy; but by the time he had crossed the Atlantic it had been decided to settle the OSR in Paris—first in two bor-rowed offices on the second floor of the United States Embassy, later in the rue Saint-Florentin on the north-east corner of the Place de la Con-corde, in the eighteenth-century mansion where Talleyrand had lived with the last of his mistresses. The European recipients of Marshall Aid, meanwhile, set up their staff headquarters in Passy, on the site of the former sixteenth-century Château de la Muette, itself touched with scandal by the Duchesse de Berry, the lively daughter of the Regent.[22]

Making mistakes, changing their minds, trying out new procedures, arguing and often wrangling, the men and women who put the Marshall Plan into practice accomplished more than was sometimes recognized a few years later, when improvization had given way to institutions and routine. Between 1948 and 1952, in addition to the 9,500 million dollars that the United States had already made available to Western Europe since World War II, the ERP supplied grants and credits totalling 13,150 million dollars. The largest sums went to the United Kingdom and her dependen-cies (3,176 million dollars), France (2,706 million dollars), Italy (1,474 million dollars) and Western Germany (1,389 million dollars). On top of this, helped by a 22-million-dollar mail subsidy, American citizens sent private relief parcels valued at more than 500 million dollars—an average of over 3 dollars a head. In the first year, half of all Marshall Aid imports into Europe consisted of food; by 1951, only a quarter. During the whole four-year programme, nearly two-thirds of the total aid was spent on food, feed, fertilizers, raw materials and semi-finished products. Fuel accounted for sixteen per cent, machinery and vehicles for seventeen per cent. More than two-thirds of all these imports came from America; but one-sixth of the aid was used to finance trade within Western Europe itself. Between 1947 and 1950, this trade more than doubled, reaching its prewar level in the last quarter of 1949, two years ahead of expectations. By the summer of 1951, Western Europe's industrial production was forty-three per cent, and farm production was ten per cent above their respective prewar totals.

Progress was far from uniform; but by then European recovery had ceased to be only a programme: it was well on the way to being achieved.[23]

Psychologically as well as financially, dollar aid was what made this progress possible. The Europeans certainly matched America's drive and imagination with their own skill and hard work. It was only under American pressure, however, that they set up a permanent body to concert their efforts. In the decade that followed, European economic co-operation was taken for granted, if not actually belittled; but in the nineteen-forties its novelty was as striking—and, to some, as disconcerting—as the 'supra-national' projects launched later by the Europe of the Six. Originally, some Governments had intended to deal with Marshall Aid on a purely tempo-rary basis. When Ernest Bevin spoke at the sixteen-nation Paris Conference on 12 July 1947, he stressed: 'We have no idea of setting up a permanent organization to rival the United Nations. It is a piece of *ad hoc* machinery to grapple with this special problem.' The CEEC report of 12 September, likewise, spoke of an 'organization ... of a temporary character ... [which] will cease to exist when the special assistance necessary for the recovery of Europe comes to an end.' It took repeated efforts by Under-Secretary Will Clayton and his colleagues, culminating on 5 January 1948 in a simultaneous *démarche* by all the US embassies in Western Europe, to persuade the recipients of Marshall Aid to negotiate and at length estab-lish, on 16 April of that year, the Organization for European Economic Co-operation (OEEC). A senior British civil servant, Sir Hugh Ellis-Rees, later Chairman of the OEEC Council, revealingly described it as 'a per-petual international conference'. But in 1948 even this was something quite new to Europe; and under its first Secretary-General, the thirty-seven year-old Robert Marjolin, an acute French economist with an American wife and a partly American education, it performed at least three out-standing and difficult tasks.[24]

The first was thrust upon it. On Saturday 5 June 1948, Averell Harriman announced to the OEEC Council that it must itself take charge of allocat-ing Marshall Aid. His audience was dumbfounded. Some, like the British, had hoped to profit by dealing direct with Washington; others had been less optimistic; but none had expected this sudden responsibility, and all foresaw trouble—especially when the funds made available by Congress for 1948–9 proved to be 500 million dollars short of Europe's requests. To cut up the cake would be difficult; to cut down the portions would be harder still. In a sixteen-nation gathering it was out of the question. On Friday 16 July, therefore, after what one participant described as 'much backstage fighting', the Council appointed a group of four national civil servants—from Britain, France, Italy and the Netherlands—to propose how the aid should be divided. Each country in turn brought them its programme for vetting; a member of one delegation has recalled how he and his colleagues 'entered the examination room with the special feeling of tension well known to anyone who has gone through examinations in private life'. The four experts then left Paris for an undisclosed address in Chantilly, twenty-five miles away, to work out their proposals in peace. When they presented them to the Council, as an eye-witness put it, 'pandemonium broke loose': for two hours, an argument raged about the merits of discussing them at all. But at length, after weeks of recrimination, a much amended version of the experts' work was accepted. The so-called 'restricted committee' method had proved its worth; and a year later, in an even graver crisis, it was used again. The following years' allocations were made more simply, by using the 1949–50 percentages; but by now the OEEC had established two of its characteristic procedures—the mutual confrontation of national programmes, and their scrutiny by a small committee acting 'extranationally' on behalf of the whole group. Necessity in the face of Congress had been the mother of the OEEC's invention.[25]

Co-operation is hard to quantify; but the OEEC's second main achievement—the liberalization of trade—is easier to measure. At the outset, trade in Western Europe was clogged by national import controls, relics of the 'thirties depression maintained and multiplied during and after World War II. Individually intended to boost home production and improve the balance of payments, the restrictions were collectively self-defeating; but few Governments would risk removing their own unless their competitors did likewise. It was not until 2 November 1949, that the OEEC countries formally committed themselves 'to remove before 15th December 1949, quantitative restrictions on at least fifty per cent of their total imports on private account [i.e. all but state trading] from the other Member countries as a group'. All but six were able to keep their promise. On 18 August 1950, the OEEC agreed on a 'Code of Liberalization' to ensure greater equity; and by the end of the year all member states but two had achieved a fifty per cent liberalization, all but three had reached sixty per cent, two had topped seventy per cent, and one had attained eight-six per cent. The years that followed saw some steps backward; but in January 1955 the minimum liberalization of private trade was raised to ninety per cent, and by the end of 1956 the average level for all imports was eighty-nine per cent. Five years later, when the OEEC was formally superseded by the Organization for Economic Co-operation and Development (OECD), liberalization had reached ninety-five per cent. By this time, the OECD method of removing restrictions from one group of products after another, instead of gradually relaxing all of them, had met a 'hard core' of difficult cases; but these were mainly agricultural, and controls on industrial imports had almost disappeared.[26]

Imports must obviously be paid for; and there would have been little point in removing restrictions on trade if nothing had been done to free intra-European payments from exchange controls. Here, too, Western Europe had been caught in a net of contradictions. Lacking gold and dollars, each country had wanted to earn them with its exports, yet none had been eager to spend them on imports. The situation was too absurd to last; but the immediate remedies found for it were purely bilateral. Pairs of trading partners agreed to meet each other's deficits with limited credits: only beyond these margins—and seldom in practice even then— would they seek payment in hard currency or cash. By 1947, nearly two-thirds of the trade within Western Europe was bound by such agreements; without a central clearing-house, it was almost a barter system. On 18 November 1947, Belgium, France, Italy, Luxembourg and the Netherlands made the first agreement on Multilateral Monetary Compensation; but this was extremely cautious. Even when extended to all the OEEC countries, its total turnover was only 10 million dollars a month. Beginning on 16 October 1948, the United States supplemented these sums by making part of Marshall Aid 'conditional' on its recipients' granting equivalent credits—'drawing rights'—to their European debtors. At first, drawing rights were strictly national; then, a year later, debtors were allowed to transfer twenty-five per cent of them to other countries. Even this extra liquidity, however, reduced net deficits and surpluses by less than 800 million dollars, and the scramble for gold and dollars went on. Not until 7 July 1950 did the OEEC countries agree on a real multilateral clearance system, the European Payments Union (EPU). That day a triumphant press release, known to its sponsors as 'The Child's Guide to the EPU', gave a layman's—or a clubman's—explanation:

If four people play bridge during an evening, they may settle their debts at the end of each rubber. But if they change partners continually, they may prefer to keep the score on a piece of paper and only settle at the end of the evening. Only the players who are net losers will pay; only the net winners will receive.

'I see,' said a reporter: 'Now they're playing bridge instead of demon patience.' Whatever the game, it moved briskly. The EPU was formally established on 19 September 1950. Soon it was handling 250 million dollars a month.[27]

However, despite these achievements, the OEEC had more success with immediate problems than with longer-term questions of investment and balanced growth. It suffered, in particular, from two related handicaps. One was Europe's inability to deal as an equal with America. The other was the lack of real unity among Europeans themselves.

The very existence of the Marshall Plan implied that Western Europe's postwar difficulties were more than merely European. Had they not been dealt with, their effects could have been very widespread; their causes, too, lay partly elsewhere. Europe's dollar deficit largely reflected North America's surplus; and a better balance in the world economy ideally required a joint policy, worked out together by both sides. As it was, America supplied advice and dollars; but in return the European countries concerted their policies only with each other. While far from one-sided, this was certainly asymmetrical. To plan their investments and overseas exports, the Europeans needed to know something of America's intentions; but American apostles of planning in Europe were disciples of *laissez-faire* in their own country; there was no United States 'plan' to act as a guide. Nor, with or without a plan, could the Europeans have much say in American policy, notwithstanding America's impact on their own. Dependent on United States dollars, they were in no position, psychologically or politically, to talk on equal terms with their powerful patron. At times, this was unpalatably obvious: when the aid requests for 1948–9 were cut, the US military representative from the British and American zones of Germany—by then merged into the 'Bizone'—caused deep resentment by insisting on its privileged status. But for the most part, the ECA combined firmness with tact and wisdom. American leadership was simply a fact of life. Paying the piper, the United States felt entitled to suggest at least some of the tunes, all the more because Congress held the purse-strings. Some Administrations, no doubt, have been glad to use Congress as a pretext for pressing their own policies; but Congressional control of Marshall Aid was genuine and thorough, and it helped to kill any real hope of joint transatlantic planning, which Europe and America could only have tackled as equals.[28]

It was here, by a strange paradox, that American leadership failed. To achieve greater influence in Washington, European countries would have had to unite; and this was what America repeatedly urged them to do. Far from feeling at ease in her lonely pre-eminence, she constantly tried to share it, reverting only fitfully to the impatient use of power. Western Europe was her obvious potential partner—another industrial society, mainly of the same stock, with a similar civilization, a comparable way of life, and analogous forms of government. Often, no doubt, there was ambivalence in Americans' views of that Old World from which so many of their ancestors had been religious, political or economic refugees. Like some exotic widow, veiled, sloe-eyed and musky, Europe had always exerted equivocal fascination; now, her charms were stale and she had been too often conquered. In the wake of two world wars, the European countries seemed so small, so backward, so disputatious, stiff with tradition and hierarchy. There was a great temptation to ascribe their troubles to defects of character, or to preach them zealous lessons from America's experience of unity. Transatlantic bluntness, real or supposed, caused as much amusement as annoyance. It was curious, one night in a garden in New Delhi, to watch the French Ambassador's face as Professor Walter Hallstein, then President of the Common Market Commission, told the story of the American business-man flying over Europe for the first time. 'That's France down below,' said his assistant. 'Don't bother me with details,' was the reply. This was no doubt apocryphal; but at least one American tourist has been known to complain: 'You come to so many frontiers when you cross Europe— why don't they all get together?' Nor have such thoughts been confined to private visitors. One day during World War II John Foster Dulles, later Secretary of State under President Eisenhower, pointed to a map of Europe and said: 'After the war all that will have to be united, other-wise nothing lasting can be built.'[29]

In the State Department, interest in European unity went back at least as far as 1942, when George Kennan unsuccessfully urged that some of the technical centralization imposed by Hitler be retained and entrusted to 'a new European federal authority'. In the same year, the Department commissioned a study group from the Council on Foreign Relations to examine 'American Interests in the Economic Unification of Europe with Respect to Trade Barriers'; but its report, which was carefully qualified, aroused little response.[30]

For several years, in fact, American official thinking on this subject was tinged with suspicion. President Truman was said to favour a United States of Europe; but it was only gradually, as hopes of 'Big Three' col-laboration dwindled, that opinion in Washington began to follow suit. The first pressures came from outside the State Department. As early as 1946, Paul Hoffman became convinced of the need to apply in Europe the production techniques made possible by America's mass market; and in January 1947, in his testimony before the Senate Committee on Foreign Relations, he elaborated his ideas for 'greater unity in the Euro-pean economy'. On 17 January, with the backing of Governor Thomas E. Dewey and Senator Vandenberg, John Foster Dulles made a speech before the National Publishers' Association in New York urging the United States to take the lead in reconstructing Europe on federal lines.

On 22 March, resolutions calling for a United States of Europe were introduced into both Houses of Congress. On 5 April, in the *New York Herald Tribune*, Walter Lippmann proposed 'not less than an economic union' in Europe.[31]

The most fully argued appeal, however, came from the State Department itself, in the memorandum by Charles Kindleberger, Harold van Buren Cleveland, and Ben T. Moore, drawn up in its final form on 12 June 1947:

There appears to be no alternative equally effective for present-day Europe. The symbols of nationalism in France and Italy and in Germany are essentially bankrupt and in danger of being captured by reactionary and neo-fascist political elements which we do not wish to support. There is a possibility of developing tremendous emotional drive in Western Europe behind the supranational idea of European unity....

To avoid injuring sensitive feelings of nationalism, our appeal should be couched in terms of a European recovery plan which stresses the raising of European production and consumption through the economic and 'functional' unification of Europe. In our propaganda and our diplomacy it will be necessary to stress (even exaggerate) the immediate economic benefits which will flow from the joint making of national economic policies and decisions.[32]

Under-Secretary Will Clayton had been even more specific in the paper he had handed to General Marshall on 27 May 1947:

This three-year grant to Europe should be based on a European plan which the principal European nations, headed by the United Kingdom, France and Italy, should work out. Such a plan should be based on a European economic federation on the order of the Belgium-Netherlands-Luxembourg Customs Union.[33]

On 23 July, George Kennan's Policy Planning Staff recommended as 'a long-term objective' what it called 'the eventual formation of a European Customs Union'. The aim, wrote Kennan later, was 'to force the Europeans to begin to think like Europeans, and not like nationalists, in their approach to the economic problems of the continent.' When the Harriman Committee at length reported, on 7 November 1947, it more tactfully made a similar point. For twenty years, Averell Harriman himself had believed that Europe needed economic unity in order to share America's advantages; now, his Committee's Report firmly underlined the benefits of removing trade barriers. The Herter Report, published on 1 May 1948, went even further, and called for a 'European federation'. Paul Hoffman and the ECA were more cautious; but time and again, in the months and years that followed, they urged the Europeans toward what Hoffman called, in a memorable homily, 'nothing less than an

E

integration of the Western European economy'. 'The substance of such integration,' he added, 'would be the formation of a single large market within which quantitative restrictions on the movement of goods, monetary barriers to the flow of payments, and eventually, all tariffs are permanently swept away.'[34]

The early history of the Marshall Plan can be read as a struggle between this American vision and the stubborn, untidy realities of Western Europe.

It began in the dry, cloudless summer of 1947, at the Paris meetings of the CEEC. On Tuesday 15 July Count Carlo Sforza, the Italian Foreign Minister, announced to what he later described as 'that frigid gathering of statesmen and economists': 'We must look for more than technical agreements; we must be willing to destroy the myths of self-sufficiency, we must limit national sovereignty; to the dogma of national independence we must add the dogma of European independence.' He went on to propose a customs union, initially between Italy and France.[35]

Before very long, the idea was broadened to include all Western Europe. Will Clayton, who had already proposed this in Washington, came to Paris at the end of the month; and the Europeans soon realized, in the words of a Dutch delegate, that 'a customs union would be one of the projects which would vitalize and catch American public opinion and imagination'. In mid-August, the CEEC's Executive Committee— the Ministers' deputies—began to discuss it; but at first their progress was slow. When Clayton remarked on this to Sir Oliver Franks, their British Chairman, Franks asked him whether a European customs union was a precondition for American aid. No, said Clayton, it was not; but he added that it would greatly improve the chances of Congressional approval. He repeated the point less bluntly at a formal meeting with all European Heads of Delegation, on Saturday 30 August 1947, when he argued that 'definite steps should be taken to diminish trade barriers, leading to an eventual abolition of all impediments to trade'.[36]

The Report that the CEEC finally produced on 22 September 1947, however, was very much more cautious. 'The advantages which the United States has enjoyed through the existence of a large domestic market with no internal trade barriers,' it declared, 'are manifest.' But from this it merely concluded that 'the idea of a Customs Union including as many European countries as possible is one which contains important possibilities for the economic future of Europe and it is in the general interest that the problems involved should receive careful and detailed study by Governments.' For this purpose, on 13 September 1947, all of them except Iceland, Norway, Sweden and Switzerland formed, and all eventually joined, a Customs Union Study Group, which began work two months later in Brussels. Out of it arose two further bodies; a Tariff Committee, later known as the Customs Committee, which laboured to collate definitions and rates of duty; and an Economic Committee to study the industrial and other problems that a customs union would involve. Thanks to the Customs Committee, nomenclature was at length partially standardized, and a permanent Customs Co-operation Council was set up; but although the Economic Committee concluded that there were 'fewer difficulties in the way of the formation of a Customs Union than might have been expected', its detailed findings were far from comprehensive. Few Governments answered its questionnaires fully; three—Ireland, Switzerland and Turkey—supplied no answers at all. Equally academic, as it turned out, was the work of the parent Study Group, whose Report of March 1948 was characteristically inconclusive:

It is not practicable at this stage to pronounce definitely on the merits and disadvantages of a Customs Union. There is a presumption, however, that such a Union would in the long run make for the greater prosperity of the countries composing it. How far it would do so would depend on the proper solution of a great many problems and the nature of the compromise reached....

In the end, after further pronouncements in a similar vein, the customs union project was abandoned. What was clearly lacking was a firm political will.[37]

By no means all of the OEEC countries were opposed to economic integration. Belgium, the Netherlands and Luxembourg had already accepted it in principle when they signed the Benelux Convention of 5 September 1944. In April 1946 they agreed to aim at an economic union, with harmonized economic policies; and its first element, the Benelux customs union, began to take effect on 1 January 1948. Italy and France, responding to Sforza's suggestion of 15 July 1947, devised a bilateral customs union known as 'Francita', whose Treaty they signed on 26 March 1949. Later in the same year, with the Treaty still unratified, they considered merging it with Benelux under the daunting name of 'Fritalux' or 'Finebel'. Denmark, Norway and Sweeden, meanwhile, spent two years discussing a Scandinavian customs union; and there was also talk—but nothing further—of similar unions between Italy and Austria and between Turkey and Greece.[38]

All these projects met with serious obstacles, and only Benelux ultimately reached its goal. The specific problems were manifold; but the basic issue in each case was very much the same. By removing the customs barriers between them and establishing a common tariff against the rest of the world, governments would give their economies the stimulus of mutual competition and the benefits of a larger home market. At the same time, however, they would surrender to the resultant union part of their national autonomy. *Vis-à-vis* its partners, each government would have lost one of the weapons of economic policy; *vis-à-vis* the rest of the world, that same weapon could now be wielded only jointly. The removal of mutual protection, moreover, would mean economic changes, some of them painful; but it would also mean a smaller range of purely national measures with which to meet them. To recover control of their economy, the members of the union would increasingly have to work together, not only on tariffs but also on other matters; tax policy, freight rates, capital movements, rates of exchange. In any but a *laissez-faire* system of devil-take-the-hindmost, the customs union would require some measure of economic union as well.[39]

No wonder that some governments were hesitant to start on what looked like a slippery slope of economic interdependence; no wonder that, once embarked, they found it a tricky run. If even tiny Benelux faced complications, an OEEC-wide customs union would have been more complicated still. Its member states would have included ex-allies, ex-neutrals and ex-enemies; former great powers and much smaller nations; imperial, ex-imperial and non-imperial countries; devotees of planning and of economic liberalism; countries nearly starving and others—the neutrals—replete with steaks and butter; some with uncontrolled inflation and at least three with strong, stable currencies; those that were members of the United Nations and one that was not; even, for that matter, republics and monarchies. To weld them all together would have been a perplexing task.[40]

It would be unjust, therefore, to blame only Great Britain, as some have done, for the failure of American plans for European economic union. Ernest Bevin responded promptly to the Marshall Plan; and British administrative expertise was invaluable in the OEEC, as was the work of devoted and skilful civil servants like Sir Oliver Franks and Eric Roll. Nor, at the outset, was Britain alone in stressing national independence. When Bevin and Bidault tried to negotiate with Molotov, both assured him that they planned no abandonment of sovereignty; and if, at the opening of the sixteen-nation CEEC conference, Bidault proclaimed that 'the hour has come to construct a Europe', his words were vague and perhaps intended chiefly to impress the US Congress.[41]

Britain, nevertheless, was in a key position. At that time, as the Herter Committee insisted, she alone possessed 'the past experience and the present economic resources and political stability necessary for bold and imaginative leadership'; yet while France, for whatever motive, was soon prepared to move toward economic union, Britain repeatedly shied away. In August 1947, after conceding that 'some or all of the participating countries might form a customs union or unions', Sir Oliver Franks sounded a note that was to become familiar: for Britain, a customs union involved special difficulties. 'These difficulties arise,' he said, 'from our links both economic and political, outside Europe, and especially with the Commonwealth', which had 'the effect of making the UK an extra-European as well as an intra-European power.' Throughout the subsequent work of the Customs Union Study Group, Britain maintained the same stand. In March 1948, when France urged that the future OEEC should have majority voting, a strong executive board, and an independent Secretary-General with real powers of decision, it was Britain in particular that insisted on weaker institutions. In the following year, during the talks that finally led to the European Payments Union, Britain likewise resisted continual American pressure for 'really effective machinery' and 'a central authority possessing adequate supranational powers'. At the end of 1949, again, Paul Hoffman and the ECA urged that the OEEC Council meet often, perhaps always, at ministerial instead of official level, and that it be headed by a political Secretary-General. About the first proposal, Britain remained sceptical; against the second she was adamant.[42]

The memory of these disputes was not effaced easily. For many Americans and continental Europeans, it entered the mythology of recent history; and it led to a lasting suspicion of Britain's actions and aims. Her insular aloofness from European union seemed all the greater because some had expected its opposite.

Just two years before the Marshall Plan, by a strange irony, the US State Department had even suspected Britain of something like what it now urged her to do. In a Briefing Book paper prepared for the Potsdam Conference in July 1945, it had warned the United States Government against a supposed 'British Plan' to establish a West European 'bloc'. 'As a "hedge" against the possible failure of Big Three collaboration in the postwar world,' it had reported, 'the British are following the policy recommended by General Smuts of strengthening their position by drawing the nations of Western Europe into closer association with the Commonwealth.' The 'plan', as proposed by Smuts to the Empire Parliamentary Association on 25 November 1943, had been to offer Belgium, Denmark, France, the Netherlands and Norway something akin to Dominion status in the Commonwealth, with 'a common foreign policy, coordination of military strategy, combined boards for finance, transport, production, supplies, resources, and raw materials, a customs union, currency arrangements, and a joint approach to civil aviation and colonial problems.' According to the Briefing Book, all this had been made clear by the British Foreign Secretary, Anthony Eden, in the House of Commons on 29 September 1944. In reality, all that he had said was: 'We have had certain informal discussions about our future relations, and these will be pursued further in due course.' 'It will give us,' he had added, 'more authority with the other great Powers if we speak for the Commonwealth and for our near neighbours in Western Europe.' His argument, as it happened, was refuted by another of the Potsdam briefing papers, aptly classified Top Secret. 'At meetings of the "Big Three",' it noted, 'Mr Churchill may occasionally, without due reflection, give the impression that he is the spokesman for the whole British Commonwealth. He is, on the contrary, only the representative of the United Kingdom.'[43]

Anthony Eden's alleged 'plan', which if anything had been tentative, was certainly short-lived; but his successor Ernest Bevin had also toyed in the past with similar notions. Visiting America in 1926, he had found, as he said later, '130,000,000 people within one economic entity, with no tariffs, with an ability among the people to move about without the boundary handicaps that apply to Europe.' On the second day of his visit he had written in his notebook:

I came to the conclusion that the road my mind has been travelling is a correct one:
  a. That Britain must have a customs union within the Empire, and
  b. With Europe as well, if possible.
  c. Or, if Colonies will not join then with Europe without colonies. . . .

He told an American reporter that within fifty years there would be a United States of Europe; and at the 1927 Trades Union Congress in Edinburgh he argued: 'If we are to deal with the problems of Europe, we have got to try to teach the people of Europe that their economic interests, their economic development have to transcend merely national boundaries.' He therefore proposed a European customs union 'to inculcate the spirit of a United States of Europe—at least on an economic basis, even if we cannot on a totally political basis.' 'We want,' he declared, 'an indivisible united nation spreading from the borders of Russia right to the borders of France.' At the 1939 Labour Party Congress, again, Bevin proposed—'even though it may involve a limitation of our sovereignty'—to 'invite countries like Scandinavia, Holland, Belgium, Russia, France and the USA who are willing to co-operate to come within our [Commonwealth] preference system' in order to achieve 'a real pooling of the whole of the colonial empires and their resources'.[44]

The ambiguities in these ideas were evident. Did 'the people of Europe' include the British? Which 'borders of Russia' were intended—East or West? Why mention 'the borders of France' and not those of Great Britain? What likeness was there among the proposed recruits to the Commonwealth preference system? Were only the 'colonial empires' to be pooled? Clearly, Bevin was never doctrinaire. Already in 1930 had had helped to draw up a report by the Trades Union Congress Economic Committee which advised against British membership of 'a European block' in favour of 'as full a development as possible of the economic relations between the constituent parts of the British Commonwealth'. Now, as Foreign Secretary, he spoke from a similar brief. Events had overtaken two of the traditional axioms of British foreign policy—naval supremacy, and a balance of power in Europe with no permanent commitment to either side. In Europe, in particular, as a State Department memorandum put it, there was 'no longer any power to balance'. The real power lay with the United States and the Soviet Union, both far beyond Britain's weight. This might have been an incentive for her to match them by pooling her resources with her neighbours; but although Bevin still at times talked of a United States of Europe, he evidently thought of it as something for export only. History, geography, language, traditional policy, the fortunes of war and the habits of the wartime alliance—all made it seem more natural and necessary to cleave not only to the Commonwealth, but also to the 'special relationship' with the United States. Some Americans did their best to discourage what they saw as an illusion; at one Anglo-American conference held in the late 'forties, a paper prepared by the British with the title 'US-UK Special Relationship' was withdrawn and then destroyed at the US delegation's request. The Commonwealth countries, likewise, gradually disabused Britain of some lingering 'imperial' assumptions. For the time being, however, British policy was slow to respond. Economically, Commonwealth preference complicated links with the continent; politically, Britain's sense of still leading her former empire and being a priviliged partner of America delayed the realization that she was no more than equal to other European countries of comparable size.[45]

One incident may serve to show the strength of Britain's arguments against joining in an economic union of Europe—as well as the weakness of their underlying premise. In June 1949 the Americans were trying hard to persuade European countries to free themselves from their tight bilateral payments system and make transferable at least some of the 'drawing rights' that creditors granted to debtors as a condition for receiving part of their Marshall Aid. Maurice Petsche, the French Finance Minister, proposed that forty per cent of 'drawing rights' should be made transferable. Britain, however, feared that this would saddle her with dollar debts, since Belgium and Switzerland would only hold a limited amount of sterling without converting it into dollars or gold. Transferability, in other words, threatened the British with convertibility—and they had vivid memories of the drain on sterling that this had caused two years earlier. Sir Stafford Cripps, the austere and astringent Chancellor of the Exchequer, put the argument persuasively to the OEEC Council on 29 June 1949, using the example of the 'drawing rights' that Britain had granted to Germany:

I take the case of a country to whom the United Kingdom has granted a credit of, let me say, 50 million dollars in sterling, that is the valuation of it. During the course of the year, owing to the United Kingdom purchasing more goods from that country, and owing to other countries outside the O.E.E.C. spending more sterling in the country, the credit on the United Kingdom is no longer required. Under the existing scheme that credit is carried forward and will be utilized in cases of necessity in future years. Under M. Petsche's scheme, 40% of that credit would become usable in some other countries, and could be used for any other purpose, necessity or non-necessity, and if so used the United Kingdom would lose 40%, that would be 20 million dollars of the conditional aid, and this, Mr Chairman, because the United Kingdom have taken every step, as they are bound to do, to liberalize their trade with that country, and to increase it. That apparently desirable action is, therefore, penalized by the loss of 20 million dollars, regardless of the requirements of the United Kingdom in dollars for her Recovery Programme. Now the only reaction which can be taken to that risk by any creditor country is to see that fewer purchases are made so that it is quite certain that the debtor country, who receives the credit, spends all the credit with the creditor country, and therefore the creditor country cannot lose dollars. The whole of the impetus, therefore, is to restrict in order not to lose dollars.

Answering Cripps shortly afterwards, Petsche pointed out that 'the United Kingdom might, by the interplay of transferability, equally well earn dollars as lose them'. As the biggest net debtor and recipient of 'drawing rights', France had an interest in her own argument; but she also had a point. Transferability meant not only risks, but opportunities; what was more, it pointed the way toward a multilateral system. Each country by itself might well be afraid to remove national controls, but if all did so together their general prosperity would increase. The British position, as Averell Harriman had already remarked, was 'unacceptable because it failed to provide, in any effective form, the stimulation to the liberalization of intra-European trade which would result from increased competition ... It would tend to make Europe a high cost area.' Indeed, understandable as was Britain's concern with her own national problems, it seemed to reveal an uncharacteristic pessimism and lack of imagination. At the time, her fears were well-founded: within less than three months, on 19 September 1949, she was obliged to devalue sterling by thirty per cent. But she seemed not to see—or, if she saw, she rejected—one sure way to enjoy the collective benefits of multilateral payments while minimizing their national risks. This would have been to accept the strong central monetary institutions proposed for Europe by Paul Hoffman and the ECA. But that was 'supranationalism', and Britain would have none of it. Even when the European Payments Union was finally established, she and the Scandinavian countries made sure that its Managing Board was subordinate in practice to the OEEC Council, and not an independent body with real power over national policies.[46]

As incidents of this type multiplied, it grew hard to avoid the conclusion that Britain's technical arguments concealed a deep-rooted feeling that somehow she was different from her continental neighbours—not merely as they all differed from each other, but in a quite special and ineradicable way. Was it pride? Was it self-absorption? Was it the concern to build a more just society at home, and a better world in general, that made continental Western Europe seem irrelevant or remote? All these there may have been; but they seemed to be reinforced by the innocent, self-protective obtuseness with which, in the early postwar era, Britain made crucial policy decisions by default, almost viscerally, without appearing to suspect that alternatives existed. By doing so, she delayed both the unification of Europe and her own chance to share in it. Where was the adventurous inventiveness that she had shown during World War II? Reassuringly, the challenge of events was soon to prove that neither she nor her Western allies had lost it.

CHAPTER SEVEN

The Age of Anxiety

For indeed it is a most lying thing that same Past Tense always: so beautiful, sad, almost Elysian-sacred, 'in the moonlight of Memory', it seems; and *seems* only. For observe: always, one most important element is surreptitiously (we not noticing it) withdrawn from the Past Time: the haggard element of Fear!   *Thomas Carlyle*[1]

I confess that I have no comprehension of the Russian character.   *Joseph Conrad*[2]

Underneath all the solid and magnificent virtues of the German race there lies a layer of nervous uncertainty.
                              Harold Nicolson[3]

ALL international meetings look rather alike. The baize-covered table with a delegation's name-card at each place, the sharpened pencils, the pads of paper, the carafes and water glasses, the microphones, the interpreters' glass-fronted cabins—all these are more or less standard. Fairly standard, too, are the aides, the civil servants, discreet ingenious men in sober suits, holding files of documents like shields. Even the ministers or heads of delegation seldom seem colourful: an ebullient Bevin or an implacable Molotov is rare. The fly on the wall, or the spy beneath the table, would have a hard time deciphering requests 'to replace Paragraph Roman two figure one little c of Conference Document seventeen by Revised Draft capital B one little f, circulated this morning by the Secretariat'. Even the active participants, drafting, expounding, arguing, bargaining, and drafting again, sometimes feel lost in a timeless bureaucratic frenzy. The long hours of committee and council meetings at the Paris headquarters of the ECA and OEEC were no exception. It was not always easy, there, to picture the bulldozers, dams, giant transformers, dredgers, looms or steel plants behind the texts, graphs and statistics. Nor was it easy, later, to remember that in these early years of recovery, Western Europe felt increasingly under siege from the East.

Molotov and the Soviet delegation had walked out of their Paris meeting with Bevin and Bidault on Wednesday 2 July 1947. By the end of the following week, the Soviet Union had begun to draw the East European countries into a tighter network of trade agreements—with Bulgaria on Thursday 10 July; with Czechoslovakia on 11 July; with Hungary on 14 July; with Jugoslavia on 25 July; with Poland on 4 August; with Rumania on 26 August. On 22 September, at Russian bidding, Communist Party representatives from Bulgaria, Czechoslovakia, Hungary, Jugoslavia, Poland, Rumania and the Soviet Union—as well as from France and Italy—met at Wilcza Gora, the country house of Wladyslaw Gomulka, Polish Deputy Premier, to set up the Cominform, or Communist Information Bureau. This, despite its name, was a partial revival of the 1919 Comintern, the Third or Communist International, which had been dissolved in May 1943 as a gesture of goodwill toward the West. It was formally established, with headquarters in Belgrade, on 5 October 1947.[4]

These moves, clearly, were in part a riposte to the Truman Doctrine and the Marshall Plan, which Stalin's emissary at the September meeting, A. A. Zhdanov, denounced as 'an embodiment of the American design to enslave Europe' and 'an attack on the principle of national sovereignty'; 'the imperialists,' he added, sought 'to unleash a new war.' His language had the characteristic shrill violence with which Communist orators seemed to outbid each other; but given Soviet beliefs about the nature of 'bourgeois' society, it was no doubt sincere. Although the East-West confrontation could be seen as the co-existence of two mutually suspicious power centres, it was never in reality free of ideological content. Each side believed that its own society was superior to the other's; each was committed in principle to converting the rest of the world. Each saw most clearly the other's imperfections; but because 'bourgeois' decadence, corruption and economic injustice were in practice less revolting than the drab, cynical ruthlessness of Stalinist dictatorship, the West might have been expected to be even more Messianic or 'imperialist' than the East. In the first postwar years, however, ideology had seemed secondary to traditional power politics: both the Soviet Union and the United States had tacitly respected, for the most part, each other's sphere of influence. Only now did each begin to take the other's slogans literally; and the combined effect was as if both had been bent on expansion all along. 'The Soviet Union,' Zhdanov told his audience at Wilcza Gora, '. . . will bend every effort in order that [the Marshall Plan] be doomed to failure . . . The Communist parties of France, Italy, Great Britain and other countries . . . must take up the standard in defence of the national independence and sovereignty of their countries.' Their first effort was to help foment, in the winter of 1947-8, a series of industrial strikes. To this extent the Marshall Plan—and more especially the Truman Doctrine—contributed to what the Cominform itself called the consolidation of 'two opposite political lines'. They were not, however, the only factors; they were also a response to moves by the USSR.[5]

Long before the Truman Doctrine was enunciated, the East European countries had made many economic agreements with each other and with the Soviet Union; and the idea of something like the Cominform had already been mooted in the Spring of 1946. By the time of the Marshall Plan, moreover, Stalin had two further reasons for tightening the reins. One was growing restiveness among the neighbouring Communist parties; the other was the natural development of what had been happening in Eastern Europe since the defeat of the Nazis[6]

For some time the files in Moscow had grown fat with evidence of what has been called 'the revolt of the First Secretaries'. In Rumania, Stalin was being warned against the ambitions of Gheorghe Gheorghiu-Dej, while his colleague Lucretiu Patrascanu, an intellectual of middle-class origins, was becoming what his accusers later described as 'an exponent of bourgeois ideology'. In Poland, Wladyslaw Gomulka was openly criticizing Soviet policy. In Hungary, Martyas Rákosi was said to be reliable, but was making accusations against Lászlo Rajk. In Czecho-slovakia, President Edvard Beneš had said as recently as 6 May 1947, that his country sought a middle way between the American and the Soviet systems. But the worst offender was Marshal Tito of Jugoslavia, later to be expelled from the Cominform. Since 1944 he had been trying to form a federation with Bulgaria; and in June 1947 he told Western newspapermen that 'the free Balkan peoples' should build 'a strong monolithic entity'. Tito's potential partner was Georgi Dimitrov, the victim and hero of Nazi persecution after the Reichstag fire of 1933, who had recently returned from exile in the Soviet Union and resumed his Bulgarian citizenship. Called upon to explain in Moscow Bulgaria's plans for alliance with Jugoslavia and a customs union with Rumania, Dimitrov faced a memorable, revealing tirade:

'Yes, but you didn't consult with us,' Stalin shouted. 'We learn about your doings in the newspapers. You chatter like women from the housetops whatever occurs to you, and then the newspapermen get hold of it.' ...

Dimitrov remonstrated, 'There are essentially no difference between the foreign policies of Bulgaria and the Soviet Union.'

Stalin, decidedly and firmly: 'There are serious differences. Why hide it? It was Lenin's practice always to recognize errors and to remove them as quickly as possible.'

Dimitrov, placatingly, almost submissively: 'True, we erred. But through errors we are learning our way in foreign politics.'

Stalin harshly and tauntingly: 'Learning! You have been in politics fifty years – and now you are correcting errors. Your trouble is not errors, but that you are taking a line different from ours.'[7]

Differences were only to be expected, since in many ways the East European countries were as various as those of the West. In language and tradition, all except Albania, Hungary and Rumania were predominantly Slav; but Czechoslovakia and Jugoslavia were each made up of at least two separate peoples. In religion, Czechoslovakia, Hungary and Poland had in the past been mainly Catholic, Bulgaria and Rumania mainly Orthodox; Jugoslavia had been mixed, and Albania seventy per cent Muslim. Politically, Czechoslovakia and Poland had been republics, the remainder monarchies. In World War II, finally, Bulgaria, Hungary and Rumania, willingly or not, had been on the side of the Axis, the others on that of the Allies. And yet, despite their differences, all had two features in common. All were in the Soviet sphere of influence: when hostilities ended, it was natural for them to enter her tutelage. But all had largely agrarian economies, which from a Marxist point of view required nursing before their backward peasantry and weak proletariat would be fully ripe for Communism. It was equally natural, therefore, that initially most of them should be governed by 'bourgeois democratic' left-wing coalitions. Even without the Truman Doctrine and the Marshall Plan, this phase would have been part of what Marx and Lenin had called 'a political transition period'. Sooner or later, the East European countries would have been expected to move toward the dictatorship of the proletariat in one-party Soviet-type regimes. The process had begun, indeed, soon after the end of hostilities. It took different forms in different countries; but in anxious Western eyes its main elements were ominously uniform.

In Poland, as has been seen, the struggle had begun while the war still continued; it merely became more open in 1945. On 4 January, the Communist-controlled 'Lublin Committee' declared itself to be 'The Provisional National Government of the Polish Republic'. Western attempts to have it reorganized on a broader basis, with democratic leaders from exile and from Poland itself, remained fruitless for several months. Meanwhile, at the end of March 1945, the Russians arrested sixteen Polish underground leaders who had been unwise enough to reveal themselves, and flew them to Moscow, to the Lubianka prison, where they awaited trial—and all but four of them, imprisonment—for alleged 'diversionist' sabotage in the rear of the Red Army. In May, however,

Stalin seemed to relent. He assured Harry Hopkins, the late President Roosevelt's Special Assistant, that Poland would have a system of parliamentary government similar to that of Belgium or Holland; and in June a number of Polish leaders—including Stanislaw Mikolajczyk from London—were invited to Moscow for consultations. On 23 June they agreed on a 're-organized' Provisional Government, to include representatives of the Peasant, Socialist, Democratic and Christian Labour parties. Of its twenty-one members, sixteen had been in the previous Provisional Government, three came from London, and two from Poland itself. Mikolajczyk was Second Deputy Premier and Minister of Agriculture and Land Reform; but much of his authority, he later complained, was usurped by the Communist Minister of Forestry. The Communists, moreover, held the key ministries, including that of Public Security; and when Mikolajczyk tried to reorganize the Peasant Party, which from being a left-wing agrarian group was turning into a centre of miscellaneous opposition to Communism, they attacked his supporters with censorship, suppression, threats and even murder. In June 1946, the Government held a referendum on three separate issues, the first of which was the abolition of the Senate; and although this was popular, Mikolajczyk urged his followers to vote against it in order to test their electoral strength. Where the Peasant Party could check the results, more than eighty per cent were in its favour; elsewhere, the Government suppressed them. When Britain and the United States reminded Poland of the definition of free elections agreed upon at Yalta, the only response was a protest against foreign interference. Police pressure against the Peasant Party continued, with arrests and raids on its headquarters. An election was at last fixed for 19 January 1947; but already in the previous September the Polish Socialists and Communists had agreed with Stalin and Molotov on the composition of the new Government. During the election campaign, Mikolajczyk and his party faced a reign of terror: many of his supporters were arrested, and in ten out of fifty-two constituencies his candidates were disqualified. Again the United States and Britain protested; again they were told that their information was false, and that they should mind their own business. The election result was a landslide, pre-arranged in flagrant contradiction of the Yalta and Potsdam agreements. The American Ambassador, Arthur Bliss Lane, resigned in protest; and Mikolajczyk, in the end, escaped to the West.[8]

In Bulgaria, the 'Fatherland Front' had seized power on the night of 8 September 1944, just as the Russians were liberating the country at the cost of more than 20,000 civilian lives. It set up a coalition government in which the Communists, the Agrarian Party and the *Zveno* military partisans were equally represented, together with Social-Democrats and Independents; the Communists, however, held the key posts of Minister of the Interior and Minister of Justice. Shortly afterwards, the Agrarian leader Dr G. M. Dimitrov, namesake of his Communist rival, returned from war work with the British in Cairo to reorganize the party as its Secretary-General. British intervention in the Greek civil war, however, made him suspect to the Communists; and on 18 January 1945, he was forced to cede his office to Nikola Petkov. By now, the Agrarian party was splitting; and in May 1945 Petkov himself was replaced by Alexander Obbov, from its pro-Communist wing. The Social-Democrats were likewise divided into three conflicting groups. On 18 June, the Fatherland Front Government announced an election for 26 August; but only the Government itself was to present lists of candidates. Six ministers demanded that opposition parties be allowed to do likewise. When they got no satisfaction, the Agrarian and Social-Democrat dissidents, Petkov and Grigor Cheshmedjiev, resigned from the Government. After Western warnings that any rigged election would indefinitely delay the peace treaty, the Government made some concessions. It even allowed the opposition to publish newspapers—which quickly reached ten times the circulation of the official press. It refused, however, to appoint non-Communist Ministers of the Interior and of Justice; and the opposition parties therefore decided to boycott the election. After some delay, it was held on 18 November with only one list of candidates; there was also some evidence of violence and threats. The Fatherland Front won three-quarters of the seats, and supplied all the members of the new Government; but as a result of further diplomatic skirmishes among the Allies, the Soviet Union 'advised' Bulgaria to appoint two opposition ministers, Petkov and the moderate Socialist Kosta Lulchev. They in turn demanded, without success, that the Ministries of the Interior and of Justice be freed from control by Communists; the dispute dragged on for nearly twelve months. Meanwhile, the Communist party was extending its grip on the country. In the summer of 1946 it purged the Bulgarian army of its *Zveno* leaders; at a referendum on 8 September, ninety-two per cent of the population voted to abolish the monarchy; and on 27 October an election was held for the Great National Assembly of the new Republic. Through the Allied Control Commission, Britain and the United States tried hard to ensure free voting in accordance with the Yalta Declaration on Liberated Europe; but intimidation, delays in the issue of voting cards, and the imprisonment of some opposition leaders and supporters made the poll something of a travesty. Many would-be electors were held up by road-blocks—one of which stopped the British Control Commission representative, General Oxley. Even so, Petkov later claimed that the Agrarian and Social Democratic opposition had won sixty per cent of the votes. The official returns gave them twenty-two per cent, with 101 seats in the Assembly. The Fatherland Front won 364 seats. Of these, 277 were held by Communists; and when Georgi Dimitrov became Premier, his Cabinet included nine Communist ministers, making the coalition a mere façade.[9]

In Rumania, King Michael had broken with the Nazis in the last week of August, 1944, arresting Marshal Ion Antonescu and appointing a coalition Government under General Sanatescu which included all four political parties—the National Liberals, the National Peasants, the Socialists and the Communists. The Red Army, meanwhile, entered and occupied Bucharest. An armistice was signed in Moscow on 12 September 1944, fixing reparations to the Soviet Union at 300 million dollars to be paid in kind over a period of six years. As a start, the Russians seized fifty per cent of Rumania's rolling stock, its whole navy, most of its merchant fleet, and much oil equipment. According to Anna Pauker, the Communist leader who was later to be Foreign Minister, there were barely a thousand Communists in the country before the Red Army arrived; and they had only one post in Sanatescu's Government. With their allies from the 'Ploughmen's Front' and left-wing splinter groups, however, they quickly formed a 'National Democratic Front'; and in November, when Sanatescu reshuffled his Cabinet after clashes with the Russians, the National Democratic Front secured more Government places. On 2 December Sanatescu resigned, to be replaced by the seventy-year-old General Radescu; but he in turn was not to last long. His main offence was to delay the land reform pressed by the Communists, which produced farm holdings so small as to be unworkable without collectivization. When the censored press attacked him, Radescu hit back with bitterly anti-Communist broadcasts and public speeches; and in January 1945 Anna Pauker and her colleague Gheorghe Gheorghiu-Dej, then on a visit to Moscow, were told to mobilize the National Democratic Front in a counter-campaign of demonstrations and strikes. Radescu, who was his own Minister of the Interior, did his best to crush them; but with help from the Red Army, the demonstrators disarmed the few Rumanian troops left in the capital, and the disorders continued. On Tuesday 27 February 1945, the Soviet Deputy Foreign Minister Andrei Vyshinsky arrived in Bucharest and asked to see King Michael, who received him that evening with his Foreign Minister Constantine Visoianu. Radescu's Government, said Vyshinsky, was incapable of keeping order: it should be replaced by one that represented 'the truly democratic forces of the country'. Next day, Vyshinsky was back again. What was the decision? The King explained that he had notified Radescu and had begun consulting party leaders with a view to replacing him. This, said Vyshinsky, was not enough. Looking at his watch, he told King Michael that he had just two hours and five minutes to announce Radescu's dismissal. By eight o'clock, a new Prime Minister must be named. Visoianu pointed out that Rumania was a constitutional monarchy, and that the King was obliged to respect its rules. Vyshinsky accused Radescu of 'protecting fascists': a royal decree of the previous day, retiring ten Rumanian officers, had been 'an unfriendly act', and must be annulled. The King agreed to rescind it, and Vyshinsky left. According to the American political representative in Bucharest, 'he slammed the door so hard that the plaster around the door frame was cracked badly.' The King went on consulting party leaders, but on the following day, Thursday 1 March 1945, Vyshinsky announced that the Soviet Union's choice for Prime Minister was Dr Petru Groza, a land-owner and former member of the pro-Communist Ploughmen's Front. The King could only acquiesce. When Groza formed his Government on Tuesday 6 March, he appointed Communists to the Ministries of the Interior, of Justice, and of Public Works. The Foreign Ministry went to Gheorghe Tatarescu, a former Liberal; the remaining posts were divided among the Ploughmen's Front, the left wing of the Social Democrats, and other splinter groups from the National Democratic Front, while the Peasant, Liberal and right-wing Socialist parties refused to join. The American and British representatives on the Allied Control Commission declared that the new Cabinet was unacceptable to their Governments; but when the King asked Groza to resign, he simply refused. The King then withdrew to his palace at Sinaia, and himself refused to sign govern-mental decrees. For several months, Groza carried on without him. Royalist demonstrations were broken up with violence, including some deaths. After further Western pressure, the Cabinet was enlarged to in-clude one representative of the National Peasant party and one of the National Liberals; and at length, on 4 February 1946, the Government was officially recognized by Britain and the United States. In preparation for the election, first to be held in May, then postponed till November, Groza's Government broke up meetings by the rival parties, threatened, injured and even killed some of their militants, stopped them from broadcasting, limited the circulation of their newspapers, and hindered the registration of their electors. The printers' union refused to work on anti-Government material, and some two hundred opposition leaders were imprisoned. At the polls on 19 November 1946, the Government coalition won 348 out of 414 seats. The Western Governments once again protested; but they felt powerless to do more.[10]

Events in Hungary followed a similar pattern. A Nazi coup on 16 October 1944 cut short a bid by the Regent, Admiral Horthy, for a separate peace; and fighting dragged on, devastating the country, until April 1945. Already in December 1944, however, a Provisional National Assembly had been formed at Debrecen near the Rumanian border, and on 22 December it approved by acclamation a Provisional National Government. In this the Communists, the Smallholders and the Social-Democrats had two portfolios each; the remainder went to smaller groups and individuals, including a few ministers and generals from the Horthy regime. The Communists held only the Ministries of Agriculture and Trade; but Communist deputy ministers and officials were influential elsewhere, especially in the Ministry of the Interior. Despite the Allied Control Commission, the Russians were the country's ultimate rulers. Under the armistice agreement signed in Moscow on 20 January 1945, Hungary had to pay 300 million dollars' worth of reparations, and a further 200 million dollars in ex-German property. When the Ministry of Finance tried to stem inflation by restricting the number of roubles in circulation, Red Army men staged a virtual armed robbery of the National Bank. The first test of popular feeling was the land reform carried out quickly and successfully in March 1945; a second took place on 2 October, when a municipal election was held in Budapest. In a capital recently freed from the rule of Nazi collaborators, the Communists and their Social-Democrat allies seemed confident of victory, and certainly played fair. To their surprise, however, the Smallholders' party, a moderately liberal group with some recent right-wing support, won fifty-one per cent of the votes and 121 of the total of 240 seats. Marshal Voroshilov, the Russian chairman of the Control Commission, thereupon pressed the Smallholders' leaders to present at next month's general election a single list of candidates drawn up jointly with the other Government coalition parties, When they refused, the Communists agreed to separate lists, but insisted that the coalition continue whatever the results at the polls. In the event, on 4 November 1945, the Smallholders won 59·9 per cent of the votes, the Communists 17·1 per cent the Social-Democrats 16·9 per cent and the National Peasant Party 5·6 per cent. Zoltán Tildy, a Smallholder, became Premier with nine other ministers from his own party, four from the Communists, four Social-Democrats and one from the National Peasant group. The Communists, however, threatened to leave the Government unless they obtained the

Ministry of the Interior. Tildy consented, and it went to Imre Nagy. On 1 February 1946, when the National Assembly declared Hungary a republic, Tildy became its first President. Desider Sulyok, the Smallholders' original candidate to succeed him as Premier, was ousted from the party under Communist pressure, and the post went to his colleague Ferenc Nagy, who had previously been President of the Assembly. While rifts among the Smallholders deepened, the Communists organized a left-wing bloc with the Social-Democrats, the National Peasant Party, and the trade unions; and when Sulyok criticized their economic policies and their control of the police, they counter-attacked him fiercely, staging demonstrations in the capital and demanding that twenty-two other members of the Smallholders' party be dismissed. The Communist Minister of the Interior, Imre Nagy, was now replaced by the formidable László Rajk, and Communist control was also extended to the Ministry of Defence. With the Communist Mátyás Rákosi as Deputy Premier, with the trade unions controlled by the Soviet-trained Stephen Kossa, with another Communist, Zoltán Vas, running the Supreme Economic Council, and with a deluge of unwanted advice pouring daily from Radio Moscow, Ferenc Nagy began to find his position untenable. By October 1946, when Sulyok's dissident Smallholders, renamed the 'Freedom Party', were officially recognized, even Nagy's wing of the party had virtually become an opposition minority. In December 1946, the Ministries of the Interior and of Defence began making a series of arrests without even informing the Premier. They claimed to have uncovered a vast conspiracy organized by the prewar nationalist group 'Hungarian Community' (*Magyar Közöségg*), which allegedly planned to reinstate the former regime. The charges against it implicated many Smallholder leaders, including Ferenc Nagy's friend and colleague Béla Kovács, who despite his parliamentary immunity was seized by the Russians on 26 February 1947, and subsequently disappeared. Three months later, while on a mission to Switzerland, Nagy himself was forced to resign under threats to his son, who had remained in Hungary. In a highly suspect election held that August, thirty-five per cent of Hungarians still voted for the opposition; but the remaining resistance, now centred in the Catholic Church, was steadily eroded. In the following year, the militant Cardinal Mindszenty was arrested and sentenced to life imprisonment. Not long afterwards the Assembly was dissolved, and a one-party election gave the Communist-dominated Government a majority of ninety per cent.[11]

If developments in Poland, Bulgaria, Rumania and Hungary were broadly similar, Finland, Albania and Jugoslavia pursued separate courses; only the prevailing winds were the same.

In Finland, once the Nazis were driven out, a new Government was formed under Juho Kusti Paasikivi, a former Conservative and now an Independent. His Cabinet included representatives of the extreme left, one of whom was a Communist; and his policy, dictated by the facts of geography, was to seek 'the best possible understanding' with the Soviet Union. At the elections of 17 and 18 March 1945, after Paasikivi had asked voters to give Parliament 'a new face', the Communist and Social-Democrat People's Democratic League won an overwhelming victory and took key posts in the new Government; the Communist Yrjoe Leino became Minister of the Interior. So great was the revulsion against the wartime past that the Soviet Union felt little need to intervene directly. Stalin, who had himself proclaimed Finland's independence at Helsinki in 1917, and who had taken the measure of Finnish toughness during the Winter War of 1939–40, decided that moderation, as he put it, was 'not kindness but common sense'. Only nine months later, at the 'War Guilt' trials, did Soviet pressure become marked. In March 1946 the seventy-nine-year-old President Mannerheim, who had been Commander-in-Chief in the Winter War, resigned for health reasons, and Paasikivi became President. The new Prime Minister, Mauno Pekkala, brought three Communists into the Cabinet, and in May of the same year began a further purge of right-wing organizations, staff officers and civil servants. There was some friction with Russia over the terms imposed by the Peace Treaty; but on 10 February 1947, the Finnish Government signed it, and settled down in watchful semi-independence.[12]

In Albania, economically the most backward of the East European countries, the Communists seized power at once through their control of the Liberation Front, later renamed the 'Democratic Front'. Essentially, this was an alliance between the peasants and partisans from the intelligentsia. Its leader was the French-educated Communist Enver Hoxha, whose Government was recognized by the Allies in November 1945. In the election held on 2 December, eighty-six per cent of the population voted for it: there were no opposition candidates at all. In January 1946, King Zog was formally deposed; and from then onward Hoxha ruled almost unchallenged as a military dictator, first under the patronage of Jugoslavia, until Tito's expulsion from the Cominform in 1948, then—until 1961—more directly under Moscow. A semblance of popular consent was supplied by referenda; but the ballot was hardly secret. Owing to the high rate of illiteracy, voters were given a ball to drop into a box with two openings marked respectively 'Yes' and 'No'. Through the 'Yes' slot, the ball fell silently into a sack; through the 'No' slot, it rattled into a tin can.[13]

In Jugoslavia, when the war ended, effective power lay with the People's Liberation Front, which now became the People's Front. This included prewar political parties, two of which—the Croatian Peasant Party and the (Serbian Peoples Peasant Party-retained apparent autonomy; the controlling organization was that of Marshal Tito's Communist partisans. In March 1945, a coalition government was formed. Stalin described the Jugoslav regime as 'something between de Gaulle's France and the Soviet Union'; but although the cabinet included politicians back from wartime exile, and although King Peter remained technically in office, there was no question at this time of establishing a Western-style democracy or constitutional monarchy. Opposition leaders were arrested or otherwise harassed; and when a general election was held on 11 November 1945, there were no opposition lists of candidates, but merely a separate ballot-box in which to express dissent. 88·6 per cent of the electorate voted, 90·5 of it for the People's Front. On 29 November the new Assembly declared Jugoslavia a republic; and on 31 January 1946, it approved a constitution closely modelled on the Soviet Constitution of 1936. That summer, Tito eliminated the remaining opposition leaders. General Draža Mihailović, the Serb patriot whose forces had fought during the war against Tito's partisans as well as against the enemy, was tried for treason and shot on 17 July 1946. Dr Dragoljub Jovanović, leader of the People's Peasant Party, who criticized the People's Front on whose ticket he had been elected, was violently attacked and threatened, removed from his University chair and from the Serbian regional Parliament, expelled by the Communists from his own party, and later arrested and tried. A similar fate befell Archbishop Stepinac, the Croatian Primate, who had failed to protest during the war when individual Croatian priests had been involved in the persecution and forcible conversion of Serbs. In October 1946 the Archbishop was sentenced to imprisonment for sixteen years.[14]

Before long, Jugoslavian nationalism was to lead to a breach with the Soviet Union: Tito was expelled from the Cominform on 28 June 1948. But if this seemed to modify the stereotype of a monolithic East European bloc, any comfort that it might have given Western observers was far outweighed by the fate of Czechoslovakia.

Here, the first postwar President was the veteran statesman Edvard

Beneš, who had been Foreign Minister under Thomas Masaryk and had succeeded him in 1935. Three years later he had resigned, bitterly disillusioned at the Munich agreement by which Britain and France had truncated his country under threats from Hitler and Mussolini. It was a betrayal that he never forgot. In 1941, when he became President of the exiled Czechoslovak Government in London, he decided that his country was too vulnerable to rely on distant Western allies, and resolved to secure the support and friendship of the Soviet Union. His diagnosis was accurate; his prescription was tragically mistaken.

In April 1945, coming from London via Moscow, Beneš set up a provisional Government at Košice, in the liberated area of Slovakia. On 5 May, Resistance workers in Prague rose against the Nazi occupation; and fearing what they had heard about Red Army behaviour, they urged the Americans—then fifty-six miles away—to come to their aid. But when General Eisenhower told the Russian Chief of Staff, General Antonov, that he was willing to do so, Antonov said no. One result was a mass slaughter among the Czech Resistance; another was the undisputed Russian occupation of Prague. It was shortly after this that the Provisional Government moved there.[15]

The Prime Minister was the left-wing Socialist Zdeněk Fierlinger; with him in the cabinet were two other Socialists, three Czech 'National Socialists' (left-wing Liberals), three Populists, three Slovak Democrats and seven Communists, three of them Slovaks. All these were members of the so-called 'National Front'. The Agrarian and other right-wing parties from the London Government were excluded; but Jan Masaryk, the son of Thomas, and like Beneš close to the 'National Socialists', continued to be Foreign Minister as he had been in London; and the independent General Ludvik Svoboda became Minister of Defence. The Communists, however, were put in charge of the Ministries of the Interior, of Education, of Agriculture, and of Information. Their strategy, as described later by their leader Klement Gottwald, now a Deputy Premier, was to exploit the 'national and democratic revolution' to attract a majority into the party. No elections were held for a full year; meanwhile, Beneš and the National Front pushed through a series of drastic reforms, expelling German minorities, redistributing farmland, and nationalizing much of Czechoslovakian industry.[16]

At length, on 26 May 1946, the country went to the polls to elect a Constituent Assembly. Some 250,000 to 300,000 alleged wartime collaborators had meanwhile been struck off the voting lists, and the land reform had helped local Communists at the expense of the Agrarian Party, which was now dissolved; but on polling day itself there was little or no malpractice. The Communists won thirty-eight per cent of the vote, and their Social-Democrat allies thirteen per cent, giving them together 153 seats in the Assembly, against 147 held by the other parties. The new government was headed by Gottwald himself; it contained two more Communists and two fewer Slovaks than before. There followed a period of comparative calm and progress. Production rose and trade developed, especially with the countries of the West. It was no doubt this that encouraged Gottwald to respond, at first, to the offer of the Marshall Plan in July 1947—a move quickly checked by Stalin, who also forestalled a new treaty of alliance with France. The resultant ill-feeling was increased by the foundation of the Cominform that October; even the Social-Democrats grew restive, and in November they ousted their former leader Fierlinger. With an election due to be held in March 1948, the Communist Party began to fear that it might not win a majority of the ballot; and it made preparations for victory by other means, campaigning for new recruits and working to extend its hold on the trade unions, the army and the police.[17]

Its hour struck in early February, 1948, when the Communist Minister of the Interior Václav Nosek dismissed eight non-Communist police commanders in Prague and replaced them with his own men. Led by the Czech 'National Socialists', a majority of the Cabinet demanded that Gottwald rescind the order. He refused. Thereupon, on Friday 20 February 1948, the twelve non-Marxist Ministers resigned from the cabinet. They hoped to overthrow the Government; but the Social-Democrats, who had originally joined in the protest, now remained in office, leaving Gottwald a quorum of thirteen. 'Believe me,' he told Masaryk afterwards, 'we have spent months thinking how to carry out the *putsch*, what excuse to use, how to do it, then those ex-Ministers handed it to us on a plate. They gave us a perfect excuse, and all that was needed was to stand there and kick them in the behind, and that is what we did.' Already, in fact, the Communists had put out feelers to Moscow: 'Our friends,' said one party official, 'have given us guarantees against any eventuality.' On Thursday 19 February Valerian Zorin, former Soviet Ambassador in Czechoslovakia and now a Vice-Minister of Foreign Affairs, had arrived in Prague unexpectedly, and extra contingents of the Red Army had entered the Soviet Zone of Austria near to the Czechoslovak frontier. With these assurances, Gottwald now asked President Beneš to accept a new Cabinet purged of 'reactionaries'. At first, Beneš hesitated. The dissenting Ministers tried to see him, to argue with Nosek, to negotiate their way back into the Cabinet; but they found the way blocked and their offices taken over. On Saturday 21 February, the Communists formed workers' militia and staged a rally of 200,000 people in the ice-bound capital. On Sunday 22 February, at a vast Congress of

Workers' Councils from all over the country, they announced a governmental programme; the Congress threatened a general strike unless Gottwald formed a cabinet to carry it out. Meanwhile, with the army confined to barracks, Communist-controlled gendarmes and security police patrolled the Prague streets. For two days, Czechoslovak students gathered in counter-demonstrations; but on Monday 23 February they were finally crushed: the Minister of the Interior claimed to have put down a reactionary plot. On Tuesday 24 February Gottwald announced his ultimatum: on the following morning, for the last time, he would submit his new Cabinet list to Benes. Meanwhile, the Communist party shut down opposition newspapers; huge crowds of workers filled Wenceslas Square, carrying red flags, shouting slogans and singing the *Internationale*. Five truckloads of armed workers seized the Social-Democrat headquarters. That same evening, the non-Communist parties threw in their hand. Next day, while workers armed with brand-new rifles marched through the streets, Beneš accepted Gottwald's conditions, and the *putsch* was complete. Two days later, the Socialist Minister of Justice Prokop Drtina tried to kill himself; and at dawn on Wednesday 10 March 1948, the pyjama-clad body of Jan Masaryk was found on the pavement under the window of his apartment in the Czernin Palace, headquarters of the Foreign Ministry. Was it suicide, as his private secretary thought, or murder? The answer remained uncertain; but the question itself was eloquent. In May, new elections were held with a single list of candidates. On 8 June, Beneš resigned. When he died in September, vast crowds attended his funeral. Their silence was more eloquent still.[18]

Western spectators of all these events, largely unable to affect them, were both indignant and alarmed. In one country after another, they saw non-Marxist parties squeezed out of office, seldom democratically, sometimes by subterfuge, most often by a combination of fraud, intimidation and force. The first step, it seemed, was for the Communists to enter left-wing coalition Governments, sooner or later securing the key ministries, including that of the Interior, and packing them with a number of their own supporters. Gradually, these bridgeheads would be enlarged. Public information would be controlled; non-Marxist newspapers would be harassed, censored or abolished; non-Communist political meetings would be shouted down or broken up; party headquarters would be sacked and party militants arrested. Industrial action—strikes, demonstrations, marches—would redouble the political pressure. Finally, at the right moment, a crisis would be stage-managed. The non-Communist parties would be routed, their electors tricked and their leaders imprisoned. From then onward, only Soviet-type 'democracy' would be allowed.

If this could happen in Eastern Europe, there seemed some chance of its being repeated in the West, and especially in Belgium, France and Italy, where the Communists were relatively strong. Armed insurrection by Communist Resistance fighters seemed the most immediate danger—although in all three cases it was precluded by the facts of power. In Belgium, the Communist-led *Front de l'Indépendance* refused to surrender its weapons at the liberation, but eventually obeyed a Government order to do so, backed by the presence of British troops. In France, sporadic uprisings by the similar *Francs-Tireurs et Partisans* were discouraged by Moscow and easily defeated. Even in Italy, where both Communist and right-wing partisans maintained private arsenals, and where many old scores were settled by violence, there was no real attempt at revolution. No less an authority than the Central Committee of the Soviet Communist Party gave the revealing explanation. 'Unfortunately,' it admitted, 'the Soviet Army could not render ... assistance to the French and Italian Communist Parties.'[19]

It was no wonder that the news from Eastern Europe made the 'bourgeois' parties in Belgium, France and Italy wary of their Communist colleagues. In each case, the Communist Party's Resistance record had helped it to win a larger showing in Parliament. In the Belgian election of 17 February 1946, it had secured 23 seats in the Chamber—more than twice its prewar representation. In France, in the first Constituent Assembly elected on 21 October 1945, it held 151 seats as against 150 for the Catholic *Mouvement Républicain Populair* (MRP) and 139 for the Socialists; in the second Constituent Assembly elected on 2 June 1946, it dropped two seats; but in the election for the National Assembly on 10 November of that year it obtained a total of 171, against 162 MRP and 102 Socialists. In the Italian Constituent Assembly, elected on 2 June 1946, the Communists won 104 seats, coming third after the Christian Democrats with 207 and the Socialists with 115. In all three countries, the Party was a power to be reckoned with; and in all of them it secured ministerial posts. Each of Belgium's first two post-Liberation Governments contained two Communist ministers, and on 31 March 1946, this number was doubled. In France, the Party held two portfolios in General de Gaulle's 1944 Provisional Government, and five in his first regular Cabinet, formed on 21 November 1945. When the General resigned in January 1946, the next two Governments each had six Communist ministers; and although these were followed in December 1946 by an all-Socialist caretaker Cabinet under Léon Blum, the

Government formed by Paul Ramadier on 22 January 1947, once more contained a five-man quota of Communists. In Italy, likewise, Communists had been members of the two successive Governments headed by Ivanoe Bonomi after the liberation of Rome, of Ferruccio Parri's Government, set up in June 1945, and of the first three cabinets formed by the Christian-Democrat leader Alcide De Gasperi as tripartite coalitions of Communists, Christian-Democrats and Socialists.[20]

Would the Communists use their new position in parliaments and governments to weaken constitutional authority, infiltrate the administration, and ultimately seize power? In Italy, Palmiro Togliatti might claim that his party had 'always declared that it does not conceive of the republican Constitution as an expedient for using the institutions of bourgeois democracy until the moment of insurrection in order to conquer the State and transform it into a Socialist State, but as a unitary pact freely concluded by the great majority of the Italian people and a basis for the organic development of national life.' However orotund and abstract, this was an echo of the Resistance hope of renovating Western society; but if it was opposed—as it was—by many vested interests, it was also vitiated by Communist actions elswhere. Not everyone saw the danger, or agreed that there was one. Many very able or idealistic Westerners continued to vote Communist as a protest, in ignorance, out of loyalty, or in stubborn hope of change. More and more, as time went on, they seemed to be sealed off in a private system of politics. Perhaps this dramatized their grievances, and the need for greater justice and equality: 'bourgeois' fear of Communism was often an incentive to reform. But it was also an excuse for disdain or repression; and those who supported the Party for years without criticism, despite Prague, despite Budapest, inevitably came to seem illogical, malevolent, venal, or blind to what was happening in the other half of Europe. Even Togliatti, moreover, had qualified this promise of moderation by saying that it applied 'for a whole historical period'. What might follow remained unstated.[21]

It was without great regret, therefore, that the governments of Belgium, France and Italy now lost their Communist ministers. It might seem that this was the mirror-image of events in Eastern Europe; but the likeness was merely superficial. In the West there was little of the chicanery, and virtually none of the terror and violence, that were used against non-Communists in the East. In at least two of the three cases, moreover, the Communists virtually excluded themselves.

In Belgium, in March 1947, the Communist ministers resigned in a dispute over coal prices and subsidies to coalmines; and on 12 March the Socialist Paul-Henri Spaak formed a new government without them. In

France, at the end of April, after several clashes on defence, economic and foreign policy, Communist ministers attacked the Ramadier Government's wage freeze—partly to placate more militant strikers at the Renault car works. On 4 May, when a vote of confidence was taken in the National Assembly, the Party voted against it; but the Communist ministers refused to leave the Government, hoping that this would force Ramadier himself to resign. Instead, he dismissed all but one of them that same evening; the other, a non-member of the Assembly, resigned next day. In Italy, finally, it was De Gasperi himself who at length dropped the Communists from his cabinet. Even before the Marshall Plan, they had denounced the 'economic imperialism' of American aid to Italy—although De Gasperi's Foreign Minister, the Socialist leader Pietro Nenni, was their chief working ally. When tension rose to breaking point, it first split the Socialist Party: in January 1947, the moderate leader Giuseppe Saragat walked out of its Rome Congress, taking with him a group of distinguished militants. Both he and Nenni now left the Cabinet; and De Gasperi himself resigned on 20 January, to form a new tripartite Government two weeks later, but with the 'Atlanticist' Count Carlo Sforza as Foreign Minister. At last, on 30 May 1947, after further quarrels and crises, De Gasperi felt strong enough to form a further cabinet, this time without either Communists or Nenni Socialists. This ensured stability until the election of the first postwar parliament, due on 18 April 1948. The Czechoslovakian coup of February 1948 turned the campaign into a suspense drama: would the Prague *putsch* be repeated in Rome? Many quite sober observers feared that it might. Both the United States and the Vatican put their weight behind De Gasperi, the former threatening to cut off aid if the Communists and Socialists won the election, the latter encouraging priests to refuse the sacraments to godless pro-Soviet voters. As it turned out, the Christian-Democrats won 48·5 per cent of the poll, compared with 35·2 per cent in the 1946 election for the Constituent Assembly. The joint Socialist-Communist ticket received 31 per cent—which, even together with the 7·1 per cent won by the Saragat Socialists, still totalled less than the 39·7 per cent obtained by Socialists and Communists in 1946. With more than 300 Christian-Democrat seats out of 574 in the Chamber, De Gasperi was urged by the Vatican to form a one-party Catholic Government. Wisely, he refused, and put together the centre coalition of Christian-Democrats, Liberals, Republicans and Saragat Social-Democrats that was to become a classical pattern in postwar Italian politics. Italy, like France and Belgium, had rounded the cape.[22]

The fear of internal subversion was exorcized; but throughout these same months events in Eastern Europe had cast still darker shadows.

Was Soviet Communism inherently expansionist? Was Stalin determined to spread it westward by the use of armed force? In his *Problems of Leninism*, he had stated the orthodox doctrine: the capitalist system included 'as an inevitable element imperialist wars'. As Lenin had written,

...The existence of the Soviet Republic side by side with imperialist states for a long time is unthinkable. One or the other must triumph in the end. And before that end supervenes a series of frightful collisions between the Soviet Republic and the bourgeois states will be inevitable.

'The bourgeois states,' added Stalin, '... send spies, assassins and wreckers into our country and are waiting for a favourable opportunity to attack it by armed force.' 'We must remember that we are surrounded by people, classes and governments who openly express their intense hatred for us. We must remember that we are at all times but a hair's breadth from every manner of invasion.' To defend itself, the Communist Party must forestall attack and overthrow non-Communist governments, beginning with the weaker countries, such as former colonial dependencies.[23]

In context, these words seemed to refer to 'the successful seizure of power' in the class struggle—to the pattern, that is, being followed in Eastern Europe. John Foster Dulles, later to be President Eisenhower's Secretary of State, himself admitted that

Class war, rather than *national* war, is taught as the preferred method of achieving Soviet Communist encirclement. That explains why Stalin can say, as he not infrequently does, that the Soviet Union and the United States, as nations, can coexist peacefully, i.e., without national war.

But the violent rhetoric of Stalin and his associates blurred the distinction. 'Many feel,' said Dulles, 'that because Soviet Communist leaders treat us as "enemies", and because their nation has a great military establishment, it necessarily follows that the Soviet Union will fight a national war against us, and that we should concentrate on military things.' Despite his later reputation as a 'Cold Warrior', Dulles preached caution. 'Whether Soviet leaders do plan a fighting war,' he added '... is by no means certain, and if we treat it as certain and make our dispositions accordingly, we may fall victim to a fatal trick play.'[24]

Western fears, then, may possibly have misread Soviet intentions: but what was significant on both sides was the climate of fear. World War II was not long over; its violent sequels were still being enacted in the 'satellite' countries; the landscape of Europe, and the minds of men, still bore its scars. Dulles, even when he spoke of peace, used the language of war. 'It is time,' he said, 'to think less of fission bombs and more of establishing justice and ending terrorism in the world.' But this very sentence was preceded by another: 'It is time to think in terms of taking the offensive in the world struggle for freedom and of rolling back the engulfing tide of despotism.' Such words confirmed the worst of Soviet suspicions, as Communist rhetoric confirmed those of the West; and mutual distrust, rightly or wrongly, was deepened by the military situation of each side. To be prepared is the duty of all military planners: unless they are themselves distrustful, they betray their trust. And the relative military strength of the West and the Soviet Union in the late 'forties inevitably increased the political tension. Since 1945, the United States had possessed the atomic bomb; they had also withdrawn many of their troops from Western Europe. The Soviet situation was precisely the opposite. Stalin's technologists had not yet produced a nuclear weapon; in compensation, the Soviet Union maintained and was developing conventional forces far greater than those of the West. Being asymmetrical, the balance of power was highly dangerous: each side's weakness faced the other's strength. The ensuing arms race was therefore run, as it were, on two separate tracks. The Soviet Union made immense efforts to build an atomic device, which it finally tested in 1949. The West, meanwhile, felt obliged to strengthen its conventional defence.[25]

In Western Europe, the first move was made by Ernest Bevin, the British Foreign Secretary. On 13 January 1948, he told General Marshall, US Secretary of State, that Britain planned to propose to France and the three Benelux countries a series of bilateral defence agreements. With President Truman's backing, Marshall answered that the United States agreed with Britain on 'the urgent need for concerted measures by the nations of Europe'. On 22 January, Bevin explained his plan to the House of Commons. After reminding his audience how the original postwar hope of a united world had come to grief, he declared that the free nations of Europe must now draw closely together. It was not, he was quick to add, a formal political union that he had in mind, but 'the closest possible relations'. 'We have then to go beyond the circle of our immediate neighbours ... and consider the question of associating other historic members of European civilization, including the new Italy, with this great conception.' Bevin put his proposal formally at the end of January. In the third week of February the Benelux countries, and particularly Paul-Henri Spaak, the Belgian Foreign Minister, urged that it be a collective regional arrangement, economic, social and cultural as well as military, rather than a series of bilateral defence pacts. Meanwhile, Czechoslovakia was in turmoil—and the ominous news from Prague helped speed the work of the diplomats. On Thursday 4 March, one week after Klement Gottwald's *putsch*, a negotiating conference met in Brussels. On Wednesday 17 March, one week after Jan Masaryk's death, Britain, France and the Benelux countries signed a brief, crisp treaty eleven articles long. Concluded for fifty years, it set up a Consultative Council of Foreign Ministers, a Military Committee, and other permanent bodies to deal with economic, social and cultural matters: one of their products was to be a Cultural Identity Card. More important was the multilateral defence commitment, pledging its signatories to aid each other against armed aggression—automatically if it occurred in Europe, after consultation if elsewhere. Unlike the Treaty of Dunkirk signed by Britain and France a year earlier, on 4 March 1947, the Brussels Treaty was not limited to defence against Germany; in this way it was the first postwar treatly implicitly to recognize a potential Soviet threat. Largely on French insistence, however, it mentioned possible aggression by Germany. The ambivalence was characteristic of the changing times.[26]

Victors and vanquished are always mutually suspicious. Which of the defeated can their conquerors trust? The openly hostile, sturdy in their defiance—or the eager, the efficient, the complaint? Are the victors themselves to be trusted? Is there arrogance in their good intentions, or a saving grace of honesty in their lapses? Can either side speak plainly? How long will it be before memories and misgivings are effaced?

After World War II, this process was slower than usual. More than most others, it had been a 'people's war'. As in World War I, conscripts had formed vast citizen armies, and bombing had brought civilians under fire. Occupation, first of Allied countries, then of the Axis, had involved whole populations; millions had been deported or imprisoned; millions had become refugees. Yet, paradoxically, some of those who had known occupation proved more tolerant than those who had escaped it: if their sufferings were greater, they at least saw the enemy at close quarters, and could distinguish between the bad and the worse.

Of all the Axis leaders, it was Hitler who had left the deepest mark on Europe. For many of the Allies, it had been the second war against Germany in two generations; for France, it had been the third. The war in the Far East had most directly affected the United States, Australia and New Zealand. Mussolini's legions had proved imperfectly martial. But the Nazis had largely lived up to their legend; and their death camps had given human evil unimagined new dimensions. Caught in collective guilt, the most conscientious Germans now wound their way through labyrinths of tortured logic to recover a necessary minimum of self-respect. Political leaders quoted Karl Jaspers; journalists wrote anguished books to explain German unpopularity, lacerating their readers only less than themselves. Yet at the same time they resented the lordly airs of their new conquerors, few of whom had had to face such appalling ethical dilemmas. To many among the Allies, in fact, the ordinary apolitical German, living his life as best he could in the interstices of disaster, seemed to have been feckless and irresponsible; his defeated democratic leaders, rightly or not, looked ineffectual and out of touch. Only after searching, frank, and painful—almost psychoanalytical—discussion of the Nazi era could real mutual trust between Germans and others again become possible. Failing that, horror at Nazi atrocities all too easily led to an understandable but still ugly form of race hatred: as anti-Semitism was defeated, anti-Germanism grew.[27]

To a generation that grew up fearing and then fighting Hitler, much that was German now had a suspect fascination. Films from the Weimar epoch were seen by one influential critic—himself of German origin—as revealing 'deep psychological dispositions': they helped, he thought, 'in the understanding of Hitler's ascent and ascendancy'.[28] Propaganda, abetted by national habit, had established some unattractive stereotypes. The stout, beer-drinking, cigar-smoking Bavarian, at home the embodiment of robust, jovial prosperity, was often seen abroad as boorish and self-indulgent; the lean, aristocratic captain of industry seemed to many non-Germans a vulpine capitalist, if not a 'Prussian militarist' in civilian clothes. German seriousness seemed heavy, German scholarship pedantic, German romanticism sentimental, German realism cruel. Wagner, like imperial architecture, spelt glory at home, but abroad was sometimes accused of bombast. The 'Deutsches Eck' at Koblenz, recommended to foreigners in search of 'the German character', to Germans meant sobriety, solidity, hard work, and the mighty Rhine; to too many others, it held all the grey menace of the Reich's sombre factories, the overcast powerhouses of the Ruhr. Even the uniforms worn by postwar German railway porters sent chills down middle-aged foreign spines. The German peaked cap recalled the Wehrmacht; a German accent in English, French or Italian revived unwelcome emotions; and even the German language risked seeming pompous, ambiguous, abstract and back-to-front.

Amid the marsh of speculation and prejudice there were a few rocks of fact. Germany, like almost every European country, had long had a hierarchical society; but whereas in most others industrialization had thrown up a new middle class of managers, here there had been no real social revolution before 1933. Discipline and hierarchy had reinforced German industriousness, making the country a great—and rival—economic power, but with a social fabric ready to split at the seams. At the same time, Germany had long been in an exposed position. For centuries —from the Counter-Reformation until after the French Revolution—its internal divisions and lack of firm natural frontiers had made it the victim of others' quarrels, an object of diplomacy and one of the spoils of war. Now, once more divided, this time between East and West, it lay across Europe like a crippled giant. Both Eastern and Western Allies were anxious to exorcize its past and potential menace; but they differed as to how it should be done.[29]

The Potsdam Conference had stipulated that 'during the occupation period, Germany shall be treated as a single economic entity', and that 'so far as is practicable there shall be uniformity of treatment of the German population throughout Germany'. The four Commanders-in-Chief who made up the Allied Control Council in Berlin were to rule 'jointly, in matters affecting Germany as a whole'. Their decisions, however, were subject to the rule of unanimity; and each of them, on instructions from his government, was to exercise 'supreme authority' in his own zone of occupation. If unity was a political aspiration, division thus became an administrative fact. France, in particular, was hostile to the establishment of a central German administration; and although the Soviet Union ostensibly agreed with the United States and Britain on the need to treat Germany as a unit, in practice it followed its own familiar policy in the Eastern zones, as it did in the Eastern sector of Berlin.[30]

Fighting in the capital had ended on Wednesday 2 May 1945. When the Americans arrived on Sunday 1 July, they found a complete apparatus of government already in place. Prominent positions had been assigned to non-Communists, but Party members were safely in control of key posts, including education and the police. Even the clocks had been set to Moscow time: dazed Berliners found that it was still dark at 7·00 a.m. on summer mornings, while at midnight it was still light. Meanwhile, in the Eastern zone as a whole, Sovietization proceeded rapidly. Early in the occupation, the Soviet Union drew from Germany some 500 million dollars a year—a striking contrast with the 700 million dollars that the United States and Britain were paying in. But not content with official reparations, the Soviet authorities amalgamated two hundred firms into large state corporations, *Sowjetische Aktiengesellschaften*, whose output they could freely exploit since they held fifty-one per cent of the shares. By mid-1946, in these and other ways, they expropriated 7,000 factories. In a drastic land reform, East Germany's large estates were broken up, and 400,000 peasants became small-holders with farms of seventeen to twenty-two acres each. At the same time, party politics in the Eastern zone began to acquire a decisive Soviet stamp. The first order issued by the Soviet Military Administration, on 10 June 1945, authorized four political parties: the Communist KPD, or *Kommunistische Partei Deutschlands;* the Socialist SPD, or *Sozialdemokratische Partei Deutschlands;* the Christian Democrat CDU, or *Christlich-Demokratische Union;* and the Liberal LDP, or *Liberal-Demokratische Partei.* In the West, permission was similarly granted by the Americans, the British, and the French; and in the following winter and spring the SPD, CDU and LDP held their first inter-zonal conferences. The KPD, however, was small; and from the autumn of 1945 onwards, partly at Soviet prompting, it began to press for amalgamation with the SPD. A number of German Socialists, including the concentration camp victim Kurt Schumacher, were supicious of the proposed merger; and on 1 March 1946, a mass meeting in Berlin came out against it. But Otto Grotewohl, the SPD's Berlin leader, had already persuaded his colleagues on the Executive to approve it; and although other Berlin Socialists organized a plebiscite which overwhelmingly opposed it—by eighty-two per cent of the votes—their protest was limited to the Western sectors, since the Russians forbade it in the East. Accordingly, on 21–22 April 1946, the East German SPD merged with the Communist Party in the new Socialist Unity Party, or SED (*Sozialistische Einheitspartei Deutschlands*), with Grotewohl and the Communist Wilhelm Pieck at its head. It was never recognized in the West. For a time, the two groups within it struggled for supremacy; but the Communists, with strong Soviet backing, maintained effective control. They made no pretence of excluding former followers of Hitler: one militant coined the appealing slogan, 'The SED—the great friend of the little Nazi.' Alongside it, paradoxically, the Soviet authorities encouraged the formation of 'anti-Fascist democratic mass organizations' of farmers, youth clubs, trade unions, women and cultural groups. These were openly political. The statutes of the trade union organization, the *Freier Deutscher Gewerkschaftsbund* (FDGB), declared as its aim 'a Socialist structure of society'; but its officials, far from being freely elected, were appointed by the Soviet authorities, then confirmed in office by the bodies that they themselves had set up.[31]

Local elections were held in the Eastern zone in September 1946, eight months after the first vote in the American zone. The SED was allowed to put up candidates in all the 11,623 local communities involved; but the CDU, which was registered in 4,200 of them, was allowed to do so in only 2,082, and the LDP, although registered in 2,200, in only 1,121. Heavy pressure was exerted on CDU leaders, three of whom were forced out of office; and in several areas, non-Marxist meetings were broken up. Partly by these means, the SED won 52·4 per cent of the votes, and the 'mass organizations' 3·3 per cent. Similar tactics were used at the provincial elections held on 20 October 1946: the SED was allotted 900 tons of newsprint for its electoral manifestos, compared with nine tons for the CDU and LDP. Even so, out of the 520 seats in the *Land* assemblies, the SED secured only 249, or 47·6 per cent: votes for the mass organizations brought the Marxist total to 265, or just over 50 per cent, against 133 for the CDU and 122 for the LDP. The precariousness of this qualified victory was made more obvious by the election results in Berlin, where inhabitants of all four sectors voted, under Allied supervision, and where the SPD was still able to put up candidates: here the SED won only 20 per cent of the votes, against 48·7 per cent for the SPD. In the Eastern zone as a whole, the SED now had an absolute majority in two of the five *Länder*–Saxony and Saxony-Anhalt; in Thüringia it had half the votes, and just under half in Brandenburg and Mecklenburg. On this basis, it took five out of nine cabinet posts in Saxony, three out of six in Saxony-Anhalt, six out of nine in Thüringia, three out of six in Brandenburg, and four out of eight in Mecklenburg. In four of the five *Länder*, moreover, it secured the Ministry of the Interior, and thereby controlled the police.[32]

In the West, meanwhile, it had become increasingly clear that the Soviet authorities were not applying the 'all-German' provisions of the Potsdam Agreement. Far from treating Germany as an economic unit, the Soviet Union had been stripping the Eastern zone of resources that should have helped Germany's recovery as a whole. Early in April 1946, General Lucius Clay, US Deputy Military Governor, came to the conclusion that so long as each zone was treated as a separate economic entity, the Americans 'were being placed in the position not only of financing reparations to the Soviet Union but also of agreeing to strip our own zone (which had insufficient industrial capacity for self-support) without getting the benefits which would come from the amalgamation of all zones.' As a second-best solution, he began to envisage economic unity among the Western zones alone. On Friday 3 May 1946, after further arguments, he stopped reparations payments to the East; and shortly afterwards he recommended to Secretary of State James Byrnes that, failing French and Soviet agreement, 'the British be approached to determine their willingness to combine their zone of occupation with ours. If the British are willing for this merger to be accomplished, the French and Russian representatives should be advised that it is our proposal to effect this merger before winter, even though we would much prefer to obtain Allied unity in the treatment of Germany as a whole.' Two months later, on Thursday 11 July 1946, Byrnes announced to the Paris four-power Conference that 'pending agreement among the four powers to implement the Potsdam agreement requiring the administration of Germany as an economic unit, the United States will join with any other occupying government or governments in Germany for the treatment of our respective zones as an economic unit'. On the following morning, the British Foreign Secretary, Ernest Bevin, announced his government's agreement in principle; and after much hard bargaining over relative occupation costs, Britain and the United States concluded a final settlement on Monday 2 December 1946. The 'Bizone'—'Bizonia' to those unafraid of Ruritanian echoes—came into being on New Year's Day, 1947.[33]

In these ways, both the Soviet Union and the Western powers were beginning to take steps, on either side of the East-West border, that ultimately led to the esablishment of two rival German Governments. Formally, each step could be seen as a riposte. Thus, on Thursday 27 February 1947, the Soviet Union lodged a protest against the formation of the Bizone; on Thursday 29 May 1947, after Soviet intransigence at the four-power Moscow Conference in March and April, the British and Americans set up the Bizone's Economic Council of fifty-two delegates from the *Land* assemblies, together with an Executive Committee representing the *Land* governments; in June, the Soviet Union established an East German Permanent Economic Commission (*Ständige Wirtschaftskommission*) of twenty-five members, a majority of them appointed by the Soviet administration, the remainder representing the trade unions and farmers' organizations. In July, the Western powers decided to extend Marshall Aid to their occupation zones of Germany. In December, while a further four-power Conference was still deadlocked in London, the Soviet authorities held the first of a series of German People's Congresses (*Volkskongresse*), composed of 2,215 delegates theoretically representing the whole of Germany—although the Western parties declined the invitation, and the non-Marxist parties in the Eastern zone were outnumbered and outmanoeuvred by the SED.[34]

It was 1948, the year of the Czechoslovak crisis, that saw the most decisive moves. Early in February, the British and Americans proposed that they meet in London with the French to discuss the future of the Bizone. On Monday 9 February, however, without waiting for French agreement, they enlarged its Economic Council to 104 members, and added an upper house, or *Länderrat*, consisting of two governmental delegates from each *Land*; at the same time, they remodelled the Executive Committee, which now grouped the heads of the various administrative agencies. This, as General Clay remarked,

...was a realistic political structure of the federal type even though it had no sovereign powers, was limited in its authority to fiscal and economic measures, and its acts were subject to Military Government approval. There was a legislature, with broad authority in fiscal and economic fields, composed of a lower house, whose members were elected by the state parliaments and were at least indirectly responsible to the people, and an upper house representing the states. There was a chairman of the Executive Committee (roughly, the chairman corresponded to a Prime Minister and the Committee to a Cabinet) responsible to the legislature.... We had the machinery for government, if not a government.

It was completed on the same day by a High Court, and on Monday 1 March 1948, by a central bank, the *Bank Deutscher Länder*, serving all three Western zones. Meanwhile, on Monday 23 February, while the Prague crisis was at its height, the French, British and Americans had begun their meeting in London, behind closed doors at India House at the bottom of Kingsway, where they invited the three Benelux countries to join them. On Saturday 6 March they announced their agreement to establish international control of the Ruhr, 'to guarantee that its economic resources are not used again for aggressive ends, and that satisfactory access to its coal, coke, and steel is ensured in the interest of a large part of the European community, including Germany.' They added that they favoured 'a federal form of Government' as 'the most appropriate to make possible the ultimate re-establishment of German unity.'[35]

The response from the East came quickly. That same day, a Soviet Note of protest was delivered to the British Government; and on Tuesday 9 March it was published by the *Tass* news agency. Next day, the Soviet Union increased the powers of the East German Economic Commission; and on Wednesday and Thursday of the following week, on 17 and 18 March, it held a second People's Congress. This promptly elected a 400-member 'People's Council', which in turn appointed a committee to draft a formal 'All-German' Constitution. Finally, on Saturday 20 March 1948, the previously affable Soviet member of the four-power Control Council in Berlin, Marshal Vassily Sokolovsky, read a long aggrieved statement to his colleagues, interrupted the British representative who began to reply to it, and declared: 'I see no sense in continuing this meeting.' He and the whole Soviet delegation then walked out of the room. There now seemed little hope of an all-German settlement. In practical terms, as General Clay put it, 'the Allied Control Council was dead.'[36]

In London, the Western powers continued their 'semi-official' talks. At length, on Tuesday 1 June 1948, the conference ended; and on the following Monday, 7 June, its conclusions were published. They recommended not only the establishment of an International Authority for the Ruhr, but also the formation of a German Constituent Assembly, whose members were to be elected by each of the Western *Länder* according to whatever procedure its legislative body chose. The Constituent Assembly was to draw up a Constitution which, in the words of the Allied communiqué,

... should contain such provisions as will enable the Germans to contribute to putting an end to the present division of Germany, not by the reconstruction of a centralized *Reich* but by the adoption of a federal form of government which satisfactorily ensures the protecton of the different States' rights while providing for sufficient central authority and guaranteeing individual rights and liberties.

The Constitution was to be submitted to the Commanders-in-Chief, who would verify its conformity to these principles; it was then to go to the various *Länder* for ratification. On 20 June, moreover, the Western Allies issued a new West German currency, the *Deutsche Mark*, which was exchanged at the rate of one DM for ten old *Reichsmark*—later reduced to 6·5 DM for 100 RM. Everyone was allowed, however, to exchange forty of his RM for forty DM, with the promise of a further twenty DM for twenty RM two months later. The instant result was a brief orgy of spending, and a renewed faith in paper money after years of quasi-barter in which cigarettes had been the hardest currency. Ludwig Erhard, the heavily-built Bavarian who as the Bizone's Director for Economic Administration had played a large part in the currency reform, shortly afterwards removed a number of price restrictions— rather startling the Allies. 'It was strictly laid down by the British and American control authorities,' he confessed later, 'that permission had to be obtained before any definite price changes could be made. The Allies never seemed to have thought it possible that someone could have the idea, not to alter price controls, but simply to remove them.' Helped by Allied appropriations and by already increasing production, these measures triggered off rapid economic growth. In 1946, the Western zones of Germany had produced thirty-three per cent of their 1936 total: by mid-1949 the proportion had risen to ninety per cent.[37]

When currency reform had first been mooted, the Soviet Union had toyed with the notion of using the new *Deutsche Mark*, and had asked the Americans for a set of printing plates. Warned by a previous experience, when the Russians had failed to account for the Allied 'military Marks' that they had printed from duplicate plates, General Clay refused their request. He proposed instead that the printing works, in the American sector of Berlin, be placed in an enclave under four-power control; but this, in turn, was rejected by the Russians. Instead, they responded with a separate currency reform in East Germany, a walk-out from the four-power *Kommandatura*, and a land blockade of the city of Berlin.[38]

Berlin had felt pinpricks earlier. On 15 December 1947, the Soviet Military Administration had begun to require permits for motorized travel into the city; on 18 January 1948, the Soviet Commandant had prohibited the transfer of property between the sectors; on 23 February, the Soviet authorities had cut by one-fifth the number of permits for goods trucks between Berlin and the West. On 29 March, they announced that from 1 April onwards permits would be required for Allied troop movements, and that private baggage would be checked. In May, the formalities were made more complex; on 10 June, civilian traffic between Berlin and the West was suspended for two days. Now, at 6.00 a.m. on Thursday 24 June 1948, all rail traffic was stopped. Shortly, the ban was extended to canal and highway traffic. By 4 August, Berlin was in a state of siege.[39]

When the blockade began, the two-and-a-half million civilians in West Berlin had food stocks for thirty-six days and coal stocks for forty-five days. Any new supplies would now have to come by air. To withstand the siege, it was estimated, Berlin would need a daily airlift of at least 4,500 tons. The United States had on hand just over one hundred twin-engined transport and troop-carrying aircraft of $2\frac{1}{2}$ tons capacity each, some of them already elderly; the British had fewer; the French had none. To meet the target with existing resources, every aircraft would have had to make the impossible total of a dozen flights a day. Nevertheless, hopeless as it seemed, the airlift began on Friday 25 June, the day after the rail blockade. By Thursday 22 July, when Clay reported to President Truman in Washington on the progress of operations, fifty-two C-54 and eighty C-47 aircraft were making two round trips daily; but they could carry only 2,400–2,500 tons a day. Truman asked Clay what risks might be involved in sending in armed land convoys. The Russians' initial reaction, Clay answered, would be to put up road blocks; and if these were dismantled, they might then resort to force. They would not, he thought, attack Allied planes with fighters; but when he asked for additional aircraft, the President's Air

Force advisers hesitated: they were anxious not to weaken Allied air strength if the Soviet Union were really bent on war. Wisely, Truman agreed with Clay in thinking that the blockade was not, as many imagined, the prelude to hostilities. He gave orders for continuing talks with the Russians and for rapid expansion of the airlift. By 20 August 1948, it was carrying 3,300 tons a day, with 4,575 tons as its biggest daily load. By 9 September, the average was 4,000 tons; by December it had reached 4,500 tons; by February 1949 it had risen to 5,500 tons; and by the Spring, it had attained 8,000 tons—as much as had previously been brought in by rail and water. On one record day, the airlift delivered nearly 13,000 tons of food, fuel, goods and raw materials.[40]

It was during these anxious months that the United States took a further decisive step in its progressive involvement with Western Europe, following the Truman Doctrine and the Marshall Plan. On Wednesday 17 March 1948, shortly after the Czechoslovakia crisis, on the same day that Britain, France and the Benelux countries signed the Brussels Treaty, President Truman hailed their newly created 'Western Union' as 'a notable step in the direction of unity in Europe for protection and preservation of its civilization'. 'This development,' he added, 'deserves our full support ... I am sure that the determination of the free countries of Europe to protect themselves will be matched by an equal determination on our part to help them to protect themselves.' He therefore urged Congress to provide for universal military training and a restoration of selective service. A few weeks later, on Friday 23 April, Ernest Bevin sent to Washington a top-secret telegram in effect proposing a North Atlantic security system; and on Tuesday 6 July, his hand strengthened by Arthur H. Vandenberg's Senate Resolution in favour of regional arrangements 'based on continuous and effective self-help and mutual aid', Truman's Under-Secretary of State Robert A. Lovett began secret talks with the Washington Ambassadors of Canada and the Brussels Treaty powers. In February 1949 these talks became formal negotiations and on Monday 4 April 1949 the North Atlantic Treaty was signed by the United States, Canada, Belgium, Denmark, France, Iceland, Italy, Luxembourg, the Netherlands, Norway, Portugal and the United Kingdom. Its essential provision was that all its signatories agreed 'that an armed attack against one or more of them shall be considered an attack against them all'. Its essential significance was that the United States had turned its back on the concept of 'Fortress America'. As Paul-Henri Spaak, later to be NATO Secretary-General, put it, 'the Monroe Doctrine was abandoned; American isolationism was dead.[41]

The almost immediate sequel to the Atlantic Pact, if not necessarily its consequence was that the Soviet Union called off the Berlin blockade.

Firmness and moderation, backed by the airlift's display of wealth and resources, had worked. On Wednesday 4 May 1949, the four occupying powers announced that it would end on Thursday 12 May. Until the last moment of the long negotiations preceding this agreement, the Soviet Union had insisted that the Western powers cease their efforts to establish a West German Government; now, it no longer made this a prior condition. Stalin recognized, no doubt, that on both sides of the East-West border the State-making process had passed the point of no return.

On Sunday 8 May 1949, in fact, the West German Constituent Assembly —renamed the 'Parliamentary Council'—adopted the Constitution, renamed the 'Grundgesetz' or 'Basic Law'; on Thursday 12 May the Allied Military Governors provisionally approved it; and in the following week it was ratified by all the Länder Assemblies with the exception of Bavaria, which would have preferred a looser confederation, but agreed to abide by the majority's decision.[42]

Almost simultaneously, on Sunday and Monday 15 and 16 May, the third East German People's Congress approved the draft Constitution submitted to it by the People's Council on the previous 19 March. This particular Congress had been voted in by what were described as 'universal, secret and direct elections'; but these had been held on the basis of a single joint list of candidates put up by the SED, the mass organizations, and the East-zone CDU and LDP. It was impossible to choose between parties, and even between candidates. In fact, 37·2 per cent of the electorate rejected the joint list; but the SED was assigned 90 seats, the mass organizations 126, and the CDU and LDP 45 each, while 15 each went to two new groups, the National Democratic Party and the Agrarian Party. Thus assembled, the Congress approved the draft Constitution, and appointed a new People's Council, seventy of whose members were deemed to represent West Germany.[43]

On Monday 23 May 1949, the West German Parliamentary Council held its last meeting, and proclaimed the adoption of the Basic Law. While the Western occupying powers made their final arrangements, drawing up an Occupation Statute to regulate their remaining duties and amalgamating the three zones under an Allied High Commission, the West Germans themselves prepared for their first postwar election. This was held on Sunday 14 August 1949, and 78·5 per cent of those eligible actually voted: of the 402 seats in the lower house, the Bundestag, the CDU won 139, the SDP 131, the Free Democratic Party 52, and the Communists and regional parties 80. On 12 September, the Parliament elected Theodor Heuss of the FDP as Federal President, and he in turn proposed as Chancellor Konrad Adenauer, former Mayor of

Cologne, who was elected by a one-vote majority, having character-istically voted for himself.[44]

On Friday 7 October 1949, without any pretence of elections, the East German People's Council set itself up as a 'Provisional People's Chamber' (*Volkskammer*) and promulgated the new Constitution. Three days later, the Eastern *Land* Assemblies selected delegates to a second legislative chamber, the *Länderkammer*; and on 11 October, at a joint meeting, the two houses elected as President of the Republic the Communist leader Wilhelm Pieck.[45]

In this way, by a fatal leapfrog process, the Eastern and Western parts of Germany moved towards separate statehood. Both the Soviet Union and the Western powers claimed that the administrative apparatus which they were respectively assembling would be suitable for the whole of Germany; but each reflected the political conceptions of its sponsors, and each move inevitably hardened the East-West division. Neither side was necessarily insincere: but what was at issue was a question of ideology, confused with a problem of power politics. The Soviet Union was primarily anxious to impose its own Marxist order on Germany, as on the rest of Eastern Europe; it was also concerned to build a buffer between itself and the West, and perhaps to recruit the resources of Germany as a whole. The Western powers hoped to install and instil Western concepts of democracy; but they also hoped to build a bulwark against the East, and to have Germany make her essential contribution to Western Europe's well-being, as later to its defence. As so often in the past, Germany was still thought of—by both sides—as part-threat, part-ally and part-prey. Which side the Germans themselves preferred was suggested by the 1½ million refugees who crossed from the East zone to the West between 1945 and September 1950;[46] but during all this time, despite the very real differences between the Eastern system of centralized, bureaucratic and pitiless 'People's Democracy' and the federal, liberal, democratic organization of West German capitalism, there remained one feature in common between East and West. The Germans, on both sides of the border, were still an object of policy; they had not yet recovered full political stature. As time went on, and as West Germany in particular grew richer, this situation became too paradoxical to last.

CHAPTER EIGHT

Europe and the Islands

The Summer holds: upon its glittering lake
Lie Europe and the islands...
W. H. Auden[1]

The waters of the Channel have run for too many years in
our blood. *William Golding*[2]

The Sage is full of anxiety and indecision in undertaking
anything, and so he is always successful. *Chuang-tzu*[3]

It is easier to induce nations to discuss problems than to
discuss politics... The only way to promote unity is to
induce people to concentrate on problems with which they
are economically confronted. *Ernest Bevin*[4]

THE Preamble to the 'Basic Law' of the German Federal Republic declared that the West German people was resolved not only 'to preserve
its national and political unity', but also 'to serve the peace of the world
as an equal partner in a united Europe'.[5]

This statement was less simple than it seemed. For many, a 'united
Europe' no doubt meant a Europe including the countries of the East.
If all of Europe were to achieve 'unity', this would help restore the
unity' of the German people, although in the two contexts the same
word meant different things. For others, 'Europe' in 1948 and 1949
already meant 'Western Europe'. Some, perhaps, saw Western European
unity as a substitute ideal to placate the Germans, robbed of national
unity; some as a means of strengthening the West with German resources, and anchoring to it the new-born Federal Republic; some as a
means of taming Germany, dissolving in a broader unit the renascent
national identity already implicit in the Basic Law's reference to 'an
equal partner'.

Most of these unstated interpretations, however, were open to question; and none of them adequately conveyed the emotional force of
'the European idea'. 'Europe'—if only as a hope of transcending
narrow national frontiers—had especial appeal to the Germans, who

had so recently explored the dark excesses of Hitler's nationalism; but others had shared very similar or worse experiences. They had seen the misery, destruction, chaos, poverty and weakness to which unbridled national sovereignty could lead. Many were determined, in varying degrees and sometimes inexplicitly, to introduce into the relations between their countries some civilizing influence like that exerted by laws and institutions within the nation-state itself. They also realized, however obscurely, that only by acting together—and perhaps only by uniting—could European countries ever recover that influence in the world that had passed, now, to the super-powers, the United States and the Soviet Union, with the People's Republic of China, still distant, just visible on the horizon. It was no coincidence that the postwar constitutions of both France and Italy also envisaged the limitation of national sovereignty. 'On conditions of reciprocity,' said the Preamble to the Constitution of the Fourth Republic, 'France will accept the limitations of sovereignty necessary to the organization and defence of peace.' 'Italy,' stated Article 11 of her 1947 Constitution, '. . . agrees, in conditions of parity with other States, to the limitations of sovereignty necessary to an order that will ensure peace and justice among Nations.' And if such pledges of principle could be made by written constitutions, practical plans and projects abounded elsewhere.[6]

'The European idea' had a venerable history, and had acquired many meanings at different times. The classical world had left on the notion of Europe the twin imprints of Greek philosophy and Roman law; Christianity had sanctified it; the medieval Empire and the Papacy had endowed it with largely misleading analogies; the Crusades had stiffened its pride and solidarity; post-medieval nostalgia and the search for perpetual peace had spawned some premature utopias; cosmopolitan culture had coloured it; the United States' example had inspired it, and Napoleon partly perverted it; Romanticism, nationalism, international Socialism and trade unionism, nineteenth-century federalism—all had contributed to the shades of meaning and connotation that the word 'Europe' inspired. There had been innumerable proposals, some harebrained, for Europe-wide States, Republics, Federations, Assemblies, Senates, Councils, Diets, Tribunals, Armies: the panoply of the *ancien régime* had been invoked to build a new international order. With the exception of the Memorandum put forward in 1930 by Aristide Briand, the French Prime Minister, it was only during and after World War II that European unity potentially became a matter of practical politics. Statesmen like Winston Churchill, Charles de Gaulle, Pope Pius XII,

Paul-Henri Spaak, Alcide De Gasperi, Robert Schuman, Johan Willem Beyen, Konrad Adenauer, Joseph Bech; Resistance leaders like Ernesto Rossi, Altiero Spinelli, Henri Frenay, Eugen Kogón, Hendrik Brugmans, Alfred Mozer; writers like Albert Camus, George Orwell, Denis de Rougemont; tireless publicists like Count Coudenhove-Kalergi—all urged, and many helped to organize, efforts to establish what Churchill memorably called, in a speech at the University of Zurich on Thursday 19 September 1946, 'a kind of United States of Europe'. Support for the idea came from many countries and most parts of the political spectrum. 'Europe', like 'unity', covered a multitude of senses; and Churchill himself was badly misunderstood by those who imagined that he proposed to include Great Britain in his European United States. At the time, however, action seemed more important than exegesis. In the winter of 1947, a number of separate organizations together set up an International Committee of the Movements for European Unity, led by Joseph Retinger, who had been right-hand man to the London Polish leader General Wladyslaw Sikorski. The Committee proceeded to organize a full-scale 'Congress of Europe' in The Hague from 7 to 10 May 1948. This brought together more than 750 statesmen, who called for political and economic union in Europe, a European Assembly and a European Court of Human Rights. There followed some weeks of frenzied backstage lobbying, during which Retinger and the national delegations pressed their governments for action on the Resolutions. France and Belgium, in particular, expressed interest; Clement Attlee, the British Prime Minister, was reluctant to commit himself at this stage. Eventually, on Tuesday 20 July, the French Foreign Minister Georges Bidault, who had attended the Hague Congress, put forward some of its proposals officially at the second session of the Consultative Council of the five-nation Brussels Treaty.[7]

What Bidault proposed was a customs and economic union among the Brussels Treaty powers and any others that wished to join them, together with a consultative European Assembly to advise the Governments on this task. Initially, the proposal made no headway, especially with Ernest Bevin, the British Foreign Secretary, who said that he was anxious about likely Communist members of such an Assembly, and would therefore prefer it to be unofficial—a club that could blackball whomever it wished. On the following day, the organizers of the Hague Congress asked each of the five Brussels powers to receive a small delegation to discuss the question. Ten days later, Bevin answered that pending further study he saw no point in an interview at the present time.

The French, however, kept up the pressure. On 28 July 1948, the Foreign Affairs Committee of the National Assembly called on the

Government to convene the European Assembly proposed by the Hague Congress, so that it might among other things prepare a draft federal constitution for Europe. On 18 August, a new French cabinet quickly gave its backing, not to this suggestion, but to a further Memorandum from the Hague Congress organizers. While admitting that 'until such time as the nations should decide to transfer some part of their sovereign rights to an international European authority, the Assembly could have no legislative or executive powers', this Memorandum distantly envisaged such an authority, and called for the Assembly to be established with all possible speed. But despite French acquiescence, the British still hung back. On 2 September, they circulated an eleven-point questionnaire whose tone was cold, sceptical and scathing: it asked, for example,

Are the [Assembly] delegates to represent the views of the Parliaments or the Governments? If the former (as the memorandum suggests) in what sense are they delegates, since the Parliaments have no corporate views on the issue nor any machinery for giving instructions to delegates? Moreover, if the delegates cannot speak for the Governments, what is expected of the Preparatory Conference and why indeed are Governments being consulted?

Reading such words more than twenty years later, one can hardly wonder at the now outmoded stereotype of the British as both insular and arrogant.[8]

On 30 September 1948, the French Government essayed some answers to the British queries; and it reaffirmed that while the proposed Assembly might ultimately become a legislature, for the present it would have a purely consultative role. If this principle were accepted now, some of the points of detail raised by the British—on whether or not overseas dependencies should be governed nationally or jointly, or whether European states should still be represented nationally at the United Nations—could reasonably be dealt with later. On 7 October, the British complained that their questions had still not been precisely answered; but at length, in the last week of October, they at least agreed to set up a committee to study further steps. There were, said Bevin, three major problems: first, 'a feeling of hesitation at the prospect of being united with the Continent without taking the Commonwealth into account'; secondly, 'the question of sovereignty' which 'seemed to his Government a particularly delicate one'; and thirdly, the 'differences between the political systems of the five countries'. Robert Schuman, the French Foreign Minister, was quick to reassure him that the French had similar anxieties, and he once more stressed the proposed Assembly's consultative status.[9]

The Study Committee accordingly met in Paris from 24 November 1948, to 15 December, when it presented several alternative proposals. The French and Belgians, in particular, favoured a Consultative Assembly of parliamentarians alongside a Committee of Ministers: but on Tuesday 18 January 1949, having asked for a twelve-day postponement of the Committee's New Year meeting, the British delegation, led by Hugh Dalton, abruptly proposed that 'the Committee of Ministers already suggested be supplemented not by an assembly but by an inter-governmental conference of delegates at which all the delegates from one country should be nominated by its government and should cast a single bloc vote.' Amid general consternation, the discussions broke down; the whole question, it was agreed, must be referred to the Council of the Brussels Treaty powers, due to meet in London at the end of the month.[10]

Opening the London meeting, Bevin did his best to explain the British proposal. What Whitehall feared were 'conflicts of competence ... between an Assembly adopting resolutions which might endanger the work of responsible bodies with well-defined tasks.' 'A free Assembly', as he aptly called it, might tread on the toes of OEEC and thereby risk 'conflicting with the concrete work of the Governments'. Unless there were bloc voting, finally, might not the votes in the Assembly run counter to national policy? To meet the first of these points, Schuman suggested that governments should control the Assembly's agenda; on the question of voting he pleaded for a flexible, pragmatic approach. After further discussion, the procedure for appointing delegates was left to each individual government; with the Ministerial Committee enjoying the right of veto on the Assembly's agenda, the proposal for bloc voting was dropped. On Monday 7 March 1949, the Brussels Treaty powers convened a conference to which they also invited Denmark, Norway, Ireland, Italy and Sweden. On Tuesday 3 May the Foreign Ministers of the ten countries met at St James's Palace, London, and two days later they formally agreed on 'The Statute of the Council of Europe'. Its main feature, they declared, was

... the establishment of a Committee of Ministers and of a Consultative Assembly, which together will form from the Council of Europe. Of these two bodies, the Committee of Ministers will provide for the development of co-operation between Governments, while the Consultative Assembly will provide a means through which the aspirations of the European peoples may be formulated and expressed, the governments thus being kept continually in touch with European public opinion.[11]

The fanfare was encouraging; and for a while its promise seemed to be kept. The Assembly met in Strasbourg on Wednesday 10 August 1949, and elected as President the eloquent, sometimes ebullient Paul-Henri Spaak. At the end of the session he declared: 'I came to Strasbourg convinced of the need for a United States of Europe. I leave with the certainty that union is possible.' Yet two years later Spaak was to resign from the Presidency in disillusion and disgust. 'If a quarter of the energy spent here in saying No,' he thundered at the Assembly, 'were used to say Yes to something positive, we should not be in the state we are in today.' Nearly two decades afterwards, looking back on his experience in the Committee of Ministers, he wrote: 'Of all the international bodies I have known, I have never found any more timorous or more impotent.'[12]

Spaak's strictures were not entirely fair. The Council of Europe was the first European organization to be avowedly political. Its Assembly's members were, in the end, appointed by parliaments; they sat in the Chamber not by national delegations, but in alphabetical order of their surnames; they were not obliged to vote in blocs. With the help of a dedicated permanent Secretariat, the Council performed—and still performs—many valuable, unsung technical tasks. The European Convention for the Protection of Human Rights, and its European Court, form a lasting monument to one of its political aims. Yet, all the same, the corridors of the *Maison de l'Europe* were paved with good intentions as much as with brown linoleum: essentially, it was to be a house of disappointed hopes. Emasculated even before the negotiations that established it, the Assembly never acquired the legislative status that the French had ultimately promised and the British immediately feared; the Committee of Ministers, empowered only to make recommendations to the member governments, was further hamstrung by its practice of taking decisions unanimously even in those few cases where this was not the rule. It was hardly surprising, with such a structure, that the Council of Europe failed to achieve the European political union that had been the goal of the Hague Congress. The truly effective thrust in this direction had to come indirectly; and it came, not from Strasbourg, but from the opposite side of France.[13]

Cognac is not only a brandy; it is also a town of some 21,000 inhabitants on the Charente river, roughly halfway between Angoulême and the Atlantic estuary of the Gironde. For centuries it has lived on brandy and the salt trade; near the stills and warehouses, especially along the river front, the walls are black with microscopic fungus caused by the alcohol fumes. It is a solid, hard-working French provincial town, quiet and modest, but well-to-do and fundamentally self-assured. It rather resembles its most distinguished citizen—Jean Omer Marie Gabriel Monnet.

Jean Monnet was born in Cognac on Friday 9 November 1888. His grandfather was a farmer who became Mayor and lived to the age of 102; his father, Jean Gabriel Monnet, founded the brandy firm that bears his name. Monnet, like his brother Gaston, was trained for the family business; at the local *lycée* he took only the first part of his *bachot*, and never went on to a university. Instead, he set out at eighteen as a brandy salesman in the Canadian backwoods, along the Vancouver railroad in boom towns like Calgary, Moose Jaw and Medicine Hat. It was there that he learned his clipped, North-American English; he learned also to appreciate transatlantic informality. One day in Calgary, when he was looking for a horse and buggy to hire, he asked a stranger for the nearest livery stable. 'Can you ride?' asked the stranger. 'Then take my horse. When you're through just hitch it up here.' This, said Monnet later, was his first lesson in the international pooling of resources.[14]

He began to apply it early in World War I. Returning to France via London, he discovered from friends in the City that Britain and France, although allies, were bidding against each other for scarce raw materials. Back in Cognac, he persuaded an influential local lawyer to introduce him to the Prime Minister of France, René Viviani. With all the assurance of his twenty-six years, Monnet urged that the Allies should set up a joint procurements system. Viviani agreed, and asked Monnet to help with the job. Already refused for military service on account of kidney trouble, he leapt at the offer, and became an official of the French Board of Trade. After two years of persistent argument, France and Britain at last set up a joint supply commission, on which Monnet himself served. By the end of the war he had made his reputation. In 1919, at the age of thirty-one, he was asked by the two Governments to become Deputy Secretary-General of the newborn League of Nations.[15]

At the League, he learned a further lesson. Raymond Poincaré, the new French Premier, believed that the only way to prevent a further war was to keep the defeated enemy under Allied domination. Monnet disagreed fundamentally, and said so. Only as equals, he thought, could nations learn to trust one another; there must be rules to guarantee their equality and institutions to see that the rules were kept. The League, as he saw it, was only a 'switchboard' keeping nations in touch with each other; and it was hampered by the unanimity rule. In 1923, Monnet resigned and went back to the family business, which was now in low water. Within two years its affairs were once more prospering.[16]

From then on, Monnet pursued a very varied international career. For a while, he worked as an associate of the Blair Foreign Corporation in New York; on its behalf he went to Warsaw to advise the Polish Government and to Bucharest to help in the stabilization of the Rumanian currency. He also became Vice-President of the Transamerica holding company, which owned the Bank of America. He made a fortune on Wall Street, then lost it in the 1929 crash. Next, the Swedish Government asked him to wind up the Kreuger match empire. It was at this time that he met and eloped with Silvia de Bondini, the painter wife of an Italian diplomat; later, he married her after a lightning Moscow divorce. In 1933 and 1934 he spent two years in China as a financial adviser, helping to reorganize the railways: to recruit nervous capital, he set up the China Finance Development Corporation, in which London, New York, Paris and Shanghai financiers were willing to stake money together and on an equal footing—whereas none would have done so on a majority basis or, less still, alone.[17]

In March, October and December 1938, and again in January 1939, Monnet went to the United States on confidential missions for the French Government, which was anxious to buy American military aircraft. When World War II broke out on 3 September 1939, he remembered his World War I experience; on that same day he sent a note to Premier Edouard Daladier proposing that France and Britain pool their supplies from the outset. Within three months, his efforts succeeded; and he himself was appointed Chairman of the Franco-British Committee for Economic Co-ordination. As R. A. Butler, then Under-Secretary of State for Foreign Affairs, told the House of Commons on 30 November 1939, Monnet had become 'the first inter-Allied official'. In this role, he ironed out many anomalies: at one point, French agents were found to have been bidding for Australian tallow against the British Ministry of Food, which itself had been bidding on behalf of France. At the same time, he went on asking questions. How many aircraft did the Allies need to match the *Luftwaffe*? How many could they build? How many should they buy in the United States? The questions were simple; but nobody knew the answers. So Monnet set out to supply them, and on that basis to have planes and engines ordered in the United States. This was the key that unlocked the American arsenal—and it had one unexpected result. At 3.00 a.m. on 17 June 1940, just before the fall of France, her representative in Washington signed over to Britain, for the token sum of one dollar, the whole French share of these American contracts. They proved invaluable later in helping Britain to withstand the Blitz.[18]

Meanwhile, during the anxious days of May and early June, 1940,

Monnet had proposed to Winston Churchill and General de Gaulle an even more radical form of international pooling—political union and joint citizenship between Britain and France. It came within a few hours of succeeding; and even when failure seemed inevitable, Monnet made a last-minute effort to persuade France to agree. Borrowing a British aircraft, he flew to Bordeaux, where the Government had taken refuge. His plane—the Sunderland flyingboat *Claire*—was big enough to carry the French Cabinet to London or North Africa; but for fear of being branded as cowardly *émigrés* or even dupes of Churchill, its members refused to leave under a British flag. Looking back three years later, in Washington, Monnet said: 'Think what it would have meant if the political offer of union had succeeded. There would have been no way of going back on it. The course of the war, the course of the world, might have been very different. We should have had the beginnings of a union of Europe.'[19]

As it was, Monnet returned to London with his flying-boat full of refugee families. He might at this point have joined General de Gaulle's Free French movement; but since Britain and America were now the essential bastions of the Allied cause, he preferred to work directly with them. With a French passport personally endorsed by Churchill, Monnet went to Washington as a British civil servant, a member of the British Supply Council. There, he played an important part in devising Roosevelt's 'Victory Program' of aircraft production, and was credited with the invention both of the slogan 'the arsenal of democracy' and of Lend-Lease. After Washington, he went to Algiers. There, he helped to reconcile General de Gaulle and General Giraud; he also became a member of the French National Liberation Committee. It was at this time that he first proposed to de Gaulle the project with which many Frenchmen still most closely associate him: the 'Monnet Plan' for the postwar modernization of France. Hitherto, much of his work had been international, trying to persuade governments to see their problems as common problems, to pool their resources and tackle together tasks that none of them could accomplish alone. Now, he hoped to apply the same principle on a national scale, bringing employers, workpeople, and government officials together round the table to work out joint targets for French recovery and growth.[20]

In 1946, appointed as France's first *Commissaire au Plan*, with modest offices in the rue Martignac administratively attached to the Prime Minister and to no one else, Monnet became for the first time rather more than a grey eminence. His small group of colleagues and assistants— men like the engineer Etienne Hirsch, the economist Pierre Uri, the rising civil servant Paul Delouvrier—formed a close-knit and mutually complementary team; many of them were to follow him in later European ventures; almost all became personal friends. All were more 'brilliant' than Monnet: but it was he who left the most lasting impression—and it was he who got things done. As a young man, he had looked un- mistakably Latin, a short, rather stocky, well-dressed figure with a dark, slightly saturnine moustache. Now, at fifty-eight, the moustache was greyer; his face was ruddy, and his watchful, hooded eyes twinkled readily under eybrows that seemed always to be impassively raised. Chiang Kai-shek had once said that there was something Chinese about Monnet; and he had certainly learned something from his days in China. A friend who lived there had advised him: 'Stop trying to understand these people—you never will. Just stick to what you want, and make your actions conform with your words.' Monnet did. He was also, still, something of a French peasant: wherever he worked, he preferred to live in the country. Outside Paris, he had bought an L-shaped con- verted farmhouse with a thatched roof; but the property was marred by an intrusive adjoining field. Monnet's predecessor had tried to buy the field from its peasant owner—but in vain. Monnet was rebuffed also, until he bought a better field elsewhere in the village, and offered it in exchange. His offer was instantly accepted: like had dealt with like.[21]

With it all, Monnet still had something of the international entre- preneur, and a merchant banker's feel and flair. As an orator, he was undistinguished: in large gatherings his small dry voice was lost. But in private he could be immensely persuasive, arguing, cajoling, asking Socratically simple questions, breaking now and then into a sharp stac- cato chuckle, tirelessly repeating his homely maxims. Clear as water, they had the deceptive strength of pure spirit: 'there is no choice'— 'we must go on'—'these are common problems'—'conditions must be changed'. 'Must'—'indispensable'—'rapid'—'concrete'–'immediate': his whole vocabulary breathed action. Action was preceded, invariably, by painstaking inquiry, long hesitation, and discussion with friends and colleagues; but it was marked by a willingness to seize every opportu- nity as soon as it came. Persistent, optimistic and restless, Monnet was unlikely to be content for long to deal only, and in isolation, with the affairs of France.[22]

Already in the later years of World War ɪɪ he had concluded that the United Nations, like the League of Nations, would also be only a 'switchboard': it would involve no real abandonment of sovereignty. 'This,' he said, 'is not going to happen on a world scale ... and let us not blind ourselves this time, by the picture of impressive machinery, to the really tough things that need to be done if we are to have peace.' The journalist who reported these reflections added: 'What are those

tough things? For Monnet, as for most Europeans, the toughest questions of all are Germany and European unity. Monnet would like to see
... the great Rhine coal and iron fields run by a European authority for
the benefit of all participating nations ... But this in turn implies a
Europe far more unified than before the war. Here he would like to
see not merely a "switchboard" association, but a true yielding of sovereignty by European nations to some kind of central union—a union that
could cut down tariffs, create a great internal European market and
prevent that race of nationalism "which is the curse of the modern
world". But where to begin? And how far to go? And could England
be brought in?'[23]

Monnet went on developing these themes in the years immediately
after the war. In private notes and in letters to friends in the French
cabinet, he pointed out that Europe could not rely indefinitely on
Marshall Aid, nor remain forever dependent on America: She must
learn to stand on her own feet. This required a form of collective effort
in which Germany's contribution could safely be included. To expect
it of OEEC, with sixteen separate and sovereign nations, was an illusion.
Only a federation, and one that included Great Britain, could ensure
Europe's rapid recovery and, in the long run, prevent war. It was an
ambitious project; but a start might be made, Monnet thought, if Britain
and France could be induced to act together. Why not begin by applying in the economic field the idea of cross-Channel union that he had
proposed in 1940?[24]

Already in January 1947, when the British and French Governments
were preparing the Dunkirk Treaty that they eventually signed on
4 March, they had set up a permanent joint Economic Committee 'to
study ... the respective reconstruction and modernization plans with
a view to preventing their conflicting with each other'. It had held its
first meeting in Paris on 18–20 January 1947, under the chairmanship of
Hervé Alphand from the French Foreign Office, with Sir Edmund Hall-
Patch at the head of the British delegation. A few days later, Monnet
visited London to talk with British officials; and at the end of April 1947,
he was invited by Sir Stafford Cripps, the Chancellor of the Exchequer,
to a further series of meetings. Afterwards he told *Agence France
Presse:* 'I did not come to London to discuss ways of harmonizing the
French and British economies, because I think that for the moment
there is only the broadest of notions [*il y a une simple vue de l'esprit*],
given present economic circumstances and the impossibility of forecasting now what the economic situation will be in the next few years.
Moreover, the French Plan is a plan for the future, aiming at an effective

increase of our resources, whereas Britain's Plan is so far limited to the allocation of her resources for 1947.'[25]

Nevertheless, close contacts continued, and Monnet did his best to encourage them. On 16 and 17 January 1948, when the French Finance Minister René Mayer met Cripps in London, they issued a joint communiqué announcing that in addition to reviewing the events of the past year they had 'examined together the problems facing them in 1948 with a view to co-ordinating as far as possible their respective policies'. These prospects were dimmed, however, by disagreement over the French devaluation on Saturday 24 January; and although talks were held at intervals on specific points of detail, more ambitious hopes lay dormant until early in 1949. Then, on 20 February, Sir Stafford Cripps visited Paris for discussions with Maurice Petsche, who was now French Finance Minister. Monnet seized the opportunity. On his suggestion, Petsche proposed that the French and British planning authorities jointly examine their respective economic plans. With Petsche's blessing, Monnet went to London to explain his proposal; and by 3 March, when Cripps was again in Paris, it had been accepted. Monnet then invited Sir Edwin Plowden, head of the UK Economic Planning Staff, to come out to Houjarray, the small village forty minutes' drive to the south-west of Paris where he had his country home.[26]

Plowden arrived on the morning of Thursday 21 April 1949, accompanied by his deputy and by Robert Hall, the Head of the Economic Section of the Cabinet Office. With Monnet were Etienne Hirsch, already familiar in wartime London as '*le Commandant Bernard*', and the mercurial Pierre Uri. The advantage of the meeting, as Monnet saw it, was its total informality. Gathered in the long, low, stone-floored drawing-room with its family *bibelots*, its paintings by Madame Monnet, and its tall french windows overlooking the fields towards Rambouillet, it was possible to discuss ideas frankly rather than negotiate from pre-arranged positions. On this friendly basis, Monnet and Plowden reviewed and compared the economic situation in Britain and France, and the plans and problems both governments had before them. Then Monnet turned to the crucial question. What would happen if the French and the British, instead of planning separately, were to draw up a joint plan? How far, in particular, would it be possible to pool the resources of the two countries for the benefit of both?[27]

To do so, Monnet knew, would mean economic as well as psychological change. Trade in Europe was still subject to heavy national controls and restrictions; and while these could hardly yet be dismantled entirely, owing to the dollar shortage, those between Britain and France would have to go if the two were to combine their resources. If they did, they might establish between them an economic union which other European countries could later join.

At this point, at first almost imperceptibly, a basic misunderstanding began to take shape. Perhaps Monnet was at fault in not making his project clear enough; perhaps his visitors found it hard to grasp its radical implications. Whatever the explanation, while Monnet was proposing a general objective and a principle, the British characteristically began discussing details and facts. Britain lacked food; France lacked coal. Could each not help to supply the other's needs?

The idea was reasonable and practical. It might well have formed part of an overall joint plan for the two economies, such as Monnet had in mind. He agreed with Plowden that they should exchange information, and study what could be done. The results, however, were disappointing. Without joint action on economic policy generally, trade by itself ran into difficulties. On 18 September 1949, Britain devalued the pound by 30·5 per cent; and although France followed suit on 19 September, the franc's parity dropped by only 22·4 per cent. The resultant discrepancy between the two currencies inflated the price of French exports to Britain, while reducing that of British exports to France. Both sides felt aggrieved, although for formally opposite reasons; the episode not only hampered the proposed exchange of food and fuel, but also weakened mutual trust. By the end of the year it had become obvious, as Etienne Hirsch wrote later, that 'the British Government was not interested in drawing up a joint plan for France and Britain, but only in a more extensive exchange of goods along traditional lines.'[28]

World events, meanwhile, were giving a new urgency to the need to unify Europe. On 23 September 1949, President Truman revealed that American experts had detected a nuclear explosion in the USSR; and next day the Soviet Union publicly acknowledged that it now possessed the atomic bomb. The 'cold war' had turned into the 'balance of terror'. Dismayed, resentful, and increasingly nervous, both East and West appeared to be growing resigned to the prospect of real war: instead of preparing for a more hopeful future, both seemed to be hypnotized by precautions against disaster. Central to their fears was divided Germany. For the time being, German reunification was impossible, since there was no prospect of agreement between the Soviet Union and the United States; in October 1949 the four occupying powers had once more failed to agree. In this situation, Germans themselves were increasingly restive: in the West, shortly after the August 1949 elections, Chancellor Adenauer had startled a press conference by announcing that the

Federal Republic hoped to join not only the Council of Europe but also the Atlantic Alliance. Under the three-power Occupation Statute, which came into force on 21 September 1949, a number of central questions— including armaments, reparations, decartelization, and foreign policy— were reserved to the Allied High Commissioners; but it was becoming clear that this could hardly last. Already there had been disagreements among the Americans, the French and the British on the International Ruhr Authority: the Americans found it too stringent, the French too lax; the British tried to placate all parties. By the Spring of 1950, more- over, the Americans were pressing hard for a greater German contribu- tion not only to Western Europe's economy, but also to her defence. In mid-April, US Secretary of State Dean Acheson proposed to Britain and France a conference of experts in London to prepare a meeting of mini- sters to be held there on 12 and 13 May. No one knew what might be its outcome; but many feared that the prospect of a re-armed independent West Germany would alarm and provoke the Russians no less than it disquieted the French.[29]

In this uncertain, uneasy and rapidly shifting situation Monnet saw both danger and opportunity. The danger was a further stiffening of 'cold war' attitudes; the opportunity might be to sublimate the German question, as it were, in the beginnings of a united Europe. A small step in this direction could lead to others, at length transforming the whole context of relations between East and West. What was essential was to change the course of events—to stop the drift. Words and plans alone would be ineffective without 'real, immediate, and dramatic action' to replace fear by hope. As usual, Monnet put his thoughts on paper, for himself and for the French Government. In late April 1950, he sent a memorandum to the Prime Minister, Georges Bidault. Then he waited, to give Bidault time to react.[30]

What Monnet urged was 'action on one limited but decisive point'— that the French Government propose 'to place the whole of Franco- German coal and steel production under a common High Authority, in an organization open to the participation of the other countries of Europe'. By this means, five years after the end of the war, Germany would again be treated as an equal; the pooling of basic resources would make war between France and Germany 'not only unthinkable but materially impossible'; the problem of controlling the Ruhr would be dissolved into that of supervising international heavy industry; and the fusion of interests thus achieved could lead to the establishment of 'an economic community', leading toward 'the European federation which is indispensable to the maintenance of peace'. Gradually, one step would lead to another, changing the whole context of the question. At each successive stage, problems that had previously seemed forever insoluble would be seen to have solutions. The essential thing was to start.[31]

This project, like most of Monnet's proposals, was the result of long reflection, debate, and repeated collective drafting; the small circle of those who helped to write it included Hirsch, Uri and Paul Reuter, Professor of Law at Aix and legal adviser to the French Foreign Office. Nor, contrary to common belief, was it entirely novel—even when Monnet himself had broached it in wartime Washington. None other than Leon Trotsky had once suggested that 'the question of the Ruhr, that is of European fuel and metal ... may perfectly well be settled in the framework of a United States of Europe'. And if Monnet had not read Trotsky, he certainly knew of the rather similar ideas put forward by Konrad Adenauer. As long ago as the 'twenties, the future German Chancellor had said that 'a lasting peace between France and Germany can only be attained through the establishment of a community of economic interests between the two countries', and he had drawn up a plan for the integration of German, French and Belgian industry. On New Year's Day, 1949, the Minister-President of North-Rhine/Westphalia, Karl Arnold, had likewise proposed, with CDU backing, 'an association with an international legal status' into which 'Germany would bring the Ruhr, France the ore resources of Lorraine, both of them the Saar, Belgium and Luxembourg their heavy industries'. Adenauer had revived this notion in January 1950 in a conversation with John J. McCloy, the American High Commissioner. Unhappy about the controls still unilaterally imposed on the Ruhr, and about France's intention to continue running the mines in the Saar, he suggested that the produce of both areas be internationalized. On 7 March, four days after the Franco-Saar Conventions which satisfied French demands at the expense of annoying Germany, Adenauer went further. In an interview with Kingsbury Smith, of the American International News Service, he proposed a political union between Germany and France, to be open also to Britain, Italy and the three Benelux countries; and he repeated the idea in further interviews and speeches on 23 March, 2 April and 18 April.[32]

The response, however, had proved disappointing. General de Gaulle, then in opposition and President of the *Rassemblement du Peuple Français*, had certainly hailed the proposal in a press conference on 16 March. 'For thirty years,' he declared, 'I have followed with interest and appreciation the words and deeds of Konrad Adenauer. I see in what this good German says a kind of echo of the appeal of Europe.' But the French Government, perhaps piqued by the fact that Adenauer's suggestions seemed chiefly to be made to Americans, had merely declared its willingness to listen to any 'concrete proposals'.[33]

What was required was action; and this was what Monnet proposed. If his project itself was not new or wholly original, his sense of timing, persuasiveness and persistence were all his own. Now, they were certainly needed. Days passed, and no news came from Bidault. Monnet decided to try another tack. One of his close associates was Bernard Clappier, at that time *Directeur de cabinet* to Robert Schuman, the French Foreign Minister. Schuman, a quiet, shrewd, stooping, rather bookish bachelor two years older than Monnet, came from Lorraine, on the disputed Eastern frontier; he had studied in Germany, and still spoke German fluently; his personal experience, his firm religious faith, and his present responsibilities, all made him likely to be sympathetic to a practical proposal for reconciling Germany and France. Monnet invited Clappier to lunch, and showed him the memorandum to Bidault. Clappier promised to take it to the minister, with a covering note in Monnet's own hand.[34]

Now once again Monnet waited. Schuman had taken the memorandum with him over the weekend of 29–30 April to his rather austere country house—not unlike a very large cottage—at Scy-Chazelles, near Metz. There, in the peace of his study, he read it and reflected. That Sunday, 30 April 1950, he made up his mind. Next day, back in Paris, he telephoned Monnet. 'I accept,' he said; 'For me, it's decided.'[35]

Throughout that week, in consultation with Schuman, Monnet and his colleagues went on putting the finishing touches to the draft text. They also sent a further copy to Bidault, but still he gave no answer; afterwards, the document was found lying in a drawer in his assistant's office. Schuman, meanwhile, wrote a brief introduction, and discussed the plan with other 'Europeans' in the Cabinet, including René Mayer, Minister of Justice, and René Pleven, Minister of Defence. Then, on the morning of Tuesday 9 May 1950, he presented it formally to the Cabinet, which authorized him to proceed. Rather to his colleagues' surprise, he did so rapidly and publicly. That same afternoon, in the gilded Salon de l'Horloge of the French Foreign Office building on the Quai d'Orsay, he read to the press what had now become 'the Schuman Declaration', proposing in effect the European Coal and Steel Community (ECSC), forerunner of the Common Market.[36]

As one of Monnet's staff confessed later, the launching of the Schuman Plan had been something like a conspiracy. Only a few people had been involved in it; and on the evening before Schuman's press conference, most of the preliminary drafts were burned. Stealth and surprise, in Monnet's view, were essential to the project; but it was equally important to ensure its instant acceptance by Germany and support by the United States. To secure Adenauer's agreement, Schuman had sent to him in Bonn, with the utmost secrecy, a private envoy who was also a close personal associate. Not until the morning of 9 May, while the French Cabinet was already in session, did he telephone Schuman to report that his mission was accomplished. Monnet, meanwhile, had kept in close touch with his friends in the American Embassy—David Bruce, the Ambassador, and William Tomlinson, a brilliant young US Treasury official, later to meet a sadly early death.[37]

The British Government, however, had not been let into the secret. Only when the French Cabinet had approved Schuman's proposal was an urgent message sent to London via the French Ambassador, René Massigli, announcing the statement to be made to the press later that day. This caused both embarrassment and annoyance—the former to US Secretary of State Dean Acheson, the latter to Ernest Bevin, the British Foreign Secretary. By a pure coincidence, Acheson had chosen to stop off in Paris on Sunday 7 May 1950, on his way to the London Foreign Ministers' Conference due to begin on the following Thursday, 11 May. Both Schuman and Monnet seized the chance to explain their project to him; and before the French Cabinet had approved it, on the morning of 9 May, he sent an 'eyes only' telegram to President Truman urging that he be authorized to express United States support. Then he left for London, where he was lunching with Ernest Bevin. When he arrived, the news had still not reached Whitehall, so he said nothing to his host. During lunch at Bevin's house, a message arrived from Massigli asking for an appointment with the Foreign Secretary that afternoon. As Acheson realized, it was to announce the Schuman Plan; but he still felt bound to keep the secret. At 4.00 p.m., when they met again, this time at the Foreign Office, Bevin was furious at having been kept in the dark. What was more, in Acheson's words, 'he bristled with hostility to Schuman's whole idea'.[38]

It can be argued that France's—and Monnet's—tactics were partly to blame. Conceivably, had Bevin been consulted earlier, it might have been just possible to launch the Schuman Plan with Britain as a full participant, laying the foundations of the future Common Market on a broader basis than that of its six founder-members. There can be no doubt that the abruptness of the French announcement irritated Whitehall. But fundamental decisions of foreign policy grow from deeper roots than passing irritation; and in the words of Kenneth Younger, who at that time was Minister of State at the Foreign Office, 'the pique was slight and faded quickly'. More important was the suspicion in London that a proposal made so suddenly could hardly be serious. More important still was what Younger himself described as 'a nation-wide attitude which could not be doubted'—a deep British unwillingness to limit national sovereignty by pooling it with that of other countries, especially in continental Europe, at a time when the Atlantic Alliance naturally seemed paramount and the Commonwealth still seemed to preclude any move by Britain towards a European union. Many times in the recent past this attitude had shown itself; and in the light of experience Monnet feared that if Britain had the chance she would automatically, almost innocently, transform the project into something quite different—a traditional, unambitious system of co-operation between independent sovereign states. Robert Schuman was especially sceptical: answering questions at his 9 May press conference, he explained that Britain, like Italy and the Benelux countries, would be invited to join in the project, but that he realized the difficulties, both technical and psychological. He had no idea, he said, what the British reply would be.[39]

The first comments in the British press, on Wednesday 10 May 1950, were very largely favourable. Only the *Daily Express* and the *Daily Worker* dissented—a conjunction of Right-wing and extreme-Left opposition that later grew familiar. But except for *The Economist*, most papers treated the Schuman Plan as economic rather than potentially political, and few called for Britain to take part. Speaking for many, the weekly *Statist* urged that she 'wait and see'. This seemed broadly to be the Government's policy: on 11 May, in the House of Commons, Prime Minister Clement Attlee declared that

... the proposals ... have far-reaching implications for the future economic structure of participating countries; and this aspect will require very careful study by His Majesty's Government and the other Governments concerned. His Majesty's Government will approach the problem in a sympathetic spirit and desire to make it clear at the outset that they welcome this French initiative to end the age-long feud with Germany and so bring unity and peace to Europe.

Next day, the London *Times* published a collective letter urging acceptance of Schuman's proposal. It signatories were members of the British Committee of the European League for Economic Co-operation (ELEC), which had been founded in 1946 by Paul Van Zeeland, former Prime Minister of Belgium: they included Julian Amery, Edward Beddington-Behrens, David Eccles, Bob Edwards, Harry Hynd, Lord Layton, Harold Macmillan and Peter Thorneycroft.[40]

There was some reason for optimism, therefore, when Monnet arrived in London on Sunday 14 May 1950, to talk over the project with Plowden and other British officials. Schuman, meanwhile, had been discussing it with Bevin in the intervals of the three-power Foreign Ministers' Conference. In all these conversations, the British asked a number of technical questions. What would be the position of cartels? Might the Schuman Plan lower the standard of living? How would it affect French planning? Would it affect the ownership of industry? What form would the proposed High Authority take?[41]

To the British, such questions seemed natural: they were astonished at how little concrete detail the Schuman Plan then contained. To Monnet, on the other hand, questions of detail were secondary. He made it clear, in the words of a UK Minute, 'that the French Government felt it desirable that the acceptance by other Governments of the principles set out in the French communiqué of 9th May should precede any working out of the practical application of their proposals.'[42]

Superficially, this looked like continental dogmatism *versus* British pragmatism; but in fact it was an insistence that immediate practical problems should not be allowed to compromise the Schuman Plan's aims and structure. For Monnet, the essential objective was to establish, in a limited field, European rules and institutions binding equally all the participating governments. In the past, Great Britain had resisted all such 'supranationality'; now, it was all the more important to commit her to the common objective lest in discussing the means she lead others —including Germany—to desert the ends. And if she refused that commitment? There had been a time when British refusal might have blocked such projects; but by now that time was past. On Monday 15 May 1950, at an Anglo-French press luncheon, Schuman had declared that France would 'pursue the project with only one other country if necessary'. Sir Stafford Cripps now put the same question to Monnet. He answered that Cripps knew his feelings towards Britain and could not doubt them, but that he himself was convinced that, always a realist, she would adjust to the facts once she saw that the plan was a success. Despite suggestions to the contrary, there can be no doubt that Monnet was sincere.[43]

Monnet left London on Friday 19 May. On the following Tuesday, 23 May 1950, he went with Clappier to Bonn. His first call was on the Allied Control Commission, where he explained the Schuman proposals and announced his intention of going to see Chancellor Adenauer with a view to opening negotiations. The Commission was broadly in agreement; but some of its members were anxious that they should be represented at the talks. This Monnet refused. The reason, as he said afterwards, was very simple: 'one cannot build Europe except on absolute equality and total liberty.' 'There will be a negotiation,' he told the Commission, 'if France and Germany sit as equals round the table without supervision of any kind.' Finally, the Commission relented, and that afternoon Monnet went to see Adenauer. After explaining the project, and securing the Chancellor's formal support for it, Monnet described his visit to London, and repeated the substance of what he had said to Cripps. Although the British had proved rather hesitant, they had the great virtue of being realists. Adenauer agreed that they were people who needed to be given a little time.[44]

Two days later, on Thursday 25 May 1950, Monnet wrote a long explanatory letter to his British friends in the hope of dispelling their anxieties. But time, for Britain, was already running out. That day, the French Government sent London a Memorandum announcing that the Federal German Government had agreed to negotiate on the Schuman Plan and had accepted the terms of a draft communiqué to be published in about a week's time. This declared:

The Governments of . . . are resolved to carry out a common action aiming at peace, European solidarity and economic and social progress by pooling their coal and steel production and by the institution of a new High Authority whose decisions will bind . . . and the countries which will adhere to it in the future.

Negotiations, on the basis of the principles and essential undertakings contained in the French proposals of 9 May last, will open on a date which will be proposed shortly by the French Government, with a view to drawing up a Treaty which will be submitted for ratification to the respective Parliaments.

The draft text, the Memorandum added, had been transmitted to the Belgian, Netherlands, Luxembourg and Italian Governments: the French Government hoped that Britain would also be able 'to participate on the same conditions in these negotiations from the outset'.[45]

By an unlucky coincidence, this message crossed with one from London sent on the same day. In this, Bevin rejected the whole idea of an international conference based on a prior commitment of principle; he proposed instead 'direct conversations between France and Germany' in which the British would like 'to participate from the outset, with the hope that, by obtaining a clearer picture of how the proposals would operate in detail, they would be able to join the scheme'.[46]

When Sir Oliver Harvey, the British Ambassador in Paris, delivered this message to the French Foreign Office, it undoubtedly caused perplexity. Britain's desire to take part in the 'conversations' and her hope of joining the 'scheme' certainly appeared encouraging; but she made no mention of the basic principle and failed, in the words of a probably inspired comment by *Agence France Presse*, 'to take account of a whole series of clarifications on the part of the French'. For the moment, Monnet advised patience. He hoped that his own letter and the French Government's message might in the meantime modify the British stand. They did—but only to harden it. On Saturday 27 May 1950, came a fresh Memorandum from Bevin. 'His Majesty's Government,' it declared,

...wish to reiterate their desire to participate in any discussion which takes place in the manner suggested in my message, and generally to adopt a positive attitude towards the French proposals. It should, however, be realized that if the French Government intend to insist on a commitment to pool resources and set up an authority with certain sovereign powers as a prior condition to joining in the talks, His Majesty's Government would reluctantly be unable to accept such a condition. His Majesty's Government would greatly regret such an outcome.

His Majesty's Government appreciate that it would not now be possible to confine the conversations to a purely Franco-German basis if some of the Governments which have been approached wished to participate on the same basis as the German Federal Government, and, further, that it might be necessary to consult such Governments before agreeing to participation in the discussions of other Governments on a different basis.[47]

The refusal, the tone and the suggestion seemed clear enough. Britain was now categorically rejecting the 'prior condition'; she seemed to resent the speed with which France had approached the other governments; and she still hoped to join the talks 'on a different basis'. And yet, even so, it remained just possible that the breach now widening between Paris and London was due to a simple mistake.

From the French point of view, the 'prior condition' was that those taking part in the talks should agree on what they were about. But this did not mean that every participant would thereby be committing itself, in advance, to pooling resources under the proposed High Authority: only the acceptance of the eventual treaty coud pledge it to that. What was at stake was a commitment of principle, not the signature of a blank cheque. Were the British afraid even to try negotiating such a treaty, for fear of being drawn into entanglements which at present they shunned? Were they over-scrupulously anxious to avoid raising false expectations? Or might they, after further explanation, agree to negotiate on the basis proposed by Monnet and Schuman, and find later that what they had feared was not so formidable after all?

It was a slim hope; but it seemed worth investigating. Next day, although it was a Sunday, René Massigli called on Kenneth Younger at the Foreign Office. 'He asked me,' Younger reported,

...if he was right in thinking that, while we are not prepared to commit ourselves now to the principle of pooling resources under an international authority possessing certain sovereign powers, we are not taking up an attitude of opposition to this principle but are prepared to enter into discussions with the object of findng a practical method of applying the principle.

I told him that I thought that roughly expressed the difference between us. We were certainly not proposing to go to these discussions with our minds set against the principles referred to, but equally we were not prepared to commit ourselves to the principle without a much clearer idea than we have at present about the way in which it is to be carried into effect. The Ambassador said that he had always felt sure that this was our attitude but had thought it better to get it confirmed by me before passing this interpretation to his Government.

He said he found my explanation reassuring since it seemed to him that our reservations would not in any way limit our effective participation in the discussions.

Younger himself, as he afterwards recalled, 'pressed hard for Britain to join the Schuman Plan Conference before finally recognizing that hardly anyone thought the conditions of participation could be accepted.' Bevin's reaction to this advice, according to one story, was: 'Splash about, young man, you'll learn to swim in time.' But even the conversation with Massigli left ambiguities unresolved. When the Ambassador tried then and there to redraft the proposed French communiqué, 'he succeeded in producing something which seemed to me to be on the whole unobjectionable,' said Younger; 'but I told him that if there was to be a single communiqué it would have to explain clearly the attitude of the different Governments.' The gap therefore remained.[48]

Prompted by Monnet, the French Government now made one last attempt to close it. On Tuesday 30 May, Schuman handed to Sir Oliver Harvey an 830-word exegesis of his proposals, pointing out that previous British Notes seemed to have misunderstood the commitment of principle stipulated by the French. This was no mere debating point: at that moment, it was still conceivable that semantics, not policy, divided the two governments. For this reason, the new French Memorandum took great pains to be clear:

The special position in these negotiations which the British Government wishes to preserve is justified in their Memorandum by the intention, said to be held by the French Government, of asking as a prior condition for full participation in the discussions, for an undertaking to pool coal and steel resources, and to set up an authority with certain sovereign powers.

As their representatives have informed the British representatives orally, the French Government wish particularly to confirm once more that these are not their intentions. As has already been made clear in the French Memorandum of 9th May, there will be no commitment except by the signature of a treaty between the States concerned and its parliamentary ratification.

In fact the aim which the French Government proposes is quite different. Knowing the practical difficulties which the discussion will have to surmount, it seems essential that they should constantly be guided by common principles. Only if the negotiations are clearly directed by agreement between participating Governments on the fundamental objectives to be reached, will it be possible to work out quickly the ways and means and the supplementary arrangements necessary for giving effect to M. Schuman's plan of 9 May. That is the meaning which should be given to the word 'undertaking' [engagement] in the second paragraph of the draft communiqué....

To carry out its task, the [High] Authority will act – within the limits of its mandate and subject to possible appeal by Governments – by virtue of a statute which will have been considered by sovereign states and ratified by Parliaments. One of the objects of the negotiations will be to lay down precisely by treaty the conditions under which the Authority shall act, the nature of its powers, and the machinery for appeal. But in order that its work may serve to develop a European community, it is essential that such an Authority should be independent both of Governments and of individual interests. This partial fusion of sovereignty is the contribution which the French proposal makes to the solution of European problems. Public opinion has recognized its importance and its novelty,

The French Government consider that the above explanations will clear up any misunderstanding about the scope of the proposed basis for negotiation. They do not think that there can be any difference of view between them and the British Government on the objectives put forward. They hope now that the British Government will consider it possible to take part in the projected negotiations on the same basis as the other Governments,[49]

All day on Wednesday 31 May 1950, Monnet and Schuman waited to hear how the British Government had reacted to these careful explanations. While they waited, the Dutch Government sent to the French Foreign Office a *note verbale* which cast further light on the point at issue. Basically, it accepted the Schuman Plan and the French draft communiqué as a basis for negotiation. 'Nevertheless,' it added, 'since this text implies the acceptance of certain principles which form the basis of the French Government's Memorandum, the Dutch Government is obliged to reserve the right to retract, during the course of the negotiations, its acceptance of these principles if their application were to prove impossible in practice.'[50]

Superficially, this appeared to confirm and justify British reservations. In reality it did the reverse. On the one hand, it made clear that the Netherlands initially accepted the Schuman Plan's basic principles; on the other, it merely spelled out more explicitly the normal right of withdrawal which, as the latest French note had made plain, was available to any participant in the talks. Would Britain, now, take a similar line?

At 10.00 p.m. that evening, Wednesday 31 May 1950, the answer came. It was as if the British Government had not received, or not understood, the French Note.

> ... It remains the view of His Majesty's Government that to subscribe to the terms of the draft communiqué enclosed in the French Government's Memorandum of 25 May would involve entering into an advance commitment to pool coal and steel resources and to set up an authority, with certain supreme powers, before there had been full opportunity of considering how these important and far-reaching proposals would work in practice. His Majesty's Government are most anxious that these proposals should be discussed and pursued but they feel unable to associate themselves with a communiqué which appears to take decisions prior to, rather than as a result of, intergovernmental discussions.

The Government therefore proposed an addition to the draft communiqué, announcing that

> ... the Government of the United Kingdom will participate in the proposed conversation in a constructive spirit and in the hope that, as a result of the discussions, there will emerge a scheme which they will be able to join. But they cannot at this stage enter into more precise commitment.[51]

Monnet's disappointment on reading these words can easily be imagined. Not only had the forthcoming negotiations become a mere 'conversation' in the British draft, but Britain's refusal to accept their basis was now to be stated in a public communiqué as well as in intergovernmental memoranda. What Britain was asking, once again, was to take part in the negotiations, but 'on a different basis' from that accepted by others. This implicitly denied the principle of equality underlying the Schuman Plan; it also had manifest dangers. 'It is obvious,' wrote Monnet in a confidential note to the French Government,

> that if Great Britain takes part in the negotiations in such a way that she is able not to propose but to dispute the principles themselves, other countries, and particularly Germany, will do the same. ... To accept British participation on these terms is therefore to resign oneself in advance to the replacement of the French proposal by a conception which would be only a travesty of it, and from which all the essential notions would have disappeared.[52]

Even so, Monnet persuaded the French Government to make one more effort. On Thursday 1 June 1950, it proposed to Britain a final revised version of the draft communiqué. Now, instead of stating that 'governments ... *are resolved* to carry out a common action ... *by* pooling

G

their coal and steel production and by the institution of a new High Authority', the draft declared that 'Governments ... *in their determination* to pursue a common action ... *have assigned to themselves as their immediate objective*' the pooling of coal and steel and the establishment of the High Authority. An objective was less binding than a 'resolve', and better expressed the distinction made in the French Note of 30 May. By this time, however, Monnet suspected that this verbal change too might well be lost on its British readers. At all events, the French Government was now explicitly prepared to proceed if necessary without waiting for Britain. For the first time, it now set a firm time-limit to further discussion: when Schuman handed the new Note to Sir Oliver Harvey, he asked that Britain's answer should reach Paris by 8.00 p.m. on the following day, Friday 2 June 1950.[53]

When intergovernmental talks are visibly leading nowhere, there comes a point at which each party begins to think less about the problems at issue than about its own public image. This stage may well have been reached earlier in London than in Paris. Its beginnings can be sensed in the stiff British Memorandum of 31 May, and are also discernible in the French note of 1 June, with its virtual ultimatum. By Friday 2 June 1950, there was little doubt left: both governments were now seeking to justify themselves rather than to convince each other.

That day, the British Government met the French deadline with a counter-proposition—'a meeting of Ministers of the countries interested at which the question of the most effective and expeditious method of discussing the problems at issue could be examined and settled.' In retrospect, it is hard to take the suggestion seriously. What it implied was just such a discussion as Monnet and Schuman feared—calling into question the basic principles which other countries had by this time accepted. First orally, in talks with Sir Oliver Harvey that same Friday, 2 June 1950, then in a written Note on the following morning, the French Government restated its position. The meeting proposed by the British, it argued, 'would have the effect of delaying the opening of the negotiations without offering any real possibility of reconciling divergent points.' With that, there was nothing to do but agree to disagree.[54]

That same day, Saturday 3 June 1950, three separate communiqués were issued. The first was from the governments of France, Germany, Italy and the three Benelux countries, announcing their intention to negotiate on the basis of Robert Schuman's proposals. The second, from the British Government, repeated its refusal to accept that basis for negotiation, recalled its latest counter-proposition, and announced that it was preparing its own 'proposals inspired by the French initiative'— although these, as it turned out, were never to be officially published.

The third communiqué came from the French Government: it promised to keep in touch with the British Government, both to inform it of the progress made and to 'take into account to the greatest possible extent' Britain's point of view, so that Britain might 'have the chance to join or associate itself with the common effort at the time when it judged this to be possible'.[55]

Appearances had been saved; but feelings were undoubtedly ruffled. At one point during the last tense hours of discussion, the British Embassy in Paris had produced a draft communiqué which spoke scornfully of 'international organizations set up with fanfares of trumpets'. Accident, too, had contributed to the difficulties. The weekend of 28 May had been Whitsun; Parliament was in recess; many ministers were out of London; Attlee and Cripps were on holiday—in France; Bevin was ill; and the deputy Prime Minister was Herbert Morrison, no outstanding expert on foreign affairs. Had circumstances been different, Britain might perhaps have joined in the Schuman negotiations on the basis proposed by France. But had she done so, it is hard to believe that she would have stayed to the end—unless the negotiations had failed in their essential object of setting up rules and institutions which, at that time, Britain found too much to accept. Monnet's and Schuman's insistence on the commitment of principle was a gamble; but it would have been an even greater gamble to accept Great Britain's proposals, since in that case the foundations of the European Community might never have been laid at all.

As it was, these few weeks in the Spring of 1950 witnessed momentous decisions, some taken by default. Significantly, the first of the three communiqués issued on 3 June 1950, when subsequently published in a British White Paper, bore the heading 'Six-Power communiqué'. It was the first official appearance of 'the Six'—those six continental countries that were later to form the Common Market. Europe was on the point of being built. For the first time since World War II, an important European initiative was being taken without Britain. Her new isolation was to last for another twenty years.

CHAPTER NINE

The Echternach Dance

All other Errors but disturb a State,
But Innovation is the Blow of Fate.
John Dryden[1]

It is in the nature of progress to appear much greater than
it really is.   *Johann Nestroy*[2]

Politics is the slow public application of reason to the
governing of mass emotion.   *Theodore H. White*[3]

ONE of the attractions of the Grand Duchy of Luxembourg—apart
from its tiny size (1,000 square miles and 350,000 round inhabitants),
its forests and castles and its *truite au bleu*—is an annual procession
held at Echternach near the eastern corner of the country. Here, on
Whit Tuesday, pilgrims gather with brass bands playing to make their
way to the tomb of St Willibrord. Their progress is halting: they move
in a dance rhythm, repeatedly taking five steps forward and three steps
back. It was appropriate that Luxembourg, the home of this sixteenth-
century survival, should become the headquarters of the Schuman Plan,
the first practical move in Europe's equally fitful progress towards unity.
Perhaps it was also appropriate that St Willibrord was British.

Six countries—Belgium, France, Germany, Italy, Luxembourg and
the Netherlands—had accepted the Schuman proposal; and on Tuesday
20 June 1950, their delegations met in Paris to work out its details, in the
same Salon de l'Horloge where Schuman had made the Declaration of
9 May. Although the trappings were traditional this was not in the ordinary sense a negotiation. In the words of the French delegation's official
report: 'It was a joint constructive effort whose aim was not to eliminate disagreements but to solve the multitude of problems ... For the
first time, the participating Governments did not seek a provisional compromise between their respective interests: they took a common view
of their common interests, and their representatives together sought ways

of reaching the goal that they had recognized as valid for all of them.' As Robert Schuman himself put it, 'the six delegations were in some sense allies, pooling their knowledge and their skill.'[4]

It was Jean Monnet, leader of the French delegation and chairman of the Schuman Plan Conference, who made this approach possible. Instead of presenting a merely French point of view, he did his best constantly to identify and defend the common interest. In this respect he foreshadowed the 'supranational' or 'extranational' role to be played later by the High Authority of the Schuman Plan and the Commission of the European Common Market. 'During the nine months that it took to turn the Schuman declaration into a treaty of one hundred articles and a number of annexes,' a Dutch delegate recalled,

he saw to it that neither the central objective, a European Community, nor the proposed method, delegation of powers to common institutions, got lost in the mass of details about coal, steel, scrap, transport, wages, cartels, distortions and discriminations. More than that, he never allowed the negotiations to become negotiations in the traditional sense. Apart from the basic objective and the method laid down in the Schuman declaration and accepted by each of the Six before negotiations began, he showed great flexibility. The delegations were not confronted with French positions, but were invited to discuss, to contribute, to help find common answers to common problems. Monnet never defended a merely national and therefore of necessity a partial view, but tried to define the general interest of the community the negotiations were establishing together. Some of the delegates, formed in the tug-of-war of economic negotiations of the 'Schachtian' decade, at first believed that they were simply being tricked when, during meetings, they saw the little group of Frenchmen around Monnet disagreeing among themselves just as much as with other delegations. How could one negotiate one nation's special interest in orderly fashion against another's, if the inviting delegation seemed to have no clear view of the national interests it wanted to defend? But Monnet's method was so contagious, the attempt to find solutions for common problems instead of defending simply one's own national interests was so liberating and exhilarating, that none of the chief delegates resisted this new approach for very long.[5]

The Schuman Plan Conference had been at work for less than a week when events on the far side of the globe gave new urgency to its underlying purpose. At dawn on Sunday 25 June 1950, North Korean troops crossed the 38th parallel dividing the north from the south of the country. Next day, the United States called a meeting of the United Nations' Security Council, which at once ordered a cease-fire—but in vain. The invading forces included almost all the North-Korean army, which comprised four divisions and three brigades of armed police; within twenty-four hours their tanks were in the suburbs of Seoul, the Southern capital; by the following day it was encircled; by Wednesday 28 June it was occupied. On 26 June, President Truman had promised aid and supplies to South Korea, and next day he had ordered General Douglas MacArthur to give naval and air support. The Security Council meanwhile condemned North Korea for its breach of the peace, and recommended that 'the members of the United Nations supply to the Republic of Korea the assistance which may be necessary to repulse armed attack and re-establish peace and international security in this area.' Before long, America and her allies were engaged in a real if limited war.[6]

From Europe, this looked doubly ominous. The Security Council's resolution had been passed—no doubt could only have been passed—in the absence of the Soviet delegation. Now, the Soviet Union rejected it, protesting against its 'illegality'. But despite this refusal to 'interfere in the affairs of other peoples', North Korea's forces were known to be using Soviet arms and equipment. Rightly or wrongly, they were also suspected of having obeyed Soviet prompting. The United States had refrained from intervening in China's Communist revolution; and on 12 January 1950, Secretary of State Dean Acheson had told the National Press Club in Washington that America's 'defensive perimeter' stretched from the Aleutians off the coast of Alaska to Japan and from there to the Ryukyu Islands East of Formosa—a ring that clearly excluded Korea. This, it was thought, had encouraged the Soviet Union to engineer the invasion from the North, although in April 1950 the US National Security Council had in fact revised its strategic doctrine and raised the military estimates from thirteen to thirty thousand million dollars so as to be able to parry any attack. Nervously uncertain of each other's intentions, the two giant powers seemed in danger of unleashing a third world war. Weak and divided, the countries of Europe could neither deter the Soviet Union nor restrain the United States. So real and widespread was the fear of war that continental housewives began hoarding sugar, rice, soap, and canned goods; in France the gold *napoléon*, index of the small speculator's sense of insecurity, rose from 3,140 to 3,500 francs in two days.[7]

But European uneasiness was specific as well as general. Korea resembled Germany. Formerly on the side of the wartime Axis, it had been divided in 1945 between the Soviet Union and the United States, who had agreed to exercise joint trusteeship and to help the inhabitants establish democratic institutions. For two years, from 1946 to 1948, the Russian and American authorities on the spot had failed to agree on the country's future, largely because the Soviet Union had resisted efforts to reunite it. In 1948, tension had grown to breaking-point, and each side had established in its own zone a government that claimed authority over both. Now, the Communist Government had gone to war with its rival. Could the same thing happen in Germany?

Optimists pointed to some crucial differences. The South Korean Government of Syngman Rhee was at once belligerent and weak: in the elections of May 1950 it had been shown to be widely unpopular. What was more, except for a 500-man military mission, the United States had withdrawn its troops from the South. But if South Korea was militarily ill-prepared, Western Germany was totally unarmed; without American troops, it would be defenceless. In Eastern Germany, there were 300,000 highly mechanized Soviet forces, backed by 54,000 German *Bereitschaften*, or armed barracks police, many of them re-cruited from the former *Wehrmacht*. In Western Germany, there were only 200,000 Allied men, poorly equipped and badly organized: the French First Army in Cologne, for example, depended as a NATO unit on the US Army Group in Heidelberg, but as a French unit took its orders from the High Command in Paris. In Western Europe as a whole, the Allies had only fourteen divisions and a thousand aircraft, compared with 175 or more Soviet divisions and 20,000 Soviet planes.[8]

Of the European countries, Britain and the Netherlands were already spending on defence a higher proportion of their national incomes than the United States. France's contribution was only slightly less. It was natural, therefore, for some Europeans to look to America for further military assistance. But America was now involved in the Korean War, and just as naturally she pressed for greater efforts from Europe. In July 1950, the five members of the Brussels Treaty agreed to increase their armaments and prolong military service; but there were obvious limits to what they could do. Britain was still policing the sizeable remnants of Empire; France had much of her army in Indochina Belgium was still committed to the Congo, and the Netherlands to West Irian; Luxembourg was sturdy but small. Europe's greatest reserve of potential military strength was the German Federal Republic; and American pressure to use it, which had already been felt earlier, now grew very rapidly. In a speech in New York on 7 May 1950, the former US Military Governor in Germany, General Lucius Clay, had first openly suggested a German contribution to Europe's defence. On 25 July, it was proposed by John J. McCloy, now American High Com-missioner in Germany. On 5 August, President Truman asked his Euro-pean Allies how Europe could improve its military arrangements: and although he avoided mentioning Germany, several susceptible French-

men—including the new Government's Defence Minister, Jules Moch—
even began to wonder whether the Pentagon might not have welcomed
the Korean War as a pretext for prodding Europe, and Germany, towards
rearmament. Moch had lost a son in World War II, and was understandably mistrustful; yet such suspicions showed not only the deep
fear of Germany, but also the uneasiness of relations between middle-
sized European countries and their powerful, distant American ally.
Fear and uneasiness grew, moreover, when later in August Chancellor
Adenauer—who himself opposed the restoration of a German national
army—requested permission to raise two to three divisions of armed
police as a counterpart to the East German *Bereitschaften*. On Saturday
9 September 1950, Truman promised to send more US troops; but three
days later, on Tuesday 12 September, when Dean Acheson met his colleagues Ernest Bevin and Robert Schuman in Washington, he formally
proposed that NATO forces should include German divisions.[9]

Schuman's reaction was frankly hostile; so, initially, was Bevin's
Acheson made it clear, however, that if there were no German defence
contribution America might oppose the establishment in Europe of
General Eisenhower's inter-Allied High Command. When the other
members of the Alliance met a few days later, most of them gave way
before American pressure; and on 16 September Bevin himself threw
in his hand. France was now in what Maurice Schumann, then a leader
of the Catholic MRP called later 'an infernal situation': her Government was unstable, she had heavy transatlantic debts, and she was in
danger of being isolated from her allies. Sooner or later, it was clear,
she would have to acquiesce. As Hubert Beuve-Méry, editor of *Le
Monde*, had written when the Alliance was concluded, 'the Atlantic
Pact contains the rearmament of Germany, like the embryo in an egg.'[10]

But if there had to be German rearmament, need there be a German
national army? Could German units, or even German individuals, not
safely serve under an Allied command? The Americans proposed that
this command should be NATO. Could it not be Europe? Why not form
a European army? Why not set up, alongside the Schuman Plan's European Coal and Steel Community, a European Defence Community of
which Germans—but not a German army—could form a part?

Such was the reasoning that led to the project for a European Defence
Community (EDC). As a practical proposal, it was put forward by Jean
Monnet; but as in the case of the Schuman Plan, the idea was not new.
Konrad Adenauer had suggested it in an interview with the *Cleveland
Plain Dealer* as early as the previous December; and in France it had
been publicized in March 1950, in a book by General Pierre Billotte. In
the first week of August, the French Socialist André Philip proposed it

in the Consultative Assembly of the Council of Europe, followed on 11 August by Winston Churchill in a motion carried by eighty-five votes to five. Later, on 8 October 1950, Arthur Koestler revived the idea in an article in the *New York Times*, suggesting a kind of European Foreign Legion with multinational platoons. But once again it was Monnet—as much a man of collective action as a man of individual ideas—who put the project to the right person at the right time. Even he, moreover, had to make two attempts before he succeeded.[11]

Characteristically, Monnet's first approach to defence was from the viewpoint of pooling resources and supplies. In August 1950, he began to discuss with his friends a joint European procurements fund. As *Commissaire au Plan*, he was anxious for France to make the best use of scarce manpower and materials; as instigator and chairman of the Schuman Plan Conference, he saw the scope for avoiding reduplication within a European Community. By September, his thoughts had crystallized further: he now envisaged a 'European' solution to the problem of rearmament. When Acheson made his proposal to rearm Germany, on 12 September 1950, Monnet grasped both the danger and the opportunity. Although slightly unwell at the time, he quickly sent a memorandum to his former assistant René Pleven, who was now French Prime Minister, and to Robert Schuman, who was negotiating in New York. What Monnet proposed was that Europe's defence should be organized collectively on the lines of the Schuman Plan for coal and steel.[12]

Schuman was all for action; but the French Government was divided, and on 22 September the delegates in New York adjourned without reaching a conclusion on the American proposal or hearing any counter-proposal from France. A further meeting was fixed, however, for 28 October 1950. Then, it seemed certain, the United States would redouble its pressure. Meanwhile, the military situation itself had begun to strengthen America's hand. General MacArthur had launched an offensive on 15 September which gave US troops their first major success in Korea; in Indochina, the French army's weakness was emphasized by a serious defeat at Cao-Bang on 8 October. It was harder, now, for Jules Moch to maintain his intransigence—especially since talks with General George C. Marshall had convinced him that the United States would welcome a 'European' defence proposal from France.[13]

This was Monnet's second opportunity, and he seized it. In a much-redrafted memorandum to Pleven, he proposed that before meeting again with her allies on 28 October, France should make a public statement refusing German rearmament on a national basis, but suggesting the formation of a European army, in a European Defence Community, in which the Germans would participate with other European nations.[14]

This time, Monnet was successful. On Tuesday 24 October 1950, Pleven presented to the French National Assembly the project for a European Defence Community that came to be known as 'the Pleven Plan'. It provided for a European army, jointly equipped and financed, with national contingents incorporated at the level of the smallest practicable unit, which was then thought to be the batallion. At the same time, member States would be able to retain their national armies, and might be authorized to supplement them at time of need by withdrawing some of their 'European' units. In charge of the European army would be a European Defence Minister, appointed by the member governments and responsible both to them and to a European Assembly. Policy directives would be laid down by a Council of Ministers from the respective member States.[15]

Bold as this seemed, the National Assembly approved it by 343 votes to 225. That night, Jules Moch called in his closest assistants and told them to produce, at top speed, a paper for the NATO meeting in four days' time. Working against the clock, they did so; but the result, as one of them confessed afterwards, was 'a disaster'. As it at length turned out, he might have said the same of the EDC project itself.[16]

For the time being, all seemed hopeful. The United States welcomed the French proposal; so did a number of her European allies. On Thursday 15 February 1951, less than four months after Pleven's speech to the National Assembly, a treaty-making conference met in Paris under the chairmanship of Hervé Alphand from the French Foreign Office; and although at first only five countries—Belgium, France, Germany, Italy and Luxembourg—were members of it, the Netherlands joined them in the following October, making the full complement of the Schuman Plan Six. Meanwhile, on 18 April 1951, the Schuman Plan Conference itself ended with the signature of the Treaty establishing the European Coal and Steel Community (ECSC). Symbolically, the document signed was printed in French by the National Printing Office, in German ink on Dutch vellum; the parchment of the cover came from Belgium, the ribbon from Italy and the glue from Luxembourg. The text provided for a common market in coal, coke, steel, iron ore and scrap, to be run by an independent nine-man High Authority, a Council of national Ministers, a seventy-eight-member Common Assembly chosen by and from the national Parliaments, and a supreme Court of Justice with seven judges and two advocates-general. Just over a year later, the Pleven Plan Conference produced the EDC Treaty, initialled on 9 May 1952—the second anniversary of the Schuman Declaration—and formally signed on 27 May, also in the Salon de l'Horloge. Instead of a European Defence Minister, the EDC was now to have a nine-man executive Commissariat similar to the ECSC High Authority, a Council of Ministers, a Court of Justice to be shared with the ECSC and a European Assembly—that of the ECSC slightly enlarged—which was to prepare further steps towards political unity. A month later, in mid-June 1952, the last of the six national parliaments ratified the ECSC Treaty. In August, after the Six had failed to agree on a site for its headquarters, the High Authority began work in Luxembourg with Monnet as its first President; and in September, without waiting for EDC to come into force, the Council of Ministers of the ECSC asked its Common Assembly to co-opt eight additional members into an 'Ad hoc Assembly' to draft the Treaty for a European Political Community. Within six months, by 10 March 1953, the draft was ready. It provided for a European Executive Council, to be known as the 'Ministers of the European Community'; a Council of national Ministers; a Court of Justice; and a Parliament consisting of a Senate whose members were to be chosen by the national parliaments, and a People's Chamber directly elected by the citizens of the Community as a whole. If blueprints were buildings, Europe was built.[17]

Unfortunately, even on paper, the construction had serious flaws. Within two years, the institutions of the Political Community were intended to inherit the tasks of the ECSC and EDC; but they also had an even broader mandate: to co-ordinate foreign policies, prepare a general common market for all goods, and guarantee constitutional order and democratic institutions within any member country, either at its own request or on a unanimous vote of the Council. Had the Political Community come into existence, this last provision might have been tested in France in May 1968: but in all probability it would have been found wanting. The draft Treaty contained more good intentions than specific provisions; on the proposed common market, in particular, it was even less explicit than the later Rome Treaty—itself an outline treaty—establishing the European Economic Community. It was hardly surprising that when the Foreign Ministers of the Six examined it, in the summer and autumn of 1953, they felt obliged to start again from the beginning. In part, this was due to the natural conservatism of governments, in part to the waning of momentum as time passed and the 'cold war' began to thaw. On Thursday 5 March 1953, just five days before the Ad hoc Assembly published its draft political treaty, Joseph Stalin died; a little over four months later, the Korean War came to an end. In a new and seemingly hopeful international climate, those who had seen the unity of Western Europe only as 'a bulwark against aggression' began to question whether it was still needed. Their doubts, and their hostility, crystallized around EDC.[18]

It had taken a year to ratify the ECSC Treaty; in all six national parliaments the debate had been heated and long. EDC was even more controversial—so much so that the German *Bundestag*, the first national assembly to approve it, did so only on 19 March 1953, ten months after the signing of the Treaty. The *Bundesrat* followed suit on 15 May; the lower house of the Dutch Parliament on 23 July; the Belgian Chamber of Deputies on 26 November; the Dutch Senate on 20 January 1954; the Belgian Senate on 12 March; and the Luxembourg Chamber of Deputies on 17 April 1954.[19]

From this slow roll-call there were two crucial absentees—Italy and France. In both countries, the delay was partly the result of government instability; but this in turn was increased by fierce opposition to EDC from the extremes of Left and Right. Even in Germany, the Social-Democrat SPD had fought it, as they had fought the Schuman Plan. They argued that to integrate the Federal Republic with the rest of Western Europe might block German reunification; but their opposition was sharpened by the antagonism that existed between Adenauer and the SPD leader Kurt Schumacher, mutilated and embittered by twelve years in Nazi concentration camps, and deeply fearful of giving his compatriots guns. In Italy and France, as in other countries, many felt the same fear; they tended to forget that EDC had been devised precisely to forestall the creation of a new German army. Communists made much of these feelings; so did Right-wing nationalists, who in addition to the German bogey disliked the prospect of committing a part of the services to a motley European army of fourteen divisions, all in some soulless European uniform. It was a strange mixture of motives—pacificism, jingoism, internationalism, fear, pride and nostalgia—that brought together in the opposition camp German Social Democrats and Italian Neo-Fascists, Communists and Gaullists, Pietro Nenni and Marshal Alphonse Juin, the Comte de Paris and Kurt Schumacher. In the long run, they might have been defeated—but for one further absentee.[20]

This, once again, was Great Britain. If Britain had joined without reservations in the Schuman Plan and the project for a European Defence Community, much of the opposition would have been weakened. The weight of Germany, which so obsessed EDC's French opponents, would have been balanced by that of another well-established democracy. France's sacrifice of sovereignty would have been matched by a colleague and rival no less proud. True, Britain's presence might have weakened the institutional structure: she might have sought to limit its 'supranational' powers. Once in, however, she would have wanted it to be efficient and democratic; she therefore might well have favoured a strong decision-making body responsible to a real European Parliament. But as it was, Britain remained aloof. Not for the last time, her absence proved embarrassing.

The original exchange of Notes between Paris and London in May and early June 1950 had seemed to hinge on the question of 'prior commitment', whether or not to accept, as a condition for taking part in the Schuman Plan Conference, the objective of a European Community and the method of delegating power to common institutions. The real stumbling-block for the British, however, was not 'prior commitment' as such, but the proposed pooling of sovereignty. As early as Tuesday 28 March 1950, Ernest Bevin had told the House of Commons that Britain could never agree to the creation of an executive organ in Europe whose mandate it would be to impose decisions on any State. The Conservatives, although they now pressed for Britain to take part in the Schuman Plan Conference, fundamentally agreed with their Labour opponents. Britain, said Winston Churchill, 'could not be an ordinary member of a federal union limited to Europe in any period which at present can be foreseen.' But it was the Labour Party Executive that took the most openly hostile stand. On Monday 12 June 1950, ten days after the Franco-British exchange of Notes and a week before the Schuman Plan delegates met in Paris, Hugh Dalton—who had recently resigned as Chancellor of the Exchequer after a 'Budget leak'—presented to the press a pamphlet that he had personally steered through to approval. 'Bevin, Cripps and I,' he wrote in his memoirs, 'were all definitely anti-Federal.' His pamphlet, misleadingly entitled *European Unity*, was no less so. Expressly rejecting 'supranationality', it recommended instead 'co-operation between responsible Governments on the basis of mutual consent'. 'No Socialist Party,' it proclaimed, '. . . could accept a system by which important fields of national policy were surrendered to a supra-national representative authority.'[21]

European Unity soon became notorious. Its chocolate-coloured cover inspired Winston Churchill to call it 'Dalton's Brown Paper'. The American press dismissed it as 'a ridiculous manifesto'; the French press was predictably incensed. Two days later the British Prime Minister, Clement Attlee, drew a careful distinction between the Party's pamphlet and the Government's policy; but the main difference seemed only to be that the Government recognized the value of the Schuman Plan for others, provided that Britain remained outside. As Jean Monnet remarked at the second session of the Schuman Plan Conference, the British attitude was on the whole sympathetic to the project, but hostile to the delegation of sovereignty to the proposed High Authority. For obvious reasons, France and the other participants were anxious to see Britain join. The British authorities would be kept fully informed of the Conference's progress; but its economic, political and moral aims would be compromised if it were to abandon the principle of a supranational authority. However, Monnet added, the British had one great virtue: they recognized facts. To act was the best way of securing their eventual support.[22]

By an irony that might have confirmed Monnet's refusal to temporize, the British Government had already instructed its senior civil servants to work out an alternative to the Schuman Plan. By a further irony, the chairman of the interdepartmental committee set up to prepare it was Monnet's friend Sir Edwin Plowden. It was he, together with Sir Edward Bridges, Sir William Strang, and Sir Roger Makins, who had been responsible for drafting the British side of the recent exchange of Notes with France. The counter-proposals that he was now asked to draw up had first been announced in the British communiqué of 3 June 1950. Two days later, *Agence France Presse* had reported from London that they would be submitted at or after the opening of the Schuman Plan Conference, where Britain, it was said, hoped to maintain 'an invisible presence'. She may also have hoped to recover the initiative if—as many in London expected—the Conference failed. Since it at length succeeded, Britain's counter-proposals came to nothing, and were never officially divulged. They were, however, radically different from the Schuman Plan. Technical rather than political, they provided for the sharing of European markets, the reduction of transport costs, the rationalization of machine-tools capacity, and the adjustment of tariffs. They envisaged the establishment of regional, national and international boards to deal with European heavy industry; but the members were to be national representatives, not independent persons responsible to the group as a whole. There would have been, in other words, no supranational authority.[23]

This was the obstacle at which the British, however well-disposed in theory, in practice repeatedly balked. Ernest Bevin and Hugh Dalton had been two notable examples: another, now, was Harold Macmillan, who eleven years later was to lead Britain to the threshold of the Common Market. Like his colleagues in the Conservative Party, he had attacked the Labour Government for its reaction to the Schuman Declaration:

it had been, said Macmillan, 'a black week for Britain, for the Empire, for Europe and for the peace of the world.' Two years earlier, on 17 September 1948, he had told the House of Commons: 'Europe needs a common currency, a free movement of goods with due regard to existing obligations and preferential arrangements of the participating countries.' On 17 August 1949, he had proposed in the Council of Europe that 'the Committee of Ministers shall be an executive authority with supranational powers'. Now, however, he appeared to change his mind. In June 1950, in a private minute to Churchill, he urged that Britain should enter the Schuman negotiations. 'Then,' he said, 'we can mould the plan to our own pattern.' On Tuesday 8 August 1950, he and David Eccles submitted to the Council of Europe a bulky memorandum which indicated what in their view that pattern should be. It proposed that any member countries wishing to do so should form a Ministerial Committee, which in turn would appoint an Authority for coal and steel. The Authority's members would be chosen from representatives of employers, trade unions and consumers; they would have votes proportional to their respective countries' coal and steel output—an arrangement advantageous to Britain. The supranational principle was to be abandoned: each country was to have the right of veto and the right to withdraw. 'One thing is certain,' said Macmillan, 'and we may as well face it. Our people are not going to hand over to any supranational authority the right to close down our pits or steelworks.' This, as it happened, was a caricature of the powers eventually granted to the ECSC's High Authority, which were far less drastic; and—as Monnet pointed out in a personal letter to Macmillan on 8 August 1950—the line of thought completely missed the point.[24]

The ensuing debate in the Council of Europe's Consultative Assembly illuminated the contrast between what Macmillan called 'Anglo-Saxon' and Continental habits:

The difference [he declared] is temperamental and intellectual. It is based on a long divergence of two states of mind and methods of argumentation. The continental tradition likes to reason *a priori* from the top downwards, from the general principles to the practical application. It is the tradition of St Thomas of Aquinas [*sic*], of the schoolmen, and of the great continental scholars and thinkers. The Anglo-Saxon likes to argue *a posteriori* from the bottom upwards, from practical experience. It is the tradition of Bacon and Newton.

It might be retorted that even Bacon and Newton based their thought on assumptions; the real difference was that these were too inexplicit to be recognized as principles. The assumption underlying British attitudes seemed to be the inalienable nature of the nation-state. But Macmillan was more subtle than his own over-simplifications. 'Of course,' he added, 'the Scottish people, who are the intellectuals of Britain, know that there is nothing to be frightened of: one should accept everything *en principe*, get around the table and start the talks.' In time of crisis, Britain would 'certainly be prepared to accept merger of sovereignty in practice if not in principle'; she might join in the unification of Europe 'in a fit of absence of mind or by a series of improvizations which would be particularly gratifying to my countrymen'. Macmillan's words hinted at the crabwise stealth with which he was later to coax Britain towards the Common Market. They also suggested that if continental Europeans could recruit Britain as an associate of the Schuman Plan, she might end up as a full member.[25]

The notion that Britain might be 'associated' with the Schuman Plan was first voiced in London in May 1950 by Robert Schuman himself. Speaking on Monday 15 May at a luncheon given by the Anglo-French press, he said:

We shall pursue the project with only one other country [*à deux*] if necessary. Besides, one can imagine varying degrees of participation and, for example as regards Great Britain, if there is not one-hundred-per-cent participation, there can be association compatible with her economic ideas and structure.

Six weeks later, on Tuesday 25 July 1950, he declared that 'if we do not manage to get the British to share our views we are determined to seek a form of association between the Authority and the United Kingdom'.[26]

'Association', although still undefined, was also mooted on the British side. On Friday 11 August 1950, speaking to the same session of the Council of Europe's Consultative Assembly that had just heard Winston Churchill's proposal for a European Army, Hugh Dalton announced that

... if agreement is reached between these six nations, we British will be most ready to consider how, and how far, Britain could be associated with any new organization which the Governments and Parliaments of these six continental countries might have approved for this most important problem of the better organization of their heavy industries.

The pledge was repeated in the House of Commons on Tuesday 7 November 1950, when Ernest Davies, Under-Secretary of State at the Foreign

Office, told a questioner that Britain was prepared, if invited, to discuss with the Six the practical means whereby she could associate herself with the proposed High Authority. Much depended, it was clear, on the content of the Schuman Plan Treaty. When at last this was signed, on 18 April 1951, the road seemed open. Speaking in Paddington on Labour Day, Tuesday 1 May 1951, the Minister of State at the Foreign Office, Kenneth Younger, revealed that the Government was studying the provisions of the Treaty to see how far Britain could become an associate. A few weeks later, on Saturday 9 June 1951, the British Ambassador in Paris, Sir Oliver Harvey, presented to Robert Schuman an official British Note to the same effect, indicating that the Government would be glad to discuss the question when the time was ripe.[27]

Still more categorical was the joint communiqué issued on Friday 14 September 1951, after three-power talks in Washington between Dean Acheson, Robert Schuman, and Herbert Morrison, who had become Britain's Foreign Secretary on 9 March, just five weeks before Ernest Bevin's death from a heart attack on 14 April 1951:

The three Ministers recognize that the initiative taken by the French Government, concerning the creation of a European Coal and Steel Community and a European Defence Community, is a step towards European unity. They welcome the Schuman Plan as a means of strengthening the economy of Western Europe and look forward to its early realization.... The Government of the United Kingdom desire to establish the closest possible association with the European continental Community at all stages of its development.

The significance of this statement was threefold. First, it made clear that America welcomed the integration of Europe, and that her welcome was acknowledged and seconded by Great Britain. British sceptics could no longer plausibly argue that the emerging European Community was incompatible with the Atlantic Alliance. Secondly, Britain now recognized the Schuman Plan as part of a political movement, not merely concerned, in Dalton's phrase, with 'the better organization of ... heavy industries'. Finally, the British Government were now pledged to 'the closest possible association' not only with the ECSC but also with EDC. Potentially, this might mean a great deal.[28]

The hope that Britain might join in the effort to unite Europe seemed to be confirmed six weeks later, on Thursday 25 October 1951, when Attlee's ailing Labour Government was replaced by a Conservative administration under Winston Churchill. Continental Europeans were encouraged by reports from London that the new government planned to set up a permanent mission to the European Coal and Steel Community. They recalled—and misremembered—Churchill's celebrated speech at the University of Zurich on 19 September 1946, urging 'a kind of United States of Europe'; they re-read—and misinterpreted—his words in the Council of Europe on 11 August 1950. 'We should make,' he had said, 'a gesture of practical and constructive guidance by declaring ourselves in favour of the immediate creation of a European army under a unified command, and in which, we should bear a worthy and honourable part.' But, as in so many political speeches, the word 'we' turned out to be misleading. In Zurich, Churchill had made it clear that Britain would support but not join a united Europe; now, her 'honourable part' was to be with but not in EDC. On Wednesday 28 November 1951, Sir David Maxwell Fyfe, the new Home Secretary, told the Council of Europe: 'I cannot promise that our eventual association with the European Defence Community will amount to full and unconditional participation because this is a matter which must be left for intergovernmental discussion elsewhere.' This sounded hopeful; at a press conference afterwards he added, 'It is quite wrong to suggest that what I said was any closing of the door.' But in Rome on the same day the new Foreign Secretary, Anthony Eden, slammed the door shut. He had asked himself, he wrote later, 'whether in practice we could join an army forming part of a European federation; I agreed with our predecessors that we could not.' To join a federation on the continent of Europe, he explained in a lecture at Columbia University on the following 11 January 1952, 'is something which we know, in our bones, we cannot do.'[29]

Even in his bones, however, Eden could hardly fail to notice that Britain's absence hindered the progress of EDC. As he wrote in a personal minute to Churchill on Saturday 1 December 1951, 'Now that the Pleven Plan is running into trouble in the countries that put it forward, we are being made the whipping boy.' It was partly for this reason that on Tuesday 18 December, after talks with the French Government in Paris, Britain promised that 'the United Kingdom Forces under the direction of the Supreme Allied Commander in Europe will be linked with those of the European Defence Community for training, supply and operations by land, sea and air.' Meeting Robert Schuman again on 1 February 1952, Eden spelled this out in more detail. The proposed 'link' would be 'particularly profitable' between the respective air forces; arrangements could be made for the exchange and loan of individuals, units and formations; and Britain would maintain troops on the continent 'for as long as is necessary'. However, when Schuman pressed for a formal treaty promising mutual aid against aggression, Eden replied that 'it was doubtful whether we could accept this. We already had the NATO commitment and I was not convinced that a further engagement was necessary.' At length, after consultation with Acheson on 13 February, he proposed instead a joint Anglo-American declaration of support if any European country threatened the peace.[30]

Shortly afterwards, the EDC Conference ran into further trouble, once more aggravated by Britain's aloofness. Germany, as the country most exposed to any attack from the East, was anxious that the European army should respond automatically to aggression against any member of the future Defence Community; but the Dutch, in particular, were reluctant to give this undertaking without a similar commitment from Britain. On Friday 14 March 1952, in the hope of solving the dilemma, the EDC Conference formally asked the British Government to conclude a mutual assistance treaty. France and the Netherlands suggested that this might be done by extending the Brussels Treaty which already linked Britain with France and the three Benelux countries, to the whole of EDC.[31]

Again, however, Eden demurred. 'This,' he told Dirk Stikker, the Dutch Foreign Minister, 'was a difficult business for us. It was natural that we should conclude the Brussels Treaty with our closest European friends and allies. To extend it to Italy and Germany, because they were members of EDC and for the forty-five years which the treaty had to run, was quite a different proposition.' He said the same to Robert Schuman. 'Once again,' he reported wearily, 'I heard the cry that for parliamentary reasons, it was necessary for Her Majesty's Government to enter into some form of treaty commitment with the European Defence Community ... Was there a danger that we should be asked to go further and join EDC?'[32]

To forestall it, Eden finally gave way. On Saturday 5 April 1952, after a further meeting of the Cabinet, the British Ambassador in Paris, Sir Oliver Harvey, announced to Schuman that the British Government would indeed conclude a formal treaty; and a first draft was put to the EDC Conference on the following Tuesday 8 April 1952.[33]

It had been a long and tiresome task to secure even this undertaking. Ultimately it turned out to be too little, too late. Meanwhile, Eden and his staff had taken another step which, however well-meant, suggested that they scarcely realized what continental 'Europeans' were trying to achieve. On Wednesday 19 March 1952, at a meeting of the Council of Europe's Committee of Ministers in the Salon de l'Horloge at the

French Foreign Office, Eden presented an Aide-mémoire largely drafted by Anthony Nutting, his Parliamentary Under-Secretary. The paper, which came to be known as 'the Eden Plan', proposed an institutional merger between the Council of Europe and the future Community of the Six. 'The essence of the plan,' wrote Nutting, '... was to make the Council of Europe the parent body ... The Committee of Ministers, the Assembly and the Secretariat of the Council of Europe would become the Committee of Ministers [sic] of the Coal and Steel Pool and the EDC.'[34]

The idea itself was not entirely novel. Something like it had been suggested by Harold Macmillan and David Eccles in 1950, in their counter-proposals to the Schuman Plan, and had been echoed by the Council of Europe's Committee of Ministers in October of that year. Now, the first reactions seemed favourable. 'As the Foreign Secretary read through his typescript giving an outline of his plan to his European colleagues,' said Nutting,

I could feel a deep sense of relief and thankfulness filling the room. Only the impassive features of the Chairman, Osten Unden of Sweden, showed no signs of emotion. He was no doubt busy trying to work out in his mind how he could square his neutral conscience with sitting in on a Committee of Ministers charged with overseeing the E.D.C. M. Bech, Luxembourg's doyen among the Foreign Ministers of Europe, beamed like a contented seal through a forest of snow white moustaches, his jubilant rotundity bearing happy witness to the delights of combining the not always arduous duties of Foreign Minister of Luxembourg with the ever pleasurable activities of the Minister for Winegrowing. Even the sphinx-like features of Dr Adenauer could not conceal a smile as he sat like a Grand Inquisitor slowly twiddling his thumbs in his lap. As for Robert Schuman, he made no attempt to hide his joy and summed up the reactions of his fellow ministers by saying that, apart from the intrinsic merits of the plan, by far the most important and encouraging aspect of it was that it represented a British initiative.[35]

Despite the ministers' smiles, it soon became clear that the Eden Plan had a number of drawbacks. Some were technical. The Council of Europe's Ministerial Committee consisted of Foreign Ministers; the Council of the ECSC comprised those concerned with economic questions, and the Council of EDC would no doubt include Ministers of Defence—a subject specifically excluded from the Council of Europe. Some of the delegates in the Council of Europe's Consultative Assembly were nominated by governments, and did not have to be members of parliament: those in the Community Assembly were to be chosen by and from their national legislatures. It might be difficult, finally, for the

Council of Europe's Secretariat, with staff from all the member countries, to handle confidential subjects for the Six.

More serious were the political problems that underlay the technical difficulties. What the Six were hoping to achieve was not just an intensified version of the Council of Europe's co-operation between separate sovereign States: it was a pooling of resources and a fusion of material interests within a Community that might gradually become a United States of Europe. This distinction the Eden Plan seemed to ignore. Under it, as Nutting himself said, 'Great Britain could play a part without being committed to the obligations of membership of any supranational agencies.' Without, that is, accepting the duties of Community membership, she and other countries would acquire the right to scrutinize, if no more, the internal affairs of the new entity that the Six were forming. For Jean Monnet and his colleagues, in Nutting's words, it would be 'like some nagging mother-in-law moving in on the newly-weds'.[36]

Although, therefore, both the Committee of Ministers and the Consultative Assembly of the Council of Europe approved the Eden Plan in principle, the Assembly's General Affairs Committee came to a different conclusion. Reporting back to the Assembly on Monday 15 September 1952, after a detailed study, it recommended instead a much more limited system of contacts. In the subsequent Council of Europe debate, Paul-Henri Spaak, Paul Reynaud and the MRP Resistance veteran Pierre-Henri Teitgen all sharply attacked the original project; and within a few months it was quietly buried. 'Tragically,' Nutting commented, 'our initiative had only aroused suspicion that we were really trying to sabotage the unity of Europe.' To some Europeans it certainly seemed so. But Monnet, whatever his private doubts, still went on looking for ways to bring Britain closer to the Community of the Six.[37]

He was already sixty-three when he took up his duties in Luxembourg as President of the ECSC High Authority; but from the first he set an exhausting pace. Lights burned until all hours in the headquarters' offices, soon established in an elderly brownstone building that had belonged to the Grand Duchy's railways. Officials' weekends were interrupted by urgent meetings: at least once, Monnet summoned an assistant from the woods, where he was enjoying a Sunday picnic with his family. Some newcomers complained that Luxembourg, despite its five night-clubs and seven cinemas, was hardly the gayest of capital cities: 'Europe won't get built in night-clubs' was Monnet's reply. One evening he himself was due to leave on holiday: hotel rooms had been booked, seats reserved and baggage packed; but the High Authority was meeting, and Monnet insisted on staying to the end. One by one, urgent messages were passed to him: the train was leaving soon—it had gone —so had the next one; but every time he brushed them aside. It was exasperating, but exhilarating; and it helped to weld together a loyal international team.[38]

The High Authority's two Vice-Presidents were Franz Etzel, a tall, cool, grey-eyed lawyer who later became German Finance Minister, and the solid but energetic Albert Coppé, a Fleming who had been Belgian Minister of Economic Affairs. The other members were Léon Daum, a small, crisp, dapper French businessman and steel expert; the bony, white-haired Paul Finet, a former Belgian foundry worker who had been first President of the International Confederation of Free Trade Unions; Enzo Giacchero, an Italian Christian-Democrat and active federalist, who walked with a limp owing to a wartime wound; Heinz Potthoff, a serious-minded ex-steelworker from Germany who had served on the International Ruhr Authority; the taut, well-groomed Dirk Spierenburg, formerly head of the Dutch delegation to the OEEC and to the Schuman Plan Conference; and the stout, fatherly Albert Wehrer from Luxembourg. All were very different, by temperament as much as by political conviction; but under Monnet's chairmanship and in the relative isolation of the Grand Duchy, they quickly acquired the habit of seeing the Community's problems as common problems, transcending any purely national point of view.[39]

They held their first, ceremonial meeting on 10 August 1952—a Sunday, and ten days after the majority of Frenchmen and others would normally have left for their month-long holidays in the sun. The British Ambassador to Luxembourg was present at the ceremony, and Monnet declared: 'We are determined to seek without delay, in direct talks, the means of fulfilling the British Government's stated intention to establish the closest association with the Community.'[40]

The British Government responded on the very next day by announcing that it was ready for talks on the subject; and ten days later, on Thursday 21 August 1952, Monnet was in London seeing the Minister of State at the Foreign Office, Selwyn Lloyd. The result was that on Monday 1 September Britain accredited to the High Authority a delegation headed by Sir Cecil Weir, a Scottish businessman and civil servant whose most recent official post had been as Chairman of the Dollar Exports Board. One of his tasks was 'to lay the foundations of an intimate and enduring association between the Community and the United Kingdom'. As a first step, he helped to establish a joint Committee between the High Authority and the British Government; and at the Committee's first meeting, on Monday 17 November 1952, Monnet explained the form of 'association' that he had in mind. It was not, he said, a trade agreement or a cartel to share out overseas markets, but a system of joint action involving rights, responsibilities and obligations undertaken in common. As well as consultation and the exchange of information, this meant joint institutions and rules to be worked out and applied together. He suggested that the British Government and the High Authority begin by taking an overall view of their future prospects—'just as if you were members of our Community'.[41]

On Tuesday 10 February 1953, the ECSC opened its 'common market' in coal, followed on Friday 1 May 1953, by the common market in steel. The way was now open, as Monnet saw it, for the drafting of a formal Treaty of Association with Great Britain; and the early versions of it prepared by the High Authority's staff showed how far-reaching Monnet's ambitions were. What he envisaged was the gradual establishment of a coal-steel common market between the Community and the United Kingdom. The question of institutions was left open; but Monnet clearly hoped that practical necessity would lead the British towards virtual or even actual membership of the ECSC—and thence, perhaps, to full membership of the political and defence Communities that were to be set up alongside it.[42]

It was important, however, not to alienate British opinion by too bold a proposal; and the project went through many drafts before Monnet and his colleagues were satisfied. Finally, on the morning of Christmas Eve, 1953, Monnet handed a formal Note to Sir Cecil Weir. In it, he no longer spoke explicitly of a 'common market' with Britain, but he came as close to his original idea as he could without raising the spectre of 'supranationality'. He proposed:

– an association between the markets, through the diminution and, if possible, the elimination of reciprocal protection and the institution of rules that each party pledges itself to respect;
– a procedure for joint action;
– joint institutions entrusted with the task of seeing that the system works, preparing joint action, and taking decisions arrived at by common accord.

The institutions, moreover, might include not only a Council of Association composed of members of the High Authority and the British Government, but also machinery for publicly discussing the Council's action and for interpreting the rules—in other words, a joint parliamentary Assembly and a Court.[43]

Monnet's letter requested a reply 'as soon as possible'; but on Thursday 21 January 1954, in answer to a parliamentary question, Anthony Eden explained that the proposal would require 'careful study and consultation with the interests concerned'. These, for contradictory reasons, were cool towards association. The British Iron and Steel Federation, representing industrialists, was suspicious of anything that might threaten further controls on private enterprise; the Government-run National Coal Board and Iron and Steel Board were reluctant to share— or diminish—their existing powers. It was hardly surprising that the British Government took four months to give a formal answer. Finally, on Thursday 29 April 1954, Weir called on Monnet with a formal invitation to go to London to discuss the 'precise form' of the future association. Within twenty-four hours, Monnet accepted, and a meeting was tentatively scheduled for early June. But then came an unforeseen obstacle, which in the end destroyed any hope that Britain's association with the Coal and Steel Community might bring her closer to—and thereby help to save EDC.[44]

For several years, Monnet had been under the strain of uninterrupted hard work and anxiety. Now, he fell seriously ill, and his doctors ordered a long rest. By the time he was better, July was almost over, and Europe was beginning its annual summer exodus. The London meeting was therefore postponed until September. When that month began, and newly bronzed officials came flocking back to Luxembourg, it was to a gloom that owed little to the Grand Duchy's climate. As an American observer put it, the Coal and Steel Community for which they worked was 'no longer the advance guard of a strong movement toward integration: it was more like an isolated outpost'. EDC was dead.[45]

The manner of its dying was undignified and dramatic; but its fate had long been foretold. Despite the encouraging example of the Coal and Steel Community, many Frenchmen were still afraid of facing Germany in EDC without Britain. In January 1953, when a further change of government brought in Georges Bidault to succeed Robert Schuman as Foreign Minister, France had demanded further concessions, including a European settlement for the Saar, still in dispute with Germany, and additional protocols to the EDC Treaty, to safeguard 'the unity and integrity of the French Army and the French Union' and ensure, in particular, that France's voting power could never be outweighed by Germany's. What was more, Bidault asked for a firmer commitment by Britain. On Thursday 12 February 1953, he and René Mayer, the new French Premier, visited London to request the British Government not only to maintain at least its existing strength on the Continent, but also to conclude a political association with the EDC

Council and Assembly. Unfortunately, in the words of a British Minister, 'their appeals fell upon deaf ears.'[46]

By now, time was running out. Under the new administration of President Eisenhower and Secretary of State John Foster Dulles, the United States continued to press hard for EDC to be ratified; in December 1953 Dulles even threatened an 'agonizing reappraisal' of American policy if it were to fail. But the death of Joseph Stalin and the subsequent softening of Soviet propaganda led many people—including Winston Churchill—to predict a 'thaw' in East-West relations; and this impression was not effaced even after Soviet tanks had crushed an uprising in East Berlin on 13 June 1953. As the hope of *détente* grew, enthusiasm for EDC waned still further.[47]

In July 1953 René Mayer fell, to be replaced by Joseph Laniel at the head of a conservative cabinet including several Gaullists. He and his Ministers promised the National Assembly that they would not seek ratification of EDC until they were assured of British association with it. Eden, at this time, was recovering from a series of operations; and when on his return to the Foreign Office Anthony Nutting pressed him for a decision, he delayed it, partly because he was preoccupied with Churchill's eagerness for East-West 'summit' talks. At length, after the abortive four-power conference in Berlin in January 1954, Britain made her offer; but it fell far short of French hopes. Instead of guaranteeing to keep her present fighting strength on the Continent, she agreed to consult with EDC before reducing it; instead of British representation in the EDC Council and Assembly, she proposed *ad hoc* discussion between Ministers; instead of integrating all her forces on the Continent with those of EDC, she promised to assign to the European army one armoured division. It was disappointing, but it was something. On Tuesday 13 April 1954, France and her partners signed an agreement along these lines.[48]

Two months later, Laniel's Government fell, and was followed on Saturday 19 June 1954 by a coalition of Radicals and Gaullists under Pierre Mendès-France. He, whatever his personal convictions, had never belonged to the comparatively small circle of the most active 'Europeans'; and for all his creative dynamism, he faced sceptical colleagues and a Parliament deeply divided over EDC. He also had urgent tasks outside Europe: to grant internal autonomy to Tunisia, and above all to fulfil his promise that he would end the war in Indochina within four weeks. Impressed but deeply uneasy, his European partners determined to do their best to keep EDC on Mendès France's tight agenda. Their efforts merely brought the latent crisis to a head.[49]

On Tuesday 22 June, three days after Mendès-France had formed his government, Paul-Henri Spaak conferred with his Benelux colleagues, and two days later they jointly proposed a meeting of the Six. The Germans and the Italians accepted; but Mendès-France was overburdened by more pressing anxieties, and Spaak therefore arranged to meet him in Paris at 12.30 p.m. on Wednesday 30 June 1954. Their conversation, interrupted by a late lunch, lasted four hours.[50]

Physically, there was little resemblance between the broad, well-padded Spaak, with his air of Churchill's understudy, and the slight, blue-chinned hooded-eyed Mendés-France. Both in their different ways, however, were nervous, proud and easily hurt; both, too, were compulsive doodlers, impatient and rhetorical behind their respective masks of calm and irony. They were too alike to find it easy to agree.[51]

Mendès-France began by explaining his own awkward position. Until recently he had been against EDC, but had thought that the French Parliament would vote for it. Today, he still had objections: the existing project was too exclusively military and anti-Soviet; it contained too few safeguards, and was too dramatic a step towards supranationality; finally, Britain was not included, and there could be no progress in Europe without her presence and active support. On balance, however, a defence Community was desirable; but now that he had come around to supporting it, he was forced to realize that Parliament would not vote for it in its present form.[52]

Spaak raised sceptical eyebrows; but Mendès-France went on. What he proposed was to try to persuade French opponents and supporters of EDC to work out and agree on a compromise solution by 20 July, when the Geneva conference on Indochina was due to conclude. If they failed, he himself would make new proposals by 15 August, so that the National Assembly could cast its vote before the end of that month. What would this involve? There were three possibilities. Parliament might ratify EDC but postpone the application of some of its provisions; it might request changes; or it might approve parts of the Treaty while rejecting others.

Spaak pointed out that Germany, Belgium, the Netherlands and Luxembourg had already ratified EDC as it stood. Were they now to have to wait for a *diktat* from the French Parliament, and start their own parliamentary procedure all over again? The Americans, he knew, were impatient for a decision: in April, Dulles had personally warned him that further delay might lead to cuts in US military aid to Europe. As an alternative solution, there was now serious talk of simply admitting Germany to NATO. If France were to water down EDC into a mere military coalition, Spaak added, he would prefer the NATO solution himself. In that case, rather than force the other European countries to reject a diluted French version of the EDC Treaty, it might be better for France simply to say 'No'. But at the very least the Six should have a chance to discuss Mendès-France's counter-proposals before he put them to Parliament. Perhaps, after all, some compromise might be possible. Mendès-France promised to try this way out, and the two men parted amicably. But they both knew that the real difficulties remained.[53]

On Tuesday 20 July 1954, only a few hours before his self-imposed time-limit, Mendès-France secured an armistice in Indochina. Some observers of the Geneva negotiations that led to it, including Raymond Aron, suspected that the Soviet Union had consented in the hope that the French Government might reciprocate by rejecting EDC. Twice— on Saturday 10 July and Wednesday 21 July—Mendès-France was closeted alone with V. M. Molotov, the Soviet Foreign Minister; but to suspect that they had a tacit understanding would no doubt be an injustice. By his own account, Mendès-France refused to link the two questions; and when at their second meeting Molotov warned him that EDC would not 'serve to bring together France and the Soviet Union', this was already twenty-four hours after the armistice agreement, and Mendès-France answered non-committally. His real difficulties were not with the Soviet Union, but with the National Assembly in France.[54]

There, supporters and opponents of EDC were as far as ever from being reconciled; and a fortnight after the Geneva Conference, Mendès-France held a series of secret cabinet meetings to expound new proposals of his own. These, he believed, could be embodied in protocols to the EDC Treaty which would only have to be signed by France's partners, whereas the French Parliament would have the chance to vote them. Briefly, they called for EDC to last as long as the Atlantic Alliance, ceasing to exist if that were denounced or if Germany were reunited; for military integration to be limited to units stationed in Germany; and for the 'supranational' clauses of the Treaty to take effect only after eight years. 'In other words,' wrote Anthony Nutting. 'Mendès-France was asking for a European army for the Germans and a French army for the French.' Even so, he failed to satisfy three Gaullist members of his cabinet—General Pierre Koenig, Maurice Lemaire and Jacques Chaban-Delmas. It was with their strictures still echoing that he left Paris for Brussels on Wednesday 18 August 1954, to present his proposals to his partners in the Six.[55]

From the start, the Brussels Conference was uneasy. The EDC Treaty had been signed two years earlier; since then, France had continually postponed ratification, and repeatedly asked for concessions; now, she was proposing changes yet again. Her new Premier, dynamic and unpredictable, was a newcomer to the circle of veterans round the table: Paul-Henri Spaak in the chair; Konrad Adenauer for Germany; Johan Willem Beyen for the Netherlands; Joseph Bech for Luxembourg; Attilio Piccioni for Italy. A few moments before the meeting opened, news came of the death of Alcide De Gasperi, Italy's greatest 'European'. To some, it seemed as if an epoch was ending.

Presenting his proposals, Mendès-France promised that the French Parliament would be able to vote them before the end of the year; but nothing else, he said, stood any chance of success. It was a story that had been heard too often to be believed; arguing the contrary, delegates pointed to articles in the French press by Robert Schuman and the Socialist leader André Philip in support of the original EDC Treaty. Spaak quoted a letter that he had received from Philip; Adenauer quoted optimistic forecasts by Maurice Faure. One after another, Beyen, Adenauer and Bech repeated a further objection—Beyen with particular vehemence: the changes that Mendès-France demanded would mean going back to all the national parliaments, with no guarantee at all that the new draft would be accepted.[56]

In the hope of finding a way out, Spaak suggested that instead of protocols to be added to the Treaty, any changes take the form of a declaration of intent. He had done his best, he said, to draft one, which he now proposed to read. It began with a preamble summarizing EDC's long history, including previous hard-fought discussions with France. As soon as Mendès-France heard this, he interrupted. It was intolerable, he exclaimed, that his country should be accused in this fashion; and he insisted that the preamble be torn up then and there. Solemnly and a little sheepishly, the delegates destroyed their copies and promised never to reveal the contents. Then, with relative calm restored, the debate continued late into the night. Next day, officials of the Six laboured to try to reconcile Mendès-France's and Spaak's proposals; and at 8.00 that evening the Ministers met again. At 11.00 p.m., Spaak proposed a brief adjournment, and retired to his office with Mendès-France. 'We shan't agree,' said Mendés-France, 'I'm convinced of it'; and he drew from his pocket a paper that he had been preparing. 'This is what I shall say when we realize we've failed,' he explained. 'I don't want to take the responsibility of breaking things off prematurely; but I can tell you that I've decided to say no.'[57]

Nothing Spaak said could shake him. Despite the concessions already made, despite last-minute pleas when the Conference resumed, despite renewed American pressure in the form of a note from Dulles delivered to Spaak at 1.00 a.m. while the meeting was still in progress, Mendès-France insisted on making his declaration. What had been offered him, he said, was still not enough to satisfy the French Parliament: to all intents and purposes, he was going away empty-handed.[58]

That Sunday, 22 August 1954, he left Brussels for London. Winston Churchill met him at the airport, and they drove together to the Prime Minister's summer residence at Chartwell. There they were met by Anthony Eden, who had returned from holiday for the occasion. As Mendès-France argued afterwards, he was unhappy that the price of Franco-German reconciliation in EDC should be a rift between France and Great Britain; but he was also anxious, no doubt, to forestall what Dulles had proposed in his note to Spaak: a conference of Benelux, Germany, Italy, the United States and Britain that would in fact have isolated France. Now, he made what one British Minister called 'a final half-hearted attempt to bring Great Britain into the EDC.' Churchill, although he had originally proposed the idea of a European army, would have none of it. 'The best way out,' he answered, would be if Mendès-France could persuade the French Parliament to ratify the existing Treaty with the declaration of intent proposed by Spaak and his partners. Its rejection, Churchill went on, would mean grave dangers to France and to the Western world. Mendès-France repeated that the French Parliament would certainly refuse to ratify it on any terms but those he was proposing. At this, Churchill and Eden together urged him to explain clearly in the debate that if EDC failed another solution would have to be found without delay. He agreed, and declared— characteristically setting a further time-limit—that this could be done within two months.[59]

Explicitly or not, what was now in prospect was a convergence of policy between the Governments of Britain and France. Both knew that the United States would insist on rearming the Germans; both were anxious to avoid too close or exclusive a link between Germany and America; both, however, were unwilling to accept—for themselves—a 'supranational' European solution. Both bore some responsibility for EDC's difficulties, as did the over-insistence of John Foster Dulles.

On Saturday 28 August 1954, despite a further last-minute compromise proposed by Spaak, Mendès-France submitted the original EDC Treaty to the French National Assembly. His speech was deliberately cool: he made it clear that he was neither endorsing EDC nor demanding a vote of confidence. Two days later, on Monday 30 August, the Assembly rejected the Treaty by 319 votes to 264 with 43 abstentions, on a merely procedural motion to postpone discussion indefinitely. Among the abstentions were Mendès-France and six of his Cabinet colleagues. Among the Noes were the Communist Party, the Gaullists, and more than half of both the Radicals and the Socialists. When the result was announced, the Opposition burst into the *Marseillaise*.[60]

God Save the Queen might have been almost as appropriate. Within two months, in fact, Britain had come to the rescue with a plan that Anthony Eden claimed later had come to him in his bath on the morning of Sunday 5 September—although it resembled the suggestion made to him two years earlier by Robert Schuman, that the Brussels Treaty should be extended to Germany and Italy. Was it also, perhaps, an echo of something that Mendès-France had said? At all events, on Wednesday 20 October 1954, Spaak, Mendès-France, Adenauer, Beyen, Bech and Gaetano Martino met with Eden in Paris to sign on Saturday 23 October an agreement enlarging the Brussels Treaty into Western European Union (WEU). It was a little more than a military alliance, and it had a consultative Assembly; but it bore no real resemblance to EDC. From Britain's point of view, its only provision that was even remotely 'supranational' was the pledge that her four divisions and her tactical air force would not be withdrawn from the Continent—except in 'an acute overseas emergency'—without the consent of a majority of WEU's member States. Germany, by contrast, faced notable constraints. The occupation régime was ended, and she was admitted to NATO; but her land contingent was limited to twelve divisions, and she was forbidden to manufacture atomic, biological or chemical weapons on her own soil.[61]

For many reasons, the establishment of WEU was a Pyrrhic victory. Those who had opposed a European army including Germans now faced the prospect of a German army within a looser, more or less traditional alliance. Those who had tried to achieve political unity in Europe by means of EDC and its attendant project for a Political Community now saw the ECSC as the sole survivor of their hopes. Those who had pressed for British participation now saw her a little more closely associated with her continental neighbours, but still not a member or even an associate of the only Community organization that remained.

At the Coal and Steel Community's headquarters in Luxembourg, some officials were frankly despondent: Europe, it seemed, had come to the end of the road. But Jean Monnet remained optimistic. Like Mendès-France, he recognized the importance of achieving economic unity as a basis for political and military integration. After a setback, the right course was to draw the lesson and continue building Europe by patient practical steps. Restored to health although no longer smoking his favourite cigars, he was now eager to press on with developing the ECSC and its association with Great Britain.

On Monday 6 September 1954, just a week after the defeat of EDC, Monnet had a preliminary talk with the head of the British Delegation, Sir Cecil Weir, and arranged to start unofficial discussions with Duncan Sandys, the Minister of Supply. Friendly as these were, they faced a number of difficulties. Already, the form of association now being worked out was far from Monnet's original idea of bringing Britain into the coal-steel common market; now, Monnet had a struggle to prevent its being weakened further still. In particular, although the British at length agreed to the High Authority's establishing a permanent delegation in London, they firmly rejected the notion of a joint Assembly and a Court. With WEU in the offing, they were anxious for quick results; but the High Authority, however 'supranational', was handicapped as always by the need to secure agreement from all the Community's member States. The French Government was by far the most difficult: Mendès-France disliked the prospect of a bilateral link between the ECSC and Great Britain, and—perhaps on the WEU analogy—would have preferred to see her represented in the Community's Council of Ministers. At length, on Wednesday 8 December 1954, after both private talks and a number of long six-nation discussions, Monnet and his colleagues were authorized to initial a draft agreement. It was formally signed in London on 21 December 1954. After ratification by all seven national Parliaments, it came into force on Friday 23 September 1955.[62]

Britain's association with the ECSC undoubtedly proved useful. It led to a steady exchange of technical data; it installed in London a Community delegation with an influential information office; and in 1957 it produced an agreement to cut steel tariffs between Britain and the Community to a level on both sides around ten per cent. For Monnet, these modest beginnings of consultation and joint action were a basis on which more ambitious projects might have been built. The British Government, however, clearly saw the Association Agreement not as a potential starting point for eventual membership, but rather—in the words of Alfred Robens, chief Opposition speaker in the debate on its ratification—as 'the model of the association which we would be ready to accept in any organizations, any communities that may be set up in Europe to deal with things other than coal and steel'.[63]

So the Echternach dance continued, five steps forward, three steps back. With only the Coal and Steel Community left, the first —'supranational'—stage in Europe's unification seemed to be over. Britain had embarked on a new relationship with the Continent, but she still retained her 'special position'. Having rejected EDC for its supranational features, she had made a practical pledge of British forces to the intergovernmental WEU. Having removed the supranational element from Monnet's original proposals of December 1953, she had taken the practical step towards tariff-cutting embodied in her Association Agreement with the ECSC. With that, for the time being, 'Europeans' had to be satisfied. There was now a pause in the dance's rhythm before progress could begin again.

CHAPTER TEN

Never So Good

What is Europe? Thought that is never contented.
Paul Hazard[1]

Greater virtues are needed to bear good fortune than bad.
François, duc de la Rochefoucauld[2]

British foreign policy has usually been content to react to
the behaviour of others. *A. J. P. Taylor*[3]

WHILE Europe's statesmen and civil servants toiled and wrangled, others
had not been idle—on farms and building sites, in factories and offices,
in schools and universities, in laboratories, hospitals and homes. The
same burst of creative energy that had begun to transform international
relations had also been changing the face of the continent and the lives
of its inhabitants. Within ten years after World War II Western
Europe had not only recovered from most of war's effects; it had
entered a new phase of unprecedented peaceful growth.

A bird's or airman's eye view of Europe now revealed a more reassuring landscape. The scars and shadows of war had largely—although
not entirely—vanished. Along the temperate latitudes stretched familiar
green miles of meadow, field and woodland, smudged but made more
prosperous by the industrial towns and suburbs that thrust across them
from north-west to south-east, through Lancashire, London, the Netherlands, Belgium, the Ruhr and Munich, up the Seine to Paris, through
Lyon, spanning the Alps to Milan, Turin, Genoa. Only the periphery,
the bleak uplands and the dry southern *maquis*, remained barren and
poor.

Spreading like webs or wheelspokes from London, Paris, Cologne,
Milan, the railways were busy again, many of them now electrified, and
soon to rival the airlines with the smooth speed and luxury of the Trans-
Europ-Express. Motorways (*Autobahnen, autoroutes, autostrade* or
express highways) were under construction, most notably in Germany,
Italy and France. The Rhine, the Weser, the Seine and Europe's other
great rivers and ship canals were once more crowded with barges; the

H

rebuilt port of Rotterdam and its older competitors—London, Antwerp, Hamburg, Bremerhaven—were once more dealing with a prewar volume of traffic, as were Liverpool and Marseilles. The busiest airports—London, Paris, Frankfurt, Rome, Copenhagen and Berlin—were each handling about a million passengers a year.[4]

People were travelling, and there were many more of them. Europeans spoke of a postwar 'baby boom', a 'population bulge', that was most marked in Finland, the Netherlands, France and Portugal. Returning servicemen had been eager to be fathers, and the birth-rate in almost all European countries had risen sharply in 1946 and 1947. No less important, many more children were now surviving: Western Europe's infant death-rate for 1955 was little more than half that for 1939, and in some countries—Denmark, Finland, Spain, Switzerland and the United Kingdom—it was rather less than half. The adult death-rate, too, was everywhere well below the 1939 level. Deaths from accidents, malignancies and stress diseases were significantly increasing; but many of the illnesses that had once been killers—typhoid, smallpox, diphtheria and other epidemic diseases—had by now been largely tamed. Tuberculosis was being brought under control; bronchitis and pneumonia were being fought with new drugs. The combined result was that by mid-1955 Western Europe's population totalled nearly 300 million. They were most densely concentrated in Britain, the Netherlands, Belgium, the Ruhr, the Rhineland, the Paris region, Lombardy and the Campagna round Naples. More than half of them—161 million—lived in France, Germany, Italy and the Benelux countries, forming the six-nation European Coal and Steel Community and, later, the Common Market. More than half of them, almost everywhere, were girls or women: only Iceland had an equal number of either sex, and only Luxembourg had fewer women than men.[5]

This increase in numbers was one reason for Western Europe's rapid economic expansion. By 1950, virtually all the member countries of OEEC had exceeded their prewar levels of production; by the beginning of 1955, all had done so. Now, Western Europe's total output was valued at more than 220 thousand million dollars. Her annual growth-rate had varied between 8·3 per cent in 1949–50 and 2·7 per cent in 1951–2; in 1954–5 it reached 6·7 per cent, well above the average for the whole decade. Since 1952, Western Europe had been enjoying a surplus in her overall balance of payments; by 1955, her total reserves of gold and foreign currency, which in 1950 had been just below eleven thousand million dollars, stood at nearly sixteen thousand million. The only major exception was the United Kingdom, whose reserves had dropped, during the same five-year period, from 3·7 to 2·2 thousand million dollars.[6]

In world trade, Western Europe's relative position had been eroded since 1938; but in the general expansion her total imports from the rest of the world had now tripled, and her total exports quadrupled. The most notable single increase was in her imports of energy, which had risen from seven per cent of her total consumption in 1937 to reach twenty-five per cent in 1955—four-fifths of it in the form of oil. Of her total imports, valued at eighteen thousand million dollars a year, nearly sixteen thousand million dollars' worth consisted of food, raw materials, fuel, ores, and base metals; of her total exports, valued at sixteen thousand million, eleven thousand million dollars' worth were capital and consumer goods and other manufactures. Western Europe, in other words, was still a workshop, in which many hands were gradually making lighter work.[7]

But her growing population was not the only reason for Europe's new prosperity. True, some countries with an ample labour force, like Germany, Italy, the Netherlands and Switzerland, were enjoying spectacular growth-rates, while Belgium, Britain and the Scandinavian countries, with limited labour supplies, grew more slowly. But France and Austria, equally hard-pressed for manpower, nevertheless expanded rapidly, the former at the cost of inflation, the latter with the aid of technical advance. This, reducing the so-called 'backlog of unexploited technology', helped expansion everywhere. From 1950 to 1955, employment in Western Europe rose by only 7 per cent, and total man-hours by only 8·2 per cent. Yet during the same period production increased by no less than 26·2 per cent, revealing a marked rise in productivity. This was made possible largely by new machinery, which in turn had required heavy capital investment. By 1955, Western Europe was investing forty-five thousand million dollars a year, or more than one-fifth of the value of its total production. Twenty per cent of these investments went to housing; but much of the rest was devoted to new industrial plant. Of the high-income countries, those with the lowest investment rates—Belgium and Great Britain—were among those with the slowest rate of growth.[8]

In all countries, investment was now partly supplied, enforced or encouraged by the State, which had come to play a far greater role in the economy. Of total government expenditure in 1955, five thousand million dollars—over eight per cent—went to direct investment, making up more than twelve per cent of total capital supplies. Most railways, central banks and airlines were virtually or wholly government-owned, and in many countries the State had a sizeable holding in heavy industry.

Altogether, government revenue and expenditure amounted to some sixty thousand million dollars.[9]

Some of this greatly increased government outlay was earmarked for defence, on which Western Europe was now spending nearly five per cent of the value of her total production. This overall figure was swollen, however, by the unusually high proportion—eight per cent—still being spent by Great Britain; for most countries, the figure was appreciably lower. A far more uniform element in government spending, and one that was more novel, was what was known in Britain as 'the Welfare State'. Primarily, this referred to the great expansion of social security: sickness and unemployment benefits, pensions and family allowances. In twenty years, the total spent on these had more than tripled: by the beginning of 1955 the average annual expenditure per head in Western Europe was 76 dollars, with the Saar the highest at 153 dollars, and Spain the lowest at 4·90 dollars. Except for Greece, Portugal and Spain, where social security was rudimentary, and Austria, Finland, Ireland and Italy, where it was still incomplete, most of Western Europe was now fully covered. Sweden and the United Kingdom had the most comprehensive systems, although in some cases Belgium, France, Germany and Luxembourg gave higher benefits. Of the total of over twenty-two thousand million dollars—not all of which, by any means, came from the State—the highest single item of expenditure was on pensions (nearly eight thousand million dollars a year), followed by medical care and sickness benefits (six thousand million), with family allowances coming third.[10]

Government spending on education had also greatly increased by 1955, although it was still only half of that devoted to defence. The average annual expenditure was 2·4 per cent of total production, with peaks of 3·4 per cent in Finland, Iceland and Sweden and troughs of 1·4 per cent in Greece and Spain and 1·2 per cent in Portugal. In absolute terms, education in Western Europe cost 5,312 million dollars in 1955, or eighteen dollars per head of population. The highest national expenditure per head was in Sweden, with 41 dollars, followed by Iceland with 31·6 and Switzerland with 30·5; Britain came fourth, together with Belgium and Luxembourg, at 25·9 dollars per head. The lowest expenditure, again, was in Portugal—two dollars and fifty cents In Western Europe as a whole, 81·8 per cent of all children between the ages of five and fourteen were at school, compared with nearly 100 per cent of American children, and only 15·9 per cent of those between fifteen and nineteen, compared with over 80 per cent in the United States. Higher education in Europe was open to only 4·5 per cent of the age-group between twenty and twenty-four. In primary schools,

Britain had the highest percentage; but secondary education was relatively most widespread in Sweden, and higher education in Denmark. In all three categories, Portugal again came last, although even there the number of secondary-school enrolments had doubled since 1938.[11]

More numerous, more healthy, better cared for, and—in some degree —better educated, more Europeans were now beginning to enjoy material prosperity. By 1955, the annual value of total production per head of population in Western Europe had reached 747 dollars; but this average was brought down by Spain, Greece and Portugal: in Belgium, Luxembourg, Sweden, Switzerland and the United Kingdom, production per head was already more than a thousand dollars a year. For the whole of Western Europe, private consumption per head—at official exchange rates—now averaged 490 dollars a year. Switzerland was in the lead with 825 dollars, followed by Belgium with 765, Sweden with 745 and the United Kingdom with 700. To cope with this growing purchasing power, thirteen million people, 10·3 per cent of the total labour force, were now engaged in wholesale and retail trade, compared with ten million or 8·9 per cent, in the nineteen-thirties. Altogether, there were just over four million stores, market stalls and mobile shops, or one for every seventy-two inhabitants. Belgium with many family businesses— and a 'Ministry of the Middle Classes' to protect them—had one for every thirty-four inhabitants; Iceland, at the other extreme, had one for every 158. Britain, once the nation of shopkeepers, had relatively fewer stores than most of her neighbours: soon, although less rapidly than Germany, she was to become a nation of supermarkets.[12]

More than half this army of retailers were sellers of food, on which Europeans were now spending an annual average of 177 dollars a head, rather more than one-third of the family budget. With the easing of supplies since the early postwar years, they had begun to eat less bread and fewer potatoes, and more fruit and meat. The annual consumption of cereals had fallen from 130 kilograms a head in 1948–9 to less than 120 in 1955; of potatoes, from over 120 kilograms to little more than 100. The consumption of fruit had risen from less than 40 kilograms to more than 60, and of meat from 30 to nearly 45. And if these had once been luxuries, Europeans could now afford others. They were now spending nearly forty dollars a head each year on household equipment, furniture and private cars, eight per cent of the family budget as against six per cent in 1949. One in five Europeans now had a radio set, as against one in ten before World War II; one in twelve had a telephone; one in twenty-five had a car. Sixteen per cent of families had television sets, fifteen per cent had washing machines, and ten per cent had refrigerators. All these numbers, moreover, were rapidly growing. In 1955 alone, two million new cars were driven on to European roads.[13]

It was two years later that Harold Macmillan told a British audience, 'Most of our people have never had it so good'; but already the so-called 'consumer society' had arrived. It contrasted sharply with the 'austerity' of the recent past. Its uglier aspects included smog, traffic jams, property speculation, horror comics, and organized appeals to prurience, vanity, snobbery and greed. To many, it seemed to be a world of advertising, public relations and expense account gluttony; of Edwardian suits and self-conscious connoisseurship; of espresso bars and vodka martinis; of 'James Bond' fantasies and after-shave lotions; of soft-faced men who had done well out of the peace. Some, who had never been poor, derided the 'materialism' of those who were eager for washing machines, refrigerators and television sets; an older generation, remembering the 'thirties depression, deplored the 'fecklessness' of families—eight out of every ten in Britain—who bought on hire purchase or deferred payment terms. What both types of critic found novel was the ability of 'working-class' people, many of them young, to afford the products of their own labour. Privileges once reserved for the few could now be shared, at least, by the many. Unit trusts introduced them to the stock exchange on the same principle as the conducted tours that offered them foreign travel. However imperfectly, frozen foods, paperbacks and do-it-yourself kits made widely available what had once been expensive or rare. It was not quite the world of equality and freedom so often imagined in wartime; but if gross inequality remained, both within European nations and between them, many more people had been freed—and freed by 'the system'—from fear and want.[14]

With a new material environment came a new mood, curiously blending 'realism' and fancy. In the various arts, the two were in counterpiont at different times. In painting, despite the isolated solidity of Renato Guttuso, 'social' or representational art was now either rare or weak. Paris was giving place to New York as the centre of finance and inspiration; and the chief thrust seemed to be inwards, toward the abstract, sensuous in the work of Nicolas de Staël or Jackson Pollock, more cerebral in the hard-edged, perhaps defensive products of the 'pop' and 'op' art that was to come. In serious music, the trend seemed to be in the same direction, influenced by the 'aleatory' methods and electronic techniques associated with Karlheinz Stockhausen; *mutatis mutandis*, popular music followed a similar course, both in the harmonic experiments of 'progressive' jazz and in the inchoate move away from tradi-

tional ballads and Dixieland imitations, towards the more insistent, re-
petitive and hypnotic rhythms of rock-and-roll and the later 'pop'.

European cinema was also growing moodier, more introspective. Immediately after World War II, its characteristic tone might have seemed
to be the romantic pessimism of Marcel Carné and his scriptwriter
Jacques Prévert, the resurrected surrealism of Jean Cocteau's *Orphée*,
or even the whimsicality of Great Britain's 'Ealing comedies'. But the
most creative talents at that time had been engaged in work that was
socially concerned, often explicitly 'neo-realist': Vittorio De Sica's
Sciuscia, *Ladri di Biciclette*, and *Umberto D*; René Clément's *La
Bataille du Rail* and *Les Jeux Interdits*; Georges Franju's short *Sang des
Bêtes*; Luchino Visconti's *La Terra Trema*; Roberto Rossellini's *Paisà*.
Then, in the early 'fifties, came a change. De Sica made his disappointing,
part-American *Stazione Termini*; Clément ventured into ironic comedy
with *Monsieur Ripois*; Franju launched into feature films; Visconti into
the historical equivocations of *Senso*; Rossellini into a series of run-of-
the-mill productions. 'Neo-realism' was to have further brief flashes;
but by 1955, broadly speaking, the most interesting talents seemed to be
those of the introverts: Michelangelo Antonioni, with *Le Amiche*, from
a story by Cesare Pavese; Ingmar Bergman, with *Smiles of a Summer
Night* and, soon, *The Seventh Seal*; Federico Fellini, with *La Strada*.
The French 'new wave' was yet to come: its future members were for
the most part making short 'documentaries' or writing film criticism;
but in this interim period their elders were already enlarging the scope of
cinema, often with mannered bravura, to admit strange dreams.

In literature and the theatre there was a similar interaction. In France,
the characteristic postwar figures seemed to be Jean-Paul Sartre, Simone
de Beauvoir and Albert Camus. All struggled to square technical philosophical concepts with the irrational brute facts of existence; but their
tortured *littérature engagée* was soon to be challenged by other
experiments, partly linguistic: Nathalie Sarraute's *Portrait d'un Inconnu*, Alain Robbe-Grillet's *Le Voyeur*, Michel Butor's *L'Emploi du
Temps*. In Italy, the 'neo-realist' work of Carlo Levi, Vasco Pratolini and
even Elio Vittorini began to be over-shadowed by the more fanciful
complexity of Italo Calvino, while Pier Paolo Pasolini moved on from
the immediacy of *Ragazzi di Vita* to more reflective ventures, recording
popular speech with an exactitude that was almost academic. The move
away from simple realism was most marked in Germany, where only
nightmares seemed capable of explaining nightmare. Older writers like
Hans Werner Richter or Gerd Gaiser having explored the limits of traditional narrative, it was left to such newcomers as Günter Grass or Uwe
Johnson to open trapdoors into darker depths.

In Britain, meanwhile, the process was partially reversed. Here, one immediate sequel to World War II seemed to have been a taste for the Gothic, if not the fey. The grotesque novels of Mervyn Peake; the fantasies of William Sansom; the juicy extravaganzas of Dylan Thomas; the charades of Christopher Fry or Ronald Duncan; the brave preciosity of Denton Welch—perhaps in this liminal territory the imagination had already sought a peacetime stimulus comparable to the demands of war. There was more than a suspicion, however, of dilettantism, of reaction against wartime drabness rather than an attempt to assimilate and reinterpret what had been deeply felt. This was especially so in the theatre. Even John Whiting, gifted and highly serious, seemed unable to engage his themes full-bloodedly; and while *Salad Days* vied for popularity with plays by Terence Rattigan, critics overpraised translations from Ugo Betti, Marcel Aymé and Jean Anouilh. Once more, the change came in the mid-'fifties. In 1953, John Wain published a 'picaresque' first novel, *Hurry On Down*, followed in 1954 by Kingsley Amis's *Lucky Jim*; in May 1956 John Osborne's *Look Back in Anger* was staged at the Royal Court Theatre. Publicists lumped these three very different writers together, to their annoyance, as 'angry young men'—chiefly because all three were equally impatient with postwar neo-gentility, but also because their idiom was vigorous and blunt. Partly concerned with English class nuances, their work seemed insulated from some of their continental colleagues' obsessions; but its robust directness, which in Amis's case owed something to the experience in the services that his generation had shared, marked a more serious—if less solemn—mood in English writing. Other examples were Robert Conquest's verse anthology, *New Lines*, which launched a short-lived 'Movement' for stricter form and greater clarity, and in particular the taut, muscular poems of Philip Larkin and Thom Gunn. At the same time, however, an equally English tradition of puckish intellectual fantasy lived on in some of the novels of Iris Murdoch and Muriel Spark.

It was in architecture, finally, that fancy and 'realism' were now most effectively blended. Much of Western Europe's postwar building, certainly, was uninspired. Identical cheap apartments or large commercial offices—both badly needed—were not promising subjects: too often, they seemed to treat human individuals as interchangeable units, belittled by sheer numbers, to be stacked like convicts in pale-grey blocks of more or less comfortable cells. But other assignments had already by 1955 produced undoubted masterpieces. Some were relatively orthodox, like the busy boxes of the Royal Festival Hall in London, Alison and Peter Smithson's stark, flatland Secondary School at Hunstanton, Norfolk, or Arne Jacobsen's icily austere Town Hall in Rodovre, Copenhagen. Others were comfortingly human, like the welcoming Lijnbaan shopping centre in Rotterdam, Michael Scott's gay and efficient bus terminal at Beresford Place in Dublin, or the colourful honeycomb of the Gröndal apartment complex in Stockholm. But the most exciting were fantastic useful monuments—Le Corbusier's horned barbaric Church of Notre-Dame du Haut at Ronchamp in the Vosges; Stazione Termini in Rome, with its roof leaping from the ruins of the pre-Christian Servian Wall; the dazzling sunflower ceiling of Pier Luigi Nervi's Casino at Chianciano Terme near Lake Trasimeno; Danzeisen and Voser's astonishing Goldzack works at Gossau in Switzerland, with its stepped and corrugated roof like a row of gigantic transparent cable-drums tipped slightly sideways. Together, such buildings as these spoke of hope and vision after the desolation of war. No: Europeans were far from finished. Indeed, they had barely begun.

Those who were working to unite Europe at this time badly needed such encouragement. By the beginning of 1955, most of their hopes had been disappointed. The OEEC, which some had once believed might be the basis of a European customs union, had become a useful but traditional body for co-operation between sovereign governments. The Council of Europe was virtually powerless. The European Coal and Steel Community, once thought of as the spearhead of unity, was now a blade without a shaft: the further projects for a European Defence Community and a European Political Community had finally been broken. Britain, it was true, had helped to form Western European Union, and had concluded an Agreement of Association with the surviving Coal and Steel Community; but Western European Union was just one more intergovernmental body, and the coal-steel Association Agreement was a means for consultation and little more. Joseph Stalin's death had reduced the incentive of fear that had once helped spur Europeans towards unity; the death of Alcide De Gasperi had removed one of Europe's foremost friends. Richer now, fat with peace, and no longer so frightened, had Europeans forgotten the hard lessons that war and poverty had taught them? Did they once more believe that their nation-states could solve their problems separately? Had they lost faith in the future they had sought to build together? It seemed so. On Thursday 11 November 1954, when Jean Monnet announced in Luxembourg that he would not seek re-election as President of the coal-steel High Authority when his mandate expired in the following February, it seemed as if a generation were passing, as if an epoch of bright, misguided hopes were coming to an end.

And yet, within less than a year, this dismal climate had been totally transformed. Fears that the Coal and Steel Community, now isolated, might fail, had proved groundless. Monnet had been replaced at the High Authority, not by some obscure technocrat, but by a political figure who was also a convinced 'European'. Above all, Europe—as the phrase went—had been 'relaunched'; and Britain too had begun to reconsider, if not yet radically to change, her policy towards it.

Monnet proposed to leave the High Authority, as he told his colleagues and the press, 'in order to be able to take part with complete freedom of action and speech in the construction of European unity'. Already, however, two days after the fatal Monday 30 August 1954, on which the French Parliament had failed to ratify the Defence Community Treaty, he had begun to discuss the prospects for reviving the European idea. On Wednesday 1 September 1954, he was in Paris consulting his friends among the 'Europeans': it was the first of a whole series of such meetings throughout that autumn and the following spring. The list of those whom he saw made an impressive roll-call: Antoine Pinay, René Pleven, Robert Schuman, Guy Mollet, Paul Ramadier, Pierre Mendès-France, Pierre-Henri Teitgen; Paul-Henri Spaak, Jean Rey, Pierre Wigny; Joseph Bech; Giuseppe Pella, Emilio Battista; Ludwig Erhard, Eugen Gerstenmaier, Walter Hallstein, Konrad Adenauer, Walter Freitag, Heinrich Imig. The two last, German trade-unionists who had come to know and trust Monnet through their work with the Coal and Steel Community, were for the time being his line of communication with the German Socialist Party, still suspicious of the moves afoot to unite Western Europe. As time went on, however, contact and understanding grew here too. Patiently, Monnet pursued his consultations, travelling repeatedly to Paris, Bonn, Brussels and Strasbourg; when he was not deep in conversation with his visitors in Luxembourg, he seemed always to be on the telephone or on the train. As the weeks went by, plans for the relaunching of Europe gradually crystallized into action.[15]

Monnet's mandate as President of the High Authority was due to expire on Thursday 10 February 1955, two years after the formal opening of the 'common market' in coal, iron ore and scrap. The anniversary date, it seemed, might be the moment for him to make a resounding political statement, a rallying-cry and a call for further action. What should that action be? One of Monnet's closest young associates, the Englishman François Duchêne, suggested at one point that Monnet should stand for the French Parliament, in order to form an explicitly 'European' party in France. If the idea ever tempted Monnet, he quickly thought better of it. What seemed far more appropriate was to form a 'European' party on a European, not a national, basis. It might be a 'European Front' or action group, composed not of individuals but of political parties and trade unions themselves.[16]

By January 1955, the idea of an action group had taken firm shape, and its proposed programme was beginning to be sketched out. At first, this included plans for further integration in the fields of energy and transport, to be achieved by extending the powers of the Coal and Steel Community; for the establishment of new Community institutions to deal with armaments and the peaceful uses of atomic energy; for direct elections to the existing Common Assembly; and for the convening of a new 'Ad hoc Assembly' to study and promote new steps towards unity. After further discussion, however, Monnet dropped the plan for an armaments pool, which was all too likely to arouse the same motley opposition as the Defence Community project. He also rebaptized his proposed action group, this time as a 'Front for the United States of Europe'. Then, in the last week of February, came a new idea, that all six Community member governments might issue a joint communiqué. What had begun as the notion of a resignation speech had turned into the plan for an action group. That in turn had led to a programme for further unification. Now it was turning into proposals for action by governments.[17]

What had made this seem feasible was a change of Government in France. Over the weekend of 5–6 February 1955. Pierre Mendès-France's cabinet, already four times reshuffled, had finally fallen; and after Antoine Pinay, Pierre Pflimlin and Christian Pineau had each in turn failed to form a Government, a cabinet headed by Edgar Faure had won a vote of confidence on Wednesday 23 February. It included several of those whom Monnet had been consulting: Pinay was Foreign Minister, Schuman Minister of Justice, and Teitgen Minister for France Overseas. With their support, it might now be possible to persuade the Six to take action; and with this in mind, Monnet once more revised and simplified his proposals. Now, they included the extension of the Coal and Steel Community to cover energy and transport; the establishment of a new Community for the peaceful uses of atomic energy; and the formation of a European Full Employment Insurance Fund.[18]

To achieve these aims, he envisaged a meeting of Foreign Ministers; and at the beginning of April, after the French *Conseil de la République* had approved the WEU agreements, Paul-Henri Spaak formally proposed that such a meeting be held in three weeks' time. Its aim, he wrote, would be

...to relaunch the European idea by extending the attributions of the Coal and Steel Community. This extension of the Community could apply to all existing forms of energy (electricity, gas and fuel) and to means of transport (railways, river traffic, roads and airlines). The pooling of efforts for the peaceful development of atomic energy could also be entrusted to an organization dependent on the E.C.S.C. In order to achieve this extension, it would be urgently necessary to organize an international conference at which the idea would be examined practically, and whose aim would also be the drafting of a treaty. The chairman of this conference could be M. Monnet.[19]

All seemed well on the way to being settled, when Monnet heard two pieces of bad news.

The first came on Tuesday 5 April 1955, in a telephone call from Hallstein in Bonn. Adenauer, who was due to receive Pinay at the end of April to discuss the Saar dispute and the canalization of the Moselle, was anxious to avoid complicating these delicate matters with a six-nation Foreign Ministers' meeting, which also threatened to clash with some speaking engagements of his own. He therefore proposed that it be delayed until the end of May, after the next session of the coal-steel Common Assembly. What was more, he felt that the question of further integration required more detailed study. The reason underlying this was that pooling atomic energy, which Monnet saw as the kernel of his project, was less popular in Germany than the prospect of freer trade, perhaps within a general common market.[20]

The second piece of bad news came a week later, from Paris. Here, the order of priorities was exactly the reverse: except with the national atomic authorities, the idea of a nuclear pool was popular, while the lowering of tariffs was not. Edgar Faure, moreover, depended on the support of the Social Republicans, who were hostile to 'supranationality' and wary of Monnet and the High Authority; as a result, his statements on Europe were understandably cautious. At a press conference on Wednesday 13 April 1955, he spoke only of 'certain formulae of European co-operation [sic] for atomic energy', and declared that the European organization of energy and transport would not necessarily be achieved within the framework of the ECSC.[21]

The next few days were anxious and uncertain. On Friday 15 April it was provisionally agreed that the Foreign Ministers' meeting would be held on 30 May; but so clouded were its prospects that Monnet was briefly tempted to seek a further postponement. Before he could do so, however, the train of events that he had helped to set in motion gave a further lurch forward. This time, the impulse came from The Hague.[22]

Johan Willem Beyen, the Netherlands' joint Foreign Minister, had long been anxious to broaden the scope of European economic integration, which had hitherto been practised and envisaged sector by sector. On 4 April 1955, he had sent to Spaak a memorandum in which he explained his reasons:

All partial integration tends to solve the difficulties in one sector by measures which harm other sectors or the consumers' interests, and it tends to exclude foreign competition. That is not the way to increase European productivity. Furthermore, sector integration does not help to strengthen the feeling of Europe's solidarity and unity in the same degree as general economic integration. To strengthen this feeling, it is essential that the notion of the European States' joint responsibility for the common good be incorporated in an organization adapted to the pursuit of the general interest, and whose executive body is responsible not to Governments but to a supranational Parliament. . . .

That is why it seems opportune for the three [Benelux] Governments to take a well-prepared initiative which might usefully be announced at the E.C.S.C. Foreign Ministers' meeting. Such an initiative would aim at establishing a supranational Community whose task it would be to achieve the economic integration of Europe in the general sense, proceeding by means of a customs union to the establishment of an economic union. By clearly defining our point of view, we shall be able to put an end to the confusion and discouragement of those who support integration; and this seems to me to be of very particular interest for the future integration of Europe.

On Thursday 21 April 1955, in a speech to the Netherlands Council of the European Movement, Beyen made these views public, and called for a study to be made of general economic integration, on supranational lines.[23]

Within twenty-four hours, Monnet had paid a lightning visit to Paul-Henri Spaak in Brussels; and on the following day, Saturday 23 April, Spaak himself was in The Hague. Together, he and Beyen agreed to ask Joseph Bech of Luxembourg to join them in submitting to the Foreign Ministers' meeting a joint Benelux Memorandum based partly on Beyen's and partly on Monnet's texts.[24]

When Pinay and Adenauer held their long-scheduled meeting on the following Friday and Saturday, 29 and 30 April, they announced their agreement that the time had come 'to give a new impulse to European co-operation', especially in the fields of transport, air navigation, aircraft-building and research on atomic energy and its peaceful uses. Beyen's speech, perhaps, had forced the pace; but the reference to 'European co-operation' was not reassuring; and it was clearly essential that the Benelux Memorandum form the agenda of the Foreign Ministers' meeting. For this, it had to be well drafted, and it had to be presented soon. From now on, Monnet kept in close touch with Spaak. At length, on Friday 6 May, Spaak announced that the reworked draft was ready. It came with a covering note: 'Herewith your child.'[25]

On Monday 9 May 1955, the fifth anniversary of the Schuman Declaration, Monnet—still 'caretaker' President of the High Authority —presented its annual Report to the Common Assembly. He said little of his projects for the future: but he took care to point out that there was no essential contradiction between extending unification to new sectors and pursuing general economic integration. In response, on the following Saturday 14 May, the Assembly unanimously voted a Resolution calling on the six Foreign Ministers, whose meeting was now fixed for 1 June, to 'charge an intergovernmental conference or conferences to work out, with the appropriate aid of the Community's institutions, the necessary draft treaties for the achievement of the next steps in European integration, of which the establishment of the European Coal and Steel Community was the beginning.' On the previous day, moreover, the Assembly had asked Monnet to 'intervene' with the six Governments to ensure that its views on social policy were heard. The 'relaunching of Europe' was thus doubly linked, so far as the Assembly could ensure it, with the existing 'supranational' institutions. For the time being, there was little more to do except wait.[26]

Eventually, on Friday 20 May, Monnet received two crucial telephone calls. The first was from Paul-Henri Spaak: the Benelux Memorandum was being officially submitted to the Foreign Ministers' Conference. The second call was from René Mayer in Paris: Edgar Faure and Antoine Pinay had just asked the French Cabinet to propose him as Monnet's successor on the High Authority. The first was a victory. The second was an irony.[27]

What was ironic was that just at this moment Monnet himself was preparing to withdraw his resignation. When he had originally announced it, in November 1954, the situation in Europe had looked bleak. Now, it was hopeful again—partly because of the influence that Monnet's position in Luxembourg had helped him to exert. There, he had material resources—offices, advisers, secretaries, drivers, telephones and telex machines, as well as an official platform: the material problems involved in all political work were easily solved. As long ago as December 1954, the ECSC's embryonic Parliament, the Common Assembly, had urged him to reconsider the decision to step down; and now it had voted two resolutions calling for the ECSC and Monnet himself to be given an active role in the 'relaunching of Europe'. Already, at the Assembly's Strasbourg session, Monnet had begun to think about staying on; and by the time he received Mayer's news on Friday 20 May 1955, he had already written the first draft of a letter on the subject to the governments of the Six.[28]

He hesitated, but not for long. The French Cabinet was due to meet on the following Wednesday, 25 May. On Saturday 21 May, Monnet sent off his letter; and three days later on Tuesday 24 May, he gave it to the press. In it he explained his reason: 'In the face of the relaunching of policy undertaken by Governments, it would not be understood if I were not to declare myself ready once again to participate directly in the development of the task undertaken, should Governments wish to confirm the desire that several of them have insistently expressed to me.'[29]

If this was a bid for re-appointment to the presidency of the High Authority, there were arguments in its favour. René Mayer, a large, bass-voiced, Mr Punch-like figure who had been a Radical Premier of France before retiring to private business, was a 'European' and had had some hand in the original Schuman Declaration; but the 'anti-Europeans' in Edgar Faure's Cabinet—particularly the Social Republicans Gaston Palewski, General Pierre Koenig and General Edouard Corniglion-Molinier—were not without weight, and there was no guarantee that they would support him. It might prove harder to oppose Monnet, the present incumbent; and even if he were rejected, the fact that he too was in the running might make it easier for Mayer to be accepted as a compromise. Such a concession by the 'Europeans' might then win them greater freedom on matters of substance when the Foreign Ministers met. The unaccustomed ambiguity of Monnet's letter, moreover, left it unclear whether he was in fact offering his services as President of the High Authority or for some other role in the 'relaunching of Europe'. At this stage, it was still uncertain whether the two would be separate or not.[30]

In the event, his offer was refused: when the French Cabinet met, on Wednesday 25 May, it chose René Mayer as France's official candidate. But on the question of substance, Monnet's action may have had some effect. At the same meeting, the Government gave a fairly broad mandate to Antoine Pinay, its delegate to the Foreign Ministers' Conference; as one of Pinay's assistants put it, France could not say 'no' to everything. Next day, Edgar Faure addressed a news conference in unusually 'European' terms. 'A true organization,' he said, 'cannot be given too loose a formula, cannot become a mere club or a conference of ambassadors. If the term "supranationality" is alarming, let us say that nevertheless it must be given powers of decision.'[31]

So far, so good. With the French Government once more co-operative, the way seemed clear for the 'relaunching of Europe'. The Foreign Ministers were due to meet in Messina on the following Wednesday and Thursday, 1 and 2 June. But now, at the last moment, came news of a further obstacle. In addition to the Memorandum from Benelux, the German Government too had submitted a draft paper which threatened to compromise the Community principle just when the French Government had at last endorsed it.

The Benelux Memorandum proposed further integration in a number of specific sectors—transport, energy, and atomic energy; it also proposed 'the establishment of a European economic community', to integrate the economy as a whole. This, like the sectors to be integrated, required 'the establishment of a common authority endowed with the necessary powers'. The German paper, on the other hand, was far more loosely worded. 'An attempt, it declared, 'must be made to achieve European economic unity', and 'close economic cooperation [*sic*] must be established between the States'; but this could be achieved by 'constituting under the responsibility of the ECSC Council of Ministers a permanent consultative organ' with limited tasks. These views were those of Ludwig Erhard, Adenauer's stout, cigar-smoking and ultra-'liberal' Minister of Economic Affairs, who deeply distrusted both *dirigisme* and 'supranationality'; but to have accepted them would have been a departure from past practice and a betrayal of existing hopes. 'Co-operation' was no substitute for integration. A 'consultative organ' responsible to the Council of Ministers, who represented the individual member States, would have been very different from the ECSC's independent High Authority, to say nothing of its Court and Assembly. Instead of continuing and developing the new method of pooling national sovereignty under common rules and common democratic institutions, begun by the Coal and Steel Community, the German Memorandum seemed to propose returning to the traditional method of intergovernmental bargaining that experience had condemned.[32]

Yet, nevertheless, the German arguments had some point. The Benelux Memorandum had called for 'a common authority'; but how, asked one of Monnet's German colleagues, could this work in the broader field of global economic integration? A body like the High Authority of the ECSC might be suitable for dealing with specific sectors, where governments could agree on fairly detailed rules in advance; but it could hardly tackle the whole range of the economy, even supposing that governments were willing to give it such broad and sweeping powers.[33]

With the benefit of hindsight, the way out of the dilemma now seems clear. In practice, the ECSC High Authority, despite its name, seldom behaved like a 'supranational' Government, ruling by *diktat*. Its essential quality was its independence, not its direct power. As an impartial body responsible to the Common Assembly for the affairs of the Community as a whole, it worked in harness—in 'dialogue', as Community jargon put it—with the Council of Ministers, whose opinion it sought more often than was legally required. A similar model, based on the High Authority's practice rather than its paper prerogatives, was at length to be adopted for the future Common Market. Here, the independent body was to be the Commission, whose most important role was to propose solutions for the problems that it alone could see from an overall Community viewpoint; the main decisions were to be taken by the Council of Ministers, with the Commission sitting in. Gradually, the Common Market was to agree on what was virtually a series of further Treaties, each prepared by the Commission with the aid of the Assembly, and voted by the Council of Ministers representing the member States. The difficulty of delegating so much authority, daunting as it seemed at the outset, was resolved by doing so gradually as successive problems were broached.

Little of this could be foreseen, however, when the Foreign Ministers' Conference opened in Messina. In the Mediterranean sunshine, they were taking a step in the dark. The setting—Sicily in Spring—was magnificent; but like many historic occasions, the meeting was less impressive at the time than it came to seem in retrospect. The delegates stayed in a former monastery, the Hotel San Domenico at Taormina, some twenty-five miles down the coast; in the late afternoon of Wednesday 1 June 1955, they drove to Messina. Their talks were to last until the early hours of Friday 3 June. Their host was the dapper Gaetano Martino, Italian Foreign Minister and Rector of Messina University. The chairman was Joseph Bech, from Luxembourg, avuncular but shrewd behind his Santa Claus moustaches. The other participants were Paul-Henri Spaak, from Belgium; Antoine Pinay, from France, brisk and punctilious; Walter Hallstein, from Germany, in a slightly crumpled lightweight suit; and Johan Willem Beyen, from the Netherlands. Each had his own preoccupations. The Benelux Ministers took turns at explaining their Memorandum. Pinay approved it in principle, but pointed out that economic integration would raise many problems, among them the height of the future Common Market's outer tariff and the levelling up of wage rates as between the member countries. Martino, submitting a Memorandum on behalf of Italy, stressed the need to harmonize taxes and social security contributions; he also called for a European fund to retrain and resettle workpeople who had to change their jobs. Hallstein, a convinced 'European' who had helped negotiate the ECSC Treaty but who as German Secretary of State was the only non-Minister heading a delegation, had the invidious task of presenting the patchy German Memorandum; but he made the most of its positive features: its call for a European atomic energy pool, and its sound analysis of what a general Common Market would involve. It was Hallstein, indeed, who towards the end of the day put the crucial question: 'Are we agreed to do something on the basis of the Six?'[34]

They were; but at first sight it looked unspectacular. When the delegates finally parted, after a candle-lit dinner in their monastery, they had voted a Resolution several pages long. It took account of all three preparatory papers, and especially of the Benelux Memorandum, much of whose wording it adopted. 'The Governments,' it declared,

... believe that the time has come to make a fresh advance towards the building of Europe. [The Benelux Memorandum had referred to its 'integration'.] They are of the opinion that this must be achieved, first of all, in the economic field.

They consider that it is necessary to work for the establishment of a united Europe by the development of common institutions, the progressive fusion of national economies, the creation of a common market and the progressive harmonisation of their social policies.

Such a policy seems to them indispensable if Europe is to maintain her position in the world, regain her influence and prestige and achieve a continuing increase in the standard of living of her population.

But by way of practical decisions, the Messina Resolution seemed mainly to advocate a series of studies—of transport, energy and atomic power, and of the gradual establishment of 'a European market, free from all customs duties and all quantitative restrictions'. 'Conferences' were to be held 'to work out treaties or other arrangements concerning the questions under consideration'; 'the preparatory work' was to be done by 'a Committee of Governmental representatives, assisted by experts, under the chairmanship of a political personality responsible for co-ordinating the work in the various fields.'[35]

To many this seemed unduly cautious. 'The Governments,' wrote Le Monde, 'have implicitly abandoned the idea of "supranationality".' 'Isn't all that very vague?' asked a journalist at Messina. 'No,' said the Ministers' patient Luxembourg Secretary-General, Christian Calmès; 'proposing a statesman to run it is a guarantee that it will work, since he'll make it a point of honour to succeed.'[36]

Calmès was to be proved right. Shortly afterwards, Paul-Henri Spaak was chosen to head the new Committee. On Saturday 9 July 1955, it held its first meeting, at the Belgian Ministry of Foreign Affairs; after that, it met in the Château de Val Duchesse, a modest mansion standing in its own grounds on the south-east outskirts of Brussels. Its mandate, although general, was fairly clear. Despite the national contrasts concealed in the Messina Resolution, the Governments had agreed on their broad objectives: the Committee's task was to discuss means, not ends. Spaak, admittedly, was no expert; but his parliamentary experience, his emotional power and oratorical skill, and above all his imposing physical presence, were invaluable as a goad. Pounding the table, imposing deadlines, threatening and cajoling, he forced the technicians to stick to the point. He was aided, moreover, by Jean Monnet and his associates. Although the Committee was composed of national delegates, it also included representatives from the High Authority—officially Dirk Spierenburg, semi-officially the ubiquitous Pierre Uri. Uri—'prodigiously brilliant, ditto vain, ditto kindly' was a colleague's private description—was still prominent in the so-called 'Monnet grapevine' that for some years had helped to disseminate 'European' ideas, information and influence. Through him and others, as well as directly, Monnet kept in close touch with the Spaak Committee's work. For Monnet himself, however, one chapter was now closing. The Messina Conference, before discussing its Resolution, had quickly dispatched the main item on its original agenda: it had appointed René Mayer to succeed Monnet as President of the High Authority.[37]

So, on Thursday 9 June 1955, Monnet had said his farewells to the staff in Luxembourg. On Friday 10 June he had officially handed over to Mayer. On Saturday evening, 11 June, his friend and assistant Max Kohnstamm had given a fork dinner for him; they had stayed up talking until 2.00 a.m. Then, on Monday 13 June, Monnet had tidied up his last official papers. He was sixty-six. He had 'launched Europe', and now had helped to 'relaunch' it. At this point, quite honourably, many men might have retired. Instead, Monnet went on his travels again, to bring together the 'Front' or 'Committee' for the United States of Europe that he had planned before the Messina meeting.[38]

His first stop was Paris. Here he saw Etienne Hirsch, Robert Marjolin, Hubert Beuve-Méry of Le Monde, Robert Schuman, Guy Mollet and Robert Bothereau of Force-Ouvrière. In London, he had talks with Campbell Secord, a Canadian engineer whose advice he sought on the proposed European atomic organization. In Bonn, he saw his trade-union friends Walter Freitag and Heinrich Imig, then Hallstein and Adenauer, then the Socialist leaders Erich Ollenhauer and Herbert

237

Wehner. In Belgium, he called on the Socialist Max Buset and a number of labour leaders, including André Renard. In the Netherlands, he saw Sicco Mansholt, Jelle Zijlstra and the president of the Dutch trade union federation. In Paris again after a brief August holiday, he had further talks with Hirsch, Marjolin, Pierre Mendès-France and Louis Armand, the *polytechnicien* who had revolutionized French state railways and who now suggested the name 'Euratom' for the proposed atomic energy pool. All this time, acceptances had been trickling in; and on Thursday 13 October 1955, after six more weeks of travel, meetings, correspondence and telephone calls, Monnet was at last able to announce the formation of his 'Action Committee for the United States of Europe'. It comprised, as corporate members, the Socialist, Christian Democrat and Liberal Parties, as well as the non-Communist trade unions, of all six member countries of the ECSC. As one anonymous commentator later said, it was 'something like the collective democratic conscience of the European Community'. Its thirty-three founder delegates included such well-known names as Guy Mollet, Erich Ollenhauer, Amintore Fanfani, Kurt Kiesinger, Théo Lefèvre, Maurice Faure, Ugo La Malfa, René Pleven, Auguste Cool and Giulio Pastore. Their first aim, they declared, would be to demonstrate 'to Governments, Parliaments, and public opinion their determination to see that the Messina Resolution of 2 June becomes a veritable step towards the United States of Europe.'[39]

Backed—and sometimes prodded—by Monnet's distinguished action group, the Spaak Committee toiled on in Val Duchesse. At length, Spaak sent Uri, the German delegate Hans von der Groeben, and one of his own Belgian assistants, to a quiet retreat in the south of France—the Grand Hôtel at St-Jean-Cap-Ferrat—with instructions to draft a final report. When it was ready and broadly approved by the Committee, Spaak presented its findings to a special session of the ECSC Assembly held in the Belgian Senate Chamber on Tuesday 13 March 1956. Just over five weeks later, on Saturday 21 April, he submitted the printed Report to the six Foreign Ministers. Meeting in Venice on Tuesday 29 May, they adopted it as a basis for formal negotiations, and the Spaak Committee turned into a Treaty-making conference, which began work in Val Duchesse on Tuesday 26 June. Here, once again, Spaak deployed all his boisterous talents to force the pace. On one typical occasion, when experts had haggled interminably about the tariff to be applied to banana imports, he deliberately lost his temper. 'I give you two hours,' he told them; 'if it's not settled by then, I shall call the press in and announce that Europe won't be built after all, because we can't agree about bananas.' Then he walked out. When he came back two hours later, the problem had been solved.[40]

Spaak's blend of chairmanship and gamesmanship was highly effective. It was helped, moreover, by two very serious crises in the summer and autumn of 1956. The first was over Suez, the second in Hungary. Both gave new impetus to the unification of Western Europe.

The origins of the Suez crisis can be traced back to the nineteenth century; but its immediate causes emerged only after World War II. Middle-Eastern politics were now polarized, both by the establishment of Israel in the midst of resentful Arab countries and by the revolution in Egypt that replaced puppet kings and pashas, first by General Mohammed Neguib, then by Colonel Gamal Abdel Nasser. Four external powers had interests in the area. For the Soviet Union and the United States, it was one focus of their global rivalry; for France and Britain, history gave the Suez Canal emotional as well as strategic and economic importance; the Suez Canal Company, moreover, was largely a French concern. All four had slightly ambiguous relationships with both Israel and Egypt. Broadly speaking, the Soviet Union backed Egypt and the United States backed Israel; but Nasser was reluctant to take sides in the 'cold war', and Russian technicians made no secret of their impatience with Arab pupils, while the United States was anxious to set up a Middle East defensive system in which Egypt would be included. France, in the throes of the Algerian War, was grimly hostile to Nasser's pan-Arab aspirations, although she retained friends and influence in Lebanon; and Britain, although on bad terms with Israel, was growing increasingly uneasy at Nasser's attempts to play off the Soviet Union against the West. The scene was set for a convergence of Israeli, French and British interests: it remained to be seen which way the United States would feel it safe to move. Tension, already latent, became acute when John Foster Dulles, the American Secretary of State, refused finance for the building of the Aswan High Dam in Upper Egypt. Britain followed suit; and on Friday 20 July 1956, Nasser retaliated by nationalizing the Suez Canal.[41]

There followed some weeks of anxious diplomacy, none of it very effective. This in itself helped dramatize the need to build Europe. Meeting in Paris on Wednesday and Thursday 19 and 20 September 1956, Monnet's new Action Committee declared: 'The events of the summer have revealed that only a United Europe can make its voice heard, and be respected, in the world of today.' Western Europe, the Committee pointed out, was 'the only great industrial region of the world that does not produce the power necessary to its development. Its life, in the near future, might be paralyzed by the cutting-off of its oil imports from the

Middle East . . . In this respect, the Suez crisis is a grave warning. Even if, as we hope, it is solved by peaceful means, this fundamental lack of balance, with its threat to peace, will remain: namely, the weakness and growing dependence of Western Europe as regards its supplies of power.' It was a fresh argument for hastening the Val Duchesse negotiations, and especially for establishing Euratom, which Monnet at that time regarded as the key feature of further integration, partly because it alone could persuade the French Government and Parliament to accept the general Common Market. The Committee therefore proposed that governments appoint 'Three Wise Men' to report on Europe's atomic energy needs and possibilities; and on Tuesday 13 November 1956, the governments did so, naming Louis Armand, Franz Etzel from the High Authority, and the bearded Italian physicist Francesco Giordani. The Report that they eventually submitted on Saturday 4 May 1957, although initially over-optimistic, certainly helped to speed the Euratom and Common Market Treaties through the national parliaments, and to that extent left its mark.[42]

But the Suez crisis gave a further and sharper thrust to events in Western Europe. When Guy Mollet had become French Prime Minister on Thursday 2 February 1956, he had been expected as a Socialist to come to terms with the Algerian rebels; yet only four days later, howled down by a crowd of Algiers settlers and bombarded with stones and rotten tomatoes, he seemed to change his mind. His attitude to the Arabs now became abruptly hostile. Before the year was out, he acquiesced in—if he did not connive at—the kidnapping of the rebel leader Mohammed Ben Bella while flying over international waters on the night of Sunday 21 October. Next day, at a secret meeting in Sèvres on Monday 22 October, he conspired with David Ben-Gurion, the Israeli Prime Minister, to make what amounted to a combined attack on Egypt. Also present were Christian Pineau, the French Foreign Minister; Maurice Bourgès-Maunoury, the Defence Minister; General Moshe Dayan, the Israeli Chief of Staff; and Shimon Peres, Secretary-General to the Israeli Ministry of Defence. Later they were joined by Mr Selwyn Lloyd, Anthony Eden's Foreign Secretary, and Mr (later Sir) Patrick Dean, then Deputy Under-Secretary at the British Foreign Office. All the principals were sworn to lifelong secrecy. It was not surprising, for they were putting the final touches to a plot that the French had suggested to Eden in an equally secret meeting at Chequers on the Sunday of the previous week. Crudely, what they planned was that Israel should invade Egypt across the Sinai Desert, and that Britain and France should intervene— supposedly to 'separate the combatants', but in fact to seize the Canal and bring Nasser to his knees.[43]

The Israelis crossed the border on Monday 29 October, and advanced across the desert with great prowess and dash. But the rest of this dubious scheme was slower to move into action, and it quickly came to grief Condemned by the United Nations and by many of the British people, threatened by the Soviet Union, and disavowed by the United States, which made no move to support sterling until £100 million had fled abroad, first Britain and then France had to call a halt and hand over to a United Nations peace-keeping force—but not before Nasser had seized a number of their assets and blocked the Suez Canal.[44]

The Suez adventure cost about 3,000 lives, many of them Egyptian. Britain lost twenty-two servicemen—and one badly shaken Prime Minister: Eden, already ill when the plot was hatched, had to step down in favour of one of its early supporters, Harold Macmillan. This, which helped make possible Macmillan's later bid for Britain to join the Common Market, was not the least of the consequences; but just as important was the effect on public opinion in Europe. For Britain, in particular, the Suez affair had shown that the United States—especially before an election—would refuse to be dragged into policies that it disapproved of. So long as Britain needed American support for the pound, her 'special relationship' with Washington was bound to be one-sided. In the long run, fears for Europe's oil supplies were to prove excessive, since the Arab States had to sell in order to live. But the relative impotence of individual European countries had been shown unmistakably—all the more so since the Suez affair coincided with that year's other serious crisis, the Soviet invasion of Hungary.[45]

Signs of unrest in the eastern half of Europe had been growing ever since the death of Joseph Stalin; but it was in 1956 that they threatened to turn into revolt. It began in Poland, where 'destalinization' in April and May brought the release of some 30,000 political prisoners, and a reduction of the sentences on 40,000 more. Then, in June and July, came a number of strikes and riots, notably in Poznań. Wladyslow Gomulka, who had been victimized under Stalin, was now re-admitted to the Communist Party, and soon became First Secretary. In this position, and confident of popular support, he was able to stand up moderately to the Soviet Union and dissuade it from using force to crush the new regime.

Hungary was less fortunate. Here, after Stalin's death, the once disgraced Imre Nagy had become Premier; but in 1955 he had again been ousted by the Stalinist Mátyás Rákosi. At this, the Hungarian Writers' Association, which had hitherto supported Rákosi, turned against him; and the Petöffi Circle of Hungarian intellectuals organized a series of mass public debates, calling for his resignation and demanding, among other things, freedom of the press. In July 1956 the Soviet Union dismissed him, partly for permitting these disorders, and replaced him by Ernö Gerö, another hard-line Party man. Against Gerö, public feeling soon grew violent; and on Tuesday 23 October, after a broadcast in which he had attacked the 'revolution', angry crowds swarmed through Budapest shouting for Imre Nagy. Outside the radio building, one group was fired on by the AVO security police: but it fought back and manhandled them when they tried to make arrests. In the City Park, another crowd pulled down and smashed the giant metal statue of Stalin: it was like a famous scene from Eisenstein's film *October*, but attacking a Communist tyrant rather than a Czar. Gerö then called in Soviet troops— but they were not enough to crush the rebellion, and three days later, on Friday 26 October, he was replaced by Nagy. For a week there was heady excitement. The one-party system was abolished; Cardinal Mindszenty was released from his long imprisonment; freedom of teaching was promised; and on Saturday 3 November a new government was formed, including two non-Communists: the former President Zoltán Tildy, and Béla Kovács, former Secretary-General of the Smallholders' Party, to which Tildy also had belonged. On the very next day, however, 6,000 Soviet tanks converged on the capital. At 5.20 p.m. that same Sunday, Nagy came to the radio to announce, 'Our troops are fighting'; but by then the situation was desperate. For nearly three hours, Budapest went on broadcasting messages and appeals for help. Then, at 8.07 p.m., the radio went silent. That was that.[46]

At the time, it was tempting to believe that if the West had not been occupied with Suez, the Soviet Union might have held back; but what evidence there is suggests the contrary. The very speed of the final invasion revealed its careful planning, and the first fighting in Budapest actually preceded the attack on Suez. Hungary, like Czechoslovakia twelve years later, had overstepped the margin allowed by Moscow: Suez provided good cover, but no pretext was needed for the Soviet Union to act. On the other hand, this sudden hardening of the 'cold war' gave Western Europeans a powerful, if crude, incentive for seeking unity. A more united Western Europe would certainly be stronger, and might well discourage aggression; and even if, in this instance, it could have done little to save Hungary, it was clear that a divided Western Europe could do even less.

Working against the clock and under these multiple pressures, the Val Duchesse negotiators completed the Euratom and Common Market

Treaties in record time. From start to finish, it took them less than ten months. At length, on Monday 25 March 1957, in the huge, ornate and crowded Sala degli Orazi e Curiazi of the Capitol in Rome, the Treaties were formally signed by the representatives of the Six—Spaak and Baron Snoy, for Belgium; Adenauer and Hallstein, for Germany; Christian Pineau and Maurice Faure, for France; Antonio Segni and Gaetano Martino, for Italy; Joseph Bech and Lambert Schaus, for Luxembourg; Joseph Luns and Johannes Linthorst Homan, for the Netherlands. The obstacle race was almost over. One by one, the national parliaments ratified the Treaties; and this process too was unwittingly assisted by the Soviet Union. On Friday 4 October 1957, Soviet technicians put into orbit the world's first artificial satellite, Sputnik 1, a 183-lb sphere nearly two feet across. It was a startling illustration of how far the countries of Western Europe lagged behind the giants; and Monnet and his friends were quick to use it as an argument for unity. Finally, in December 1957, the Rome Treaties cleared their last parliamentary hurdle; and on Wednesday 1 January 1958, they came into force.

On Monday and Tuesday of the following week, 6 and 7 January, the Foreign Ministers of the Six met in Paris to decide where Euratom and the Common Market should have their headquarters, and to appoint the Presidents and members of their respective Commissions. The latter task proved easier than the former. In 1952, the ECSC had settled in Luxembourg in default of a ministerial decision; now, it might have seemed logical for the new institutions to be set up alongside it, perhaps in a 'European District' on the model of Washington, DC. For a time, Monnet in particular canvassed this solution; but Luxembourg opinion, backed, it was said, by the Grand Duchess Charlotte and the Church, was already very conscious of the High Authority's busy presence, and it feared a fresh influx of impatient foreigners. When the Government finally changed its mind, the chance had passed. Brussels, a larger and more lively capital with better communications, was now firmly in the running: not for nothing had the negotiations been conducted at Val Duchesse. Eventually, after long discussion, the ministers decided that the new Community authorities should meet in Brussels and Luxembourg alternately. For a few weeks, this was attempted: the High Authority vacated some of its offices, and welcomed its new colleagues with a nervously eager embrace. But so much travelling quickly proved impracticable, and Brussels soon became the Commissions' *de facto* new home. At first, both Euratom and the Common Market were lodged in the same narrow, white-stone-faced building in rue Belliard. When they moved in, the lower floors were still not completed, and strangers wandered in and out of half-furnished offices to the tap of workmen's hammers and the buzz of drills. Within a few months, however, the Common Market Commission moved into roomier quarters in a similar new white building, appropriately located in the Avenue de la Joyeuse Entrée.[47]

As President of the Euratom Commission, the ministers appointed Louis Armand. Its Vice-President was Enrico Medi, a highly volatile Italian physicist; the other three members were Paul Hubert De Groote, a lean, laconic former minister and Rector of Brussels Free University; Heinz Krekeler, who had been German Ambassador in Washington; and Emanuel Sassen, a former minister from the Netherlands who looked a little like Robert Boothby, and whose bulk and vocal power had been well known in the ECSC's Common Assembly.

The Common Market Commission had nine members to Euratom's five. Walter Hallstein became its President—a fifty-six-year-old bachelor who had been Rector of Frankfurt University before his appointment by Adenauer to the head of the German Foreign Office. Shy, rather solitary, sober-suited and bespectacled, with thinning hair above a C. P. Snow-like brow, he seemed very much the law professor, author of works like *Die Berichtigung des Gesellschaftskapitals* and *Wiederherstellung des Privatrechts*. But like most of his generation, he had lived through much more than the academic world could teach. As a boy growing up in the Rhineland, he had been told by one schoolmaster that the French across the frontier were his hereditary enemies. In 1944, conscripted into the German army, he had found himself fighting them. He was captured in Normandy by the Americans, and spent the rest of the war in Louisiana, where he organized a prison-camp 'university', and was nearly murdered for his pains by Nazi fellow-captives. Since World War II he had been an active 'European', and had represented Germany both at the Schuman Plan negotiations that had set up the ECSC, and at the recent Messina Conference. At times, his respect for law and protocol seemed rigid; but it sprang from a deep revulsion against anarchy and tyranny. Later, he was to sacrifice his own post to his concern for principle. Meanwhile, he set to work with immense dedication. A serious, introspective man who saw few of even his senior staff regularly, he nevertheless made it a point to accept speaking engagements. He was anxious to put the Commission on the map, in public view; perhaps, also, on the platform he felt both shielded and released. There was certainly a duality within him. Deskbound, he looked back nostalgically to early skiing holidays. His official car was a grey Mercedes, but a convertible with red leather upholstery. And although work seemed to be his only hobby, he delighted in the theatre and in Berlin cabaret: at one official fancy-dress party, he astonished his fellow-guests by coming disguised as a tramp.[48]

His colleagues made a piquant contrast. There were three Vice-Presidents—Sicco Mansholt, a tall, weatherbeaten Dutch Socialist, with a brown bald head who had won fame as a Resistance leader and as a postwar Minister of Agriculture, although his hobby was sailing, not farming; Piero Malvestiti, a stocky, plump Italian Christian Democrat who later became President of the ECSC High Authority, and who as a staunch Catholic favoured what he called 'a Guelph party in Europe'; and Jean Monnet's ex-colleague Robert Marjolin, formerly of OEEC, still at forty-six looking like a youthful college lecturer with his bright eyes behind dark-framed glasses, his springy step and his quick, wincing smile. The other members of the Commission were Hans von der Groeben, co-author of the Spaak Report, slightly resembling a younger, less Asiatic Adenauer; Robert Lemaignen, a gnarled, middle-aged French industrialist; the solid and dapper Giuseppe Petrilli, later to be head of IRI, the Italian state holding company; Michel Rasquin, a gaunt Socialist militant and former minister from Luxembourg; and Jean Rey, a friendly, lively, optimistic Belgian with heavy spectacles and a rapid, pouncing voice that made many of his remarks sound like successful tongue-twisters. A lawyer by profession and a Liberal in politics, Rey had been a prisoner-of-war in Germany and had later become Minister of Economic Affairs. In a country split by the language dispute between Walloons and Flemings, and repeatedly the victim of its bigger neighbours' quarrels, it was natural for him to be a federalist. Eventually he was to succeed Hallstein as President of the European Commission.[49]

Among the nine Common Market Commissioners, there were Catholics and Protestants, Socialists, Christian Democrats and Liberals. Several had served in the Resistance; several had been in prison-camps. Nearly all spoke French, and at least four spoke fluent English. At first they hardly knew each other. Lemaignen wrote eloquently later of the novelty and bewilderment of working in so mixed a group; and Malvestiti went so far as to have duplicated the speech that he planned to make at one of its early meetings, as if at some formal conference. But before long, in the small, deliberately cramped room near Hallstein's office on the top floor where the Commission met every Wednesday like a national cabinet, the atmosphere grew more relaxed and intimate. It was just as well. Looking out across the wintry roofs of Brussels, all nine felt the weight of what lay ahead. Backed by the Court of Justice and the 142-man European 'Parliament', working in harness with the Council of Ministers that represented the national governments, their

245

task was nothing less than to fuse six economies into one. They had just over a decade in which to do it.[50]

It was eight years since Jean Monnet had launched what became the Schuman Plan. It was six years since the Coal and Steel Community had been set up in Luxembourg. It was four years since EDC had been defeated. Now, Europe was on the move again, but in a different world. In the age of anxiety of the early nineteen-fifties, defence had seemed the key to Western Europe's unity: but with peace taken more and more for granted, and new prosperity beckoning, the hope of an American-sized Common Market was doubly attractive—as a means to greater wealth and a basis for political union. After the wild oats of EDC, it was a return to the more modest principles of the Schuman Declaration. 'Thus will be realized ... the fusion of interests which is indispensable to the establishment of an economic community; thus will be introduced the germ of a broader and deeper community between countries long opposed to one another by bloody conflicts.' In those early months of 1958, Monnet's and Schuman's vision seemed to be coming true.[51]

For the moment, only one thing marred it: Great Britain still stood apart. This was one of Monnet's failures. Shortly after the Messina Conference, he had had another. Staying in Scotland with Sir Cecil Weir, his friend from the British Delegation in Luxembourg, he had tried his hand at an unaccustomed pastime. That night, he had noted in his diary: 'I try to catch salmon in stream, without success.' For salmon, the close-time came soon afterwards; but there was no close season for Britain. Monnet had always believed that facts, not ideas, would eventually draw her into uniting Europe; and now, as the Common Market took shape in Brussels, at Val Duchesse and then in the Avenue de la Joyeuse Entrée, there came from across the Channel the first, hesitant signs that he was right.

CHAPTER ELEVEN

The Lion and the Unicorn

> The lion and the unicorn
> Were fighting for the crown.
> *Nursery Rhyme*[1]

> I don't care to belong to any club that will have me as a
> member.   *Groucho Marx*[2]

> We are no longer strong enough to stand alone, and if we
> fail to bring a Western European Union into being, we shall
> be obliged, in the long run, to subordinate our policy to
> that of one Great Power or the other.   *George Orwell*[3]

BRITAIN was not always an island. In the tertiary geological era, an
isthmus blocked the Straits of Dover; even today, over part of the Col-
bart, the ridge in mid-Channel between Dungeness and Ambleteuse,
there are only six feet of water at low tide. Ever since the eighteen-
hundreds, attempts have been made to bridge the Channel or to tunnel
under it. Militarily, modern landing vessels, aircraft and missiles have
reduced it to little more than a ditch. But in the late nineteen-fifties, the
eighteen miles of choppy sea between Dover and Cap Gris Nez still formed
a psychological barrier, despite the five million people who were crossing
it every year. Then, Britain was still tempted to think of Continental
Europe, as in the London *Times* of the period, under the general heading
of 'Overseas'. To many British people, other European countries seemed
no less alien than other continents, and in some respects more distant
than English-speaking members of the Commonwealth on the opposite
side of the planet.[4]

In the Messina Resolution of June 1955, the Foreign Ministers of the
Six promised to invite Britain, as a member of WEU and an associate of
the ECSC, to join the Spaak Committee set up to prepare the Common
Market and Euratom. When Harold Macmillan, as British Foreign
Secretary, accepted the invitation, he was careful to reserve his govern-
ment's position. 'There are, as you are no doubt aware,' he wrote, 'special

difficulties for this country in any proposal for "a European common market". They [the British Government] will be happy to examine, without prior commitment and on their merits, the many problems which are likely to emerge from the studies and in doing so will be guided by the hope of reaching solutions which are in the interests of all parties concerned.' The Government accordingly sent to the Spaak Committee the forty-nine-year-old R. F. Bretherton, a professional economist and amateur entomologist who was now Under-Secretary at the Board of Trade.[5]

At the Committee's first meeting, he pointed out that he was neither a delegate nor an observer, but a 'representative'—presumably to stress Britain's midway position of being neither 'in' nor 'out'. From the start, as Spaak put it, he was 'discreet and sceptical': 'While other countries' representatives took up their task with enthusiasm, he remained silent most of the time. When he intervened in the discussions, it was to express doubt whether his country could accept the ideas on which agreement seemed to be emerging.'[6]

This was already discouraging, and worse was to come. On Tuesday 6 September 1955, the Foreign Ministers met at Noordwijk on the Dutch coast to discuss the Committee's progress; but although the British Foreign Secretary was invited, he failed to appear. Then, in the second half of October, when the experts at Val Duchesse produced their first report, it revealed two basic clashes between the British and their colleagues. First, Britain opposed the idea of a common market based on a customs union: she preferred a free trade area, whose member States would retain their own existing tariffs on imports from non-members. Secondly, Britain wanted no new European institutions: she relied on the methods and machinery of the existing OEEC. 'Existing' was in both cases the key word: above all, she wished to avoid change.[7]

On Monday 7 November 1955, Spaak held a meeting of the heads of delegations to review the work of the experts. When Bretherton was called upon to comment, he again reserved the British position until further details were clarified; but he argued that it would be difficult for Britain, as a member of the Commonwealth, to join a European common market. On Euratom he was a little less chilling; but he still could make no formal promises. In reply, Spaak voiced the general disappointment that Britain was unwilling to go beyond intergovernmental co-operation as practised in OEEC. He added that the experts' work was now completed, and that the next step was for the delegations to prepare a report for the Foreign Ministers. This, he made clear, would involve a political decision to proceed on the basis of the Messina Resolution. For Britain, it was the moment of choice. As it turned out, her choice was fateful. Bretherton returned to London, and the Spaak Committee continued on the basis of the Six.[8]

Once again, Britain had missed an opportunity. Both she and the future Common Market were to pay for the mistake. But at the time it seemed natural. The Six had plagued Britain to join EDC, and at the very least to form some link with it; yet when she had done so, EDC had failed. The new venture looked no closer to succeeding; unlike EDC, moreover, it seemed to be a matter of economics and trade, hardly enough to call for 'supranational' institutions distinct from those of OEEC.

Mixed with British scepticism, there was also a measure of hostility, less to Euratom than to the Common Market. On Thursday 17 November 1955, the British Government announced that it was unable to join the proposed atomic organization, partly because of its supranational institutions, partly because Britain's civil nuclear programme was closely linked with defence, and partly because of existing bilateral links with Australia, Canada and the United States. It added, however, that it had no desire to hinder the creation of Euratom if the Messina countries wished to proceed.[9]

The Common Market was another matter. Here, too, Britain repeatedly stressed that she was not opposed to the project; but to Continental Europeans, some of her actions seemed to belie her words. Anthony Eden, then British Prime Minister, made no secret of his fear that 'these associations could lead to a high tariff group in Europe', and spoke of American 'enthusiasm' for them in terms that showed how little he shared it. And a very clear demonstration of British policy was given on Tuesday 6 December 1955, not in the Spaak Committee, but at a special unofficial meeting of the Heads of Delegation of OEEC, convened by the President in office, Sir Hugh Ellis-Rees.[10]

There was uncertainty and disquiet, said Ellis-Rees, about the future of OEEC. It was clear from the Messina resolution, as from the later work of the Spaak Committee, that the Six's objectives were mainly political. It was also clear that they could lead to a reduplication of the work of OEEC and other bodies—something that the United Kingdom had repeatedly and officially opposed. Britain was not opposed to a greater political unity among the Six; but if they used economic means to achieve this end, it raised a problem for the other members of OEEC, none of whom had had the slightest hand in drawing up the Spaak Committee's reports. Given the difficulties that the Six must face, were they likely to achieve their economic aims more rapidly than

OEEC could do by other means? As at present envisaged, the European Common Market would be an exclusive group, and could lead to the formation of a discriminatory bloc, nullifying part of OEEC's multi-lateral work. There was a danger that Western Europe might find itself divided into two camps. There was no question of proposing that the Six should cease their discussions, or hold them within the OEEC frame-work; but the relations between the Messina enterprise and the other member countries should be discussed by all the interested parties, with a view to general agreements to be worked out gradually through OEEC. The British Chancellor of the Exchequer, Mr R. A. Butler, would make some proposals on these lines for discussion by the OEEC Ministers at their meeting in February 1956.[11]

Mr Butler was renowned for his skilful use of ambiguity; and something of it seemed to pervade this statement by the Treasury's former Under-Secretary. In many respects, it was thoroughly reasonable. Was Britain opposed to a European Common Market? No: but she drew attention to its dangers. Did she believe that OEEC should take over the Six's project? No: but something might be worked out.

The type of arrangement that might be proposed was beginning to be clear in the case of Euratom. On Friday 10 June 1955, just a week after the Messina Conference, OEEC had set up a working party on atomic energy. It reported back in January 1956; but Ellis-Rees, at the December meeting, was able to refer already to a plan whereby OEEC member States might collaborate or not, according to their needs and resources, in achieving well-defined aims. This was a fair description of what was to become OEEC's European Nuclear Energy Agency (ENEA). With far smaller resources than Euratom, it was to do well. But in the case of the Common Market, something far more elaborate was in prospect; and again it was highly ambiguous.[12]

In public, Britain repeated that while she could not join a European common market because of her Commonwealth commitments, she had no wish to thwart it. In private, in a Memorandum to the German Government on Monday 19 December 1955, she appeared to suggest that Germany should break off the Spaak Committee negotiations and instead hold talks within OEEC.[13]

Spaak, informed of what seemed to him like an attempt to sabotage his efforts, was predictably incensed. In a calmer mood, he composed a long letter to Anthony Eden, which he finally sent on Tuesday 7 February 1956. After recalling the unhappy history of EDC and the hopes aroused by Britain's association agreement with the European Coal and Steel

Community, he described the progress made since Messina. 'But now,' he added,

…some weeks ago, a new and important event occurred, which may have very grave consequences for the future. Great Britain has not only declared that she will not associate herself with what may come into existence, but has added that she is against it. This is no longer benevolent and slightly sceptical neutrality, but hostility clearly expressed.

From the sides I hear the echoes of this opposition. I regret it and I should like to speak about it very frankly.

Let me summarize once again the many reasons that lead me to seek the integration of Europe.

First of all, this I believe is the real way to solve the German problem … A Germany which is integrated in European entities, and, through them, in the Atlantic Pact, will have defended herself against an individualism that too rapidly takes the form of nationalism, whose effects we know, and at the same time against the temptation to approach the Russians by herself in an attempt to solve with them, directly, the problems in dispute, without taking account of the general interests of the West. …

To this political conceptions are added some economic considerations. …

It seems clear to me that in this field the future belongs to the large communities of mankind. Automation, the progress of technology, the increase of production and productivity – all, to give their best results, require large markets. The Americans have achieved a material standard of living very much higher than that of European countries. Russia has announced a new Five-Year Plan. Even if we discount some of it as bluff, the size of its objectives is disquieting. What have we got to set alongside it? Not much, I am afraid. …

I recognize very willingly that if a European economic union is set up, with six countries and more than 150 million inhabitants, this raises serious problems for its neighbours – even if, as is the case, the union in question rejects all idea of self-sufficiency or excessive protectionism. To that, I might answer that our union is not exclusive, that on the contrary it is open to those who wish to join it, and that this applies above all to Great Britain. But I know that this reply is inappropriate, because Great Britain does not intend to join.

There remains, therefore, the subsidiary solution of an agreement between the new union and Great Britain. Is such an agreement possible? Quite clearly, the question must be thoroughly explored. What I dread is that Great Britain, by throwing her considerable weight into the balance of the talks, may succeed in wrecking our great projects and obliging us to accept the *fait accompli* of a negative policy, whose consequences for the future would I think be disastrous from all points of view.

If Great Britain is really afraid of our European ventures, would it not be better to discuss the subject frankly between ourselves? And is W.E.U. not the place where such discussions might be held?[14]

I

A few days later, on Monday 13 February 1956, Spaak received an answer which he later described as 'cordial but vague'. Shortly afterwards, Eden suggested that he talk with Harold Macmillan, who had now succeeded Butler at the Treasury. For Whitehall, clearly, the 're-launching of Europe', although recognized as political, was still at this stage to be treated as economic, and referred to the Board of Trade and the Treasury rather than to the Foreign Office—still less to the Ministry of Defence. Nothing was made of Spaak's suggestion that talks be held in WEU, where Britain and the Six were closeted together. Instead, Britain continued to prefer the heterogeneous OEEC, whose eighteen member States ranged from members of NATO to neutrals, and from highly industrialized democracies to countries that both economically and politically were far less favoured. As one of Spaak's former assistants remarked, if Britain feared that the Six were 'dividing Europe', it was hard to claim that OEEC had united it.[15]

Ironies apart, however, the British response to the Six's plans was not completely negative. During the early meetings of the Spaak Committee, Britain had mooted the possibility of establishing a free trade area in Europe; and on Wednesday and Thursday 14 and 15 March 1956, the British economist James Meade published two articles on the subject in the *Manchester Guardian* that some believed to have been officially inspired. Finally, on Thursday 5 July 1956, less than six weeks after the Spaak Report had been accepted by the six Foreign Ministers as a basis for negotiating Euratom and the Common Market, Sir Edward Boyle, then Economic Secretary to the Treasury, announced to the House of Commons that the Government was re-appraising the whole of its European policy. What this meant became clear some days later, at the July meeting of the OEEC Council of Ministers. There, with strong British backing, the Secretary-General René Sergent proposed a working party to study the possibility of setting up a free trade area embracing all the OEEC countries, and including as one of its constituents the Common Market of the Six.[16]

In retrospect, many people—including Spaak himself—came to believe that the proposed Free Trade Area would have dissolved the Common Market, as some of them put it, 'like a lump of sugar in a British cup of tea'. But the belief was slow in growing. When James Meade's articles were published, they were hailed by several of Monnet's associates, including one or two who were later very critical of the plan. Monnet himself favoured it: on Thursday 20 September 1956, the Action Committee called on Governments to 'do all that lies in their power to hasten the conclusion of the Treaty for the European Common Market, and the completion of the studies undertaken in OEEC for the inclusion of this Common Market in a free trade area comprising the United Kingdom and the other members of OEEC.' Even Walter Hallstein, as late as January 1958, when he had just been appointed President of the Common Market Commission, was to describe the Free Trade Area as its 'necessary supplement'.[17]

The OEEC working party duly reported back in January 1957; and on the 15th of that month Paul-Henri Spaak paid a visit to London to see the new Chancellor of the Exchequer, Peter Thorneycroft. The negotiations for Euratom and the Common Market were by this time far advanced; but Britain was anxious to ensure that the Common Market should not be set up before the Free Trade Area. Spaak pointed out that it would be impossible to hold up the negotiations, which the British conceded: he therefore suggested that if by the end of them Britain or other countries detected anything in the draft Treaty that seemed incompatible with a Free Trade Area, they should inform the Six. He further proposed that the Treaty contain a revision clause to cover the possibility of change if other countries were associated—although it would require unanimous agreement and parliamentary ratification. He then turned to the content of the proposed Free Trade Area. Fresh from his experiences in Brussels, he pointed out that to be effective it would have to deal with other barriers besides customs tariffs. The British seemed largely to agree. They refused, however, to include agriculture in the free trade system; as a compensation, they offered to maintain benevolent neutrality if the Common Market's own agricultural policy came under fire from other exporting countries in such international bodies as the General Agreement on Tariffs and Trade (GATT).[18]

The impression that Spaak brought back from his London talks was discouraging. The technical difficulty of establishing a free trade area, already considerable, now looked even greater than before. Agriculture was to be excluded: this would deny outlets, in particular, to France and Italy, which as high-tariff countries would be making large concessions in the industrial field. Britain was worried at the prospect that the Six's colonies and ex-colonies might be linked with the Common Market; yet she herself proposed to stand at the crossroads of the Free Trade Area and the Commonwealth preference system, enjoying commercial privileges that her partners were denied. There was vagueness about the innumerable non-tariff problems with which the Brussels negotiators had grown familiar; revenue duties, subsidies to home industries, export rebates, tax discrimination, health and safety requirements, differential freight rates, cartels, monopolies and price-rings.

There was hesitancy about institutions. There was doubt about the possible diversion of trade: how could imports through the low-tariff countries be prevented from slipping across the frontier into neighbouring higher-tariff markets, unless there were a system of certificates of origin, which itself might be open to fraud? There was anxiety about the cohesion of the Common Market: if free trade—the most obvious of its benefits—were to be offered without the discipline of a common tariff, common rules and common institutions, might not its member States slide gradually into this convenient commercial arrangement, without ever approaching the economic union that was their formal goal? Finally, there was doubt about America. Was it reasonable for the OEEC countries—who were not embarking on economic or political union—to grant each other special privileges and establish tariff discrimination against the dollar area, just at the time when their newly favourable balance of payments position required them to remove the quota discrimination that the United States had accepted while they were poor? Washington welcomed the Common Market as a step towards European unity; but although it maintained a diplomatic silence, it was obviously embarrassed by the Free Trade Area proposal.

These difficulties were real. With many other technical problems, they occupied the negotiators for eighteen months, from the spring of 1957 until November 1958—first in expert committees of OEEC, then in a full-scale conference under the buoyant chairmanship of Reginald Maudling, who was also head of the British negotiating team. Conceivably, the problems might have been solved, and the Free Trade Area might have come into being—but for the dramatic events that now shook France and were soon to shake Europe itself.

At 3.00 p.m. on Tuesday 13 May 1958, the sturdy, silver-haired Pierre Pflimlin, Catholic Mayor of Strasbourg, rose in the National Assembly to make his investiture speech as Prime Minister of France. Appointed by President René Coty to end a further month-long Government crisis, he faced a country torn apart by the three-and-a-half years of the Algerian War, an army on the brink of mutiny, and an unnerving multiplicity of threats, rumours, and genuine plots. Rightly or wrongly, both the settlers and the soldiers in Algeria suspected Pflimlin of being about to make terms with the Algerian rebels.[19]

Just two hours later, in Algiers, open riot broke out. A general strike was in progress, and the hot afternoon streets were crowded with young men. Unexpectedly, a mob of students and schoolboys attacked the Government Building, and invaded it with the help of paratroops supposedly called in to disperse them. When General Raoul Salan, the Army Commander-in-Chief, tried to restore order he was howled down. Thereupon, the paratroop general Jacques Massu announced the formation of a Committee of Public Safety; he also telegraphed Paris, demanding a government that would keep Algeria French. On the following day, Massu issued an appeal to the sixty-seven-year-old General de Gaulle to return to power; and Salan, prompted by a Gaullist plotter, half-inadvertently echoed this appeal next morning by ending a speech with the cry of 'Vive de Gaulle!' De Gaulle had already heard from the conspirators, and with this he felt free to act. From his country retreat at Colombey-les-Deux-Eglises, he put himself forward as 'ready to assume the powers of the Republic'. After four more days of uproar in Algiers and suspense in Paris, he gave a resounding press conference, stating his views on Algeria in terms designed to appeal to both sides. Then, once more, he waited. On Sunday 25 May the blow fell: the Right-wing rebels seized the island of Corsica. The Government ordered the French navy to recapture it—but next day, in the face of a virtual refusal, it had to rescind the order. On Tuesday 27 May, after secret contacts with Pflimlin and with Guy Mollet, the Socialist leader, de Gaulle announced that he had begun 'the regular process necessary to establish a republican Government capable of restoring the unity and independence of the country'. In fact, to be on the safe side, he was also still in touch with the army insurrectionists. Next day, President Coty told the party leaders that they must choose between de Gaulle and a Popular Front Government that would surely spark off a revolt by the army. His own choice was now clear. On Thursday 29 May, he announced that he was asking de Gaulle to form a Government of National Safety; and on the evening of Sunday 1 June 1958, with the necessary support of Guy Mollet's Socialists, de Gaulle was voted into office after an absence of over twelve years.[20]

At sixty-seven, de Gaulle described himself as an 'old man, worn by suffering, detached from human concerns, feeling the approach of eternal cold, but never weary of watching in the shadows for the gleam of hope'. It was the peroration of his war memoirs, following similar evocations of France and the whole earth; perhaps he added it after his return to power. As a literary artist whom critics compared to Bossuet and Pascal, he expressed very nobly the bleakness of his vision; but his rhetoric left a sense of strain and artifice. At worst, the grandeur of the style obscured the poverty of the content: too often, he was writing beyond his means.[21]

The same applied to many of de Gaulle's actions. His greatest skill was to use the grand manner to conceal his lack of resources. It was an art that he had learned in wartime London. Then, as now, his triumphs were essentially literary and histrionic: his broadcast appeal in June 1940; his masterly playing of the 1958 crisis; his later handling of the 'barricades' rebellion, crushed largely by a single broadcast; finally, the four-minute speech with which he ended the disorders of May 1968. He was never quite without weapons: but to deploy them he used the power of words. Each time he had the courage, when lesser men were faltering, to stand up straight and say 'No'.

So astonished were some of his contemporaries that they looked for hidden subtleties in de Gaulle's political philosophy. They found them in his tactics: the shrewd, patient timing, the weighing of odds, the manipulation of rivalries, the feel for French public opinion, the sense of others' weaknesses, the use of hints, vague promises, ambiguous threats. But those who sought to construct a complicated system out of de Gaulle's twisting and turnings—his nods and winks to first one potential partner, then another—were fundamentally mistaken. In domestic as in foreign policy, de Gaulle's ideas were few and simple. Like his very great virtues, they were those of a soldier. He believed in efficiency, and he believed in France. To be efficient, it was essential to use the latest material techniques; it was also essential to practise the military art of 'man management', partly by television, partly by profit-sharing, partly by the traditional wiles of leadership. Democracy was another matter. France had suffered from its excesses; and France must be restored. In the world of modern technology, this meant international co-operation. But no alliances could be eternally binding; no interests could be superior to the national interest; no pretended 'merger of sovereignty' must tie the hands of France. And now, once again, 'France' meant General Charles de Gaulle.

His return to power cast a cold shadow in the spring sunshine of Brussels. His views were well known. He and his party had opposed the Schuman Plan, the Common Market and Euratom; his new Prime Minister, Michel Debré, had passionately attacked the Spaak Report, and had been as fiercely attacked in his turn by Paul-Henri Spaak. At the same time, however, 'Europeans' had read de Gaulle's memoires, and had noted that at one point during World War II he had spoken of 'a strategic and economic federation' in Western Europe, 'to which Great Britain might be attached'. The options, it seemed, were open. De Gaulle might well be persuaded to continue French support for the

Common Market—provided that it showed clear advantages to France.[22]

The proposed Free Trade Area fulfilled no such condition. Lacking a single outer tariff, it would impose no collective discipline on its members; lacking an agreement on agriculture, it would provide no extra market for French farm produce; including Great Britain—and in a privileged position—it would challenge the tacit leadership that in the Common Market seemed to belong to France. For all these reasons, and not solely for fear of rivalry, de Gaulle decided to halt the negotiations. On the evening of Friday 14 November 1958, the French Minister of Information, Jacques Soustelle, announced to the press that 'it has become clear to France that it is not possible to set up the Free Trade Area as wished by the British'. France's partners protested; but her opinion was shared by many of the Brussels Commission, although for different reasons. After much argument, two special reports by the Commission, and an American-sponsored re-organization of OEEC which turned it into an 'Atlantic' body (OECD, the Organization for Economic Co-operation and Development) with the US and Canada as full members, the hope of a Europe-wide Free Trade Area was finally buried. The lion and the unicorn had fought their first battle. Helped by some 'Europeans', who feared the dissolvent effects of the Free Trade Area no less than the disruptive potential of General de Gaulle, the unicorn—for the time being—had won.

The second battle began three years later. In the meantime, the situation had changed. Britain, her hopes of a large Free Trade Area vanishing, had begun to form a small one: in Stockholm, on Friday 20 November 1959, she signed the Convention establishing the EFTA, or European Free Trade Association, comprising Austria, Denmark, Norway, Portugal, Sweden and Switzerland, in addition to Britain herself. This was partly a salvage operation, to secure whatever benefits were possible on a smaller and more scattered basis. In this respect it succeeded: eventually, it was to remove its internal tariff barriers more quickly than the Common Market, although many non-tariff obstacles remained. But in so far as EFTA was intended to bring pressure on the Common Market for a revival of the old Free Trade Area, in its early years it had very little success. It certainly dramatized the so-called 'division of Europe', and news of its formation played some part in proposals for world-wide tariff-cutting made by the US Under-Secretary of State, C. Douglas Dillon, shortly before the EFTA Convention was formally signed. But America continued to treat EFTA with extravagant coolness;

and in the longer term its chief significance may have been as a stage in Britain's gradually greater involvement with the European continent.[23]

The Common Market, meanwhile, had survived the fears aroused by de Gaulle's return to office. By pushing through a 17·5 per cent devaluation of the franc on 27 December 1958, de Gaulle had actually made it possible for France to join in the first Common Market tariff reductions, due on 1 January 1959, without requesting a waiver. On 12 May 1960, the six member States agreed to the Commission's proposal to speed up the tariff-cutting process; and by mid-1961 the tariff barriers between them had been almost halved, while quota restrictions on industrial products were on their way to disappearing. Overall production had increased by twenty per cent, and trade within the Common Market by seventy per cent. There was no watertight proof that this was due to the cutting of tariffs; but it seemed significant that trade with non-member countries had grown only half as fast. Already, in June and July 1959, two members of OEEC had drawn their own conclusions: Greece and Turkey had both applied for association with the Six.[24]

A similar process of rethinking had been going on in London. In October 1959, Harold Macmillan's government had been returned with an increased majority. Cartoonists were fond of portraying Macmillan as a slightly seedy Edwardian with almost heraldic moustaches; but under the archaic camouflage he was alert and sensitive, as much aware in Europe as in Africa of what he called 'the wind of change'. His manner was in part at least a sop to human conservatism, as misleading as De Gaulle's reassurance that he had 'understood' the Algiers settlers. There was no real paradox, therefore, in Macmillan's being responsible for Britain's first decisive step towards uniting Europe. It was only unfortunate in being too cautious and too well disguised.

The first sign of change came on Thursday 21 January 1960, at a meeting of the Consultative Assembly of the Council of Europe, when Selwyn Lloyd, the British Foreign Secretary, went so far as to admit: 'I believe we made a mistake in not taking part in the negotiations which led to the formation of the Coal and Steel Community.' In March, Macmillan went to Washington, and was startled to find how strongly the US Administration backed the Common Market, if necessary to detriment of any 'special relationship' with Britain: when, referring presumably to EFTA, he tactlessly recalled the 'peripheral coalition' against Napoleon, his remarks were promptly leaked to the *Washington Post*. In April, the British Government announced that it could no longer afford to build the 'Blue Streak' military rocket; in May, Nikita Khrushchev broke up the long-heralded 'summit' meeting in Paris after President Eisenhower had admitted, with undiplomatic candour, his responsibility for the high-level 'U-2' photographic reconnaisance aircraft, one of which had just been shot down near Sverdlovsk in the Urals. Both incidents set off a train of newspaper comment about Britain's relative impotence in world affairs and her inability by herself to match American technology. As a remedy, both *The Economist* and *The Observer* now began to advocate joining the Common Market. A similar conclusion was beginning to emerge from the Economic Steering Committee which the Government had set up under Sir Frank Lee, Permanent Secretary at the Treasury, to make a confidential study of the whole subject.[25]

In June 1960 the Cabinet itself edged a little further in this direction. Speaking in Paris at the Assembly of Western European Union, John Profumo, then Minister of State at the Foreign Office, affirmed that 'the British Government, without regard to all that has happened in the last few years, will certainly be ready to consider anew the proposal that Britain should join Euratom, and indeed, the European Coal and Steel Community as well.'[26]

Jean Monnet had been watching these developments with a mixture of anxiety and hope. Long after de Gaulle had rejected the old Free Trade Area, Monnet and the Action Committee had continued to press for multilateral links between Britain and the Common Market, first in a European framework, then in a broader context that would not exclude the United States. Now, on Monday 11 July 1960, the Committee made an unequivocal response to Profumo's statement. 'The acceleration of the Common Market,' it declared,

... has shown the United Kingdom and the other European countries that there is now no going back on European integration, that it is beneficial, and also open to all.

Today it is possible to envisage the participation of all in the common task of uniting Europe.

Accordingly the Action Committee, echoing the wishes of the vast majority of citizens in our countries, earnestly hopes that the United Kingdom and the other European countries will simultaneously become members of the Coal and Steel Community, Euratom, and the Common Market, which are three facets of a single reality. This reality is the emerging European economic union that is paving the way for a political unity, the exact nature of which cannot now be foreseen.[27]

The British Government was not slow to take the point: it realized the difficulty of joining two of the Community organizations without joining the third. On Monday 25 July 1960, when the House of Commons debated the question, Selwyn Lloyd reviewed the three main groups of problems that seemed to be raised by Common Market membership—the Commonwealth, agriculture and EFTA—in terms that revealed how far the discussion in Cabinet had gone. 'I have not pronounced against us going into some form of European institution,' he added, 'but we have to be careful what these institutions are, what they are to do, and what would be our responsibilities in the matter.' In fact, the Cabinet was still divided.[28]

Conversations at that time in Whitehall and Westminster revealed several reasons for Britain's hesitation. Some ministers and officials still questioned whether a united Western Europe was desirable or possible. Others, while accepting it as an objective, doubted whether Britain could actually join the Common Market without deserting and offending her partners in the Commonwealth and EFTA. A third group, finally, now urged British entry, but feared a possible rebuff. There seemed no likelihood of a quick decision—until two events in the second half of 1960 combined to tip the scales. First, the Common Market Six began discussing political union. Secondly, John Fitzgerald Kennedy was elected President of the United States.

The impetus for political talks in Europe came from General de Gaulle. In a radio broadcast on Tuesday 31 May 1960, he had said:

To help to build Western Europe into a political, economic, cultural, and human group, organized for action, progress, and defence is the aim of the French Government. Already West Germany, Italy, the Netherlands, Belgium, and Luxembourg are co-operating directly with her in several fields. In particular the Common Market of the Six will on 31 December become a practical reality [when it was planned to make an extra internal tariff cut and begin establishing the common tariff on imports from outside]. Of course, the participants do not want this organization to injure the other countries of Europe, and we must expect a way to be found of accommodating their interests. Also, of course, the nations which are becoming associated must not cease to be themselves, and the path to be followed must be that of organized co-operation between states, while waiting to achieve, perhaps, an imposing confederation.

Listening in Brussels to this speech, some 'Europeans' were suspicious. It was not so long since the General and his followers had denounced the 'relaunching of Europe'; and as recently as 17 September 1958, he had formerly proposed to Eisenhower and Macmillan a Franco-British-American directorate of NATO that would have made impossible any equitable European Defence Community. The 'organized co-operation between states' might mean little more than a traditional alliance, no doubt to be led by France; and although the term 'confederation' was indeed imposing, it might well be a means of short-circuiting the Common Market's more truly federal institutions.[29]

Not everyone was so pessimistic. The only difference between a federation and a confederation, said some, was a French three-letter word. Others pointed out that even in a United States of Europe nations would never 'cease to be themselves'. If de Gaulle was seriously proposing co-operation among the Six on foreign policy, 'culture', and defence, his partners should seize the opportunity; it might not be 'political union', but it could be a step towards it. All that was essential was to ensure that the new moves strengthened rather than weakened the Common Market's structure, and that they took place within the Atlantic Alliance rather than seeking to establish an autonomous 'third force'.

On Friday 29 July 1960, de Gaulle expounded his ideas to Dr Adenauer at Rambouillet, the magnificent fifteenth-century chateau thirty miles south-west of Paris where Francis I had died. At the end of August, he saw J. E. De Quay and Joseph Luns, respectively Dutch Prime Minister and Foreign Minister; in early September he saw Amintore Fanfani and Antonio Segni, their Italian counterparts; later in the month he talked with Gaston Eyskens and Pierre Wigny from Belgium, and with Pierre Werner and Eugène Schaus from Luxembourg. After further diplomatic contacts, De Gaulle and Adenauer met again on Thursday 9 February 1961; and on the Friday and Saturday the 'Heads of State or Government'—President de Gaulle and the Prime Ministers—and the Foreign Ministers of the Six held a so-called 'little summit' meeting to study, as they put it, 'suitable means of organizing closer political co-operation. The establishment of links in other spheres will provide future bases for a progressively developing union. This union, for the moment confined to the Member States of the European Economic Community, could subsequently extend its boundaries.' To make more concrete proposals, they set up an intergovernmental committee; and although the Dutch delegation there feared 'that the system of European institutions might be compromised by the creation of a political superstructure of an intergovernmental character', when the Six held their next summit meeting, in Bonn on Tuesday 18 July 1961, they had smoothed over the cracks. They decided, in the words of their final communiqué, 'to give shape to the will for political union already implicit in the Treaties establishing the European Communities', and they set up a new committee to draft a political treaty.[30]

This committee—usually known as the 'Fouchet Committee' after its first chairman, the French representative Christian Fouchet, although it was later chaired by Attilio Cattani from Italy—at length disbanded without reaching agreement. It was divided, in particular, about Europe's place in the Atlantic Alliance, about British membership of the proposed 'political union', and about the need for a revision clause whereby the new institutions might be strengthened. If the Fouchet Committee had succeeded in its task, it might conceivably have helped avoid some of the later friction between the French Government and its partners. But it might equally have weakened the Common Market; and the institutions that it proposed to establish were themselves so feeble that they seemed unlikely to promote unity on subjects so intractable as foreign policy and defence. The first draft treaty put forward by France, her partners' counter-proposal, a second French draft, and a compromise text canvassed just before the talks ended, all spoke of a 'European Political Commission'; yet this would have consisted, not of independent persons like the members of the Common Market Commission, but simply of national representatives. All four drafts, not unnaturally, proposed a traditional Council of Ministers; but only that prepared by France's partners envisaged majority voting, and then only if all members of the Council unanimously agreed to it. All four mentioned the European Parliament; but none explicitly proposed that it be directly elected or have any specific powers. Neither French draft, finally, mentioned a Court of Justice; and although this was proposed by France's partners, it was virtually dropped from the final text. Broadly speaking, the Fouchet Committee retained Community terminology, but only to disguise its desertion of Community principles.[31]

At the time, this in no way discomfited the British Government; but far more disquieting was Britain's exclusion from the Six's plans. Only by joining the Common Market, it seemed, could she be sure of taking part in any collective political venture, and recovering as a member of the future union a share in the world influence she could no longer command alone.

Britain's relative loss of power was becoming very evident in her relations with Washington, where the 'special relationship' was obviously less prized than in London. The US Presidential election of November 1960, which brought Kennedy to the White House in place of Eisenhower, accentuated this fact. Far from weakening America's support for the Common Market and her hope that Britain would join it, Kennedy and his team made them more articulate and active. The francophile Douglas Dillon, rather to Eisenhower's annoyance, stayed on with the new Administration; and other convinced 'Europeans' came in. Robert Bowie became a consultant to the new Secretary of State, Dean Rusk; McGeorge Bundy, the editor of Dean Acheson's speeches, became the President's special adviser on National Security Affairs; Paul Nitze became Assistant Secretary for International Security Affairs in the Pentagon; and the tough, genial George Ball, a close friend and associate of Jean Monnet's, became Under-Secretary of State for Economic Affairs, later succeeding Chester Bowles as Under-Secretary. He brought into his office three youngish State Department officials who were all energetic, gifted, and equally 'European': Robert Schaetzel, Stanley Cleveland and Arthur Hartman.[32]

From this array of talent on 'Fluff Row'—the State Department's top-level carpeted corridors—came a strong new impetus in America's relationship with Europe. Journalists later called it 'the Grand Design', although it was no more than a reinvigorated version of what had been United States policy since World War II. It sought essentially what Kennedy called 'an open partnership' between the United States and uniting Europe—'a relationship,' as Jean Monnet's Action Committee said later, 'of two separate but equally powerful entities, each bearing its share of common responsibilities in the world'. Kennedy, again, was to echo these words just one week afterwards; the 'dialogue of continents' seemed to have begun. Its most concrete expression was the US Trade Expansion Act, leading at long last to the 'Kennedy Round' of tariff negotiations, whereby the United States, the Common Market and other countries eventually made tariff cuts of more than thirty per cent—and in some cases, of fifty per cent—on 40,000 million dollars' worth of annual trade.[33]

Under a technicality in the Trade Expansion Act, the US President's tariff-cutting powers would have been even greater had Britain joined the Common Market. It was drafted, in fact, with this in mind. Although Kennedy and his advisers stopped short of actual pressure, their eagerness for Britain to join the Common Market was very obvious. In London on Thursday 30 March 1961, Edward Heath, the Lord Privy Seal, asked George Ball what America's attitude would be if she did. Ball answered that he had not discussed the question with the President. Nevertheless, he said,

...if Britain is now prepared to recognize that the Rome Treaty is not a static document but a process that could eventually lead to an evolving European community – something in the nature of a European federation – and if Britain can make the great national decision to join Europe on those terms, I am confident that my Government will regard this as a major contribution to Western solidarity and the stability of the free world. So long as Britain remains outside the European Community, she is a force for division

263

rather than cohesion, since she is like a giant lodestone drawing with unequal degrees of force on each member State. But if Great Britain now decides to participate in the formidable efforts to unite Europe, she can, and I am sure will, apply her unique political genius – in which we have great confidence – toward the creation of a unity that can transform the Western world.

Harold Macmillan received a similar answer early in April when he put the same question to President Kennedy. So—somewhat to his surprise —did Walter Hallstein, President of the Common Market Commission, when he was in Washington in mid-May, 1961.[34]

By this time the British Government was approaching a decision. In the last week of June, 1961, the Ministerial Council of EFTA met in London and resolved that, if negotiations with the Common Market took place,

> ...the European Free Trade Association, the obligations created by the Convention between the Members, and the momentum towards integration within the Association, would be maintained at least until satisfactory arrangements have been worked out in negotiations to meet the various legitimate interests of all Members of EFTA, and thus enable them all to participate from the same date in an integrated European Market.

Britain pledged herself, in other words, not to make use of the denunciation clause allowing any member State to leave EFTA after twelve month's notice, and not to join the Common Market until all her EFTA partners were either about to join or about to make free-trade arrangements with it. At the time, it seemed a far-reaching commitment. No such promises were made, however, to the Commonwealth countries. In the hope of forestalling criticism, five British ministers visited their capitals, mostly during the first half of July; but the ensuing communiqués were inexplicit and brief.[35]

At last, on Monday 31 July 1961, Harold Macmillan made his announcement to the House of Commons. One observer noted that it was delivered 'in a surprisingly uninspired way'; but more important than Macmillan's fatigued manner was the substance of what he said. Britain was to ask for negotiations with the European Economic Community to see if mutually acceptable conditions could be worked out for British membership. 'No British Government,' he explained,

> ...could join the European Economic Community without prior negotiation with a view to meeting the needs of the Commonwealth countries, of our European Free Trade Association partners, and of British agriculture consistently with the broad principles and purposes which have inspired the concept of European unity and which are embodied in the Rome Treaty.

'The ultimate decision whether to join or not,' he added,

> must depend on the result of the negotiations.... No agreement will be entered into until it has been approved by the House after full consultation with other Commonwealth countries by whatever procedure they may generally agree.[36]

To Jean Monnet and his associates, Macmillan's announcement seemed curiously bitter-sweet. On the one hand, it was the culmination of their hopes and efforts; yet on the other it confirmed some lingering fears. Monnet knew very well the material problems involved in British entry; but to solve them he had for some time been urging a different procedural approach. His advice on the subject has been summarized as 'sign now, negotiate later'. This does it some injustice. More properly, what he was proposing may be described as 'decide now, negotiate on essentials, sign, then solve the other problems from within the Common Market'.[37]

His argument was roughly as follows. Speed, as in many important matters, was essential. An opportunity once lost might not recur for a long time; and when it recurred it might not be recognized. There was no certainty that General de Gaulle would welcome or even grudgingly accept British entry into the Common Market; and a long negotiation would make it easier for him to refuse. Delay, moreover, would only increase the number of new agreements within the Common Market that Britain would face when she finally entered: the sooner she joined, the more say she would have in the shape the Common Market took. Finally, the institutions themselves—the Commission, the Council of Ministers, the Court and the European Parliament—had been devised for the specific purpose of solving the member States' problems. To try to solve them from outside, without the help of the institutions, would be to start off on the wrong foot. Once Britain was in, however, her national concerns would be part of the Common Market's problems, which all its members had an interest in solving.

Monnet recognized, however, that some problems would brook no delay. British agriculture, he thought, had little to fear from competition with that of the Six; and if Britain joined the Community quickly enough, she could help shape its farm policy. Food imports from the former Dominions were more difficult, although here again early entry would enable Britain to influence policy. For New Zealand, and particularly for its butter, some standstill arrangement would have to be worked out, pending a permanent solution to be negotiated by the enlarged Common Market. For tropical primary products, the principle should be that Commonwealth producers in Africa deserved the same right of association with the Common Market as was offered to its founder-member's ex-colonies. For raw materials and manufactures, Britain would have to adopt the common outer tariff of the Six; but the duty on some products might be left to be settled by the institutions of the Common Market once Britain had joined. Finally, if some EFTA countries failed to join or associate with the Common Market, any trade problems that might arise for them would have to be discussed within OECD. What was above all essential, however, was that the number of questions to be settled before Britain's entry be reduced to a minimum, and that a firm decision be taken to join.[38]

Seen from London, there were several objections to such a course. First, it could be claimed that the provisions of the Rome Treaty, although mainly institutional and procedural, were also partly substantive: they included some precise agreements on material problems raised by one or other of the founder-members. The most obvious instance was the association with the Common Market of France's former colonies. Could Britain not claim something analogous for India, Ceylon and Pakistan? Her responsibilities to the Commonwealth covered a far broader area than the overseas commitments of any of the Six; and although it might be argued that this made the problem far more difficult, the ethical principle was surely the same. By a similar token, the change involved for Britain in joining the Common Market could be considered more drastic than that undergone by any of the Six. Leaving aside the fact that she had not been defeated in war or invaded for the past nine centuries, leaving aside her Commonwealth ties and responsibilities, there were many technical differences between her legislative, judicial and economic situation and those of the Six. In British law, for instance, no Parliament could bind its successors: some constitutional contortion would therefore be necessary for the House of Commons to ratify the Common Market Treaty, with no expiry date and no denunciation clause. British law was in many respects different from that of continental countries; this too would take time to adjust. Britain's national currency, unlike those of the Six, was still—however falteringly—a world reserve currency; her system of farm support, with low food prices and high subsidies to producers, was diametrically opposite to that of most of the Six; and while all the latter had been touched however unwillingly, by the Napoleonic Code and the metric system, Britain had resisted Napoleon and missed his equivocal legacy.

Some of these objections had force, and in a perfect world they might have been sustained. But the world was far from perfect, and Britain had to make a choice. If she was not a founder-member of the Common Market, this was no fault of the Six; she must do her best to fit into the club as they had made it—although once inside she would find its rules more flexible than they looked. If she retained responsibilities as a leading member of the Commonwealth, the Common Market itself had comparable responsibilities as a leading industrial power. The Commonwealth preference system, together with the sterling area, could in this context be regarded as partial and imperfect attempts to solve world problems which the Common Market also faced. Britain's entry would merely re-state them in more pressing terms; and their ultimate solution could only be sought by the enlarged Common Market with the aid of the United States. Finally, if Britain's changeover to Common Market membership caused her considerable upheaval, there was no question of her entering without a transition period in which to adapt herself. On the specific question of agriculture, where the adjustment problem seemed most acute, even the addition of Britain to the Common Market would not radically change the balance of supply and demand or the ratio of agriculture to industry. It would be understandable, therefore, if the Six asked Britain to accept the broad principles of what they themselves proposed as an agricultural policy—although the sooner she entered the greater say she would have.

Warnings and suggestions of this sort continued to reach London from a variety of quarters; but it was not easy for the British Government to respond. On Tuesday 1 August 1961, Edward Heath told the WEU Council: 'We shall be seeking the support of public opinion not just for British application for negotiations to join the European Economic Community but for the whole great enterprise which from now on we are, I trust, going to pursue together.' But if this suggested that in Heath's mind at least the decision of principle was already taken, it remained formally necessary to keep up the 'exploratory' stance. Characteristically, Macmillan's policy seemed to be to back into Europe. This was one reason that it failed.[39]

On Thursday 10 August 1961, Great Britain formally requested the opening of negotiations. She was accompanied by Denmark, but overtaken by Ireland, which had applied to negotiate on 1 August. On Tuesday 10 October, after further discussion among the Six, their ministers met with Heath in Paris to hear a preliminary statement of Britain's case. It was in the same Salon de l'Horloge at the Quai d'Orsay that had seen so many European gatherings since the afternoon a decade ago when Robert Schuman had made his Declaration of 9 May 1950.

In many respects, Heath's speech was heartening:

> In saying that we wish to join the E.E.C., we mean that we desire to become full, whole-hearted and active members of the European Community in its widest sense and to go forward with you in the building of a new Europe.... In particular, we accept without qualification the objectives laid down in Articles 2 and 3 of the Treaty of Rome, including the elimination of internal tariffs, a common customs tariff, a common commercial policy, and a common agricultural policy.
>
> We are ready to accept, and to play our full part in, the institutions established under Article 4 and other Articles of the Treaty....
>
> We are anxious that our accession to the Treaty should not tend to slow up the progress towards harmonization....
>
> We are also ready, once we enter the Community, to make, in a single operation, the same cuts in tariffs on trade between Member States as you will have yourselves made by that date. In addition, we are prepared to move our M.F.N. [non-Commonwealth] tariff towards the new common tariff by a step equivalent to that which you have already taken....
>
> We fully share the aims and objectives, political and otherwise, of those who drew up this Declaration [the Bonn Declaration on 'political union' of 18 July 1961], and we shall be anxious, once we are members of the Community, to work with you in a positive spirit to reinforce the unity which you have already achieved....
>
> We in the United Kingdom will regard the successful conclusion of these negotiations as a point of departure, not as the end of the road....[40]

This sounded far from 'exploratory'; but the substance of Heath's speech was more disappointing. It would not be quite true to say that he gave away nothing in Paris that had not been announced in London: he did, after all, agree to make the tariff changes already gradually applied by the Six. The rest of his statement, however, gave the impression of trying to perpetuate in another form the economic and trading patterns that were crystallized in the Commonwealth and EFTA. By ingeniously adapting various provisions of the Rome Treaty, the speech implied, it would be possible for Britain to avoid—as the Six had avoided—imposing a tariff on trade where none had been in force before. The EFTA countries would join the Common Market or become associated with it in a free trade area; the African, Asian, and other 'developing continue their exports as before. Only on one point did Heath's statements; 'comparable outlets' would be found in the enlarged Common Market for foodstuffs from the former dominions, so that they could continue their exports as before. Only on one point did Heath's statement seem to allow for movement from this position of principle, hint-ing that it was a negotiating posture and not an inflexible stance. On manufactures from the Commonwealth, apart from those for which Britain proposed nil duties in the common outer tariff, he admitted that 'we recognize that indefinite and unlimited continuation of free entry over the whole of this field may not be regarded as compatible with the development of the Common Market, and we are willing to discuss ways of reconciling these two conflicting considerations.' In other respects, the system he initially proposed, if accepted by the Six, would have amounted not so much to Britain's joining the Common Market as to her embracing it and perhaps dissolving it in a quasi-worldwide system of free trade that would have included the whole of Western Europe, most of Africa, and all the rest of the British Commonwealth —discriminating, in other words, against the United States, Japan, Latin America and non-Commonwealth 'developing countries'. Clearly, this was impossible; and the main task of the negotiations was to force a slow retreat from this initial bargaining position towards a series of agreements much more like those that Monnet and his associates had already suggested.[41]

The negotiations formally began in Brussels on Wednesday 8 November 1961, in a long narrow room at the top of Belgium's brand-new Foreign Ministry building in the rue des Quatre Bras. The British delegation sat at one end, in front of the interpreters' cabins; the President and Secretariat sat far away at the other, with the member States' and the Commission's delegations spread out along the sides. This led to problems. It was winter; the building was new, and was being dried out. The windows were therefore tight shut, and the central heating was oppressively efficient. Not only this, but several of the British had brought their pipes. It was not surprising that they pleaded for fresh air. At their request, windows were briskly opened. but then stealthily shut by those unlucky enough to be sitting in front of them. After several weeks of this running battle, the Belgians found a solution: directly above the British delegation they installed a ventilator pipe big enough to contain several spies or journalists. The tobacco-smoke vanished, the windows stayed shut, and the British delegation had its fresh air. In the euphoria of those early days, the incident seemed to symbolize all that the negotiators hoped.[42]

As the weeks went on, however, euphoria diminished. The British team was impressive: at ministerial level it was led by the bulky, shrewd and popular Edward Heath, a master of his dossiers; at official level, by the scholarly Sir Pierson Dixon, British Ambassador in Paris. It included Sir Eric Roll, Sir Roderick Barclay, Sir Henry Lintott, and Sir William Gorell Barnes—known collectively, because of their air trips to London, as 'the flying knights.' But despite this deployment of very able officials, the talks were extremely slow. Later, it was tempting to blame this on delaying tactics by the French delegation, whose leader at ministerial level was Maurice Couve de Murville, de Gaulle's icy Foreign Minister. But Couve de Murville's deputy was Bernard Clappier, who had been Robert Schuman's *Directeur de cabinet*; and although he was in a highly delicate position, he in fact played scrupulously fair. Nor, finally, could the Common Market Commission be accused of obstruction. Headed at official level by an outstandingly able young Frenchman, Jean-François Deniau, who was later to be a Commission Member, it in fact produced all but one of the technical solutions that were found for Britain's problems before the end.[43]

It was April 1962, in fact, before the negotiators did more than elaborate fact-finding. By then, the Common Market had made further strides. At 5.32 a.m. on the morning of Sunday 14 January 1962, after several all-night sessions and at least one ministerial heart attack, it had settled the broad lines of its farm support system, and had moved into the second four-year stage of its transition period—having 'stopped the clock' at midnight on 31 December to maintain the legal fiction that it was on time. The agricultural agreement, strongly pressed by France, put paid to British and 'European' hopes that Britain would be able to help shape the Common Market's farm arrangements. As Heath complained, it was like negotiating on a moving staircase.[44]

However, from April 1962 onwards, the beginnings of solutions could be seen to emerge. The breakthrough came over manufactured goods imported from Canada, Australia and New Zealand. On these, Britain agreed to phase out Commonwealth Preference and gradually apply the common outer tariff; the Common Market, meanwhile, agreed to consult on trade matters with the countries concerned. The process of transition was to be completed by 1970, but the steps involved were to be less steep than those prescribed by the Treaty of Rome.

A similar solution was found for imports from India, Pakistan and Ceylon. Here too Commonwealth Preference was to be tapered off, but even more gradually. The enlarged Common Market was to give guarantees for Indian and Pakistani exports of textiles, and was to remove the tariff on tea: it was also to negotiate comprehensive trade agreements with all three countries to help promote their economic development.

To Commonwealth countries in Africa and the Caribbean, the enlarged Common Market offered association on the lines of that enjoyed by the ex-colonies of the Six. For those that might refuse association, comprehensive trade agreements were on offer, similar but not identical to those proposed to India, Pakistan and Ceylon.

On agricultural imports from the temperate zones of the Commonwealth, full agreement was never reached; but what was envisaged was a tapering-off of Commonwealth Preference, accompanied by world-wide support agreements among the major supplying and importing countries —or, if they proved unco-operative, with Commonwealth countries alone.[45]

When the negotiating conference broke up for the summer recess in the early hours of Sunday 5 August 1962, some crucial aspects of these and other Commonwealth problems—as well as those of EFTA—still remained to be settled. From September to the end of the year, however, the negotiators concentrated chiefly on the subject of home agriculture. Of all the main issues that the conference confronted, this seemed the least intractable technically. British farmers were efficient; the Common Market had not yet fixed the majority of its common price levels; complication rather than difficulty seemed to be the snag. But all parties, including the British, were inclined to be intransigent: on one occasion, delegates wasted a whole afternoon scoring debating points at each other's—and their own—expense. In principle, Britain accepted the Common Market's farm support system; one major point at issue, however, was whether she should adopt the transitional measures it included, or have a special transitional regime of her own. Several of the Six, and France in particular, feared that this might give her a privileged position, from which she would be hard to dislodge. These questions were stubbornly debated for several weeks. Finally, in December 1962, in the hope of breaking the apparent deadlock, the conference agreed to do what it might usefully have done from the beginning: it gave the Common Market Commission the task of finding common solutions instead of simply advising the Six on how they should negotiate with Britain. Under Sicco Mansholt, the Commission Vice-President chiefly responsible for agriculture, a special Ministerial Committee of Investigation sped through a sea of statistics and technical expertise, emerging in the early hours of Tuesday 15 January 1963, with a voluminous but at last unanimous report. With this as a basis and the new working method as a model, it almost looked as if the Brussels negotiations might soon be completed. But by that time most people knew that they were dead.[46]

They had lasted nearly fourteen months. This was hardly the rapid progress that Monnet and his friends had urged. Instead of settling only a few questions before entering the Common Market, Britain had tried to solve the bulk of them. Instead of proposing solutions like those suggested by the 'Europeans', the British delegation had been obliged, for domestic political reasons, to let itself be forced towards them, step by step. When the solutions emerged, they all had a similar pattern: in each case, Britain was given time to adapt to the Common Market's framework, while the Common Market accepted joint responsibility with Britain for what had once been mainly British concerns. In other words, the negotiation had simply provided transitional solutions—the steps whereby Britain would move from the Commonwealth Preference system into the Common Market. All the long-term solutions—trade agreements, and so on—were left to be dealt with by the enlarged Common Market. This looked very like what Monnet had suggested at the outset; but to get there had taken fourteen precious months.

It was not time alone, however, but General de Gaulle that killed the Brussels negotiations. Their length and detail no doubt gave him his opportunity; but the responsibility was his. On Monday 14 January 1963, he told a press conference in Paris:

England in fact is insular, maritime, bound by her trade, her markets, her supplies, to countries that are very diverse and often very far away ... The nature, the structure, the situation that are peculiar to England are very different from those of the continental countries. How can England, as she lives, as she produces, as she trades, be incorporated into the Common Market as it was conceived and as it works?

The question was rhetorical; but if de Gaulle had expected the Brussels talks to cease forthwith, he was disappointed. In the rue des Quatre Bras, while officials in the corridors were listening to the General's words on pocket transistor radios, their colleagues in the conference-room worked on, that day and the next. Then, on the evening of Wednesday 16 January 1963, Maurice Couve de Murville proposed to his colleagues of the Six that they discuss whether and how the negotiations should continue; and next day he formally requested their adjournment. For hours of tense argument, the other five and the Commission fought to keep the talks open; but all that they could secure was a postponement of the final blow. At last, on Tuesday 29 January, after further sharp exchanges, the seven delegations and the Commission met once again in the long familiar conference room that had heard so many speeches, so many arguments about canned salmon and East India kips, so many weak jokes and flowery compliments. Now, euphoria had given place to bitterness. One by one, the ministers made their farewell speeches: one German delegate sat weeping; Couve de Murville looked hunted and old.[47]

On one reckoning, this was the second battle between the lion and the unicorn; and again the unicorn had won. As Walter Hallstein commented afterwards, 'When the negotiations were suspended ... it could not fairly be said that they had already failed on technical grounds, or that they were already on the verge of success. There is no need to conclude from the negotiations themselves, therefore, that future British membership has been proved to be unworkable: far from it.' Britain had been denied a hearing, and condemned for the existence of those very problems that she was negotiating to solve. It was true that de Gaulle had suggested an interim 'association' between her and the Common Market; but this disdainful consolation-prize amounted to little more than non-voting second-class citizenship, if that.

No less important than the fact of de Gaulle's veto was its motivation, real or supposed. In part, this may well have been fear of British rivalry in an enterprise that even before de Gaulle's return to office had been greatly influenced by France. Over the weekend of 15 and 16 December 1962, de Gaulle and Macmillan had already had a chilly meeting at Rambouillet, which now lived up to Marie Antoinette's description of it as a 'crapaudière' (or toad-hole). Here, de Gaulle had virtually warned Macmillan that he planned to halt the negotiations; he also dropped a delicate hint about Anglo-French collaboration on missiles, to which Macmillan made no response. But it seems likely that de Gaulle's growing impatience was increased by suspicion of America, and by the feeling that Britain, as Gaullists frequently put it, was 'an American Trojan Horse'.[48]

The pretext for this reproach was the Nassau meeting between Macmillan and Kennedy on 18–21 December 1962. Ever since the Cuba missile crisis of October, de Gaulle had been even more painfully aware of America's nuclear supremacy, and ever more concerned to even the balance between the United States and Europe. France was struggling to build a nuclear arsenal; Britain was clinging to the remnants of her own: logically, there might have been a case for co-operation. But Britain was also relying on America, which had promised her the Skybolt air-ground missile—until Friday 9 November 1962, when the US Defence Secretary Robert McNamara telephoned his British counterpart Peter Thorneycroft to announce that he was thinking of abandoning it. With Britain's 'independent deterrent' thus threatened, Macmillan flew to the Bahamas to try to reverse the American decision—having told de Gaulle that weekend what he hoped to do. He came back, not with a British Skybolt, but with a NATO Polaris missile, available to Britain under special circumstances, and offered also to France. De Gaulle, scenting American 'hegemony', indignantly refused the offer; and it no doubt confirmed him in his suspicion of Britain.[49]

This additional encouragement to de Gaulle to halt the Brussels negotiations might have been avoided if they had not been so slow. It might also have been prevented. To have taken up De Gaulle's hint of bilateral Anglo-French co-operation on military matters might well have been unwise: it would certainly have troubled the Germans, and possibly the United States. But with the benefit of hindsight it certainly seems to have been inappropriate to talk so fulsomely about sharing the aims of the Bonn Declaration, while acting as if the bid to join the Common Market and to help unite Europe were quite distinct from matters of defence. If, as some suggested directly after the veto, the British Government had announced that it would make over its nuclear missile forces to any future combined European component in NATO, it might have saved its own hopes of joining the Common Market, helped Europe towards unity, and tied it more closely to the United States. But as things were, it merely retired to lick wounds. There were more to come.[50]

The year 1963 had begun in hope; it ended as a year of disaster. Britain was excluded from the Common Market; Kennedy had been killed, and the Grand Design seemed to have died with him; Adenauer had at last stepped down in Germany; in Britain, Harold Macmillan had retired in the wake of the Profumo scandal. No less dismaying was the state of the Common Market. General de Gaulle's veto had plunged it into a crisis from which it was not to recover for several years.

There was nothing technically illegal, of course, in General de Gaulle's having blackballed a would-be new member: everyone had the same right. But the manner of the veto—unannounced, undiscussed, unjustified—made it almost unconstitutional, a breach of unwritten law. The result was a crisis of confidence; and it was heightened by the almost simultaneous conclusion of the Franco-German Treaty of Friendship, signed in Paris on Tuesday 22 January 1963, by Adenauer and General de Gaulle. This closely resembled an earlier French draft of a treaty for 'political union' that had come before the Fouchet Committee. In reality, it merely sealed—and claimed the credit for—the reconciliation of the two countries that had already been achieved within the European Community; it also pleased its two elderly signatories, no doubt for subtly different reasons. But in the eyes of the smaller Community countries in particular, it threatened to pervert the Common Market's fair workings by establishing prior Franco-German consultation even on subjects due to be discussed later in the Council of the Six. As it was, the Bundestag, encouraged by some official 'Europeans', insisted on voting in a Preamble to the Treaty which drew most of its sting. But within the Community, resentment against de Gaulle was now very powerful, and the Common Market ground almost to a halt. At length, in the spring of 1963, reprisals gave way to a method of work that Gerhard Schroeder, then German Foreign Minister, described as 'synchronization'. Essentially, this meant horse-trading. Its most obvious instance was the tacit agreement to synchronize progress on the Kennedy Round of tariff negotiations—of special interest to Germany, Belgium and Holland, with work on the farm support system—of special interest to France.

'Synchronization' had been practised before in the Common Market: there had always been some degree of package deals. But whereas in the past a country making a concession had sometimes been prepared to wait for 'compensation' in the future, the watchword now was 'payment on the nail'. In practice, this was not always workable: the bulk of the Common Market's farm policy was in fact agreed on long before the end of the Kennedy Round. But the principle was now half-respectable; and the contagion spread.

It can, in fact, be blamed for the next serious crisis, or the next instalment of the same crisis, which occurred in 1965. Then, the Commission itself attempted to promote a package deal compounded of three connected elements: the completion of the farm finance regulations, sought in particular by France; the independent financing of the Common Market out of its own resources, most desired by the Commission; and the granting of greater power to the European Parliament, demanded by the Parliament itself and by the Netherlands. Crudely, the Commission tried to make General de Gaulle pay a 'supranational' price for his agricultural settlement.[51]

As might have been expected, the trick failed to work. At midnight on Wednesday 30 June 1965, Maurice Couve de Murville, who was then chairman of the Council of Ministers, broke up the meeting—refusing to 'stop the clock'—because it had not settled the farm finance question on time. Thereupon, the French Government virtually boycotted the Common Market for seven months. At length, after de Gaulle had been forced into a run-off in the Presidential elections of December 1965, partly owing to the efforts of the 'European' candidate Jean Lecanuet, a so-called 'Gentlemen's Disagreement' was patched up. By this, de Gaulle did his best to cripple the Commission and eliminate majority voting from the Common Market, while the other five member States, showing unexpected cohesion partly under German leadership, did their best to resist. France reserved her 'right' to the veto, despite the text of the Treaty; the 'Five' reserved their right to overrule her. The most unfortunate victim of the whole affair was Walter Hallstein. The French Government's resentment led it to object to a further renewal of his mandate as President of the Common Market Commission; the German Government persuaded France to agree to appoint him for a shorter time than the statutory two years. Since this would have contravened the Treaty, Hallstein refused to accept it. His legalism had courage.

Hallstein's successor was Jean Rey, fresh from his success in negotiating for the Common Market in the Kennedy Round. He took his place on 1 July 1967 at the head of a Commission larger than Hallstein's, for by now the three Community organizations—the ECSC, Euratom, and the Common Market—had been merged under the terms of a Treaty signed in Brussels on 8 April 1965. Its ratification had been held up by the crisis; but now the way ahead once more seemed clear. The time had come, moreover, for a third brief round in the battle of the lion and the unicorn. On Wednesday 10 May 1967, Harold Wilson, Britain's Labour Prime Minister, lodged her formal application to become a member of the Common Market.[52]

The process that had led the Labour Party to this decision was similar to that which had moved the Conservatives before them. Elected in October 1964, the Labour Government had been expected to canvass 'Commonwealth', 'EFTA', and even 'neutralist' solutions to Britain's twin problems of slow economic growth and waning political influence. As early as February 1965, however, Harold Wilson had declared that if favourable conditions arose, Britain would be prepared to negotiate for membership of the Common Market, provided that essential British and Commonwealth interests could be assured. This was an echo of the 'five conditions' put forward by the late Hugh Gaitskell during the first Common Market negotiations: safeguards for the Commonwealth, adequate arrangements for the other EFTA countries, suitable arrangements for British agriculture, freedom to pursue an independent foreign policy, and freedom to carry out national economic planning. At one time, these had seemed incompatible with Common Market membership; but times had changed. The 1961–3 negotiations had suggested how the Commonwealth and EFTA might be safeguarded. British agriculture, as such, had little to fear; and de Gaulle had demonstrated how easily national planning and a national foreign policy could be conducted by a full member of the Common Market. What was more, experience had changed the perspective. The Commonwealth remained a vital British interest; but trouble in Rhodesia and Nigeria, if nowhere else, had shown the limits of its cohesive force. Britain remained bound to EFTA; but her partners there had understandably reacted when she had felt herself obliged by the sterling crisis in October 1964 to slap a fifteen per cent surcharge on all British imports. The United States, meanwhile, had contributed to the rethinking process. Lyndon Johnson, Kennedy's very different successor, had for some months pressed very hard the proposal for a mixed-manned multilateral NATO force of surface ships carrying Polaris missiles—the MLF—a project that had originated under Eisenhower and been developed by Kennedy, but never so much. Well-meaning as this was, it underlined Britain's reduced status; and when Johnson abruptly dropped the MLF project in 1965, this caused some relief in Britain. But America was not the only source of not always welcome pressure. Equally powerful were the international bankers—the so-called 'gnomes of Zurich'—whose influence on British national planning was at least as strong as the Common Market's would have been on Britain as a member. Finally, although Wilson was cautious in referring to European defence problems, the cutdown of British forces 'East of Suez', forced by economic necessity, was a further factor pointing towards Europe, as was the unpopularity, among many Labour Party members, of American military policy in South-East Asia.[53]

There was, moreover, one new element in the European equation that had not been so prominent in the past. This was technology. In essence, it had lain at the root of the Spaak Report: aircraft and atomic power, Spaak had said, required technical resources on a European scale. But more recent years had seen a growing realization that rapid economic growth now depended on high-technology industries; and these in turn depended not only on large markets, but also on large-scale government expenditure. Space and computers were the most obvious example where the United States had leapt ahead for this reason. Could Europe do the same? If she failed to, America would surely dominate her industries. One French author nicknamed the problem 'the American challenge': the slogan, and the book of that title, had immense success.[54]

Others looked at the problem rather differently. Technology, in their eyes, was not an end in itself. What was important was to master it. Unless Europe did so, she would risk something worse than comparative backwardness: blind market forces would ensure that technology reached her, probably from America, but certainly out of her control. Individual European firms would be too small to withstand American takeovers; individual European countries might be no match for American corporations. To ensure that the quality of life should not suffer in a secondhand technological revolution, it was essential for Europeans to be rich, strong and united enough to make their new society civilized, and get their human priorities right.

Such was some of the thinking that lay behind Britain's second application to join the Common Market. Like the first, but more quickly, it was rebuffed. On Tuesday 3 October 1967, the European Commission, at the request of the Council of Ministers, gave its Preliminary Opinion on Britain's application for membership. It concluded:

... in order to dispel the uncertainty which still attaches in particular to certain fundamental points, negotiations should be opened in the most appropriate forms with the States which have applied for membership, in order to examine in more detail, as is indeed necessary, the problems brought out in this document and to see whether arrangements can be made under which the indispensable cohesion and dynamism will be maintained in an enlarged Community.

Eight weeks later, on Monday 27 November 1967, General de Gaulle gave another of his press conferences. This time, he stressed 'the impossibility of bringing the Great Britain of today into the Common Market as it stands'. Finally, on 19 December 1967, the Council Ministers issued a sadly revealing communiqué. 'Five member States,' it declared, 'subscribed to the point of view of the Commission.' France did not.

One member State ... expressed the opinion that this enlargement [of the Community] would modify profoundly the nature and the ways of administering the communities. . . .
One member State considered that the process of restoring the British economy must be completed for Britain's application to be considered.

The unicorn had won a third round.[55]

But triumphs, like sorrows, are not always lasting. Before long, General de Gaulle himself was in difficulties. His personal magic had first seemed tarnished when he faced the run-off in the December 1965 election. In January 1966, he had ousted Valery Giscard d'Estaing from the French Finance Ministry, and started a running battle between the Gaullists and their 'Independent Republican' allies. In March 1966, he had further alienated sections of French opinion by withdrawing France from NATO; in June he had paid an inconclusive visit to the Soviet Union; in August, in Djibouti, riots had forced him to cancel a speech. In the legislative elections of March 1967, the Gaullists had lost forty seats; in June, despite the General's admonitions, Israel had launched the six-day war. In July, the General had visited Quebec, cried 'Vive le Québec libre!' and found himself persona non grata in Ottawa. In

November he had alienated many Frenchmen—including civil servants and army officers—by making a verbal attack on Jewry. Then, in May 1968, France was rocked by student disorders and strikes. For a while, the General faltered. When he recovered, with the assurance of army backing, he made a brilliant four-minute broadcast which helped set off a carefully orchestrated movement of support. Now, for nearly twelve months, French political life remained calm. But the May disorders had shaken confidence; the closing months of 1968 saw France's reserves falling and a serious currency crisis. Then, in April 1969, the General staked his career on a referendum; and he lost. Promptly, without fuss, he retired; and Georges Pompidou was voted into his place.

Almost simultaneously, Jean Monnet's Action Committee held a further meeting, this time in Brussels. Now, it included the British Labour, Conservative and Liberal Parties, all of them formally committed to 'European' cause. It had before it reports on the main problems of British entry into the Common Market: agriculture, monetary policy, technology and institutions. Without exception, the conclusion of their authors was that these problems could be solved.[56]

After the slow stagnation of the late nineteen-sixties, then, the unification of Western Europe seemed due to make fresh progress. The archaic battle between the lion and the unicorn could be forgotten; and General de Gaulle's departure was only one of the reasons. Another was a quickening sense that the world was once more insecure. In the Middle East, in Asia, in Africa, in Latin America, violence had exploded; it was still very close to the surface. Two past giants—Japan and China—were re-emerging in a new guise, one as a rival, the other as a potential threat. Under President Nixon, the United States, so long Western Europe's protector, was still deeply involved in South-East Asia, and was planning to reduce her European garrison. Relations with Eastern Europe, which had thawed under Khrushchev, were chilly and uncertain under Brezhnev and Kosygin: the Soviet invasion of Prague in August 1968 was a grim commemoration of Czechoslovakia's fate twenty years earlier, and a repetition of Hungary's in 1956. With hopes of liberalization in Eastern Europe fading yet again, unity in the West seemed more than ever essential for a true *détente*. This was made very clear when Willy Brandt's Social Democrats came to power in Germany after the elections of 28 September 1969. Although renowned—and in some quarters vilified—for his *Ostpolitik* of cautious contact with Eastern Europe, Brandt repeatedly stressed that this, like German re-unification, would only be possible within a European Community. On this point, if on no other, Konrad Adenauer would have agreed with him.[57]

The European response to these incentives was less rapid than might have been hoped. The Common Market's morale had been sapped by years of crisis; the farm prices imposed by the professional lobbies had caused mountainous surpluses; and the absence of a common monetary policy had led to grave imbalance. At the 'summit' meeting of the Six's Heads of State or Government, together with their Foreign Ministers, on 1 and 2 December 1969, in the Hague, it was agreed that economic and monetary union must be pursued, and political union studied; but practical progress was slow. Early in 1970, the Community settled its financial arrangements for the common farm policy, giving marginal budgetary powers to the European Parliament; in the summer, talks began with a view to British membership. How fast and how far they would go depended largely — but not entirely — on Great Britain.

What obstacles stood between her and a uniting Europe? Lingering doubts in Britain were understandable. After so many rebuffs, it was natural to fear another; after living so long on food bought at dumping prices in the world market, it was painful to face the prospect of paying continental farmer's excessive costs. Lingering doubts were natural also in the Community: Britain, after all, was a late convert to the cause. But in the longer perspective, the very real difficulties of this transitional phase were unimportant compared with the opportunities that were now at hand. Even the fact that European unity remained half-finished was in some respects encouraging: with economic union only beginning, and common defence and foreign policies still unformed, new recruits to the task of unifying Europe had a real chance to share in the shaping of their common future. The present problems might seem daunting; but the possibilities were immense.

CHAPTER TWELVE

Remembering the Future

The best Qualification of a Prophet is to have a good Memory.   *George Savile, first Marquess of Halifax*[1]

To-morrow is an old deceiver, and his cheat never grows stale.   *Dr Samuel Johnson*[2]

If you have built castles in the air, your work need not be lost; that is where they should be. Now put the foundations under them.   *Henry David Thoreau*[3]

THIS book began with a retrospect; it ends with a reminder. The past thirty years have brought Europe and the world an immense distance. A further generation will bring them into the twenty-first century. The talismanic year 2000 is surprisingly near. Numerology apart, moreover, the future is already bearing down upon us far more rapidly than we often realize. To secure its benefits and forestall some of its dangers, we have no option but to look ahead.

Speculation about what may be in store for us has lately become a growth industry; disused Utopias pile up yearly, yet future-snobbery still abounds. It can hardly be surprising that prophets are often at a loss when they are not at loggerheads, since the extrapolation of current trends—one standard procedure for forecasts—is more than usually mis-leading in times of turmoil. Such is the pace of change at present that many curves on the graph of 'progress'—for the growth of world steel production, of energy consumption, of accumulated explosive power—are now almost vertical, apparently heading for infinity within a few decades. This makes estimates rough-and-ready, and in many cases physically absurd. They also ignore the inevitability of the unexpected and the seemingly impossible. But if predictions, like compasses, are almost always out of true, this is no reason for renouncing them. At least they tell us something about the present day.

Science and technology, in all likelihood, will continue to act as the

281

ploughshare of future change. Increasingly, the distinction between them, as between their once separate disciplines, is becoming blurred. 'Spin-off' is a characteristic feature of defence research, which has constant repercussions on civil technology; in this field, further spectacular results may be expected. But similar forces are at work among the 'pure' sciences. Radio-astronomy provides one example; inter-disciplinary co-operation in the study and design of materials is another; and equally symptomatic are such terms as the familiar 'bio-chemistry' and the less familiar 'biometry' and 'bio-physics'. The relatively recent exploration of the genetic code, indeed, is only one of the developments in biology that are likely to have profound and disturbing effects on human life.

Here, a number of tendencies may well converge. Man-machine symbiosis, already beginning with the improvement of artificial limbs and organs, may ultimately be completed by connecting miniaturized electronic units to the central nervous system; one day, for instance, there may be built-in radar for the blind. Some hereditary disabilities may be removed by 'clonal' reproduction or by the chemical modification of the genes. Viral and bacterial diseases may increasingly be checked by immunization. A start may be made on creating a primitive form of artificial life, if only by the self-reproduction of molecules; tissue culture, meanwhile, may extend its success in facilitating further grafts of organs and the transfusion of cells. It may be that in this direction a cure will at length be found for cancer; and if, as may be hoped, arterial and degenerative diseases can be treated bio-chemically, some progress will have been made toward solving the problems of ageing. Intelligence, likewise, may prove amenable to physical or chemical treatment. Non-narcotic drugs may be more widely used to reduce or eliminate some of the forms of mental illness or personality disorder at present treated—or left untreated—by other means; medicine may also find ways of raising the level of mental perception for specific tasks or of improving intelligence permanently.

Together with simpler contraception and more effective ways of increasing fertility, all these developments will give men and women, or those who can afford them, far greater control over processes once thought ineluctable; they will become forbiddingly responsible for their own bodies and minds. Misused, power of this order would have alarming possibilities. Even used with wisdom, it will present a very considerable challenge in philosophy, ethics, and politics. Who is to benefit first from the new discoveries—or to be their human guinea-pigs? Whose authority should be required for operations on the genes, on the brain, on a foetus, on an ovum? If intelligence is a matter of medicine, what becomes of competitive examinations? If ageing can be postponed indefinately, what becomes of the world's population? Will individuals one day have to decide whether and when to die?

If biology may thus come to transform the framework of ordinary living, the progress of space research is doing so already. Seriously envisaged for the future are exploits even more striking than the first launchings of artificial satellites or the landings on the moon. Before long, systems will be devised for the regular rescue of cosmonauts. Not much later, a scientific research station may be established in orbit, followed by the development of rockets and orbital vehicles that can be serviced for re-use. Manned overflights of Mars and Venus seem likely in the nineteen-seventies, as is the establishment of a base on the moon. In the following decade, if not earlier, the first men may land on Mars. By the year 2000, rocket probes will probably have taken place outside the solar system, research stations may have been set up on some of the nearer planets, and the moon may well be the scene of mining operations. The early years of the twenty-first century may see a permanent base on Mars, a manned overflight of Pluto, and even perhaps some landings on the satellites of Jupiter. 'Colonizing the planets' is a grandiose term for these sparse ventures into immensity; but the earliest European explorers of other continents, after all, were almost as few.

The exploration of space is affecting life on earth in at least two senses. Most immediately, its impact is practical. Artificial satellites will soon make possible truly world-wide television, as well as a marked improvement in weather forecasts. The actual control of weather will take much longer; but there seems every prospect of its being achieved —if only, at first, for military purposes—in the early 'eighties. By the turn of the century, high-altitude 'space' gliders may well be in use for ballistic commercial transport.

No less real, however, are the psychological repercussions of space research. It already seems incongruous to see the moon as a 'white goddess' now that machinery has been installed on it. Yet the function of myth is hardly to describe external reality, but rather to embody and respond to human fears and longings. Although known to be 'untrue', it may come closer to everyday experience of the universe than a God's-eye view of the 'objective' models of science; and whenever spectacular experiments or discoveries seem to break with such experience, the result is a psychological wrench. Similar dissociation or alienation was felt, more obviously, in the nineteenth century, when the findings of Darwin and Huxley appeared to clash with the revealed truth of the Bible. Abruptly, the normal tension between different 'levels' of awareness becomes a strain. We find it harder than ever to see

283

K

life as a whole, to keep simultaneously in focus the versions of reality perceived by the different components of our nature: the relatively in-efficient two-legged machine, the intelligent animal that eats and defe-cates, the primitive human being afraid of the dark and of loneliness; the sensitive and quasi-autonomous but often unreliable computer, the reveller, the hero, the lover, the scientist, the citizen, the solitary dreamer. When these seeming contradictions become unbearable, we tend to deny or ignore one or other mode of perception. Some take refuge in a smug and simple scientism: they reduce once distant mysteries to prosaic terminal problems, coldly eyeing the conquered moon. In this way, the very magnitude of man's achievements in space may revive a geocentric self-importance that became anachronistic with Copernicus. Most scientists, however, are wary of complacency: they retain a sense of wonder, humility and scepticism, knowing that they will never do more than laboriously nibble at the edges of the cosmos. Partly for this reason, and partly because research into outer space seems at once irrelevant and menacing, others again react to it with what one alert semi-layman described as 'a certain sort of bored astonishment'.[4] One further result of the space race, therefore, may be a slightly forced reassertion of private, personal values in a world where the individual feels increasingly lost.

Equally disturbing to habitual assumptions is the further growth of the computer. Here, the next generation will see a double development: far greater sophistication in computers themselves, and a vast extension of their use. These alone may prove quite as revolutionary as anything in computer development over the past twenty years.

One of the many nervous jokes made about computers in their early days was the stock description of them as 'high-speed idiots'. As far as speed is concerned, the immense acceleration of data processing that has taken place in the last generation is unlikely to be repeated in the future. Even so, computer speeds may yet increase more than a hundred-fold during the next few decades. What is almost certain, moreover, is that by the end of the century, and probably long before it, computers will in some respects have ceased to be idiots. If present progress con-tinues, they will soon be far better able to learn from experience; and they may become capable of asking unexpected questions, sustaining a provocative dialogue, and taking the initiative. When this happens, a computer's 'intelligence' may be less clearly limited by that of its pro-grammer or its designer; and some will not need programming at all. They will still, of course, be essentially calculating machines of very great complexity; they may lack such human attributes as 'intuition', moral sense and persuasive power; nor is a 'sub-conscious' likely to be built into them—unless, perhaps, their designers can work under hypnosis. But despite these ultimate limitations, the computers of the future will be very much more like so-called 'thinking machines', and their speed will help to compensate, as now, for their residual naïvety. Perhaps it would be wise to avoid endowing such mechanical 'brains' with efficient and powerful mechanical 'bodies'.

Even without such shadowy possibilities, the fairly primitive computers now in use have begun to have an immense influence on human affairs. This will grow very rapidly. Computers themselves are unlikely to become much larger, although their capacity will increase: on the contrary, their physical size is shrinking. Already, it is claimed, a six-foot cube could theoretically store the sum total of recorded knowledge; and for less ambitious purposes, micro-circuitry may yet make possible computers little larger than transistor radio sets. Coupled with their mass production, expected by the 'eighties, this could open up some remarkable prospects. One is the development of a national, continental or global grid system of data storage, into which individual computers could be plugged to retrieve tailor-made information. This could have obvious applications for economic planning, for the stock exchange, for tax calculation, for legal advice, for marketing, and for scientific and other abstracts; it might also extend to automatic translation and interpretation, which in turn could be linked with an audio-visual telephone service, and with more responsive teaching machines. Nor need the flow of data be all one way. In some car factories, customers' individual orders have long been fed in at the start of the assembly line, on which all conceivable variants of each model travel nose to tail. With more sophisticated automation systems, custom-built mass production of this sort could be carried further, and into many other fields. Ultimately, its methods might be applied to politics, with automated polling at elections and quick referenda on specific issues, each elector dialling his vote from his own home.

Once again, however, there is no need to enter the realm of speculation to realize computers' potential impact. Transport, in particular, offers rapidly increasing scope. Ships have been built with computer-controlled engines; before long, they may have automated systems for collision warning, reckonings and stability control. Airline bookings are already largely computerized; so is movement control at the major airports. The 'seventies may well see the surveillance of air traffic extended to cover all aircraft in flight over a broad area, and not merely within a short radius of the tower. On the railways, moreover, surveillance may be replaced by remote control. Automated signalling and automatic coupling are already commonplace; within the next generation, the remote control of goods trains may begin with the processing of the original way-bill and only end with the trans-shipment of the containers for local delivery by road. The roads themselves, meanwhile, seem likely to change more slowly. Car design, it is true, may increasingly incorporate automatic features, and fully automatic underground parking lots are already being built. But human resistance to regimentation seems likely to delay the financing of automatic highways, where vehicles travel at fixed intervals under the control of a central computer system to which they can switch in at will. The social cost of road accidents will presumably have to rise even higher before such projects are seen to be economic.

Major innovations in transport will themselves involve both new materials and new forms of energy conversion or storage. High-speed express trains travelling in the region of 150 m.p.h., require special steel rails with stronger embankments and sleepers. Any successful electric car will need a cheap, light and compact accumulator or fuel cell system; and submarine freight transport, which promises high efficiency, will almost certainly rely on nuclear power. Controlled thermonuclear fusion, as distinct from fission, may be achieved experimentally within the next two decades; and the end of the century should see its first adoption on an industrial scale. By that time, the world's energy consumption may have increased tenfold,[5] and a growing proportion of men's needs will have to be met by nuclear power, perhaps marginally supplemented by the conversion of solar heat into electricity. Of the fossil fuels, coal and oil may by then increasingly be used as chemical raw materials, since these, like energy, will be in very great demand. Many of the mineral resources that can be tapped by present methods may be in danger of exhaustion early in the twenty-first century.[6] The threat, if genuine, is less alarming than it sounds. Necessity is the mother of invention, and has often proved the mother of prospecting. Over the coming decades, materials science will undoubtedly develop new synthetic substances, many of them stronger, lighter and more flexible than those already in use; while some raw material and chemical needs may be met by deep drilling for molten magma, by mining the ocean bed, and by extracting metals from sea-water—this last, perhaps, as one of the by-products of dealination research.

With such technological change in prospect, 'scientific' Utopias and anti-Utopias have become an all too familiar literary form.

Switching on the domestic robot before leaving his plastic, tenant-owned apartment block, the man of the year 2000 – let us call him 'John Future'

– entrains on the high-speed monorail for the downtown section of his vast linear city. On the journey he buys some groceries; the store in the club car automatically debits his bank. This morning he has no need of the train's office facilities, for he delta-winged in last night from a five-hour conference in the antipodes, and got his overnight work done in the supersonic V.T.O.L. rocket. Through the panoramic window he can see that the city council has programmed a fine crisp day as usual, although weather control seems anachronistic now that industry is moving to the tropics to leave the temperate zones free for the automated ploughlands and prairies that the Farmer Giles of the twenty-first century runs from the console of his 'Sunnybrook-X' computer. Arriving at the office, John Future dials for the business page of his favourite newspaper, plays back the taped cassettes of the morning's mail, then settles down with the colour-TV phone for a planning discussion with his colleagues in Greater Paris, Novosibirsk, and the Osaka-Kyoto-Kobe urban complex. A friendly argument soon develops between them and their computer, which has meanwhile been analysing forward market trends. As usual, the computer – they fondly call it 'Old Know-all' – has the last word. The conference over, John Future spends a half-hour study period with his teaching machine switched into the Further Education (Western Hemisphere) Network, then his day's chores are done. Ready for relaxation, he hops the continuous conveyor belt out to the company's riding stables. His wife has arranged for a deputy to pilot her hovercar ambulance on the noon shift so that they can lunch together at an exclusive old-world cafeteria in one of the rural reservations. After the quiet clean air of the city, the din and dirt of the countryside are refreshing, although John's great-grandfather told him when they last played squash together that there was once more wildlife around. Over lunch—a luxury meal of fresh fish and newly fried potatoes—the Futures discuss their coming vacation. John is keen to try one of the new low-budget Adventure Weekends with the Club Lunaire, leaving the children to play 'Independent Nations' at a Living History Camp. His wife, something of a stay-at-home, wants to split the time between Acapulco and Isfahan. 'But we do that *every* month,' objects John. Before a row can blow up, they both reach in their handbags and take their Darby and Joan pills. By coffee-time, all's well once more.[7]

Most of these things are possible, and some of them are very likely. But what makes such vignettes so unconvincing—apart from their prose and characterization—is their reluctance to admit that the imagined society of the future will be only slowly, painfully and patchily achieved. All ages are 'ages of transition', and the future is no exception. Even within the industrialized nations, many of the possibilities theoretically open to 'twenty-first century man' will in fact be available only to a minority. Few cities will be built from nothing: most of them, as in the past, will grow up piecemeal around surviving buildings on existing sites. New forms of transport will coexist with the old. Forecasting by computers may make possible faster economic growth, but lack of capital will continue to delay many public investment projects. New machines will be resisted for fear of unemployment; new jobs and re-training will have to be provided for those displaced. Apprenticeship courses, like education in general, will have to turn out growing numbers of electronics and other engineers to service ever more complex apparatus—until it can either service itself unaided or be replaced so cheaply as to become expendable. A few manual jobs that could be mechanized may continue for a time to be done by human beings: in one of the world's most modern automatic rolling mills, I myself have seen a solitary workman rubber-stamping the finished steel by hand. Some such tasks—many of them in the open air or the country—may be highly prized by those unwilling or unable to undertake others. In the factories, it may well be possible to adopt a thirty-hour week, forty weeks a year, and thirty-five years in a lifetime;[8] but this reduction of working hours, however modest, may not be universal. The organization of an increasingly prosperous mass-consumption society will demand a great deal of bureaucracy; and contrary to some predictions, not all of it seems likely to be automated. Even in the twenty-first century, offices will still probably employ enough people to keep them comfortably untidy: paperwork will still create paperwork, even if it takes the form of punched cards. Many of the staff, moreover, relieved of routine drudgery by the help of business machines, will act as intermediaries with the public, explaining procedures, meeting requests and complaints, settling priorities, and solving human problems within the growing complexities of large-scale administration. Such responsibilities will require not only high intelligence, technical knowledge, and judgment, but above all integrity, self-confidence, and the power of initiative in emergencies. This will be all the more necessary since power failures and electrical faults, despite all fail-safe systems and replacement circuits, will now and then produce unprecedented chaos.

Even without such technical imperfections, society will face some inevitable snags. The 'problem of leisure', which greatly agitates those restless enough to fret about the distant future, may well turn out to be exaggerated. If the devil finds work for idle hands, man runs him a close second. Many people spend all their existing spare time in physical activity for which they would claim high wages if it were labelled 'work'—using antiquated forms of transport (sailing or riding), propelling various projectiles (golf, tennis, cricket, football, motoring), or manufacturing items of furniture on an uneconomic scale. There seems

no reason to believe that the appetite for these pursuits is easily sur-
feited. For the majority, the problem is not one of too much leisure, but
of too much work; and more time for recreation will mean more work
for those in the industries that service it. Increasingly, too, as human
knowledge accumulates and becomes more readily available, self-educa-
tion and refresher courses will compete for men's hours of freedom.

What is far more serious is the problem of numbers. In the field of
leisure, this means clogged roads, spoiled countryside, teeming holiday-
resorts, crowded moorings and meat-soup swimming pools. For a time,
at least, the congestion could be relieved by staggering vacation times
throughout the year and by exploiting still more distant regions; but life
at home, for many people, will also become less private as numbers
grow. More crowded cities will offer less separate living space, and will
need more elaborate social engineering; this will require more comprehensive statistics, which better communications will help to assemble,
digging deeper into individual lives. Whatever the political complexion
of future governments, technology will inevitably emphasize the collective aspects of existence: a big corporation, just because it deals
mechanically with very large numbers, is bound to seem in many ways
as impersonal as the state.

This need not imply excessive standardization. Only in the primitive
stages of a successful mass society may the individual have to put up
with unimaginative minor officials, identical speculative houses and
apartments, and the ubiquitous tastelessness of pre-cooked, pre-sliced,
pre-wrapped, pre-masticated supermarket food. The better the machine,
whether social or industrial, the better its products can be adapted to
individual and even eccentric preferences. But total eccentricity, like the
illusion of total privacy, will certainly become increasingly expensive.
Personal service, custom-made tailoring, an isolated country cottage,
and home-grown fruit and vegetables may more and more be regarded as
luxury items, for special occasions only. Their day-to-day substitutes
may be of even higher quality, as the products of today's best chain-
stores sometimes show; but the knowledge that their variety has limits
may be frustrating in itself.

Comfortable, close-knit, and of necessity well-ordered, the society of
the future may well have to guard against its appearing too tame. More
and more, it will be vital to find outlets for men's natural anti-social
impulses. Authorized rebellion, clearly, is a contradiction in terms.
'Adventure playgrounds', despite their uses, will hardly satisfy the truly
adventurous; and there are limits to the effective outlets that society
itself can provide. Space travel, sometimes mooted as a safety-valve, is a

highly organized and disciplined collective venture, sharing many draw-backs with the environment it purports to escape. Private flying, polar exploration and solitary ocean cruising may recruit some stalwarts; big-game hunting or mercenary soldiering may attract others. But the real difficulty lies with those whose energies fall short of such endeavours, while yet overflowing the limits of an ever more tutelary state. Fifty years ago, William James foresaw the problem and proposed 'instead of military conscription, a conscription of the whole youthful population to form for a certain number of years a part of the army enlisted against *Nature*'—a kind of compulsory Peace Corps. Whatever the solution, a continuing task for the industrialized nations will certainly be to treat their social and psychological casualties, to cope with crime and viol-ence, and to find what James described as 'the moral equivalent of war'.[9]

In all these ways 'the society of the year 2000' seems likely to con-found its simpler prophets. Even more fundamentally, it will still be limited to a minority of mankind. In default of really drastic action, and perhaps in spite of it, twenty-first century prosperity and dark-age poverty will continue to coexist on a shrinking planet; and the num-bers of the poor and hungry will almost certainly grow.

Recent estimates of the world's population in the year 2000 have varied very widely. In 1945, one expert arrived at the figure of 3·3 thousand million; two others, in 1953, suggested 3·2 thousand million. Today, thirty years ahead of schedule, these numbers have already been attained. The next forecast was 6·3 thousand million, made by the United Nations in 1958: on that reckoning, the year 2000 would see as many people in non-Soviet Asia as now inhabit the entire globe. More recently, Rand Corporation experts have scaled down this estimate to 5·1 thousand million. But the reason that some of them gave was dis-quieting: they grimly predicted, for the less developed countries, a greater number of deaths from lack of food.[10]

Birth control may help to avert this catastrophe; but if it should prove impracticable or unacceptable, ways could still be found of pro-ducing food for six thousand million people. Insecticides, pesticides, fungicides, growth promotion agents and retardants, antibiotics and artificial fertilizers can greatly improve crop yields, especially in the less developed countries. Irrigation can help convert into foodstuffs some of the solar energy now wasted in the deserts, while reafforestation can curb their spread. Reclamation of the jungle could bring new areas under cultivation; water conservancy could more effectively harness the monsoons. Such measures as these might produce enough basic calories to ward off widespread famine; but because of the slowness of traditional livestock-breeding and the competition for fodder, the shortage of protein may have to be met by other means. These might include 'sea farms' for large-scale fish rearing, by analogy with oyster-beds; collecting and possibly cultivating certain forms of plankton, including the tiny shrimp-like krill; and even, perhaps, manufacturing foodstuffs chemically by the synthesis of proteins in cell-free systems.

Despite the cost and difficulty of many of these projects, the biggest obstacles may not be technological, but human. By the end of the century, some of today's less developed countries may have profited from others' experience and by-passed the first industrial revolution, With the aid of nuclear power and computers, they may have taken a short-cut into advanced technology, and some of their manufactured output may well be highly competitive. But their economies are almost certain to have developed lop-sidedly, with all the familiar contrasts that traditionally astonish the visitor, like the sight of barefoot women working as building labourers at India's Trombay centre for nuclear research. Having joined the technology race at a stage when industry employs more machines and fewer workmen, such countries may find themselves saddled with a rural rather than an urban proletariat, impoverished peasants increasingly unable to produce enough food. Even in the richer nations, agriculture has until recently been a poor relation, only slowly mechanized, and never able to match the productive growth of industry. Short of intensive, laborious and electorally unrewarding efforts, it may lag even further behind in the developing countries; and their raw material producers, at the same time, will face even sharper competition from synthetics. If the gap between rich and poor nations is not to grow wider, therefore, it may prove necessary to reverse some of the accepted patterns of world trade. Instead of acting as quarries and home farms for the older industrialized nations, the less developed countries will have to import more food from them, meeting part of the bill by selling them more sophisticated manufactures.

The change, if it occurs, will not be rapid. For a long time to come, the richer countries may still have unsaleable agriculture surpluses. As the world's population grows, however, they may well have to increase their production of certain foodstuffs, gearing it more closely to the less developed countries' needs rather than to their present-day purchasing power. If the recipient countries are to pay for their food imports— as ultimately they must—their manufactures will have to be given easier access to the markets of the richer countries. In some this will mean social and even political upheaval unless expansion continues fast enough to absorb the shock. Meanwhile, the less developed countries will have to develop livelier market research and salesmanship, and ensure that the food they receive in fact reaches the needy members of their own population. The latter in turn may have to be persuaded to accept an at first unfamiliar diet: wheat and beans instead of rice, for example, or fishmeal, krill, and even synthetic proteins. Finally, a vast campaign of education, land reform and investment will be needed to bring agriculture in these countries more nearly abreast of the industrial development and population growth to be expected in the decades to come.

To achieve this, habits and conventions in rich and poor countries alike will have to change. Piecemeal, perhaps, the change may be said to be beginning: more positive stockage policy, food aid, and the gradual disappearance of tariffs among the industrialized countries may already be signs of the times. But time presses; and unless more systematic and resolute efforts are made to meet a future that is already forseeable, the results could be disastrous. In many places, famine is nearer than we think. At present, *vis-à-vis* the less developed countries, we are all in some degree practitioners of *aparthied*. Is our condemnation of it in others an oblique and cathartic criticism of ourselves?

Such are some of the shadows that mar the prospect of the future; but the darkest of all is the shadow of possible war. It would be naïve to imagine that in the midst of other technical progress, military technology will stand still. Some of its products, admittedly, may be welcomed: 'non-mortal' means of persuasion and riot control, such as water guns and tear gases; effective nuclear bomb shelters; and anti-submarine defence. But less innocuous are some of the other developments already conceivable: an anti-ballistic missile race, kiloton 'tactical' nuclear weapons, hydrogen bombs in orbit, and biological agents for killing and incapacitating, affecting men's sanity or sapping the will to resist. War, never clean, will grow dirtier. Even now it could virtually destroy civilization.

General and controlled disarmament might seem the obvious safeguard; yet for at least twenty years it has proved impossible to achieve. Unilateral national disarmament has a few advocates: their opponents usually reply with variations on the couplet

> Pale Ebenezer thought it wrong to fight,
> But Roaring Bill, who killed him, thought it right.

Equally fruitless, so far, have been attempts to secure general disarmament in the nuclear field alone. One effective move in this broad direction is the 1968 treaty on non-proliferation, whose 'nuclear' signatories have promised not to pass on atomic weapons to others, while the 'non-nuclear' powers agreed not to aquire them. Despite the very real dangers that the treaty is intended to parry, it too has run into snags. Some non-nuclear powers have proved reluctant to accept it, fearing that their existing inferiority of status might become permanent, that inspection of their peaceful atomic plant might reveal industrial secrets, or that their dangerous neighbours might sign and then break their word. Others disliked on principle the whole notion of discrimination that underlies the treaty, and feared that it might kill the hope of a united Europe's one day equalling the United States. Finally, none of the three nuclear powers backing the treaty, seems remotely likely to pass on nuclear weapons, while the other two powers that possess them —France and Communist China—have both refused to sign. However, like the Strategic Arms Limitation Talks (SALT) that began in 1969 in Helsinki, the non-proliferation treaty at least had the great advantage of keeping the United States and the Soviet Union talking peaceably together —so long as they refrain from settling the fate of other countries over their heads.

Will any of these efforts come to effective fruition in the near future? Past experience suggests that they may not, or that, if they do, their success will be only partial. There seems little hope of eliminating the instruments of war without tackling its basic causes, since these are precisely what makes agreement so difficult. If complete disarmament were possible, it would no longer be necessary. For the present, the most that seems likely is a series of conventions, probably tacit, to restrict new armaments, to maintain existing de facto spheres of influence, to limit anti-ballistic missiles and perhaps to demilitarize space. These, if achieved, would be very far from negligible; and they might bring world peace. At the very least, they would further acknowledge the common interest in avoiding a large-scale conflict, and they might succeed in staving it off. But smaller conflicts seem all too likely. In Latin America, economic progress is strengthening the demand for social changes that are long overdue; the inevitable upshot is political unrest. In the southern areas of Africa, continued white rule may lead to future explosions; to the north, new states are settling in with difficulty, often at odds with their neighbours, and sometimes a prey to civil war. The Middle East remains a potential battleground. Parts of south-east Asia have not known peace for over twenty years. The rise of Communist China, meanwhile, has added a third term to the East-West power equation. None of the giants may intentionally join battle; but they might be involved in war by their respective allies. Continuing insecurity, therefore, appears to be inescapable in the decades ahead.

Headlong, overcrowded, disunited and dangerous, the world of the future may look forbidding; but for those with the zest and energy to face it, the prospect is surely a challenge. Now, as never before, men hold their destiny in their own hands. Will they succumb to *hubris*, or to squabbling over their new-found and future riches? Or will they have the wisdom, skill and patience to devise a less unjust and uneasy form of international society, and a better way of settling disputes than by going to war? To these questions, Europe may furnish the modest beginnings of an answer.

Most of the world's present evils are familiar from Europe's history: disease and famine; the contrast of poverty and riches; tyranny and anarchy; commercial rivalry and pitiless war. Very gradually, Europeans have begun to overcome them. Since World War II, in particular, they have deliberately fostered a community of material interests between formerly implacable enemies. First in the European Coal and Steel Community, then in Euratom and the Common Market, six European countries have accepted the discipline of common rules and institutions, tempering the sovereignty of the nation-state. Often reluctantly, they have begun to apply to their dealings with each other those principles of law and order that in civilized communities keep the peace and settle disputes between private citizens. Haltingly, imperfectly, and in a limited field, they have begun to establish a new form of international society.

Already, this has had broader repercussions. Increasingly united by the institutions of the European Community, its members are beginning to act as one in their economic dealings with the rest of the world. In tariff negotiations, in international monetary discussions, their collective action has succeeded where individual efforts would have failed; and with British membership, this new European entity could be more effective still. The United States, although it also fears the rivalry of a prosperous united Europe, has welcomed its beginnings and sought to establish with it a new relationship of equals, healthier, closer and more enduring than the present traditional alliance of many smaller countries with one giant. Progress toward this goal has been slow and not without friction; but the momentum of economic interest and political necessity remains powerful: Europe and America have far more in common than their obvious differences suggest. Gradually, as Europe gropes its way towards political unity, its 'equal partnership' with

America could develop in a similar direction. As equals, the United States and Europe could exert a moderating influence on each others' foreign policies. As partners, they could be more self-confident in their dealings with the Soviet Union and Communist China, without the suspicion and uneasiness prompted by either's trying to act alone. Less tempted, because less able, to pursue its old policy of dividing the West, the East might be more prepared to come to terms with it. Unity in Europe, partnership across the Atlantic, and genuine peaceful coexistence between East and West would bind the world together in a network of institutions and agreements; national disruptive action would be more difficult, and less of a danger to peace. Within Europe, the barriers created by the 'cold war' could be diminished: allowed once more to travel freely across the frontier, the German people could be in practice reunited without reviving a German *Reich*. In the wider world, the new international climate could put fresh life into the United Nations, and at last make it possible for East and West to co-operate on tasks that neither, however powerful, can successfully tackle without the other. Foremost among them would be a concerted effort to prevent famine, to eliminate disease and poverty, and to keep the peace.

Could the unification of Europe really begin such a process? Is the thought not simply a pipe-dream, a typically European form of optimistic pride? With unity still incomplete in Western Europe, is there any real hope of reconciling East and West?

A generation ago, this question could have been asked of France and Germany. A true forecast, then, of present-day Western Europe would have seemed absurdly visionary. Yet visions of the future are what move men to act. And there is surely something noble about the vision of Europe, for so long a source of civilization and of conflict, so worn and weathered by history, so strong in spirit, so measured and so free, recovering its self-respect after so much shame and agony, achieving unity and assurance without losing its diversity, standing up once more for the old virtues—courage, wisdom, generosity, tolerance—in a world that so badly needs them, as Europe needed them in 1945.

Guilt is a paralysing legacy, and it was harder than ever for Europeans to build the future when burdened by their recent past. Quite quickly, they cleared away the ruins; eagerly, and in some ways blindly, they grasped at a prosperity greater than they had ever known. Above all, patiently and doggedly, they began to civilize the relations between states by means of laws and institutions similar to those that keep the peace between fellow-citizens. Their task is far from ended. Performed in committees and councils instead of on the battlefield, disputing percentages and protocols instead of human lives, it seems undramatic and slow. But if there is one respect in which Europe today differs from the Europe of the past, this is its willingness, however fitful, to limit the self-righteousness of nations—its sense that a common interest binds even those who passionately disagree. World War II has often been called the last European civil war. That this can be said without irony is due to the efforts of those who set out to realize their vision of Europe; who failed; and who yet succeeded, because their aim was so high. The struggle continues. Its most appropriate epigraph was written in the year that Jean Monnet was born:

Men fight and lose the battle, and the thing they fought for comes about in spite of their defeat, and when it comes turns out to be not what they meant, and other men have to fight for what they meant under another name.[12]

Today, the name is Europe. Tomorrow, it could be the world.

REFERENCES

CHAPTER I. A GENERATION OF CHANGE

1. *Averroës et l'Averroisme* (Paris, 1861), p. v (transl. R.M.)
2. *La Civilisation de 1975* (Paris, 1964) p. 7 (transl. R.M.)
3. *Table Talk and Omniana* (London, 1917), p. 434
4. Cf. Dwight D. Eisenhower, *Mandate for Change 1953–1956* (Signet edition, New York, 1965), p. 548
5. Christopher Isherwood, *Prater Violet* (London, 1946), p. 5
6. J. & F. Fourastié, *Les arts ménagers* (Paris, 1950), p. 73; estimate based on Reader's Digest European Surveys, *Products and People* (London, 1963), tables 5 and 55
7. Office Statistique des Communautés Européennes, *Statistiques de base de la Communauté: Comparaison avec certains pays européens, le Canada, les Etats-Unis d'Amérique et l'Union des Républiques Socialistes Soviétiques* (Brussels/Luxembourg, 1967), p. 152
8. E. G. Couzens & V. E. Yarsley, *Plastics in the Service of Man* (London, 1965), pp. 289–90; cf. the same authors' *Plastics* (London, 1941), pp. 154–8
9. Norman Lansdell, *The Atom and the Energy Revolution* (London, 1958), 60; Bertrand Goldschmidt, *L'Aventure atomique* (Paris, 1962), p. 94; Office Statistique des Commuautés Européennes, *op. cit.* (n. 7, *supra*), p. 70
10. Sir George Thomson, *The Foreseeable Future* (Cambridge, 1955), p. 88. Léo Moulin, *La Société de demain dans l'Europe d'aujourd'hui* (Paris, 1966), pp. 29–30, appraises Thomson's predictions and those of W. Ley. For a convenient summary of space chronology and statistics, cf. D. & M. Frémy, *Quid?* (Paris, 1968), pp. 263–9. Further statistics from the U.S. National Aeronautics and Space Administration (NASA) and the Space Department of the Royal Aircraft Establishment, Farnborough, England
11. Jean Fourastié, *Les 40.000 heures* (Paris, 1965), p. 18
12. T. S. Ashton, *The Industrial Revolution 1760–1830* (Oxford, 1948), p. 99
13. A. J. P. Taylor, *English History 1914–1945* (Oxford, 1965), p. 132 n. 2
14. Lord Strang, *Home and Abroad* (London, 1956), p. 137; Taylor, *op. cit.*, p. 426 n. 2
15. Robert Murphy, *Diplomat Among Warriors* (London, 1964), pp. 258–9
16. Harry S. Truman, *Memoirs*, Vol. I, *1945: Year of Decisions* (Signet edition. New York, 1965), p. 444
17. Eisenhower, *op. cit.* (n. 4, *supra*), p. 586; *Waging Peace 1956–1961* (London, 1966), p. 415
18. Frémy, *op. cit.* (n. 10, *supra*), p. 959; Organisation for Economic Co-operation and Development (O.E.C.D.), *Tourism in O.E.C.D. Member Countries 1966* (Paris, 1966), p. 28; Wilfred Owen, 'The Transport Revolution', in J. Frederic Dewhurst and others, *Europe's Needs and Resources* (New York, 1961), pp. 279–311 (p. 293); cf. also Bernard Dutoit, *L'Aviation et l'Europe* (Lausanne, 1959), *passim*

19. Fourastié, *op. cit.* (n. 11, *supra*), p. 17; Frémy, *op. cit.* (n. 10, *supra*), pp. 957–8, 988–9; *The Times* (London), 5 January 1967, p. 1; John Montgomery, *The Fifties* (London, 1965), p. 233

20. Dewhurst, *op. cit* (n. 18, *supra*), appendices, pp. 913, 919

21. Cf. Peter Townsend, *The Family Life of Old People* (London, 1957), *passim*

22. Andrew Shonfield, *The Attack on World Poverty* (London, 1960), p. 15, J. Fourastié & C. Vimont, *Histoire de demain* (3rd ed., Paris 1964), pp. 85, 122–3; Hubert d'Hérouville, *L'économie mondiale* (4th ed., Paris, 1960), p. 12; Fritz Baade, *The Race of the Year 2000* (London, 1963), pp. 6–7, quoting L. Dudley Stamp, *Our Underdeveloped World* (London, 1952), p. 24; United Nations, *The Future Growth of World Population* (New York, 1958), *passim*; Carlo M. Cipolla, *The Economic History of World Population* (revised ed., London, 1964), pp. 91–106. The Italian edition of this last, *Uomini, tecniche, economie* (Milan, 1966), pp. 96–113, contains more recent figures

23. P. Lamartine Yates, *Food, Land and Manpower in Western Europe* (London, 1960), pp. 198–9; J. Fourastié, *La Civilisation de 1975* (Paris, 1964), p. 96; d'Hérouville, *op. cit.*, p. 51; John O. Coppock, 'Land and Agricultural Resources' in Dewhurst, *op. cit.* (n. 18, *supra*), pp. 479–519 (pp. 494–5); d'Hérouville, *op. cit.*, p. 70; Dennis Gabor, *Inventing the Future* (London, 1963), pp. 75–85; Fourastié & Vimont, *op. cit.*, pp. 43–58

24. Cipolla, *Uomini, tecniche, economie* (Milan, 1966), pp. 50, 69; Office Statistique des Communautés Européennes, *op. cit.* (n. 7, *supra*), p. 78; J. Fourastié, *La Civilisation de 1975* (Paris, 1964), p. 83; d'Hérouville, *op. cit.* (n. 22, *supra*), pp. 64, 82; Office Statistique des Communautés Européenes, *Commerce extérieur: Statistique mensuelle* (Brussels/Luxembourg, monthly), *passim*; d'Hérouville, *op. cit.*, p. 90; Fourastié, *op. cit.*, p. 59; Fourastié, *Idées Majeures* (Paris, 1966), p. 99; Massimo Salvadori, 'Capitalism in Postwar Europe', in Dewhurst, *op. cit.* (n. 18, *supra*), pp. 734–58 (p. 734); Angus Maddison, *Economic Growth in the West* (London, 1964), p. 220; P. Lamartine Yates, 'Social Security', in Dewhurst, *op. cit.*, pp. 375–403 (p. 400); Yates, 'Education', in Dewhurst, *op. cit.*, pp. 312–43 (p. 333); Maddison, *op. cit.*, p. 228; Dewhurst, 'Needs and Resources: Summary', in *op. cit.*, pp. 862–88 (p. 868); Dewhurst, 'Manpower', in *op. cit.*, pp. 61–106 (p. 76); Maddison, *op cit.*, p. 240; John O. Coppock, 'Government Expenditure and Operations', in Dewhurst, *op. cit.*, pp. 404–42; Fourastié, *Le grand espoir du XXe siècle* (Edition définitive, Paris, 1963), p. 160; Dewhurst, 'Consumption Levels and Patterns', in *op. cit.*, pp. 143–78 (p. 171); Yates, *Food, Land and Manpower in Western Europe* (London, 1960), pp. 32–4; Yates, 'Household Operations', in Dewhurst, *op. cit.*, pp. 246–78 (p. 265); Dewhurst, *op. cit.*, appendices, pp. 1012–13; extrapolation from Office Statistique des Communautés Européennes, *Statistiques de base* (cf. n. 7, *supra*), p. 151

25. Cf. Gabor, *op. cit.* (n. 23, *supra*), pp. 23–4; C. Northcote Parkinson, *Parkinson's Law or the Pursuit of Progress* (London, 1958), chapter 1

26. Cf. Andrew Shonfield, *Modern Capitalism* (London, 1965), pp. 376–7, 385, 421–7

27. Robert Triffin, *The World Money Maze* (New Haven, Connecticut, and London, 1966), p. 349

28. Alexis de Tocqueville, *Democracy in America*, transl. Henry Reeve (Oxford, 1946), pp. 286–7

29. Pierre George, *Géographie industrielle du monde* (Paris, 1957), pp. 67–9

30. Office Statistique des Communautés Européennes, *Statistiques de base* (cf. n. 7, *supra*), pp. 43, 64, 80, 82, 90, 143–53

31. André Gide, *Retour de l'U.R.S.S.* (Paris, 1936), p. 14

32. League of Nations, *Industrialization and Free Trade* (Geneva, 1945), II, A. 10, p. 13; Norman S. Buchanan & Friedrich A. Lutz, *Rebuilding the World Economy* (New York, 1947), p. 185; Richard Mayne, *The Community of Europe* (London, 1962; New York, 1963), pp. 61–2

33. Leonard Beaton, *Must the Bomb Spread?* (London, 1966), pp. 42, 47, 141

34. Buchanan & Lutz, *loc. cit.* (cf. n. 32, *supra*)

35. Organisation for Economic Co-operation and Development (O.E.C.D.), *Economic Surveys, Japan* (Paris, December 1965), pp. 6, 7; Office Statistique des Communautés Européennes, *Statistiques de base* (7e. édition, Brussels/Luxembourg, 1967), pp. 15, 64, 80, 90, 91; Norman Macrae, 'The Risen Sun', in *The Economist*, vol. CCXXIII, Nos. 6457 & 6458 (London, 27 May–2 June & 3–9 June 1967); cf. *International Management*, December 1967, pp. 41–3

36. J. Fourastié, *Les 40.000 heures* (Paris, 1965), pp. 17–18; Institute of Strategic Studies, *The Military Balance 1968–69* (London, 1969); Jean Cocteau, *Portrait d'un inconnu* (Paris, 1953), p. 31

37. Cf. Evan Luard (ed.), *The Cold War: a Reappraisal* (London, 1964) and André Fontaine, *Histoire de la guerre froide* (2 vols., Paris, 1965 and 1967). For the traditional 'Western' view, cf. David Rees, *The Age of Containment* (London, 1967); for the opposite, D. F. Fleming, *The Cold War and its Origins 1917–1960* (2 vols., London, 1961) and David Horowitz, *From Yalta to Vietnam* (revised edition, London, 1967). Louis J. Halle, *The Cold War as History* (London, 1967) is a scrupulous attempt to see the issue from both sides. On later changes, cf. especially Ghita Ionescu, *The Break-up of the Soviet Empire in Eastern Europe* (London, 1965), Edward Crankshaw, *The New Cold War: Moscow v. Pekin* (revised edition, London, 1965) and Peter Bender, *Offensive Entspannung* (Cologne/Berlin, 1964)

38. M. M. Postan, *An Economic History of Western Europe 1945–1964* (London, 1967), pp. 12, 16; Alfred Nydegger, 'Foreign Trade and Capital Movements', in Dewhurst, *op. cit.* (n. 18, *supra*), pp. 635–73 (p. 655); Dewhurst, *op. cit.*, appendices, pp. 1097–8; 1103–4

39. Cipolla, *op. cit.* (n. 24, *supra*), p. 60; d'Hérouville, *op. cit.* (n. 22, *supra*), p. 87; Albert Kervyn, 'Exchange and Currency Problems', in Dewhurst, *op. cit.*, pp. 674–707 (p. 707); Dewhurst, *op. cit.*, appendices, pp. 1106–7

40. D. Swann & D. L. McLachlan, *Concentration or Competition: A European Dilemma* (London, 1967), p. 19; Frémy, *op. cit.* (n. 10, *supra*), pp. 397–9

CHAPTER 2. THE WASTE LAND

1. *Table Talk*, ed. S. W. Swinger (3rd ed., London, 1860), p. 210
2. 'Alle Tage', from *Die gestundete Zeit* (1953), reprinted in Horst Bingel (ed), *Deutsche Lyrik: Gedichte seit 1945* (DTV edition, Munich, 1963), p. 9 (transl. R.M.)
3. *La Pelle* (Economica Vallecchi edition, Florence, 1965), p. 36 (transl. R.M.)
4. Lionel Trilling, *The Middle of the Journey* (Penguin edition, London, 1963), p. 313
5. Harry C. Butcher, *My Three Years with Eisenhower* (New York, 1946), p. 836
6. P. E. Schramm (ed.), *Die Niederlage 1945* (DTV edition, Munich, 1962), pp. 433 & 451n.; William D. Leahy, *I Was There* (New York, 1950), pp. 357–8; Dwight D. Eisenhower, *Crusade in Europe* (Dolphin edition, New York, 1961), p. 453; Harry S. Truman, *Memoirs*, Vol. I, *1945: Year of Decisions* (Signet edition, New York, 1965), p. 230; John Toland, *The Last Hundred Days* (Bantam edition, New York, 1967), p. 644; Butcher, *op. cit.* (n. 5, *supra*), p. 834
7. Field-Marshal the Viscount Montgomery of Alamein, K.G., *Memoirs* (Fontana edition, London, 1960), pp. 345–50; Dönitz Diary, 7 May 1945, in Schramm, *op. cit.*, p. 433; Leahy, *loc. cit.* and Eisenhower, *op. cit.*, p. 455, both corrected and greatly amplified by Toland, *op. cit.*, pp. 644–7 (n. 5, *supra*). On the Caserta surrender, cf. Allen Dulles, *The Secret Surrender* (London, 1967)
8. Leahy, *op. cit.*, p. 361; Toland, *op. cit.*, p. 647; Truman, *op. cit.*, p. 232; Leahy, *op. cit.*, p. 359 (n. 6, *supra*)
9. Truman, *op. cit.*, p. 231; Leahy, *op. cit.*, pp. 362–3; Arthur Bryant, *Triumph in the West 1943–1946* (Allanbrooke War Diaries, vol. II), (Fontana edition, London, 1965), p. 357; Toland, *op. cit.*, pp. 647, 654n; cf. *The Papers of Dwight David Eisenhower: The War Years* (5 Vols. Baltimore, 1970), *passim*
10. Private information; Robert Murphy, *Diplomat Among Warriors* (London, 1964), pp. 296–7; Bryant, *loc. cit.*; Toland, *op. cit.*, p. 645; Philip E. Mosely, 'Dismemberment of Germany', in *Foreign Affairs*, vol. XXVIII, No. 3 (April, 1950), pp. 487–98, reprinted in *Ibid.*, *The Kremlin in World Politics* (Vintage books edition, New York, 1960), pp. 131–54 (pp. 148–52)
11. Toland, *op. cit.*, pp. 657–60 and Schramm, *op. cit.*, pp. 454–5 (n. 6, *supra*); Cornelius Ryan, *The Last Battle* (London, 1966), photograph in plates between pp. 320 and 321; Butcher, *op. cit.* (n. 5, *supra*), p. 844
12. Murphy, *op. cit.* (n. 10, *supra*), p. 298; H. R. Trevor-Roper, *The Last Days of Hitler* (revised Pan edition, London, 1962), p. 240; Schramm, *op. cit.* (n. 6, *supra*), pp. 413–17, 420, 429, 434
13. Schramm, *op. cit.*, pp. 419, 431–2, 433, 441–2; Trevor-Roper, *op. cit.*,

pp. 236, 237, 255; Lionel Kochan, *The Struggle for Germany 1914–1945* (Edinburgh, 1963), pp. 94–6, 127; Rebecca West, *The Meaning of Treason* (revised Penguin edition, London, 1965), p. 127; Murphy, *op. cit.*, pp. 297–300. Cf. also Walter Lüdde-Neurath, *Die Regierung Dönitz* (Göttingen, 1950) & Carl Dönitz, *Zehn Jahre und zwanzig Tage* (Bonne, 1958), *passim*

14. On the Eastern campaign, cf. Alan Clark, *Barbarossa* (Penguin revised edition, London, 1966); on Russian behaviour in Germany, Ryan, *op. cit.* (n. 11, *supra*), and Anon., *A Woman in Berlin*, transl. James Stern (London, 1965); on Russia's defensive expansion', Louis J. Halle, *The Cold War as History* (London, 1967), esp. pp. 11–19; on the effects of 'unconditional surrender', Jean Laloy, *Entre guerres et paix 1945–1965* (Paris, 1966), esp. pp. 32–3, 67

15. Jacques Dumaine, *Quai d'Orsay 1945–1951*, transl. Alan Davidson (London, 1958), p. 226

16. U.N. Economic Commission for Europe, *The European Housing Problem: a Preliminary Review* (E/ECE/110, Geneva, 1949); R. G. Hawtrey, 'The Economic Consequences of the War', in A. & V. M. Toynbee (ed.), *The Realignment of Europe* (London, 1955), pp. 36–51 (p. 39); Michael Balfour, 'Germany', in A. Toynbee (ed.), *Four-Power Control in Germany and Austria 1945–1946* (London, 1956), pp. 1–265 (p. 7); John Gunther, *Inside Russia Today* (London, 1958), p. 65; Paul Alpert, *Twentieth-Century Economic History of Europe* (New York, 1951), pp. 253–4; Bruno Foa, *Monetary Reconstruction in Italy* (New York, 1949), p. 23; Katharine Duff, 'Liberated Italy: from September 1943 to February 1947', in A. & V. M. Toynbee, *op. cit.*, pp. 409–53 (p. 441)

17. John Lukacs, *Decline and Rise of Europe* (New York, 1965), p. 15; R. C. Mowat, *Ruin and Resurgence 1939–1965* (London, 1966), pp. 85–94; Balfour, *op. cit.* (n. 16, *supra*), pp. 7–8; Truman, *op. cit.* (n. 6, *supra*), p. 378; Lucius D. Clay, *Decision in Germany* (London, 1950), pp. 21, 32; Eugene Davidson, *The Death and Life of Germany* (London, 1959), p. 66; J.-F. Angelloz, 'En Allemagne: Berlin–Hambourg', in *Mercure de France*, No. 1007 (Paris, 1 July 1947), pp. 456–66 (p. 457)

18. Balfour, *op. cit.* p. 9, & Alpert, *op. cit.*, p. 251 (n. 16, *supra*), G. R. Gayre, *Italy in Transition* (London, 1946), pp. 26–7; Robert Aron, *Histoire de la libération de la France* (*Livre de poche* edition, Paris, 1967), vol. i, p. 466; David Thomson, *Europe Since Napoleon* (2nd ed. revised, London, 1962), p. 775

19. Hawtrey, *op. cit.*, p. 39, Balfour, *op. cit.*, p. 9, Alpert, *op. cit.*, p. 252 (n. 16, *supra*); Clay, *op. cit.*, p. 188, Davidson, *op. cit.*, p. 70 (n. 17, *supra*)

20. Marcel Jouanique & Lucien Morice, *La Navigation intérieure en France* (Paris, 1951), p. 16; Hawtrey, *op. cit.*, pp. 40, 42, Balfour, *op. cit.*, p. 9, Alpert, *op. cit.*, p. 252 (n. 16, *supra*); Theodore H. White, *Fire in the Ashes: Europe in Mid-Century* (New York, 1953), p. 140; Muriel Grindrod, *The Rebuilding of Italy* (London, 1955), p. 38

21. Hawtrey, *op. cit.*, p. 40, Balfour, *op. cit.*, p. 11, Alpert, *op. cit.*, pp. 252–3 (n. 16, *supra*); Grindrod, *op. cit.*, pp. 39, 155; White, *loc. cit.* (n. 20,

supra); Norman Kogan, *A Political History of Postwar Italy* (London, 1966), p. 43

22. Howard K. Smith, *The State of Europe* (London, 1950), p. 10; Alpert, *op. cit.* (n. 16, *supra*), p. 254; Italy, Instituto Poligrafico dello Stato, *Lo Sviluppo dell'Economia Italiana* (Rome, 1952), p. 3; Grindrod, *op. cit.* (n. 20, *supra*), pp. 38–9; Libero Lenti, *Inventario dell'economia italiana* (Milan, 1966), pp. 20–4; A. J. P. Taylor, *English History 1914–1945* (Oxford, 1965), p. 599; Hawtrey, *op. cit.* (n. 16, *supra*), pp. 41–2, 47–8; T. Balogh, 'The International Aspect', in G. D. N. Worswick & P. H. Ady, *The British Economy 1945–1950* (Oxford, 1952), pp. 476–510; Anthony Harrison, *The Framework of Economic Activity* (London, 1967), p. 83; Norman S. Buchanan & Friedrich A. Lutz, *Rebuilding the World Economy* (New York, 1947), p. 78; Balfour, *op. cit.* (n. 15, *supra*), p. 9; J.F., 'De l'économie de guerre à l'économie de paix', in *Mercure de France* No.1010 (Paris, 1 October 1947), pp. 198–205; 'Christopher Felix', *The Spy and his Masters* (London, 1963), p. 173

23. Cf. Michel van der Plas, *Mooie Vrede: een documentaire over Nederland in de jaren 1945–1950* (Utrecht, 1966), p. 15

24. Hawtrey, *op. cit.*, p. 38, Alpert, *op. cit.*, p. 253, Duff, *loc. cit.* (n. 15, *supra*), Truman *op cit.*, (n. 6, *supra*), p. 252

25. Hawtrey, *loc. cit.*, Alpert, *op. cit.*, p. 255 (n. 16, *supra*); J.F. *op. cit.*, (n. 22, *supra*), p. 203; H. Riemans, *Perspectief voor Nederland* (Amsterdam, 1957), p. 63

26. Janet Flanner, *Paris Journal 1944–1965* (London, 1966), p. 5; Aron, *op. cit.* (n. 18, *supra*), pp. 464–5; Edmund Wilson, *Europe Without Baedeker* (London, 1948), p. 146; Smith, *op. cit.* (n. 22, *supra*), p. 215

27. United Nations, Economic and Social Council, *Preliminary Report of the Temporary Sub-Commission on Economic Reconstruction of Devastated Areas* (18 September 1946), 26–7; Hawtrey, *op. cit.* (n. 16, *supra*), pp. 38–9; René Masseyeff, *La Faim* (Paris, 1956), p. 92; Smith, *op. cit.* (n. 22, *supra*), p. 170

28. Smith, *op. cit.* (n. 22, *supra*), p. 10; D. & M. Frémy, *Quid?* (Paris, 1968), pp. 493–5, J. Frederic Dewhurst, 'Population', in J. Frederic Dewhurst & associates, *Europe's Needs and Resources* (New York, 1961), 32–60 (p. 32, n. 1); Balfour, *op. cit.* (n. 16, *supra*), p. 10; United Nations, Economic Commission for Europe, *Growth and Stagnation in the European Economy* (Geneva, 1954), p. 236; D. V. Glass & E. Grebenik. 'World Population, 1800–1950', in H. J. Habakkuk & M. Postan (ed.), *The Cambridge Economic History of Europe*, vol. II, *The Industrial Revolutions and After: Incomes, Population and Technological Change* (Cambridge, 1965), pp. 56–138 (p. 61)

29. Malcolm J. Proudfoot, *European Refugees: 1939–52* (London, 1957), pp. 303–17; Eugen Kogón, *Der SS-Staat und das System der deutschen Konzentrationslager* (Munich, 1946), transl. as *The Theory and Practice of Hell* (New York, 1951); Gerald Reitlinger, *The Final Solution: the Attempt to Exterminate the Jews of Europe, 1939–1945* (London, 1953); *ibid.*, The

SS: Alibi of a Nation (London, 1956); *Trial of the Major War Criminals before the International Military Tribunal*, 42 vols (Nuremberg, 1947-9); *Trials of War Criminals before the Nuremberg Military Tribunals*, 15 vols (Washington, 1951–2); Alan Moorehead, 'Glimpses of Germany: II – Belsen', in *Horizon*, vol. XII, No. 67 (London, July 1945), pp. 26–35; William L. Shirer, *The Rise and Fall of the Third Reich* (Crest edition, New York, 1962), pp. 1234–88; Rudolf Hoess, *Commandant of Auschwitz*, transl. Constantine FitzGibbon (London, 1959); Constantine FitzGibbon, 'Auschwitz', in *Random Thoughts of a Fascist Hyena* (London, 1963), pp. 33–57; Robert Merle, *La Mort est mon métier* (Paris, 1953); Jean-François Steiner, *Treblinka* (Paris, 1966)

30. Proudfoot, *op. cit.* (n. 29, *supra*), pp. 32, 34; Davidson, *op. cit.* (n. 17, *supra*), p. 53; Joseph B. Schechtman, *European Population Transfers, 1939–1945* (New York, 1946), pp. vii, viii; *ibid.*, *The Refugee in the World: Displacement and Integration* (New York/London, 1963), pp. 3, 13, 47; Montgomery, *op. cit.* (n. 7, *supra*), p. 407; Clay, *op. cit.* (n. 16, *supra*), p. 15; Balfour, *op. cit.* (n. 16, *supra*), p. 13

31. Schechtman, *The Refugee in the World* (n. 30, *supra*), p. 14; Elizabeth Wiskemann, *Germany's Eastern Neighbours* (London 1957), pp. 121–2; Robert Kee, *Refugee World* (London, 1961), p. 21; Inez Holden, 'U.N.R.R.A. in Germany', in Reginald Moore & Edward Lane (ed.), *The Windmill* (London, 1946), pp. 13–32 (pp. 15–16); Proudfoot, *op. cit.* (n. 29, *supra*), pp. 170–5; Peter Rodd, 'The Psychology of Refugees', in *Horizon*, vol. X, No. 59 (London, November 1944), pp. 312–19

32. Malaparte, *op. cit.* (n. 3, *supra*), p. 68; René Fallet, *Banlieue Sud-Est* (*Livre de poche* edition, Paris, 1967), pp. 109–11 (transl. R.M.)

33. Wyndham Lewis, *The Writer and the Absolute* (London, 1952), p. 68; Proudfoot, *op. cit.* (n. 29, *supra*), pp. 128–9, 175–8, 313; Ryan, *op. cit.* (n. 11, *supra*), pp. 361–3, 366–7, 382–9; van der Plas, *op. cit.* (n. 23, *supra*), pp. 77–135; Aron, *op. cit.* (n. 18, *supra*), p. 455; *ibid.*, *Histoire de l'épuration*, vol. I (Paris, 1967), p. 433; M. R. D. Foot, *SOE in France* (London, 1966), pp. 418–23; Anon., *op. cit.* (n. 14, *supra*), *passim*; Peter Novick, *The Resistance versus Vichy* (London, 1968), pp. 71, 202–8

34. Shirer *op. cit.* (n. 28, *supra*), p. 1482

35. Thomson, *op. cit.* (n. 18, *supra*), p. 877

36. G. M. Gilbert, *Nuremberg Diary* (New York, 1947), p. 31; Davidson, *op. cit.* (n. 17, *supra*), p. 108, n. 1

37. Whitney R. Harris, *Tyranny on Trial: the Evidence at Nuremberg* (Dallas, 1954), p. 16, Robert H. Jackson, *Report* (Department of State Publication 3080, Washington, 1949), pp. 340–4; Davidson, *op. cit.* (n. 17, *supra*), pp. 105, n. 107, 122, n. 3; Gordon Young, *The Fall and Rise of Alfred Krupp* (London, 1960), p. 81

38. Young, *op. cit.* (n. 37, *supra*), p. 88

39. For an example perhaps deliberately paradoxical, cf. A. J. P. Taylor, *The Origins of the Second World War* (Penguin edition with Foreword. London, 1964), pp. 96ff

40. *The New York Times*, 9 August 1932; *Trial of Major War Criminals* (n. 29, *supra*), vols. II, p. 154, XIX, pp. 399, 448; Jackson, *op. cit.* (n. 37, *supra*), p. 295; Davidson, *op. cit.* (n. 17, *supra*), pp. 102, nn. 7, 8, 9; 117, n. 1. On the Nuremberg trial in general, and particularly its atmosphere, cf. also R. W. Cooper, *The Nuremberg Trials* (London 1946)

41. Wilson, *op. cit.* (n. 26, *supra*), p. 24

CHAPTER 3. THE NEW FRONTIER

1. Milovan Djilas, *Conversations with Stalin*, transl. Michael B. Petrovich (Penguin edition, London, 1963), p. 90

2. *Memoirs*, vol. I, *1945: Year of Decisions* (Signet edition, New York, 1965), p. 354

3. *Through the Looking-Glass and what Alice Found There* (Miniature edition, London, 1908), p. 153

4. John Toland, *The Last Hundred Days* (Bantam edition, New York, 1967), pp. 500–9, which misprints the date as 26 April (p. 502); Cornelius Ryan, *The Last Battle* (London, 1966), pp. 371–2; Dwight D. Eisenhower, *Crusade in Europe* (Dolphin edition, New York, 1961), p. 434; Arthur Bryant, *Triumph in the West 1943–1946* (Alanbrooke War Diaries, vol. II (Fontana edition, London, 1965), p. 353; Chester Wilmot, *The Struggle for Europe* (Fontana edition, London, 1959), p. 802

5. John Colville, Churchill's assistant private secretary, quoted by Lord Moran, *Churchill: The Struggle for Survival* (Boston, 1966), p. 194

6. Cf. Ludwig Dehio, *The Precarious Balance*, transl. Charles Fullman (New York, 1962), esp. pp. 247–88; Wilfrid Knapp, 'The Partition of Europe' in Evan Luard (ed.), *The Cold War: A Reappraisal* (London, 1964), pp. 45–61; John Lukacs, *Decline and Rise of Europe* (New York, 1965), pp. 25–56

7. D. F. Fleming, *The Cold War and its Origins 1917–1960* (London, 1961), vol. I, pp. 145–8

8. Sidney Lowery, 'Poland', in A. & V. M. Toynbee (ed.), *The Realignment of Europe* (London, 1955), pp. 126–245 (pp. 164–82); Hugh Seton-Watson, *The East European Revolution* (London, 1950), pp. 83–98, 104–5; Fitzroy Maclean, *Disputed Barricade* (London, 1957), p. 291; W. H. McNeill, 'Greece, 1944–1946', in Toynbee, *op. cit.*, pp. 389–408 (p. 392); Winston Churchill, *The Second World War* (Cassell paperback edition, vol. XI, *The Tide of Victory*, London, 1964), pp. 187, 188, 203

9. Churchill, *op. cit.* (n. 8, *supra*), p. 200; Moran, *op. cit.* (n. 5, *supra*), p. 207

10. Churchill, *op. cit.* (n. 8, *supra*), pp. 200–1; André Fontaine, *Histoire de la guerre froide*, vol. I (Paris, 1965), p. 246

11. Polish Government in Exile, *Facts and Documents Concerning Polish Prisoners of War, Captured by the U.S.S.R. during the 1939 Campaign* (London, 1944); Joseph Mackiewicz, *The Katyn Wood Murders* (London, 1951); Lowery, *op. cit.* (n. 8, *supra*), pp. 138–47; Jean Laloy, *Entre guerres et paix 1945–1965* (Paris, 1966), pp. 68–9

12. Stanislaw Mikolajczyk, *The Pattern of Soviet Domination* (London, 1948), pp. 78–87, 102, 328; Churchill, *op. cit.* (n. 8, *supra*), p. 208; Laloy, *op. cit.* (n. 11, *supra*), pp. 70–2; Lowery, *op. cit.* (n. 8, *supra*), pp. 171–3, 177–8

13. Mikolajczyk, *op. cit.* (n. 12, *supra*), pp. 103–8; Churchill, *op. cit.* (n. 8, *supra*), p. 200; Jan Ciechanowski, *Defeat in Victory* (New York, 1947), pp. 328–9, 338; Wladyslaw Anders, *An Army in Exile* (London, 1949), pp. 237–9, 243; James F. Byrnes, *Speaking Frankly* (New York, 1947), p. 29; William D. Leahy, *I Was There* (New York, 1950), p. 249; Robert E. Sherwood, *Roosevelt and Hopkins: An Intimate History* (New York, 1948), pp. 833–4; Lowery, *op. cit.* (n. 8, *supra*), pp. 182–4

14. Ciechanowski, *op. cit.* (n. 13, *supra*), pp. 333–4, 342–3, 345; Mikolajczyk, *op. cit.* (n. 12, *supra*), pp. 109–11, 114; Anders, *op. cit.* (n. 13, *supra*), pp. 240–2; Churchill, *op. cit.* (n. 8, *supra*), pp. 208, 210, 212–13; Hansard, *House of Commons debates*, 5th series, vol. 404, cols. 493–5 & vol. 406, cols. 1478–578; Lowery, *op. cit.* (n. 8, *supra*), pp. 184–9

15. Lowery, *op. cit.* (n. 8, *supra*), pp. 191–4, 202 n. 1, 206 n. 5; U.K. Foreign Office, *Report of the Crimea Conference* (Cmd. 6598, London, 1945); Leahy, *op. cit.* (n. 13, *supra*), p. 370

16. Laloy, *op. cit.* (n. 11, *supra*), p. 95

17. McNeill, *op. cit.* (n. 8, *supra*), pp. 393–8; Hugh Seton-Watson, 'Yugoslavia', in Toynbee, *op. cit.* (n. 8, *supra*), pp. 352–71 (p. 359); Byrnes, *op. cit.* (n. 13, *supra*), p. 31

18. Cf. Knapp, *op. cit.* (n. 6, *supra*), p. 46

19. *Foreign Relations of the United States*, 1943, vol. I, pp. 708–10, 762–3; *Correspondence between the Chairman of the Council of Ministers of the U.S.S.R. and the Presidents of the U.S.A. and the Prime Ministers of Great Britain during the Great Patriotic War of 1941–45* (Moscow, 1957), vol. I, No. 186, p. 154; Laloy, *op. cit.* (n. 11, *supra*), pp. 43, 52–3

20. Laloy, *op. cit.* (n. 11, *supra*), pp. 42–5; Norman Kogan, *A Political History of Postwar Italy* (London, 1966), pp. 4–5; L. M. Goodrich & M. J. Carroll (ed.), *Documents on American Foreign Relations, 1943–1944* (Boston, 1945), p. 228; Hansard, *House of Commons debates*, 5th series, vol. 392, col. 99; Katharine Duff, 'Liberated Italy: from September 1943 to February 1947', in Toynbee, *op. cit.* (n. 8, *supra*), pp. 409–53 (pp. 418–20); Peirgiovanni Permoli, *La Costituente e i Partiti Politici Italiani* (Rocca San Casciano, 1966), pp. 70–6

21. Lionel Kochan, *The Struggle for Germany 1914–1945* (Edinburgh, 1963), pp. 79–80, 84, 89–90; *Foreign Relations of the United States, Diplomatic Papers: The Conferences at Cairo and Teheran, 1943* (Washington, 1961), pp. 600–1; Laloy, *op. cit.* (n. 11, *supra*), pp. 103–4; Arthur Conte, *Yalta ou le partage du monde* ('J'ai lu' edition, Paris, 1965), p. 332; *Pravda*, 10 May, 1945; *Foreign Relations of the United States, Diplomatic Papers: The Conference of Berlin, 1945* (Washington, 1960), vol. II, p. 61

22. *Foreign Relations of the United States, 1942: Europe, Vol. III*, pp. 517–18; Kochan, *op. cit.* (n. 21, *supra*), pp. 80 82, 84; *The Conferences at Cairo*

and Teheran, 1943 (n. 21, *supra*), *loc. cit.*; Lukacs, *op. cit.* (n. 6, *supra*), p. 36; Laloy, *op. cit.* (n. 11, *supra*), p. 62

23. Eugene Davidson, *The Death and Life of Germany* (London, 1959), pp. 6–10; Cordell Hull, *Memoirs* (New York, 1948), vol. 11, pp. 1265–6; Sumner Welles, *The Time for Decision* (New York, 1944), pp. 336–61; *The Conferences at Cairo and Teheran, 1943* (n. 21, *supra*), *loc. cit.*; Leahy, *op. cit.* (n. 13, *supra*), p. 186; Lukacs, *op. cit.*, (n. 6, *supra*), pp. 32–3; Robert Murphy, *Diplomat Among Warriors* (London, 1964), p. 281

24. Ray S. Cline, *Washington Command Post: The Operations Division* (Washington, 1951), p. 217; Herbert Feis, *Churchill, Roosevelt, Stalin: The War They Waged and the Peace They Sought* (Princeton, 1957), p. 360; Sir Llewellyn Woodward, *British Foreign Policy in the Second World War* (London, 1962), p. 438; Laloy, *op. cit.* (n. 11, *supra*), pp. 31, 55, 56 n. 1; Hull, *op. cit.* (n. 23, *supra*), pp. 1255–6, 1285; Kochan, *op. cit.* (n. 21, *supra*), p. 86; Edgar McInnis, Richard Hiscocks & Robert Spencer, *The Shaping of Postwar Germany* (Toronto/London, 1960), pp. 93–4

25. Philip Mosely, 'The Occupation of Germany', in *Foreign Affairs*, vol. XXVIII, No. 4 (July, 1950), pp. 580–604, reprinted in *Ibid., The Kremlin in World Politics* (Vintage books edition, New York, 1960), pp. 155–88 (p. 157 n. 4); *The Conferences at Cairo and Teheran, 1943* (n. 21, *supra*), p. 183; *Foreign Relations of the United States, 1943* vol. 1 (Washington, 1963), pp. 720–1; Laloy, *op. cit.* (n. 6, *supra*), pp. 55–6; Kochan, *op. cit.* (n. 21, *supra*), p. 86

26. Winston Churchill, *The Second World War* (Cassell paperback edition, vol. XII, *Triumph and Tragedy*, London, 1964), p. 159; Feis, *op. cit.* (n. 24, *supra*), p. 360; John L. Snell, *Wartime Origins of the East-West Dilemma over Germany* (New Orleans, 1959), p. 46

27. Lord Strang, *Home and Abroad* (London, 1956), pp. 203, 204, 207, 208, 212, 220; Nikolaus Pevsner, *The Buildings of England: London, Vol. I: The Cities of London and Westminster* (London, 1957), p. 447; Mosely, *op. cit.* (n. 25, *supra*), and 'Dismemberment of Germany', in *Foreign Affairs*, vol. XXVIII, No. 3 (April, 1950), pp. 487–98, also reprinted in *Ibid., The Kremlin in World Politics* (n. 25, *supra*); *Foreign Relations of the United States, 1944*, vol. 1, pp. 17ff; E. F. Penrose, *Economic Planning for Peace* (Princeton 1953), *passim.*

28. Woodward, *op. cit.* (n. 24, *supra*), p. 442; Mosely, *The Kremlin in World Politics* (n. 25, *supra*), p. 168; Sir Frederick Morgan, *Overture to Overlord* (London, 1950), p. 124; Strang, *op. cit.* (n. 27, *supra*), p. 218

29. Strang, *op. cit.* (n. 27, *supra*), pp. 213–14; Ryan, *op. cit.* (n. 4, *supra*), pp. 125–6; Mosely, *op. cit.* (n. 25, *supra*), pp. 169–71; Kochan, *op. cit.* (n. 21, *supra*), p. 87

30. Strang, *op. cit.* (n. 27, *supra*), pp. 213–15; Moseley, *op. cit.* (n. 25, *supra*), pp. 167, 171

31. Ryan, *op. cit.* (n. 4, *supra*), pp. 115–29, 134 (reproduction of *National Geographic* map); *Foreign Relations of the United States, Diplomatic Papers 1944*, vol. 1: *General* (Washington, 1966), pp. 195–6 (with inset

map); Murphy, *op. cit.* (n. 23, *supra*), pp. 284–7; Dwight D. Eisenhower, *Waging Peace 1956–1961* (London, 1966), p. 335, n. 5

32. Private information; Mosely, *The Kremlin in World Politics* (n. 25, *supra*), pp. 171–3; George Kennan, *Memoirs 1925–1950* (London, 1968), pp. 168–71

33. Mosely, *The Kremlin in World Politics* (n. 25, *supra*), pp. 166–7; Ryan, *op. cit.* (n. 4, *supra*), pp. 124–5; *Foreign Relations of the United States, Diplomatic Papers 1944* (n. 31, *supra*), pp. 100–9

34. Strang, *op. cit.* (n. 27, *supra*), p. 215

35. *Foreign Relations of the United States, Diplomatic Papers: The Conference at Malta and Yalta, 1945* (Washington, 1955), pp. 612, 624; Kochan, *op. cit.* (n. 21, *supra*), p. 86

36. Private information; Murphy, *op. cit.* (n. 23, *supra*), p. 281; Churchill, *op. cit.* (n. 26, *supra*), p. 159

37. Byrnes, *op. cit.* (n. 13, *supra*), pp. 50–2, 54–5, 60; R. H. Markham, *Rumania under the Soviet Yoke* (Boston, 1949), pp. 207–12; Lowery, *op. cit.* (n. 8, *supra*), pp. 210–14; Churchill, *op. cit.* (n. 26, *supra*), p. 124

38. Ryan, *op. cit.* (n. 4, *supra*), pp. 133–5. On friction, cf. Churchill, *op. cit.* (n. 26, *supra*), pp. 114–25, 156–68, 200–2; Dwight D. Eisenhower, *Crusade in Europe* (Dolphin edition, New York, 1961), pp. 325–6, 419–27; Field-Marshal the Viscount Montgomery of Alamein, K.G., *Memoirs* (Fontana edition, London, 1960), pp. 281–3, 287–90, 341–2; Bryant, *op. cit.* (n. 4, *supra*), pp. 346–53; Omar Bradley, *A Soldier's Story* (London, 1952), p. 537; Wilmot, *op. cit.* (n. 4, *supra*), pp. 553–62, 606–9, 612–4, 782–3, 788–95, 815–16

39. Montgomery, *op. cit.* (n. 38, *supra*), pp. 281, 290, 294; Eisenhower, *op. cit.* (n. 38, *supra*), pp. 326–7

40. Bryant, *op. cit.* (n. 4, *supra*), pp. 347, 350; Montgomery, *op. cit.* (n. 38, *supra*), p. 341; Ryan, *op. cit.* (n. 4, *supra*), p. 185; Eisenhower, *op. cit.* (n. 38, *supra*), pp. 419–20

41. Churchill, *op. cit.* (n. 26, *supra*), pp. 117–25; Bryant, *op. cit.* (n. 4, *supra*), pp. 347–51; Eisenhower, *op. cit.* (n. 38, *supra*), p. 422; Ryan, *op. cit.* (n. 4, *supra*), pp. 178, 180

42. Churchill, *op. cit.* (n. 26, *supra*), p. 117; Ryan, *op. cit.* (n. 4, *supra*), pp. 186–95

43. Bryant, *op. cit.* (n. 4, *supra*), p. 353; Ryan, *op. cit.* (n. 4, *supra*), pp. 252–3, 259–60; Wilmot, *op. cit.* (n. 4, *supra*), pp. 791–4; Leahy, *op. cit.* (n. 13, *supra*), p. 351; F. C. Pogue, 'The Decision to Halt on the Elbe, 1945', in Greenfield and Kent (ed.) *Command Decisions* (London, 1960)

44. Leahy, *op. cit.* (n. 13, *supra*), pp. 349–50; Churchill, *op. cit.* (n. 26, *supra*), p. 161; Truman, *op. cit.* (n. 2, *supra*), pp. 237–45

CHAPTER 4. SELF-HELP

1. *Terre des hommes* (*Livre de poche* edition, Paris, 1961), p. 59, quoting his fellow-pilot Guillaumet on his survival after a forced landing in the Andes (transl. R.M.)

THE RECOVERY OF EUROPE

2. *Maximen und Reflexionen,* ed. Paul Stöcklein (Munich, 1963), p. 111 (transl. R.M.)

3. *Self-Help: with Illustration of Conduct and Perseverance* (New edition, London, 1887), p. 1

4. Hansard, *House of Commons debates,* 5th series, vol. 364, cols. 1161–2; Arnold Toynbee, 'Introductory Note' to F. Ashton-Gwatkin, 'The United Nations Relief and Rehabilitation Administration', in A. & V. M. Toynbee, *The Realignment of Europe* (London, 1955), pp. 51–125 (p. 52)

5. Ashton-Gwatkin, *op. cit.* (n. 4, *supra*), pp. 72–4, 77, 83–4, 102–7, 110; George Woodbridge & others, *UNRRA: The History of the United Nations Relief and Rehabilitation Administration* (3 vols., New York, 1950), vol. II, pp. 320, 451–2; Inez Holden, 'U.N.R.R.A. in Germany', in Reginald Moore & Edward Lane (ed.), *The Windmill* (London, 1946), pp. 14–32 (pp. 21, 31); Edmund Wilson, *Europe Without Baedeker* (London, 1948), pp. 205–6

6. Ashton-Gwatkin, *op. cit.* (n. 4, *supra*), pp. 53–4, 62, 68

7. Ashton-Gwatkin, *op. cit.* (n. 4, *supra*), pp. 68, 70, 77–8, 89, 111–17; *UNRRA* Council, 1st Session, Resolution 14, Section 16; Woodbridge, *op. cit.* (n. 5, *supra*), vol. I, pp. 81–3, vol. III, pp. 33ff; Richard Mayne, *The Community of Europe* (London, 1962; New York, 1963), pp. 59–60

8. Ashton-Gwatkin, *op. cit.* (n. 4, *supra*), p. 104; Woodbridge, *op. cit.* (n. 5, *supra*), vol. III, pp. 428–97

9. Ashton-Gwatkin, *op. cit.* (n. 4, *supra*), pp. 77, 78, 88

10. Cf. Saul Friedländer, *Hitler et les Etats-Unis, 1939–41* (Geneva, 1963), revised by the author and translated by Aline B. & Alexander Werth as *Prelude to Downfall: Hitler and the United States 1939–1941* (New York, 1967), pp. 165–75

11. Allan Nevins, *America in World Affairs* (Oxford, 1941), pp. 131–2; A. J. P. Taylor, *English History 1914–45* (Oxford, 1965), pp. 513, 533; R. G. Hawtrey, 'The Economic Consequences of the War', in A. & V. M. Toynbee, *op. cit.* (n. 4, *supra*), pp. 36–51 (p. 45); Norman S. Buchanan & Friedrich A. Lutz, *Rebuilding the World Economy* (New York, 1947), pp. 78–9; J.-B. Duroselle, *De Wilson à Roosevelt: politique extérieure des Etats-Unis* (Paris, 1960), p. 310; Harry S. Truman, *Memoirs,* vol. I, *1945: Year of Decisions* (Signet edition, New York, 1965), p. 262

12. L. M. Goodrich & M. J. Carroll (ed.), *Documents on American Foreign Relations, July 1942 – June 1943* (Boston, 1944), pp. 264–5; Ashton-Gwatkin, *op. cit.* (n. 4, *supra*), p. 66

13. William D. Leahy, *I Was There* (New York, 1950), pp. 272–3, 280

14. Nevins, *op. cit.* (n. 11, *supra*), p. 132; Harry Dexter White, Memorandum on meeting in Hull's office, 20 September 1944, in *Foreign Relations of the United States, Diplomatic Papers: The Conference at Malta and Yalta* (Washington, 1955), pp. 136–9

15. White, *loc. cit.* (n. 14, *supra*), Truman, *op. cit.* (n. 11, *supra*), pp. 257–8

16. Truman, *op. cit.* (n. 11, *supra*), pp. 254–5

17. Truman, *op. cit.* (n. 11, *supra*), pp. 255–8; James F. Byrnes, *Speaking Frankly* (New York, 1947), p. 62

18. Truman, *op. cit.* (n. 11, *supra*), pp. 255–6, 260, 524; Leahy, *op. cit.* (n. 13, *supra*), p. 414; Hawtrey, *op. cit.* (n. 11, *supra*), p. 42 n. 2

19. R. F. Harrod, *The Life of John Maynard Keynes* (London, 1951), p. 595

20. Harrod, *op. cit.* (n. 19, *supra*), p. 596; T. Balogh, 'The International Aspect', in G.D.N. Worswick & P. H. Ady (ed.), *The British Economy 1945–50* (Oxford, 1952), pp. 476–510 (p. 490); Hugh Dalton, *High Tide and After: Memoirs 1945–1960* (London, 1962), p. 68

21. Dalton, *loc. cit.* (n. 20, *supra*), Harrod, *op. cit.* (n. 19, *supra*), p. 595

22. R. N. Gardner, *Sterling-Dollar Diplomacy* (Oxford, 1956), p. 186 & n.; Buchanan & Lutz, *op. cit.* (n. 11, *supra*), p. 78

23. Truman, *op. cit.* (n. 11, *supra*), p. 524; P. J. D. Wiles, 'Prewar and War-time Controls', in Worswick & Ady, *op. cit.* (n. 20, *supra*), pp. 125–58 (pp. 153–4); Dalton, *op. cit.* (n. 20, *supra*), pp. 71–2

24. Dalton, *op. cit.* (n. 20, *supra*), pp. 70, 73–4, 75 n. 1; Harrod, *op. cit.* (n. 19, *supra*), pp. 596–7

25. Hawtrey, *op. cit.* (n. 11, *supra*), pp. 47–8

26. Balogh, *loc. cit.* (n. 20, *supra*); Dalton, *op. cit.* (n. 20, *supra*), p. 81

27. Dalton, *op. cit.* (n. 20, *supra*), p. 73

28. Woodbridge, *op. cit.* (n. 5, *supra*), vol. I, pp. 327–31; Ashton-Gwatkin, *op. cit.* (n. 4, *supra*), pp. 92–3; Susan Cooper, 'Snoek Piquante', in Michael Sissons and Philip French (ed.), *Age of Austerity 1945–51* (Penguin edition, London, 1964), pp. 35–57 (pp. 38–42)

29. Francis Williams, *A Prime Minister Remembers: The War and Post-war Memoirs of the Rt. Hon. Earl Attlee, K.G., P.C., O.M., C.H.* (London, 1961), pp. 135–48; Truman, *op. cit.* (n. 11, *supra*), p. 514

30. Truman, *op. cit.* (n. 11, *supra*), pp. 512, 513, 515–16, 519–22; *Ibid.*, vol. II, *1946–1952: Years of Trial and Hope* (Signet edition, New York, 1956), p. 389; Williams, *op. cit.* (n. 29, *supra*), p. 140

31. Williams, *op. cit.* (n. 29, *supra*), pp. 135, 138–9

32. Winston Churchill, *The Second World War* (Cassell paperback edition, vol. XII, *Triumph and Tragedy*, London, 1964), p. 164; Lucius D. Clay, *Decision in Germany* (London, 1950), p. 265; Eugene Davidson, *The Death and Life of Germany* (London, 1959), p. 135; Williams, *op. cit.* (n. 29, *supra*), p. 148

33. Byrnes, *op. cit.* (n. 17, *supra*), p. 182; Cordell Hull, *Memoirs* (New York, 1948), vol. II, p. 1603; Henry L. Stimson & McGeorge Bundy, *On Active Service in Peace and War* (New York, 1947), p. 573

34. Byrnes, *op. cit.* (n. 17, *supra*), p. 181; Henry Morgenthau, *Germany is our Problem* (New York, 1945), pp. 12–15; Ernest F. Penrose, *Economic Planning for the Peace* (Princeton, 1953), pp. 244–50; Michael Balfour, 'Germany', in A. Toynbee (ed.), *Four-Power Control in Germany and Austria 1945–1946* (London, 1956), pp. 1–255 (p. 19); *Le Monde* (Paris, 8 February, 1967), p. 19

35. Stimson & Bundy, *op. cit.* (n. 33, *supra*), p. 578; Morgenthau, letter to

Edward R. Stettinius, 20 September 1944, quoted by H. Freeman Matthews, Deputy Director of Office of European Affairs, U.S. State Department, in Memorandum of 20 September 1944, reprinted in *The Conferences at Malta and Yalta* (n. 14, *supra*), p. 134; Lord Moran, *Churchill: The Struggle for Survival* (Boston, 1966), p. 190; Edmund Burke, *Speech moving his Resolutions for Conciliation with the Colonies, 22 March, 1775*, in *Select Works* (ed. E. J. Payne, Oxford, 1874), vol. I, p. 192: 'I do not know the method of drawing up an indictment against a whole people.'

36. Cf. C. P. Snow, *Science and Government* (Four Square edition, London, 1963), p. 26; R. F. Harrod, *The Prof* (London, 1959), *passim*; The Earl of Birkenhead, *The Professor and the Prime Minister* (Boston, 1962), *passim*; Davidson, *op. cit.* (n. 32, *supra*), p. 37; Moran, *op. cit.* (n. 35, *supra*), pp. 191–2; Byrnes, *op. cit.* (n. 17, *supra*), p. 184

37. Churchill, *op. cit.* (n. 32, *supra*), pp. 19–20; *Ibid*, vol. XI, *The Tide of Victory*, p. 138

38. Davidson, *op. cit.* (n. 32, *supra*), pp. 6–14; Department of State *Bulletin*, vol. XIII, (Washington, 1945), pp. 596–607; Stimson & Bundy, *op. cit.* (n. 33, *supra*), p. 570; Clay, *op. cit.* (n. 32, *supra*), pp. 6, 11, 17–18; Theodore H. White, *Fire in the Ashes* (New York, 1953), pp. 138–40

39. Byrnes, *op. cit.* (n. 17, *supra*), pp. 28–9; U.K. Foreign Office, *Protocol of the Proceedings of the Berlin Conference, 2 August, 1945* (H.M.S.O., Cmd. 7087, London, 1947), pp. 7–8; Balfour, *op. cit.* (n. 34, *supra*), pp. 77–8, 87; Clay, *op. cit.* (n. 32, *supra*), pp. 120–1; William Henry Chamberlin, *The German Phoenix* (London, 1964), p. 35; Howard K. Smith, *The State of Europe* (London, 1950), pp. 104, 107; Nicolas Nabokov, *Old Friends and New Music* (London, 1951), p. 211; John P. Nettl, *The Eastern Zone and Soviet Policy in Germany* (London, 1951), p. 204; Mayne, *op. cit.* (n. 7, *supra*), p. 59

40. Henry C. Wallich, *Mainsprings of the German Revival* (New Haven, 1955), p. 370; Chamberlin, *op. cit.* (n. 39, *supra*), p. 71; Clay, *op. cit.* (n. 32, *supra*), p. 124

41. Karl W. Roskamp, *Capital Formation in West Germany* (Detroit, 1965), p. 39; personal knowledge

42. Konrad Adenauer, *Erinnerungen 1945–1953* (Stuttgart, 1965), pp. 36–7; Robert F. Kennedy, *Just Friends and Brave Enemies* (Popular Library edition, New York, 1963), pp. 139–40; Harold Zink, *The United States in Germany, 1944–1955* (New York, 1957), p. 136; Chamberlin, *op. cit.* n. 39, *supra*), pp. 40–2; Davidson, *op. cit.* (n. 32, *supra*), pp. 84–5; Field-Marshal the Viscount Montgomery of Alamein, K.G., *Memoirs* (Fontana edition, London, 1960), p. 380

43. Balfour, *op. cit.* (n. 34, *supra*), pp. 169–265; Raymond Ebsworth, *Restoring Democracy in Germany: The British Contribution* (London, 1960), *passim*; Clay, *op. cit.* (n. 32, *supra*), pp. 67–70, 98–9, 258–62, 287–8, 298–302

44. Balfour, *op. cit.* (n. 34, *supra*), pp. 203–4, 212–15, 219–26, 231; H. H. Wollenberg, *Fifty Years of German Film* (transl. Ernst Sigler, London,

1948), p. 47; William L. Shirer, *The Rise and Fall of the Third Reich* (Crest Books edition, New York, 1962), p. 333; Ebsworth, *op. cit.* (n. 43, *supra*), p. 22

45. Simone de Beauvoir, *La Force des Choses* (Paris, 1963), p. 14 (transl. R.M.)
46. Federico Chabod, *L'Italia Contemporanea 1918–1948* (Piccola biblioteca Einaudi edition, Turin, 1965), p. 133 (transl. R.M.); Michel van der Plas, *Moie Vrede: een documentaire over Nederland in de jaren 1945–1950* (Utrecht, 1966), p. 142 (transl. R.M.); Margot Lyon, 'The Christian Democratic Parties and Politics', in *Journal of Contemporary History*, vol. II No. 4 (London, October 1967), pp. 69–87; Peter H. Merkl, *Germany Yesterday and Tomorrow* (New York, 1965), p. 204; Dalton, *op. cit.* (n. 20, *supra*), p. 3
47. M. M. Postan, *An Economic History of Western Europe 1945–1964* (London, 1967), pp. 217–29; Vera Lutz, 'The French "Miracle" ', in Jossleyn Hennessy, Vera Lutz & Guiseppe Scimone, *Economic 'Miracles'* (London, 1964), pp. 75–167 (pp. 79–80)
48. Paul Alpert, *Twentieth-Century Economic History of Europe* (New York, 1951), pp. 289–90; David Thomson, *Europe Since Napoleon* (London, revised ed., 1963), pp. 775–6

CHAPTER 5. THE RELUCTANT ST GEORGE

1. *High Tide and After: Memoirs 1945–1960* (London, 1962), p. 187
2. *Autobiography* (Everyman edition, London, 1948), p. 118
3. *1066 and All That* (26th edition, London, 1938), p. 115
4. Harry S. Truman, *Memoirs*, vol. II, *1946–1952: Years of Trial and Hope* (Signet edition, New York, 1965), p. 122; Joseph Marion Jones, *The Fifteen Weeks* (Harbinger edition, New York, 1964), pp. 3–4; David Watt, 'Withdrawal from Greece', in Michael Sissons & Philip French (ed.), *Age of Austerity 1945–1941* (Penguin edition, London, 1964), pp. 106–31 (p. 107); Dalton, *op. cit.* (n. 1, *supra*), p. 208; Dean Acheson, *Present at the Creation* (London, 1970), p. 217
5. Jones, *op. cit.* (n. 4, *supra*), pp. 5, 59–77; Dalton, *op. cit.* (n. 1, *supra*). p. 206; personal knowledge; George F. Kennan, *Memoirs 1925–1950* (London, 1968), pp. 316–17
6. Truman, *op. cit.* (n. 4, *supra*), pp. 221–2
7. Dalton, *op. cit.* pp. 187–8, 193, 199, 201–3, 210; Watt, *op. cit.* p. 106; Howard K. Smith, *The State of Europe* (London, 1950), pp. 20–1
8. Dalton, *op. cit.* (n. 1, *supra*), pp. 206–7
9. Dalton, *op. cit.* (n. 1, *supra*), pp. 220–1, 257, 259–60, 262 & n. 2
10. *Ibid.*, pp. 193, 197, 221
11. Maulana Abul Kalam Azad, *India Wins Freedom* (Bombay, 1959), pp. 57ff; Taya Zinkin, *India* (London, 1965), pp. 73ff; Ronald Segal, *The Crisis of India* (London, 1965), pp. 115ff. Cf. also Michael Brecher, *Nehru: A Political Biography* (Oxford, 1953); V. P. Menon, *The Transfer of Power in India* (Bombay, 1961); Penderal Moon, *Divide and Quit* (London, 1962)

12. Personal knowledge
13. Jones, *op. cit.* (n. 4, *supra*), p. 44
14. Harry S. Truman, *Memoirs*, vol. I, *1945: Year of Decisions* (Signet edition, New York, 1965), pp. 464–5; William D. Leahy, *I Was There* (New York, 1950), p. 430; Barbara Ward, *The West at Bay* (New York, 1948), p. 14
15. David J. Dallin, *The Big Three: United States, Britain, Russia* (New Haven, 1945); Cf. also John Mander, *Great Britain or Little England?* (London, 1963), pp. 26–30
16. James F. Byrnes, *All In One Lifetime* (London, 1960), pp. 368–9, 400–2; Jones, *op. cit.* (n. 4, *supra*), p. 54; Truman, *Memoirs*, vol. II (n. 4, *supra*), p. 125; *Ibid.*, vol. I (n. 14, *supra*), pp. 86–7, 98–9, 606; Watt, *op. cit.* (n. 4, *supra*), p. 121; D. F. Fleming, *The Cold War and its Origins 1917–1960* (London, 1961), vol. I, pp. 441–2
17. Private information
18. Jones, *op. cit.* (n. 4, *supra*), p. 3
19. *Ibid.*, pp. 129, 132, 136–8, 144–7; Kennan, *op. cit.* (n. 5, *supra*), p. 314; Truman, *Memoirs*, vol. II (n. 4, *supra*), pp. 122–3, 126–7; Acheson, *op. cit.* (n. 4, *supra*), pp. 217–19
20. Truman, *Memoirs*, vol. II (n. 4, *supra*), pp. 127–8; Jones, *op. cit.* (n. 4, *supra*), pp. 76–7, 269–74; Acheson, *op. cit.* (n. 4, *supra*), pp. 220–3
21. Jones, *op. cit.* (n. 4, *supra*), pp. 160–1; U.N. General Assembly, *Resolution of 13 December, 1946*
22. Jones, *op. cit.* (n. 4, *supra*), pp. 154–5, 163; Kennan, *op. cit.* (n. 5, *supra*), pp. 314–15, 317
23. *Ibid.*, pp. 320–2
24. Jones, *op. cit.* (n. 4, *supra*), p. 190; Kennan, *op. cit.* (n. 5, *supra*), p. 321
25. Ward, *op. cit.* (n. 14, *supra*), pp. 10–14; Harry Bayard Price, *The Marshall Plan and Its Meaning* (Ithaca, New York, 1955), pp. 29–32; Howard S. Ellis, *The Economics of Freedom* (New York, 1950), p. 62; Organisation for European Economic Co-operation, *Second Report* (Paris, 1950), p. 21; R. Mayne, *The Community of Europe* (London, 1962 & New York, 1963), pp. 74–5
26. Theodore H. White, *Fire in the Ashes* (New York, 1953), pp. 45, 135; Ward, *op. cit.* (n. 14, *supra*), pp. 17, 160–1; United Nations, Economic Commission for Europe, *Growth and Stagnation in the European Economy* (Geneva, 1954), p. 255; Norman J. G. Pounds & William N. Parker, *Coal and Steel in Western Europe* (Bloomington, Indiana, 1957), p. 296
27. Personal knowledge; Ward, *op. cit.* (n. 14, *supra*), p. 12; Price, *op. cit*, Eugene Davidson, *The Death and Life of Germany* (London, 1959), p. 172
28. Price, *op. cit.* (n. 25, *supra*), p. 9; E. F. Penrose, *Economic Planning for Peace* (Princeton, 1953), *passim*
29. Asher Isaacs, *International Trade: Tariff and Commercial Policies* (Chicago, 1948), pp. 790–7, 816–17; Mayne, *op. cit.* (n. 25, *supra*), pp. 73–4; Jones, *op. cit.* (n. 4, *supra*), pp. 207, 233
30. Personal knowledge; Jones, *op. cit.* (n. 4, *supra*), pp. 199–201, 242–4; Max Beloff, *The United States and the Unity of Europe* (London, 1963),

pp. 15–18; Ernst H. van der Beugel, *From Marshall Aid to Atlantic Partnership* (Amsterdam/London/New York, 1966), pp. 44–6

31. Jones, *op cit.* (n. 4, *supra*), pp. 199–201, 228; Lippmann in *New York Herald Tribune*, 20 March 1947; van der Beugel, *op. cit.* (n. 30, *supra*), p. 39; Truman, *Memoirs*, vol. I, *1945: Year of Decisions* (Signet edition, New York, 1965), pp. 519–22

32. Donald Watt, 'Germany', in Evan Luard (ed.), *The Cold War: A Reappraisal* (London, 1964), pp. 84–119 (pp. 99)

33. Watt, *op. cit.* (n. 32, *supra*), pp. 100–103; Philip E. Mosely, 'Some Soviet Techniques of Negotiation', in Raymond Dennett & Joseph E. Johnson (ed.), *Negotiating with the Russians* (Boston, Mass., 1951), pp. 271–303; *L'Année Politique 1946* (Paris, 1947), pp. 399–401; *L'Année Politique 1947* (Paris, 1948), pp. 49–58, 79–88; Lucius D. Clay, *Decision in Germany* (London, 1950), p. 151; van der Beugel, *op. cit.* (n. 30, *supra*), p. 34; Jones, *op. cit.* (n. 4, *supra*), pp. 221–3

34. Kennan, *op. cit.* (n. 5, *supra*), pp. 325–6

35. Kennan, *op. cit.* (n. 5, *supra*), pp. 330, 332–3

36. Jones, *op. cit.* (n. 4, *supra*), pp. 206–7; text of speech, *Ibid.*, pp. 274–81; Acheson, *op. cit.* (n. 4, *supra*), pp. 227–30

37. Jones, *op. cit.* (n. 4, *supra*), pp. 249–52; Kennan, *op. cit.* (n. 5, *supra*), pp. 335–8, 341; Price, *op. cit.* pp. 22–3 ('Western' omitted on p. 22)

38. Jones, *op. cit.* (n. 4, *supra*), pp. 246–8; Beloff, *op. cit.* (n. 30, *supra*), p. 19

39. Kennan, *op. cit.* (n. 5, *supra*), p. 342; Price, *op. cit.* (n 25, *supra*), pp. 23–4; Jones, *op. cit.* (n. 4, *supra*), pp. 31–3, 249, 252–5

40. Full text in Jones, *op. cit.* (n. 4, *supra*), pp. 281–4; cf. Policy Planning Staff memorandum quoted on p. 101, *supra*

41. Price, *op. cit.* (n. 25, *supra*), pp. 24–7

42. Jones, *op. cit.* (n. 4, *supra*), pp. 212, 255–6; Leonard Miall, 'How the Marshall Plan Started', in *The Listener* (London, 4 May 1961), pp. 779–80

43. Jones, *op. cit.* (n. 4, *supra*), p. 256; Price, *op. cit.* (n. 25, *supra*), p. 27; Hansard, House of Commons, vol. 438 (19 June 1947), cols. 2353–4; Dean Acheson, *Sketches from Life* (New York, 1961), p. 2

44. *L'Année Politique 1947* (Paris, 1948), pp. 134–5, 352

CHAPTER 6. EUROPE OF THE STATES

1. *A Midsummer-Night's Dream*, Act III, Scene 2, lines 208–10

2. *Introductio ad Prudentiam* (2nd edition, London, 1740), vol. II, p. 131

3. *L'Ancien régime et la révolution*, Book I, Chap. i, last sentence (transl. R.M.)

4. *L'Année politique 1947* (Paris, 1948), pp. 134–5, 353; *The Times* (London), 14 and 20 June 1947; Ministère des Affaires Etrangères, *Documents de la Conférence des Ministres des Affaires Etrangères de la France, du Royaume Uni et de l'URSS tenue à Paris du 27 juin au 3 juillet 1947* (Paris, 1947), pp. 15–16

5. *L'Année politique 1947* (Paris, 1948), pp. 135, 353–4 (Bidault, transl. R.M.); *The Times* (London), 24 June 1947; D. F. Fleming, *The Cold War and its Origins 1917–1960* (London, 1961), vol. I, p. 479

6. *Pravda* (Moscow), 16 and 25 June 1947; Fleming, *loc. cit.* (n. 5, *supra*); Harry Bayard Price, *The Marshall Plan and its Meaning* (Ithaca, New York, 1955), p. 28; *L'Année politique 1947* (Paris, 1948), p. 136; Ministère des Affaires Etrangères, *op. cit.* (n. 4, *supra*), pp. 38–42

7. Price, *op. cit.* (n. 6, *supra*), p. 27; Fleming, *loc. cit.* (n. 5, *supra*)

8. Ministère des Affaires Etrangères, *op. cit.* (n. 4, *supra*), pp. 44–6

9. *Ibid.*, p. 49

10. Ministère des Affaires Etrangères, *op. cit.* (n. 4, *supra*), pp. 52–3; official translation except for 'voluntarily' (replacing official 'willingly') in second sentence

11. *Ibid.*, pp. 58–61; Fleming, *op. cit.* (n. 5, *supra*), pp. 479–80

12. Ministère des Affaires Etrangères, *op. cit.*, pp. 62–5; *L'Année politique 1947* (Paris, 1948), p. 137 (transl. R.M.)

13. *Ibid.*, p. 354 (transl. R.M.)

14. Price, *op. cit.* (n. 6, *supra*), p. 28; Ernst H. van der Beugel, *From Marshall Aid to Atlantic Partnership* (Amsterdam/London/New York, 1966), p. 62; William C. Mallalieu, 'The Origins of the Marshall Plan', in *Political Science Quarterly*, vol. LXIII (1958), pp. 483–91; Hubert Ripska, *Czechoslovakia Enslaved* (London, 1950), pp. 52–3

15. W. W. Rostow, *The United States in the World Arena* (New York, 1960), p. 211, quoted by David Horowitz, *From Yalta to Vietnam* (Penguin edition, 1967, of *The Free World Colossus* (London, 1965), p. 72; cf. also Fleming, *loc. cit.* (n. 11, *supra*)

16. Theodore H. White, *Fire in the Ashes* (New York, 1953), pp. 39–40; Price, *op. cit.* (n. 6, *supra*), pp. 27–8 (interview with Dean Acheson); Fleming, *loc. cit.* (n. 11, *supra*)

17. Private information

18. Price, *op. cit.* (n. 6, *supra*), pp. 26, 36–7, 39–48, 50–5, 61; Committee of European Economic Co-operation, vol. I, *General Report* (Paris/London, 1947); William Diebold, Jr., *Trade and Payments in Western Europe* (New York, 1952), p. 25; van der Beugel, *op. cit.* (n. 14, *supra*), pp. 86–9, 97–8, 174; Robert A. Dahl, *Congress and Foreign Policy* (New York, 1950), pp. 128–30

19. Price, *op. cit.* (n. 6, *supra*), pp. 63–5; Arthur H. Vandenberg, Jr. (ed.), *The Private Papers of Senator Vandenberg* (Boston, 1952), p. 389

20. Price, *op. cit.* (n. 6, *supra*), p. 70; David M. Crawford, 'United States Foreign Assistance Legislation, 1947–1948', in *Yale Law Journal*, May 1949, pp. 877–921

21. Price, *op. cit.* (n. 6, *supra*), pp. 71–3; Paul G. Hoffman, *Peace Can Be Won* (New York, 1951), p. 87

22. Price, *op. cit.* (n. 6, *supra*), pp. 76–7; White, *op. cit.* (n. 16, *supra*), p. 60

23. U.S. Department of Commerce, *Foreign Aid by the United States Govern-*

ment 1940–1951, Supplement to the *Survey of Current Business* (Washington, 1952), pp. 7, 12, 57, 60–1; Price, *op. cit.* (n. 6, *supra*), pp. 88–90

24. *New York Times*, 13 July 1947; Committee of European Economic Co-operation, *op. cit.* (n. 18, *supra*), p. 22; van der Beugel, *op. cit.* (n. 14, *supra*), pp. 80, 127–8; Price, *op. cit.* (n. 6, *supra*), p. 285; personal knowledge

25. van der Beugel, *op. cit.* (n. 14, *supra*), pp. 147, 149–65

26. Organisation for European Economic Co-operation, 9th Report, *A Decade of Co-operation: Achievements and Perspectives* (Paris, 1958), pp. 55, 60, 61; Diebold, *op. cit.* (n. 18, *supra*), pp. 164–6; Michael Palmer & others, *European Unity: A Survey of the European Organisations* (London, 1968), pp. 101–2; R. Mayne, *The Community of Europe* (London, 1962; New York, 1963), p. 76

27. Organisation for European Economic Co-operation, *op. cit.* (n. 26, *supra*), pp. 76–8; Robert Triffin, *Europe and the Money Muddle* (New Haven, Conn., 1957), p. 153; Diebold, *op. cit.* (n. 18, *supra*), p. 64; O.E.E.C. Information Department, Mimeographed document Press D (50) 14, 7 July 1950; private information; M. J. Colebrook, *Dialogue of the Deaf: Franco–British Relations and European Integration 1945–1950* (unpublished thesis, Geneva 1968), Chapter II B, 'The Payments Issue'

28. G. D. N. Worswick, 'The British Economy 1945–50', in G. D. N. Worswick and P. H. Ady (ed.), *The British Economy 1945–1950* (Oxford, 1952), pp. 1–34 (pp. 32–4); William Adams Brown, Jr. and Redvers Opie, *American Foreign Assistance* (Washington, 1953), p. 201; van der Beugel, *op. cit.* (n. 14, *supra*), pp. 152–6, 169

29. Personal knowledge; Georgette Elgey, *Histoire de la IVe République*, vol. II, *La République des Contradictions 1951–1954* (Paris, 1968), pp. 207–8. Cf. also Marcus Cunliffe, 'Europe and America', in *Encounter*, vol. XVII, No. 6 (London, December 1961), pp. 19–29, and Melvin J. Lasky, 'America and Europe', in *Encounter*, vol. XVIII, No. 1 (London, January 1961), pp. 66–82

30. George F. Kennan, *Memoirs 1925–1950* (London, 1967), p. 417; Max Beloff, *The United States and the Unity of Europe* (London, 1963), pp. 2–3

31. Beloff, *op. cit.* (n. 30, *supra*), pp. 7, 11, 14; Count Coudenhove-Kalergi, *An Idea Conquers the World* (London, 1953), p. 260; private information; U.S. Senate, 2nd Session, Part II, p. 54; John C. Campbell, *The United States in World Affairs 1945–1947* (New York, 1947), p. 471; Joseph Marion Jones, *The Fifteen Weeks* (Harbinger edition, New York, 1964), p. 220; van der Beugel, *op. cit.* (n. 14, *supra*), p. 39

32. Cf. p. 97–8. *supra*; Beloff, *op cit.* (n. 30, *supra*), pp. 15–18; van der Beugel, *op. cit.* (n. 14, *supra*), pp. 44–6

33. Cf. p. 102, *supra*; Jones, *op. cit.* (n. 31, *supra*), pp. 246–8; Beloff, *op. cit.* (n. 30, *supra*), pp. 19–20

34. Cf. Chapter V, p. 101, *supra*; Beloff, *op. cit.* (n. 30, *supra*), p. 23; Kennan, *op. cit.* (n. 30, *supra*), p. 337; private information; Price, *op. cit.* (n. 6, *supra*), p. 44; van der Beugel, *op. cit.* (n. 14, *supra*), pp. 86, 88, 90–1, 182–3; *European Recovery and American Aid*, Report by the President's

L

Committee on Foreign Aid (Washington, D.C., 1947); U.S. Select Committee on Foreign Aid, *Final Report on Foreign Aid*, House of Representatives, 80th Congress, 2nd Session, 1948; Paul Hoffman, speech to the O.E.E.C. Ministerial Council, 31 October 1949, O.E.E.C. Document C (49) 176

35. Sforza in *Relazioni Internazionali*, 24 January 1948, p. 57 (transl. R.M.); Diebold, *op. cit.* (n. 18, *supra*), p. 354

36. Private information; van der Beugel, *op. cit.* (n. 14, *supra*), pp. 74, 78–80

37. Committee of European Economic Co-operation, vol. I, *General Report* (Paris/London, 1947), pp. 19–20; Diebold, *op. cit.* (n. 18, *supra*), pp. 305–11; European Customs Union Study Group (E.C.U.S.G.), *General Report of the Economic Committee* (mimeographed, Brussels, October 1948), vol. I, p. 11; E.C.U.S.G., *First Report* (mimeographed, Brussels, March 1948), p. 91

38. Diebold, *op. cit.* (n. 18, *supra*), pp. 377–83

39. *Customs Unions: A League of Nations Contribution to the Study of Customs Union Problems* (New York, 1947), pp. 47, 75; J. E. Meade, *Problems of Economic Union* (London, 1953), pp. 9ff, 82; Jacob Viner, *The Customs Union Issue* (New York/London, 1950), p. 41; Pierre Uri, 'The meaning of economic integration', in *Aspects of European Integration* (London/Paris, 1962), pp. 1–2; Walter Hallstein, *United Europe: Challenge and Opportunity* (Cambridge, Mass./Oxford, England, 1962), pp. 30–57; Mayne, *op. cit.* (n. 26, *supra*), pp. 119–28; *Ibid.*, 'Economic Integration in the New Europe', in Stephen Graubard (ed.), *A New Europe?* (Boston, Mass., 1964), pp. 174–99 (pp. 175–9)

40. Cf. van der Beugel, *op. cit.* (n. 14, *supra*), pp. 68–9

41. Ministère des Affaires Etrangères, *op. cit.* (n. 4, *supra*), pp. 44–6, 52–3; *New York Times*, 13 July 1947

42. van der Beugel, *op. cit.* (n. 14, *supra*), pp. 92, 132; *The Times* (London), 16 August 1947; private information; Beloff, *op. cit.* (n. 30, *supra*), p. 45

43. *Foreign Relations of the United States, Diplomatic Papers: The Conference of Berlin, 1945* (Washington, 1960), vol. I, pp. 253, 256–7 (Documents 223 & 224, Briefing Book papers of 4 July 1945, Summaries and Recommendations); Jan Christian Smuts, *Thoughts on a New World* (Empire Parliamentary Association, London, 1943); Hansard, House of Commons, 5th Series, vol. 403, vols. 704–6

44. Alan Bullock, *The Life and Times of Ernest Bevin* vol. I (London, 1960), pp. 360–1, 371, 387–8, 633; *Milwaukee Leader*, 6 November 1926. In the first quotation above 'an ability' is interpolated: Bullock, *op. cit.*, p. 387, quoting the T.U.C. *Report*, reads 'a mobility', which seems likely to have been a mis-hearing or an error of transcription by the T.U.C. secretariat

45. Bullock, *op. cit.* (n. 44, *supra*), pp. 440–2; F. S. Northedge, *British Foreign Policy: The Process of Readjustment 1945–1961* (London, 1962), pp. 13–32; *Foreign Relations of the United States, Diplomatic Papers: The Conference of Berlin, 1945* (Washington, 1960), vol. I, p. 258 (Memorandum of 28 June 1945); Hansard, House of Commons, 5th Series, vol. 416, cols. 759–846; vol. 427, cols. 1487–1623; vol. 446, cols. 383–622; vol. 450, colls. 1105–

1222; vol. 456, cols. 89–107; Mayne, *op. cit.* (n. 26, *supra*), pp. 132–7; private information

46. Diebold, *op. cit.* (n. 18, *supra*), pp. 40–1, 64–70; Colebrook, *loc. cit.* (n. 27, *supra*), O.E.E.C., *Memorandum by the Chancellor of the Exchequer, Consultative Group of Ministers*, CGM(49)16 Annexe I, Paris, 1 June 1949; O.E.E.C., *Memorandum by the French Minister of Finance and Economic Affairs*, Consultative Group of Ministers, CGM(49)16, Annexe II, Paris, 2 June 1949; O.E.E.C., *Present Positions on the Principles of the Payments Scheme for the 1949–50 Financial Year*, CGM(49)16, 27 June 1949; O.E.E.C., *54th Council Meeting* (Ministerial Level), C/M(49)11, 29 June to 1 July 1949

CHAPTER 7. THE AGE OF ANXIETY

1. *The French Revolution* (London, 1837), vol. III, p. 112
2. *Under Western Eyes* (9th Edition, London, 1924), p. 8
3. *Diplomacy* (2nd edition, Oxford, 1950), p. 140
4. Kenneth Ingram, *History of the Cold War* (London, 1955), pp. 20–1; David Horowitz, *From Yalta to Vietnam* (Penguin edition, 1967, of *The Free World Colossus*, London, 1965), p. 74; Anton Zischka, *The Other Europeans* (English translation by Brian Battershaw, London, 1962, of *Auch Das ist Europa*, Gütersloh, 1960), p. 243
5. Louis J. Halle, *The Cold War as History* (London, 1967), p. 151; Frederick L. Schuman, *Russia Since 1917* (New York, 1957), pp. 362–3
6. Sidney Lowery, 'Poland' in A. & V. M. Toynbee (ed.), *The Realignment of Europe* (London, 1955), pp. 126–245 (pp. 216–17); *Ibid.*, 'Hungary', in A. & V. M. Toynbee, *op. cit.*, pp. 317–32 (p. 324); Hugh Seton-Watson, 'Yugoslavia', in A. & V. M. Toynbee, *op. cit.*, pp. 352–71 (pp. 363–4, 369); *Ibid.*, 'Albania', in A. & V. M. Toynbee, *op. cit.*, pp. 371–6 (pp. 374–5); Elisabeth Wiskemann, 'Czechoslovakia: Spring 1945 to the Signing of the Peace Treaties, February 1947', in A. & V. M. Toynbee, *op. cit.*, pp. 376–88 (p. 387); Milovan Djilas, *Conversations with Stalin* (transl. from the Serbo-Croat by Michael B. Petrovich, Penguin edition, London, 1963), p. 100
7. Ghita Ionescu, *The Break-up of the Soviet Empire in Eastern Europe* (London, 1965), pp. 29–31; Hugh Seton-Watson, *The East European Revolution* (London, 1950), p. 314; *Ibid.*, 'Yugoslavia', in A. & V. M. Toynbee, *op. cit.* (n. 6, *supra*), pp. 352–71 (pp. 365–7); Djilas, *op. cit.* (n. 6, *supra*), pp. 136–7 (10 February 1948)
8. Cf. Chapter III, pp. 47–8, *supra*; Sidney Lowery, 'Poland', in A. & V. M. Toynbee, *op. cit.* (n. 6, *supra*), pp. 126–245 (pp. 194–242); R. E. Sherwood, *Roosevelt and Hopkins: An Intimate History* (New York, 1948), pp. 887–912; Stanislaw Mikolajczyk, *The Pattern of Soviet Domination* (London, 1948), pp. 147–9, 180–212; Seton-Watson, *op. cit.* (n. 7, *supra*), pp. 171–9; R. C. Mowat, *Ruin and Resurgence, 1939–1965* (London, 1966). pp. 162–4

9. Sidney Lowery, 'Bulgaria', in A. & V. M. Toynbee, *op. cit.* (n. 6, *supra*), pp. 301–17; Zischka, *op. cit.* (n. 4, *supra*), p. 120; Mowat, *op. cit.* (n. 8, *supra*), pp. 164–5; Seton-Watson, *op. cit.* (n. 7, *supra*), pp. 211–19; *Ibid.*, *Nationalism and Communism* (London, 1964), pp. 93–7; U.S. Military Intelligence, *The Communist Bloc in Europe* (H.Q., U.S. Army Europe, 10 March 1959), pp. 292–3

10. Sidney Lowery, 'Rumania', in A. & V. M. Toynbee, *op. cit.* (n. 6, *supra*), pp. 285–301; D. F. Fleming, *The Cold War and its Origins 1917–1960* (London, 1961), vol. 1, p. 208; A. Cretzianu (ed.), *Captive Rumania* (New York, 1956), pp. 51, 56; Mowat, *op. cit.* (n. 8, *supra*), pp. 168–71; James F. Byrnes, *Speaking Frankly* (London, 1947), pp. 50–2; Zischka, *op. cit.* (n. 4, *supra*), p. 142; Seton-Watson, *Nationalism and Communism* (n. 9, *supra*), p. 98

11. Sidney Lowery, 'Hungary', in A. & V. M. Toynbee, *op. cit.* (n. 6, *supra*), pp. 317–32; Ferenc Nagy, *The Struggle Behind the Iron Curtain* (London, 1948), pp. 52, 101, 112, 145–51, 159–64, 311–70; P. E. Zinner, *Revolution in Hungary* (New York, 1962), pp. 33, 37; Zischka, *op. cit.* (n. 4, *supra*), p. 186; U.S. Military Intelligence, *op. cit.* (n. 9, *supra*), pp. 261–3; Mowat, *op. cit.* (n. 8, *supra*), pp. 165–8; Seton-Watson, *op. cit.* (n. 10, *supra*), pp. 146–53

12. Sidney Lowery, 'Finland', in A. & V. M. Toynbee, *op. cit.* (n. 6, *supra*), pp. 261–85 (pp. 277–84); Isaac Deutscher, *Stalin: A Political Biography* (revised Pelican edition, London, 1966), pp. 187, 435; Howard K. Smith, *The State of Europe* (London, 1950), pp. 363–7

13. Hugh Seton-Watson, 'Albania', in A. & V. M. Toynbee, *op. cit.* (n. 6, *supra*), pp. 371–6; Zischka, *op. cit.* (n. 4, *supra*), p. 89

14. Hugh Seton-Watson, 'Yugoslavia', in A. & V. M. Toynbee, *op. cit.* (n. 6, *supra*), pp. 352–71; Mowat, *op. cit.* (n. 8, *supra*), pp. 275–8; Djilas, *op. cit.* (n. 6, *supra*), p. 90

15. Wiskemann, *op. cit.* (n. 6, *supra*), pp. 376–7; Mowat, *op. cit.* (n. 8, *supra*), p. 178; Hubert Ripka, *Czechoslovakia Enslaved* (London, 1950), p. 38; Dwight D. Eisenhower, *Crusade in Europe* (Dolphin edition, New York, 1961), p. 442

16. Wiskemann, *op. cit.* (n. 6, *supra*), pp. 377–8; P. E. Zinner, *Communist Strategy and Tactics in Czechoslovakia 1914–48* (London, 1963), pp. 118–19, 174; W. Jaksch, *Europe's Road to Potsdam* (London, 1963), pp. 429ff; Mowat, *op. cit.* (n. 8, *supra*), p. 179

17. Wiskemann, *op. cit.* (n. 6, *supra*), pp. 380–7; Hubert Ripka, *Eastern Europe in the Post-War World* (London, 1961), p. 73; Jaksch, *op. cit.* (n. 16, *supra*), p. 434; Mowat, *op. cit.* (n. 8, *supra*), pp. 180–1; Zinner, *op. cit.* (n, 16, *supra*), pp. 124, 156

18. Mowat, *op. cit.* (n. 8, *supra*), pp. 182–3; Celia Phelps, 'The Death of Jan Masaryk: An Interview with his Private Secretary', in R. Macdonald & M. West (ed.), *Eurovista '69* (St Andrews, 1969), pp. 11–12; Howard K. Smith, *The State of Europe* (London, 1950), pp. 334–47; André Fontaine, *Histoire de la guerre froide*, vol. 1 (Paris, 1965), pp. 399–403

19. Peter Novick, *The Resistance Versus Vichy* (London, 1968), pp. 72–6; John Steward Ambler, *The French Army in Politics 1945–1962* (Columbus, Ohio, 1966), pp. 79–81; M. R. D. Foot, *SOE in France* (London, 1966), pp. 444–5; Crane Brinton, *The Americans and the French* (Cambridge, Mass., 1968), p. 91; Viscount Chilston, 'Western Europe', in A. & V. M. Toynbee, *op. cit.* (n. 6, *supra*, pp. 523–53) (pp. 540, 542); Katharine Duff, 'Italy', in A. & V. M. Toynbee, *op. cit.* (n. 6, *supra*), pp. 409–53 (pp. 427, 432); Norman Kogan, *A Political History of Postwar Italy* (London, 1966), p. 10; Royal Institute of International Affairs, *The Soviet–Yugoslav Dispute* (London, 1948), p. 51; Ripka, *op. cit.* (n. 17, *supra*), p. 68 (Soviet letter of 4 May 1948 to Central Committee of Jugoslav Communist Party)

20. Chilston, *op. cit.* (n. 19, *supra*), pp. 513 n. 1, 520, 539, 545, 548 & n. 1; *L'Année politique 1946* (Paris, 1947), pp. 11–12, 145, 158, 285; Duff, *op. cit.* (n. 19, *supra*), pp. 426, 429; W. Hilton-Young, *The Italian Left* (London, 1949), pp. 184–5, 187, 189; Maxime Mourin, *Histoire des Nations Européennes*, vol. III (Paris, 1963), pp. 115–17; *L'Année politique 1944–1945* (Paris, 1946), pp. 5, 352; *L'Année politique 1947* (Paris, 1948), pp. 7–8; Piergiovanni Permoli, *La Costituente e i Partiti Politici Italiani* (Rocca San Casciano, 1966), pp. 85–91, 114–23; Federico Chabod, *L'Italia Contemporanea (1918–1948)* (9th edition, Turin, 1965), pp. 143, 161–2

21. Sergio Bologna et al. (ed.), *Fascismo e antifascismo: Lezioni e testimonianze* (Milan, 1962), vol. II, *1936–1948*, p. 645 (transl. R.M.)

22. Mourin, *op. cit.* (n. 20, *supra*), pp. 116–17; Chilston, *op. cit.* (n. 19, *supra*), p. 551; *L'Année politique 1947* (Paris, 1948), pp. 39–43, 65–6, 91–3; Hilton-Young, *op. cit.* (n. 20, *supra*), pp. 191–4; Kogan, *op. cit.* (n. 19, *supra*), 47–53; H. Stuart Hughes, *The United States and Italy* (Cambridge, Mass., 1953), pp. 155–9; Chabod, *op. cit.* (n. 20, *supra*), pp. 161–9; personal knowledge

23. J. V. Stalin, *Problems of Leninism* (11th edition, Moscow, 1940), pp. 3, 52, 79, 156–7, 657

24. John Foster Dulles, *War or Peace* (New York, 1950), pp. 12–13

25. *Ibid.*, p. 175; F. W. Mulley, *The Politics of Western Defence* (London, 1962), pp. 32–46

26. Harry S. Truman, *Memoirs*, vol. II, *1946–1952: Years of Trial and Hope* (Signet edition, New York, 1965), p. 280; Ernst H. van der Beugel, *From Marshall Aid to Atlantic Partnership* (Amsterdam/London/New York, 1966), pp. 121–2; Paul Stehlin, *Retour à zéro* (Paris, 1968), pp. 47–9; *L'Année politique 1948* (Paris, 1949), pp. 14–15, 33–4, 44–6, 381–2 (Text of Brussels Treaty); personal knowledge

27. Cf. Heinrich von Brentano, *Speech on denazification*, July 4, 1947, reprinted in *Ibid.*, *Deutschland, Europa und die Welt*, transl. by Edward Fitzgerald as *Germany and Europe: Reflections on German Foreign Policy* (London, 1964), pp. 19–29 (p. 22); Hermann Eich, *The Unloved Germans*, transl. by Michael Glenny (London, 1965); Gudrun Tempel, *Deutschland? Aber Wo Liegt Es?*, transl. by Sophie Wilkins as *Speaking Frankly About*

the Germans (London, 1963); Hans Herzfeld, 'The Splitting of Berlin in 1948', in Charles B. Robson (transl. & ed.), Berlin – Pivot of German Destiny (Chapel Hill, North Carolina, 1960), pp. 47–66 (p. 52); personal knowledge

28. Siegfried Kracauer, From Caligari to Hitler: a Psychological History of the German Film (Princeton, 1947), pp. v, 11

29. Cf. Rolf Dahrendorf, Gesellschaft und Demokratie in Deutschland (Munich, 1965), passim; Enzo Bettiza, L'Altra Germania (Milan, 1968), pp. 20–1

30. Potsdam final communiqué, paras. III A 1, III B 14; Ernst Deuerlein (ed.), Potsdam 1945 (Munich, 1963),pp. 350, 357

31. Eugene Davidson, The Death and Life of Germany (London, 1959), pp. 70–1, 74, 76, 132–3, 140, 179; German Federal Government, Germany Reports (Wiesbaden, 1953), p. 70; Thilo Vogelsang, Das geteilte Deutschland (Munich, 1966), pp. 53–6; Wolfgang Leonhard, Die Revolution entlässt ihre Kinder (Cologne/Berlin, 1955), p. 448; Michael Balfour, 'Germany', in A. Toynbee (ed.), Four-Power Control in Germany and Austria 1945–1946 (London, 1956), pp. 3–265 (pp. 205–7, 239–40); Gordon Schaffer, Russian Zone, (London, 1947), p. 72

32. Davidson, op. cit. (n. 31, supra), p. 141 and n. 2; Lucius D. Clay, Decision in Germany (London, 1950), pp. 88–91; Richard Lukas, Zehn Jahre Sowjetische Besatzungszone Deutschlands (Mainz/Wiesbaden/Düsseldorf, 1955), p. 17; William Henry Chamberlin, The German Phoenix (London, 1964), p. 126; German Federal Government, op. cit. (n. 31, supra), p. 71; Richard Hiscocks, 'Divided Germany', in Edgar McInnis (ed.), The Shaping of Postwar Germany (London/Toronto, 1960), pp. 57–89 (p. 69); Balfour, op. cit (n. 30, supra), pp. 208–9

33. Cf. pp. 78–9, supra; Clay, op. cit. (n. 32, supra), pp. 78, 121; Byrnes, op. cit. (n. 10, supra), pp. 195–7; Elmer Plischke, Contemporary Government of Germany (London, 1964), p. 18

34. Clay, op. cit. (n. 32, supra), p. 174; Plischke, op. cit. (n. 33, supra), p. 183; German Federal Government, op. cit. (n. 31, supra), p. 71

35. L'Année politique 1948 (Paris, 1949), pp. 31–2, 46–7; Clay, op. cit. (n. 32, supra), pp. 180–1

36. L'Année politique 1948 (Paris, 1949), p. 47; Alfred Grosser, La République Fédérale d'Allemagne (Paris, 1963), p. 15; Plischke, op. cit. (n. 33, supra), p. 184; Clay, op. cit. (n. 32, supra), pp. 355–6; Wolfgang Heidelmeyer & Guenter Hindrichs (ed.), Documents on Berlin 1943–1963 (Second ed., revised, Munich, 1963), pp. 55–6

37. L'Année politique 1948 (Paris, 1949), pp. 107–9, 400–3; Davidson, op. cit. (n. 31, supra), pp. 223–4; Ludwig Erhard, Wohlstand für Alle, transl. by E. T. Roberts & J. B. Wood as Prosperity Through Competition (London, 2nd ed., 1959), pp. 13–14; Grosser, op. cit. (n. 36, supra), p. 69; personal knowledge

38. Clay, op. cit. (n. 32, supra), pp. 63, 208–9

39. William H. Conland, Berlin: Beset and Bedevilled (New York, 1963), pp. 239–41; Clay, op. cit. (n. 32, supra), pp. 358–62

40. Clay, *op. cit.* (n. 32, *supra*), pp. 365–6, 376, 381–2, 386; Truman, *op. cit.* (n. 26, *supra*), pp. 149–53

41. Truman, *op. cit.* (n. 26, *supra*), pp. 278–9, 281–8; North Atlantic Treaty, Article 5; Paul-Henri Spaak, *Combats Inachevés*, vol. 1 (Paris, 1969), p. 263

42. Plischke, *op. cit.* (n. 33, *supra*), p. 23 & n. 7

43. German Federal Government, *op. cit.* (n. 31, *supra*), p. 72; Plischke, *op. cit.* (n. 33, *supra*), p. 185

44. Plischke, *op. cit.* (n. 33, *supra*), pp. 23–5

45. Plischke, *op. cit.* (n. 33, *supra*), pp. 185–6

46. German Federal Government, *op. cit.* (n. 31, *supra*), p. 112

CHAPTER 8. EUROPE AND THE ISLANDS

1. *The Dog Beneath the Skin* (with Christopher Isherwood, London, 1935), p. 11

2. *The Hot Gates* (Pocket Books edition, New York, 1967), p. 37

3. *The Texts*, Book XXVI

4. Verbatim note of a discussion at Chatham House, February 1939, quoted by Alan Bullock, *The Life and Times of Ernest Bevin*, vol. 1 (London, 1960), pp. 631–2

5. Fritz Nova, *Contemporary European Governments* (Baltimore/Dublin, 1963), p. 603

6. *Constitution of the Fourth Republic*, in Philip M. Williams, *Crisis and Compromise: Politics in the Fourth Republic* (London, 1964), pp. 478–92 (p. 479); *Costituzione della Repubblica Italiana*, in Senato della Repubblica/Camera dei Deputati, *Manuale Parlamentare, Legislatura IV* (Rome, 1964), pp. 13–54 (p. 16) (transl. R.M.)

7. R. Mayne, *The Community of Europe* (London, 1962; New York, 1963), pp. 29–52, 68–9, 78–80; Denys Hay, *Europe: the Emergence of an Idea* (Edinburgh, 1957); Federico Chabod, *Storia dell'idea dell'Europa* (Universale ed., Bari, 1967); Achille Albonetti, *Préhistoire des Etats-Unis d'Europe* (Paris, 1963); Bernard Voyenne, *Petite histoire de l'idée européene* (Paris, 1965); J.-B. Duroselle, *L'Idée européene dans l'Histoire* (Paris, 1965); Hendrik Brugmans, *L'Idée européene 1918–1965* (Bruges, 1965); Lord Gladwyn, *The European Idea* (London, 1966); Altiero Spinelli, 'European Union in the Resistance', in *Government & Opposition*, vol. II, No. 3 (April–July, 1967), pp. 321–9; Denis de Rougement, 'The Campaign of the European Congresses', *Ibid.*, pp. 329–49

8. *L'Année politique 1948* (Paris, 1949), p. 126; *Le Monde*, 22 July 1948, p. 2; private information; Royal Institute of International Affairs, *Survey of International Affairs, 1947–1948*, pp. 143–4; European Movement, *The European Movement and the Council of Europe* (London, 1949), p. 52; private information

9. Private information

10. *L'Année politique 1948* (Paris, 1949), pp. 217, 236; Royal Institute of International Affairs, *op. cit.* (n. 8, *supra*), p. 145; *Ibid, Survey of International Affairs 1949–1950*, p. 169; private information

11. Private information; Royal Institute of International Affairs, *op. cit.* (n. 10, *supra*), p. 170; European Movement, *op. cit.* (n. 8, *supra*), pp. 61–2

12. Mayne, *op. cit.* (n. 7, *supra*); personal knowledge; Paul-Henri Spaak, *Combats Inachevés*, vol. II, (Paris, 1969), pp. 28, 51

13. Mayne, *op. cit.* (n. 7, *supra*), pp. 81–4

14. Merry & Serge Bromberger, *Les Coulisses de l'Europe* (Paris, 1968), pp. 9–12; 'Then Will It Live...', *Time*, vol. LXXVIII, No. 14 6 October 1961), pp. 20–7 (p. 23); R. Mayne, 'The Role of Jean Monnet', *Government and Opposition*, vol. II, No. 3 (April-July, 1967), pp. 349–71 (pp. 352–3); *Ibid.*, 'Jean Monnet – Portrait of a European', *The Listener*, vol. LXXX, No. 2072 (12 December 1968), pp. 787–9 (p. 787)

15. Bromberger, *op. cit.* (n. 14, *supra*), pp. 14–20; *Time, loc. cit.* (n. 14, *supra*), Mayne, *locc. citt.* (n. 14, *supra*)

16. Personal knowledge; Mayne, *locc. citt.* (n. 14, *supra*); John Davenport, 'M Jean Monnet of Cognac', *Fortune*, vol. XXX, No. 2 (August, 1944), pp. 121–126; Bromberger, *op. cit.* (n. 14, *supra*), pp. 20–1; Time, *loc. cit.* (n. 14, *supra*)

17. Bromberger, *op. cit.* (n. 14, *supra*), pp. 21–6; *Time, loc. cit.*; Mayne, *locc. citt.*; private information; personal knowledge

18. Private information; John M. Haight, 'France, the United States, and the Munich Crisis', *Journal of Modern History*, vol. XXXII, No. 1 (December 1960), pp. 340–58; *Ibid.*, 'Roosevelt and the Aftermath of the Quarantine Speech', *Review of Politics*, vol. XXIV, No. 2 (April 1962), pp. 233–59; *Ibid.*, 'Les Négociations françaises pour la fourniture d'avions américains (I), *Forces Aériennes Françaises*, No. 198 (December, 1963), pp. 807–39; *Ibid.*, 'France's First War Mission to the United States', *The Airpower Historian*, vol. XI, No. 1 (January 1964), pp. 11–15; *Ibid.*, 'Les Négociations relatives aux achats d'avions américains par la France pendant la période qui précéda immédiatement la guerre', *La Revue de l'Histoire de la 2e Guerre Mondiale*, No. 58 (April 1965), pp. 1–34; *Ibid.*, 'Jean Monnet and the Opening of the American Arsenal', paper to the Franco-American Historical Colloquium, September 1964; *The Times* (London), 28 November 1939; W. K. Hancock & M. M. Gowing, *British War Economy* (London, 1949), pp. 192 n. 1, 195

19. Private information; Max Beloff, 'The Anglo-French Union Project of June 1940', *Mélanges Pierre Renouvin* (Paris, 1966), pp. 199–219; Winston Churchill, *The Second World War* (Cassell paperback edition, London, 1964), vol. III, pp. 183–7; Charles de Gaulle, *Mémoires de Guerre* (Livre de poche edition, Paris, 1959), vol. I, pp. 80–7; J.-R. Tournoux, *Secrets d'Etats*, vol. II : *Pétain et de Gaulle* (Paris, 1964), pp. 426–41; Davenport, *loc. cit.* (n. 16, *supra*)

20. *Time, loc. cit.* (n. 14, *supra*); Mayne, *locc. citt.* (n. 14, *supra*); Bromberger, *op. cit.* (n. 14, *supra*), pp. 37–66; Robert Murphy, *Diplomat Among*

Warriors (London, 1964), pp. 223–8; Harold Macmillan, *The Blast of War 1939–1945* (London, 1967), pp. 297–8, 300, 312, 317–19, 321, 328–31; Georgette Elgey, *La République des Illusions* (Paris, 1965), pp. 413–34

21. Private information; personal knowledge; Elgey, *loc. cit.* (n. 20, *supra*); Bromberger, *op. cit.* (n. 14, *supra*), pp. 14, 26
22. Personal knowledge; Mayne, *op. cit.* (n. 7, *supra*), pp. 90–1
23. Davenport, *loc. cit.* (n. 16, *supra*)
24. Private information
25. *L'Année politique 1947* (Paris, 1948), pp. 31, 351; Agence France Presse dispatch 30 April 1947
26. *L'Année politique 1948* (Paris, 1949), pp. 12–14, 67, 87, 196–7, 236; *L'Année politique 1949* (Paris, 1950), pp. 456–7; Bromberger, *op. cit.* (n. 14, *supra*), pp. 96–7; Elgey, *op. cit.* (n. 20, *supra*), pp. 439–40; Etienne Hirsch, 'L'Angleterre fera-t-elle antichambre?', *Les Calviers de la République*, No. 51 (January, 1963), pp. 9–16
27. Private information; personal knowledge
28. Private information; Bromberger, *loc. cit.* (n. 14, *supra*), Elgey, *loc. cit.* (n. 20, *supra*), *L'Année politique 1949* (Paris, 1950), pp. 160–1; Hirsch, *loc. cit.* (n. 26, *supra*)
29. *L'Année politique 1949* (Paris, 1950). p. 167; Don Cook, *Floodtide in Europe* (New York, 1965), pp. 110–12; *L'Année politique 1950* (Paris, 1951), p. 93; Mayne, 'The Role of Jean Monnet' (n. 14, *supra*), p. 356
30. Private information; Pierre Gerbet, 'La Genèse du Plan Schuman', *Revue Française de Science Politique*, vol. VI, No. 3 (Paris, 1956), pp. 525–53 (p. 544); Elgey, *op. cit.* (n. 20, *supra*), p. 445; Bromberger, *op. cit.* (n. 14, *supra*), p. 119
31. Quotations from the Schuman Declaration of 9 May 1950, based on Monnet's drafts; text in *L'Année politique 1950* (Paris, 1951), pp. 306–7 (transl. R.M.)
32. Mayne, *op. cit.* (n. 7, *supra*), pp. 43, 90–1; Bromberger, *op. cit.* (n. 14, *supra*), pp. 116–19; Fritz Stern, 'Adenauer and a Crisis in Weimar Democracy', *Political Science Quarterly* (March 1958), p. 22, n. 55; William Diebold, Jr., *The Schuman Plan* (New York, 1959), pp. 25–6, 35–6; Konrad Adenauer, *Erinnerungen 1945–1953* (Stuttgart, 1965), pp. 41, 303, 311–16; Regierung des Landes Nordrhein-Westfalen *et al.*, *Das Abkommen über die Errichtung einer Internazionalen Ruhrbehörde* (Düsseldorf, 1949), p. 5; *L'Année politique 1950* (Paris, 1951), pp. 63, 93–4
33. *Ibid.*, pp. 93–4 Bromberger, *op. cit.* (n. 14, *supra*), pp. 114–15
34. Personal knowledge; Bromberger, *op. cit.* (n. 14, *supra*), pp. 103–4, 121–2; Elgey, *op. cit.* (n. 20, *supra*), p. 445–6
35. Jean Monnet, *Allocution à Scy-Chazelles le 3 octobre 1965* (mimeographed, Paris, 1965); Robert Schuman, *Pour l'Europe* (Paris, 1963), p. 207
36. Bromberger, *op. cit.* (n. 14, *supra*), pp. 121–3 (but with dates confused); Elgey, *op. cit.* (n. 20, *supra*), pp. 445–7; Mayne, *op. cit.* (n. 7, *supra*), pp. 85–91; private information

37. François Fontaine, *La Nation frein* (Paris, 1965), pp. 99–101; Bromberger, *loc. cit.* (n. 36, *supra*); Elgey, *loc. cit.* (n. 36, *supra*); Cook, *op. cit.* (n. 29, *supra*), pp. 124–5; private information

38. Dean Acheson, *Sketches from Life* (New York, 1961), pp. 35–9; *Ibid., Present at the Creation* (London, 1970), pp. 382–6

39. Ulrich Sahm, 'Grossbritanniens Haltung zum Schuman-Plan', in Walter Hallstein and Hans-Jürgen Schlochauer (edd.), *Zur Integration Europas: Festschrift für Carl Friedrich Ophüls* (Karlsruhe, 1965), pp. 153–65; transl. as 'Britain and Europe, 1950', in *International Affairs*, vol. XLIII, No. 1 (London, January, 1967), pp. 12–24, with a comment by Kenneth Younger, *Ibid.*, pp. 24–8 (pp. 24, 26); *Keesing's Contemporary Archives*, 1950 p. 10705

40. Gilles Anouil, *La Grande-Bretagne et la Communauté Européenne du Charbon et de l'Acier* (Issoudun, 1960), pp. 45–7; *Anglo-French Discussions regarding French proposals for the Western European Coal, Iron and Steel Industries, May-June, 1950* (H.M.S.O. Cm. 7970), p. 5; *The Times* (London), 12 May 1950

41. Cmd. 7970 (Cf. n. 40, *supra*), p. 6; private information

42. Cmd. 7970 (Cf. n. 40, *supra*), p. 6; *Hansard*, vol. 475, col. 587 (1950)

43. Raymond Racine, *Vers une Europe nouvelle par le Plan Schuman* (Neuchâtel, 1954), pp. 62ff; Hirsch, *op. cit.* (n. 26, *supra*), p. 10; private information

44. Cmd. 7970 (Cf. n. 40, *supra*), p. 6; Jean Monnet, *Interview with German television* (typescript, Paris, 21 July 1965), pp. 2–3; private information; Adenauer, *op. cit.* (n. 32, *supra*), pp. 336–7

45. Private information; Cmd. 7970 (Cf. n. 40, *supra*), pp. 7–9, translation corrected from original version in *La Documentation Française*, No. 1339 (13 June 1950), pp. 4–5

46. Cmd. 7970 (Cf. n. 40, *supra*), pp. 6–7

47. *Agence France Presse* dispatch of 25 May 1950; Cmd. 7970, p. 8

48. Cmd. 7970 (Cf. n. 40, *supra*), p. 9; Younger in *International Affairs*, *loc. cit.* (n. 40, *supra*), p. 27

49. Private information; Cmd. 7970 (Cf. n. 40, *supra*), pp. 9–11, translation and punctuation corrected from original version in *La Documentation Française*, *loc. cit.* (n. 45, *supra*), pp. 5–6

50. *Note verbale de l'Ambassadeur des Pays-Bas*, 31 May 1950; cf. Mayne, *op. cit.* (n. 14, *supra*), pp. 359–60

51. Cmd. 7970 (Cf. n. 40, *supra*), pp. 11–12

52. Elgey, *op. cit.* (n. 20, *supra*), pp. 448–9 (transl. R.M.)

53. Cmd. 7970 (Cf. n. 40, *supra*), p. 12

54. Cmd. 7970 (Cf. n. 40, *supra*), pp. 13–14

55. *Ibid.*, pp. 14–15, translation corrected from *La Documentation Française*, *loc. cit.* (n. 45, *supra*), p. 8

CHAPTER 9. THE ECHTERNACH DANCE

1. *Absalom and Achitophel* (London, 1681), lines 799–800
2. Motto to Ludwig Wittgenstein, *Philosophical Investigations* (Oxford, 1953) (transl. R. M.)
3. *The Making of the President 1960* (Cardinal edition, New York, 1961), p. 429
4. République Française, Ministère des Affaires Etrangères, *Rapport de la délégation française sur le Traité instituant la Communauté Européenes du Charbon et de l'Acier et la Convention relatives aux dispositions transitoires signés à Paris le 18 avril 1951* (Paris, October, 1951), pp. 11–12; Schuman, lecture at the College of Europe, Bruges, 1953
5. Max Kohnstamm, 'The European Tide', in Stephen R. Graubard (ed.), *A New Europe?* (Boston, 1964), pp. 140–73 (pp. 151–2)
6. André Fontaine, *Histoire de la guerre froide*, vol. II (Paris, 1967), pp. 13–22; *L'Année politique 1950* (Paris, 1951), pp. 144–5, 364 (Security Council resolution of 27 June 1950)
7. *L'Année politique 1950* (Paris, 1951), p. 145; Fontaine *op. cit.* (n. 6, *supra*), p. 14; Philip Mosely, *The Kremlin in World Politics* (Vintage Books edition, New York, 1960), p. 327; Barbara Ward, *Policy for the West* (New York, 1951), p. 101, n. 2; Georgette Elgey, *La République des Illusions* (Paris, 1965), p. 458; personal knowledge
8. *L'Année politique 1950* (Paris, 1951), p. 144; Fontaine, *op. cit.* (n. 6, *supra*), p. 19; Elgey, *op. cit.* (n. 7, *supra*), p. 460; Drew Middleton, *The Defense of Western Europe* (New York, 1952), pp. 76–7; Royal Institute of International Affairs, *Britain in Western Europe* (London, 1956), p. 25; Paul-Henri Spaak, *Combats Inachevés* (Paris, 1965), vol. I, p. 269
9. Ward, *op. cit.* (n. 7, *supra*), p. 101, n. 1; Fontaine, *op. cit.* (n. 6, *supra*), p. 47; Elgey, *op. cit.* (n. 7, *supra*), p. 461; Jacques Fauvet, *La IV ème République* (Paris, 1959), p. 168; Jules Moch, *Histoire du réarmement allemand depuis 1950* (Paris, 1965), pp. 46–7; Royal Institute of International Affairs, *op. cit.* (n. 8, *supra*), p. 26; Konrad Adenauer, *Erinnerungen 1945–1953* (Stuttgart, 1965), pp. 350–62
10. Fontaine, *loc. cit.* (n. 9, *supra*); Elgey, *op. cit.* (n. 7, *supra*), p. 462; 'Sirius' (Beuve-Méry) in *Le Monde* (Paris, 6 April 1948)
11. *The Plain Dealer* (Cleveland, Ohio, 3 December 1949); Adenauer, *op. cit.* (n. 9, *supra*), pp. 341–9; Pierre Billotte, *Le Temps du choix* (Paris, 1950), *passim*; Richard Mayne, *The Community of Europe* (London, 1962; New York, 1963), p. 101; Arthur Koestler, *The Trail of the Dinosaur* (London, 1955), pp. 204–14
12. Private information
13. Moch, *op. cit* (n. 11, *supra*), pp. 60–139; Elgey, *op. cit.* (n. 7, *supra*), pp. 461–3
14. Private information; Elgey, *op. cit.* (n. 7, *supra*), p. 462; Merry and Serge Bromberger, *Les Coulisses de l'Europe* (Paris, 1968), pp. 132–8

15. Présidence du Conseil, Secrétariat-Général du Gouvernement, *L'Organisation de l'Europe Occidentale (1948–1955)*, (Paris, 19 July 1955), p. 45
16. *Ibid.*; Paul Stehlin, *Retour à Zero* (Paris, 1968), pp. 83–4
17. Présidence du Conseil, *op. cit.* (n. 15, *supra*), pp. 45–6, 48–56, 61–5; Mayne, *op. cit.* (n. 11, *supra*), pp. 102–3; *Ibid., The Institutions of the European Community* (London, 1968), p. 11
18. Mayne, *op. cit.* (n. 11, *supra*), p. 103; Présidence du Conseil, *op. cit.* (n. 15, *supra*), p. 63
19. *Ibid.*, p. 46
20. Personal knowledge; Mayne, *op. cit.* (n. 11, *supra*), p. 104; *Ibid.*, 'Castellammare and E.D.C.', *New Statesman* (London, 14 April 1954); Daniel Lerner & Raymond Aron (edd.), *France Defeats EDC* (New York, 1957), *passim*

    Cf. Chapter VIII, *supra*; *Hansard*, House of Commons, 1950, vol. 472, col. 320; Ulrich Sahm, 'Grossbritanniens Haltung zum Schuman-Plan', in Walter Hallstein & Hans-Jürgen Schlochauer (edd.), *Zur Integration Europas: Festschrift für Carl Friedrich Ophüls* (Karlsruhe, 1965), pp. 153–65 (p. 158), transl. as 'Britain and Europe, 1950', in *International Affairs*, vol. XLIII, No. 1 (London, January 1967), pp. 12–24 (p. 17); Churchill, speech in the House of Commons, 27 June 1950; *L'Année politique 1950* (Paris, 1951), p. 140; Hugh Dalton, *High Tide and After: Memoirs 1945–1960* (London, 1962), p. 334; National Executive Committee of the British Labour Party, *European Unity* (London, May 1950), p. 8
22. R. C. Mowat, *Ruin and Resurgence 1939–1965* (London, 1966), p. 227; *L'Année politique 1950* (Paris, 1951), pp. 140–1; official minutes of the Schuman Plan Conference, unpublished
23. Sahm, *op. cit.* (n. 21, *supra*), pp. 161–2 (original), 20–21 (translation); *Anglo-French Discussions regarding French proposals for the Western European Coal, Iron and Steel Industries, May-June, 1950* (H.M.S.O., Cmd. 7970), p. 15; *Europa-Archiv*, 1950, p. 3173; *Hansard*, House of Commons, 1950, vol. 476 (15 June, 1950), cols. 551, 554; Gilles Anouil, *La Grande-Bretagne et la Communauté Européenne du Charbon et de l'Acier* (Issoudun, 1960), pp. 91–2; Raymond Racine, *Vers une Europe Nouvelle par le Plan Schuman* (Neuchâtel, 1954), p. 66; A.F.P. dispatch of 4.00 p.m., 5 June 1950; *Le Monde* (Paris, 7 & 20 June 1950); private information
24. Cf. Chapter VI, *supra*; Anthony Sampson, *Macmillan: A Study in Ambiguity* (Pelican edition, London, 1968), pp. 90–92; Harold Macmillan, *Tides of Fortune 1945–1955* (London, 1969), pp. 193–5, 204; Council of Europe, *Documents de Séance*, 1950, pp. 719–24; Anouil, *op. cit.* (n. 8, *supra*), pp. 93–5; Nora Beloff, *The General Says No* (London, 1963), pp. 58–9
25. Sampson, *loc. cit.* (n. 24, *supra*); Beloff, *op. cit.* (n. 24, *supra*), pp. 59–60
26. Anouil, *loc. cit.* (n. 23, *supra*); Racine, *loc. cit.* (n. 23, *supra*); *Le Monde* (Paris, 27 July 1950)
27. Council of Europe, Consultative Assembly, 2nd Session, *Reports*, Part I, p. 136; *Hansard*, House of Commons, 1950, vol. 476 (7 November 1950); A.F.P. dispatch, 1 May 1951; private information

28. H. J. Heiser, *British Policy with regard to the unification efforts on the European Continent* (Leyden, 1959), p. 41; the Rt Hon. Sir Anthony Eden, K.G., P.C., M.C., *Memoirs: Full Circle* (London, 1960), pp. 31–2; *The Times* (London 14 July 1950), editorial

29. Associated Press dispatch from London, 23 November 1951; R. S. Churchill (ed.), *The Sinews of Peace: Postwar Speeches by Winston S. Churchill* (London, 1948), p. 199; Eden, *op. cit.* (n. 28, *supra*), pp. 30, 32–3, 36; Council of Europe, Consultative Assembly, *Official Report*, 3rd Session, 1951, pp. 513–14; Mayne, *op. cit.* (n. 11, *supra*), pp. 79, 138

30. Eden, *op. cit.* (n. 28, *supra*), pp. 34–5, 37–8, 40–41

31. Eden, *op. cit.* (n. 28, *supra*), pp. 42–4

32. *Ibid.*

33. *Ibid.*, p. 44

34. Conseil de l'Europe, Assemblée Consultative, 4ème Session ordinaire, AS (4) 11 : *Demande d'avis du Comité des Ministres sur les meilleurs moyens de mettre en application les propositions du Royaume-Uni* (Strasbourg, 24 May 1952); Eden, *op. cit.* (n. 28, *supra*), pp. 47–8; Anthony Nutting, *Europe Will Not Wait* (London, 1960), p. 42

35. Nutting, *op. cit.* (n. 34, *supra*), p. 43

36. Nutting, *op. cit.* (n. 34, *supra*), pp. 42, 44

37. Council of Europe, *Documents*, 4th Session, Document 33, pp. 409–29; Anouil, *op. cit.* (n. 23, *supra*), pp. 115–17; Nutting, *op. cit.* (n. 34, *supra*), p. 46

38. Private information; personal knowledge

39. Personal knowledge

40. Anouil, *op. ct.* (n. 23, *supra*), p. 121; private information

41. *Le Monde* (Paris, 13 August 1952); Anouil, *op. cit.* (n. 23, *supra*), pp. 121–6; private information

42. Private information; High Authority Information Service, *Chronology of Association with the United Kingdom* (Luxembourg, 16 October 1954)

43. Private information; High Authority, *Correspondance concernant les relations entre la Communauté Européenne du Charbon et de l'Acier et le Royaume-Uni* (Luxembourg, 3 May 1954), pp. 1–5

44. *Hansard*, House of Commons, 1954, vol. 552, col. 190; British Iron and Steel Federation, *Monthly Statistical Bulletin* (London, March 1954); private information; High Authority, *loc. cit.* (n. 43, *supra*)

45. Private information; William Diebold, Jr., *The Schuman Plan* (New York, 1959), p. 641

46. Arnold J. Zurcher, *The Struggle to Unite Europe 1940–1958* (New York, 1958), pp. 114–18; *New York Times*, 4 March 1953; Nutting, *op. cit.* (n. 34, *supra*), pp. 47–8

47. *New York Times*, 15 December 1953; Nutting, *loc. cit.* (n. 46, *supra*)

48. Nutting, *op. cit.* (n. 34, *supra*), pp. 50, 55–6, 59–64

49. Mayne, *op. cit.* (n. 11, *supra*), pp. 104–5; *Ibid.*, 'Le Rouge et le Noir', *New Statesman* (London, 26 June 1954)

50. Pierre Rouanet, *Mendès-France au Pouvoir 1954–1955* (Paris, 1965), pp. 220–2; Spaak, *op. cit.* (n. 8, *supra*), pp. 276–7

51. Personal knowledge; private information

52. Spaak, *op. cit.* (n. 8, *supra*), p. 278; Pierre Mendès-France in *Le Figaro* (Paris, 17 February 1969)

53. Rouanet, *op. cit.* (n. 50, *supra*), pp. 224–31; Spaak, *op. cit.* (n. 8, *supra*), pp. 277–80

54. Mayne, *op. cit.* (n. 11, *supra*), pp. 104–5; Daniel Lerner and Raymond Aron (ed.), *France Defeats E.D.C.* (New York, 1957), p. 17; Rouanet, *op. cit.* (n. 50, *supra*), pp. 122–3, 231–40

55. Rouanet, *op. cit.* (n. 50, *supra*), pp. 248–54; Nutting, *op. cit.* (n. 34, *supra*), p. 67

56. Spaak, *op. cit.* (n. 8, *supra*), pp. 286–7; Rouanet, *op. cit.* (n. 50, *supra*), pp. 255–63

57. Spaak, *op. cit.* (n. 8, *supra*), pp. 287–90; Rouanet, *op. cit.* (n. 50, *supra*), pp. 263–75; Mendès-France, *loc. cit.* (n. 52, *supra*)

58. Spaak, *op. cit.* (n. 8, *supra*), pp. 290–5; Rouanet, *op. cit.* (n. 50, *supra*), pp. 265–75

59. Spaak, *op. cit.* (n. 8, *supra*), pp. 295–7; Rouanet, *op. cit.* (n. 50, *supra*), pp. 276–81; Mendès-France, *loc. cit.* (n. 52, *supra*); Nutting, *op. cit.* (n. 34, *supra*), p. 67

60. Spaak, *op. cit.* (n. 8, *supra*), pp. 297–9; Mayne, *op. cit.* (n. 11, *supra*), p. 105; Zurcher, *op. cit.* (n. 46, *supra*), p. 124

61. Eden, *op. cit.* (n. 28, *supra*), p. 151; *Documents agreed on by the Conference of Ministers held in Paris, 20-23 October 1954* (London, H.M.S.O., Cmd. 9304, November 1950)

62. Private information; Anouil, *op. cit.* (n. 23, *supra*), pp. 174, 184

63. *Bulletin from the European Coal and Steel Community*, vol. IV, No. 5 (London, November 1957), p. 4; High Authority, *Sixth General Report*, vol. I (Luxembourg, 1958), pp. 83–5; *Hansard*, House of Commons, 21 February 1955, col. 897

CHAPTER 10. NEVER SO GOOD

1. *La Crise de la conscience européenne* (*Idées* edition, Paris, 1968), vol. II, p. 295 (transl. R.M.)

2. *Maximes*, ed. F. C. Green (Cambridge, 1945), p. 60, No. 25 (transl. R.M.)

3. *English History 1914–1945* (Oxford, 1965), p. 425

4. *Statistiques des aéroports de l' Europe de l'Ouest* (Paris, annual), *passim*

5. J. Frederic Dewhurst and others, *Europe's Needs and Resources* (New York, 1961), pp. 36, 40, 50, 347–53; European Economic Community, Commission, *Report on the Economic Situation in the Countries of the Community* (Brussels, September 1958), pp. 23, 30; European Community Information Service, *The Community in Maps* (Brussels/Luxembourg, 1967), map 2

REFERENCES

6. Charles P. Kindleberger, *Europe's Postwar Growth: The Role of Labor Supply* (Cambridge, Massachusetts, 1967), *passim*; Dewhurst, *op. cit.* (n. 5, *supra*), pp. 17, 27, 120, 676, 706; O.E.E.C. *General Statistics* (Paris, July 1960); I.M.F. *International Financial Statistics* (Washington, June 1960)

7. Dewhurst, *op. cit.* (n. 5, *supra*), pp. 576, 651, 655, 1106–7, 1145–6

8. Kindleberger, *op. cit.* (n. 6, *supra*), pp. 24–86; Dewhurst, *op. cit.* (n. 5, *supra*), pp. 113, 444–5; Angus Maddison, *Economic Growth in the West* (New York/London, 1964), pp. 76–98; Jossleyn Hennessy and others, *Economic 'Miracles'* (London, 1964), *passim*

9. Dewhurst, *op. cit.* (n. 5, *supra*), pp. 407, 431, 433, 437, 439

10. Dewhurst, *op. cit.* (n. 5, *supra*), pp. 138, 378–9, 398–9, 413

11. Dewhurst, *op. cit.* (n. 5, *supra*), pp. 138, 313, 315, 330; Raymond Poignant, *L'Enseignement dans les pays du Marché commun* (Paris, 1965), pp. 28, 76

12. Dewhurst, *op. cit.* (n. 5, *supra*), pp. 123, 146; James B. Jeffreys & Derek Knee, *Retailing in Europe* (London, 1962), pp. 8, 24–5, 106–7

13. Dewhurst, *op. cit.* (n. 5, *supra*), pp. 147, 185, 189, 258, 265–6, 306; O.E.E.C., *Agricultural and Food Statistics* (Paris, 1956 and 1959)

14. Harold Macmillan, speech to an open-air rally at Bedford, 20 July 1957; John Montgomery, *The Fifties* (London, 1965), p. 270; Clive Irving and others, *Scandal '63* (London, 1963), p. 3

15. Statement to the High Authority on 9 November 1954, the Council of Ministers and the press on 11 November, and the Common Assembly on 30 November; *Débats de l'Assemblée Commune*, No. 7 (Luxembourg, 1955), p. 21; private information

16. Private information

17. Private information

18. Private information

19. Private information; Paul-Henri Spaak, *Combats Inachevés*, vol. II (Paris, 1969), pp. 62–3 (transl. R.M.)

20. Private information

21. *L'Année politique 1955* (Paris, 1956), p. 381

22. Private information

23. Spaak, *op. cit.* (n. 19, *supra*), pp. 64–5 (transl. R.M.); *L'Année politique 1955* (Paris, 1956), p. 382

24. *L'Année politique 1955* (Paris, 1956), p. 382

25. *L'Année politique 1955* (Paris, 1956), pp. 375–6; private information

26. *L'Année politique 1955* (Paris, 1956), pp. 409–13

27. Private information

28. Private information

29. *L'Année politique 1955* (Paris, 1956), p. 415

30. Personal knowledge; R. Mayne, 'The Role of Jean Monnet', in *Government and Opposition* vol. II, No. 3 (April-July, 1967), pp. 349–71 (pp. 366–7)

31. *L'Année politique 1955* (Paris, 1956), p. 416; Miriam Camps, *Britain and the European Community 1955–1963* (London, 1964), p. 23; Merry & Serge Bromberger, *Les Coulisses de l'Europe* (Paris, 1968), p. 193

32. Benelux Memorandum in *L'Année politique 1955* (Paris, 1956), pp. 714–16; German Memorandum, *Ibid.*, pp. 716–17 (transl. R.M.)

33. Private information

34. Personal knowledge; private information; Bromberger, *loc. cit.* (n. 31, *supra*); Camps, *op. cit.* (n. 31, *supra*), pp. 24–9; Jean Lecerf, *Histoire de l'unité européenne* (Paris, 1965), pp. 56–9

35. Lecerf, *op. cit.* (n. 34, *supra*), p. 60; Messina Resolution in British White Paper (Cmd. 9525, H.M.S.O., London, July 1955), pp. 7–9, and Camps, *op. cit.* (n. 31, *supra*), pp. 520–2

36. *Le Monde* (Paris, 5-6 June 1955); Camps, *op. cit.* (n. 31, *supra*), pp. 28–9; Lecerf, *op. cit.* (n. 34, *supra*), pp. 60–1

37. Personal knowledge; private information; R. Mayne, *The Community of Europe* (London, 1962; New York, 1963), pp. 108–9

38. Private information

39. Private information; Action Committee for the United States of Europe, *Statements and Declarations 1955–67* (London, 1969), pp. 7–11; 'Setting the Pace for Unity', in *Common Market*, vol. IV, No. 6 (The Hague, June 1964), pp. 104–6 (p. 106); Walter Yondorf, 'Monnet and the Action Committee: the Formative Period of the European Communities', in *International Organization*, vol. XIX, No. 4 (1965), pp. 885–912; Mayne, 'The Role of Jean Monnet', *op. cit.* (n. 30, *supra*), pp. 367–71; Mayne, *The Community of Europe, op. cit.* (n. 37, *supra*), pp. 109–10

40. Spaak, *op. cit.* (n. 19, *supra*), pp. 85, 89; Bromberger, *op. cit.* (n. 31, *supra*), p. 218; personal knowledge

41. On Suez, cf. Hugh Thomas, *The Suez Affair* (London, 1967); Anthony Nutting, *No end of a lesson* (London, 1967); Anthony Moncrieff (ed.), *Suez ten years after* (London, 1967); Henri Azeau, *Le piège de Suez* (Paris, 1964); Terence Robertson, *Crisis* (London, 1965); Merry and Serge Bromberger, *Les Secrets de l'expédition d'Egypte* (Paris, 1957); also private information

42. Action Committee, *op. cit.* (n. 39, *supra*), pp. 17–19; Mayne, *op. cit.* (n. 37, *supra*), pp. 112–13; *A Target for Euratom, Report submitted by Mr. Louis Armand, Mr. Franz Etzel and Mr. Francesco Giordani at the request of the governments of Belgium, France, German Federal Republic, Italy, Luxembourg and the Netherlands* ([Luxembourg], May 1957)

43. John Steward Ambler, *The French Army in Politics 1945–1962* (Columbus, Ohio, 1966), pp. 214, 228; Thomas, *op. cit.* (n. 41, *supra*), pp. 112–15; Nutting, *op. cit.* (n. 41, *supra*), pp. 90–9, 101; Moncrieff, *op. cit.* (n. 41, *supra*), pp. 93–4

44. Moncrieff, *op. cit.* (n. 41, *supra*), p. 25; Thomas, *op. cit.* (n. 41, *supra*), pp. 145–7

45. Thomas, *op. cit.* (n. 41, *supra*), p. 151

46. P. E. Zinner, *Revolution in Hungary* (New York, 1962), pp. 135, 182, 223, 226 & *passim*; Moncrieff, *op. cit.* (n. 41, *supra*), pp. 118–26; Anton Zischka, *The Other Europeans* (English translation by Brian Battershaw, London, 1962, of *Auch Das ist Europa*, Gütersloh, 1960), pp. 190–9; R. C. Mowat,

Ruin and Resurgence 1939–1965 (London, 1966), pp. 305–12; L. B. Bain, *The Reluctant Satellites* (New York, 1960), *passim*; Doris Scarlett, *Window onto Hungary* (Bradford, mimeographed, n.d.), *passim*

47. Personal knowledge; private information; Mayne, *op. cit.* (n. 37, *supra*), pp. 109, 113; Ibid., *The Institutions of the European Community* (London, 1968), pp. 60–1

48. Personal knowledge; private information

49. Personal knowledge; private information; Piero Malvestiti, *Parte guelfa in Europa* (Milan, 1945)

50. Personal knowledge; Rogert Lemaignen, *L'Europe au berceau: souvenirs d'un technocrate* (Paris, 1964)

51. Schuman Declaration in *L'Année politique 1950* (Paris, 1951), pp. 306–7 (transl. R.M.)

CHAPTER II. THE LION AND THE UNICORN

1. Iona & Peter Opie (ed.), *The Oxford Dictionary of Nursery Rhymes* (2nd edition, Oxford, 1952), p. 269

2. *Groucho and Me* (Dell Books edition, New York, 1960), p. 240

3. 'In Defence of Comrade Zilliacus', in *Collected Essays, Journalism, and Letters* (ed. by Sonia Orwell & Ian Angus (London, 1968), vol. IV, pp. 395–400 (p. 398)

4. Deryck Abel, *Channel Underground* (London, 1961), pp. 7–8, 46, 68–9; O. M. Watts (ed.) *Stanford's General Chart of the English Channel, Eastern Section* (London, 1969)

5. *Correspondence arising out of the Meeting of the Foreign Ministers of the Governments of Belgium, France, the Federal Republic of Germany, Italy, Luxembourg and the Netherlands held at Messina on 1–2 June 1955* (H.M.S.O., Cmd. 9525, London, July 1955)

6. Miriam Camps, *Britain and the European Community 1955–1963* (London, 1964), p. 30; Paul-Henri Spaak, *Combats Inachevés*, vol. II (Paris, 1969), p. 73 (transl. R.M.)

7. Camps, *op. cit.* (n. 6, *supra*), pp. 33, 34

8. Camps, *op. cit.* (n. 6, *supra*), pp. 43–5

9. Private information

10. Private information; the Rt. Hon. Sir Anthony Eden, K.G., P.C., M.C., *Memoirs: Full Circle* (London, 1960), p. 337

11. Private information

12. Private information; Christopher Layton, *European Advanced Technology: A Programme for Integration* (London, 1969), p. 106

13. Spaak, *op. cit.* (n. 6, *supra*), pp. 74–5

14. Spaak, *op. cit.* (n. 6, *supra*), pp. 75–9 (transl. R.M.)

15. Personal knowledge; Spaak, *op. cit.* (n. 6, *supra*), pp. 80–1

16. *The Manchester Guardian* (Manchester, 14 and 15 March 1956); Camps, *op. cit.* (n. 6, *supra*), p. 95 and n. 6, pp. 96–9

17. Spaak, *op. cit.* (n. 6, *supra*), p. 82; personal knowledge; Action Committee

for the United States of Europe, *Statements and Declarations 1955–67* (London, 1969), p. 17; R. Mayne, *The Community of Europe* (London, 1962 & New York, 1963), p. 141

18. Private information

19. *L'Année politique 1958* (Paris, 1959), p. 54; personal knowledge

20. Merry and Serge Bromberger, *Les 13 Complots du 13 Mai* (Paris, 1959), *passim*; *L'Année politique 1958* (Paris, 1959), pp. 57–71; Aidan Crawley, *De Gaulle* (London, 1969), pp. 332–53; Alexander Werth, *De Gaulle: a Political Biography* (Third edition, London, 1969), pp. 11–52; Paul-Marie de la Gorce, *De Gaulle entre deux mondes* (Paris, 1964); pp. 535–6

21. Charles de Gaulle, *Mémoires de Guerre*, vol. III, *Le Salut* (Livre de poche edition, Paris, 1961), p. 337

22. Charles de Gaulle, *op. cit.* (n. 21, *supra*), vol. II, *L'Unité* (Livre de poche edition, Paris, 1960), p. 481

23. Mayne, *op. cit.* (n. 17 *supra*), pp. 144–6

24. Mayne, *op. cit.* (n. 17 *supra*), pp. 15–17, 143

25. Council of Europe, *Debates, Eleventh Ordinary Session* (Strasbourg, January 1960), pp. 760–4; The *Economist* (London, 11 June 1960); The *Observer* (London, 3 July 1960); Camps, *op. cit.* (n. 6, *supra*), pp. 278, 280–1, 283–4, 287

26. W.E.U., *Debates, Sixth Ordinary Session, First Part* (June, 1960), p. 137; Camps *op. cit.* (n. 6, *supra*), p. 298

27. Action Committee, *op. cit.* (n. 17, *supra*), p. 50

28. *Hansard, House of Commons* (25 July 1960), cols. 1099–1218; Camps. *op. cit.* (n. 6, *supra*), p. 298

29. *L'Année politique 1960* (Paris, 1961), pp. 647–9; on NATO, cf. esp. Spaak, *op. cit.* (n. 6, *supra*), pp. 180–7

30. European Parliament, Political Committee, *Towards Political Union: A Selection of Documents with a Foreword by Mr Emilio Battista* (London, January 1964), pp. 6–11; Camps, *op. cit.* (n. 6, *supra*), pp. 302–12, 329; R. Mayne, *The Institutions of the European Community* (London, 1968), p. 74

31. Mayne, *op. cit.* (n. 30, *supra*), pp. 74–7; Miriam Camps, *What Kind of Europe?* (London, 1965), pp. 89–116; *Ibid.*, *European Unification in the Sixties* (New York, 1966), pp. 27, 126, 223, 225

32. Dwight D. Eisenhower, *Waging Peace* (London, 1966), p. 603; Joseph Kraft, *The Grand Design: From Common Market to Atlantic Partnership* (New York, 1962), pp. 24–5; personal knowledge

33. Kraft, *op. cit.* (n. 32, *supra*), title; J. F. Kennedy, *Message to Congress*, 25 January 1962; *Ibid.*, *Speech at Philadelphia*, 4 July 1962; Action Committee, *op. cit.* (n. 17, *supra*), pp. 64–5 (Joint Declaration of 26 June 1962)

34. George W. Ball, *The Discipline of Power* (Boston, 1968), pp. 78–9; Camps, *op. cit.* (n. 6, *supra*), pp. 336–7; personal knowledge

35. EFTA, *Bulletin* (Geneva, July 1961), p. 8; *Commonwealth Consultations on Britain's Relations with the European Economic Community* (H.M.S.O., Cmd. 1449, London, July 1961); Camps, *op. cit.* (n. 6, *supra*), pp. 338–56

36. *Hansard, House of Commons,* vol. 645, no. 159 (31 July 1961), cols. 928–31
37. Camps. *op. cit.* (n. 6, *supra*), pp. 287, 357
38. Private information
39. Private information
40. *The United Kingdom and the European Economic Community* (H.M.S.O., Cmd. 1565, London, November 1961)
41. *Ibid.*
42. Personal knowledge. Cf. Camps, *op. cit.* (n. 6, *supra*), pp. 367–506; Nora Beloff, *The General Says No* (London, 1963), pp. 113–71
43. Personal knowledge. Cf. Piers Dixon, *Double Diploma: The Life of Sir Pierson Dixon, Don and Diplomat* (London, 1968), pp. 279–314
44. Personal knowledge
45. E.E.C. Commission, *Report to the European Parliament on the State of the Negotiations with the United Kingdom* (Brussels, 26 February 1963)
46. Personal knowledge
47. Personal knowledge; *L'Année politique 1963* (Paris, 1964), p. 400 (transl. R.M.)
48. Robert Kleiman, *Atlantic Crisis* (New York, 1964), pp. 48–9
49. *Ibid.,* pp. 50–61
50. Private information
51. Mayne, *op. cit.* (n. 30, *supra*), pp. 42–50; John Newhouse, *Collision in Brussels* (London, 1968), *passim*
52. Uwe Kitzinger, *The Second Try: Labour and the EEC* (London, 1968), p. 177
53. Pierre Uri (ed.), *From Commonwealth to Common Market* (London, 1968), pp. 51–88
54. Jean-Jacques Servan-Schreiber, *Le défi américain* (Paris, 1967)
55. Texts in Kitzinger, *op. cit.* (n. 52, *supra*), pp. 299, 316, 317, 319
56. *Problems of British entry into the EEC: Reports to the Action Committee for the United States of Europe* (London, September 1969)
57. Cf. Z. E. B. Zeman, *Prague Springs: A Report on Czechoslovakia 1968* (London, 1969); Willy Brandt, *A Peace Policy for Europe* (London, 1969)

CHAPTER 12. REMEMBERING THE FUTURE

1. 'Miscellaneous Thoughts and Reflections', in *Complete Works,* ed. by Walter Raleigh (Oxford, 1912), p. 249
2. *Letters,* ed. by G. B. Hill (London, 1897), vol. 1, p. 221
3. *Walden* (Scott Library edition, London, n.d. [1905?]), p. 321
4. Dr Jonathan Miller, in Henry Brandon, *Conversations With* (London, 1966), p. 253
5. Fritz Baade, *The Race to the Year 2000* (London, 1962), p. 122
6. Dennis Gabor, *Inventing the Future* (London, 1963), pp. 49–50; Penguin edition (London, 1964), p. 42
7. This example, perhaps needless to say, is imaginary
8. This thesis is developed in Jean Fourastié, *Les 40,000 heures* (Paris, 1965)
9. William James, 'The Moral Equivalent of War', in *Memories and Studies* (London, 1911)

10. 1945 estimate by Frank W. Notestein; W. S. & E. S. Woytinsky, *World Population and Production: Trends and Outlook* (New York, 1953), pp. 257–62; United Nations, *The Future Growth of World Population* (New York, 1958); J. Fourastié & C. Vimont, *Histoire de demain* (3rd ed., Paris, 1964), pp. 14–17; 'Les savants scrutent l'avenir', in *Réalités* (Paris, September and October, 1965); NATO Defense College, Course 30, Segment 3, *The Way Ahead* (Rome, 1967), pp. 33–50 (pp. 38, 47)
11. NATO Defense College, *op. cit.* (n. 10, *supra*), pp. 44–6
12. William Morris, *The Dream of John Ball*, chap. IV, in G. D. H. Cole (ed.) William Morris, *Stories in Prose, Stories in Verse, Shorter Poems, Lectures and Essays* (London, 1948), p. 214

BIBLIOGRAPHY

Abel, Deryck. *Channel Underground*. London, 1961.

Abendroth, Wolfgang. *Sozialgeschichte der Europäischer Arbeiterbewegung*. Frankfurt-am-Main, 1965.

Abosch, Heinz. *The Menace of the Miracle*. London, 1962.

Acheson, Dean. *Sketches from Life*. New York, 1961.

Present at the Creation. London, 1970.

Action Committee for the United States of Europe. *Statements and Declarations 1955–1957*. London, 1969.

Adenauer, Konrad. *Erinnerungen 1945–1953*. Stuttgart, 1965.

Erinnerungen 1953–1955. Stuttgart, 1966.

Erinnerungen 1955–1959. Stuttgart, 1967.

'Adstans'. *Alcide De Gasperi nella Politica Estera Italiana*. Milan, 1953.

Agar, Herbert. *A Time for Greatness*. London, 1944.

Agence France Presse. *Dispatches*.

Agenor.

The Air-Power Historian.

Albenski, Henry S., and Pettit, Lawrence K. (eds.). *European Political Processes*. Boston, Mass., 1967.

Albonetti, Achille. *Préhistoire des Etats-Unis d'Europe*. Paris, 1963.

Albrecht-Carrié, René. *The Unity of Europe*. London, 1966.

Allais, Maurice. *L'Europe unie, route de la prosperité*. Paris, 1960.

Allen, H. C. *The Anglo-American Predicament*. London, 1960.

Allen, James Jay. *The European Common Market and the G.A.T.T.* Washington, 1960.

Alperovitz, Gar. *Atomic Diplomacy: Hiroshima and Potsdam*. London, 1966.

Alpert, Paul. *Twentieth-Century Economic History of Europe*. New York, 1951.

Ambler, John Steward. *The French Army in Politics 1945–1962*. Columbus, Ohio, 1966.

Anders, Wladyslaw. *An Army in Exile*. London, 1949.

Andrews, William G. (ed.). *European Politics 1: The Restless Search*. Princeton, N.J., 1966.

L'Année Politique. Paris, annual.

Anonymous (transl. James Stern). *A Woman in Berlin*. London, 1965.

Anouil, Gilles. *La Grande-Bretagne et la Communauté Européenne du Charbon et de l'Acier*. Issoudun, 1960.

Armand, Louis, and Drancourt, Michel. *Le Pari européen*. Paris, 1968.

Plaidoyer pour l'avenir. Paris, 1961.

and Etzel, Franz, and Giordani, Francesco. *A Target for Euratom*. Luxembourg, 1957.

Aron, Raymond. *Démocratie et totalitarisme*. Paris, 1965.

Dimensions de la conscience historique. Paris, 1960.

Dix-huit leçons sur la société industrielle. Paris, 1962.

La Lutte des classes. Paris, 1964.

L'Opium des intellectuels. Paris, 1955.

Trois essais sur l'âge industriel. Paris, 1966.

Aron, Robert, *Histoire de l'épuration*, Vol. 1. Paris, 1967.

Histoire de la libération de la France. Pocket edition, Paris, 1967.

Ashcroft, Edward. *De Gaulle*. London, 1952.

Ashton, T. S. *The Industrial Revolution 1760–1830*. Oxford, 1948.

Aubrey, Henry G. *Atlantic Economic Co-operation*. London/New York, 1967.

Behind the Veil of International Money. New York, 1969.

Azad, Maulana Abul Kalam. *India Wins Freedom*. Bombay, 1959.

Azeau, Henri. *Le piège de Suez*. Paris, 1964.

Baade, Fritz (transl. Ernest Pavel). *The Race to the Year 2000*. London, 1963.

Bagrit, Leon. *The Age of Automation*. Paperback edition, London, 1965.

Bain, L. B. *The Reluctant Satellites*. New York, 1960.

Bank for International Settlements. *Eight European Central Banks*. London, 1963.

Ball, George W. *The Discipline of Power*. Boston, Mass., 1968.

Ball, M. Margaret. *Nato and the European Unity Movement*. New York, 1959.

Barraclough, Geoffrey. *An Introduction to Contemporary History*. London, 1964.

The Origins of Modern Germany. Oxford, 1946.

Bartoli, Domenico. *La Fine della Monarchia*. Milan, 1947.

Barzanti, Sergio. *The Underdeveloped Areas within the Common Market*. Princeton, N.J., 1965.

Basile, Joseph. *Les Atoufs de L'Europe*. Paris, 1970.

Bayliss, Brian T. *European Transport*. London, 1965.

Beaton, Leonard. *Must the Bomb Spread?* London, 1966.

The Politics of Arms Control. New York, 1969.

and Maddox, John. *The Spread of Nuclear Weapons*. London, 1962.

Beaufre, André. *Introduction à la stratégie*. Paris, 1963.

Beaumont, P. de. *La IVe République: politique intérieure et européenne*. Brussels, 1960.

Beauvoir, Simone de. *La Force des choses*. Paris, 1963.

Beddington-Behrens, Edward. *Is There Any Choice? Britain Must Join Europe*. London, 1966.

Bedell Smith, W. *Moscow Mission 1946–1949*. London, 1950.

Beever, R. Colin. *European Unity and the Trade Union Movement*. Leyden, 1961.

Trade Unions and Free Labour Movement in the EEC. London, 1969.

Bell, Coral. *Negotiation from Strength*. London, 1962.

Bellotto, Adriano. *La Televisione Inutile*. Milan, 1962.

Beloff, Max. *Europe and the Europeans*. London, 1957.

The Future of British Foreign Policy. London, 1969.

New Dimensions in Foreign Policy. London, 1961.

The United States and the Unity of Europe. London, 1963.

Beloff, Nora. *The General Says No.* London, 1963.

Bender, Peter. *Offensive Entspannung.* Cologne/Berlin, 1964.

Benoit, Emile. *Europe at Sixes and Sevens.* New York, 1961.

and Boulding, Kenneth E. (eds.). *Disarmament and the Economy.* New York, 1963.

Berliner, Joseph S. *Soviet Economic Aid.* New York, 1958.

Bettini, Emilio (ed.). *Il Trattato contro la Proliferazione Nucleare.* Bologna, 1968.

Bettiza, Enzo. *L'Altra Germania.* Milan, 1968.

Birkenhead, The Earl of. *The Professor and the Prime Minister.* Boston, Mass., 1962.

Birrenbach, Kurt. *Die Zukunft der Atlantischen Gemeinschaft.* Freiburg-im-Breisgau, 1962.

Black, C. E. *The Transformation of Russian Society.* Cambridge, Mass., 1960.

Blanc, André. *L'Economie des Balkans.* Paris, 1965.

Géographie des Balkans. Paris, 1965.

Blijstra, R. *Nederlandse Bouwkunst na 1900.* Utrecht/Antwerp, 1962.

Boarman, Patrick. *Germany's Economic Dilemma: Inflation and the Balance of Payments.* New Haven, Conn./London, 1964.

Bocca Giorgio. *I Giovani Leoni del Neocapitalismo.* Bari, 1963.

Bölling, K. (transl. Jean Steinberg). *Republic in Suspense: Politics, Parties, and Personalities in Post-War Germany.* London, 1964.

Bologna, Sergio, and others (eds.). *Fascismo e Antifascismo: Lezioni e Testimonianze.* 2 volumes, Milan, 1962.

Bonanni, Massimo (ed.). *La Politica Estera della Repubblica Italiana.* 3 volumes, Milan, 1967.

Bowie, Robert R., and Friedrich, Carl J. (eds.). *Studies in Federalism.* Boston, Mass., 1954.

and Geiger, Theodore. *The European Economic Community and the United States,* Washington, 1961.

Bradley, Omar. *A Soldier's Story.* London, 1962.

Brandt, Willy. *A Peace Policy for Europe.* London, 1969.

Brecher, Michael. *Nehru: A Political Biography.* Oxford, 1953.

Brentano, Heinrich von. *Deutschland, Europa, und die Welt* (transl. Edward Fitzgerald as *Germany and Europe: Reflections on German Foreign Policy*). London, 1964.

Brinton, Crane. *The Americans and the French.* Cambridge, Mass., 1968.

British Iron and Steel Federation. *Monthly Statistical Bulletin.*

Broad, Roger, and Jarrett, Robert. *Community Europe.* London, 1967.

Bromberger, Merry and Serge. *Les Coulisses de l'Europe.* Paris, 1968.

Les Secrets de l'expédition de Suez. Paris, 1957.

Les 13 complots du 13 mai. Paris, 1959.

Brown, J. F. *The New Eastern Europe.* New York, 1966.

Brown, William Adams, Jr., and Opie, Redvers. *American Foreign Assistance* Washington, 1953.

Brugmans, Henri. *L'Idée européenne 1918–1965*. Bruges, 1965.
  Les Origines de la civilisation européenne. Liege, 1958.
Bruhat, Jean. *Histoire de l'U.R.S.S.* 7th edition, Paris, 1964.
Bryant, Arthur. *Triumph in the West 1943–1946*. Paperback edition, London, 1965.
Brzezinski, Zbigniew. *Alternative to Partition*. New York, 1965.
Buchan, Alastair (ed.). *Europe's Future, Europe's Choices*. London, 1969.
Buchanan, Norman S., and Lutz, Friedrich A. *Rebuilding the World Economy*. New York, 1947.
Buckley, Christopher. *The Road to Rome*. London, 1945.
Bullock, Alan. *Hitler: A Study in Tyranny*. Paperback edition, London, 1962.
  The Life and Times of Ernest Bevin. London, 1960.
Butcher, Harry C. *My Three Years with Eisenhower*. New York, 1964.
Byrnes, James F. *All in One Lifetime*. London, 1960.
  Speaking Frankly. New York, 1947.

Les Cahiers de la République.
Calder, Nigel (ed.). *The World in 1984*. 2 volumes, London, 1965.
Callender, Harold. *A Preface to Peace*. New York, 1944.
Calleo, David. *Britain's Future*. London, 1968.
  Europe's Future. New York, 1965.
Calmann, John (ed.). *Western Europe: A Handbook*. London, 1967.
Calzini, Paolo (ed.). *Evoluzione delle Economie Orientali e Prospettive degli Scambi Est-ovest*. Rome, 1968.
Campbell, Alan, and Thompson, Dennis. *Common Market Law*. London, 1962.
Campbell, John C. *The United States in World Affairs 1945–1947*. New York, 1947.
Camps, Miriam. *Britain and the European Community 1955–1963*. London, 1963.
  European Unification in the Sixties. New York, 1966.
  What Kind of Europe? London, 1965.
Carlyle, Margaret. *The Awakening of Southern Italy*. London, 1962.
  Modern Italy. London, 1957.
Carr, E. H. *The Soviet Impact on the Western World*. London, 1946.
Carter, W. Horsfall. *Speaking European*. London, 1966.
Cartier, Raymond. *Les 19 Europes*. Paris, 1960.
Catlin, George E. G. *The Atlantic Commonwealth*. London, 1969.
Cattaneo, Carlo. *I Problemi dello Stato Italiano*. Verona, 1966.
Caute, David. *The Left in Europe Since 1789*. London, 1966.
Cavallari, Alberto. *L'Europa su Misura*. Florence, 1963.
Ceccarini, Ennio, and others. *La Nato nell'era della Distensione*. Bologna, 1966.
Céré, Roger. *Entre la guerre et la paix*. Paris, 1962.
Chabod, Federico. *L'Italia Contemporanea 1918–1948*. Paperback edition, Turin, 1965.
  Storia dell' Idea dell' Europa. Paperback edition, Bari, 1967.
Chamberlin, William Henry. *The German Phoenix*. London, 1964.

Charpentier, Maryse (ed.). *Dossier de l'Europe des Six*. Paris, 1969.

Churchill, R. S. (ed.). *The Sinews of Peace: Postwar Speeches by Winston S. Churchill*. London, 1948.

Churchill, Winston S. *The Second World War*. 12-volume paperback edition, London, 1964.

Ciechanowski, Jan. *Defeat in Victory*. New York, 1947.

Cipolla, Carlo M. *The Economic History of World Population*. Paperback edition, London, 1964.

Clark, Alan. *Barbarossa*. Paperback edition, London, 1966.

Clark, Douglas. *Three Days to Catastrophe*. London, 1966.

Clarke, Arthur C. *Profiles of the Future*. London, 1962.

Clay, Lucius D. *Decision in Germany*. London, 1950.

Cleveland, Harold Van B. *The Atlantic Idea and its European Rivals*. New York, 1966.

Cline, Ray S. *Washington Command Post: The Operations Division*. Washington, 1951.

Cole, J. P. *Geography of World Affairs*. London, 1959.

Colebrook, M. J. *Dialogue of the Deaf: Franco–British Relations and European Integration 1945–1950*. Unpublished thesis, Geneva, 1968.

Colombo, Arturo. *Rapporto sull Universita Italiana*. Milan, 1962.

Committee of Economic Co-operation. *General Report*. Paris/London, 1957. *Common Market*.

Conland, William H. *Berlin: Beset and Bedevilled*. New York, 1963.

Conquest, Robert. *Common Sense About Russia*. London, 1961.

Conte, Arthur. *Yalta ou le partage du monde*. Pocket edition, Paris, 1965.

Cook, Don. *Floodtide in Europe*. New York, 1965.

Coombes, David. *Towards a European Civil Service*. London, 1968. *Politics and Bureaucracy in the European Community*. London, 1970.

Cooper, R. W. *The Nuremberg Trials*. London, 1946.

Corbett, J. P. *Europe and the Social Order*. Leyden, 1959.

Correspondence between the Chairman of the Council of Ministers of the U.S.S.R. and the Presidents of the U.S.A. and the Prime Minister of Great Britain during the Great Patriotic War of 1941–1945. Moscow, 1957.

Coston, Henry. *L'Europe des banquiers*. Paris, 1963.

Coudenhove-Kalergi, Richard. *An Idea Conquers the World*. London, 1953.

Council of Europe. *Debates*. *Dix Ans de Coopération Européenne*. Strasbourg, 1958.

Couzens, E. G., and Yarsley, V. E. *Plastics*. London, 1941. *Plastics in the Service of Man*. London, 1965.

Crankshaw, Edward. *Krushchev's Russia*, London, 1959. *The New Cold War: Moscow v. Pekin*. London, 1965.

Crawley, Aidan. *De Gaulle*. London, 1969.

Cretzianu, A. (ed.). *Captive Rumania*. New York, 1965.

Criddle, Brian. *Socialists and European Integration*. London, 1969.

Crozier, Michel. *Le monde des employés de bureau*. Paris, 1965.

Curzon, Gerald. *Multilateral Commercial Diplomacy*. London, 1965.

Dahl, Robert A. *Congress and Foreign Policy*. New York, 1950.

Dahrendorf, Rolf. *Gesellschaft und Demokratie in Deutschland*. Munich, 1865.

Dallin, David J. *The Big Three: The United States, Britain, Russia*. New Haven, Conn., 1945.

Dalton, Hugh. *High Tide and After: Memoirs 1945–1960*. London, 1962.

Davidson, Eugene. *The Death and Life of Germany*. London, 1959.

Davis, Melton S. *All Rome Trembled*. London, 1957.

Davison, W. Phillips. *The Berlin Blockade*. Princeton, N.J., 1958.

Deakin, F. W. *The Last Days of Mussolini*. Paperback edition, London, 1966.

De Gasperi, Maria. *De Gasperi, Uomo Solo*. Milan, 1965.

de Gaulle, Charles. *Mémoires de guerre*. 3 volumes, Paris, 1954–9.

Dehio, Ludwig (transl. Charles Fullman). *The Precarious Balance*. New York, 1962.

Del Bo, Dino. *Traguardo Europa*. Florence, 1966.

Dell, Sidney. *Trade Blocs and Common Markets*. London, 1963.

Deniau, J. F. *The Common Market*. Second edition, London, 1961.

Dennett, Raymond, and Johnson, Joseph E. (ed.). *Negotiating with the Russians*. Boston, 1951.

Denton, Geoffrey. *Planning in the E.E.C.* London, 1967.

⸺ (ed.). *Economic Integration in Europe*. London, 1969.

de Rougemont, Denis. *The Meaning of Europe*. London, 1965.

Despicht, Nigel. *The Transport Policy of the European Communities*. London, 1969.

Deuerlein, Ernst. (ed.). *Potsdam 1945*. Munich, 1963.

Deutsch, Karl W., and others. *Political Community and the North Atlantic Area*. Princeton, N.J., 1957.

Deutscher, Isaac. *Stalin: A Political Biography*. Revised paperback edition, London, 1966.

Dewhurst, J. Frederick, and others. *Europe's Needs and Resources*. New York, 1961.

d'Hérouville, Hubert. *La Communauté économique atlantique*. Third edition, Paris, 1964.

⸺ *L'Economie méditerranéenne*. Paris, 1958.

⸺ *L'Economie mondiale*. Fourth edition, Paris, 1960.

Diebold, William, Jr. *The Schuman Plan*. New York, 1959.

⸺ *Trade and Payments in Western Europe*. New York, 1952.

Dill, M. *Germany: A Modern History*. Michigan, 1961.

Dixon, Piers. *Double Diplomat: The Life of Sir Pierson Dixon, Don and Diplomat*. London, 1968.

Djilas, Milovan (transl. Michael B. Petrovitch). *Conversations with Stalin*. Paperback edition, London, 1963.

La Documentation Française.

Dolci, Danilo. *Conversazioni Contadini*. Turin, 1962.

⸺ (transl. R. Munroe). *The Outlaws of Partinico*. London, 1960.

⸺ (transl. P. D. Cummins). *Poverty in Sicily*. London, 1959.

Dönitz, Karl. *Zehn Jahre und Zwanzig Tage*. Bonn, 1958.

Donnelly, Desmond. *Struggle for the World*. London, 1965.

Donnison, F. S. V. *Civil Affairs and Military Government: N.W. Europe 1944–1946*. New York, 1961.

Dosser, Douglas, and Han, S. S. *Taxes in the E.E.C. and Britain: The Problem of Harmonization*. London, 1968.

Drouin, Pierre. *L'Europe du marché commun*. Paris, 1963.

Dulles, Allen. *The Secret Surrender*. London, 1967.

Dulles, E. L. *The Bank for International Settlements at Work*. New York, 1932.

Dulles, John Foster. *War or Peace*. New York, 1950.

Dumaine, Jacques (transl. Alan Davidson). *Quai d'Orsay 1945–1951*. London, 1958.

Duroselle, J.-B. *De Wilson à Roosevelt: politique extérieure des Etats-Unis*. Paris, 1960.

L'Idée européenne dans l'histoire. Paris, 1965.

Dutoit, Bernard, *L'Aviation et l'Europe*. Lausanne, 1959.

Ebsworth, Raymond. *Restoring Democracy in Germany: The British Contribution*. London, 1960.

The Economist.

Eden, The Rt. Honourable Sir Anthony, K.G., P.C., M.C. *Memoirs: Full Circle*. London, 1960.

Eich, Hermann (transl. Michael Glenny). *The Unloved Germans*. London, 1965.

Einaudi, M., and Goguel, F. *Christian Democracy in Italy and France*. Notre Dame, Indiana, 1952.

Einzig, Paul. *The Euro-Dollar System*. London, 1964.

Foreign Dollar Loans in Europe. London, 1965.

Eisenhower, Dwight D. *Crusade in Europe*. Paperback edition, New York, 1961.

Mandate for Change. Paperback edition, New York, 1961.

The Papers of Dwight David Eisenhower: The War Years. 5 vols., Baltimore, 1970.

Waging Peace. London, 1966.

Elgey, Georgette. *Histoire de la IVe République, Volume I: La Republique des illusions*. Paris, 1965.

Volume II: La République des contradictions. Paris, 1968.

Ellis, Howard S. *The Economics of Freedom*. New York, 1950.

Encounter.

Erhard, Ludwig. *Deutschlands Rückkehr zum Weltmarkt*. Düsseldorf, 1953.

(transl. J. A. Arengo Jones and J. S. Thomson). *The Economics of Success*. London, 1963.

(transl. Edith Temple Roberts and J. B. Wood). *Prosperity Through Competition*. Second edition, London, 1959.

Etzioni, Amitai. *Political Unification: a comparative study of leaders and forces*. New York, 1965.

European Coal and Steel Community. *Bulletin*.

Common Assembly. *Debates*.

Correspondance concernant les relations entre la Communauté Européenne du Charbon et de l'Acier et le Royaume-Uni. Luxembourg, 1954.
General Reports.
European Community Information Service. *The Community in Maps.* Brussels/ Luxembourg, 1967.
European Customs Union Study Group. *First Report.* Brussels, March 1948.
General Report of the Economic Committee. Brussels, October 1948.
European Economic Community, Commission. *Report on the Economic Situation in the Countries of the Community.* Brussels, 1958.
Report to the European Parliament on the State of the Negotiations with the United Kingdom. Brussels, 1963.
European Free Trade Association. *Bulletin.*
European Movement. *The Economic Future of Europe.* London, 1954.
The European Movement and the Council of Europe. London, 1949.
European Parliament. *Debates.*
Political Committee. *Towards Political Union: A Selection of Documents with a Foreword by Mr Emilio Battista.* London, 1964.

Fabra, Paul, *Y a-t-il un marché commun?* Paris, 1965.
Faculté des Lettres et Sciences Humaines de Paris. *Mélanges Pierre Renouvin.* Paris, 1966.
Fauvet, Jacques. *La IVième République.* Paris, 1959.
Feis, Herbert. *Between War and Pace: The Potsdam Conference.* London, 1960.
Churchill, Roosevelt, Stalin: The War They Waged and the Peace They Sought. Princeton, N.J., 1957.
Fejtö, François. *Budapest '56.* Paris, 1966.
'Felix, Christopher.' *The Spy and his Masters.* London, 1963.
Le Figaro.
Fitz Gibbon, Constantine. *Random Thoughts of a Fascist Hyena.* London, 1963.
Flanner, Janet. *Paris Journal 1944–1965.* London, 1966.
Fleming, D. F. *The Cold War and its Origins 1917–1960.* Two volumes, London, 1961.
Florinsky, Michael T. *Integrated Europe:* New York, 1955.
Foa, Bruno. *Monetary Reconstruction in Italy.* New York, 1949.
Fontaine, André. *Histoire de la guerre froide.* Two volumes, Paris, 1965–7.
Fontaine, François. *La Nation frein.* Paris, 1956.
Foot, M. R. D. *S.O.E. in France.* London, 1966.
Forces Aériennes Françaises.
Foreign Affairs.
Foreign Relations of the United States, 1942: Europe Vol. III.
1943: Vol. I.
1944: Vol. I.
Diplomatic Papers: The Conference of Berlin, 1945. Washington, 1960.
The Conferences at Cairo and Teheran, 1943. Washington, 1961.
The Conferences at Malta and Yalta, 1945. Washington, 1955.

Fortune.

Fougeyrollas, Pierre. *Pour une France fédérale.* Paris, 1968.

Fourastié, J. *La Civilisation de 1975.* Paris, 1964.

  Le Grand espoir du XXe siècle. Paris, 1963.

  Idées majeures. Paris, 1966.

  Les 40,000 heures. Paris, 1965.

  and F. *Les arts ménagers.* Paris, 1950.

  and Vimont, C. *Histoire de demain.* Third editon, Paris, 1964.

Fraenkel, H. *Farewell to Germany.* London, 1959.

Frank, Isaiah. *The European Common Market.* New York, 1961.

Frankel, Joseph. *International Relations.* London, 1964.

Frankel, P. H. *Mattei: Oil and Power Politics.* London, 1966.

Fremy, D., and M. *Quid?* Paris, annual.

Freymond, Jacques. *The Saar Conflict 1945–1955.* London/New York, 1960.

  Western Europe Since the War. London/New York, 1964.

Friedländer, Saul. *Hitler et les Etats-Unis 1939–1941.* Geneva, 1963. (Revised by the author and transl. Aline B. & Alexander Werth as *Prelude to Downfall: Hitler and the United States 1939–1941.* New York, 1967).

Friedmann, Georges. *Le Travail en miettes.* Paris, 1964.

Fulop, Christina. *Competition for Consumers.* London, 1964.

Gabor, Dennis. *Inventing the Future.* London, 1963.

Galante, Pierre and Miller, Jack. *The Berlin Wall.* London, 1965.

Galli, Giorgio. *Il Bipartismo Imperfetto.* Bologna, 1966.

  and Facchi, Paolo. *La Sinistra Democristiana.* Milan, 1962.

Gardini, T. L. *Towards the New Italy.* London, 1943.

Gardner, R. N. *Sterling-Dollar Diplomacy.* Oxford, 1956.

Gayre, G. R. *Italy in Transition.* London, 1946.

George, Pierre. *Géographie industrielle du monde.* Paris, 1957.

  Géographie de l'Italie. Paris, 1964.

German Federal Government. *Germany Reports.* Wiesbaden, 1953.

Giacchero, Enzo. *Il Mezzogiorno nel Mercato Italiano.* Luxembourg, 1957.

Gide, André *Retour de l'U.R.S.S.* Paris, 1936.

Gilbert, G. M. *Nuremberg Diary.* New York, 1947.

Gilbert, Martin. *The European Powers 1900–45.* London, 1965.

Ginestet, Pierre. *L'Assemblée parlementaire européenne.* Paris, 1959.

Giordano, Renato. *Il Mercato Comune e i suoi Problemi.* Rome, 1958.

Gladwyn, Lord. *The European Idea.* London, 1966.

  De Gaulle's Europe. London, 1969.

Golay, J. F. *The Founding of the Federal Republic of Germany.* Chicago, 1958.

Goldschmidt, Bertrand. *L'Aventure atomique.* Paris, 1962.

  Les Rivalités atomiques. Paris, 1967.

Gollancz, Victor. *In Darkest Germany.* London, 1947.

Goodrich, L. M. and Carroll, M. J. (eds.). *Documents on American Foreign Relations July 1942–June 1943.* Boston, 1945.

  Documents on American Foreign Relations 1943–1944. Boston, 1945.

Gorce, Paul-Marie de la. *De Gaulle entre deux mondes*. Paris, 1964.

Gorell Barnes, Sir William. *Europe and the Developing World*. London. 1967.

Government and Opposition.

Graham, B. D. *The French Socialists and Tripartisme 1944–1947*. London, 1965.

Granick, David. *The European Executive*. New York, 1962.

Graubard, Stephen R. (ed.). *A New Europe?* Boston, Mass., 1964.

Grindrod, Muriel. *Italy*. London, 1964.

   The Rebuilding of Italy. London, 1955.

Grosser, Alfred. *La IVe République et sa politique extérieure*. Paris, 1961.

   La République Fédérale d'Allemagne. Paris, 1963.

The Guardian.

Gunther, John. *Inside Europe Today*. Revised edition, New York, 1962.

   Inside Russia Today. London, 1958.

Guyard, Jacques. *Le Miracle français*. Paris, 1965.

Haas, Ernst B. *The Uniting of Europe*. Revised edition, Stanford, Calif., 1968.

Habakkuk, H. J., and Postan, M. M. (eds.). *The Cambridge Economic History of Europe, Vol. VI*. Cambridge, 1965.

Halecki, Oscar. *The Limits and Divisions of European History*. London, 1950.

Halle, Louis J. *The Cold War as History*. London, 1967.

Hallstein, Walter. *United Europe: Challenge and Opportunity*. Cambridge, Mass./Oxford, 1962.

   and Schlochauer, Hans-Jürgen (eds.). *Zur Integration Europas: Festschrift für Carl-Friedrich Ophüls*. Karlsruhe, 1965.

Hambis, Louis. *La Sibérie*. Paris, 1957.

Hancock, W. K. and Gowing, M. M. *British War Economy*. London, 1949.

Hansard. *Parliamentary Debates.*

Harris, Whitney R. *Tyranny on Trial: the Evidence at Nuremberg*. Dallas, 1954.

Harrison, Anthony. *The Framework of Economic Activity*. London, 1967.

Harrod, R. F. *The Life of John Maynard Keynes*. London, 1951.

   The Prof. London, 1959.

Hartmann, Frederick H. *Germany Between East and West: The Reunification Problem*. Englewood Cliffs, N.J., 1965.

Hartog, F. *European Trade Cycle Policy*. Leyden, 1959.

Haviland, H. Field, Jr. (ed.). *The United States and the Western Community*. Haverford, Pa., 1957.

Hay, Denys. *Europe: The Emergence of an Idea*. Edinburgh, 1957.

Heidelberg, Franz C. *Das Europäische Parlament*. Baden-Baden/Bonn/Frankfurt-am-Main, 1959.

   Die Berlin-Frage. Frankfurt/Strasbourg, 1965.

Heidelmeyer, Wolfgang and Hindrich, Günter (eds.). *Documents on Berlin 1943–1963*. Second edition, revised, Munich, 1963.

Heidenheimer, A. T. *Adenauer and the C.D.U.* The Hague, 1960.

Heinemann, Dannie N. *Esquisse d'une Europe nouvelle*. Brussels, 1931.

Heiser, H. J. *British Policy with regard to the Unification Efforts on the European Continent*. Leyden, 1959.

Henig, Stanley, and Pinder, John (eds.). *European Political Parties*. London, 1969.

Hennessy, Jossleyn; Lutz, Vera, and Scimone, Giuseppe. *Economic 'Miracles'*. London, 1964.

Héraud, Guy. *Peuples et langues d'Europe*. Paris, 1966.

Herz, Martin. *Beginnings of the Cold War*. Bloomington, Ind., 1966.

Hildebrand, George H. *Growth and Structure in the Economy of Modern Italy*. Cambridge, Mass., 1965.

Hinshaw, Randall. *The European Community and American Trade*. New York, 1964.

   (ed.). *Monetary Reform and the Price of Gold*. Baltimore, 1967.

Hirsch, Fred. *Money International*. London, 1967.

Hodgkins, Jordan A. *Soviet Power: Energy Resources, Production, and Potentials*. Englewood Cliffs, N.J., 1961.

Hoehler, Fred. K. *Europe's Homeless Millions*. New York, 1945.

Hoess, Rudolf (transl. Constantine Fitz Gibbon). *Commandant of Auschwitz*. London, 1959.

Hoffmann, Paul G. *Peace Can Be Won*. New York, 1951.

Hoffmann, Stanley and others. *France: Change and Tradition*. London, 1963.
Horizon.

Hornstein, Erika von (ed.). *Beyond the Berlin Wall*. London, 1962

Horowitz, David. *From Yalta to Vietnam*. London, 1967.

Howard, Michael. *Disengagement in Europe*. London, 1958.

Hudson, G. F. *The Hard and Bitter Peace*. London, 1966.

Hughes, H. Stuart. *Contemporary Europe: A History*. Englewood Cliffs, N.J., 1961.
   The United States and Italy. Cambridge, Mass., 1953.

Huizinga, J. H. *Confessions of a European in England*. London, 1958.
   Mr Europe. London, 1961.

Hull, Cordell. *Memoirs*. Two volumes, New York/London, 1948.

Huntley, James R. *The Nato Story*. New York, 1965.

Ingram, Kenneth. *History of the Cold War*. London, 1955.

Institute for Strategic Studies. *Adelphi Papers*.
   The Military Balance. London, annual.

International Affairs.

International Monetary Fund. *International Financial Statistics*.

International Organization.

Ionescu, Chita. *The Break-up of the Soviet Empire in Eastern Europe*. London, 1965.

Irving, Clive and others. *Scandal '63*. London, 1963.

Irving, David. *The Destruction of Dresden*. Paperback edition, London, 1966.

Isaacs, Asher. *International Trade: Tariffs and Commercial Policies*, Chicago. 1948.

Isolera, Italo. *Roma Moderna*. Turin, 1962.

Istituto Poligrafico dello Stato. *Lo Sviluppo dell'economia Italiana.* Rome, 1952.

Jacobsen, Hans-Adolf and Stenzl, Otto (eds.). *Deutschland und die Welt.* Munich, 1964.
Jaksch, W. *Europe's Road to Potsdam.* London, 1963.
Jackson, Robert A. *Report.* Washington, 1949.
Jasny, N. *The Soviet Economy During the Plan Era.* Stanford, 1951.
Jay, Douglas. *After the Common Market.* London, 1968.
Jefferys, James B. and Knee, Derek. *Retailing in Europe.* London, 1962.
Jennings, W. Ivor. *A Federation for Western Europe.* Cambridge, 1940.
Jones, Joseph Marion. *The Fifteen Weeks.* Paperback edition, New York. 1964.
Jouanique, Marcel and Morice, Lucien. *La Navigation intérieure en France.* Paris, 1951.
Journal of Contemporary History.
Journal of Modern History.
Jouvenel, Bertrand de. *Quelle Europe?* Paris, 1947.
Junckerstorff, H. K. *International Manual on the European Economic Community.* St. Louis, Mo., 1963.

Kahn, Herman and Wiener, Anthony J. *The Year 2000.* New York, 1967.
Kee, Robert. *Refugee World.* London, 1961.
Keesing's Contemporary Archives.
Kennan, George F. *American Diplomacy 1900–1950.* London, 1952.
  Memoirs 1925–1950. London, 1968.
  Russia and the West. New York, 1962.
Kennedy, John F. *Why England Slept.* Paperback edition, New York, 1962.
Kennedy, Robert F. *Just Friends and Brave Enemies.* Paperback edition, New York, 1963.
Kidder Smith, G. E. *The New Architecture of Europe.* London, 1962.
Kimball, Warren F. *The Most Unsordid Act: Lend-Lease 1939–1941.* Baltimore, 1969.
Kindleberger, Charles P. *Economic Growth in France and Britain 1851–1950.* Cambridge, Mass., 1964
  Europe's Postwar Growth: The Role of Labor Supply. Cambridge, Mass., 1967.
Kissinger, Henry. *The Necessity for Choice.* Paperback edition, New York, 1962.
  The Troubled Partnership. Paperback edition, New York, 1965.
Kitzinger, U. W. *Britain, Europe, and Beyond.* Leyden, 1964.
  The Challenge of the Common Market. Oxford, 1961.
  German Electoral Politics. Oxford, 1960.
  (ed.). *The Second Try: Labour and the E.E.C.* London, 1968.
Kleiman, Robert. *Atlantic Crisis.* New York, 1964.
Kochan, Lionel. *The Struggle for Germany 1914–1945.* Edinburgh, 1963.
Koestler, Arthur. *The Trail of the Dinosaur.* London, 1955.

Kogan, Norman. *A Political History of Postwar Italy*. London, 1966.

Kogon, Eugen. *Der SS-Staat und das System der deutschen Konzentrationslager*. Munich, 1946.

Kracauer, Siegfried. *From Caligari to Hitler*. Princeton, N.J., 1947.

Kraft, Joseph. *The Grand Design: from Common Market to Atlantic Partnership*. New York, 1962.

Kumar, Dharma. *India and the European Economic Community*. Bombay, 1966.

Laloy, Jean. *Entre guerres et paix 1945–1965*. Paris, 1966.

Lambert, John. *Britain in a Federal Europe*. London, 1968.

Lamfalussy, Alexander. *The United Kingdom and the Six*. London, 1963.

Lansdell, Norman. *The Atom and the Energy Revolution*. London, 1958.

La Palombara, Joseph. *Interest Groups in Italian Politics*. Princeton, N.J., 1964.

Lapie, Pierre-Olivier. *Les trois communautés*. Paris, 1960.

Laqueur, Walter. *Europe since Hitler*. London, 1970
   Russia and Germany: A Century of Conflict. London, 1965.

Laurat, Lucien. *Bilan de vingt-cinq ans de plans quinquennaux*. Paris, 1955.

Lavrillère, Jacques. *L'Industrie des banquiers*. Paris, 1966.

Layton, Christopher. *European Advanced Technology: A Programme for Integration*. London, 1969.

League of Nations. *Industrialization and Free Trade*. Geneva, 1945.

Leahy, William D. *I Was There*. New York, 1950.

Lecerf, Jean. *Histoire de l'unité européenne*. Paris, 1965.

Lechat, Paul. *Italie*. Paris, 1954.

Ledre, C. *Robert Schuman*. Paris, 1954.

Leith, C. K., and others. *World Minerals and World Peace*. Washington, 1943.

Lekachman, Robert. *The Age of Keynes*. London, 1967.

Lemaignen, Robert. *L'Europe au berceau*. Paris, 1964.

Lenti Libero. *Inventario dell'Economia Italiana*. Milan, 1966.

Leonhard, Wolfgang. *Die Revolution entlässt ihre Kinder*. Cologne/Berlin, 1955.

Leonhardt, Rudolf Walter. *This Germany*. Greenwich, Conn., 1964.

Lerner, Daniel, and Aron, Raymond. *France Defeats E.D.C.* New York, 1957.

Lewis, Norman. *The Honoured Society*. London, 1964.

Lichtheim, George. *Europe and America*. London, 1963.

Lindsay, Kenneth. *European Assemblies*. New York, 1960.

Lippmann, Walter. *The Communist World and Ours*. London, 1959.
   Western Unity and the Common Market. Boston, 1962.

The Listener.

Lister, Louis. *Europe's Coal and Steel Community*. New York, 1960.

Locatelli, Silvio. *Konrad Adenauer*. Milan, 1965.

Luard, Evan (ed.). *The Cold War: A Reappraisal*. London, 1964.

Lüdde-Neurath, Walter. *Die Regierung Dönitz*. Göttingen, 1950.

Lukacs, John. *Decline and Rise of Europe*. New York, 1965.

M

Lukas, Richard. *Zehn Jahre Sowjetische Besatzungszone Deutschlands*. Mainz/ Wiesbaden/Düsseldorf, 1955.
Lyon, Margot. *Belgium*. London, 1970

Macdonald, R. and West, M. *Eurovista '69*. St Andrews, 1969.
McInnis, Edgar; Hiscocks, Richard and Spencer, Robert. *The Shaping of Postwar Germany*. Toronto/London, 1960.
Mackay, R. W. G. *Towards a United States of Europe*. London, 1961.
Mackiewicz, Joseph. *The Katyn Wood Murders*. London, 1951.
Maclean, Fitzroy. *Disputed Barricade*. London, 1957.
MacLennan, Malcolm. *French Planning: Some Lessons for Britain*. London, 1963.
Macmahon, Arthur W. (ed.). *Federalism: Mature and Emergent*. New York, 1955.
Macmillan, Harold. *Memoirs. Vol II: The Blast of War 1939–1945*. London, 1967.
   III: Tides of Fortune 1945–1955. London, 1969.
McNeill, W. H. *The Rise of the West*. Chicago, 1963.
Madariaga, Salvador de. *Portrait of Europe*. New edition, London, 1967.
Maddison, Angus. *Economic Growth in the West*. New York/London, 1964.
Mahotière, Stuart de la. *Towards One Europe*. London, 1970.
Maillet, Pierre. *La Croissance économique*. Paris, 1966.
Malvestiti, Piero. *Parte Guelfa in Europa*. Milan, 1945.
Mander, John. *Berlin: Hostage for the West*. London, 1962.
   Great Britain or Little England? London, 1963.
Marc, Alexandre. *L'Europe, terre décisive*. Paris, 1959.
Markevitch, Igor (transl. Darina Silone). *Made in Italy*. London, 1949.
Markham, R. H. *Rumania under the Soviet Yoke*. Boston, Mass., 1949.
Martin, Laurence W. (ed.). *Diplomacy in Modern European History*. New York, 1966.
Mason, Henry L. *The European Coal and Steel Community*. The Hague, 1955.
Masseyeff, René. *La Faim*. Paris, 1956.
Massip, Roger. *Voici l'Europe*. Paris, 1958.
Mathijsen, Pierre. *Le Droit de la Communauté Européenne du Charbon et de l'Acier*. The Hague, 1958.
Maxwell, Gavin. *God Protect Me From My Friends*. London, 1956.
Mayne, Richard. *The Community of Europe*. London, 1962.
   The Institutions of the European Community. London, 1968.
Meade, J. E. *Negotiations for Benelux*. Princeton, N.J., 1957.
   Problems of Economic Union. London, 1953.
Meinecke, F. *The German Catastrophe*. Cambridge, Mass., 1950.
Meisel, J. H. *The Fall of the Republic*. Michigan, 1962.
Menon, V. P. *The Transfer of Power in India*. Bombay, 1961.
Mercure de France.
Merkl, Peter H. *Germany Yesterday and Tomorrow*. New York, 1965.
Meyer, F. V. *The Seven*. London, 1960.

Middleton, Drew. *Crisis in the West*. London, 1965.
 The Defense of Western Europe. New York, 1952.
 The Supreme Choice. London, 1963.
Midgley, John. *Germany*. London, 1968.
Mikolajczyk, Stanislaw. *The Pattern of Soviet Domination*. London, 1948.
Miles, W. (ed.). *The Forrestal Diaries*. London, 1952.
The Milwaukee Leader.
Ministère des Affaires Etrangères. *Documents de la conférence des Ministres des Affaires Etrangères de la France, du Royaume-Uni, et de l'U.R.S.S. tenue à Paris du 27 juin au 3 juillet 1947*. Paris, 1947.
Moch, Jules. *Histoire du réarmement allemand depuis 1950*. Paris, 1965.
Moncrieff, Anthony (ed). *Britain and the Common Market 1967*. London, 1967.
 Suez Ten Years After. London, 1967.
Le Monde.
Monnet, Jean. *Les Etats-Unis d'Europe ont commencé*. Paris, 1955.
Montgomery of Alamein, Field-Marshal the Viscount, K. G. *Memoirs*. Paperback edition, London, 1960.
Montgomery, John. *The Fifties*. London, 1965.
Moon, Penderel. *Divide and Quit*. London, 1962.
Moonman, Eric (ed.), *Science and Technology in Europe*. London, 1968.
Moore, Ben T. *Nato and the Future of Europe*. New York, 1958.
Moore, Reginald, and Lane, Edward (eds.). *The Windmill*, London, 1946.
Moran, Lord. *Churchill: The Struggle for Survival*. London, 1966.
Morandi, Rudolfo. *Storia della Grande Industria in Italia*. Turin, 1966.
Morgan, Sir Frederick. *Overture to Overlord*. London, 1950.
Morgenthau, Henry. *Germany is our Problem*. New York, 1945.
Morris, James. *The World Bank: A Prospect*. London, 1958.
Mosely, Philip E. *The Kremlin in World Politics*. Paperback edition, New York, 1960.
 The Soviet Union Since Khrushchev. New York, 1966.
Moulin, Léo. *La Société de demain dans l'Europe d'aujourd'hui*. Paris, 1966.
Moulton, Harold G. and Pasvolsky, Leo. *War Debts and World Prosperity*. Washington, 1932.
Mourin, Maxime. *Histoire des nations européennes*, Vol. III. Paris, 1963.
Mowat, R. C. *Ruin and Resurgence 1939–1965*. London, 1966.
Muhlen, Norbert. *The Survivors: A Report on the Jews in Germany Today*. New York, 1962.
Mulley, F. W. *The Politics of Western Defence*. London, 1962.
Murphy, Robert. *Diplomat Among Warriors*. London, 1964.

Nabokov, Nicolas. *Old Friends and New Music*. London, 1951.
Nagy, Ferenc. *The Struggle Behind the Iron Curtain*. London, 1948.
Nettl, John P. *The Eastern Zone and Soviet Policy in Germany*. London, 1951.
Neuvecelle, Jean. *Eglise capitale Vatican*. Paris, 1954.
Nevins, Allan. *America in World Affairs*. Oxford, 1941.
Newhouse, John. *Collision in Brussels*. London, 1968.

The New Statesman.

The New York Herald-Tribune.

The New York Times.

North Atlantic Treaty Organization, Defence College. *The Way Ahead.* Rome, 1967.

Northedge, F. S. *British Foreign Policy: The Process of Readjustment 1945–1961.* London, 1962.

Northrop, F. S. C. *European Union and United States Foreign Policy.* New York, 1954.

Nova, Fritz. *Contemporary European Governments.* Baltimore/Dublin, 1963.

Novick, Peter. *The Resistance versus Vichy.* London, 1968.

Nutting, Anthony. *Europe Will Not Wait.* London, 1960.

   No End of a Lesson. London, 1967.

The Observer.

Office Statistique des Communautés Européennes. *Commerce Extérieur: Statistique Mensuelle.*

   Statistiques de base de la Communauté Européenne: Comparaison avec certains pays européens, le Canada, les Etats-Unis d'Amérique, et l'U.R.S.S. Brussels/Luxembourg, annual.

Ogburn, W. F. (ed.). *Technology and International Relations.* Chicago, 1949.

Olivi, Bino. *L'Europa Difficile.* Milan, 1964.

Organisation for Economic Co-operation and Development. *Economic Surveys. Tourism in O.E.C.D. Member Countries 1966.* Paris, 1966.

Organisation for European Economic Cooperation. *Council Meetings, Reports. Memorandum by the Chancellor of the Exchequer.* Paris, 1 June, 1949.

   Memorandum by the French Minister of Finance and Economic Affairs. Paris, 2 June, 1949.

   Present Positions on the Principles of the Payments Scheme for the 1949–50 Financial Year. Paris, June 27, 1949.

   Reports.

Orwell, George. *Collected Essays, Journalism, and Letters* (ed. Sonia Orwell and Ian Angus). Four volumes, London, 1968.

Palmer, Michael, and others. *European Unity: A Survey of the European Organizations.* London, 1968.

Pantaleone, Michele. *Mafia e Politica.* Turin, 1962.

Paranque, Régis. *La Semaine de trente heures.* Paris, 1964.

Parker, Geoffrey. *The Logic of Unity.* London, 1969.

Parkinson, C. Northcote. *Parkinson's Law.* London, 1958.

Payne, R. *General Marshall.* London, 1952.

Penrose, E. F. *Economic Planning for the Peace.* Princeton, N.J., 1953.

'Pentad'. *The Remaking of Italy.* London, 1941.

Permoli, Piergiovanni. *La Costituente e i Partiti Politici Italiani.* Rocca San Casciano, 1966.

Pevsner, Nikolaus. *The Buildings of England: London, Vol. I: The Cities of London and Westminster*. London, 1957.

Peyret, Henry. *La Stratégie des trusts*. Paris, 1961.

Pflimlin, Pierre, and Legrand-Lane, Raymond. *L'Europe Communautaire*, Paris, 1966.

Phillips, Cabell. *The Truman Presidency*. New York, 1966.

Pickles, Dorothy. *The Fifth French Republic*. Third edition, London, 1965.

Pickles, William. *Not with Europe: The Political Case for Staying Out*. London, 1962.

Pinder, John. *Britain and the Common Market*. London, 1961.

Europe Against De Gaulle. London, 1963.

and Pryce, Roy. *Europe After De Gaulle*. London, 1969.

Pingaud, Bernard. *Hollande*. Paris, 1954.

Pisani, Edgard and others. *Problems of British Entry into the E.E.C.: Reports to the Action Committee for the United States of Europe*. London, 1969.

Plischke, Elmer. *Contemporary Government of Germany*. London, 1964.

Summit Diplomacy. College Park, Md., 1958.

Poignant, Raymond. *L'Enseignement dans les pays du marché commun*. Paris, 1965.

Polish Government in Exile. *Facts and Documents Concerning Polish Prisoners of War Captured by the U.S.S.R. During the 1939 Campaign*, London, 1944.

Political and Economic Planning (London). *Aspects of European Integration*. London/Paris, 1962.

European Organizations. London, 1959.

The Political Science Quarterly.

Poos, Jacques F. *Luxembourg et le marché commun*. Luxembourg/Lausanne, 1961.

Posner, M. V., and Woolf, S. J. *Italian Public Enterprise*. London, 1967.

Postan, M. M. *An Economic History of Western Europe 1945–1964*. London, 1967.

Pounds, Norman J. G. *The Economic Pattern of Modern Germany*. London, 1963.

and Kingsbury, Robert C. *An Atlas of European Affairs*. London, 1964.

and Parker, William N. *Coal and Steel in Western Europe*. Bloomington, Ind., 1957.

Pravda.

Présidence du Conseil, Secrétariat-General du Gouvernement. *L'Organisation de l'Europe occidentale (1948–1955)*. Paris, 1955.

Price, Harry Bayard. *The Marshall Plan and Its Meaning*. Ithaca, N.Y., 1955.

Proudfoot, Malcolm J. *European Refugees 1939–52*. London, 1957.

Pryce, Roy. *The Political Future of the European Community*. London, 1962.

Quin, Claude; Boniface, Jean, and Gaussel, Alain. *Les Consommateurs*. Paris, 1965.

Racine, Raymond. *Vers une Europe nouvelle par le Plan Schuman*. Neuchâtel, 1954.

Reader's Digest European Surveys. *Products and People*. London, 1963.

Réalités.

Reed, Laurance. *Europe in a Shrinking World*. London, 1967.
  Ocean-Space: Europe's New Frontier. London, 1969.

Rees, David. *The Age of Containment*. London, 1967.

Regierung des Landes Nordrhein-Westfalen and others. *Das Abkommen über die Errichtung einer Internazionalen Ruhrbehörde*. Düsseldorf, 1949.

Reitlinger, Gerald. *The Final Solution: The Attempt to Exterminate the Jews of Europe 1939–1945*. London, 1953.
  The SS: Alibi of a Nation. London, 1956.

Relazioni Internazionali.

Repubblica Italiana, Senato dell Repubblica/Camera dei Deputati. *Manuali Parlamentari*.

République Française, Ministère des Affaires Etrangères. *Rapport de la délégation française sur le Traité instituant la Communauté Européenne du Charbon et de l'Acier et la Convention relative au dispositions transitoires signés à Paris le 18 avril 1951*. Paris, 1951.

The Review of Politics.

La Revue Française de Science Politique.

La Revue de l'Histoire de la 2e Guerre Mondiale.

Reynaud, Paul. *La Politique étrangère du Gaullisme*. Paris, 1964.

Riemans, H. *Perspectief voor Nederland*. Amsterdam, 1957.

Ripka, Hubert. *Czechoslovakia Enslaved*. London, 1950.
  Eastern Europe in the Postwar World. London, 1961.

Robertson, A. H. *European Institutions*. New York, 1959.

Robertson, Terence. *Crisis*. London, 1965.

Robson, Charles B. (transl. and ed.). *Berlin – Pivot of German Destiny*. Chapel Hill, N.C., 1960.

Rodens, Franz. *Konrad Adenauer*. Munich/Zurich, 1965.

Rogow, Arnold. *Victim of Destiny*. London, 1966.

Romano, Salvatore F. *Storia della Mafia*. Paperback edition, Verona, 1966.

Roskamp, Karl W. *Capital Formation in West Germany*. Detroit, 1965.

Rostow, W. W. *The United States in the World Arena*. New York, 1960.

Rothstein, Andrew. *A History of the U.S.S.R.* London, 1950.

Rouanet, Pierre. *Mendès-France au pouvoir 1954–1955*. Paris, 1965.

Rovan, Joseph. *L'Europe*. Paris, 1966.

Royal Institute of International Affairs. *Britain in Western Europe*. London, 1956.
  The Soviet-Yugoslav Dispute. London, 1948.
  Surveys of International Affairs.

Rueff, Jacques, and others. *Le Marché commun et ses problèmes*. Paris, 1958.

Ryan, Cornelius. *The Last Battle*. London, 1966.

Sampson, Anthony. *Macmillan: A Study in Ambiguity*. Paperback edition, London, 1968.

The New Europeans. London, 1968.

Sannwald, Rolf, and Stohler, Jacques. *Wirtschaftliche Integration*. Basel/Tübingen, 1958.

Sayers, R. S. (ed.). *Banking in Western Europe*. Oxford, 1962.

Scarlett, Doris. *Window onto Hungary*. Bradford, n.d.

Schaffer, Gordon. *Russian Zone*. London, 1947.

Scheingold, Stuart A. *The Rule of Law in European Integration*. New Haven, Conn./London, 1965.

Schlachter, Gustav. *The Italian South*. New York, 1965.

Schlechtman, Joseph B. *European Population Transfers 1939–1945*. New York, 1946.

The Refugee in the World: Displacement and Integration. New York/London, 1963.

Schoenbrun, David. *As France Goes*. London, 1957.

Schramm, P. E. (ed.). *Die Niederlage 1945*. Paperback edition, Munich, 1962.

Schuman, Robert. *Pour l'Europe*. Paris, 1963.

Schur, Val, and Curzon, Gerard (eds.). *East-West Trade*. London, 1965.

Schwab-Felisch, Hans (ed.). *Der Ruf*. Munich, 1962.

Scitovsky, Tibor. *Economic Theory and Western European Integration*. London, 1958.

Scott, John. *Democracy is Not Enough*. New York, 1960.

The Soviet World. New York, 1966.

Seale, Patrick, and McConville, Maureen. *French Revolution 1968*. London, 1968.

Segal, Ronald. *The Crisis of India*. London, 1965.

Servan-Schreiber, Jean-Jacques. *Le Défi americain*. Paris, 1967.

Seton-Watson, Hugh. *The East European Revolution*. London, 1950.

From Stalin to Malenkov. London, 1953.

Nationalism and Communism. London, 1964.

The New Imperialism. London, 1961.

The Pattern of Communist Revolution. London, 1953.

Shanks, Michael, and Lambert, John. *Britain and the New Europe*. London, 1962.

Sherwood, Robert E. *Roosevelt and Hopkins: An Intimate History*. New York, 1948.

Shirer, William L. *The Rise and Fall of the Third Reich*. Paperback edition, Greenwich, Conn., 1962.

Shonfield, Andrew. *The Attack on World Poverty*. London, 1960.

British Economic Policy Since the War. Revised edition, London, 1959.

Modern Capitalism. London, 1965.

Siegfried, A. *De la IVe à la Ve République*. Paris, 1958.

Siegler, Heinrich von. *Dokumentation der Europäischen Integration 1946–1961 mit besonderer Berücksichtigung des Verhältnisses EWG-EFTA*. Bonn/Vienna/Zurich, 1961.

Silbermann, Alphons. *Vom Wohnen der Deutschen*. Frankfurt/Hamburg, 1966.
Silvestri, Stefano (ed.). *Il Mediterraneo: Economia, Politica, Strategia*. Rome/ Bologna, 1968.
Simpson, E. S. *Coal and the Power Industries in Postwar Britain*. London, 1966.
Sissons, Michael, and French, Philip (eds.). *Age of Austerity 1945–51*. Paperback edition, London, 1964.
Smith, Howard K. *The State of Europe*. London, 1950.
Smuts, Jan Christian. *Thoughts on a New World*. London, 1943.
Snell, John L. *The Meaning of Yalta*. New York, 1956.
  Wartime Origins of the East-West Dilemma over Germany. New Orleans, 1959.
Snow, C. P. *Science and Government*. Paperback edition, London, 1963.
Snoy et d'Oppuers, Baron. *La Formation du Zollverein (1815–1867): une leçon pour l'Europe contemporaine*. Brussels, 1957.
Spaak, Paul-Henri. *Combats Inachevés*. Two volumes, Paris, 1969.
  Why Nato? London, 1959.
Spanier, J. W. *American Foreign Policy Since World War Two*. New York, 1960.
Speier, Hans. *Divided Berlin*. London, 1961.
Spinelli, Altiero. *Rapporto sull'Europa*. Milan, 1965.
Stalin, Joseph V. *Correspondence with Churchill, Attlee, Roosevelt, and Truman*, London, 1952.
  Problems of Leninism. Eleventh edition, Moscow, 1940.
Stamp, L. Dudley. *Our Underdeveloped World*. London, 1952.
Steel, Ronald. *The End of Alliance*. London, 1964.
Stehlin, Paul. *Retour à zéro*. Paris, 1968.
Steiner, Jean-François. *Treblinka*. Paris, 1966.
Sternberg, Fritz. *Wer beherrscht die zweite Hälfte des 20. Jahrhunderts?* Paperback edition, Munich, 1963.
Stettinius, E. R. *Roosevelt and the Russians*. London, 1950.
Stimson, Henry L., and Bundy, McGeorge. *On Active Service in Peace and War*. New York, 1947.
Stolper, Wolfgang. *Germany Between East and West*. Washington, 1960.
Strang, Lord. *Home and Abroad*. London, 1956.
Strange, Susan. *The Sterling Problem and the Six*. London, 1967.
Strauss, E. *Common Sense About the Common Market*. London, 1958.
  European Reckoning. London, 1962.
Strauss, Franz-Josef. *The Grand Design*. London, 1965.
Swann, D., and McLachlan, D. L. *Concentration or Competition: A European Dilemma*. London, 1967.
Szokoloczy-Syllaba, Janos. *Les Organisations professionnelles françaises et le marché commun*. Paris, 1965.

Taber, George M. *John F. Kennedy and a United Europe*. Bruges, 1969.
Taylor, A. J. P. *English History 1914–1945*. Oxford, 1965.
  Europe: Grandeur and Decline. London, 1967.

The Origins of the Second World War. Paperback edition, London, 1964.

Tempel, Gudrun (transl. Sophie Wilkins). *Speaking Frankly About the Germans.* London, 1963.

Thomas, Hugh. *The Spanish Civil War.* Paperback edition, London, 1965.
The Suez Affair. London, 1967.

Thomson, David. *Democracy in France Since 1870.* Fifth edition, London, 1969.
Europe Since Napoleon. Second edition, London, 1962.

Thomson, George. *The Foreseeable Future.* Cambridge, 1955.

Time.

The Times.

Tocqueville, Alexis de (transl. Henry Reeve). *Democracy in America.* Oxford, 1946.

Toland, John. *The Last Hundred Days.* Paperback edition, New York, 1967.

Tournoux, J.-R. *Secrets d'Etat, Vol. II: Pétain et de Gaulle.* Paris, 1964.
La Tragédie du Général. Paris, 1967.

Townsend, Peter. *The Family Life of Old People.* London, 1957.

Toynbee, A. (ed.). *Four-Power Control in Germany and Austria 1945–1946.* London, 1956.
and V.M. (eds.). *The Realignment of Europe.* London, 1955.

Trempont, Jacques. *L'Unification de l'Europe.* Amiens/Brussels, 1955.

Trevor-Roper, H. R. *The Last Days of Hitler.* Revised paperback edition, London, 1962.

Trial of the Major War Criminals before the International Military Tribunal. Forty-two volumes, Nuremberg, 1947–9.

Trials of War Criminals before the Nuremberg Military Tribunals. Fifteen volumes, Washington, 1951–2.

Triffin, Robert. *Europe and the Money Muddle.* New Haven, Conn., 1957.
The World Money Maze. New Haven, Conn., 1966.

Truman, Harry S. *Memoirs.* Two volumes, Paperback edition, New York, 1965.

United Kingdom Foreign Office. *Protocol of the Proceedings of the Berlin Conference, 2nd August 1945.* London, 1947.
Report of the Crimea Conference. London, 1945.
H.M.S.O. *Anglo-French Discussions regarding the French Proposals for the Western European Coal, Iron, and Steel Industries, May–June 1950.* London, 1950.
Commonwealth Consultations on Britain's Relations with the European Economic Community. London, 1961.
Correspondence arising out of the meeting of the Foreign Ministers of the Governments of Belgium, France, the Federal Republic of Germany, Italy, Luxembourg, and the Netherlands, held at Messina on 1–2 June 1955. London, 1955.
Documents agreed on by the Conference of Ministers held in Paris, October 20–23, 1954. London, 1954.
The United Kingdom and the European Economic Community. London, 1961.

United Nations. *Customs Unions: A League of Nations Contribution to the Study of Customs Union Problems*. New York, 1947.
The Future Growth of World Population. New York, 1958.
Economic Commission for Europe. *The European Housing Problem: a Preliminary Review*. Geneva, 1949.
Growth and Stagnation in the European Economy. Geneva, 1954.
Economic and Social Council. *Preliminary Report of the Temporary Sub-Committee on Economic Reconstruction of Devastated Areas*. Geneva, 1946.
General Assembly. *Resolutions*.
United States, Department of Commerce. *Foreign Aid by the United States Government 1940–1951*. Washington, 1952.
Department of State. *Bulletin*.
Military Intelligence. *The Communist Bloc in Europe*. Headquarters, U.S. Army in Europe, 1959.
Presidential Committee on Foreign Aid. *European Recovery and American Aid*. Washington, 1947.
Select Committee on Foreign Aid. *Final Report on Foreign Aid*. Washington, 1948.
Uri, Pierre. *Partnership for Progress*. New York, 1963.
(ed.). *From Commonwealth to Common Market*. London, 1968.
Urwin, D. W. *Western Europe Since 1945*. London, 1968.

Valentine, D. G. *The Court of Justice of the European Coal and Steel Community*. The Hague, 1954.
Valentino, Nino. *L'Elezione di Segni*. Milan, 1963.
Vallette, Geneviève, and Bouillon, Jacques. *Munich 1938*. Paris, 1964.
Vandenberg, Arthur H., Jr. (ed.). *The Private Papers of Senator Vandenberg*. Boston, Mass.
van der Beugel, Ernst. *From Marshall Aid to Atlantic Partnership*. Amsterdam/London/NewYork, 1966.
Van der Molen, G. H. J., and others (eds.). *The United Nations: Ten Years' Legal Progress*. The Hague, 1956.
van der Plas, Michel. *Mooie Vrede: een documentaire over Nederland in de jaren 1945–1950*. Utrecht, 1966.
Vaussard, Maurice. *Histoire de l'Italie contemporaine 1870–1946*. Paris, 1950.
Verburg, M. C. *Nederland in de europese ruimte*. Amsterdam, 1966.
Vernay, Alain. *Les Paradis fiscaux*. Paris, 1968.
Viansson-Ponté, Pierre. *Les Politiques*. Paris, 1967.
Viner, Jacob. *The Customs Union Issue*. New York, 1950.
Vogelsang, Thilo. *Das geteilte Deutschland*. Munich, 1966.
Votaw, Dow. *The Six-Legged Dog: Mattei and E.N.I. – a Study in Power*. Berkeley/Los Angeles, 1964.
Voyenne, Bernard. *Histoire de l'idée européenne*. Paris, 1964.

Wall, Edward. *Europe: Unification and Law*. London, 1969.

Wallich, Henry C. *Mainsprings of German Revival.* New Haven, Conn., 1955.

Walsh, W. B. *Russia and the Soviet Union.* Michigan, 1958.

Ward, Barbara. *Policy for the West.* New York, 1951.

The West at Bay. New York, 1948.

Warley, T. K. *Agriculture: The Cost of Joining the Common Market.* London, 1967.

Waterlow, Charlotte. *Tribe, State, and Community.* London, 1967.

Watt, D. C. *Britain Looks At Germany.* London, 1965.

Watts, O. M. *Stanford's General Chart of the English Channel.* London, 1969.

Weil, Gordon L. (ed.), *A Handbook on the European Economic Community.* Washington/New York/London, 1965.

Welles, Sumner. *The Time for Decision.* New York, 1944.

Where we are Heading. London, 1946.

Wellisz, Stanislaw. *The Economics of the Soviet Bloc.* New York, 1964.

Werth, Alexander. *De Gaulle: A Political Biography.* Third edition, London, 1969.

The Strange History of Pierre Mendès France. London, 1957.

West, Rebecca. *The Meaning of Treason.* Revised edition, London, 1965.

Western European Union, Assembly. *Debates.*

Reports.

White, Theodore H. *Fire in the Ashes: Europe in Mid-Century.* New York, 1953.

Williams, Francis. *A Prime Minister Remembers: The War and Postwar Memoirs of the Rt. Hon. Earl Attlee, K.G., P.C., O.M., C.H.* London, 1961.

Williams, Gertrude. *Apprenticeship in Europe.* London, 1963.

Williams, Philip M. *Crisis and Compromise: Politics in the Fourth Republic.* London, 1964.

and Harrison, M. *De Gaulle's Republic.* London, 1960.

Willis, F. Roy. *France, Germany, and the New Europe, 1945–1967.* London, 1969.

Wilmot, Chester. *The Struggle for Europe.* Paperback edition, London, 1959.

Wilson, Edmund. *Europe Without Baedeker.* London, 1948.

Wiskemann, Elisabeth. *Europe of the Dictators 1919–1945.* London, 1966.

Germany's Eastern Neighbours. London, 1957.

Italy. London, 1947.

Wollenberg, H. H. *Fifty Years of German Film.* London, 1948.

Woodbridge, George, and others. *U.N.R.R.A.: The History of the United Nations Relief and Rehabilitation Administration.* Three volumes, New York, 1950.

Woodward, Sir Llewellyn. *British Foreign Policy in the Second World War.* London, 1962.

Worswick, G. D. N., and Ady, P. H. (eds.). *The British Economy 1945–1950.* Oxford, 1952.

Woytinsky, W. S., and E. S. *World Population and Production: Trends and Outlook.* New York, 1953.

The Yale Law Journal.

Yates, P. Lamartine. *Food, Land, and Manpower in Western Europe*. London, 1960.

Young, Gordon. *The Fall and Rise of Alfried Krupp*. London, 1960.

Young, Wayland. *The Italian Left*. London, 1949.

The Montesi Scandal. London, 1959.

Zaring, J. L. *Decision for Europe*, Baltimore, 1969.

Zebot, Cyril A. *The Economics of Competitive Coexistence: Convergence Through Growth*. New York, 1964.

Zeman, Z. E. B. *Prague Spring: A Report on Czechoslovakia 1968*. London, 1969.

Zink, Harold. *American Military Government in Germany*. New York, 1947.

The United States in Germany 1944–1955. New York, 1957.

Zinkin, Taya. *India*. London, 1965.

Zinner, P. E. *Communist Strategy and Tactics in Czechoslovakia 1914–1948*. London, 1963.

Revolution in Hungary. New York, 1962.

Zischka, Anton (transl. Brian Battershaw). *The Other Europeans*. London, 1962.

Zurcher, Arnold J. *The Struggle to Unite Europe 1940–1958*. New York, 1958.

Index

359

Stockton - Billingham
LIBRARY
Technical College